Praise for *Guardian of the Vision:*

"The Merlin mystique and the fascinating rivalry of Elizabeth and Mary, Queen of Scots underpins this entertaining blend of fantasy and history, which invites comparison with Mary Stewart and Marion Zimmer Bradley. The battle for good over evil is a common theme in fantasy, but Radford's comfortable command of history keeps this one from becoming boring."   —*Publishers Weekly*

"Radford's latest historical fantasy continues the tale begun in *Guardian of the Balance* and *Guardian of the Trust* and displays the author's meticulous research as well as her gift for graceful storytelling."   —*Library Journal*

"The third installment in the Merlin's Descendants series places a magical spin to true historic events. Irene Radford enchantingly brings to life the early Elizabethan era so that the audience will think that the author contains Merlin's genes. The battles on the mundane and mystical planes propel the story line forward, but the characters make the novel so fascinating that the good, the bad, and the ugly compel the reader into a one sitting session."
—*Book Browser*

GUARDIAN
OF THE
VISION

Also by
Irene Radford

The Dragon Nimbus
THE GLASS DRAGON
THE PERFECT PRINCESS
THE LONELIEST MAGICIAN
THE WIZARD'S TREASURE

The Dragon Nimbus History
THE DRAGON'S TOUCHSTONE
THE LAST BATTLEMAGE
THE RENEGADE DRAGON

The Star Gods
THE HIDDEN DRAGON

Merlin's Descendants
GUARDIAN OF THE BALANCE
GUARDIAN OF THE TRUST
GUARDIAN OF THE VISION
GUARDIAN OF THE PROMISE*

*Coming soon in hardcover from DAW

IRENE RADFORD

GUARDIAN OF THE VISION

Merlin's Descendants:
Volume Three

DAW BOOKS, INC.
DONALD A. WOLLHEIM, FOUNDER
375 Hudson Street, New York, NY 10014

ELIZABETH R. WOLLHEIM
SHEILA E. GILBERT
PUBLISHERS
www.dawbooks.com

First paperback printing, May 2002
1 2 3 4 5 6 7 8 9 10

DAW TRADEMARK REGISTERED
U.S. PAT. OFF. AND FOREIGN COUNTRIES
—MARCA REGISTRADA
HECHO EN U.S.A.

PRINTED IN THE U.S.A.

In Memory of
Michael Gilbert
July 20, 1947–August 14, 2000

Descendants of Henry VII

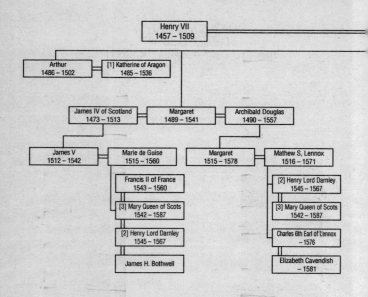

Henry VII
1457 – 1509

Arthur
1486 – 1502

[1] Katherine of Aragon
1485 – 1536

James IV of Scotland
1473 – 1513

Margaret
1489 – 1541

Archibald Douglas
1490 – 1557

James V
1512 – 1542

Marie de Guise
1515 – 1560

Margaret
1515 – 1578

Mathew S, Lennox
1516 – 1571

Francis II of France
1543 – 1560

[2] Henry Lord Darnley
1545 – 1567

[3] Mary Queen of Scots
1542 – 1587

[3] Mary Queen of Scots
1542 – 1587

[2] Henry Lord Darnley
1545 – 1567

Charles 6th Earl of Lennox
– 1576

James H. Bothwell

Elizabeth Cavendish
– 1581

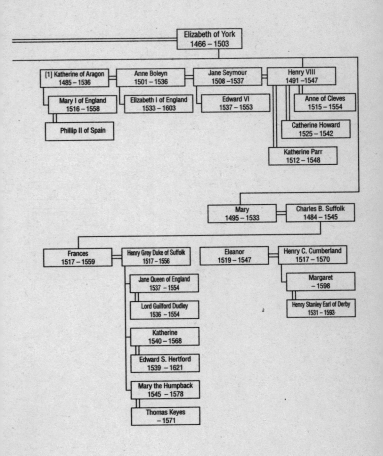

AUTHOR'S NOTES AND ACKNOWLEDGMENTS

This book was not written to confirm Hollywood's version of history or the personalities involved. I have tried to portray historical characters as they appear to me from my research. Very quickly I learned that one cannot sympathize with both Elizabeth I and Mary Queen of Scots (Marie in the first portion of the book since she signed her personal correspondence that way). Both women had their strengths and their weaknesses. Both were products of their times. Their conflict remains the subject of heated debate.

As much as possible I have stuck to an accurate chronology of events. Actual historical personages are noted in the Cast of Characters with a "*." I have also included a family tree of the Tudor family to help keep the many convoluted relationships straight. I may have oversimplified the diplomatic and theological conflicts. The number of references on these topics is formidable. I invite you to visit your local library and read more.

There is no proof that Elizabeth ever bore a child, any child, before or after her ascension to the throne. However, rumors persist to this day. Robert Dudley's wife, Amy Robsart, did die under mysterious circumstances. Many people throughout the centuries have believed that Death is an actual entity that walks the Earth in search of his next candidate. Perhaps Amy did have a rendezvous with her destiny.

Modern Jesuits have a reputation for careful scientific research and logical debate. The Society of Jesus Christ (Jesuits) was founded in 1540 by Ignatius Loyola. This order reported only to the Pope. Their mission was to bring lapsed Catholics and Protestants back into the fold. Jesuits worked actively with the Inquisition. They considered themselves crusaders and warriors of Christ. Their logic and emphasis on education came about as a result of countering the arguments of their enemies, the Protestants. Officially they arrived in England in 1578 with their literature and persuasive arguments. Rumors of forays into England by individual Jesuits litter history books, letters, and diaries of the period.

When I first embarked upon the quest of writing this book, many friends and family members chortled, "Oh, good, you get to go play with Shakespeare." Sorry. The first theater was not built in London until 1576. William Shakespeare did not travel to London and begin his outstanding career until 1588 or 1589. By 1592 he was an established actor and playwright. That is well after the scope of this book. But the beautiful language of Shakespeare has made a tremendous impact upon Western culture. How many wonderful phrases from his work have become clichés! "Into the breach!" "This is the winter of our discontent." "The undiscovered country (Death)." "A rose by any other name." The list goes on and on. This is a period when the English language had not been codified. When scholars did, soon after, apply rules of spelling and grammar, they imposed the logic of pure Latin upon a polyglot language that defied rules. There seem to be more exceptions to the rule than cases that behave. Without the restrictions of other languages, English exploded during Elizabeth's reign with new words, like "numerous," "idiom," "penetrate," "savage," "jovial," and "negotiation." The printing press and the Reformation brought literacy and education to the masses. The English reveled in poetry, history, and mythology. Any attempt I might make to imitate this glorious form of speech without overburdening the reader and the text with far too many words would be pitiful. I haven't even tried. I apologize if my characters speak too much like your next door neighbor. But if they do, perhaps they will become more real and you can empathize with their plight.

The Abbey of Whitefriars in London was the last legal sanctuary in England until this, too, was abolished by Act of Parliament in 1697. I put a glass factory in the old sanctuary somewhat earlier than history records. Since ownership of the place was in dispute, an entrepreneur like Brother Jeremy might very well have set up a short-lived factory and brought a measure of order to the chaotic world of refugees from the law. A glassworks at Whitefriars ran continuously from 1680 to 1923 when it was moved to a more modern factory. Records exist for the Battle of the Glasshouse in 1732 when the inhabitants defeated a Royal Navy Press gang with molten glass and white-hot tools. A white-robed monk remains the company logo—now owned by Caithness Glass of Perth, Scotland. Thanks must go to Heather Robbie, secretary of the Paperweight Collectors Society, Caithness Glass, Ltd., for invaluable information on the early glassworks.

No book of this length and scope, and on this deadline, could be written and researched alone. Many thanks to the reference librarians at the University of Portland, Portland, Oregon. They dived into the work of answering my obscure questions with enthusiasm above and beyond the call of duty. I just hope they still giggle when I call them for help on the next book. As usual, Mike Moscoe helped me sort out some of the religious issues, history, and practices. The Reverend Richard Toll of St. John's Episcopal Church, Milwaukie, Oregon, also came forth with books, insights, and clarifications. Beth Gilligan is always good for searching the Web for useful and fun facts that add life to the historical world I tried to create. Judith Glad is a wonder with English Lit and found the song sung by Meg in Chapter 11. It dates from 1240 A.D. I've done my best to clean up the Middle English to make it readable to a modern audience, without destroying the rhyme. Some phrases had to remain the same. Big brother James H. Radford (Ph.D candidate at Old Dominion University, Norfolk, Virginia) is the political scientist in the family and graciously loaned me his bonehead government notes on the emergence of the nation state. I'm glad he understands it. The other brother, Ed, is always good for long walks and longer conversations that helped me work through character and plot knots. And last but definitely not least, I owe a lot to Karen Lewis, best friend, coconspirator . . . er . . . plotter, and insightful reader. I can't write without her.

As always I need to thank my editor, Sheila Gilbert, who trusts me more than I trust myself to get the job done, and on time. The same goes for my agent, Carol McCleary, of the Wilshire Literary Agency. I'd be lost, personally and professionally, without her.

A pilgrimage is more a spiritual journey than a physical

one. Like Griffin Kirkwood, I have toiled down many false paths before finding the one that led to this story. My own faith has come into question and reaffirmed itself along slightly different lines than intended. But it works for me. I do not wish anyone to accept my beliefs without their own pilgrimage. Griffin's journey brings to light many questions I do not feel qualified to answer. I can only hope the questions raised help my readers sort through their own life's journey.

The popular mystical romanticism that currently surrounds the Knights Templar and their connection to modern Freemasonry and ancient mystery schools is one that in my humble opinion has not been fully researched. Perhaps, because of the spiritual nature of this cult, it cannot be subjected to standard methods of documentation. Following that path is an interesting quest. And it is the journey that is important, not the objective. Each book I write is a journey. I hope you can enjoy it with me.

Irene Radford
Welches, Oregon
October, 2000

CAST OF CHARACTERS
*denotes historical figure

The Descendants of Merlin:

Raven: 1498–1558. Sir Brian's mother. She holds the title of the Pendragon at the beginning of the book.

Sir Brian Kirkwood: b. 1517. Griffin and Donovan's father, Baron of Kirkwood.

Griffin Kirkwood: b. 1535. Inheritor of the powers and responsibilities of the Pendragon, rejects them for the priesthood.

Donovan Kirkwood: b. 1535. His twin brother. He desperately wants magic and the responsibilities of the Pendragon, but without one cannot have the other.

Meg Kirkwood: b. 1536. Sister of Griffin and Donovan. Brutally raped by the Douglas clan in a border raid. Her mind never heals.

Fiona: b. 1542. Younger sister of Griffin and Donovan. Practical and decisive.

Peregrine and Gaspar: b. 1551? Illegitimate children that may have been sired by either Griffin or Donovan, accepted into the family at birth, and raised at Kirkenwood.

Lady Katherine: 1542–1558. Donovan's first wife. Daughter of a Carlisle merchant.

Mary Elizabeth Kirkwood (Betsy): b. 1558. Donovan's eldest legitimate child.

Lady Martha St. Clare: 1532–1563. Donovan's second wife.

Griffin and Henry Kirkwood: b. 1561. Donovan's twin sons by Martha.

Their Familiars:

Helwriaeth: (Mighty Hunter). Griffin's wolfhound familiar.

Newynog: (Hungry). Raven's dog. Helwriaeth's only female pup has the same name.

Coffa: (Remembrance). Newynog's pup.

Descendants of Henry Tudor—King Henry VII of England:

*Henry VII: 1457–1509. First Tudor King, grandfather of Elizabeth I.

*Henry VIII: 1491–1547. King who implemented religious reform in England.

*Edward Tudor: b. 1537. Edward VI, King of England. Ruled 1547–1553.

*Mary Tudor: b. 1516. Queen of England. Ruled 1554–58.

*King Philip of Spain: b.? Mary's husband, brought the Inquisition to England.

*Elizabeth Tudor: b. 1533. Queen of England, 1558–1603.

*Mary Queen of Scots: 1542–1587. Crowned Queen of Scots soon after her birth. Raised in France. First husband *Francis, Dauphin of France.

Robin: Illegitimate son of Elizabeth and Dudley, fostered in the village of Hatfield.

*Lady Jane Grey: 1537–1554. Descended from Henry VII by his youngest daughter Mary. Put on the throne at the death of her cousin Edward VI by her father-in-law. Reigned nine days before Edward's sisters, Mary and Elizabeth, deposed her.

Katherine Grey: 1540–1568. Sister of Lady Jane Grey and contender for the throne of England. Married *Edward Seymour, Earl of Hertford.

Henry Stewart: 1545–1567. Lord Darnley, grandson of Henry VII by Margaret Tudor's second marriage. Second husband of Mary Queen of Scots.

The House of Valois—Rulers of France:

Catherine de Médici: 1519–1589. Daughter of the Florentine family of bankers. Married to *Henry Valois—Henri II d. 1559—King of France. Mother of three kings of France, none of whom produced heirs.

Henri II: Duc d'Orléans. Married Catherine de Médici 1533. King 1547–1559.

Francis II: born? probably around 1542. King of France July 1559–December 6, 1560. Raised with Mary Queen of Scots from age of five and married her.

Charles IX: 1550–1574. King upon Francis' death in 1560.

Henry III: b.? Duc d'Alençon. Youngest son of Catherine de Médici. Ascended throne of France May 30, 1574.

Descendants of Nimuë:

Roanna: b. 1537. Rose. Peasant held captive by Lord Douglas. Widow of Giles, Count de Planchet.

Gran: Roanna's maternal grandmother and mentor.

Raisa: 1538–1558. Roanna's sister.

House de Guise of France:

Marie de Guise: d. 1560. Widow of *King James V of Scotland. Regent for her daughter, Mary Queen of Scots.

Duc Francis de Guise: d. 1563. Uncle to Marie Stuart, Queen of Scots, and brother of the regent of Scotland.

Charlotte de Guise: Sister to Duc Francis, Countess Lafabvre.

Duc Henri de Guise: d. December 23, 1588. Son of Francis, cousin to Marie Stuart, Queen of Scots, and Captain General of the Holy League.

Charles de Guise: Cardinal of Lorraine and brother to Francis.

The Stuarts of Scotland:

Mary Queen of Scots: See above.

James Stuart: d. 1570. Earl of Moray, illegitimate son of *James V of Scotland, premier lord of the land. Later regent for *James VI.

James V: 1512–1542. Father of Mary Queen of Scots and husband of *Marie de Guise.

Others:

Father Manuel: b. 1530. Spanish priest assigned to Kirkenwood.

Eustachius du Bellay: Bishop of Paris 1551–1564 when he resigned his office. Griffin's superior sends him to England as a spy.

Father Peter: b. 1508. English priest assigned to Kirkenwood, probably inherited the position from his father, a Protestant. Like Donovan, espouses the Catholic faith because it is politically correct this year.

Bernard: Reve and blacksmith for village of Kirkenwood.

Malcolm: Sergeant-at-arms of Kirkenwood.

Callum: Man-at-arms of Kirkenwood.

Dr. John Dee: 1527–1608. Preeminent English mystic, scholar, alchemist (scientist) of his day.

Mistress Dee: d. 1580. John's mother.

Earl of Ruthven: d. ? Member of Marie de Guise's privy council.

Joseph the Mercer from Lincoln and Michael the Brewer from Stratford: Donovan's cronies in Parliament.

Robert Dudley: 1533–1588. The love of Queen Elizabeth's life. Master of the Horse, later elevated to the peerage as Baron of Denbigh and Earl of Leicester.

Ambrose Dudley: 1531–1590. Brother to Robert. Viscount Lisle and Earl of Warwick.

Micah: Gypsy who brings his family to Griffin on the road.

George: his son.

Edward de Vere: d.? Earl of Oxford. Secret Catholic. Declared his faith in 1580, seduced one of Elizabeth's maids in 1580 as well. An eccentric and free spirit. Married Anne Cecil, Lord Burghley's fifteen-year-old daughter.

Millie from the Manor: Gives Griffin directions to a candle-maker in Oxford who will shelter him for a time.

Jonathan the Candlemaker: Offers hospitality to Griffin in Oxford.

Henry Hastings: 1536–1595. Third Earl Huntington. Descended from Edward III. Had a claim to the throne, not ambitious enough to pursue it. Married to *Katherine Dudley, sister of Robert Dudley.

Thomas Howard: d. 1572. Fourth Duke of Norfolk. Open Catholic who conspired with Marie Queen of Scots to depose (by assassination) Elizabeth. Executed for treason.

John Dudley: 1502–1553. Duke of Northumberland. Lord Protector of England during minority reign of Edward VI. Father-in-law to Jane Grey.

Guilford Dudley: 1536–1554. Fourth son of *John, Duke of Northumberland, and husband to *Jane Grey.

William Cecil: d.? Lord Burleigh. Elizabeth's Secretary of State and chief adviser.

Charles Mattingly and Mathew de Lisle: Younger sons of Protestant lords who are sympathetic to Norfolk's cause and bid for power.

Sir Bartholomew Digby and Lord Edward Binghamton: Catholics in Norfolk's entourage. True Catholics seeking religious freedom for themselves.

Fr. Thomas Greene: 1529–1589. Rector of parish church, Hatfield.

Beatrice Green: 1532–1599. The rector of Hatfield's wife.

Ralph: Gatekeeper of Whitefriars.

Brother Jeremy: Master of Whitefriars.

Carola and Gareth: Young couple Griffin marries in Whitefriars. She is the daughter of Brother Jeremy, very young and tiny. He is a hulking brute who blows glass.

Thomas Randolph: An expert on Scottish Affairs and Elizabeth I's agent.

Deirdre: One-eyed crone with many ancient secrets.

Michael and Jonah: Grandsons of Deirdre of the Apothecary Hall.

Will Somers: Favorite fool of Henry VIII. Faithful to the king long after his death.

GUARDIAN
OF THE
VISION

Merlin's Descendants:

Volume Three

Prologue

23 April, 1553, St. George's Day, sixth year of the reign of our most sovereign King Edward VI, of England, Ireland, Wales, and France. The border hills beyond Carlisle.

I TURNED my face into the rising wind. My hair whipped away from my eyes. The bite of salt stung my cheeks and chin. My horse shied and tried to turn east, away from the approaching storm. I mastered his headstrong grasp of the bit and surged forward, north and west into the storm and toward our target.

I reveled in the savage lash of my primal element. It matched my anger in ferocity. The rain would come soon, covering the tracks of the two dozen mounted men who rode with me. We would be across the crumbling remnants of Hadrian's Wall when the storm crashed around us. Our quarry retreated just beyond the border of Scotland, close enough to menace our home, far enough to be beyond our king's laws and justice.

Justice. The thought hammered at the minds of my men.

The outlaws would lose their refuge tonight, and Meg would be avenged.

Our sister could regain her wits without fear.

To my right, Donovan, my twin, raised his hands to the storm, seeking to draw its power into himself. He could not, of course. I had inherited the magical talent from our grandmother that skipped my father and my twin.

With the wonders of magic comes responsibility, Grandmother Raven's voice pounded inside my head.

I ignored her. This was man's business. Meg must be avenged.

1

Peace is man's business. There is always an alternative to war.

"Shut up, Raven!" I spoke into the wind, letting my element carry my opinion home.

You know I am right. You question everything I say, challenge the traditions I pound into your thick skull, Griffin Kirkwood. Now you must question yourself.

"Not in this, Raven. Not in this. We must avenge Meg. She cannot heal unless we bring her attackers to justice."

I heard her mental snort of disgust. An inkling of doubt crept into my mind.

Helwriaeth, my wolfhound, mighty warrior that she was, let loose with the triumphant battle cry that I kept trapped within my throat. Seven more wolfhounds took up the trumpeting challenge. The sound rolled around the hills and vales as thunder.

"Quiet the dogs, Griffin," Da snarled at me. "Those black raiders outnumber us and are well armed. We need surprise this night."

I could surprise our enemies more effectively than Da and other mundanes who needed the silence and darkness of the night. But Grandmother Raven had warned us not to use magic to defeat our enemies.

Was a spell for invisibility black magic?

War is black magic, Raven's voice reminded me like a sharp caw released with the thunder.

They started it! I replied instinctively.

Silence.

Raven's silence was always the worst reprimand she could give me.

I should be the one to break the mindless quest for vengeful violence. I knew it without Raven's biting words in my head. I would be the Pendragon when she died. 'Twas my responsibility.

I needed to halt our forward plunge and think about this.

Donovan showed me the layout of the enemy village through our unique mind-to-mind communication. I instantly knew their vulnerabilities as well as their strengths.

"I know how to plan a raid," he said with his voice. He grinned at me again. "I tumbled one of the maids yesterday while I scouted the terrain."

"There." Da pulled his horse to a halt atop a low ridge.

He pointed to the broken silhouette of a destroyed castle on the next higher ridge. Only bats and ghosts threatened us from the ancient stronghold. But below it, nestled into the sheltered vale between us and the abandoned fortress, lay a cluster of thatched cottages. Two or three lights winked at us from behind closed shutters.

"The girl lives in the end cottage. Says she has a sister who's just as accommodating." Donovan grinned again. An image of hair the color of faded red autumn leaves and soft gray eyes came and went so fast I nearly lost the picture of her. She'd been eager for Donovan's attentions and not a virgin.

Our sister Meg had not been willing and had prized her virginity.

"Remember, Donovan, what they did to your sister. To *us!* " Da hissed at us both. He had four other daughters, by his three wives, But Meg was special. Meg was . . .

Not Meg anymore. The Scots must pay for what they did to her.

"All the more reason to plant our bastards in the bellies of their daughters." Donovan kneed his horse forward, level with Da. "An eye for an eye!" But his mental images were heated by lust rather than anger. Did the girl manipulate his emotions from a distance, or was she truly the answer to his randy prayers?

"These raiders are so vile, their own lord begged us to clean out this viper's nest. Paid us, too." Da's eyes gleamed in the dim light from our shielded lanterns. He was spoiling for a fight. Any fight. The Scots and Meg were merely an excuse.

Donovan looked at Da strangely at that statement. His clear and logical thinking tried to question something about Lord Douglas. Something . . .

Da raised his hand and signaled me forward. I, with my preternatural sight, led our little troop down the hillside. Helwriaeth came behind me, sniffing the true path for the rest of the pack. Youngster though she was, she kept the dogs quiet. War dogs one and all; they knew their business sometimes better than we.

By the time the ground leveled out beneath us, I had guessed why Lord Douglas wanted us to raid his own village. He wanted to steal something valuable from them, using the raid as cover, to blame us for his perfidy. He would trap and slaughter us at the same time, silencing our witness. I raised one hand to stop the others. We needed to go back, before Lord Douglas trapped us. I thought I knew a better way.

In the back of my head, I felt Raven smile. *There is always a better way.*

Lightning flashed and thunder rolled at that moment, unleashing the full fury of the storm upon our heads. In the flare of blue-white light, with my senses extended, I saw a score of mounted men waiting atop the next hill. Not our men.

Da pressed forward, too eager for the fray to exercise caution.

"Da, wait!" I called to him quietly, using magic as well as good sense to persuade him.

He ignored me. I raised my hand again, wanting a spell to hold him in place, not knowing how to do that.

The storm raged. More lightning and thunder ripped the skies apart. Energy crackled from the sky to my upthrust hand.

It grabbed hold of me. My mind fled. Power shot through me. Fire shot from my hand to thatch.

The largest cottage in the village burst into flames with a mighty explosion. Blinded, I rocked back in my saddle.

Power drained from me along with strength and will.

The leader of the border raiders resided in the now blazing cottage. 'Twas he who had led the men who stole and murdered within the boundaries of Kirkenwood. 'Twas he who raped Meg in the hut where she had gone as midwife. He had murdered the new mother and her babe. 'Twas he who would be the first to die this night.

By my hand.

Smoke blinded me. The smell of burning hair and flesh gagged in my throat. I doubled over in pain at the passing of a life.

Helwriaeth let loose another howl. Sadness ripped through me. I wanted to lift my head and match her note for note. But while she exulted, I mourned.

Endless moments of burning agony ripped through me/ my victim. We couldn't breathe. Pain. PAIN.

And then nothing.

A silent numbness descended.

I looked upon the scene as if from a different body, a different mind.

And then the raiders were upon us. Cold steel clashed with cold steel. Crossbow bolts flew through the air. Smoke choked us. Horses reared and screamed. The dogs lunged, jaws snapping. I saw one break the leg of a riderless horse with his massive jaws.

All around me the confusion and noise of battle circled, leaving me isolated. And yet I was vastly aware of every life within the village, natives and invaders. I doubled over in empathic pain every time a life fled.

Raven had warned me. Sometime, when I least expected it, my powers would mature and grow into their full potential. I had to be cautious. I had to control that moment. And now . . . I shared each death with agonizing clarity.

The echoes and cries disappeared. My ears became as numb as the rest of me. I looked down upon it all and saw myself sitting dumbly upon my horse, inert, in the middle of the fray.

Donovan dragged a young woman from the end cottage. He held her easily with one arm around her throat. His other hand fumbled to release his now swollen codpiece. She screamed and kicked. She clawed at him. Not the willing maid of yesterday. Her gray eyes widened with panic and fear.

I shared the emotions with her and nearly fled the scene. Meg's plight became more real. For a moment I relived her rape. I felt the shame, the stabbing pain, the humiliation and degradation. My privates withered.

Behind Donovan another maid, perhaps a year younger, with hair to match her sister's, slammed an iron griddle into the back of his head. He sprawled headlong in the dirt, his clothing half undone and his foul deed incomplete. He was in danger of being trampled by our own men.

Donovan's victim stared at me—or the spirit of me that hung above my body—from beneath Donovan's inert body. Our gazes locked, hearts beating in the same erratic rhythm. The soulless depth of her gray eyes drew me in, threatened to drown me in her anger and despair. I knew her then for kin. Kin in talent if not blood.

"I will remember," she said quietly.

I heard each syllable distinctly.

The two women fled into the arms of a waiting wall of warriors I did not recognize.

The men of the Black Douglas of Hermitage Castle.

He wanted the girl. He wanted her talents as well as her body.

My soul sank with a sickening lurch. My head reeled. I looked out upon the world through my own eyes. Ghostly double images superimposed upon real ones.

"Donovan!" I screamed with my mind and my voice as I kneed my horse closer to my fallen twin.

Friend and foe alike impeded me. With every pounding hoof I feared for my twin's life.

I honed the link of communication with Donovan to a fine barb and aimed it to rouse him. He moaned and stirred. The pain in his neck and behind his eyes became my pain. Under this new onslaught, my heart stuttered and nearly failed.

Light flared all around us, bright white, smelling of strange acids. The sharp and deafening bang of gunfire.

"Donovan!" I cried again in panic. Who among us could afford enough powder to fire an arquebus? Who had the time to mount one upon a tripod and aim it? None of our men carried firearms, preferring cold steel to the expensive toys of clockmakers.

Lord Douglas had stockpiles of black powder stolen from a hundred raids across the border. Rumor placed at least three wheellock weapons in his possession.

All grew unnaturally still around me. I lost the ever-present awareness of Donovan in my mind. Helwriaeth's comforting touch faded as well. I no longer sat atop a horse. The battle, the fires, the screams from the hurt and dying disappeared.

I stood alone and lost in the midst of the terrible light. Columns of white heat rose all around in an unbroken circle. No exit, no entrance.

Sweat slicked my body. I smelled my own fear.

I turned around and around, seeking escape, seeking answers, seeking . . . anything but this circle of blinding whiteness.

A golden sword with a jeweled hilt hung before my eyes.

Ancient runes engraved on the blade burned red with power. All light seemd to radiate from that magical blade.

I knew that sword from my lessons and my dreams. It came from the past and lived on in the future. I knew the otherworldly power it contained. Only a chosen few wielded it with impunity.

I lunged for the weapon. It eluded me.

Again I reached, with my mind as well as my hands. Again it backed away before I could so much as brush the blade with my fingertips.

Then it shifted, molded, shrank, became three crowns one atop the other, forming a vague miter suspended within a pillar of blue flames. I had seen a simpler version of that crown before, on the head of a bishop at a great mourning procession in the streets of Carlisle after the death of the old king.

Da had bowed to the authority of the man wearing that mitered crown. Grandmother Raven had not.

But these visionary crowns were older, more powerful, filled with wisdom and kindness. I knew they came from God.

"Holy Mary, Mother of God," I breathed.

I think I fell to my knees, hands clasped before me in prayer. Even with my eyes closed, the vision of the crowns and sword and the eldritch flames remained clear and bright within my mind.

The crowns grew brighter. Behind them, the sword hung suspended, its hilt forming a cross.

"I must become a man of God in support of the Holy Father in Rome," I murmured. Only that could explain the triple crown. "I must defend the church from her enemies."

I must defy family tradition and honor one religion over another. We had survived the persecutions of Henry VIII's reformation of the church by switching allegiance quite readily. Mostly we realized that God had many names and no matter what we called Him, He would listen. I knew that when Edward VI died of a sickening of the lungs—as surely he must soon—we would survive his sister Mary's restoration of the Catholic church just as easily.

But if I embraced the church, I must renounce the magic that governed much of my life; I must renounce any claim to being the Pendragon of Britain.

Raven would never forgive me.

Chapter 1

Kirkenwood Castle, 24 April 1553, just after dawn.

"YOU planned to do this all along," Donovan accused me. We had returned to our home at Kirkenwood from the raid in the early hours of the morning. Lord Douglas had carried off all of the surviving villagers: men, women, and children. He'd left us the sheep—most of them stolen from our lands to begin with—a few dead bodies, and burning houses. Nothing more.

We had returned home to the news that Meg had roused from her fever and her fear of every shadow and movement. But her seeming recovery was marred by the sense that she had retreated into the mind of a small child, unknowing of her ordeal. Unaware of her betrothed, her duties as midwife, and the life she had lived between the ages of five and sixteen.

Raven had been unable to break through the walls of forgetfulness Meg had built. I had been unable to heal her with my magic or my love.

Now I packed in preparation to leave for France. No Catholic seminaries remained in England. Helwriaeth slumbered at the foot of the bed I had shared with Donovan from earliest memory, but never would again. I must be gone before sunset. I already ached as if a part of my gut had been cut out by an enemy sword.

Occasionally Helwriaeth opened one eye a bit to see if I was ready to lead her on the next adventure. Until then, she'd rest and store her energy. I had no doubt that she would follow me even if Da tried to cage and muzzle her. She was my dog, my familiar. She and her dam, Raven's familiar Newynog, had chosen me.

I had yet to confront Raven with my decision. I would rather cut out my own tongue than disappoint her. But God had called and I must obey. His authority was greater than Raven's—but no one dared tell her that.

"That is my doublet!" Donovan grabbed the padded and embroidered red velvet out of my hands.

Hard to tell which garment belonged to me and which to him; we both wore everything in the wardrobe. We'd never questioned possession before. How could one own something exclusive to the other? We were the same person. Until now.

I'd not need red velvet in the seminary.

"You planned to betray your inheritance, Raven's trust in you. You planned to betray me!" Donovan turned his back to me, clenching and unclenching his fists, tightening his shoulders, and stalking rapidly to the shuttered arrow-slit window.

"I didn't plan to become a priest. I planned to follow Da as Baron of Kirkenwood and Raven as Pendragon," I said calmly. My air of projected calm and control was at war with the jumping inside my stomach and the quivering in my chest. "But God called me, and I cannot refuse the call."

"If you did not plan this, then why have you always questioned all that Raven has taught us? Why did you pay greater heed to Father Peter's lessons than to Raven's?" Donovan screamed as he circled our room. He was never one to stand still and listen. He constantly moved, mentally and physically. He would rather yell than speak in normal tones or whisper.

"I questioned everything, as Raven taught us both to do."

"You never questioned who fathered Peregrine and Gaspar, the two bastards you claim."

"I accepted responsibility for the boys' education and well-being because I am the eldest, am . . . was . . . Da's heir. But there is no telling which of us fathered the boys. We shared their mothers equally, as we have shared everything." Da had never curbed our randy exploits. Indeed, he had encouraged them as proof of our virility and strength. All he asked was that we take responsibility for our actions, as befitting warriors and leaders.

"We shared everything but your secret desire to be a priest, Griffin." Donovan spat bitterly. "Everything but your magical talent. How are you going to explain *that* to your new masters in the church? Witchcraft is considered heresy, you know. How are you going to humble yourself to be the lowliest servant when you have been raised to be the master?"

"Is not the master more a servant to his people and the land than those who tend him?" That's the way it should be. But few barons of my acquaintance recognized the ancient responsibilities.

"And who is to replace you here with your questioning mind and your single-minded dedication to find answers no matter where the quest leads you?" Raven stood in the doorway, black hair hanging loose down her back, swept away from her face with silver combs that matched the silver streak running from her right temple the full length of the thick mane. She held her staff—taller than herself by a head and a half—with the black crystal atop it in a white-knuckled fist.

Her mouth and nostrils looked pinched and strained. A bit of blue showed through her paler than normal skin. Her suddenly diminished posture and careworn face—a face I had always considered ageless—frightened me.

Helwriaeth leaped up to greet my grandmother and Newynog, the wolfhound at her heels, dam to my own dog. The fact that Helwriaeth had come to me rather than Raven meant that Raven would not live to see Newynog whelp another litter.

I almost faltered in my resolve. Raven had not long to live. How long? Only she and God knew the answer to that.

Perhaps the dogs knew as well. Was I prepared to abandon her—more mother to us than grandmother. Mentor, tutor, refuge. She was all of that and more.

And then something sharp flashed across my mind, and I knew I could not allow this woman or my twin to have their way. I must follow my own path.

"My twin has the same training as I, both as our father's heir to the barony and heir to you as the Pendragon of Britain, the Guardian of a proud heritage and . . ."

"The Guardian of peace and harmony in Britain," she finished for me. And then she added, "But the Pendragon is more. The Pendragon is responsible for maintaining a balance and harmony with the forces of nature. Only when that balance and harmony are controlled, then will the mundane duties of the Pendragon fall into place. We lost so much during the wars between the white rose of York and the red rose of Lancaster, and through the religious wars of Henry VIII. You must not jeopardize all that I have done to restore peace to Britain." She pounded her staff into the stone floor for emphasis. With each lifting her tool seemed heavier.

Her right fist clenched, and she brought it to her chest.

I knew how much pain I gave her. My magic as well as eighteen years under her tutelage showed me every nuance of her mood. And yet I must follow my own path, not hers.

"Donovan shared every aspect of my training. Even when you tried, you could not keep certain aspects of it secret from him. We are one soul in two bodies," I protested. Instinctively, my spine stiffened and my jaw firmed. I knew better than to try to argue with Raven without conviction.

"Your twin has not the ability to control nature, to seek out the harmonies, to work magic," Raven said sadly. "If you leave now, you rip his soul apart as well as your own."

Donovan stopped pacing. I felt his anger rising in him like a storm-driven tide.

"I am sorry to disappoint you, Raven. But this is something I must do." Donovan had been right, I'd wanted this for a long time. I had always been fascinated with the church and its mysteries. I had always longed for a deep communion with God that only the church seemed to offer me. Raven's Goddess seemed too remote, too ineffectual, too lost.

"If you leave Kirkenwood today, you may not return while I live." Raven turned her back on me and marched across the gallery above the hall. She disappeared into the shadows, little more than a shadow herself.

The Episcopal Palais of Notre Dame de Paris, home and administrative center for His Grace, the most Catholic

Bishop of Paris, Eustachius du Bellay, 21 June, before dawn of the Summer Solstice, 1558.

Bloodstained waves crashed over me. I gasped for air, desperately swimming upward toward light and life.

A sharp stab of mental pain in the back of my head partially roused me. I was aware of the hard bed beneath my back and the bare walls around me. Details of time and residence in my body rather than as a part of the sea winds remained elusive.

I tasted another presence in the wind.

"Raven?"

Her beloved face rose up before my mind's eye, more careworn and paler than I remembered. An astral wind stirred her raven-black hair. White streaked it at both temples and crown now.

Five years since I'd seen her or heard from her, and now she stalked my dreams with visions of blood and disaster.

You waste time, Griffin Kirkwood, she spat.

"Grandmother Raven." I reached out a hand to her. It passed through her ethereal image.

You must put aside sentiment, Griffin. Time passes too swiftly. Queen Mary lies dying. She rejected me as adviser, as anything more than a meddlesome beldame. She declared the heritage of the Pendragon outdated, heretical, and useless to her.

My grandmother paused a moment in her grief. I knew her disappointment as well as her current urgency. Dreams and astral winds stripped away mundane barriers.

Queen Mary will linger several months yet in her illness, but she cannot recover. In the meantime, forces gather to rend England into scattered baronies that want to be kingdoms.

"As in Arthur's day." My history lessons came back to me as if she had slammed a heavy tome into my forehead. Peace and unity in Britain had not come easily to fractious and independent barons who resented the authority of the crown, the church, anyone—including the Pendragon.

As in Arthur's day. In King John's day. Any day the monarch does not keep a firm grasp upon the barons' ability to make war among themselves. She sighed heavily with regret. *You must come home and help me. With you by my*

*side we can put Elizabeth on the throne and restore peace
before Mary dies. You can make sure that Elizabeth ac-
knowledges and heeds the Pendragon as part of her kingdom. But we cannot approach her until she takes the throne.
The Pendragon cannot make himself known to the heirs, lest
he seem to choose the next monarch. That is why we lost
contact with the crown during the wars. Now we can work
with the princes again to maintain peace and unity. We can
ease the struggle of transition.*

"I cannot, Raven. I have taken vows." My mind burned
with a flash of resentment toward her. I conquered the
emotion, too elated that she had reached out to me to
bother with past hurts.

*Vows to a foreign church, foreign princes, have never
bound such as we!* She sounded disgusted.

"Then it is about time they did and that we honor any
vow we take."

*You do not understand. Have all my lessons been washed
away by this church that demands total control of every
aspect of life, including your private thoughts?*

"The church has opened paths of enlightenment to me
that you kept closed."

*You must find your own enlightenment. Draw upon my
lessons and learn.*

She almost faded from my half-dreamed view.

"You came to me with a purpose, Raven. State it." My
words were too abrupt, too filled with five years of hurt
at her silence. That she could suffer equal pain from our
separation did not enter my mind at this juncture.

Vaguely I sensed the dawn outside my shuttered window.
She had not long to state her mission before sunlight and
daily routines broke our connection across a thousand miles
of land and sea.

*Come home, Griffin. Now. Stand at my side and help me
halt the forces of chaos. A demon is loose, and I no longer
have the strength to contain it.*

"Demons I can only fight from here with faith and
prayer. I am no exorcist to send it back to hell. There are
others better qualified to help you."

"There is *NO* one else!" Her words came through quite
audibly, telling me of her agitation and desperation. *You
are the only one who can succeed me. Donovan does not*

*live up to your example. Come home now and you will be
the next Pendragon. Keep Helwriaeth close by your side.
She will sense the presence of the demon before you can.*

Hope leaped in my breast. Raven could reconnect me to
my family. The gaping hole of loneliness would close. Only
Helwriaeth had stood by me these last five years. Only my
familiar wolfhound had anchored me to sanity and purpose.

In all those years, only Meg's mind had reached out to
me from home. And she, after her rape by the Scottish
raiders had reverted to the mind of a small child, barely
sane, lacking understanding. But she told me of daily life
at Kirkenwood, kept me informed when Da died, when
Donovan took a wife, how many ewes birthed twins, and
when the sun rose clear and bright over the standing stones
outside of the castle.

*As the Pendragon, the church will recognize your author-
ity and grant dispensation for your possession and use of
magic,* Raven said resignedly. *I have documentation of pre-
cedence. But without the authority only I can grant you, as
symbolized by my ring and staff, the church must condemn you.*

"I will find a way to come to you, Grandmother."

"My name is *Raven!* I am Grandmother to all Britain
not just to you and your worthless siblings. As you must
become Father and Grandfather—the Merlin."

"I will find a way to come to you, Raven. Soon."

*Do not delay. The demon is loose. My efforts to contain
it bleed the life from me.*

I awoke to a bright summer day in Paris with birds singing and river traffic making its usual din. As if it were just
another ordinary day.

Chapter 2

La Palais de la Louvre, Paris, France, the court of Dauphin Francis and his wife, Marie, Queen of Scots and of England, 21 June in the Year of Our Lord 1558.

"PÉRE Griffin, you do not join the court in our *jeste*." Queen Marie smiled and fluttered her eyelashes at me in obvious flirtation. "Perhaps your Jesuit masters have drained all the laughter from you and replaced it with cold sober logic?"

I kept my eyes lowered. I was no Jesuit and resented Marie's reference to their harsh and unforgiving theology. I also resented her summons when I should be seeking permission to go home.

The jester's joke about a priest making lewd advances to a notorious courtesan in the confessional had been tasteless and nearly obscene, not worthy of attention much less the rolls of laughter erupting around the court. I was surprised the jester would dare tell the tale in the presence of Charles de Guise, Cardinal of Lorraine. I was more surprised Marie's uncle laughed as loud and long as the rest of the court.

Marie's small white teeth showed beneath prettily colored lips. Her soft brown eyes and clear, pale skin glowed with intense vitality. The bejeweled gown in bright emerald green highlighted her red-gold hair.

She glittered and outshone her frail husband, Francis, seated at her side, as well as her sallow mother-in-law, Catherine de Médici, seated on the other side of her son.

Marie's maternal uncles, Charles the Cardinal of Lorraine and Duc Francis de Guise, the two most powerful nonroyals in France, stood behind their niece.

The jester now played a lute in the corner and sang a

lilting tune of how Marie attracted light by her simple presence.

"There are many things in life to laugh about, Madame." I bowed low in deference to protocol. After all, I, barely twenty-three and a newly ordained priest in my black *soutane,* devoid of lace, ornamentation, or padding, should have felt gratitude and awe at my invitation to court. Even the priceless ivory-and-gold family rosary that hung at my waist could not rival the gaudy attire and jewels of the court.

Marie frowned at my words.

"There is the laughter of intense joy," I explained. "There is the hysterical laughter of panic. Or the loving laughter when tickling a child. But to laugh *at* a jester's mockery of a person and the institution of the Holy Mother Church seems somehow . . ." I lifted my hand in a fluttering gesture of indecision rather than risk a word that might insult.

The court stilled around me. Several gaudily dressed men backed away lest my *faux pas* taint them as well.

The jester struck several discordant notes to accent the mood of the room.

A retreating courtier tripped over Helwriaeth at my feet. He flailed his arms wildly and went down on one knee. The jester let loose with another ditty about tripping over a bitch's skirts.

They all laughed again. Except for Queen Catherine de Médici, mother-in-law to Marie, near regent for the ailing King Henri II and the true power in France. That formidable woman did not have much of a sense of humor.

Queen Marie sobered first among her glittering array of courtiers. They stilled their mirth from one heartbeat to the next.

Helwriaeth cowered against my leg. She smelled danger on the sweat of these people. My own awareness heightened along with the dog's.

The court milled around, waiting upon the pleasure of one queen or the other. Both held the power of life and death over every one of us.

"You must wonder why we have summoned you to court, Pére Griffin." Queen Marie's eyes narrowed in calculation.

I merely nodded acceptance of this change of subject.

"We have heard from our learned Bishop of Paris, Eustachius du Bellay, that you have been blessed with visions." Her impeccable French accent hardened to betray a trace of the Scots she had spoken until the age of five.

Her frail husband touched her hand as if he needed to remind her of something. Marie glared at the hand until Francis removed it.

The cardinal standing behind the young queen frowned. Modern priests were supposed to extol the visions of saints in the past, not have them in modern times. I'd walked a narrow line between reverence and excommunication for five years.

Catherine de Médici frowned at Marie.

The young queen tossed her head in dismissal of the older woman's silent reprimand. Her veils drifted around her pretty shoulders, drawing attention to her long and graceful neck and the mass of red-gold hair. Every movement became an artificial study in highlighting her beauty.

And then my gaze met hers. Her dancing eyes lightened my heart and drew me deep into her enthrallment. Marie, by the Grace of God, Queen of Scots, possessed a kind of magic of her own.

I shook off her spell and nodded, acknowledging her statement. I needed a moment to regain my senses. Even then I could not speak of the cursed talent that plagued me. I'd had only two visions while awake since coming to France, both within the first few months. But I could not control my dreams.

I could not shake the heaviness of those dreams except under the brightest of sunshine. Raven called me home through my dreams.

"We wish you to give us your vision of the health of our dear cousin Queen Mary Tudor of England."

I chilled. Magic crowded my vision, threatening to show me things. Why now, when I had been free of this curse for nearly four years? My last vision had come on the day of Protestant King Edward's death and Catholic Mary Tudor's ascension to the throne of England five years ago. I'd seen flame and death and bitter rejection of the queen.

And now, I knew from Raven's visitation through my dreams, that Mary ailed as well.

"Visions are not mine to command, Majesty. God shows

me what He needs me to know, nothing more. Nothing less. As important as Queen Mary Tudor's health is to the continuance of the true faith in England, I have not seen her in any of my dreams."

But I knew that my dreams of towering, bloodstained waves centered on England. When? Now? The future? Or in the past? I had no way of knowing. Yet.

Past and future tended to work in circles reflecting each other.

"But surely one who is so blessed can pray for a vision of such import," Queen Catherine de Médici countered. Her face remained devoid of expression. I had no way to measure her displeasure.

"I can always pray," I agreed. "Whether God answers the prayers of a humble priest is another matter."

"Surely God will want to forewarn us of the ill health of our sister queen, so that we may prepare to keep England Catholic," Queen Catherine said. "If we are not prepared, then the heretical bastard Elizabeth, daughter of the whore of Babylon, will come to the throne and discard the true faith as easily as she discards her lovers!"

"I left all of my ties to England and to my family behind when I chose the church," I admitted. Helwriaeth and I both ached with loneliness over the separation from home.

Now we had a chance and a reason to go home. If only this interview would end and I could approach my bishop.

Brightness crowded closer around the edges of my consciousness. I sensed a *presence* that had not been there a few moments ago. Helwriaeth sensed it as well. She wanted out of this room and away from the newcomer. So did I. I locked my knees and ground my teeth together, fighting for stability.

I focused all of my willpower on remaining in place.

"Ye moost go back!" a new voice proclaimed, the presence I had sensed. The thick Scots accent just barely pronounced the French words so that the rarefied courtiers could understand them.

But Marie understood them. And so did I. We both looked long and hard at the new figure.

An imposing broad man stomped into the room. His muted brown-and-gray tartan draped into a traditional belted plaid over a saffron shirt proclaimed his Scottish origins better than his accent. I did not recognize the clan pattern in his clothing. Possibly Douglas, but not quite. The apparition carried a staff topped with a battered goat skull. The light from a candelabra at his elbow cast a shadow on the skull that shifted the planes and angles into a Celtic cross with a sparsely engraved circle joining the four arms. He moved forward. The next rack of candles made the shadow appear a dragon's head, yet another showed the glowing red eyes of a demon where once an innocent stock animal had looked upon the world.

My eyes, aided by Helwriaeth's senses, knew all those images to be illusions. My dog's hackles raised, and she emitted a low growl from deep in her chest. The hairs on the back of my neck and arms rose in atavistic warning.

"Who dares disturb our royal presence?" Queen Catherine rose from her chair. Outrage flared from her. The court absorbed her emotion and mimicked it.

"Ye moost go back tae Scotland, lassie," the man pronounced again staring directly at Marie.

Marie shook her head in denial.

"Wi' oot ye, chaos devours the land." He slammed the butt of his staff into the parquet flooring. Hard wood against harder wood echoed and emphasized his words.

"Nonsense, our mother rules over a peaceful Scotland as our regent," Marie returned.

"Return now, lassie, or ye'll have no Scotland to rule over!" The man raised his staff and spun in a circle.

Briefly, his gray eyes caught mine in an intense gaze. I'd seen those eyes before. Who was he?

Then, in a flash of foul smelling smoke, he disappeared. "Return now, Mary Queen of Scots, a'fore it's too late." His words lingered long after his departure.

As the smoke and sparks cleared, everyone gasped and stared where he had been. Helwriaeth and I caught a flicker of movement through a narrow postern doorway. Helwriaeth agreed with me that the man was a charlatan, not the demon we had first feared.

"Guards, seize that man," Catherine ordered.

Another flurry of movement around the edges of my vision. Darkness crowded out the light of the hundred and more candles in the room. The floor seemed to rock like the deck of a ship at sea.

I spread my arms for balance. Helwriaeth lunged upward, bracing me.

"He spreads chaos with his words," I choked out. "He is chaos."

And then the room faded around me, replaced by a bloodstained sea, and a mighty storm that ripped masts from many hundreds of ships. Waves towered above me. Cannons roared. Men died.

And in the midst of it all stood Marie, Queen of Scots, leading a long line of men to the gallows.

Chapter 3

La Palais de la Louvre, Paris, France.

THE sound of many feet pounding the older stone passages of the palais thundered ever closer. Quickly Roanna doffed her enveloping disguise of belted plaid-and-saffron shirt and dropped it down the garderobe. The next time a servant flushed the indoor privy with a bucket of water, her costume would wash into the nearest stream and float through the muck into the Seine.

She smoothed the long skirts of her coarse woolen gown and tugged at the bodice to release her breasts from the tight bands. Enough cleavage showed to convince any searcher she couldn't possibly be a man in disguise. Her clumsy boots, that had added several inches to her height, followed the woolen tartan into the garderobe.

"Go home, Griffin Kirkwood," she whispered as she paused, a little breathless, within the shadows of a cross corridor. She wrapped a tendril of compulsion around her words. "I need you at home where you can no longer defy me or my master's will."

Her lungs burned and her heart beat too quickly after running through the labyrinth of rooms to reach the servants' passages. Those who pursued her had become as lost as she. Now she need only gain the kitchen.

She breathed shallowly, trying to keep out the stench of city middens wafting through the open windows. People were not meant to live packed together in a city like rats. She longed for the clean crisp air of home. This gentle air that never truly chilled, never truly cleansed itself of the miasma of unwashed bodies, ripening waste, and rancid cooking odors made people soft and vulnerable.

An annoying drizzle made the outside cobbles slick but wasn't intense enough to wash away the muck and dirt. She'd have to watch her step.

"Go home to Kirkenwood, Pére Griffin," she whispered again while she waited for her heart to resume a normal rhythm. She'd studied Father Griffin, heir to the Pendragon of Britain, for a long time from a distance. More beautiful to look upon in person than in her scrying bowl, she nearly lost her purpose just to stare at him. But her master had prodded her into action at the last moment. She knew Father Griffin would have to accept her challenge—even though she had overtly directed it toward Queen Marie. She and her master needed Griffin at Kirkenwood. In Paris, surrounded by his faith and the forces in the mystery cult at the cathedral, he had power he did not know he tapped. She had to remove him from that power.

If Marie Queen of Scots wandered back to Scotland at the same time, so much the better. Her master would be pleased with this day's work.

Gran would be pleased, too, if she had lived. "You taught me well, Gran. I'll fulfill your legacy and pass it on to my own daughter and granddaughter."

Carefully she rested her staff—salvaged from her grandmother's few belongings—across her shoulders and ran lightly in the direction her nose told her led to the kitchen.

Once within the cavernous room, she counted upon the chaos and noise of food preparation to cover her presence. Heat blasted her from the roaring hearths with their attached ovens. Sweat beaded her brow and bosom. She mussed her hair so she would look as if she'd been hard at work. Then she dropped her shoulders and neck as if her spine curved that way naturally. With a bland kerchief over her bright hair, she merged with the flow of people, hoisted a slop bucket onto each end of her staff and continued toward the door. The goat skull on one end of the staff faded into the shadows with a thought.

"You there!" a man shouted at her.

Ten paces to go. Only ten paces away from freedom from this horrid place.

Sudden and complete quiet descended upon the kitchen. Roanna felt the gazes of those around her centering on her back. Her skin crawled from waist to nape and back again. She froze in place.

"What you got in them buckets?" A guard plowed through the milling groups of workers. His accent was as thick as the one she had used earlier, but he spoke with the soft slurring of the southern provinces of France rather than the rolling burr of the Highlands across the North Sea.

His stern countenance seemed to push people out of his way even before his massive shoulders forced a pathway. Three more men followed in his wake.

Each of them carried a pike and an unsheathed short sword.

Roanna turned around slowly, forcing her eyes to take on the vacant stare of someone whose brain moved less swiftly than their body.

"Look at me when I speak to you, girl!" the first man shouted. He must be the sergeant, or whatever rank these foreign heathens used to designate minor leadership.

With trembling chin she obeyed his command, fixing her gaze on his left shoulder. She let her eyes wander aimlessly with puzzlement.

"What you got in them buckets?" he asked again.

Roanna didn't answer. Instead she searched the room for someone in authority. No one met her gaze.

Without someone to speak for her, she tilted her shoulders so the left bucket swung closer to the guard.

He took one whiff and reared back at the smell of decaying vegetables and discarded animal entrails.

A chuckle rippled around the room. The guard frowned his displeasure and the workers quieted once more.

"Anyone give you anything to put in those buckets?" he asked.

Roanna shook her head and shrugged her shoulders. The staff tilted and threatened to upset the buckets on his scuffed boots.

He backed away from her. "Go on, then, dump them in the midden where they belong. The rest of you get back to work," he growled.

Fifteen people resumed interrupted chores with studied busyness.

Roanna retreated happily out the door and up the seven steps to the courtyard. The sergeant followed her as if to

make certain she dumped the buckets where she was supposed to. She shuffled her feet and hung her head lower
as she made her way toward the enclosing wall, uncertain
where the actual midden was. She hadn't had time to scout
the area beforehand.

Her nose led her to the reeking compost heap in the far
right corner near the back of the stable. She lowered the
staff and buckets to the ground, then ducked out of the
yoke they created, glancing over toward the kitchen door.
Sergeant Grim-face retreated down the steps, back to the
kitchen. Methodically she went about her chore as if it
taxed her mind. She lingered a few more moments, edging
farther away from the kitchen until she guessed the guards
sought their quarry elsewhere.

Whistling a sprightly jig, she grabbed her staff and made
her way out the postern to the lane that led into the city.
The staff with its distinctive goat skull might identify her,
but she'd not return home without the one thing she had
inherited from her gran.

One alley twisted into another. People filled the narrow
byways with their bodies and carts, their shouts, and their
smell. Within a quarter mile, Roanna could no longer see
the walls of the Louvre. Ducking behind a laden cart—the
owner argued vehemently with a customer at the other end
of the conveyance—she pulled a man's doublet from beneath her skirts and donned it over her bodice. Two more
quick movements and she stuffed her skirts into breeches,
giving them a fashionable padded look. Next a feathered
cap to hide her bright curls.

One illusion at a time. Her gran had taught her well until
her death shortly after Roanna had turned sixteen. "Your
lessons will live on, Gran," she promised the spirit of the
old woman who'd raised her. With one last look around
she blinked three times and wiggled her fingers in an arcane
gesture. The long staff took on the appearance of an elegant walking stick.

A dull throbbing sound became the fierce pounding of footsteps. Within a few heartbeats they grew louder yet. Sergeant
Grim-face in his gaudy uniform of scarlet and gold rounded the
corner of the building with a full dozen men in similar grab.
They peered into every nook and cranny as they passed.

She could take them down easily in a brawl—lessons

from her brothers and her master rather than Gran. But that would alert the world that she was their quarry. She needed to be gone from this smelly city soon.

The locals scuttled away, abandoning carts and packages in their haste.

One of the guards jabbed his pike into a lump of discarded cloth in the middle of the open sewer that ran down the center of the street. He lifted the cloth slightly and threw it back into the puddle, wrinkling his nose.

Roanna stepped out into the street in front of the men, as if strolling from one task to the next. They nearly bowled her over in their haste to seek a man wearing a Scottish tartan and carrying a long staff. She jumped away from them, muddying her mannish boots. *"Merde!"* she cursed, kicking some of the noisome muck from the gutter after them.

The soldiers banged on the door of the first tavern they encountered without a backward glance at her. The landlord had rooms to let above, but Roanna had vacated them early this morning. She'd left nothing behind. When the frightened serving wench opened the door a crack, the entire troop forced their way in. Denizens of the city farther along the street retreated behind closed doors and latched shutters.

When the guards were out of sight, Roanna firmly clutched the smooth rowan wood of her staff, forcing herself to breathe easily. While the locals still hid from the armed men who answered only to Queen Catherine de Médici, and the armed men questioned the inhabitants of the tavern, she sauntered toward the river and the docks.

Softly she chuckled to herself. So easy to fool the foolish. But she had no illusions that Pére Griffin Kirkwood would be tricked so easily.

"Come home soon, priest. I need you to witness the death of the Pendragon."

The Cathedral of Notre Dame de Paris the next day.

"I need you in England, Pére Griffin," Bishop Eustachius du Bellay of Paris said as he paced before the window of his office.

Helwriaeth's ears pricked upward. My heart beat faster. I could go home and claim the ring of the Pendragon! I could reconcile with Raven and Donovan.

Bishop du Bellay looked down into the courtyard of his palace, avoiding the frowning glances of his assistants sitting in the far corner. The purple buttons and piping on his *soutane* seemed to glow in the light from the long windows.

The bevy of secretaries and clerks in the corner frowned at me.

"I would happily return to my homeland, Your Grace." I bowed slightly, keeping a bland face lest I broadcast my joy at this new mission and thus jinx it. "Do you have a parish for me to minister to?"

"You have all of England to minister to," Bishop du Bellay replied succinctly.

I raised my eyebrows at that. I also instinctively looked to Helwriaeth, who sat quietly with her head on her paws. If the bishop emitted a strong emotion behind that placid mask of wisdom, my familiar would pick up on it. She lifted her head from her paws, tongue lolling in doggy laughter. She cared not for protocol and courtly politics, only that we were going home.

Then I abruptly severed my contact with Helwriaeth. This magic intruded upon the privacy of my superior. I had to be careful not to use magic until I had the ring and the dispensation from the church.

Keeping my vow to hold my magic in check had been the hardest part of my five years of study to become a priest.

Helwriaeth whined slightly and lifted her head, upset that I had broken our mental contact.

I did not look into her eyes, lest I weaken in my resolve.

"Queen Mary Tudor is dying, Pére Griffin. Protestant Elizabeth will be her heir. France needs your eyes and ears to report on everything that happens in England. Many of the faithful have turned their backs upon the church because of the extremes Mary and her husband, Philip of Spain, have allowed with the Inquisition. None of us like torture and burnings—though Mary and Philip seem to have rejoiced overmuch at the number of heretics they executed."

My vision of flame and death upon Mary's ascension to

the throne had come true. Nearly three hundred dead by the latest count.

My bishop mopped his brow with a lace-edged kerchief, then tucked it up his sleeve. He finally looked at me, and I saw some of the sorrow in his eyes.

"The misguided must be returned to the true faith, Pére Griffin. Mary and Philip have proved that torture and murder do not work on the stubborn English."

"I will do as bid, Your Grace. What will be my authority?" My attention drifted to the whispered conversation in the corner among the bishop's secretaries and assistants. I wished this conversation could have been conducted in private. But princes of the church had as little privacy as princes of the realm.

I ran the beads of my rosary through my fingers, a nervous habit I had picked up in seminary whenever my vocation or my magical talent was questioned—usually both in the same sentence. The gold decade beads of the rosary felt warm in comparison to the cool ivory of the lesser beads.

"You will have private letters that give you the authority to spy for me, and dispensation to put aside your clerical garb when necessary."

The whispers grew to a hubbub and several scowls were aimed directly at me. Helwriaeth emitted a low growl in response. Her ears remained pricked, and the tips of her pointed teeth became visible within her beard. One of the secretaries reared back as if stung.

"And publicly?" I had to keep my attention on the bishop, the man in charge, not on the bevy of underlings.

"You are a visionary, Pére Griffin. That makes many of the unimaginative churchmen is this country . . . uncomfortable." He shot a sharp glance toward the men gathered in the corner.

The underlings dropped their gazes—but did not cease their low murmuring.

"Therefore, you are officially *persona non grata* in France and thus have no reason to wear your *soutane*—if you deem it wise to put it aside—but privately you will be my spy."

"Your Grace!" a secretary rose in protest, followed by two of the other more senior assistants. "By order of the Council of Vienne two hundred years ago, all clerics must wear a cassock or *soutane* upon fear of excommunication. Besides, he is too young, untried." *Controversial*.

He didn't have to speak the last word aloud.

"Because God has granted him visions?" Bishop du Bellay lifted one bushy eyebrow in a mocking gesture. "You question God's gifts?"

"We question the authenticity of these visions." Two more men rose to join the building wall of resistance.

"Send someone more reliable, Your Grace."

"Send someone with experience in these matters." That man spoke French as if his first language had been English, and he had made several trips to England on the bishop's business.

"Like yourself, Pére Gerard?" This time both of the bishop's eyebrows rose, giving him a wide-eyed look above his beaklike nose that reminded me of the cranky old raven who perched upon the well at Kirkenwood. I almost laughed at the image. He and Grandmother Raven would make a formidable pair, God forbid they ever meet.

But too much was at stake here. These men threatened my career, questioned my very vocation.

A great trembling began in my knees and spread rapidly to my gut. A darkness crowded my vision.

"Not now," I whispered. "I need my wits about me *now*."

Helwriaeth slunk over to my side, pressing herself hard against my thigh. Her solid weight anchored me a little. But the swirling blackness around my sight increased.

During my first year at seminary I had convinced my superiors that these episodes were epileptic fits and I needed the dog to bring me back. But then one fateful day I had babbled while still entranced. The truth became known. My confessor had almost ordered Helwriaeth killed, but my friends convinced him I still needed the dog to guide me through the God-given visions.

Now I needed her to help sniff out the demon that Raven fought against.

"See, even now his familiar seeks him out. This man is a magician, not a priest." The secretary pointed an accusing finger at Helwriaeth. She growled at him.

"I am a priest. I honor my vows," I ground out between clenched teeth.

"Then get rid of the dog." The secretary approached me.

Helwriaeth snapped at him. He jerked away.

"Gentlemen!" The bishop called us all to order. "You will *obey* me in this. All of you."

"We insist that our objections be noted, Your Grace." The secretary stood his ground between me and the bishop.

I dropped to my knees and held my hands up in prayer. The act gave me a measure of control over the vision crowding my sight.

"Pére Griffin?" Bishop du Bellay asked, peering around his secretary. "Do you ail?"

"The . . . English . . . will . . . kill . . . Marie." Peals of mad laughter followed my words. Storms and waves and blood washed over me again. Marie led a growing line of men toward the gallows. She placed nooses about all their necks, including her own.

I had to go home. Now.

Chapter 4

Autumnal Equinox 1558. Early afternoon. The woods beside the kirk of Kirkenwood Grange, northern England.

DONOVAN Kirkwood, Baron of Kirkenwood these past two years, listened to the shrill barking of a squirrel high in a nearby oak tree. He rested his back against the smooth bark of an ancient sycamore.

"Concentrate on your breathing, Donovan," Grandmother Raven commanded him. "Forget the squirrel. He protests your presence because you do not belong here. You must make him believe he is wrong. Breathe!" She pounded her staff against the turf. The black crystal atop it refracted the afternoon sunshine into an arcing prism.

Donovan drew air deep into his lungs, letting it fill his body before releasing. He counted the time it took to empty his system. Seven heartbeats. Too long. But it felt so good to expel the used-up air he couldn't do it on Raven's count of three. He felt lighter.

"Breathe!" Raven commanded again. The white streak in her dark hair had spread to frost all of her thick mane. She had aged dramatically since Griffin had deserted the family, betrayed his responsibility to his heritage. In her frustration she appeared decades older than her true age.

Donovan lost all trace of his concentration with a sudden fear that his beloved grandmother could ever succumb to old age.

"On my count since you can't manage on your own," Raven commanded. "Now inhale, one, two, three, hold, two, three, release, two, three."

Donovan tried to comply. Three counts wasn't enough to either breathe in or breathe out.

"I am not a child, Raven," he protested and opened his eyes. "I can breathe on my own."

"How can you expect to control the forces of nature if you cannot control your own breath?" Raven rose clumsily, leaning heavily on her familiar and her staff. Once straightened, she loomed over him, tall and proud. She had inherited Kirkenwood from her father, passing the title to her eldest son and then her grandson. No man in the north was her superior, few her equal.

And she hated being called Grandmother or Nanna. Even Da had called her Raven rather than Mother or Mama.

Newynog, her wolfhound familiar, lurched to her feet as well. She favored one hind leg due to joint disease. Had old age caught up with them both?

Donovan rose to his feet in one smooth motion, uncrossing his legs as his balance shifted. Raven had taught him this graceful maneuver easily. Balancing his body was one thing. Controlling magic another. He hadn't yet earned a wolfhound familiar as Raven and Griffin had.

God's Wounds! but Griffin should have stayed. He had sacrificed everything in order to become a priest. Why? What was so important about a little education and an ordination ritual that Raven could not confer something similar—or better—upon him?

"Five years I've tried to teach you. Five years! And you have regressed. When Griffin was here to guide you, you controlled your breathing, you could combine chants and burning herbs to produce partial spells. Without your twin you are useless." Raven pounded her staff into the earth.

Donovan thought he felt the ground tremble in sympathetic vibration running through his bare feet.

"I'm sorry, Raven. I'll try again." Anger burned deep within him. He didn't need Griffin. Griffin had betrayed the family. Now Donovan held it together. Griffin had best not come home. Donovan wouldn't allow him to disrupt life at Kirkenwood with his faith and his power.

Donovan fought to control his anger, sinking again into his cross-legged pose, hands resting on his knees, palms turned up. He took a deep breath on three counts, held it three, and released it on another three.

He opened his eyes, wanting to share his triumph with his teacher.

"Too little, too late, Donovan. You can't repeat it two breaths in a row. Perhaps, if I inscribe a smaller circle and isolate you from the world, you can concentrate." She dug the tip of her staff into the turf and began walking a circle around him and his tree.

"Perhaps you could mix a potion that will release my talent?" Donovan asked hopefully. He knew that if he ever tapped his abilities once, he'd be able to find them again. He had had some success with potions.

"An artificial solution at best. You'd grow dependent upon the drugs before you learned anything of import. I wish Griffin had come home when I called him. He broke that promise as he broke all of his previous ones." She sighed heavily, as if she could not draw enough air or expel it. "I'll have to concentrate my energies in training Meg to follow me as Pendragon." She drooped, looking suddenly smaller, less formidable in her old age.

They both stilled at the portent of her words. Meg had never recovered after the Scottish raid five years ago. Her mind had found solace in the past, she still spoke and acted as a five-year-old. The healing magic she had once commanded with ease had turned into parlor tricks to delight her childish mind: flames at the end of her finger, communing with the numerous kitchen cats, predicting the fall of dice. Nothing more useful.

Though she did claim that Griffin spoke to her in his dreams.

If my twin can reach across the miles to speak with Meg, why can't he call me as well!

"We both know that Meg cannot manage the responsibilities of the Pendragon," he said quietly, swallowing his disappointment.

"She can attract a familiar." Raven stroked Newynog's ears with affection. "There was another female pup in the same litter as Helwriaeth. She is not yet too old to breed and keep the line of wolfhounds continuous. The familiar might heal Meg's mind."

Newynog looked up at Raven with adoring eyes and a wide grin.

Donovan offered his hand to add his caresses. Newynog

ignored him. The dogs all ignored him, even the hunting and breeding stock they did not sell to nobility throughout Europe.

"There is more to being the Pendragon than possession of a wolfhound. The Pendragon must command magic, the familiar is only an enhancer and a conduit of that power." Raven pounded her staff again. "Without the magic . . ."

"You and I have the knowledge, Raven. You have taught me well. I know the how and why. I just can't do. I can pass that knowledge on to the next generation and the next if you but name me your heir."

Raven turned her back on him and stalked through the underbrush toward the lake beside the kirk at the base of the cliff. The ferns and shrubs seemed to part for her, making a path where none existed.

She had chosen this location for their studies in direct defiance of the church laws and the Spanish priest who sought reasons to denounce her. Queen Bloody Mary Tudor had sent the Spaniard as a spy for the Inquisition after Raven had contacted her with information about the Pendragon. Mary had rejected Raven's overtures. Undoubtedly, Mary had not kept the information secret. She would have told her Spanish confessor and her Spanish husband. The Spanish Inquisition now wanted to put an end to the rumors of a new Merlin.

In five years, Raven had yet to be caught or accused of anything more dire than a knowledge of herbs for medicinal uses. She had known Father Manuel for what he was and not been lulled by his platitudes of benevolence.

"Knowledge and theory are not enough." Raven continued pounding her staff into the ground, as if she needed its support for every step. "I wish Griffin would come home," she sighed, leaning heavily upon the tall shaft of oak topped by a black crystal as big as a man's fist.

"So do I, Raven. I miss him terribly some days. Other days I hate him for betraying the family, for betraying England. He's a priest, attached to the court of the Queen of Scots in France. He is our enemy now."

"I am surprised that Newynog gave him one of her pups. She would know if he were capable of betrayal. Our wolfhounds have a greater instinct for the truth of someone's heart than we mere mortals."

Donovan still burned with jealousy every time he remembered the morning he and his twin had awakened to find Newynog staring at them. She clutched one of her newly-weaned pups by the scruff of the neck. Those massive jaws could break a man's bones with one bite, or rip out the throat of a wolf. Yet she managed the squirming morsel of fur with great gentleness.

When both boys had come fully awake, Newynog placed her baby on Griffin's chest, licked it once, and departed. The message was clear, Griffin had been chosen to succeed Raven as the Pendragon. The dogs always knew and bestowed a puppy from their last litter upon the successor.

That Raven and Newynog had lived another six years amazed everyone—but Newynog had not bred again. Donovan expected every morning to wake and find his beloved mentor had died in her sleep.

And still she stalked through Kirkenwood, pounding her staff with each step, a terror to all of the servants and Donovan's new wife, unwilling to give up until she found a successor to replace the disgraced Griffin.

"Perhaps your next son," Raven said on a huge sigh. "Peregrine and Gaspar, your bastard boys show no sign of talent, and they might be Griffin's get. I'll have none of him following in my footsteps. He did not come home when he promised."

"My son is not yet born."

"Within the month. I'll know if he has magic the moment he is born. If he does have magic, then I can pass in peace. If not, I'll have to endure this weary life a little longer."

Raven's steps took her within yards of the kirk. Donovan searched the area for signs that either of the two priests assigned to Kirkenwood might be eavesdropping. Since Mary Tudor had come to the throne shortly after Griffin left England, the Catholic priests were everywhere, spying on everything and everyone. Their Inquisition had followed hot on the heels of Mary's husband from Spain. No one—literally no one—was safe from their prying, their suspicion, their innuendo, and their greed. The Inquisitors were not above inventing charges and evidence if they felt threatened or if their chosen victim possessed land or money that the church would seize.

However, they seemed to want true proof that Raven was the Pendragon before denouncing her.

Raven defied them at every turn. Still they hesitated to act against her.

Donovan, and his father before him, remained safe from the burnings by attending Mass every day and diligently keeping their section of the border safe from raiding Scots—notorious Protestants and, therefore, minions of Satan. The French would have a hard time invading England through Scotland on Donovan's section of the border.

Queen Mary Tudor couldn't die soon enough and make room for Princess Elizabeth who would surely support the Protestant cause and banish the priests.

"Raven, mind your words. Even talking about magic is dangerous, let alone admitting you have it," he hissed at her, as much to quiet her heretical words as his treasonous thoughts.

"I'll mind my words when I face the Goddess upon my death. Till then I speak my mind. That's another reason you'll never truly be the Pendragon, Donovan. You are a coward." She pounded her staff into the ground again to punctuate each word. "No true Pendragon has ever bowed to the authority of any church." Her eyes blazed. Her strong hand spasmed around the staff.

And then she collapsed at the edge of the pool. The water seemed to reach out to enfold her.

"Raven!" Donovan raced to her side. Gently he cradled her head in his lap. "Breathe, Raven. Breathe in one, two, three, breathe out, one, two, three. Just like you taught me. Raven, breathe." A tight band of pressure and pain seemed to encircle his chest. He forced himself to breathe on the same rhythm he dictated to his grandmother.

Paris and points west, late Summer 1558.

I left France as soon as I could, delayed by many senior clergy and royal ministers who opposed both me and my mission. I needed to go home. Raven needed me. But I had vowed obedience to God, and the princes of His church kept me in Paris much longer than I desired.

Raven had not contacted me in my dreams again, and I had not been able to find her with my mind. I would not use a scrying spell until I had the ring of the Pendragon and dispensation from my church to work magic.

My ship anchored unquestioned in the harbor of Leith outside Edinburgh. French ships met too much suspicion in England for me to disembark there unchallenged. Scotland, even though largely Protestant, still honored their alliance with France. From there, it was a simple matter of buying a horse and riding across the border at one of the wild unguarded places between castle keeps. I knew the secret pathways well from my youth. We had raided the Scots as easily as they had raided us.

I still spent hours on my knees repenting the wild escapades of my youth. How many men had I killed before my eighteenth birthday? I couldn't remember and regretted each and every one of them.

That last time my full empathic talent forced me to share the deaths I had caused. That time I had known the true consequences of my actions.

If I had remained at Kirkenwood, I would have been forced to continue the life of a warrior, killing even more men, dying a bit more with the passing of each life in battle. Only as a priest of the church could I rightfully seek a life of peace upon the border.

"Every action returns to you threefold," Raven had warned me time and again.

Now I believed her.

Though I had severed my ties to home, the place drew me as my first refuge. Time and distance had weakened my connection to Donovan but not my regret at the distance that separated us. My first year in France he had written me every month, alternately begging and demanding that I return home and claim the heritage of the Pendragon. Many times I had been tempted to give up my new vocation for the old. Memory of the awesome vision of a sword of power, three crowns, and a circle of fiery pillars kept me in France, lonely but determined. I tried again and again

to explain my position to my twin. He did not want to
understand.

The rift between us grew wider with every letter until
we no longer tried to repair our relationship and ceased
writing.

Tired and dusty, I arrived at the circle of standing stones
below Kirkenwood in midafternoon on the day of the Equinox. I dismounted outside the barrier of stones and the
village they protected. Many of the houses incorporated
fallen stones into the walls of their homes. The circle was
as much a part of their everyday life as breathing. So, too,
was the magic the stones harbored and symbolized.

Apprehension rode heavy on my shoulders. This place had
been old long before the Romans came to Britain. Old, long
before my family began to keep records. It reeked of pagan
gods and ancient magics alien to my vocation as a priest.

Yet I must cross this barrier to enter Kirkenwood. Five
years ago, I had welcomed the tingle of power deep within
my bones whenever I touched one of the stones. I had
looked eagerly for the faces hidden within the whorls of
granite. Today I feared those unsubtle reminders that I had
nearly lost them all.

I'd get them back when I had Raven's ring and dispensation to work magic.

Helwriaeth dashed into the center of the circle barking
her eager return. A few village women poked their heads
out of their doors to see who disturbed their day—the men
were mostly in the fields surrounding the village and tor of
Kirkenwood. Bernard, the village reeve and blacksmith put
down his hammer and approached me with his characteristic plodding but deliberate walk.

"So ye've come back," he said succinctly. Slight changes
in my appearance and my sober clothing must have alerted
him that I was not Donovan, laird of the castle.

"Aye," I replied, eyeing the stones. I still hadn't stepped
within their circle of protection. Their solidity reminded me
of the pillars of fire of my vision. A reminder only, not an
echo of portent that something momentous would occur here.

"Reckon on staying long?" Bernard wiped his sooty
hands on his leather apron. He spread his legs and stood
between the two easternmost stones, guarding the gateway.

"I don't know. I've come to make peace with Raven and to breed my dog."

"Then you'd best get down to the kirk. She and yer brother are in the woods some'eres nearby." He stepped aside. The most invitation I'd likely receive from him. I wasn't barred from the village, but I wasn't truly welcome either.

Because I was a priest? Or because I had renounced my claim—and my responsibilities—to Kirkenwood?

One deep breath and then another and I finally had the courage to take that last step into the stone circle. Careful not to actually touch the stones I followed Bernard onto the village green. No power teased my senses. Breathing easier, I stared lovingly at the stones. Perhaps I had mastered my yearning to work magic and the stones no longer spoke to me.

Slowly I turned a circle, counting each of the sixty stones that remained standing. Another forty had fallen, some of those broken up. I knew from old that the diameter of the circle was almost a mile. Outside the stones a formal ditch encircled them. The village had grown in the past century, filling in the green, but leaving the tallest stone at the exact center within a sacred clear space. I'd never known anyone but Raven and myself, and perhaps Meg before the Scottish raid had destroyed her mind, to approach that center stone. Everyone else nodded slightly to it before giving it a wide berth.

Deep within the patterns of color in the granite on the perimeter, I picked out the images of faces. Legend claimed that the spirit of King Arthur Pendragon of antiquity inhabited the stone that faced due east. I vaguely saw the outlines of a face there. My imagination had to work harder than usual to find it. In the stone facing west, the old magician Merlin seemed to have left that stone. A raven croaked as it flew past. I looked up. My gaze lingered on the tops of the stones. Empty. Slowly, I turned another circle, inspecting each stone from bottom to top. A faint ring of magical fire, in Raven's signature color of red, should have lit and connected them with radiating lines from the center stone to the cardinal directions.

Empty.

"Raven!" I screamed in alarm and dashed through the village, into the woods. I followed the familiar path across the ditch and downhill, around the tor to the bottom of the steep cliff, unheeding of overgrowth and tree roots that tried to trip me. My breath came in short painful gasps. "Raven!" I cried again.

I saw Donovan and our grandmother at the edge of the pool. A dark-skinned man hovered in the shadows of the church's porch. I ignored him. Raven's limp figure, Donovan cradling her head in his lap, confirmed my worst fears. 'Twas Raven's personality and power that lit the stones and kept their protection of the village active. 'Twas she who bound us all together.

"Give the ring of the Pendragon to your unborn son," she gasped to Donovan. "I choose your son to follow me." She opened her eyes wide one last time and her spirit passed beyond, leaving her body an insubstantial husk, minus the personality that had given it grandeur and grace.

Newynog lay down beside her and howled her loss.

Donovan wept.

A wisp of light rose above her frail body, hovered for a moment and drifted across the lake.

A great hole opened in my heart. Raven. My connection to the past, my anchor in the present, and my hope for a future had rested on her proud shoulders for many years. And now she was gone.

Just gone. No violent death throes. No great speeches. Just gone. Bequeathing the ring of the Pendragon, my heritage—my salvation—to my brother's unborn son.

Without the ancient responsibilities that bound us to the earth and sought the protection of all England, keeping out invaders and raising up the strongest monarch, I had no excuse for the magic within me. I had no reason to fling the power building within me at my enemies—at England's enemies. The church would never give me dispensation to use that magic without the ring.

"No!" I whispered. "Raven, you can't." Tears flowed down my cheeks unchecked. I fell to my knees, deflated and alone.

Automatically I reached for my rosary and began reciting prayers for the dead.

"Heretic!" the small man by the church said with avid gloating. His Spanish accent thickened the words, making them seem more menacing. "Magician, I condemn thee to death." He pointed an accusing finger straight at my heart.

Chapter 5

The kirk of Kirkenwood, Autumnal Equinox 1558.

A SWIFT flash of something burning and bright stabbed Donovan's mind. He broke away from his all-encompassing grief and looked up.

"Heretic! Magician!"

Donovan looked around for the source of the accusation.

Father Manuel screamed all of his wrath and contempt for Donovan and Raven. His voice echoed across the water, amplified and seemed to climb the escarpment to the keep atop the tor.

Donovan cringed, knowing he must face his accuser with the truth. With Raven's passing, he could no longer hide behind a mask of acceptance of the Roman Church. He had to face what he truly believed and acknowledge it.

Fear and confusion turned his knees to water. What did he truly believe? Could he put all of Kirkenwood at risk by giving voice to vague thoughts?

Father Manuel flapped his arms, alternately pointing at him and then invoking his deity to send forth lightning to smite him. His black robes, cut to the Jesuit Order, crossed over at the front and bound by a long sash, made him appear larger than his slight frame. His wrath lent his swarthy face color. He almost seemed to lift himself off the ground and fly forward rather than walk as any normal mortal would.

Before Donovan could react, a menacing growl sounded directly behind him. Then a huge ball of brindled fur bounded past him. Father Manuel recoiled an instant before the wolfhound knocked him flat, landing with front paws in the middle of the priest's chest. It growled again and bared its teeth, aiming for the man's throat.

Briefly, Donovan wondered which of the hounds had broken free of its kennel or handler to come to his rescue. Raven's Newynog lay beside her limp body, quietly mourning in her own way, oblivious to the threat from the priest.

"Get it off me! Witchbeast!" Father Manuel screamed, twisting and flailing under the dog's weight.

"Helwriaeth, hold."

"Helwriaeth?" No dog in the Kirkwood kennels had that name. None since . . . since . . . "Griffin?" Donovan eased away from Raven's limp body to rise and face his twin. "Griffin," he stated again flatly. A curious numbness settled over him like a cold blanket. Responsibility lifted its heavy weight from his shoulders. Griffin would tell him what to do—as he had always done.

Then his mind burned once more with five years of pain and loneliness. He'd never welcome his twin at Kirkenwood.

"Who are you, Priest, that you dare accuse the laird's family without evidence?" Griffin's voice boomed across the water of the nearby lake, overcoming the remnants of Father Manuel's echoing accusation. Had Griffin used his magic to augment his aura of authority? And why did he not wear the ordinary cassock of a priest?

Donovan's brother had come home to steal the lands, titles, and heritage of the Pendragon from Donovan's grasp. He'd timed his arrival so that Raven could not oppose him. No one could stop a man of Griffin's power.

Jealousy burned deep within Donovan. He was the laird. He had stayed home to nurture the land and the people of Kirkwood. The magic should have been his as well as the position of Pendragon! He fingered the signet ring in his pocket that Raven had given him in trust for his unborn son. Almost he slipped it onto his finger. Almost.

He couldn't betray Raven's trust. Griffin had betrayed the family enough for both of them.

"Father in Heaven, protect my soul from these unholy witches," Father Manuel prayed, eyes closed. His hands clawed the earth.

Helwriaeth growled again. No one moved.

"Get this beast off me!"

"When you tell me what prompted you to make these

vile accusations," Griffin growled in much the same tone as his dog.

"I heard the old witch. I heard her invoke Satan with her dying breath. And she passed her cursed legacy to this one!" The priest's eyes crossed as he finally focused on Donovan and Griffin, then they widened in horror as he confronted the reality of their identical faces.

Donovan wanted to giggle. He and Griffin had played many wonderful pranks as children, confusing the adults who easily mistook one twin for the other. Only Raven could tell them apart when they chose deception. Even then she had to take a few moments of study to be sure of their identities.

But then he and Griffin had barely been aware that they were different people, had different goals, dreams, and life paths.

He sobered instantly. The Spaniard would see their likeness as more evidence of witchcraft. He'd do his best to send the entire clan to the stake. Kirkenwood would be forfeit to the church and the crown. This vulnerable stretch of the border would become unguarded. The Scots and their French allies could walk across.

The French. Griffin had spent the last five years in France becoming a priest. Was he friend or enemy to England? Donovan already knew him to be an enemy of the family.

"Liar," Griffin growled at the priest, sounding very much like his dog. Helwriaeth opened her massive jaws, drooling onto the priest's throat, right where she obviously wanted to clamp her teeth.

"I am a priest of the Society of Jesus, a warrior for Christ. I cannot lie."

"Liar," Donovan and Griffin said together.

"I heard her," Father Manuel protested. "She gave you the ring of the Pendragon. She made you the Pendragon!"

"Liar," Donovan said again.

"Nigh on five years you've waited for this moment, Spanish dog," Griffin growled. He must have read the priest's mind.

"And when he could not gather evidence against us, he manufactured his own," Donovan concluded his brother's statement.

"My words will be heard by my superiors in the church!" Father Manuel screeched.

"So will mine," Griffin added.

"You will have to gather an army to bring us down, Spaniard." Donovan placed himself at Manuel's head, forcing the man to strain his neck to look at him. "Think you that you can gather enough Spanish cannon to breach the walls of Kirkenwood? Think you that you can bring back your hated Jesuits to condemn us *before* Queen Mary dies and Protestant Elizabeth takes the throne?"

"You will have to act quickly, foreigner," Griffin took up the litany. "Once Queen Mary joins our Savior in Heaven, none of your kind will be welcome in England. Cardinal de Guise in France will be very interested in the lengths the Jesuits are prepared to go to impose their fanaticism over the entire church, and not just to reclaim those lost to the Protestant Reformation."

"Cardinal . . . Cardinal de Guise, uncle to Marie Queen of Scots?" Manuel's accent thickened.

Griffin merely nodded.

Donovan could almost see the foreign priest's mind spinning. His jaw trembled. At the sound of his own teeth chattering he clamped them tight.

"Helwriaeth, off," Griffin commanded. The dog looked to her master as if reluctant to obey. "I said 'off,' Helwriaeth."

Slowly the animal removed her paws and weight from Manuel's chest. The priest took one deep breath in relief until he realized the dog's mouth remained dangerously close to his throat.

"You cannot threaten a priest of the Holy Order of . . ."

"You cannot fling groundless accusations about," Donovan said. "As laird of Kirkenwood I could bring you to trial, Spaniard. But I won't—yet. Leave us to grieve the passing of our beloved grandmother. If you are still within the borders of my lands by the time we bury her with our ancestors, you will be brought to trial."

"You have no authority over me, witch."

"Perhaps. Perhaps not." Griffin tucked his hands into the sleeves of his doublet in imitation of the posture used by Father Peter, the family priest who had been pushed aside by the Spaniard.

"Who are you, twin of the witch? Everyone knows that one of a set of twins is a demon in a human body."

Griffin flinched at the statement. Donovan almost felt a moment of sympathy. But that passed as quickly as a burning arrow across his mind.

"That is a myth created by witch hunters who need excuses to burn an enemy," Griffin snorted.

Donovan cringed this time. He'd heard the same legend all his life.

"And you do not need to know who I am or from whom I derive my authority." Griffin withdrew his left hand from his sleeve and passed it in an arcane gesture Donovan did not recognize before making a cross of benediction over Manuel.

The Spaniard's eyes opened wide and he hastened to cross himself with his right hand. His left reached for the rosary at his belt.

What secret brotherhood had Griffin joined during these last five, silent years?

"I want this man gone from my land," Donovan said, not quite sure if he meant the foreign priest or this brother he no longer knew.

"You can't evict him. He is responsible only to the Pope. 'Tis the law," Griffin replied sternly. He turned his attention away from their captive. "We do not have the right to punish or restrain him, merely to refute his accusations with hard evidence in a trial presided over by priests."

"No man should be above the law, and 'tis wrong to falsely accuse another."

"You are a witch!" Manual insisted. "I heard the old witch bequeath her pact with Satan to you and your son,"

Donovan bit his cheeks at the irony of the accusation. "I have no magic, foreigner. Tell him, Griffin, that I have no magic, never have and probably never will. Your accusations are false, Spanish dog. I'll have your tongue for them. That is the law."

"By Queen Mary's laws, and the laws of the church, the accusation demands a trial," Griffin said.

For the first time, Donovan sensed fear in his twin.

"I'll not stand trial on the basis of this man's lies." A physical trial. The Spaniard would bind his arms close to his body with stout ropes and throw him into this pool. If he drowned, he'd be proclaimed innocent. If he floated and survived, they'd drag him to the stake and burn him. Either way, he'd die and the Jesuits would gain control of Kirkenwood. Who would protect Kate and the baby then?

"There is a way to prove my brother's innocence without a public trial, without automatic forfeit of his life. A trial will only humiliate the Jesuits when their vigilance looks like irrational fanaticism," I said. My mind focused clearly on the rosary still in Father Manuel's hands. All the light around the lake seemed to home in on the intricate silver crucifix dangling from the ornate beads of silver and ebony. A loud hum in the back of my mind drowned out all other thoughts but the prayers I needed to recite upon my own rosary.

"Fire or water is the only proof of innocence from the taint of Satan." Father Manuel spat out Helwriaeth's drool.

"Heel," I commanded my dog.

She looked at me with a puzzled expression as if she asked, "Who, me?"

I snapped my fingers impatiently and sharply gestured her to my left side. With one last growl and show of teeth, Helwriaeth trotted to stand where I commanded.

Father Manuel scooted back and up in a crablike motion that sent his robes askew and exposed his skinny legs. Not for him the rough sandals of a mendicant monk. He wore very expensive black cordovan leather boots.

"Kiss the priest's rosary, Donovan," I said quietly when the Spaniard had reached his feet.

"I won't touch anything this Spanish dog possesses," Donovan snarled.

"Just do it, Donovan. Refusal only reinforces his accusation." I let loose a long sigh. "Why must you always be so stubborn?"

"No more stubborn than you. If I must kiss a rosary, I'd rather kiss yours." Donovan caught my gaze. For a moment we shared the image of the ancient family keepsake that had belonged to King Arthur Pendragon.

I pulled the gold-and-ivory artifact from my belt pouch. Da had replaced the beads ten years ago when he gave it to me, acknowledging me as heir to Kirkenwood. I'd kept it when I relinquished my claims on the lands and titles for a vocation in the church.

"I do not trust a rosary you carry, twin of the witch," Father Manuel said quietly. He stared longingly at the gold and ivory glinting in the afternoon sunshine. His fingers made grasping motions. "I have no proof that it has been properly blessed. Satan may have corrupted it."

I made certain the golden Celtic cross remained firmly in my palm. This fanatic might decide that anything but a Spanish crucifix on a rosary was tainted.

"This is ridiculous," Donovan sighed.

"I agree. But it must be done, brother. Kiss his rosary and be done with it. The blessed cross will burn anyone who has made a pact with Satan."

"I do not trust the Spaniard's rosary to be free of that taint," Donovan insisted. "I will kneel at the altar of the church and kiss the reliquary there if you insist, but I will not touch *his* rosary."

"Very well. Will you accept this act of faith, Father Manuel?"

He nodded, still eyeing my rosary with greed. I shifted my grip on the precious prayer beads so that the cross dangled, swinging slightly. He fixed his gaze upon it as if enthralled.

Did he know the origins of this particular artifact? If he did, then it, as well as the destruction of the Pendragon, might very well be part of his quest.

Donovan stomped into the stone church that backed up against the cliffs. Its foundations remained dry, stabilized by bedrock. The spring-fed lake kept a constant level summer and winter, never encroaching farther upon the land.

The hum in the back of my mind intensified. I recognized it as otherworldly in origin. Instinctively I clamped down on it, forcing it out of me, as I did all magic.

At the porch Donovan turned to look out across the lake. He must sense the presence as did I.

"Raven," he said.

"I'll carry her inside. You and Father Manuel finish your business."

My hands and belly shook with trepidation as I approached the lakeside and my grandmother's body. The hum intensified, became music.

Rather than look across the water, I composed Raven's limbs into a resemblance of peace and closed her eyes. Briefly, grief replaced my awareness of whomever—or whatever—inhabited the water that had been sacred long before Christians came to Britain.

Raven filled every memory I had of home. Raven twirling her staff in a complex ritual before slamming the crystal end into the face of a raider. Raven chortling with joy as she baptized her granddaughter in a free-flowing creek. Raven communing with the cranky old bird that always perched upon the well of Kirkenwood, making it move out of the way for her when it pecked anyone else who tried to draw water. Raven gathering Donovan and me into her arms, letting us cry, crying herself in helplessness, as we watched my mother die. Raven leading the Mayday festivities, dancing around the flower-crowned pole in only her shift.

A tear touched my eye. Grief filled my throat.

"Why, Raven? Why did you give up on me and bequeath the ring to Donovan's unborn son?"

As I lifted her frail body in my arms, a dozen brightly colored sparks danced before my eyes. I blinked away the tears that nearly blinded me. The sparks remained.

"Not now," I whispered. "Why now?" For these were no ordinary insects.

Look! a dozen voices proclaimed.

Ripples spread across the lake from the center. The incessant hum grew into a dozen awed voices joined in song. The singing grew louder, bouncing off the water and the cliffs. Light concentrated on a shimmering form beneath the water.

I clutched Raven's body closer against my chest, almost as a talisman against . . .

"Jesus, give me strength to fight this temptation. Lead me along the right path. Without the ring I have only You to help me fight the evil Raven saw coming." Deliberately I stepped away from the lake. Three steps and then five. Two dozen paces more and I climbed the three steps to the porch of the kirk.

Only then did I pause to look back at the phenomenon within the lake.

A lady rose from the water clasping a magnificent sword—the weapon of my visions—against her breasts. Runes of fire rippled along the blade. Bright jewels in the hilt beckoned me to take Excalibur, make it my own, use it to fight against the forces of chaos that threatened Britain.

"I'm sorry, Lady. I am now a man of peace. I must fight my battles with prayer and words, without magic."

Sadly I bowed my head, hiding my tears of regret from my brother and the all-too-observant priest within.

They knelt before the altar, unaware of the miracle I had rejected.

Chapter 6

The forest beside the kirk of Kirkenwood Tor, two days later.

"RAVEN deserved a funeral pyre," Donovan whispered to me as he threw a handful of dirt atop her shrouded body. "At least they did not trap her spirit in a stone coffin or within one of the caves behind the church. She'd want her body to feed the earth."

I should have been appalled that my twin would suggest a pagan fire. Church fathers had decided long ago that Christians must be buried with their bodies intact so that they could enter Heaven. I cared not how we put her to rest. I knew her spirit soared free of the pain and worry and duty that had chained her to this life.

Regret became a deep ache in my gut. Regret that I had come too late to minister to Raven in her last moments and to make peace with her. Why had she bypassed me as the next Pendragon, taking the risk of passing her authority to an unborn child? She had called me home, and I came. Why had she rejected me?

You obeyed the church rather than me!

Was that Raven's voice reprimanding me from the grave? The amount of hurt she conveyed in those few words stabbed me deeply.

"We have not burned our dead since the time of King Arthur," I said to Donovan, putting aside the voice in my imagination. I knew Raven would have wanted cremation rather than burial. But some demon deep within me kept me from offering even the semblance of agreement with my twin.

Why had such restraint come between us? If only I could . . .

His harsh expression and a lightning flash of resentment across my mind kept me quiet.

"We need to defy custom once more and give Raven what she wanted, what she believed." Donovan wrapped his fist around his short sword—more a piece of ceremonial regalia than a weapon—as if he could slay custom as he would a Scottish raider.

Raven had not believed as I did. Her faith had always centered around a loving Goddess and maintaining a balance between people and the forces of nature. She had never bowed her head in prayer. Rather she had faced the four elements and the four cardinal directions as an equal partner.

Would she have accepted last rites if I had arrived in time? Would she ever have accepted my decision to take religious orders? My dreams told me desperation had driven her to accept my decision. Desperation to contain the Demon of Chaos.

Father Peter intoned a final prayer as each member of the family added a handful of dirt atop the coffin. Father Manuel had conveniently absented himself from the funeral, but not from the barony. The Spaniard did not deem Raven worthy of his God.

I had wanted to assist during the sacred rite, but my orders from my bishop kept me in disguise as a layman.

God has many names. She answers to all of them. Raven's voice whispered deep into my mind, devoid of the hurt and resentment I had heard earlier. Was either voice real, or were they both spawned by my own guilt and need to reconcile with my grandmother?

"Mon Dieu!" I breathed and reached for Helwriaeth. She leaned into me, concerned only with the uncertainty in me. No spirit from beyond troubled her.

Donovan did not look up from his silent contemplation of Raven's grave.

I glanced at each of the family members who lingered around the open hole in the earth. None of them looked as if they had heard the otherworldly communication.

"Just my imagination. Certainly God has many names, every language pronounces the word differently. They all refer to the same God," I said under my breath, needing to reassure myself with words.

"The crypt beneath the church is full," Donovan continued. "This small burial plot is crowded as well. The time has come to start a new tradition and commit our dead to the funeral pyre."

The family had started a cemetery in the woods between the kirk and the village in the last century. They'd cleared a circle amongst the towering trees. The huge pillars of timeless life reminded me briefly of my vision of crowns and swords and pillars of fire.

Life is a circle. Out of death comes life. All life must die. Look to the circles for guidance.

I reeled a moment under the impact of Raven's words. Vision teased the edges of my mind, the voice of the Lady of the Lake rose in a triumphant hymn.

I wove my fingers through Helwriaeth's ruff in an effort to ward off the vision.

For a brief moment, I saw the entire forest cleared, the village spread beyond the confines of the circle of standing stones right up to the lake, strangers in stranger garb wandering among the stones with casual disrespect, the keep abandoned . . .

My knees buckled. I gripped Helwriaeth's ruff until she whimpered. The knuckles of my other hand whitened where I clenched my missal.

"Griff?" Donovan clutched my elbow. The sharp pressure of his fingers digging into my upper arm brought me back to my own time and place.

"Nothing." I shook myself free of the vision, grateful that I knew I would not live to see the transformation.

My twin removed his hand too quickly, as if he regretted his instinctive concern for me. For two days he and I had edged around each other, polite, cautious, neither one of us willing to bridge the distance five years of separation had put between us. Every time we came close to polite conversation, bitter invective replaced the words of reconciliation I hoped to say.

Father Peter opened his arms wide, symbolically embracing the mourners and the deceased. "Go in peace to love and serve the Lord," he intoned. A beatific smile spread across his face, lifting the care of decades from his visage.

He never seemed to age or grow frail. From my earliest memories he had been a constant in life at Kirkenwood, more so than Raven. All else might change, including Raven's death, but Father Peter remained a good shepherd to all within his care.

His loving influence had probably guided me toward my true vocation within the church long before I acknowledged it that night of fire and vision. I had spent many hours of my youth talking to him, praying with him, exploring my faith with him, and finding truth within the church.

Raven's faith had not given me the peace and stillness within that I craved.

The family dispersed, sisters and their husbands, aunts, uncles, and cousins, all drawing strength from each other. They wandered back toward the keep in groups of two and three, murmuring softly, weeping, shoulders drooping. Meg drifted among them like a ghost, ignored and unwelcome in her madness. Fiona, a younger sister by Da's last wife, eventually took Meg's arm and guided her back to the keep.

"Donovan, Griffin, I would speak with you privately," Father Peter said as I finished my last prayer for Raven. He jerked his head toward the deep woodland at the other end of the lake.

"Has the Spaniard left for Carlisle yet?" I asked. I could think of only one reason why our family priest would not select the sanctity of the church for a private conversation. He did not want this conversation overheard.

"Our Spanish guest is still here," Father Peter replied. "I heard him throwing his luggage around his room before dawn. He did not seem very happy when we broke our fast this morning and he did not join me for early Mass before that." A half smile lighted his face.

"May I presume he does not anticipate success in bringing the Inquisition to Kirkenwood?" A deep thrumming in my ears kept my attention focused on the center of the lake.

"Apparently so. My bishop already has my report that Donovan proved his innocence of witchcraft when he kissed the reliquary of St. Dyfrig and did not burn or turn into a shrieking demon. The Spaniard, though, does not trust one of our own saints. He wants to repeat the ritual in Carlisle with a better known reliquary."

"Ah." I could think of no other reply while the Lady of the Lake sang to me.

My twin whistled a derisive tune under his breath.

I looked at him sharply. He avoided my gaze.

One hundred paces farther along the path, Father Peter came to an abrupt halt. He looked long and hard back across the lake where the water narrowed into a creek.

The otherworldly hymn quieted.

Regret hung heavy in my heart. I could accomplish much good in this world with a sword of power in my hand. But the power came from otherworlds, other gods. I could not wield it and remain a priest. And despite Bishop du Bellay's dispensation to maintain a guise of disgrace, I was still a priest. I still wanted to be a priest.

I needed to find answers to life's questions and solve its problems peacefully and not with violence.

"Which one of you received the ring of the Pendragon from your grandmother? There is a ritual I must perform to confirm the passage of the title," Father Peter said after a long silence.

Donovan and I studied each other for a longer moment. His bluer-than-blue eyes reflected nothing back to me. I couldn't read him, couldn't anticipate his actions or his motives. I had only the truth. The truth that remained his to tell.

At last Donovan pulled a leather thong around his neck free of his shirt. The ring suspended there caught the afternoon sun, flashing dark red shards of light at the deepest part of the lake.

Something in me sensed a stirring within the depths of the pool. The Lady awakening again? So soon? Would she offer the sword once more? Did I have the courage to reject her gift again?

I think I stepped toward the water, in anticipation.

Father Peter stopped me with a hard hand on my arm. "If your grandmother gave the ring to Donovan, she had her reasons. You cannot claim it now," he said gently.

"But she didn't give it to him. She entrusted it to him on behalf of his unborn son," I replied. The otherworldly sense of the Lady left me as abruptly as it had come.

"She couldn't have!" Father Peter gasped.

"She could and she did," Donovan insisted. "She did not trust my twin since he betrayed . . ." he hesitated, obviously unwilling to insult Father Peter. But he'd openly insulted me several times in the last two days for becoming a priest. "He betrayed her trust when he left home. And she had no luck training me to take her place. So she bequeathed our heritage to the next generation. 'Tis not unheard of."

"The responsibilities often skip generations, but never without the younger being fully trained by the older. Your son is not yet born, Donovan. Britain has no Pendragon. Britain may not have a Pendragon for many, many years to come. Our queen is dying, the transition of power may not be easy. We need a Pendragon now, as much as ever before. What are we to do?" Father Peter wrung his hands and bit his lower lip. "For over one thousand years the Kirkwoods and the Griffin clan before them have guarded secrets and worked gently and subtly to protect Britain from invasion by the forces of chaos. We eased the chaos of dynastic rivalry during the Wars of the Roses as much as possible, keeping the strongest king on the throne. Yet we could not stop the wars, could not avert the loss of faith in our mission. Now, when Elizabeth will truly need help to guide her in keeping the peace between religions, we are lost once more. What are we to do without a Pendragon?"

"Newynog and Helwriaeth chose me to succeed. Raven trained me to follow her." I could not keep the resentment out of my voice. I needed the ring to justify the presence of magic in my body and mind.

"You have not bred your wolfhound. She is six years old, possibly too old to breed. I fear the Pendragon and the line of familiars died with your grandmother," Father Peter said sadly. "What are we to do?"

"I will train my son to follow in Raven's footsteps," Donovan stated. "As she wished. The line has not died, there is merely a pause between. I am the guardian of the heritage if not the actual Pendragon."

"There is no reason why I cannot assume the role of the Pendragon now, and then pass it to one of Donovan's heirs when the time comes. The dogs chose me."

The humming in the back of my head started up again.

The lake began to ripple outward from some disturbance beneath the surface. The Lady stirred.

My magic answered her call, filling me with energy.

"But your grandmother did not give you the ring. The ring must pass directly from the hand of one Pendragon to the next. 'Tis a tradition that has not been violated in centuries," Father Peter insisted.

Wavelets lapped the edges of the lake, sending the water higher and higher against the dry land.

The power within me begged for release.

I forced it down. Without the sanction the title of the Pendragon would give me, I could not work magic. The church, my vows of obedience, were adamant that I could not work magic. 'Twas the only way to save my soul.

But time and again in previous generations Church Fathers had made exceptions for the Pendragon. I had to have the ring, undergo the ritual before I could respond to the Lady of the Lake and her mystical sword.

"Raven gave the ring in trust to my twin. We shared the same womb, we are as like to each other as two people can be. Until I was seven years old, I did not know that he and I were separate people." A note of desperation crept into my voice. The magic grew stronger along with the voice of the Lady.

Couldn't Donovan and Father Peter hear her call? Didn't they feel the allure of the sword that only she could bestow upon a Pendragon?

"Entrusting the ring to Donovan as guardian is almost the same as giving it to me," I finished.

"But she said specifically, that I must hold it in trust for my son." Donovan turned angry eyes upon me. "You betrayed her trust when you became a priest. You broke your promise to her when you failed to return after she called you home."

I flinched from the emotions roiling in him. When had he become so angry, so bitter?

At the same time I did.

"This is something that the two of you must resolve between yourselves," Father Peter said sadly. "I cannot interfere. But I will advise you both, that if Donovan's first child does not flourish or is born female, then the ring should go to Griffin."

"A daughter can become the Pendragon," Donovan insisted.

"But your grandmother said your son would follow her. In this day and age when strong women are discarded and shunned, I must believe that the responsibilities of the next Pendragon should go to a male, as should the title of Baron of Kirkenwood. We face many difficult challenges . . ."

"The villagers prepare a pagan bonfire!" Father Manuel burst through the woods, shouting.

The magic in me heightened my perceptions. I could almost see smoke curling from his ears. His aura wavered in chaotic layers of mixed colors.

"They prepare a funeral pyre for the old woman. This blasphemy must be stopped. This barony must be cleansed!"

"Raven is safely buried beside her first husband, the father of my father." I pushed the other two men aside to face Father Manuel. His fanaticism had grown tiresome. "If the villagers build a bonfire, they do it only in memory of a beloved elder."

" 'Tis a pagan ritual that must be stopped. I saw them place a shrouded body among the branches. I saw . . ."

"They burn the dog," Donovan said with humor lighting his eyes. "Raven's favorite pet could not live without her. Would you rather they buried the dog alongside the mistress in consecrated ground?" He cocked one eyebrow in a gesture I knew well from my mirror.

Father Manuel clenched his fists. His shoulders slumped, and he looked smaller, less dangerous. He had no outlet for his outrage. Something dangerous simmered beneath the surface of his emotions. "I will see you all burned at the stake for your sins." He turned on his heel and departed the same way he had come.

"I think the two of you need to settle the issue of the ring quickly. Only an acknowledged Pendragon can combat the—evil—that has come to us," Father Peter said.

The voice of the Lady of the Lake agreed with him.

Donovan glared at me and retreated toward the village bonfire, stuffing the ring back beneath his shirt.

Chapter 7

Hermitage Castle, southwest Scotland, two days after the Autumnal Equinox, 1558.

ROANNA knelt before the hearth in Lord Douglas' private solar, waiting. She had given the old man his posset of mulled wine and herbs. In a few moments the ache in his joints would ease and he would look out at the world with more cheerful, if less focused, eyes. Her potion also slowly weakened his heart, causing him more pain and promising a well-deserved long and lingering death.

His weakened heart and aching joints made him feel the cold more than ever. The thick stone walls of Hermitage Castle kept out the constant cold wind, but sunshine never warmed these rooms. He needed the fire stirred frequently. She pretended to freshen the glowing peat bricks while she waited for Laird James Douglas to fall asleep, but she truly used the time to stare deeply into the flames.

Images within the glowing coals took her back six years to the time Gran guided her through a different watching spell . . .

"Watch the flickering deep within the coals, Roanna," Gran had admonished. "Don't think of the pretty glass beads your young swain brought ye last raid. Think of the fire. 'Tis your element. Bond with it. Let it guide you over the miles."

Roanna breathed deeply, clearing her mind of the delicious games she had played with young Rabbie's cock when he brought her the string of beads. She had thanked him well. He'd bring her more treasures next time he raided across the border.

But the power she enjoyed over Rabbie—men were always slaves to their manhood—was nothing compared to the power she employed gazing into a fire. She'd been watching their enemy for two years now without Gran's help.

"I see the elder lady pacing the ramparts, watching for her men to come home," Roanna murmured. Lady Raven Kirkwood was a familiar sight in the fire images. An aura of bright red spread out from her beautiful face and flowing black hair. The element of fire, and therefore Roanna found her easily in the smoldering bricks of peat.

"And do you see the men she watches for?" Gran asked. She spun the shaft of her staff between her hands as she would a spindle. The goat skull atop the staff made a whirring noise as air passed rapidly through the nasal passages and open mouth.

The repetitive sound helped focus her vision. "I see a black-haired man, her son, and two youths with dark auburn hair, his sons, as like as two grains of barley laid side by side," Roanna said quietly, almost afraid to alert the three men to her watching. One of the twins looked up into the air, sniffing, as if alerted to her presence on the wind. He had a wolfhound pup at his heels. The dog pressed close to his side. And then the young man's midnight blue eyes seemed to lock onto her, peering deep within her soul. Roanna quickly pushed her inner sight to a different vantage point, farther away from the young man.

She couldn't withdraw entirely. The young man, perhaps two years older than herself, called to something deep within her. His gaze excited her more than Rabbie's most intimate touch.

"And can you see where the son and grandsons of Lady Raven abide?" Gran asked.

"In a forest of stone." Roanna had never ventured more than two miles from her home village. She knew this must be a city but had no way of knowing which city or how far away.

"Edinburgh. Lord Brian has taken his boys to see the regent." Gran made little whistling noises through her teeth.

"I don't think so." Roanna barely dared correct her mentor. But Gran was old and set in her ways. Her ideas were limited by her lack of knowledge of the world beyond their village and their laird. "They are English. They consider Queen Marie de Guise a foreigner, an enemy." Roanna had learned that much at least from listening to the men talk while planning a raid. "Carlisle, mayhap. To sell their wool." 'Twas early summer, the time for shearing. That seemed logical.

"A city. A full day's ride from Kirkenwood. We have time." Gran stopped spinning her staff and picked up her small pack and basket, the one she used to gather herbs and stones in the hills around their home. Roanna had done most of the gathering these last three years as part of her lessons, and to relieve her aging grandmother of the stooping and carrying.

Roanna knew all of the medicinal uses for the herbs. She'd used them often when the men returned from raids, broken and bleeding, or after the Kirkwood clan raided them. Upon occasion, Gran had dispatched men in great pain and too badly wounded to recover. Twice she had offered her knife to Roanna with the promise of great power from the act of mercy.

Always Roanna refused.

"Where are we going, Gran?" Roanna gathered her own basket and pack. Only when she hefted them did she realize Gran had already filled them: the pack with a change of clothing and food for two days' journeying; the basket with foul smelling herbs, a mortar and pestle, and three rare stones. Their destination involved an interesting spell.

She sorted through the ingredients: foxglove, tansy, a blue agate . . . "This is not a love spell," she muttered under her breath.

"Nah, I used the love spell on Raven Kirkwood's da when I came of age. But I have something greater planned for you, Roanna. Your power is beyond mine. As is your beauty. You shall have a special task."

"What?" Roanna breathed shallowly. Anticipation curled her toes and made her head light.

"We go to confront our greatest enemy, the Pendragon of Britain!" Gran chortled. "At last our line of wisewomen will be vindicated!"

They mounted sturdy ponies and rode south for many hours. Gran did not stop to gather sprigs of medicinal herbs or to trap a rabbit or grouse for their dinner. She rode forward, never looking to the side, as if she already saw the walls of Kirkenwood Castle just over the next hill.

Roanna spotted the asymmetrical pile of stones atop the tor first. 'Twas an ugly castle, built of dark stones, ancient, and brooding. Each generation had added walls and extensions, height to this tower, a gatehouse to that one. A body could easily lose herself in the labyrinth. Perhaps more than one had lost her soul in there as well.

Then she saw the standing stones, tall and straight, forming a broad circle at the base of the tor. The village sheltered within the circle. Bustling people wandered in and out of houses and stalls in the middle of the circle. They left a small open area around the tallest stone at the exact center of the stones. Market day. Many people wandering in from afar. No one would question one old crone and her granddaughter come to purchase . . .

Roanna looked to her grandmother for inspiration.

" 'Tis your rite of passage, Roanna. You make the excuses, you find the reasons to get close to your prey. 'Tisn't meant to be easy."

"Seducing the old lord would have been easy," Roanna retorted. Gran hadn't truly prepared her for this. No hints that something unusual was to happen this day. No suggestions that a rite of passage was necessary.

"Seduction is easy for one of your beauty and power, Roanna. But for me? I had to work hard to attract any man. For you? You find it hard to take a life, to make the sacrifices to maintain your power, our heritage. For hundreds of generations the women of our family have waited for this moment. Now you must find a way to bespell the ingredients I provided and give them to Raven Kirkwood in such a way that she never suspects magic saps her lifeblood and damages her heart beyond repair." Gran's voice rose in intensity and volume. Her eyes narrowed, and her withered face flushed with emotion.

Roanna wanted to back away from her vehemence. "I must kill this woman," she said around a lump in her throat.

And then the power flared within her. Stronger than the strongest ale, or even the rare sip of *usquebaugh*. She wanted that power and knew it would not come fully to her until she conquered her reluctance to take a life.

"She will linger long. She will not die in my presence. I can do this today. Then no one will be my master, not even Gran."

But Griffin Kirkwood had come to his grandmother with his overly-curious dog and interrupted the spell. She had mistaken the forest of stone of Kirkenwood's massive walls for a city. The spell had been weak. Roanna had not yet benefited from Raven's death.

The next week the Kirkwood clan had raided Roanna's village and murdered Gran. And she was forced to bow to a different master.

. . . Lord Douglas might consider himself to be her lord and master now. But he'd never know how quickly she had thrown off the shackles of his control. She acknowledged a different master in secret, pretending obedience to Douglas only so long as she needed his castle as a refuge.

Soon. Soon. The Pendragon could not live much longer. Then Roanna would be free and in control of her power. Only then.

If only she could be certain of *when!*

Images of another fire rose before her eyes. The flickering figures outlined in her flames danced to a slow and mournful tune, walking the circle deosil, along the path of the sun. Men, women, and children sang in unison, speeding a soul along its chosen path after death.

"Ah, the Pendragon has succumbed." Roanna sighed deeply, releasing years of pent-up tightness. But why had she not felt a surge of power, a sense of completeness? Her fists clenched. She forced them to relax.

Griffin Kirkwood had foiled her five years ago. Never again. She would control him as her master controlled her.

"You have witnessed the death of the Pendragon, Father Griffin. Now no one replaces her. No one! I have only to wait a little longer to avenge myself of the wrongs you heaped upon me." She wanted to leap up and dance joyously.

"Roanna, what is taking so long? I'm still cold," Douglas whined. Five years ago, when he'd taken Roanna captive, he'd been a strong and vigorous man of middle years. Now he aged and sickened by the day.

She half-smiled to herself, pleased that she aided his decline. The same spell she had used on Raven worked much more effectively on the lord.

A new figure joined the dancing people Roanna saw among the flames. Griffin Kirkwood, the man who should be the Pendragon, so different from the brother who stood beside him, and yet so alike. She needed to watch them. She needed to know how they dealt with the loss of their grandmother. She needed . . .

"Tend to my father, witch." Jamie Douglas cuffed her ear.

Roanna lost her balance and reached out with her hands to keep from falling. Her palm landed on the hearth. Heat seared through bare flesh. She jerked her hand away and fell heavily backward, banging her head on the edge of a stool, knees buckled awkwardly beneath her.

Stars rang around the edges of her vision while blackness encroached. She fought to keep her cries within her throat. A meek whimper escaped.

Where had the young laird come from? She had been so engrossed in her visions within the flames she had not heard him enter. Embarrassment sent new heat to her face. Never should she allow such a thing to happen. Control lay in awareness of all that happened around her. Control lay in anticipating the actions and reactions of her enemies.

In the back of her head, her master laughed heartily at her plight.

Control lies in manipulating the forces of chaos! he chortled.

Roanna gritted her teeth and struggled upright. "Your servants have neglected to cut and dry enough peat to build the fire higher," she said evenly. She would not give the young tyrant the satisfaction of seeing her hurt and out of control. Bad enough that the old tyrant had seen her cry and listened to her pleas for mercy the first time he raped her. He'd left her bruised and bleeding in spirit as well as body. But not broken. 'Twould take a stronger man than James Douglas to break her.

Griffin Kirkwood perhaps? Her master chortled, always

aware of her innermost thoughts and fears and ready to pounce upon them.

Never!

Laird Jamie raised his fist as if to repeat his stunning blow.

Roanna flinched in anticipation of the coming pain.

When he resorts to the chaos of violence, you are in control, her master's voice came to her clearly.

She swallowed her fear and stared at the young man in defiance.

Use the pain. Pain is power.

Jamie lowered his fist. Uncertainty flashed across his sneering visage.

In the five years Roanna had been held prisoner by this clan, she had never known anyone to defy Jamie or his father beyond the first blow. Clearly he did not know how to react.

Good.

Roanna hummed a subtly discordant tune in the back of her throat. She wove the odd notes through his confusion. Garish, clashing colors sparkled around the edges of her vision. The fire, the old laird, the room receded. She isolated Jamie and herself in a web of chaos.

His eyes took on a glazed look.

She would not falter with this spell as she had with Raven. She had grown beyond that stumbling hesitation that weakened the spell and her power.

"Your father is old and ill. You truly rule this castle, Jamie. You rule your clan, this march of the border. As long as your father lives, you will never be called master. You will always have to answer to his disordered whims. He cannot live long. But as long as he lives, you will never be master."

Jamie nodded mutely; eyes still unfocused. Building anger drew his mouth into a frown and brought color to his high cheekbones and his outsized nose.

"When you are master at Hermitage Castle, I will become your willing mistress." She added incentive to her suggestion. Deliberately she tugged on the neck ties of her shift, allowing him to glimpse the tops of her breasts. "You will own your father's most prized possession."

Roanna smiled to herself. So easy to manipulate this man. Unlike his bullheaded father, Jamie had a receptive mind. But she could manipulate the old man's body with spells and poisons, and her hands and mouth upon his cock.

Slowly she brought order to the clashing colored clouds around the edges of her perceptions. Jamie's eyes cleared.

Roanna clenched her fist at her side.

The old laird gasped and clutched at his heart.

Jamie focused on the old man.

Roanna released her fist and ducked out of the room before either man remembered to hit her. As she tripped down the stairs to the hall, she heard two mighty roars of rage: one from the old laird, one from the new.

In the back of her mind, her true master laughed wildly.

Chapter 8

Kirkenwood Village, evening, two days after the Autumnal Equinox, 1558.

I WATCHED from the ramparts of the keep as the bonfire burned late into the night. The villagers had piled branches high at the base of the center stone, where they had always built bonfires, set the Maypole, celebrated the circle of life for centuries. Sparks flew upward to the heavens, like so many bright faeries. My gaze followed their path, seeking solace and answers in the wheel of stars. They continued their orderly march across the firmament.

If the stars held any answers, they did not reveal them to me. I had not studied astrology and the other sciences during my years at seminary. Perhaps, if I consulted an expert, I'd find answers? Queen Mary Tudor had recently released Dr. John Dee from prison after he saw her death and Elizabeth's ascension in his charts. I decided to consult him. He was, after all, the foremost astrologer and magician of our time. If anyone knew how to justify the use of magic within the teachings of the church 'twas he. His prediction of change in the monarchy seemed to be coming true. The latest reports from London indicated Mary could not last long.

Would the Spanish priests scuttle home to Philip once Elizabeth ruled England? I had difficulty believing the Spaniards worshiped the same loving and forgiving God that I did.

God has many names. She answers to all of them. Had I really heard Raven whisper those words to me earlier today?

Below me, the villagers drank mead and ale in Raven's

honor. They sang. They danced. The movements and songs started slow and mournful, gaining in momentum and energy as they worked through their grief. Gradually they brought forth old songs and stories that my grandmother had known in her youth. They remembered the good times and celebrated her life as well as mourned her death.

Helwriaeth joined them, weaving in and out of their pattern dances. She paused frequently and faced the bonfire. I didn't need to see her close up to know her nose worked at the strange mingling of scents.

Many villagers wept openly for Raven and her dog. They all seemed to touch Helwriaeth—the presiding familiar—at some point in the dance.

An era passed with Raven and Newynog. No elder woman or healer remained at the keep to watch over the people and the land of Kirkenwood. Donovan had already proved himself a capable laird. But he was just a man, without the healer's touch and without the authority of the Pendragon. Meg had the healing touch but was trapped in the mind of a child.

I wanted to join my people in their dance and in their grief. Raven deserved this celebration. I should join them. If they accepted me as my grandmother's successor, could I legitimately claim her ring and my heritage? Would Donovan give it up? I set my footsteps for the courtyard, determined to add my blessing to the village ceremony.

Donovan blocked my passage through the hall. "Where is Helwriaeth?" he asked.

"In the village. She chose to stand guard over the bonfire."

"She shows signs of coming into heat. You will breed her here." An order not a request. "We need her blood to continue the line of wolfhounds." The Kirkwood family had earned a great deal of money from the breeding and selling of the noble hunting dogs.

"I had planned to breed her to one of our wolfhounds. In the last five years I could not dilute the blood of her pups with a lesser dog."

As soon as I could confirm her pregnancy, I'd leave and seek out Dr. John Dee. Even if the villagers proclaimed me Raven's successor, I needed to consult the astrologer about England's future. I also had the mission from my bishop to gather information.

"Helwriaeth remains here until the pups are weaned. The pups will not leave Kirkenwood."

I hesitated. Life with my twin would not be comfortable as long as he treated me as a hostile traitor. "I will not be separated from my familiar. Raven herself insisted I need her by my side."

Donovan's face flushed as red as if he'd lingered too close to the bonfire for too long. The great vein in his neck stood out, pulsing wildly. "I'll not have you in my household for three months or more!"

Why could we agree on nothing? We had been so close in our youth. My memory took me back eleven years. We were so close . . .

"Quickly, we have to change clothes," Donovan said as he dragged me into the little alcove off the Hall that we shared until we were fourteen when our two oldest sisters married and moved with their husbands (two brothers who owned a fleet of fishing boats) to York. After the wedding we occupied their room off the gallery. At the time of this memory, that was still two years away and the alcove was our private refuge.

"How are we going to convince Raven that I am you and you are me. She's the only one who can tell us apart," I said as I ripped off my doublet.

"Raven saw us this morning. I was wearing the red and you the yellow. We change clothes, so she'll assume at first glance that I am you."

"When she takes you down to the lair, you'll have to act like me. You can't pace and you can't blurt out the first words that come into your head."

"I know. But you'll tell me the answers, won't you?"

"Of course. I'll speak the words of the spells through you. I'll work the magic though. Once you feel how it is done, you can do it yourself next time."

With nothing more important on our twelve-year-old minds than finally sharing the one thing that made us different, we presented ourselves to Raven as the bells rang high noon. She seemed distracted that day, concerned with our current stepmother and her latest miscarriage. So far, Fiona—a puny and squalling girl of five years—was the only offspring of that marriage. Da was anxious for more boys to inherit Kirkenwood should anything happen to Donovan or me. We couldn't believe anything could harm us and didn't care for more siblings—five sisters was enough. We only wanted to share my magic.

"Griffin, did you memorize the lessons I gave you yester-eve?" Raven asked peremptorily as she loomed over us.

We had grown this past summer, topping all of our older sisters in height and approaching equality with Da. But I didn't think we would ever stand taller or straighter or more commanding than our grandmother. In reality we already topped her by two inches.

"Yes, Raven," Donovan replied succinctly and respectfully. As I would have done, and I didn't have to prompt him.

"Come, then. Show me." Raven took his arm and led him toward the secret door in the gallery.

I followed, as Donovan always did.

"Not this time, Donovan. You will not be able to comprehend this lesson." Raven held up her hand to halt me on the stairs to the gallery. She still had not looked closely at either of us.

I swallowed my laughter. "Yes, Raven," I replied putting a high level of resentment and anger in my voice.

I don't sound like that! Donovan's thoughts came to me.

Yes, you do, I informed him, almost bursting with my own mirth.

I hung back as ordered, watching until Raven turned toward the darkest corner of the gallery. On the other side of that wall was the large northeast tower—the direction from which most raids came. Only a select few members of the family knew that a long passage ran through the center of the twenty-foot-thick wall. Beneath the hall the dank tunnel split. One branch led downward, into a series of caves that eventually opened up behind the kirk by the pool at the base of the tor—a secret escape route should the castle ever fall to besiegers. The other branch of the tunnel ended in a room beneath the gatehouse. This room was Raven's workshop, library, and retreat from the noise and bustle of an overcrowded castle.

Two stories beneath ground, and separated from the rest of the world by thick stone walls, floors, and ceilings, Raven's lair might have existed in another world. She and I had spent many wonderful days in the lair studying magic and history, languages and sciences. Sometimes she allowed Donovan to join us. He grasped the concepts of science and herb lore quite readily. I had a greater gift for languages and history. Magic jumped from my fingertips at a thought. Donovan could mix potions and chant proper spells with ease, but his results were limited to the interaction of the ingredients.

The moment Raven closed and latched the low door, I raced up the stairs and pressed myself against the wall beside the entry. Slowly I counted to one hundred. Just as I was about to lift the latch, I heard a faint cough on the other side of the door. Raven knew I would follow and waited to reprimand me. I stayed put.

Another one hundred heartbeats and I knew the passageway was clear, even without Donovan's confirmation in my mind. Silently I crept behind Raven and my brother. When they entered the lair and latched that door, I slid down, back against the wall, legs crossed, and opened my mind to my brother.

"Now, Griffin, in what language must you recite this spell?" Raven asked my brother.

I had trouble keeping from bursting out loud with my adolescent mirth.

Uh, Griffin, what language? Donovan demanded.

"The spell is written in Greek, but that is a translation of the original Welsh. I think it will work better in Welsh," I whispered. He heard my thoughts but not my words.

"Very good, Griffin," Raven told Donovan when he had repeated my words. "You found the essence of the spell in the words rather than merely learning them by rote. Now recite them for me while adding each of the ingredients mentioned to the brazier."

I sensed Raven leaning back in her chair, watching as Donovan rummaged around the crowded shelves for ingredients.

"The hellebore is on the top shelf in a blue bowl. The wolfbane is in a blue bottle on the third shelf, far to the right." I closed my eyes and pictured the little room, memorizing the reach to each shelf and corner. I fed those muscle memories to my twin. A grunt of satisfaction told me he found each of the nine herbs required to sprinkle around a sheep paddock to keep predators away.

Now the hard part. I had to focus deeply to push my magic through Donovan as well as my words. I breathed deeply, inhaled three counts, hold three, exhale three. The dank smells, the deep chill embedded in the stones at my back and rump, the flickering oil lamps Raven had lit along the passage—all of them faded from my awareness. I seemed to float above my body, through the latched door, into Raven's lair. With a physical effort, I forced my astral self to sink into Donovan's body, to become him. We'd done this before, practicing for this ultimate joke on the one person who could not be fooled by ordinary tricks.

I laid my ghostly hands upon Donovan's shoulders, preparing to push myself deeper. Donovan's mental barriers were down. He was ready. I was ready.

"Halt!" Raven commanded.

I fell back into my body outside the lair. The chill stones seemed to burn through my back and butt. Every part of me ached from the cold and the backlash of the spell gone wrong.

But my contact with Donovan remained intact.

Raven stared directly into Donovan's eyes. "You are not Griffin." She jumped up from her chair to confront my twin. I heard her resounding slap upon his face before I felt Donovan recoil. My own cheek burned in sympathy as well as my ears in embarrassment.

"How dare you attempt to fool me, you ungrateful wretches?" She flung the door open, grabbed my collar, and yanked me into the lair. "Answer me. How dared you?"

"How did you know?" Donovan asked.

"I know. You have not the aura of a magician. Now answer me, Griffin, how dared you try to trick me?"

"We needed to share the magic, Raven," I apologized.

"No, you didn't. You wanted to fool me as you fool your father and stepmother. You wanted control over forces you do not know how to handle. Go now, both of you. Out of my sight. I am terribly disappointed in both of you."

Her hurt stabbed me deeply. Donovan hung his head. We trooped out of the lair with heavy feet and dampened spirits.

Halfway up the passage our normal exuberance returned full force. We diverted off to the cave system, laughing, running, and slapping each other on the back.

No more. We faced each other as adults with animosity and resentment that neither of us wanted to put aside. I wondered briefly if unnatural forces kept us apart. But I quickly dismissed that idea.

"I take orders from the Pope and my bishop, not from you," I told him, firming my resolve to defy him.

"You must stay unless you choose to leave Helwriaeth with me." He sounded more desperate than angry. Why? What forces drove him? Drove us?

Anger flared. My face heated, I clenched my fists. I longed to knock him flat. "My familiar will not stay without me." I needed her by my side to sniff out the demon Raven had warned me about. Demons were devious, easily tricking human senses. But a dog's nose could distinguish the truth.

"If she chooses to stay . . ."

"We both know she won't." She couldn't. She had already chosen me as only a Pendragon can be chosen. For her to stay would mean that Donovan had a better claim.

"Do you really want me here for three or four more months?" I asked, looking my twin directly in the eyes.

His thoughts remained elusive, as they never had before I left for France. A moment of regret for that lost closeness almost weakened my resolve to challenge him at every turn for possession of the ring of the Pendragon and all it symbolized.

"You may remain with the dog. But stay out of my way. Now I must attend my wife. Her labor has begun. Fitting that my son will be born on the day we buried Raven. We will not be without a Pendragon long." Donovan turned on his heel and marched back into the laird's solar above the hall.

"I request the privilege of christening the babe," I called after him.

"Your church considers you disgraced. You must stand in line behind Father Peter, Father Manuel, and any other priest I can find for the honor."

I retreated to the village.

The scent of woodsmoke filled my head the moment I stepped beyond the gates of Kirkenwood. Firelight twisted the shadows of the standing stones into dancing figures to match the movements of the villagers. I could well imagine that my ancestors had joined the circling celebration.

Helwriaeth bounced to my side. I ruffled her ears, holding her close against my side. She leaned her weight into me. We took comfort and warmth from each other.

Before joining the dancing, the drinking, and the reminiscing I walked behind the stones, touching each. A faint vibration caressed my hand at the third stone. Merlin's Stone we called it. Arylwren's Stone, beside her father, the Merlin, reached out and greeted me before I even touched it. Arthur's Stone, at the western edge, looking east into the village gave off an intense hum in harmony with the music of the Lady of the Lake. The music of the villagers shifted subtly to blend with it. The entire earth seemed to hum along with the music, with the Lady, with me.

I closed my eyes absorbing the life of the stones. If I reached with one of my senses, or just a hand, I could touch anyone, anything in the world. Peace settled on my shoulders. Once before, on the day I celebrated Mass for the first time, I had felt a similar unity with all life.

I opened my eyes. New clarity and sharpness flooded all of my senses. There! Three stones north of where I stood, Raven's face smiled at me from within the granite. Only then did I lift my eyes toward the tops of the stones where they pierced the night sky, outlined in sparks from the fire.

A faint shimmer of blue stretched out from the central stone and the bonfire to the tops of each of the ring stones. The fire spread out from the stones in all directions in a bright indigo web to the far corners of Britain.

I had replaced Raven's red network of life with my own blue.

I let go a long-held breath. Raven had died, but the stones lived. My ancestors lived on in the memory of the stones.

A spell is nothing more than a prayer, Raven's voice whispered to me. Raven's voice, augmented by dozens of other voices, in nearly dead languages, my own English and French, and variations I knew must come in future generations.

The blue fire that connected each of the stones to the center and to each other glowed brighter. I saw a web of fire that united Britain. My balance tilted. Sharp shards of light pierced my eyes. A united Britain. No borders, no barriers, no warfare.

Only a Pendragon could push politicians, the church, and the warriors to agree to peaceful compromise. King Arthur had envisioned it. Merlin had advised him how to achieve it. Others had tried and failed. I had the opportunity to try once more.

War was coming. I'd seen it in my dreams time and again. Horrible war with blood and death, destruction of the land and the people. War that centered on Scotland and its queen—not Marie de Guise, the regent, but her daughter in France, Marie Stuart, Queen of Scots. Here in the north, with this web of unity and power emanating from the stones, I was in a unique position to stop the war.

Britain unified.

That unification needed an active and strong Pendragon.

But I was not the Pendragon. Would never be without the ring of my ancestors, now held by my brother. No one would recognize my authority without the ring.

And then I remembered a long-ago lesson in magic. Only the Pendragon could activate the web of fire within the stones. Only the Pendragon heard the advice of our ancestors within the stones.

With or without the ring and the ritual, I was the Pendragon. I had been chosen by Raven and the wolfhounds, and perhaps by God, to wield magic on Britain's behalf. Only I could plant the seeds of peace and unity, banishing chaos, within this fractured land.

But I was a priest, forbidden contact with otherworldly powers at the peril of my immortal soul. I had chosen the church over my country and my family.

The church had failed to unite anything in Britain.

I, as the ordained delegate of the church, had to do whatever was necessary to achieve peace. Could I?

Chapter 9

Hermitage Castle.

"YOU are the laird now, Jamie," Roanna said firmly. The old man lay in state in the family chapel. The women of the household tore their hair and smeared ashes on their brows.

Roanna hadn't time for pretending grief for the man who had aided the Kirkwoods in destroying everything she valued, everything she loved.

Jamie, still in his late teens, lifted his head from deep contemplation of the bottom of his ale cup. Guilt shadowed his aura. Roanna smiled. She could almost see her true master hiding in that darkness.

Red rimmed Jamie's eyes and blotched his prominent nose. All of his features seemed too large for his gangling frame. He'd grow into his nose and hands and feet eventually. If Roanna let him live that long.

"The safety of your family, this castle, these lands are your responsibility now," she added.

"Mine." Jamie nodded sullenly. "No more Da to take them away from me."

"Yer father is dead, Jamie. He won't tell you what to do anymore. You have to decide."

"Decide what?" His words slurred, and his head nodded again. If she didn't hurry and push him to a decision, he'd fall asleep and opportunity would pass them by.

She leaned over him, bracing her hands upon the table where his ale mug rested. By lifting her shoulders just so, her bodice gaped, exposing her breasts almost to the nipples.

His attention fixed upon her body.

"You must defend your lands and your honor, Jamie." Roanna circled his chair in the drafty hall of Hermitage

Castle. She wove a web of seduction and compulsion as she circled widdershins. "You must stop the rumors that you murdered your father." She had begun the rumors among the women before the old man's body was cold. "The English spread those rumors so they can weaken your hold on your land and castle."

"Defend against the bloody English raiders."

" 'Tis five years since the Kirkwood twins burned my village—your village. Five years the deaths of your people have gone unavenged." There had been eight raids and retaliations across the border in that time, but Roanna still needed justice for Gran's death.

"Five years. Vengeance." His eyes brightened a bit, and he sat up straighter.

"Your father was weak and ill. He allowed the English to sully his honor. Your honor. He deserved to die at the hands of his only son. You must make the English pay for that raid. Now."

"I must bury my father first." Jamie slumped back into his guilt-ridden depression. He reached for the pitcher of ale on the high table.

Roanna pushed it out of his reach. "You must prove yourself a strong and able leader to silence those whispers." As long as Jamie believed he had murdered his own father, he was vulnerable to her.

"Da's heart failed," Jamie repeated the story Roanna had fed him.

"Of course it did." She smiled knowingly.

Jamie looked away, flushing with guilt.

"I'll not have my honor sullied with vile rumors." He shook himself and firmed his prominent chin. His overlarge hands clutched the arms of the laird's chair until his knuckles turned white.

"Then prove yourself an able laird. Lead your men on a raid this night. The Kirkwoods buried their grandmother today. They are distracted. Their defenses are weak. Take back your honor. Burn their castle and home village to the ground tonight."

"Saddle my horse. Call the men to arms."

Kirkenwood.

Donovan accepted the squalling infant reluctantly. A girl.

"Raven, you promised me a boy." He leaned his head back, eyes scrunched closed. "What do I do now?"

No one answered him.

Down in the village, the music of flute, drum, and bagpipe, of chimes and plucked strings grew louder. The rhythm demanded a celebration of life. An old woman had died. A new child had been born. The circle of life continued.

"You promised me a son!" Would the villagers continue to dance and sing so vigorously when they found out the laird had failed to prove his vigor by siring a son first time out? Peregrine and Gaspar, his bastard boys in the nursery, didn't count.

After a long moment he became aware that the midwife still stood before him. Donovan opened his eyes and lowered his head. His daughter continued to squirm and squall in his uncertain hands.

"You are disappointed, Milord," the woman stated blandly.

"A man always hopes for a son and heir the first time." A son to accept the ring of the Pendragon.

Give the ring to your son. Raven had been most specific.

How could she have been so wrong? Raven always knew the sex of a child long before the birth.

If she was wrong about this, could she have been wrong about entrusting the ring to him, bypassing Griffin? Could she have been lashing out in hurt when she denied Griffin the ring? He'd never known Raven to let her personal feelings interfere with important decisions. Yet . . .

"Lady Katherine is strong and healthy, Milord Donovan. There will be more children," the midwife said. A little more enthusiasm crept into her voice.

"I will see my wife now." Donovan returned the infant to the woman.

She accepted it eagerly, cooing to it, cradling it gently. Immediately the crying ceased.

"Lady Katherine is resting. Do not stay long," the midwife said sternly.

Donovan pushed his way into the bedchamber. Hundreds

of candles lit the room, dimming the moonlight streaming through the glass window beyond the bed. The hearth blazed with more light and heat. Sweat beaded his brow before he'd measured three paces. He paused a moment to snuff a few of the candles. The room was still too hot.

Then he became aware of sobs and a second voice murmuring quiet comfort.

"Kate?" he asked quietly as he thrust aside the tapestried bed hangings. Frustration burned low in his gut, feeling very much like anger.

The sobs grew louder.

"I'm sorry, Donny. I failed you," Kate wailed. Sweat darkened her blonde hair and left it in matted tendrils around her face and shoulders. Shadows under her eyes and fatigue lines around her mouth replaced the lush prettiness of her youth.

He didn't like seeing her like this. His pretty Kate should be laughing and teasing him out of his own black humor. He hoped she'd recover soon. Perhaps another expensive luxury like the glass window would hasten her healing. Eighteen panes, or lights as the Londoners called them, set in lead had cost him most of his store of gold, but Kate loved the sunlight. Donovan found her most alluring while she sat in the padded window embrasure, basking in the light like a cat.

"Hush, little one," Meg soothed, wiping Kate's brow with a cool rag. "You must rest so that you have milk to feed the babe." The first coherent sentences Mad Meg had spoken in five years. Perhaps she grew out of the protective loop that trapped her mind.

Kate cried louder, flinging herself onto her side, arms draped over her head.

Something nearly broke inside Donovan. He'd loved Kate in an offhand sort of way for a long time. Even without her impressive dowry he would probably have married her. But he did wish she'd take an interest in the world beyond their bedchamber. Her father had seen no benefit to wasting money on her education. He'd saved it all for her marriage portion instead.

Donovan's father had certainly looked no further than the dowry when he negotiated the marriage contract less then a week after Griffin had departed. Kate had been only eleven at the time. They'd waited four years to marry and beget a child.

Kate's sobs touched him in a way he'd never thought of her before, soft, vulnerable, his responsibility. She had given him a child.

He liked the idea of having a daughter, a miniature version of her mother with blonde hair and big brown eyes—but with the Kirkwood intelligence and curiosity. A little girl he could share the wonders of the forest and the awesome power of magic with. He'd teach her to read by the light of the glass window.

The next baby would be a boy. Raven had promised him a son to pass on the heritage of the Pendragon. Next time. He needn't worry yet.

Gently he perched on the edge of the bed and caressed Kate's damp hair. "Whisht, my love. Hush your tears now. We have a bonny lassie. You needn't fear you've disappointed me."

"Truly, Donny?" Kate lifted her head. Tears shone in her lovely eyes. He kissed them away.

"Truly, Kate. I'm happy with our daughter."

"Good, you've stopped crying," Meg said, adding her own caress to Kate's hair. "Crying invites demons. Can't have demons sniffing around our baby." She resorted to her childish voice and aimless prattling.

Donovan sighed and allowed his sister Meg to continue her half-sung and disjointed phrases.

"Sleep now, Kate. Sleep and grow strong again." He kissed the top of her head and retreated.

Griffin awaited him outside the door.

"Will you give me the ring of the Pendragon now?" Griffin asked. His hands clenched and released in an uncharacteristic agitation. Donovan expected his twin to begin pacing the floor and pounding the walls: actions Donovan resorted to. From earliest childhood, Griffin had had an intense inner calm—from his years spent on his knees in prayer, no doubt. Donovan did not have the time or patience to emulate his brother. But he tried. "I will follow Raven's instructions to the letter." He walked past his brother.

Then the anger he'd been hiding boiled to the surface.

"It's all your fault, Griffin. If you hadn't come home, the Gods would have granted me a son."

Griffin crossed himself, like a good Christian.

"Yes, we are pagans here, Father Griffin. Pagans who have learned to survive with the hypocrisy of your Christian God and His priests. We will continue to survive with or without you." Donovan sneered and headed for the stables. He needed a long hard ride across the moors. "May the Gods help any Scots or priests who get in my way."

I fell into my bed too tired to stand anymore, too restless to sleep. I knew Donovan rode recklessly over the hills, whipping his mount to dangerous speeds. He'd killed more than one horse on these wild rides. At least the dogs had enough sense not to follow him.

If anything should happen to him tonight . . . I did not want to think about how we would all cope without a laird and without a Pendragon. With only an infant female heir, Queen Mary would demand that the barony revert to the crown. She could turn this stronghold of pagans over to the church. I would not be the one to administer the lands, care for the people, or protect the border—unless I renounced my vows and claimed the lands and title for myself. Could I? Would I?

A morsel of hope blossomed in my chest. If my twin died, I could rightly claim the heritage I had given up for the church. I could take the magical sword proffered by the Lady of the Lake.

For that to happen, my twin had to die. If that happened, I would have to become once more a warlord who killed other men without thought. I'd never achieve the vision of peace and unity I had experienced in the web of light among the standing stones.

"Come back safely, Donovan," I pleaded, trying desperately to reopen the channels of communication. My thoughts drifted away as mist in the sunshine.

I climbed off the low cot and stumbled to the *prie dieu*

in the corner. I nearly fell to my knees in my fatigue. Resolutely, I folded my hands over my rosary in a gesture of supplication. Memorized prayers came to my lips. Beads passed through my fingers. My mind and heart spun in ever-widening circles of confusion and despair.

The deep peace of communion with God eluded me. Answers remained hidden. I could not make a decision.

After a time, I knew I'd not find sleep or ease until Donovan returned and the world righted itself again. By the light of a guttering candle, I dressed, grateful for the warmth of my knitted hose beneath my padded trunks. I had to leave off the silk-lined wool of my soutane until I'd finished my mission for Bishop du Bellay and once more walked the world openly as a priest. My long, fur-lined coat blocked a little more of the chill. In Paris, I'd rarely worn the coat except in deep winter. Here in the north, I found it barely adequate during the first days of autumn.

For a moment I longed for the softer climate of Paris, for the lively discussions of the students gathered around a great master, for the soft breads, rich cheese, and delicate sauces of their cuisine. What in St. Justin's name was I doing here in the harsh and unforgiving north?

I was on a mission from my bishop.

"Helwriaeth?" I called. Her absence left a vacancy in the back of my neck. She had taken herself off to the kennels to select a mate, or mates. I had returned home none too soon for that portion of my mission.

Alone, I paced the ramparts of the sprawling castle. Sleepy guards roused slightly at my passing. I waved them off, content to be alone with my thoughts. If anything arose that required the guards' attention, I'd see it before they would. My keen night vision had not deserted me during my years in Paris.

The great wheel of the stars marked the passage of time. I studied them again and again, seeking answers in the web of light that seemed to reach down and touch the energy of the stones. The faint vibration along those mysterious lines hummed in my body.

How could I feel so connected to everything in this life and not know how to proceed? I was the Pendragon in all but name, yet without authority.

The vibration along the lines of light changed with my

increasing agitation. I walked faster. I scanned the stars. I scanned the hills. I stared at the web of light along the tops of the stones.

My body hummed. Energy coursed through my veins, needing an outlet, needing a sword to swing. I looked toward the kirk and the lake. The Lady remained quiet. No luminescent sword shone beneath the surface of the water.

Blood pounded in my ears, taking on the rhythm of hoofbeats.

Hoofbeats in the distance.

"Raiders!" I screamed. "Raiders from the north!"

Chapter 10

The border hills between England and Scotland, near Kirkenwood.

DONOVAN crested a hillock and drew his horse to a halt. His thighs trembled with fatigue; his hands shook. The animal's sides heaved between his legs, winded but not yet blown. Both he and the horse smelled of sweat. The anger bled out of him.

Seeking landmarks, he scanned the moonlit horizon. Rolling hills, creased by sharp corries blanketed with heather, an outcropping here and there. Nothing looked familiar. A strange acrid scent lay atop the sweeter green smell of shrubs and peat bogs. It made his nostrils flare.

How far had he come? Too far. He should be back at the keep with Kate and his new daughter.

Warmth infused his heart once more at the thought of holding his child, watching her grow, and mature. He had so much to teach her, to share with her. His mouth sagged open in sheer awe at the magnificence of what he and Kate had created. He hadn't been with their mothers when his two illegitimate sons were born—he was convinced that he had sired them and not Griffin. He loved both Peregrine and Gaspar and spent a lot of time with them but felt distanced from them in many ways. Now he wanted to experience every moment of the baby's life.

There was time yet to beget a legitimate son. 'Twas the babe who had come who was important right now.

Slowly he turned the horse's head, content to let it find its own way home.

Halfway down the hillside the horse balked. It backed and shied. Donovan fought the reins. He urged the animal toward home with knees, voice, and reins.

The horse shook his head, making the bridle jingle loudly in the still night air.

A new figure rose up out of the heather directly in front of him. "Witch!" Father Manuel's voice carried clearly across the moors. His Spanish accent sounded strange, out of place. It echoed almost as if he spoke into a hollow tube, or across the portal from the netherworld.

Donovan caught a brief glimpse of red sparkles surrounding him. Like the auras Raven had tried to teach him to read. "What?" he breathed out. "What are you doing here, in the middle of nowhere, in the middle of the night? You should be on your knees in a kirk or riding like a Gadarene Pig toward Carlisle."

"Witch, riding your witch horse along the path of the moonlight with the elves. You've lost your soul to the Wild Hunt," Father Manuel intoned. He raised a long staff and swung it at Donovan.

Not a staff, a pike!

The horse reared at the flash of moonlight on the broad blade at the tip of the weapon.

"Since when do priests carry pikes as walking staffs?" Donovan snarled, reaching for his ever-present sword. He'd replaced the short ceremonial blade with a longer, more useful one. He sliced the air with it in warning.

Father Manuel blocked the blow with the pole of his weapon.

"Out of my way, priest. You no longer have a place here." Donovan parried.

"Die, you heathen dog," the priest said, almost as if he recited the words. He lunged under Donovan's guard. The pike blade bit into the thick wool of Donovan's doublet.

Sucking air through his teeth, Donovan caught the pike with his sword, twisted and pushed it out of range.

The priest recovered too quickly for an untrained man of peace. He twirled and came back with another blow perilously close to Donovan's neck.

Donovan smelled his own fear. The night breeze chilled him. And then warmth surged through him. His vision focused on his opponent. The sword became one with his arm, engaging the pike almost before he thought through his moves.

In three quick thrusts, Donovan disarmed the priest and jumped off his horse.

The Spaniard lunged, throwing them both onto the ground. They grappled. Donovan clung to his sword as his opponent clawed at his wrist with talonlike fingers. The priest roared his rage. His mouth opened like a great maw revealing daggerlike teeth. He grew to twice his normal size, bursting the seams of his cassock. His arms lengthened, grew a pelt of coarse hair, his legs bent and swelled into lizard limbs with the power of a dragon.

Burning sulfur permeated the air.

"Who are you?" Donovan breathed as he sent his left fist into the demon's jaw.

The beast reared back in surprise. *I am Tryblith, the Demon of Chaos, and I shall drink the blood of all who defy me and the church I have gathered to my bosom as my tool. Know this and fear me before you die.* It opened its mouth, once more aiming its incisors for the great neck vein of its prey.

Donovan rammed the sword upward deep into Tryblith's belly.

The image dissolved into the surprised visage of the Spanish priest. He clutched at the gaping wound. Blood flowed freely through his grasping fingers. Father Manuel rolled over and stared at the star-spangled heavens.

"You are truly cursed now, witch. You have killed a priest of God." His eyes glazed over, blood bubbled from his mouth, his bowels released.

But you have not killed me. I can never die. The seeds of chaos are sown! The demon's voice reverberated across the hilltops like a battle cry of the damned.

"To arms!" I ran to the bell tower on the northeast corner of the castle. Putting all my weight onto the bell rope, I rang the three-times-three alarm.

All around me, guards rushed to their stations, pulling on bits of clothing as they ran.

Down in the courtyard, people milled, shouting questions.

Villagers rushed up the hill to the safety of the keep. Guards tried to close the gate to keep them out.

Donovan was not there to direct them. They had never believed they could think for themselves.

"Malcolm," I called to a soldier pelting up the turret stairs toward me. "You and one other open the pedestrian gate for the villagers. One or two at a time to enter. Detain anyone you do not know. People first, sheep after, if there's time."

The soldier touched his forehead in acknowledgment and reversed his course. A moment later he had obeyed me. The villagers streamed into the courtyard, adding more confusion to the melee. The panicky livestock followed, contributing frightened bellows and noisome droppings. A man-at-arms stepped without looking, slipped and landed face first in the muck. He came up cursing and spitting.

"Fiona!" I called to my youngest sister. "Herd the livestock into a corner. Organize the women. Boiling water, bandages, food, and drink. You know what to do." She nodded and proceeded as if she had prepared for battle a dozen times in her sixteen years. She probably had. She was the laird's daughter and was allowed to think.

"Reinforce the gates, both ends of the gatehouse tunnel," I told Malcolm as he closed and barred the pedestrian portal within the huge gates. "Ten men above the gatehouse with bows and full quivers." Again the men jumped to my command.

All they needed was direction. Neither the nobles nor the church wanted them to believe they could do anything on their own—even pray.

Where was Donovan to lead them? 'Twas his place, not mine. Unless they believed me to be my twin.

For tonight, I must be. Tonight I must violate my conscience and order men to battle. I would instigate death.

Jesus, forgive me.

The smell of oily smoke announced the first attack, a flaming missile into the stable thatch. Every other building in the complex had slate tiles. Someone knew the layout and our vulnerabilities.

Fire bloomed and grew, thankful for the fuel within the thatch. The elemental force stretched and invited me to join with it, glory in the freedom of feeding on the thatch.

Cool Air on my face broke the enthrallment of Fire. I teetered dangerously close to the edge of the ramparts.

Had I truly lost myself in Fire's allure enough to try leaping to the stable roof?

Whoever had aimed the flaming arrow had fueled it with magic.

I could quench the fire. Raven had taught me how. I suppressed the yearning to throw my magic at an enemy. I held it back. The spell would exhaust me, leave me vulnerable to the next attack. The element of Water worked as well to counter the element of Fire as magic did.

Women screamed. Sheep bleated. Horses whinnied. Flames continued crackling.

Then came the thud of a battering ram against the outer gate.

Roanna sighted along the cloth yard arrow fitted into her longbow. A single window made up of eighteen glass panes awaited her aim. Not many soldiers or raiders in the border country used a longbow. The land was too harsh to support large trees for the weapons to be made locally. She had made a point of acquiring one on her travels for her master. Her magic-heightened senses made her aim true and gave strength to her arms and shoulders.

The death of the priest had fueled her talent. Her master thrived on blood and shared generously of his power.

She'd have to remember to throw the body in the river when she finished this night's business.

With this weapon she could reach well beyond the limitations of swords and pikes. Her arrows could wreak more devastation with more accuracy and speed than even the arquebus and wheellock firearms.

Even now, Jamie directed setting up the tripod to support the arquebus. They'd aim for the guards atop the gatehouse. But they'd be lucky to get off a single shot before having to retreat and reload.

Roanna's first arrow had landed in the thatch of the stable, as she planned. The defenders of Kirkenwood would be forced to turn their attention to putting out the fire and rescuing their horses. Horses were too valuable to be allowed to burn, too large and dangerous to be allowed to panic within the confines of the bailey.

They'd need more than water to extinguish her fire born of nether-world elements.

Now for the blow that would devastate them most.

"Light the tip," she commanded the lad tending a fire beside her.

He brought a flaming brand up to the oil-soaked rag wrapped around the arrowhead.

"What are you doing here, Roanna?" Jamie knocked the brand aside before it ignited the rag.

"I'm making the destruction of the Kirkwoods easier for you," she stated, keeping her target in sight.

"I don't need help from a woman," Jamie spat. "Get back with the loot wagons where it is safe. I don't want anything to happen to my pet witch." He grabbed her around the waist and lifted her off the ground. When he put her down, she faced downhill in the opposite direction from her target.

"Rabbit brain! I had them in my sights." She whirled around to seek out Kirkenwood's biggest vanity and vulnerability.

"I don't need you, Roanna. I only let you come because you plagued me nearly to death. The Kirkwood and the Douglas clans have been battling and feuding for more generations than you can imagine. I know how to do this. Now go back with the empty wagons until I call you." He pushed her gently in the direction he wanted her to go.

"My family has been feuding with the clan of the Pendragon for longer than even you can imagine, Jamie Douglas. By right of inheritance, Kirkenwood should be mine. My ancestors were ousted by the daughter of the Merlin and her bastards. I will have my vengeance tonight and not be limited by your piddling vision of victory."

Her true master had hinted at the secrets of her ancestry. She had ferreted out confirmation of those few hints from local gossip and legend, augmented by half remembered stories Gran had told her.

Roanna took a deep breath. Behind her she heard the sounds of the battering ram. A mere distraction while Jamie directed the looting of the village and the fields.

In the back of her head she heard the laughter of her master. He grew stronger with the chaos of battle.

She would give him more chaos. But first she must tend to aiming her bow.

"I will have more than some livestock and stores of grain this night. I want the death of the two who could be the next Pendragon. Kirkenwood will be heirless by dawn."

She took another breath and willed herself to disappear among the shadows.

Jamie left her knoll just beyond the deep ditch that encircled the village and the standing stones. He marched behind his second line of troops toward the loot they anticipated.

Roanna smiled to herself. She knew better than to try to penetrate the stones with magic. The women of her family were very familiar with the web of light that repulsed her kind and their spells.

But Raven Kirkwood was dead. The web of light had died with her. Donovan had no magic to reignite it. Griffin Kirkwood refused to use his magic. She was safe.

Yet still she hesitated to penetrate the circle.

With the longbow she could send her magic over the top of the stones into the keep. The old lady who had ruled the clan for three generations hadn't bothered to armor the keep with magic. She'd trusted too much in the stones.

"Light the arrow," Roanna commanded the lad by the fire.

He jumped and crossed himself. His hands shook and he dropped his stick into the dry grasses. Autumn rains had not yet dampened them to keep the fire from spreading. Embers smoldered. He moved to stamp them out.

"Let them burn. Let the entire moor burn. Now light my arrow." Roanna laughed.

"Y . . . yes, milady." He crossed himself again.

Roanna sighted along her arrow one more time. The rooftops of the sprawling castle came into her view. She focused more closely. "I need the hall." There! The large three-story building in the center with smaller rooms growing out of its sides. And above the hall, the laird's bed-chamber with the lady's solar above that.

Lord Donovan Kirkwood, Baron of Kirkenwood had squandered precious coins to create a glass window to please his bride.

Roanna's magic sensed the glass before her eyes saw firelight reflecting off it. She trusted her extra senses and released the arrow.

Magic guided the missile. A heartbeat later, the glass exploded in oily smoke.

Her master laughed deep and long. She joined him in his mirth.

Chapter 11

Kirkenwood ramparts near dawn.

"BOILING water to the ramparts above the gatehouse!" I directed the women.

Moments later the people of Kirkenwood dumped buckets, crocks, and cauldrons of scalding water onto the men wielding the battering ram.

Screams followed the streams of water.

I heard a dull thunk as our attackers dropped the pointed log in the dirt. More screams followed as men tore at their armor. Boiled leather and mail could not protect against scald burns that seeped into every seam and crevice. They would know pain, but they should not die.

Where was Donovan? I asked myself over and over. 'Twas his responsibility to direct the defense of Kirkenwood. I was a priest, a man of peace. If I caused the death of a man, my magic would kill me as well.

Below my post by the bell tower, Fiona directed the women and children in carrying water from the well to the stable roof. Smoke and steam rose in choking clouds following each dousing. The fire spread rather than diminished under the onslaught of its opposing element.

In the corner of the bailey our horses paced and reared, frightened by the smoke, needing to escape it by running back into the security of their stable—the very source of their fear. Three boys blindfolded and soothed the animals as best they could.

Helwriaeth pranced and barked in the center of it all. She wanted to attack and rip out a few throats.

So did I.

Then Meg wandered into the melee. She sang, turning in circles, arms spread to embrace the fire she danced around.

Summer has come in
Loud sings the cuckoo
Groweth sed, and blossemeth med,
And springth the wude now
Sing cuckoo

Ewe bleteth after lamb;
Loweth after calve cow
Bullock springs up, bucke verteth,
Merrie sing cuckoo!

Cuckoo, cuckoo, well sings thee, cuckoo.
Now cease thu flayer flu.
Sing cuckoo flu, sing cuckoo!
Sing cuckoo, Sing cuckoo, now!

The next bucket of water made the fire retreat.

I breathed a huge sigh of relief. Meg had taken the decision away from me. I made the sign of the cross over her from a distance, blessing her mad innocence. She could not comprehend that she sinned. But in saving others, she saved herself.

Below all the noise and confusion, another sound penetrated my thoughts. A quiet scrape of wood against stone.

"Archers to the north face," I directed as I ran to the new threat. I placed my foot on the top rung and shoved. The scaling ladder teetered backward. Three raiders jumped free, rolling into their comrades and the gorse. Arrows pelted them, forcing them back into the scrub.

I coughed out more smoke as I slapped an archer on the back, grateful for their quick attention to orders.

"Not a very well organized attack, sir," the archer muttered as he scanned the tor below the castle. "We had time to get all the people and much of the stores to safety. They'll not get away with much."

Indeed, in the growing light of dawn I watched two dozen men scuttle away empty-handed.

I didn't trust their retreat. Raids across the border had been a way of life and an income for too many centuries.

"Who sent these men?" I asked. In the distance I heard curses and invocations against demons. I saw men running recklessly through the gorse and heather, heedless of turned ankles and scraped knees. Did others wait to renew the attack? All of those sights and sounds and smells avoided a curious vacancy on the knoll to the east of the village, an emptiness that was as out of place as the ineffectiveness of the attack.

The archer beside me shrugged his shoulders, keeping his bow nocked and his eyes alert. "Could be the Kerrs. 'Tis a bit far afield for them, but they've been known to push further west when the pickings are lean in their usual territory."

I wondered if the notoriously left-handed family would think differently than right-handed people, and if I could detect the reversal if I engaged my magical senses. I'd avoided using my talent so far, best to keep it resting.

Smoldering impatiently.

"Heard rumors that Old James Douglas' heart is near to giving out," the archer continued. "Could be young Jamie trying to make a name for himself to avoid a clan fight when the old man dies. Then, too, they could be McGregors. Those Highland outlaws will raid anywhere without reason."

"Keep alert. They may come back the moment we let our defenses down." I left the archer to his musings. That vacancy on the knoll worried me.

I kept my senses open as I made my way back to the gatehouse. As the attackers retreated, I became aware of their absence—as if their minds withdrew from mine.

The vacancy on the knoll remained. Someone hid there. Someone who did not want to be found by magic or mundane means. I'd have missed that *nothingness* if I hadn't suspected deviousness and been looking for the unusual.

Smoke still hung heavy in the air. The noise in the bailey lessened. The fright of the horses no longer chafed my skin like a hair shirt. My family and the villagers could clean up the aftermath of the attack without my help.

I concentrated on the crest of the knoll. Aeons ago, the people who had erected the standing stones and dug the surrounding ditch had thrown the excess dirt there—more concerned with the sacredness of the stones and the perfection of the circle than with defense. Or perhaps it had a sacred purpose lost to us over the centuries. Other generations had used the back side of the small hill to dump their garbage. Boulders cleared from fields for plowing had added more bulk to it. Now it stood as tall as the tallest of the stones.

Slowly, the rising sun threw shadows. Shapes formed that had nothing to do with the outline of the hill. I caught a hint of smoke and embers. The summer had been drier than normal, the autumnal rains not yet begun in earnest. The normal grass and shrubs had a dull, brownish tint to the edges. Were they dry enough to invite the fire to spread?

My magical instincts reached out to quench the fire. I drew them back, as I had with the other fires in the castle. I needed all of my strength and alertness to counter the threat that lingered on the hill.

I found a suggestion of hair the color of autumn leaves and deep gray eyes that penetrated all the way to my soul. I needed to reach out to the mind behind those eyes, join with it, share my life with it. . . .

Mad laughter pulsed against my mind, stabbing me behind the eyes with lances of knowledge too painful to absorb.

The world tilted around me. My sense of up and down, right and left swirled in an onslaught of noise dominated by the laughter.

I slammed my eyes shut, pressing clenched fists hard against them. "Holy Jesus, protect me from this vision." I made the sign of the cross and reached for the rosary. One by one I recited my prayers.

The world straightened beneath my feet.

I opened my eyes. A blossom of fire, like a rose burst into full bloom overnight, appeared in midair atop the knoll. It grew and grew until I realized that unseen hands had launched it from a bow.

Time slowed.

A hideous figure emerged from the blankness behind the fire. Taller than a tall man by half, its long arms hung to its knees. The upper half of him—definitely male with exaggerated and engorged genitals—was covered in a hairy pelt. His curiously bent legs reminded me of a lizard, encased in scintillating scales. It opened its great dragon maw to reveal daggerlike teeth as it laughed and reached for me with greedy hunger.

The demon danced about the knoll in triumphant glee.

The flaming arrow spread heat to my face.

Desperate, I reached up with my hand as I ducked the flaming missile.

Pain seared my hand and my eyes. Darkness encroached through the blinding pain.

I dropped the arrow, still burning, to the stone ramparts. It sputtered. I stepped aside, lest the remnants of the flame ignite my coat. A roughness in the stonework seemed to reach out and grab my foot. I stumbled to my knees.

I tried opening my eyes. Blackness filled my vision. Demon fire had robbed me of my sight.

Donovan smelled the smoke from half a league away. "My daughter!" he cried in alarm. "Kate?" he added.

He dug his spurs into the horse's flanks. The spent beast gathered his legs under him in a valiant effort to find one last burst of speed and . . . fell to his knees.

"God's blood!" Donovan leaped free of his mount. Quickly he ran his hands along the horse's neck and flank. Too hot by half.

He didn't want to have to dispatch the beast here and now. Did he dare leave him? He had to get to the keep. Now.

"Take it easy, Bran," Donovan cooed. "Up on your feet now." He coaxed the horse up. The big gelding stumbled to stand, legs splayed, head drooping.

"Rest now, Bran. I'll be back for you." Donovan took off at a run.

Fear propelled him forward. Blood pounded in his ears. His legs pumped. His focus narrowed to the placement of his feet and the thickening smoke.

"Not the baby. Don't take Kate and the baby," he pleaded with whichever gods might listen.

He found a game trail winding through the forest. He knew it of old. The going was easier here. Deer, wolves, badgers, and boar followed this route to the lake.

Birds that had begun to chirp in the light of false dawn

fell silent as he thrashed through the crowding underbrush. A greater stillness settled upon the land. Waiting for the sun. Donovan did not have time to stop and listen.

"God's blood, I should never have left the keep!" he cursed.

But then he'd never have encountered the demon. He'd never have known the true perfidy of the Papist Church.

Too many long moments later he paused at the edge of the forest, looking out over the lake. Now he took the time to listen. His heart thundered in his ears. He counted one hundred heartbeats.

The forest should come to life again. He counted another one hundred heartbeats.

Still the creatures of the trees kept silent. Even the lake did not ripple.

A stray breeze cleared his nose of the ever-present smoke. He smelled something feral, something sweating in fear . . .

He smelled a man, or men, lying in wait.

Slowly, silently, Donovan drew his sword, still crusted with the blood of the demon/priest. He wished for one of the dogs to aid him. A dog would give him the advantage over a single attacker, even if the thieving Scot were better armed. A dog would give him a chance to survive if more than one man awaited him.

Whatever his fate, he could not allow these men to watch him go into the kirk and not come out again. They'd know a back door into Kirkenwood existed and not rest until they found it.

Before Donovan could decide to step into the clearing, two men rose up out of the mass of ferns. "A Douglas!" they shouted their battle cry. Each brandished a battle ax and a short sword. Both looked tired, hungry, and desperate.

Donovan wrestled and kicked a stout branch free of a nearby deadfall. He ducked the slashing blow from the first raider—a big, black-haired man in leather armor—and came up swinging the staff into the man's gut. Black-hair doubled over coughing. His companion—a wiry redhead with a full beard, wearing a mail shirt—hesitated, keeping one step beyond the reach of Donovan's new weapon.

Heedless of Black-hair behind him, Donovan charged

forward. He swung the staff in a complex pattern. Red backed off, not knowing when or how Donovan would strike. Donovan feinted left. The Scot struck right. Donovan caught his ax on the back swing. The sharp blade sliced through the branch, but the blow threw Red off-balance. He backed up three more steps. Donovan shifted the staff to his left hand, still twirling it. He kept the blade in his right, brandishing it in tight circles to make sure Black didn't sneak up on him from the rear.

"Die, Scottish scum," Donovan yelled, jabbing at Red with the staff and Black with the sword.

Red stumbled over a rock and fell into the lake, arms flailing.

Donovan didn't wait for the splash to confirm his fall. He whirled on Black. His shortened staff slammed down on a vulnerable wrist. Black's ax fell from slack fingers. Donovan thrust his blade deep into the man's gut. The demon blood would poison him if the wound didn't kill him.

He wiped the blade on the grass and headed for the kirk and the tunnel into the depths of Kirkenwood.

His face met the dirt before a coldly sharp pain slashed across his left thigh. He twisted, raising his sword. Red loomed over him, ax raised for a killing blow.

Chapter 12

Kirkenwood ramparts, just after dawn.

I BRACED myself against the stonework with my right hand while I pinched the bridge of my nose with my left. Carefully I touched all around my eyes, seeking a wound. My fingers remained dry. No blood. No sharp pain met my probe.

Gradually shadows filtered through to my left eye. Shapes took on outlines. The rising sun proved too bright for my damaged vision. When I shielded my eyes with my hand, my left eye focused well enough but only in shades of gray. My right eye perceived only a too-bright whiteness.

I had the sense that if I had not caught the arrow, had let it fly and fall to the ground, it would have inflicted greater damage to one and all within Kirkenwood.

Why had the stones not warned me of the approaching demon?

They had. My night of sleeplessness, my indecision. The stones had been speaking to me. I did not know how to listen. Raven would have known.

In that moment, I knew myself unworthy of her heritage.

With shaking knees, doubts, guilt, and unbalanced perception of distance and depth, I made my way back down the stairs to the bailey. Twice I nearly overstepped the open stairs and fell to the ground below. By the time I reached solid ground my knees shook, my head and neck ached, and my stomach wanted to revolt. I nearly crawled, trying to keep everything under control.

"Griffin, where are you hurt?" Fiona met me as I emerged from the stairs.

"My eyes." I croaked out the words, still shaken by my trek downward.

"Can ye see?" She touched my eyelids carefully with cool fingers. No magical healing followed her touch. She didn't have Meg's talent. Meg didn't have the wits to use hers.

"I can see enough for now. How many have we lost? What is the damage? Have the enemy retreated? Malcolm can lead a party to follow and make sure they return to their own lands." Only a few days at home and already I thought and reacted like the warrior I'd trained to be for eighteen years.

When would I think and act like a priest?

"The horses are near-useless with panic, but they'll be better off running than closed in a roofless stable that smells of smoke and fear. Malcolm is already mounting a squad to pursue the raiders." Fiona took my hand and led me across the bailey toward the keep.

"You did not answer my first question, Fiona." I stopped short. Something was terribly wrong.

My limited vision was still grainy with brightness. Details eluded me. I could see the gaping black holes that made a ruin of the stable roof. I saw the movement of many people bustling about, cleaning up.

"You have to come, Griffin. We need you to . . . to . . ." Fiona choked on the last words.

Then I remembered the crash of broken glass after the second flaming arrow.

The women began to keen within the keep. Their mourning wail sent shivers up and down my spine.

"Who?"

Donovan rolled, heedless of the pain in his left leg. The icy cold slash turned to fire, shooting up into his gut. Heat drained from his head as light fled from his vision.

"I'll kill you, you son of a midden whore." He slashed blindly with his sword until it met resistance.

Red grunted. His eyes glazed as he stared at the blade

sticking out of his gut. He clutched at the wound with both hands. Blood and innards spilled from between his fingers.

The rank smell of death filled the clearing.

"God's breath I hope 'tis yours and not mine," Donovan whispered between gritted teeth.

A moment of blackness crossed his mind and his eyes. He had something to do. Something important. Something . . .

The burning pain in his leg brought him back to awareness. He had to get through the jagged tunnel and up the ladder to the passage that ran through the curtain wall between the gallery and the gatehouse.

Strength drained from him along with his blood in the crippling wound.

Resolutely he probed it with his fingers. The bone did not protrude. He bled heavily, but it didn't gush or spout.

Through waves of pain and dizziness, he forced himself to sit. After a moment, he had enough sense to attack the hem of his shirt with his still bloody sword. The fine linen tore easily. He wadded one wide strip over the wound. Another to bind it in place.

Then he fell back on his elbows, too weak to move.

He rode out the dizziness. After interminable moments he rolled onto his right knee and two hands. Dragging his injured leg, he crawled toward the church.

The five steps up to the porch presented a formidable barrier. Donovan breathed deeply three times, making sure he cleared his lungs with each exhalation. On the fourth breath he lifted his right hand onto the first step. A long pause while he breathed again. Left hand and right knee climbed fairly easily. Hands up one more step, knee poised and ready to lift. Then he was faced with the prospect of pulling up his wounded left leg over the stone wall.

"I can do this," he promised himself. "For the baby and Kate, I have to do this." Though what good he'd be to the defenders of the keep, he didn't know. Gritting his teeth and scrunching his eyes closed he hoisted himself as high as he could to keep the wound from scraping against the stones.

Not high enough.

With a loud moan and shaking limbs he collapsed against the first step.

"Milord?" Father Peter whispered from a crack in the doorway. A waft of incense followed the opening of the door.

Donovan always associated that particular scent—whispering of fresh greens, clean earth, and beautiful flowers—with the tall, slender priest. Father Manuel preferred a heavier, more oppressive incense for his churchly rituals. No more. He'd killed Father Manuel, but not the demon that inhabited his body.

Father Peter must have assessed Donovan's condition for he thrust open the door and rushed to Donovan's side. "Holy Mother of God, bless you, my boy." The priest crossed himself and bowed his head. Then he slid his arms under Donovan and lifted.

"You needn't carry me, Father," Donovan protested, amazed that the tall and lean man who must be fifty years old, at least, could manage his weight.

"You're in no shape to negotiate the tunnel, lad." Father Peter didn't even breathe hard.

"You know about the tunnel?"

"Aye."

"How?"

"I've lived near on top of it for most of my life. And I've the same blood as you." Indeed, he bore a hawkish nose similar to most of the men of the family. Somehow Donovan and Griffin had escaped the curse of the prominent beak that dominated the face and dwarfed the eyes.

"I know." This priest was Donovan's second cousin twice removed. The living at Kirkenwood always went to a relative who could trace his descent to Arthur and the Merlin, the same as the laird and the Pendragon.

Father Peter chuckled lightly. " 'Tis my right to know the secrets of the Pendragons, in and out of the confessional. Should anything happen to you, then I must ensure the preservation of certain records and knowledge." He shouldered the door open all the way and then slipped inside.

Donovan warily searched the nave and altar for signs of lurking hostile Scots.

"Ye needn't worry about the Spaniard. He departed early this evening, all huffed up with indignation about the pyre for the dog. I dared not confront alone those two godless raiders who have been lurking about since midnight."

A long silence stretched between them. Did the enemy suspect the true importance to the location of the village kirk, so far removed from the village?

"I had to ensure that no one tried to discover the tunnel. I pray that Father Manuel did not suspect its existence and alert the raiders."

"You didn' . . . don't trust the Spaniard any more than I do."

"I consider the secret of this back door as sacred as the confessional."

"Put me down, Father Peter. I must do this on my own." Donovan fingered the little knife tucked up his sleeve. He found his balance on one foot and tested his weight on the other. He couldn't travel far, but the leg would support him the short distance to the monastic cells beside the church. He had to make certain the demon did not reanimate the foreign priest's body and return here.

"What are you thinking, Laird Donovan?" Father Peter asked sternly.

Donovan flipped the knife, catching it by the blade between two fingers. The weighted staghorn hilt perfectly balanced the blade for throwing. It also provided a convenient bludgeon. "Making certain that we are alone."

Father Peter dropped his head, mumbling a prayer or a plea for forgiveness. Donovan didn't hear the specifics. He took one cautious step along the nave toward the crossing. Then another. Cold sweat broke out on his brow and back. If only he had something to hold onto, take the weight off the wound. He began to shake with the effort of moving. His leg hurt abominably but held . . .

Until he turned right just before the altar, toward the residence. His leg buckled, and he stumbled. Father Peter was there in a heartbeat, catching him beneath the arms to break his fall.

"Kate, the baby, I've got to go to them, protect them," Donovan panted, still trying to crawl forward.

"You're as weak as your newborn daughter." Father Peter tsked. "Very well. I shall tend to this. Stay here and make certain no one follows me. I'll send healers and a litter for you when we can."

"I must . . ."

"You must survive. I will send for you." Father Peter eased Donovan back onto the stone floor. As quietly as a mist he disappeared through the locked gate leading to the crypt. Had he even unlocked and opened the decorative iron bars?

"Father Peter . . ." Donovan called the man back. But he was gone. Only a drift of incense suggested he'd been there at all.

Donovan tried crawling again. He had to get to the keep. Too many people depended upon him. His daughter. His wife. Even Mad Meg needed him.

The wound shot fire up his spine and down to his toes with every movement. Time passed. Each movement became slower. He lapsed into unconsciousness. How long?

"So, you have come crawling back to God to beg forgiveness of your sins in your final hour of life." Father Manuel's sneering voice roused Donovan from his swoon. He loomed over Donovan; the sword wound still gaped, still spilled blood. His black robes blended with the shadows like an avenging angel of death.

No, a demon of death. The man was dead. This but a shade conjured from Donovan's fevered brain.

Donovan looked up at him and saw only contempt in the man's face, no trace of mercy or pity.

"You are dead, Spanish dog."

Father Manuel crossed himself in a parody of the Christian invocation.

"Your soul is already condemned. You brought death to the doorstep of sacred ground. You murdered a priest, murdered honest soldiers rather than trust your soul to God's mercy."

"You are desperate to condemn me on any grounds— even false ones. Do you fear hell so much you seek to take me with you?" Donovan allowed his body to relax and gather strength for the ordeal to come. He had few choices left.

"You condemn yourself. But I see that God is ready to take your life and judge your soul. I need do nothing further except to see why Father Peter secretes himself in the crypt now when our adversaries are dead. He should have taken refuge there immediately."

"Not while I live." Donovan rose up and lunged at Father Manuel with all of his remaining strength. The surge of blood through his muscles sent knife blades of pain to his wound. Dizziness gave him the sensation of flying.

And then the shade of the priest disappeared. The reek of burning sulfur remained.

"Son of donkey spawn!" Donovan cursed. "May your balls rot, impious cur." He pounded the stone flooring where the ghost or demon had stood.

Time stretched before him. He knew nothing but the pain. Perhaps he slept, perhaps he fainted again.

"Donovan!" Father Peter cried from the narthex—the opposite direction from where he had disappeared. How long ago?

"Donovan. You must come with me. Now. You are needed at the keep."

The words chilled Donovan to the core. "What has happened?" He rolled onto his back.

The ghost did not return.

"Callum, help his lordship onto the litter. I do not believe he has the strength to walk to the keep on his own," Father Peter ordered.

A heaviness grew out of Donovan's belly. He'd wasted valuable energy on a ghost.

The family priest waved two cowed servants into the kirk. The men carried a rough litter made of two pike handles and a blanket.

"The keep, Father? My family? What happened?" Donovan suffered the rough ministrations of his men as they helped him slide onto the litter.

"Best prepare yourself for the worst, Donovan."

"Not knowing is worse. Tell me what happened."

"Scottish raiders attacked with fire in the dark hours before dawn. They did not breach the castle."

Donovan exhaled heavily. The castle was safe. "The village?"

"Your brother sounded the alarm in time. They all found refuge within the walls. Most of the sheep and chickens as well."

"Then what tragedy has put that scowl upon your face?" Donovan nearly shouted. Better than screaming in pain as the men jostled his leg in lifting the litter.

"A flaming arrow penetrated the glass window of the laird's bedchamber."

Chill silence descended upon Donovan. He opened his mouth to speak and had to close it again.

"My daughter?"

"Meg saved the babe from the smoke."

"K—Kate?"

"The arrow penetrated her heart."

Chapter 13

Hermitage Castle, the next night.

ROANNA shivered in the midnight air as she paced the ramparts. "Dreams. Only dreams," she murmured to herself over and over.

You have had this dream before, her master reminded her.

"I have lived this dream before. But no more. I have grown beyond it."

If you have grown beyond it, why do you continue to dream it?

"Because you will not let me forget."

You summoned me, but you did not call my name. You cannot control me, no matter what you desire. I have taught you magic, languages, history. I have given you your family heritage. And still you fight me. You will have the dream as a reminder of what you owe me as long as you resist. Her master's voice took on a menacing quality. He didn't usually resort to threats against her. He didn't have to.

Once more Roanna lived through that time five years ago. . . .

Blood trickled down the inside of her leg. Her torn shift no longer covered her left breast. Bruises blanketed her arms and face and belly. Her swollen lips oozed more blood. One eye, her left she thought but couldn't be sure which was right and which left anymore, refused to open.

She stumbled from the rough pallet where Laird Douglas snored. His soft penis sagged out of his codpiece. He'd been in such a hurry to plunge into her he'd ripped the points of his clothing and couldn't refasten his nethergarments. The smell of sour wine permeated the dank cell and his body.

Roanna retched. She sank to her knees, coughing up bile. When her body rejected nothing more, she got to her feet by clinging to the wall. One step, then two. She did not hurt any more walking than she had lying down or retching. A third step brought her to the door. The laird hadn't even bothered to lock it. He'd been so certain that his rape of her would cow her into willing submission, he could not imagine her continued defiance. Or so he had told her, time and time again as he pounded his fists into her. Her talent with fire and vision was his to command and no one else's.

Never again. Gran had warned her that men would demand submission. Roanna had grown up expecting to be raped. But, Holy Mother, she never expected it to hurt this much.

"You may have broken my body, Lord James Douglas, but you shall never possess or break my spirit." She repeated the litany of strength as she crept out of the tiny room.

All of the Douglas family and retainers slept in the great hall. Roanna tiptoed around them. Then, at the opposite tower from her cell, she pushed open the stiff door and climbed the turret stair. No one moved, no one stopped her. They were all drunk and sated on booty from her village. She imagined the Kirkwood raiders sprawled in their own hall in a similar state.

They would all die. As Raven must die from the spell she had cast a few weeks ago. The men would die weak and mewling in their beds like women, and the women would die by fire and sword, but only after they endured the same hurt and humiliation she suffered. She vowed it.

At the top of the tower she breathed deeply of the cool air three hours before dawn. The darkest hour of the night. Gran had told her that she must perform this spell at the dark of the moon, when only a little starlight and no external fire lit the path she must walk.

Gathering her anger into magical energy, Roanna walked a pentagram upon the lookout tower. Tiny flamelets burst from her heels as she defined the five points. The blood of her rape dripped and mingled with the bits of fire, fueling them. They grew, joined together, and spread along the lines of her path. She closed the central sigil with dragging feet and a heaviness in her chest. She had to hurry and complete this spell before she lost her strength and her will.

Slowly she enclosed the pentagram within a circle. The bits of fire following her grew. The heaviness left her feet and her head. Dizziness threatened to topple her over the top of the tower. She bent over, dropping her head below the parapet and closed her eyes. But only for a moment. With the swirling patterns of darkness before her eyes under control, she continued to close the circle.

"Beginning and end, one meets the other. Time past becomes time future. The present enfolds both," she chanted.

Fire flared up to her knees all along the lines of her sigil. She felt the heat but did not burn. Power flowed upward, clearing her head and brightening her vision. She could see all the way to the North Sea and deep into the bowels of the earth.

Once more she walked the enclosing circle of her pentagram, seeking a deeper darkness within the black night. Seeking the nameless folds of evil that engulfed the light of life.

There! To the southwest. A portal to the netherworld.

"Come to me, O Demon, born of darkness, bringer of pain. Heed my call and come to me!" she called into the night, careful to stand outside the pentagram but within the circle. "Come to my sigil of power. Come to the center and join with me."

What is my name? A voice boomed out of the night directly into her mind.

The intensity stabbed her between the eyes from behind and pounded into her temples. She focused the pain, pushed it downward until she started bleeding again. The warm red liquid flowed down her leg to add its power to the fire of the pentagram.

"I know not your name. I care not if you have a name. I ask that you join my quest for vengeance. Be my aide, be my power, be my life!" she intoned the ritual words with more enthusiasm than Gran had taught her. Gran's warnings of consequences seemed overcautious. "I will have my revenge on James Douglas and his clan. I will have the life of the Pendragon and her heirs. Death and destruction to them all, threefold for what they have done to me and mine.''

Then I will come to you. The voice in her head was still too loud and it seemed to laugh at her, at her mission, at the pitiful lives of mere mortals.

Flames rose up once more, blasting Roanna with the heat and fumes from hell. She tried to step away, but the power in the circle stopped her. She held her breath and pinched her nose from the burning smell of sulfur. She threw an arm up to protect her vulnerable eyes.

And she gloried in the power that infused her. She need only reach out and close her fist. James Douglas' heart would stop.

Do not murder that one just yet, the demon said. His voice took on more natural tones, as if he spoke from right in front of her instead of across the portal of time to another dimension.

Cautiously she lowered her arm from in front of her eyes and peeked at the center of her working.

Flames rose in a tower, sending sparks into the depth of night. On the eastern horizon, the faintest glimmer of light foretold the dawn. She had to finish this before the sun emerged from its nightly sleep.

What do you see within the flames, Roanna Flame-hair?

"I see a head, two arms, two legs. Only the vaguest of outlines."

And so shall you only see until I have gained in power. Together we will bring chaos to Britain. Only the pain and death of chaos will weaken the seal on my portal. When Britain succumbs to flames, when Britain's cathedrals and castles are reduced to ashes, then and only then will I emerge triumphant!

"And until then?"

You are my instrument of destruction.

"Let us begin with Laird James Douglas. Then I will depart this place and live free of all men and their controls."

We will begin with chaos. You must drive a wedge between the Kirkwood twins. Together they can undo all that you and I desire. Separate, they are useless.

"Done." Roanna turned and faced southwest, in the direction of Kirkenwood. She gathered power into her hands forming a ball of astral fire. For a few moments she tossed it back and forth between her hands, letting it grow and expand as she allowed words to form.

> *Fire burn a clear path,*
> *Fire burn away the bonds,*
> *Fire sear the vessels,*
> *Let these two joined by birth and thoughts*
> *Never more meet in mind*
> *Or reconciliation.*

She drew back her arm and launched the ball of fire upward into the heavens. Fueled by her magic the fire sped upward seemingly forever until her mundane senses could not find it. But her magic knew it flew across the moors, over the burns, down the corries to lodge in Kirkenwood, deep within the hearts of two brothers.

Her knees sagged with exhaustion, all the magic gone.

You need to refuel your power if you are to use my knowledge, the demon whispered as if he, too, were depleted by her spell. *You must also have enough power to slip away unnoticed and return with your grandmother's staff. The staff did not burn with the village. It is necessary to focus your power.*

"What must I do?" Deep satisfaction almost made up for her exhaustion.

I need a blood sacrifice, but not the laird. His death so soon after the raid will brand you as a witch. You will burn at the stake. And though I will gain power from your pain and death, 'twill not be enough to free me of my portal. You must live.

"What blood sacrifice do you need?" Roanna swallowed her revulsion. What was the death of another when Douglas and Kirkwood had conspired to raze her village and murder her family?

We will begin with one of the prisoners. The one the young laird ravishes as we speak will do. She is half dead with humiliation as it is. You show great power and strength in pushing aside the silly emotions that kill that one.

"My sister," Roanna said flatly.

She will not survive the night. Give her the mercy of a quick end.

"And then I will leave this place of evil."

*And then you will serve the laird patiently while I teach
you what you must know to survive in the world. You will
learn to infiltrate the courts of power and sow the seeds of
chaos among the rich and powerful.*

"I will not stay here!"

You will do as I command.

Searing pain blinded Roanna. She dropped to her knees
clutching her temples.

*Remember this next time you attempt to wrest control
from me. For I am the Demon of Chaos. You have not
called my name in your summons. Therefore I may use you
and you must obey.*

The road to Edinburgh, 28 September 1558.

Roanna sighed heavily and reined in her horse. Laird Jamie
kept his mount to a plodding gait, slowing the small procession to a snail's pace.

She'd had to pry him, quaking and shivering, out of the
fastness of Hermitage Castle. He had to claim his inheritance from Queen Regent Marie de Guise in Edinburgh
before he lost it to a more ambitious and smarter rival.

She needed to remove herself from Hermitage Castle,
permanently, to escape the dreams and memories.

And her failure. Both of the twins lived. Raven was dead.
Lord Brian Kirkwood was dead. Lord James Douglas was
dead. But Donovan and Griffin remained alive.

She needed time far away from the borders to contem-
plate what she had done wrong and correct it.

Since Jamie had bungled the attack on Kirkenwood, he
feared reprisal. The English as well as his own relatives
posed a continuing threat until Marie de Guise confirmed
his right to the title.

"Maybe next time you will listen to me and follow the
battle plan," she sneered at him. "Griffin Kirkwood still
lives." Her scrying bowl showed her only shadows and
clouds. She had no way to tell if her arrows had any effect
upon Kirkenwood at all.

"Griffin is a priest. He's worthless. 'Tis Donovan I fear. He'll come at me with twice the men I command." Jamie sat back on his saddle even further. His horse slowed. He looked around them anxiously, as if he expected Donovan Kirkwood to jump out of the nearest clump of heather. "Hermitage Castle is impervious to attack. We can withstand a long siege there. Perhaps we'd best return."

"Griffin Kirkwood is a powerful magician. He'll come after me rather than you with all the magic at his disposal. Hermitage Castle is impervious to mundane attacks from the English. But no castle can withstand Griffin Kirkwood. We must hie to Edinburgh. He can't kill us if he can't find us." Even as she spoke, she concentrated upon a spell that would blur their trail.

"The only reason I keep you is so your magic will protect me, make me stronger than my enemies. Can't you just . . . just do something?" Panic tinged Jamie's voice. He stopped his horse completely and looked about frantically.

Roanna sighed again. What had she done, tying herself—however temporarily—to this weakling? Thankfully she only needed him for a short time to come.

For now, she could not hasten ahead of him and maintain a semblance of servitude. She still needed the protection of the Douglas name in order to move into society. From there . . . ?

Next time, Griffin Kirkwood, I will be better prepared for you.

How hard could she prod Jamie now before he rebelled and retreated? She needed to get to Edinburgh and the queen regent. Jamie had succumbed to her whispers before the raid. Then he had shut her out of his mind quite effectively.

She wished her grandmother had told her more about a victim's resistance. But Gran's knowledge had died with her on the night the Kirkwood raiders had burned her village and let the Black Douglas take Roanna captive.

The old laird hadn't the courage to kidnap her on his own. Allied with the Kirkwoods, he had a magician to attack from one side while he set up a trap on the only escape route. He'd known that in the confusion and grief over the loss of Gran, Roanna's powers would be weakened enough to allow her to be captured.

Roanna had made certain the old laird's death was slower and more painful than Gran's.

"The battle goes to the bold," she muttered. Not that
the family motto had done them much good the night her
village had burned. "I'll have Jamie back under my control
before I throw him to the wolves at court." Three deep
breaths brought her anger to a low simmer, where she'd
kept it for five years. She could manage her emotions at
that level. As long as her demon did not awaken her memories and her guilt.

"My lord, what ails you?" Roanna asked mildly, as if she
truly cared. "Perhaps we should stop for the night and
enter the city at daylight?"

Jamie's face darkened. Fear conflicted with anger in his
aura.

"We ride. I'll sleep this night with a roof over my head."
He scanned the hilltops behind them and the pastures
ahead of them for signs of ambush. A raven flew overhead,
croaking his displeasure at the world.

Jamie started, reaching for his sword. His skin paled, and
sweat dotted his brow.

"Coward," Roanna said under her breath. " 'Tis only one
raven. The omen of death is three." *Unless this is the shade
of Raven Kirkwood come to spy upon us for Griffin, the
next Pendragon.* Then she forced a sweet smile upon her
face. "Shall I ride ahead with your steward to secure lodging?" Her face felt like it would crack from the false smile.
Until she had secured another place for herself, she had to
keep up the illusion of loyalty to a powerful border laird.

Jamie had not offered marriage in return for her services
in bed. Nor had she suggested it. Jamie was but a single
stepping stone on her life path. She aimed higher.

The queen regent did not yet know it, but she needed a
soothsayer. Roanna intended to stand beside Marie de
Guise and advise her to strike at England with warfare at
every turn. By the time Protestant Elizabeth took the
throne of England, she wouldn't have an England to rule.

Soon Roanna would wear the ring of the Pendragon. Her
master had promised.

The Demon of Chaos chortled in the back of her mind.

*Power comes from chaos. Strife builds magic. When you
wear the ring of the Pendragon, I, Tryblith, will be free.*

Chapter 14

Kirkenwood, Autumn 1558.

MY vision returned to me in bits and pieces. Most days I could see only dark shapes against a painfully bright background.

I sat for days watching my brother writhe within the depths of a fever. We stitched and poulticed the wound, dosed him with willow bark tea and feverfew, and prayed. I added extract of mummy to the poultice to draw out the blood poison, the most powerful tool in any apothecary's stores. I had purchased the drug in Paris, carefully inspecting the Egyptian corpse. Though I trusted the apothecary, even the best of them had been duped by the corpses of criminals dipped in pitch to make them appear mummified. Charlatan drugs had no effect upon wounds or taken internally. Some could do more harm than no treatment at all.

Donovan wandered in and out of his senses.

"Die, Spanish pig," he raved over and over again.

I knew who he meant and tried to keep my twin's words secret. But the women who bathed him and changed the dressings heard as much or more than I did.

I tried to persuade Meg to work her magic on him. In the past, she had commanded miracles of healing. Now she refused to acknowledge anyone but Baby Betsy, Donovan's daughter. She sat for hours crooning to the baby, releasing the child only to the wet nurse. She'd held her when Father Peter baptized her, too, acting godmother. We named the baby Mary Elizabeth, for the queen and her sister, since Donovan remained too incoherent to request otherwise.

Mad Meg worked no magic that I saw from the moment she took possession of our niece.

Father Peter officiated at the funeral mass for Kate. I no longer trusted myself to read the office, and my emotions put blocks on my memory. The entire family and village turned out for the ceremony. They filled the kirk and spilled over into the clearing around the lake and cemetery.

I should have attended. But someone had to watch over Donovan. In France, as well as the other modern and civilized parts of England, men did not attend the funeral of a woman, and women did not attend the funeral of a man. Elders of the family seemed exempt from the tradition. Raven had passed into the category of Crone, no longer capable of bearing children, and therefore no longer just a woman. My training rebelled against tainting the sacred rite of Kate's funeral with the presence of the opposite sex.

My heart wanted to grieve with the people of Kirkenwood. I wanted to belong with them. But, since the raid, I knew I must complete the mission of my bishop. I needed to be at the hub of politics in London. If the Scots raided here accompanied by a magician, then England was not safe.

The Spanish would rally to their English allies. The French must then retaliate to protect their Scottish allies. War and chaos would follow throughout our island and across the Continent.

But I could not leave yet. Until Donovan recovered, I must act the laird, giving these people guidance and protection. None of my many cousins and in-laws seemed qualified or trained to lead an entire barony.

I was sitting beside Donovan's bed, trying to read with one eye, when the first storm of autumn struck. Helwriaeth snored lightly at my feet. Her belly swelled with the new life inside her. The household set about putting up shutters and building the fires higher.

For once Meg left her chair by the hearth in the hall. She wandered about talking to Baby Betsy, spending a few moments watching each of the scurrying servants and family as they went about their chores. I watched her from the top of the stairs by the laird's bedchamber. At last she climbed those stairs, still talking to Betsy in a language all her own.

I knew I should put a stop to the nonsense words lest

the baby grow up thinking it proper speech. How could I force Mad Meg to speak coherent words and phrases? No one had heard anything but gibberish and baby talk from her for five years.

"Pretty baby, Meg's baby, pretty Betsy." Meg sang the words over and over.

The tune caught in the back of my throat and refused to let go. I hummed it along with my sister, wishing I had a timbrel or pipe to accompany us. Lacking an instrument, I tapped my foot to her lively rhythm. The true lyrics to the tune remained just at the edge of my memory. Fruitlessly, I sought the words. All I could think of was "Pretty baby one, Meg's baby two, pretty Betsy three." Together, Meg and I sang and counted her steps up to where I stood. The words sounded a little twisted stretched out to fit the notes.

Meg hesitated at thirteen, repeated twelve slowly. The tune became a dirge.

A pain slashed through my right eye. The world tilted slightly. I closed my eyes tightly, waiting for the dizziness to pass. When I looked at my sister again, she shimmered within a halo of bright golden light. The vivid reds, blues, and greens of the painted design on the whitewashed walls and ceilings jumped at me in startling detail. I had experienced these brief moments of clear vision before. Did I fall into another realm where color had more meaning than words? I scrunched my eyes closed, almost hoping that when I opened them again, the intense colors would go away.

They didn't.

Then the tune I'd been trying to remember hit me as sharply as the clear vision. I choked on the lyrics.

> *Welcome Death to our home,*
> *Life ends for all,*
> *Welcome Death now.*

"What do you mean, Meg?" I shuddered. Superstition held that death lived in the wind. He stalked his victims as he wore down their strength.

The church denounced the superstition. It persisted outside the cities, especially here in the north where the wind was a near constant companion.

My magic had always had an affinity with the element of
Air, manifested in the wind.

"Pretty Betsy, pretty Betsy," Meg chanted over and over
without a tune. Her previous song had stalled.

"What do you mean singing that song, Meg?" I asked
again.

My sister stopped three steps below me. She swayed from
foot to foot and refused to look at me.

"For once in your life, Meg, look at me and tell me
the truth."

She raised her deep blue eyes, softened by tears and her
vague concentration. "Betsy's da blames himself," she said,
dropping all hint of the baby voice she had used for five
years. "He called Death and now Death beats at our door."
Having purged herself of the revelation, she dropped her
gaze once more to the baby and resumed her song, "Pretty
baby fourteen, Meg's baby fifteen, Pretty Betsy sixteen."
She'd skipped the unlucky thirteen.

Deep in my heart I knew Mad Meg had spoken the truth.
Donovan had given up and wanted to die. But my twin had
too much to live for, a new baby, a barony. Why would he
call Death?

He had lost a wife. Had he truly loved Kate that deeply?
I knew he held a deep affection for her. Was it more? Was
she his soul mate?

The world tilted once more, and details faded from my
vision. I was left with only shades of gray in the left eye
and vague outlines in the right. Using both together, I could
see well enough to negotiate around the keep.

"Come with me, Meg." I clasped her elbow and guided
her into the large bedchamber above the hall. A gallery
ran around the perimeter of the rest of the hall, a place
for musicians, or seating for extra retainers when the hall
filled. Otherwise the ceiling of the hall reached all the way
to the smoke darkened rafters thirty feet above the floor.
I had placed a cot in the laird's chamber for myself while
Donovan was besieged with fever.

"Where?" Meg's eyes cleared for half a heartbeat, almost
as if she understood.

"Betsy needs to meet her da." I escorted her gently forward, keeping myself poised to grab her if she decided to
bolt.

No, she would make no decision. She reacted only, depending upon her instincts to protect her mind and body.

"My da died. Fiona told me so. Fiona let me kiss him good-bye before the angels came and took him," Meg said in her baby voice.

"Yes, your da is with the angels now, Meg. Do you know that he was my da, too, and Donovan's?"

She scrunched her face in confusion. I noticed hollows in her cheeks and shadows around her eyes—an adult face without the vague softness of the child she wanted to be.

"Yes, Meg. You are my sister. You are Donovan's sister and Betsy's aunt. Do you remember the time Donovan and I showed you the tunnel beneath the family chapel?"

She nodded happily. A smile brought light to her eyes, banishing the confusion for a time.

"Do you remember how I tripped and twisted my ankle?"

She shook her head, negating my statement. She pouted, trying to revert to her normal blissful state. But memory held her captive. She'd been thirteen at the time, Donovan and I barely a year older. She could not reconcile the memories of an adolescent with her need to remain a tot.

"You laid your hands upon my ankle and made the swelling and pain go away," I persisted. "You healed torn muscle and ligaments so that I could walk again. Otherwise, you and Donovan would have had to carry me all the way up the steep stairs, through the crowded crypt back into the chapel."

"No, no, no. Not Meg. Meg never did that." She tried to jerk away from me, but I held her arms tightly.

"Yes, you did, Meg. And I need you to do the same again. I need you to lay your hands upon Donovan's wound and take the fever away. You can do it, Meg. It's a good thing you do. It's a miracle only you can perform."

"You can do it if you want," she said with absolute, adult certainty. Then she relaxed and slithered out of my grasp. "Baby Betsy help." She thrust the infant into my arms and ran lightly around the gallery. She disappeared into the shadows at the far end. I knew she sought the entrance to the secret passage.

What would she do there among Raven's treasures and the family archives?

Donovan moaned and thrashed about as if he wrestled
with an unseen opponent. If Death had found him, Donovan was not yet ready to follow him into the netherworld.

If I was going to do anything, I had to do it now.

A spell is nothing more than a prayer, Raven's ghost whispered to me.

"I will not work magic, but I can pray." Resolutely, I set
the baby into her cradle and lifted my twin's wasted form
into my arms. I made my way down the stairs, across the
hall to a side door. The two steps down into the chapel
nearly tripped me, with my burden and my faulty vision. I
approached the altar, stumbling and awkward. I should
have reverence and awe in my posture as well as my mind.

Humbled, I lay my brother at the altar rail. There I knelt
and began my prayers, requesting God to help Donovan in
his fight to live. I begged forgiveness for my presumption
that only Meg and her magic could heal him. I cried for
the rift between me and my twin.

Cold crept into my joints. My fingertips and toes ached.
My knees turned to jelly. My back and arms grew stiff.
And still I prayed.

I sought answers to all of the questions and doubts my
return to England had raised within me. I prayed the entire
rosary through three times when I ran out of specific en-
treaties. I prostrated myself and prayed again.

The cold stone floor became a burning ache within my
chest.

"Your will, not my own," I breathed exhaustedly and
slumped into unconsciousness.

Time must have passed. I did not acknowledge it. "Griffin." Fiona shook my shoulder gently. "Griffin, wake up."

"Donovan?" I lifted my head, blinking against the brightness of the candle my sister carried.

"His fever has broken. He sleeps," she said quietly. "You
healed him! I thought only Meg could do that."

Two women fussed over Donovan while four men prepared a litter to carry him back to his bed.

" 'Twas the will of God," I replied meekly. "I cannot
work healing magic, even if I would work magic. Only God
has the right to work a miracle." I dropped my head against
the cold floor stones again. *Thank you, Lord.*

"Come to supper, Griffin. You've been in here all night

and a full day. The storm has blown itself out while you worked this spell."

I mumbled something, not certain I could face food yet. A long mug of beer would help revive me, though. Stiffly, I pushed myself to my knees.

" 'Twas no spell, Fiona. Merely's God's will."

"Does that explain the eldritch blue glow that filled the chapel for a night and a day?" She made the sign of the cross and took a step away from me. "I remember Raven, Griffin. I know what this family is about. I recognize magic when I see it. Why can't you?"

"My faith . . . 'Twas God's will," I insisted. I stood and faced her, determined to make her see the truth of my words.

"Griffin, your eyes," Fiona gasped as she reared away from me.

I pressed my fingers against them. They came away wet, but not with blood. My fingers remained pale in the candlelight.

"The film is gone from them." My sister knelt beside me, holding the candle closer as she grabbed my chin and inspected my face. "Can you see?"

"Not with that light blinding me to all else."

She moved the candle aside. After a moment my eyes adjusted to the dim room. The vigil light above the altar glowed faintly in its red bowl. I could detect no other colors without more light.

"It's probably just a temporary clearing, I've had them before."

"Come into the hall. We're laying the evening meal, and all of the sconces are lit."

The servants preceded us. A cheer went up among the gathered family and retainers when they saw Donovan's face, pale and wan, but no longer dry and flushed with fever.

I hesitated upon the top step, waiting for my balance to tilt and my vision to go gray again. After several long moments, Fiona pushed me into the hall. I blinked and stared about. My left eye saw colors again! Normal colors. Outlines remained fuzzy, but the cloud of gray had disappeared. My right eye saw less than the left, but more than it had yesterday.

Thank you, Lord. Now I can go about your work commanded to me by my bishop.

Not yet, Raven whispered. *You need your familiar to warn you of the demon. You must stay here with Helwriaeth for a time yet.*

Chapter 15

White Horse Inn, Edinburgh, Scotland, late autumn 1558.

ROANNA fluffed the modest ruff of lace on Jamie's collar. Just a narrow edging of needle lace attached directly to the shirt, not nearly grand enough for court. Not even a tiny bit of embroidery or lace on his shirt either, merely a few colored threads sewn around the hems of his coat. But it would have to do. Jamie hadn't the time or money to purchase more lace. Roanna had learned much of court fashion when she'd spent an entire morning spying on the popinjays who sought audience with Queen Regent Marie de Guise. Roanna had been able to pad Jamie's trousers properly and shorten them to a bit above the knee. His doublet and fur-lined coat were old-fashioned, but well made—they'd belonged to his father during his prime. She'd altered them to fit Jamie's slighter frame. He no longer looked quite the country bumpkin. Just—half finished.

Now if she could just keep him from acting like the rude border ruffian he truly was, she'd have her *entrée* to the queen.

"Stand up straight, Jamie, and remember to bend your right knee when you bow before Her Maj . . . Her Grace." She had to remember that, in Scotland, the monarchs ruled by the grace of God and not through their own majesty. She'd spent too much time in Paris and London on errands for Tryblith and almost forgotten the local protocol.

"I don't see why I have to bow to anyone—especially a woman, and a foreign woman at that. I am Laird of the Clan Douglas, a proud and ancient family. More ancient than hers."

"She is the queen regent, widow of James V and mother

121

to Marie Queen of Scots. I'll be right behind you to remind you."

"I'd rather swear my loyalty to the real queen. Scotland would be in less turmoil, lord fighting lord, all the lords protesting the queen, the church fighting all of them, the Earl of Moray manipulating them all as if he were the true king and not the queen's bastard brother. Marie should just come home." Jamie pouted. Not a pretty sight.

"Marie is married to the heir of France. She brings us a great alliance with the marriage. Her mother is learned and able. Now pay your respects to her properly. Remember to doff your cap when you bow. I'll curtsy first."

"No, you won't."

"What?" Roanna dropped her hands from his arm where she had been fussing with a loose bit of embroidery on his coat, trying to make it lie flat.

"I go alone. You're just a peasant, and a whore. You have no place at court." Jamie stalked out of their rented room at the White Horse Inn. All the visiting nobility who did not own a house in Edinburgh paid exorbitant prices for a drafty cubicle here. Located at the eastern end of the Royal Mile, convenience to Holyrood Palace made up for the heavy price.

Stunned, Roanna didn't rush to follow him.

"My blood is more ancient and proud than either yours or the queen's, Jamie Douglas," Roanna said when she regained her wits. "I'll attend court on another's arm, if not yours."

In the common room of the White Horse, a number of nobles took their ease with mugs of ale, or the newly fashionable beer made from imported hops. Some even drank mulled wine. Spices and honey must mask the vinegary taste. Roanna could tell by the smell alone that the stuff was undrinkable. Any of them could escort her into the palace. But she could not seduce them here. The women who frequented the tavern were common doxies who expected no more than a few coins, a hot meal, and a long draught of ale. No nobleman would consider taking one of them to court.

Roanna considered entering the palace through the servants' doors. She might gain the queen's ear through a reputation for soothsaying. It would take time to establish herself. She did not have time.

Cancerous demons ate greedily at the English queen's innards. Roanna wished she and Tryblith had introduced the disease to Mary Tudor's barren and twisted womb. They would have gained much power from her pain. More important that she die and her nobles fight over her successor. Tryblith needed to feed upon that chaos. Roanna planned to have Scottish and French troops poised on the border the moment Elizabeth claimed her sister's throne.

The Equinox had passed. Mary Tudor would not long survive Samhain, or All Hallows Eve as the Christians called it. Roanna needed to begin her campaign now.

Jamie Douglas was only a minor border lord. She should start higher. Lord Moray, illegitimate son of the queen regent's late husband held the loyalty of a large number of lords and clan chieftains. He rode to court from his home outside the city about this time every day.

Roanna settled a rich cloak of damask and fur about her shoulders. It had belonged to Jamie's mother and fit her admirably, as did the rose-colored bodice, sleeves, and skirt. A faded green farthingale petticoat peaked out from the folds of the skirt. The padded rolls at shoulder and wrist echoed the farthingale. Her shift boasted only a modest amount of lace at cuff and collar, but enough to lend credence to her claim to nobility. A feathered fan that could substitute as a mask completed her ensemble.

She rang the bell to summon a maid. Within moments she bribed the girl to don Roanna's usual cloak of sturdy heather brown wool and follow her into the bustling Royal Mile—the street that descended from the fastness of the castle atop its crag to the more comfortable palace at the foot of the hill.

She paused at the arched entrance to the inn's courtyard, fronting on the street. Tall houses made a canyon of the road. Narrow closes and alleyways between some of the buildings gave access to the Grassmarket on the south or the Norloch opposite. Behind the palace rose Arthur's Seat, a small mountain. Earl James Moray, the most powerful lord in Scotland, could approach the palace by a long and twisting road traversing the Grassmarket, where the poor

of the city dwelt. More likely he would cross the Norloch
by the fine arched bridge. It met the Royal Mile closer to
the castle than the palace, but gave access to either. Moray
would come from there.

Roanna turned right, seeking the best place to meet the
lord. Quickly she scanned the neighborhood. Ah, here the
houses of the wealthy pressed close to the cobblestones,
narrowing the street considerably. Their upper stories extended over the ground floor, blocking much of the weak
and damp light. The perpetual drizzle further hampered
visibility.

"Perfect," Roanna announced. She tapped the fan
against her wrist, watching how the feathers quivered.

"Milady?" The maid tugged on Roanna's cloak. " 'Tisn't
safe to stop here, Milady. We must go back." She backed
up against the granite wall of the nearest building, looking
anxiously about.

"We will remain here until I decide to go." She'd gladly
dispense with the timid creature's presence, but convention
demanded that no gently bred lady ventured out in public
alone. She needed the maid to protect her reputation for
the coming meeting.

"But, milady, there are cutpurses and . . . and . . ." The
maid's eyes went wide with imagined terrors. The black
pupil nearly blocked out the soft brown iris.

"We won't be long," Roanna reassured her. "Not long at
all," she added when she heard the clatter of many horses
prancing on the cobbles uphill from her post.

She breathed deeply, carefully clearing her lungs with
each exhalation. Once, twice, thrice, she drew in deep lung-
fuls of air. Her eyes crossed and the world became misty
around the edges of her vision. She focused on the gaily
caparisoned horse leading the cavalcade. The bay gelding
bobbed its head and rolled its eyes, barely curbed by the
cruel bit.

"Too many people too close to you, my lovey?" Roanna
whispered as the men and horses approached. She pressed
the illusion of two dozen roughly clad men upon the stupid
beast. Then she surrounded the illusion with layer after
layer of chaos. The gelding balked and shied.

Red sparkles infiltrated the illusory cloud around its
head.

"Too many smells and sounds you do not understand."
The horse bunched his feet and arched his back, ready to
bolt headlong away from the source of his fear, with or
without his rider.

"A terrible place for a fire." In Roanna's mind, and the
horse's, the image of flames and smoke rose up from the
cobbles.

The gelding reared, pawing at its greatest fear. The
horses behind it caught a whiff of its panic and reacted.

People screamed, ducking away from the shod hooves.
Horses screamed in reply, frightened more by the unexpected sounds. Riders struck at their horses with short
quirts and spurs. Two men fell to the ground. Roanna
heard bones crack as they struck the stones of the roadway.
Crazed townsfolk dashed hither and thither screaming at
the top of their lungs. She smiled.

Chaos reigned.

Tryblith laughed long and loud. She was surprised that
the people around her did not hear the demon and cringe
in fear.

Just before the lead gelding bolted, Roanna touched its
mind once more. She dived under slashing hooves. As the
gelding came down from its latest attempt to rid itself of
its rider, she grabbed the reins.

"Easy, boy. Settle down. Roanna will protect you." She
trapped the horse's gaze with her own. It pulled against her
restraint. "Quiet," she said more firmly. One by one she
removed each of the delusions she had shown him.

He snorted and pawed, still restless, still fighting her
control.

"Quiet now, there's nothing to fear." Roanna reached a
tentative hand to caress his nose.

She blew gently across his nostrils, letting him catch her
scent, hold it close, and acknowledge it.

"That's it, know me, and know I will let nothing hurt you."

The horse remained restive, shifting its weight from hoof
to hoof in an irregular rhythm. Roanna kept a firm grip
upon its bridle. The other horses settled a bit, continuing
to prance.

"Many thanks, milady. You took a terrible chance,"
Lord Moray said without a trace of distress. He dismounted in one smooth movement, a man who had grown

up riding the finest horseflesh his father's royal stables could provide.

"Milord." Roanna dipped a curtsy, as deep as she could and still maintain control of the horse. She allowed a tinge of French to color her Scots. James Stewart, Earl of Moray, illegitimate half brother to the queen, raised one eyebrow in question. She guessed that her knowledge of French was more thorough than his. Tryblith had taught her well.

"And may I know to whom I owe my limbs and head if not my life?" Lord Moray took her hand and raised it to his lips. Roanna had to come up from her curtsy or have her arm yanked from its socket. She dared raise her eyes as well. She looked up and up and further up to his intent gaze. He stood over six feet in height, with sandy hair and deep brown eyes. A fine figure of a man with lean muscles and well-proportioned features.

"Roanna Douglas," she said, bobbing her head. She heard the maid twitter behind her. Lord Moray had set more than one young maid's heart aflutter. Rumor claimed he was immune to them. An ordained priest turned Puritan lord, he had not succumbed to any of the ladies, highborn or low. Yet.

"Douglas? The borders abound with Douglases. I have met all of the presiding lords and none of them have presented a daughter named Roanna at court." He let his hand drift down the horse's neck and nose to rest atop hers on the bridle.

"The Lords of Hermitage Castle are not known for admitting all of their assets or vulnerabilities."

"Aye. A reticent lot. Still, I would think yer family would have put you on the marriage market with a very high bride price." He stooped a little, bringing his face closer to hers.

A little closer, Tryblith cautioned her. *Let him get just a wee bit closer.*

" 'Tis why my cousin has brought me to Edinburgh this day, milord. He is to present me at court this evening."

"Does yer cousin not know that the queen regent sees no one after supper? She retires early."

"I . . . No, milord, I did not know."

"Perhaps your cousin has a suitor for you already. Or mayhap he wishes to keep you to himself?"

Roanna gasped and clutched her throat. She closed her

eyes and pushed extra blood to her face to imitate a maidenly blush.

Lord Moray brushed a stray wisp of hair away from her cheek. He bent a little more, gazing directly into her eyes. *Now!*

Roanna stared back fixedly. She opened her mind, giving him glimpses of the imaginary fire and flashing hooves his horse had shied from.

He reared back, blinking rapidly.

Roanna forced the blood out of her face, letting it grow cool and clammy. She swayed and clung tighter to the bridle. "Milord. Oh, milord, you must flee this place. English sorcerers. Assassins one and all sent by their Catholic queen." She whirled about, frantically waving her hands. "I see it all now. An English sorcerer lies in wait for you, milord. He failed this time. He'll try again." She stumbled to her knees, clutching her head.

"Roanna?" The mightiest lord in the land knelt beside her, cradling her face between his big hands. "What is this nonsense, Roanna?"

"A vision, milord. 'Tis a curse I was born with. A curse my uncle tried to hide by sending me to a French convent when my mother died, though he professed the Protestant faith. He sent me to the good sisters hoping they would beat the devil out of me or kill me trying. I'm sorry. So very sorry that this curse came upon me in your presence."

She jerked herself to her feet and staggered toward the now pale and shaking maid. "We must return to the inn. Now." Roanna insisted. She did not look back as she rushed down the sloping street. On her seventh step she pretended to stumble. A strong hand clutched her elbow.

"Thank you, Meagan," she whispered, still not looking behind her, though she knew Meagan's hands were never as large or strong as the ones that now held her shoulders.

"Do not run away, milady. Seeing the truth where none dare look is a gift. 'Tis not the first time the English have tried to conquer brave Scotland through foul assassination. You saved my life today. I will introduce you to the queen this afternoon. She and I both have need of your gift. God sent you here to protect Scotland."

Not God. A demon named Tryblith. The Demon of Chaos.

Chapter 16

Kirkenwood, October 1558.

WHILE Donovan recovered from the ravages of fever, I concentrated on maintaining the defenses of Kirkenwood. I increased patrols of our land, especially along the broken and disintegrating portions of Hadrian's Wall.

Raids from Scotland increased over the next six weeks, well organized raids that encroached deeper and deeper into England. But they left Kirkenwood alone. The crops were in. Winter storms had not yet cut us off from the rest of the world. This was prime raiding season. Only late spring, when the lambs were fat and sheep's wool long, offered better loot. In all the long history of Kirkenwood, I could find no record of so peaceful an autumn. Had Lord Douglas of Hermitage (the elder or the younger) lost his nerve?

Once Donovan decided to live, he recovered from the fever quite rapidly. He turned his face to the wall whenever I entered his room. He clutched the ring of the Pendragon as if he feared I'd steal it from about his neck. I refused to steal the artifact. It had to be given freely or it carried no authority.

One time he did speak, softly, when I had left the room to retrieve my missal and then returned quietly. He must have believed me gone.

"Why, Griffin?" he mumbled to the wall. "Why have you cast your lot with the demons that destroy England? I can't accept your blessing or your healing as long as you work for the demon church."

At first I thought him feverish again. The more I thought about his words, the more I wondered if he, too, had seen the same demon as I the night of battle. But how could he mistake the demon for Holy Mother Church?

I retreated to the lair—the hidden room filled with the family archives and other treasures from the past. I needed more information if I ever hoped to combat the demon. The beast with the hairy torso, dragon maw, and lizard legs had much to answer for. Combatting it had drained vitality from Raven to the point of death, nearly blinded me, and killed Donovan's wife.

My reading led me down many paths. I found documents about the now heretical Knights Templar. I found accounts of the Synod of Whitby that ousted the Culdee or Irish version of Christianity. I found a copy of the apocryphal Gospel of St. Thomas. All of these documents claimed authority from the teachings of James the Just, first Bishop of Jerusalem, supposed brother of Our Lord Jesus. They bypassed the teaching of Paul and the wisdom of Rome. In each of them I found a common theme: Any faithful follower of Christ could approach God on his own, without the barrier of the church.

My faith rocked, nearly shattered, then righted itself. Heretical. All of these teachings had been banned by Holy Mother Church for a reason. The church was not a barrier, but a guide for the uneducated and unenlightened.

Who has kept the faithful uneducated and unenlightened? Raven whispered to me.

"The church has changed. The reformists showed us our corruption and we corrected it."

How can the church change from its fundamental purpose of control? Control over the actions and thoughts of every person in the world, true believers and heretics alike?

"We need the church to provide a sense of unity in God's light," I argued as I had been taught.

No one can allow their religion or their church to become a barrier between themselves and God.

"That is not the issue I came to learn about. I need to know more of the demon that led raiders to our door, Raven. Lead me to a cure for demons."

Would I never be free of my grandmother's haunting?

I remembered an incident. When Donovan and I were eight. . . .

*　　*　　*

Raven awaited us. She stood on the third stair, stern and forbidding, black tresses with their single white streak at one temple, flowing down her back. It seemed to crackle with the lightning of her indignation. My twin and I bounced into the hall ready to wash and change for the dinner being laid in the hall. We giggled and hushed each other as we recounted every aspect of our eight-year-old games.

"You both owe me an apology," she whispered harshly.

"Ap . . . apology?" I gulped.

"You have neglected your lessons for play. Others suffer in consequence." Her frown made me ache that I could hurt her so deeply by an unthinking act.

"How?" Donovan asked more boldly, seemingly unaffected by our grandmother's disappointment. But I knew he hurt deep inside as well. He couldn't hide his true emotions from me.

"You have both enjoyed yourselves immensely without thought of the consequences."

"Consequences?" I couldn't imagine anything bad coming from an afternoon in the village as we chased a ball around with our feet.

And then I recalled one of my first lessons in magic. What you give, whether good or evil, comes back threefold. This morning I had rushed to finish my magical exercises so I could play. I'd left a spell unfinished, and ungrounded. A simple calling of a bird to my hand. I had run off to play before dismissing the young bird. It would not leave my hand no matter how I tried to scare it away. Within a few hours it drooped from exhaustion and thirst. Children's balls, dogs, sheep, flying dust, the other children, everything I encountered followed me around, clung to me, and would not leave.

At first Donovan and I laughed at all of the extras hanging off me.

Then it became a burden. And still the bird clung to my wrist, confused and terrified.

Finally I dismissed the bird and concluded the spell with a prayer of thanks to whatever god allowed me to call it. The bird flew away and dropped into the verge of grass by the central standing stone. There it died as its frantic heart beat its last.

I cried for the bird and for my own unthinking. But then the ball game started up and I ran off to play and forget.

"There are always consequences," I murmured. "I am sorry, Raven. I shall not forget again."

"Be certain that if you ever do forget this lesson, either of you, I shall haunt you in the same way dirt and toys and animals clung to you until you finished and grounded the spell."

Raven would haunt me forever, or until I measured up to her expectations.

I accepted her comments about God and religion, tucking them away in the back of my mind to ferment and grow into a cohesive thought. Then I concentrated upon my quest.

Still . . .

Journal after journal of my ancestors led me to believe that without the ring of the Pendragon and all it represented, I had no hope of containing any demon.

The ring comes to you when you are ready to wield the authority. It gives nothing.

"Go away, Raven. I haven't time to listen to you." I left the lair for the day, too unsettled to concentrate. Raven did not bother me again. For a time.

Several days later I found a reference in the journal of Lord Henry Griffin from the time of the Crusades. He described the denizen of the netherworld in great detail with hints of possession of a human body on All Hallow's Eve—Samhain in the old religion. His description of the dragon head with huge dagger teeth, the hairy pelt on the upper body, exaggerated male genitalia, and reptilian lower extremities fit my own vision of the beast.

I faced Tryblith, the Demon of Chaos, bringer of death, destruction, and pain. It fed on the chaos of war. Border raids were just the beginning.

My ancestors had sealed the demon behind a portal. The generations of civil war, now called the Wars of the Roses, must have weakened the magic that kept Tryblith at bay. Now he sought a host, preferably one of his own blood from a previous possession, to sow the seeds of chaos and break the seal.

Before I could prevent Tryblith from triggering armed

conflict across borders and within England, I had to find his host. I needed to be in London, the center of political conflict, the site where war would begin.

Even knowing the demon's name—a source of great power—would not help me without my full magical powers and the authority of all my ancestors backing me.

I couldn't leave until Donovan resumed his duties as Laird of Kirkenwood. Nor could I leave without Helwriaeth. I needed her keen nose and extra perceptions to sniff out the demon. Her puppies weighed too heavily in her belly for her to travel. Once she whelped, I still had to wait for her offspring to be weaned.

My fist hit the desk, bouncing scrolls, books, herbs, crystals, and other paraphernalia into greater disorder.

Outwardly, Donovan's left leg healed. My right eye remained damaged.

Then the day came when he tried to get out of bed. I was with him despite his resentment. I felt it my duty to visit him each day, to offer prayers, and tend to his personal hygiene when he would let me. I talked. He stared at the wall and ignored me. But one day I caught him sitting up, gingerly testing his injured leg upon the step up to the high bed.

With clenched jaw and scrunched eyes he tried to stand and immediately collapsed upon the floor. I rushed to assist him.

"God's arse, but that hurts!" he shouted when I tried to straighten his injured limb.

Helwriaeth tried to help, too. Her body made bulky with pregnancy just got in the way until I told her to sit and stay. She looked at me with big imploring eyes. I immediately felt guilty—as she intended—for hurting her feelings.

"Try to stand again. Lean on me." I slid my hands beneath Donovan's shoulders and hoisted him up. He'd lost a lot of weight during the weeks of fever and recovery, and presented no burden to me.

"I have leaned upon you most of my life and I tire of it," he snapped.

I looked at him sharply. When I thought about our childhood, I remembered how he always deferred to me, letting me take the lead, make the decisions, take the blame. We prepared for me to become the Pendragon.

Now we vied for the honor and the responsibility.

If I had chosen a different life path, I would *be* the Pendragon now and he would never have questioned my right to the magic, the title, the power. I would march into battle with Tryblith alone and possibly die trying, alone.

Perhaps I had made the right choice after all, if for no other reason than to force Donovan and myself to find other ways of approaching the problem of the Demon of Chaos.

"This assistance is not the same as during our youth, Donovan. This time I shall only steady you until you find your own balance."

He grimaced at me but allowed me to help him up.

I steadied my twin with gentle hands. When he could stand on his own, I backed away—as I did five years ago when I left for France. He stood with most of his weight upon his sound right leg.

Holding his hands slightly away from his body for better balance, he tried taking a step and promptly crumpled again. This time his curses nearly turned the air blue.

"If you are trying to shock my priestly sensibilities, I've heard all those phrases before, little brother. Some in the confessional, some outside. I invented a few of them myself. Shall I give you penance for them now or reserve the privilege for Father Peter?"

"I have too many priests in this household," he snarled.

Helwriaeth nuzzled him with a cold nose and rough tongue. He batted her away. She sulked to my side.

I reached to help him up again. He shied away from my touch.

"I'll do this on my own or die trying."

Silently I watched his contortions as he rolled over and pulled himself upright, bracing himself with the bed hangings. Helwriaeth offered her shoulder as a convenient handhold. Donovan stared into her eyes for a long moment before consenting to lean upon her.

"Will you give me one of your pups to help me?" he asked her as he ruffled her ears.

I sensed Helwriaeth's hesitation. She understood the request and did not know how to answer. The future was not hers to see.

Something flickered around the edges of my vision. I stilled myself, waiting for the vision of events to come.

"Baby Betsy needs to see her da," Meg caroled from the doorway. Her entrance shattered whatever portent was about to visit me.

I exhaled deeply, barely aware that I had held my breath in anticipation. In all the weeks I had been home, not once had I fallen prey to the visions. Had Meg always interrupted them?

"See how Baby Betsy smiles." Meg smiled, too. The candlelight seemed to settle on her golden hair, bound up in a copper filigree caul. The entire room seemed brighter for her presence. I looked at my sister with new perspective. Perhaps she did protect me from myself. Until I had the ring of the Pendragon, these visions and my magic remained anathema to me. I should take her with me when I left, let her grow into herself away from the scene of her ravishment.

Donovan sat on the edge of the bed, holding his hands out to receive his daughter. The baby chuckled and waved her arms about as she tugged on her da's beard.

"Come, Helwriaeth." My dog and I were no longer needed. "Let's find a crutch for Donovan."

But Helwriaeth had other ideas. She pushed me around the gallery toward the secret door. I resisted her nudging and tried to go down the stairs. A wolfhound is not a beast to argue with, even when she is calm. She pressed her considerable weight and strength against me until I must yield or fall down.

My fingers found the outline of the door hidden within the paneling when my eyes failed to discern anything out of the ordinary. Raven had shown Donovan and me the entrance to her lair in the winter of our ninth year. The cobwebs and the dark and the secrecy of the journey awed us more than the actual secret room.

"What do you expect to find down here, Helwriaeth?" I asked as she preceded me onto the stone landing just inside the doorway. I grabbed the flint and iron kept there to strike a spark onto the rush torch stashed there as well. Helwriaeth had already waddled halfway down the first flight of stairs by the time I joined her. She swayed on down the next flight to the lair at a slower pace.

Helwriaeth snuffled about the room. Her nose reached

high and low. Finally she stood upon her hind legs and nudged a musty book bound in leather without inscription. "Is this what you want me to read?"

Her tongue lolled and she grinned at me, drooling happily into her beard.

I plucked the little tome from the shelf and settled into a chair by the desk. I needed to light several oil lamps from the rushlight before I had could see the tiny writing. Black ink had faded to a greenish brown. The parchment pages were brittle to the touch. But the writer had selected good unused sheets. If she had written upon pieces that had been used and scraped clean, a frequent practice, their very thinness would have made them too fragile to touch after so many years. Clearly she intended the book to last long enough to be read by her descendants.

I looked at the first date. *Fifteen June, in the year of Our Lord 1215.*

Nearly three hundred and fifty years ago. The date tickled my mind until I recalled that King John had signed a great charter that day that outlined duties and responsibilities of the monarchs of England toward their barons—an economic treaty of peace.

He had also established the beginnings of Parliament, begun the codification of English law, and established uniform weights and measures and many other innovations that fateful day. A momentous beginning date for this journal.

Mama says that my papa signed the document today, and so I shall begin my document of journal today as well.

The journal began in a childish hand in rough Latin, easier for me to understand than Anglo-Saxon or archaic French. She wrote in the ancient Secretary hand rather than the modern Italian hand, adding more difficulty to my reading. A quick look through the coming pages and I knew the writer to be Henrietta Carlotta Griffin, illegitimate daughter of Lady Resmiranda Griffin, Baroness of Kirkenwood, and King John. She thought of herself as Hetty. She had inherited the barony by decree of her father.

The names were almost as familiar to me as my own. Raven had made me read the chronicles of Resmiranda, Hetty's mother, as a lesson in perseverance and survival.

If you want to be the Pendragon, you must begin to act like one! Raven's voice haunted me once more.

I settled in to read the life of the last of my clan to carry the name Griffin. King John's dying wish to Hetty's mother had been that the family take the name Kirkwood and finally rid him of the meddlesome Griffins. By tradition the eldest son of the Baron of Kirkenwood was always named Griffin to maintain the connection.

The name change had not helped John's son, Henry III. His half sister Hetty had plagued him mercilessly throughout his long reign. Several times I laughed out loud at how Hetty had railed at Henry whenever she disagreed with him. She had manipulated him, threatened, and cajoled, all for the safety of England. For fifty-six years England had flourished and maintained the peace most of the time. (I reminded myself that war during this period was a way of life, much as the border raids had become during my own lifetime.) But Hetty had pushed Henry to seek a middle way, only going to battle when *no* other options remained.

Henry had tried ignoring his meddlesome sister, but she always found ways to keep him in line with her vision of what England should be—strong, prosperous, walking a diplomatic tightrope, and as free of strife as God and the elements allowed.

She had been an active and effective Pendragon, more so than many of her descendants. I needed to emulate her.

If you want to be the Pendragon, then act like one! Raven commanded me.

I could not stay locked away in Kirkwood grieving for Raven and my brother any longer. I had to journey to the capital where politicians, diplomats, nobles, and clerics decided the fate of England. I had to become one of them.

Helwriaeth nudged my hand. She reminded me that she could not travel so far until after her pups were born and weaned.

Nor could I leave until Donovan could move about more freely.

What was the demon Tryblith up to? Would I be able to find him in time?

Chapter 17

Kirkenwood.

DONOVAN stumped about the castle on a crutch, yelling at any who crossed his path. Helwriaeth and I did our best to avoid him. She was not so agile as she used to be and slept most of the day. She grew fat with puppies. Donovan seemed to take her fertility as a personal insult. But then he seemed to take all life as an insult—except for his daughter. He and Meg spent hours playing with Baby Betsy, bathing her, changing her, tending her simple needs, just watching her sleep.

I spent as many hours as possible in the lair reading. I learned quite a bit about my ancestors. Some of their greatest feats had been accomplished with persuasion, diplomacy, and economic pressure. I did not have to compromise my soul by using magic to be a Pendragon!

My eyes rebelled after about two hours of reading. At the end of every session my head ached and I could not focus my vision. I had to hang onto Helwriaeth's ruff just to find my way back up the stairs. For hours afterward I had to lie quietly with cold compresses over my eyes. Meg sang to me and held my hand. She treated me as she did the baby, a pet to croon over. I vowed again to take her away from here, find a way to heal her.

Presumptuous of you, Raven admonished me.

I wondered when she would cease to haunt me.

When you take up your responsibilities as you were meant to. As I taught you to.

Raven had never minced her words. I thought again of King Henry III and his half sister Hetty. He should have known never to tangle with a female Pendragon.

And who will be the Pendragon now?

"I'm trying, Raven," I whispered into the darkness. "I can't leave until Helwriaeth whelps and the pups are weaned. You told me yourself, to keep her close, that I need her to sniff out the demon."

I thought I heard an indignant snort. A long silence, then, *Time is running short.*

"I know, Raven. I know." Tomorrow I would write letters to the list of contacts my bishop had given me. I added Dr. John Dee, magician, physician, and astrologer, to my list. Other scientists occurred to me as well.

But Helwriaeth had other plans for the morrow. On the day before All Hallows Eve she whelped her puppies. We shared so much, I had often wondered if she would share this miracle of giving life with me.

I followed her all over the castle as she sought an appropriate nest. She tried Donovan's bed and mine. Neither suited her. The stable smelled wrong and was too drafty for newborns. The kitchen looked promising until a harried scullery lad stepped on her tail. Then she removed herself in a huff and sniffed every corner of every room. At last she stood by the door to the tunnel.

"You don't really want to go down there, do you?"

I almost heard her call me a stupid male. Swallowing a grin, I opened the door for her. She plunged down the two flights of stairs without waiting for me. I had to hurry to catch up with her. In her haste to make a nest for herself and the babies about to burst upon the world, Helwriaeth knocked over Raven's staff, a cauldron, and nearly set a stack of clean parchment alight when the brazier tipped. I burned my hand righting my only source of heat down here.

Helwriaeth grabbed in her teeth the blanket I kept in the lair to ward off the chill in my shoulders or knees. She tossed it to the floor, stepped into the middle of it, circled three times and plunked down, ready to get on with her business.

I sat beside her, petting her, talking to her, watching in amazement as baby after baby emerged into the world—all of them sired by purebred wolfhounds in our kennels. I had no idea if she had mated once or a dozen times.

As Helwriaeth licked each pup clean and guided it to

her teats to feed, I shared a tremendous sense of satisfaction and completeness. Between births she laid her head in my lap, panting. I had never loved her more.

Five pups wriggled about seeking the most advantageous teat. All of them appeared perfect miniatures of their mother. A long time passed. I thought her birthing over. Five pups only. All males. Wolfhounds usually birthed ten or twelve. But Helwriaeth was old for a first litter. Old to be whelping at all. Without another female, the direct line of Pendragon familiars would end.

Had the line of the Pendragon ended as well?

Then a sixth puppy was born dead. And the seventh and eighth—all female. I cried as Helwriaeth frantically licked them, trying to stimulate tiny hearts into beating and tiny lungs into breathing.

At last she pushed each one aside and laid her head back in my lap. We both grieved at the loss while rejoicing in the lives she had produced.

And then when we both thought no more pups would come, came the ninth, a scrawny female who mewled her distress and hunger from the moment she gasped her first breath.

Helwriaeth took her daughter by the scruff of the neck and placed her in my hand a moment before letting her feed.

"She's hungry, Helwriaeth."

Helwriaeth knew. But some things were more important. A tingle ran up my hand, through my arm to my heart, binding me to the mewling scrap of life. This hungry puppy was as much mine as hers.

"We must call her Newynog," I agreed with my familiar. After all, the name meant hungry in the ancient tongue of Britain. Resmiranda's familiar had been Newynog, as had Raven's. An honorable name.

Only then did Helwriaeth allow her daughter and her successor to nurse. Newynog pushed three of her brothers aside in order to find the best teat, the alpha position.

Holyrood Palace, Edinburgh Scotland, 22 November 1558.

Roanna raised her hands to cast a sleep spell upon the guards outside the doors of Queen Regent Marie's Privy Council Chamber.

"What am I doing?" she asked herself silently.

Do it! Tryblith demanded. His compulsion wove around Roanna's mind, robbing her of the ability to make decisions.

She watched her hands rise again, power tingling in her fingertips.

"No!" she exhaled sharply through her teeth. " 'Tis not the best way."

I do not care about best. I need chaos. I need to feed upon chaos. I am tired of patience and subtlety.

"This will create chaos. Chaos against me. We will be cast out. Jamie Douglas went home weeks ago. Without a protector I can do nothing in the city. I'll be alone, begging on the streets. You might like that, but I won't." Roanna dropped her hands, tangling her fingers into the stiff brocade of the ropa Lord Moray had given her. He had not yet succumbed to her spells sufficiently to give her jewels— jewels that could be sold or traded for rent and food should she decide to leave court on her own.

We must act. The English queen nears death. The Scots must be poised for war before then. They must. I weaken on this diet of minor strife and bickering.

"All will fall into place. Let me do this my way!"

As we did the night you murdered your sister!

" 'Twas not murder. Raisa begged me for death. She could not live with herself after Young Jamie Douglas used her so mercilessly." Roanna shuddered at the awful memory. Of her sister's rasping pleas for death. At the horrible smell emanating from her body. If Roanna had not plunged the knife into her heart, Raisa would have lingered a few more days at best, but in horrible pain. Not just a pain of her body, but of her spirit as well.

'Twas not murder and therefore useless to me. I should have gained tremendous power that night. Instead you merely sustained me.

"But I did not control you. I did not call your name

at the summoning, so I will never truly control you," she said bitterly.

Nor I you.

Even though she had discovered the demon's name now—French alchemists had amazing collections of writings on demonology—she had missed the opportunity of control out of ignorance.

Next time she would know better.

"I will eavesdrop in my own way. I will not murder in such a way that I am caught and burned at the stake. Who will host you if I die before you have enough power to break the seal of your portal and fully form in this world?"

The compulsion fell from Roanna's mind like a heavy cloak dropped to the floor. Suddenly lighter, cooler, with more freedom of movement, she rose up on her toes and fled the anteroom outside the Privy Council Chamber.

In a few moments she crept through the servants' pathways of Holyrood Palace more silently than the mice that lived behind the paneled walls. An abundance of dark wood deepened the shadows. The English painted their paneling above the wainscoting white with pretty flower patterns and captured the light. The royal Scots seemed as fond of gloom in their décor as in their weather.

"Eavesdropping is better than a forced entrance," she reassured the demon. "These people respond better to whispers in the ear than logical arguments. You don't like logic, remember?"

She felt Tryblith sulking.

A few more steps brought her to a door that led to the back of the audience chamber. Only the queen and her closest advisers used this door to come and go without having to weave through throngs of courtiers and petitioners in the outer rooms. Roanna suspected that even the most trusted servants did not know that adjacent to the door lay another portal. Beyond the hidden doorway lay a tiny secret room, just big enough for one person to press an eye to a peephole. Queen Marie sometimes used this spyhole to eavesdrop on her councillors. She did not trust them— many of them Protestants who owed their primary loyalty to Lord Moray—any more than they trusted her, a foreign Catholic.

Roanna slipped into the room and closed the door behind her. Soft voices came from the other side of the paneling. She looked through the peep, pressing one ear to the wood to catch every nuance of the conversation.

From here you could assassinate the queen, Tryblith almost chortled.

"Not yet. Elizabeth must declare herself a Protestant first. When she does, the Catholics will proclaim Marie Stuart, Queen of Scots, the true queen of England as well as Scotland and France. That will give you war aplenty," she whispered, keeping her voice barely audible so that Tryblith alone could hear her.

"The Dauphin of France is a weakling!" a lord shouted within the Privy Chamber. "We made a mistake allowing you to marry our queen to that limp puppet of *his* mother."

"The alliance with France is very important," Queen Marie de Guise replied. As regent, she had never had full control of the barons and clan chieftains of Scotland. But she had managed to keep the country and the government working for seventeen years, despite Moray's attempts to displace her.

Roanna looked more closely. The queen sat two places to the right of the spyhole. The man who had shouted sat with his back to her. She couldn't decide which earldom he held. He sounded like Ruthven.

"I have just returned from the court of France, and I tell you, everyone in Paris knows the marriage has not been consummated. The Frenchy will never get an heir on our queen. We need an heir!" That must be Maitland sitting across from Marie, Roanna decided. He traveled more frequently than the hidebound others.

"I assure you that my cousin is healthy enough to perform his duties as the next king of France as well as husband to my daughter." Tight lines drew Marie's mouth down. More lines radiated from her tired eyes.

"You are more tired now than you have ever been," Roanna whispered to the queen regent. "You do not have to listen to their rantings. You are the queen!" Roanna spun her words into an alluring tendril of magic. She could almost see the wisp of chaotically-colored smoke curling around the queen and into her ears.

"I say we annul the useless French marriage and bring

our queen home." A west Highland lord pounded the table with his burly fist. "Time she married a Scottish laird who will get a dozen sons on her. We don't need the French."

Marie stiffened her spine and narrowed her eyes. Her upper lip lifted in a silent snarl.

"Think for yourself," Roanna whispered to the half-civilized man with an untrimmed beard and unruly red hair that clashed with the reds of his tartan. She had to make her spell more blunt to penetrate his thick skull. He didn't like listening to anyone and resisted her spell.

"I refuse to petition the Pope for an annulment. The alliance with France is a good one," Marie snapped. "I refuse to listen to this drivel. You are dismissed one and all." She half stood.

"Defy her!" Roanna ordered.

All of the lords remained seated.

"The English threw off the yoke of the Bishop of Rome during the reign of their beloved Henry VIII. We did as well twenty-eight years ago," Moray reminded them. "We have the right to annul the marriage without approval from Rome."

"Marie Stuart, your queen, and I, Marie de Guise, your queen regent, are faithful daughters of the true Church. I will hear no more of this. All of you are dismissed. You will be gone from court by dawn."

"Your Grace," a breathless page said from the door. "Urgent messages from London." He bowed low, revealing a mudstained courier behind him. The newcomer limped into the council chamber carrying a leather pouch, the kind used to transfer important documents.

Roanna held her breath.

"Can it be?"

"Your Grace," the courier recited wearily. "Mary Tudor, Queen of England died two weeks ago in the evening hours of seventeen November in the year of our Lord 1558."

Yes. YES! Finally . . . Tryblith giggled. Roanna felt him cavort in his sealed prison as well as in the back of her mind. *Yes! Chaos will reign once more.*

Chapter 18

Kirkenwood, 5 December, 1558.

"THE Queen is dead. Long live the Queen!" Donovan proclaimed to the assembled household in the hall.

A round of enthusiastic cheers greeted the news. Only Griffin refrained from joining the back-slapping joy of the family and retainers. He stood in the back, frowning, hands folded. His rosary, the gold-and-ivory one he had inherited from the family, swung slightly as he rocked from foot to foot, the only sign of his agitation.

"Has Elizabeth accepted the crown?" Fiona asked. She leaned forward eagerly, almost overbalancing.

"She has indeed accepted the crown and commanded all of her barons and commons to attend her first Parliament on the twenty-fifth day of January." Donovan began calculating the supplies and journey time. If he hurried, he could attend the coronation on the fifteenth as well. That would mean riding fast with minimum baggage and no women. He'd have to leave Baby Betsy here, though he dreaded parting from her ever. She was too small to risk on such a long journey at this time of year.

"And what is the new queen's position regarding the church?" Griffin asked. His quiet words seemed to ring around the hall, echoing and intensifying. For a moment he sounded very much like the Spaniard. Would that demon never cease haunting Donovan?

"Queen Elizabeth has not had time to address this issue, but on my own authority I feel confident that all agents of foreign powers—including agents of the Pope, of which you are one—must report to their superiors in their home country. You will return, brother, to Paris and your bishop. I

144

expect you to leave before dawn." Donovan breathed out, releasing much of his pent up tension.

Griffin opened his mouth as if to protest that he was priest no longer.

"You are still a priest, whether you admit it or not, Griffin. You pray too often and raise your hand in blessing as if you had the right to. Forget your lies and admit that you spy for Rome." Donovan glared at his twin. Griffin clamped his mouth shut and returned the stare with equal stubbornness.

Donovan couldn't allow his frustration with Griffin to color the joy of the day. The power of Spain in England had broken. Father Manuel and his Inquisition no longer had authority. The demon must stop haunting him now. And he would make certain all of the Catholic demons fled England as well, even his once-beloved brother. He'd make life very uncomfortable for the demon loosed upon England by the church. Peace and order and unity were the only weapons to combat chaos.

"You do not have the authority to order me to do anything, Lord Kirkwood." Griffin stood his ground. "I answer only to my bishop and my conscience."

"Then go to your bishop in Paris, for I do not recognize the authority of a foreign bishop—especially the Bishop of Rome."

Another round of cheers drowned out Griffin's reply—if he made any. Triumph and relief swelled in Donovan's breast. He was free of his brother! And he still held the ring of the Pendragon in trust.

He might never see his twin again.

He looked back to his brother for one more moment of gloating or heartbreak. He didn't know which emotion dominated.

Griffin was nowhere in the crowd.

Where was he? Probably in the lair with those bloody dogs, or on his knees in the chapel. That man spent more time praying than anyone Donovan had ever met.

"True Englishmen bow to no foreign princes," Donovan proclaimed and stumped down from the dais with his crutch. Oh, how he longed to cast it off as he had the yoke of Papal dominance. Rather than weave his way through the crowd, Donovan retreated up the stairs.

Fiona followed close on his heels, hurling questions. "Is there time to make a new gown for the coronation before we go, or should I purchase one in London? We will need to send runners to a minimum of eight manors between here and the capital requesting hospitality. I really do not want to stay in inns, Donovan. How many ladies may I take? Should we take Meg and the baby or leave them home?"

"God's blood, Fiona!" The words exploded from Donovan. He immediately regretted the harshness of his tone. His sister cringed away, a hand to her breast as if she needed to calm a heart racing with fear.

"Fiona," he said more gently. "The coronation is only a little over a month away, Parliament meets a scant ten days later. There is not time for me to take a large group of retainers. The roads are bad and the weather worse. You must stay here in safety and secure Kirkenwood."

"But Griffin can do that," she protested. "This is a coronation! I might not live to see another. You deny me the opportunity. . . ."

"He's right, Fiona," Griffin said quietly from the top of the stairs. "The journey will be perilous. Kirkenwood needs you to stay and protect Meg and Baby Betsy."

"You have a bad habit of sneaking up on me," Donovan stated flatly. He would not allow his brother to see how frightened he had been, expecting to see the ghost of the murdered Father Manuel ready to push him down the stairs to his own death.

"I did not mean to startle you, brother. This news comes as no surprise. I dreamed of the courier and his message on the day Queen Mary died. Journey plans have been a part of my waking thoughts every moment. I have spent the last fortnight in prayer for the soul of Queen Mary." Griffin bowed his head over his clasped hands as if he continued those prayers. His gold-and-ivory rosary—the rosary of the Pendragons—dangled from his fingers. His cheeks were gaunt and his eyes haggard. Had the man slept or eaten in the past fortnight?

"You could not share the portentous news or your plans with me?"

"Few trust dreams. I had to wait for the courier to confirm the news. We must talk."

Burying his resentment, Donovan followed his twin to

the bedchamber, closing the door in Fiona's eager face. Excitement replaced his bitterness toward Griffin. Tingles ran up and down his spine.

"Fate has given you the opportunity to rid yourself of your chains to Rome, Griffin. Elizabeth is queen. We don't have to be Catholic anymore," Donovan said. He began pacing, ignoring the crutch and his weak leg as thoughts flew furiously around his mind.

There was so much he wanted to do—without fearing the Inquisition breathing over his shoulder. He could experiment with alchemy. If Raven's exercises could not open his talent, perhaps science could. Or special concoctions of herbs and potions. Then he could claim the ring of the Pendragon for himself and not wait for a son to be born.

Of course he did have Peregrine and Gaspar. But either of the illegitimate boys might not be his get. And Raven had declared them both unfit for magical training.

"Do you think so little of me, Donovan, to believe that I will change my religion as quickly as we change monarchs? My faith and loyalty to the true church cannot be commanded by others." Griffin truly looked shocked.

"The need to spout safe phrases of faith have passed, Griffin. Cast off the yoke of Rome and join me in rebuilding England free of foreign powers and demons."

"The time has come for the truly faithful to stand firm. Politics cannot dictate faith."

"But it does, as long as we allow a foreign bishop to tell us what to believe." He couldn't fathom Griffin's narrow view of life.

"Do you think Elizabeth will not tell you what you may or may not believe?" Griffin raised one eyebrow, giving the impression he looked down upon his twin from a superior position though they matched each other in height, breadth, coloring, and stubbornness.

"She is English, born and bred. What she decrees will be right for England."

"And was not Mary's faith also right?"

"Mary was half Spanish, married to a Spaniard. She nearly bankrupted England to pay for Philip of Spain's wars. She did not know what was right."

"But she, too, was our queen, anointed and blessed in solemn ritual."

Donovan spat into the hearth. Just thinking of pretending to be Catholic these past five years left a sour taste in his mouth.

"Foreign ritual. Join me, Griffin." He almost begged for the sense of togetherness they had shared as youths. But he could not share anything with Griffin until his twin threw off the Popish Church and the demon that controlled it.

"No. The time has come when we must embrace our true faith, and not flit from church to church because of politics." Sadness made Griffin's shoulders droop. "By the laws of the Holy Catholic Church, Elizabeth is a bastard and not eligible for the crown. By the laws of primogeniture, Mary Queen of Scots is the true queen of England."

"Another foreigner," Donovan spat. "She's more French than Scottish or English. Her mother is French, she was raised in France, and she's married to the Dauphin of France. Elizabeth is the only true English queen. By our laws she is legitimate!"

"Henry declared her bastard when he executed her mother, Anne Boleyn, for adultery, incest, and treason," Griffin insisted.

"Henry also declared Mary bastard when he divorced Katherine of Aragon in order to marry Anne Boleyn. You embraced Katherine's daughter, also bastard, as the true queen."

"Based upon my faith."

"And I embrace Elizabeth as my true queen based upon my faith."

"You have no faith," Griffin said sadly. He turned his back on Donovan and began fingering the rosary.

"I believe in many things, Griffin. I used to believe in the strength of what we could accomplish together. Join me in casting off the trappings of Rome." He had to try one last plea.

"And if I do not?"

"Then you must leave Kirkenwood forever." Donovan began to tremble with agitation and fear that Griffin might actually go. Heat flushed his face. He clenched his teeth. So did Griffin.

"Will you give me the ring of the Pendragon, as is my right?" Griffin asked. His voice remained toneless. He gave no clues to his true emotions and he did not make use of the mind-to-mind contact they'd shared as youths.

Flames seemed to rise in Donovan's mind. He needed to lash out at his brother. Only when he banished Griffin from his life would the flashes of light and pain go away.

"The ring was not bequeathed to you."

"Nor to you."

Impasse. They stared at each other long and hard, mirrors of determination.

At last Griffin sighed in defeat. "I will depart when the wolfhound pups are weaned, as I promised."

"You'll leave all six of them—including the female."

"That is Helwriaeth's decision, not mine."

"You will leave them all, or I will see you in Hell!"

"So be it."

Chapter 19

Holyrood Palace, Edinburgh, Scotland, 16 December, 1558.

ROANNA waved away the queen's hairdresser. Marie de Guise sat before her dressing table, eyes closed, face composed almost as if she slept. Roanna assumed the same rhythm of the hairbrush as the woman she dismissed. Deftly she gathered the gray-streaked black locks into an elaborate coil.

"The church fathers have found another English sorcerer," Roanna said quietly. "He had an exotic poison from Moorish lands in his wallet. He was trying to bribe a page to put it in your wine." Lies. All of it lies. But Marie would not question the information. She expected to be assassinated by the English. Or the Spanish. Or the Protestants of her own country.

"Lord Moray has taken the sorcerer to prison. He will be tried and found guilty of high treason. The page is to be rewarded for reporting the crime," Roanna continued her story. She had to be careful not to embellish too much. Liars were caught on details.

"Send the page to me. I will reward him myself," Marie said quietly. Her face remained calm. She hadn't even opened her eyes yet.

Roanna bit her lip a moment, wondering what excuse she could give to avoid presenting the fictional page. She planted a thought into the queen's mind instead.

"I will receive him privately in the travers behind the Council Chamber. I do not wish to advertise to the world that I am a target ripe for assassination."

Roanna mouthed the phrases two words ahead of the queen.

"I shall arrange it for you, Your Grace." She'd dress up as the page herself, with a mild illusion altering her face, and receive the award. She'd add the jewel or the coin to her stash of pilfered funds. Lord Moray had rewarded her for services in his bed only with rich clothing, suitable as a retainer at court. Others had been more generous; the least athletic and skilled in bed proved to be the most generous.

I do not need gold to set me free, Roanna, Tryblith reminded her. *I need war. I need to feed on death and destruction to give me the strength to break the seals that bind me to the netherworld. Force her to make war upon England!*

The demon's words bit into Roanna's mind as if she'd been hit with a mace. She almost lost her balance reeling under the force of his compulsion.

You murdered your sister for this. Do not make her death a senseless act.

"Ouch!" Marie reached up to yank her hair free of Roanna's fierce grip.

"My apologies, Your Grace." Gently, Roanna massaged the queen's injured scalp. When Marie closed her eyes again under the lulling ministration, Roanna broached the subject uppermost on Tryblith's mind.

"The English are weak right now. Queen Mary left them with heavy debts. Debts the people resent because she sent all their money to Spain to pay for King Philip's wars." Truthful statements forming a foundation for a temple of more lies. "The English people want that money back from the crown. Elizabeth has not yet had time to consolidate her power. No one trusts her. And yet she continues her sister's attempts to assassinate you. She thinks that if she can conquer Scotland while your daughter abides in France, then she can placate her people."

Marie's eyes were open now, staring ahead into some vision she did not share with her soothsayer.

Roanna paused to take a deep breath. Tryblith chattered in the back of her mind, upsetting her balance again. She stuffed the queen's hair into a jeweled caul before she damaged it any further with Tryblith's eagerness. "I have seen it in a vision, Your Grace. You can only protect Scotland and yourself by invading England. You must bring war unto them before they swarm over you like a tide of locusts."

"I must think on this." Marie de Guise rose up to her most regal height, topping Roanna by half a handspan in height and decades in dignity.

"Do not think too long, Your Grace. The English will mobilize in an eye blink. Elizabeth seeks to make them believe that Scotland is the source of all of their troubles."

"The Earl of Moray has a silver tongue. I shall send him to London with coronation gifts. War is not launched in a day. Neither is peace." Without another word Marie exited her dressing room.

Roanna and Tryblith seethed.

"If war is so important to your release, why did you not break free while the House of York and the House of Lancaster fought each other for the crown of England?" she asked the demon.

The time was not right. The seals around my portal were still too strong. The wars between the red rose and the white weakened the seals. Now I need only one more great bloodbath and I will be free. You will be queen of my new kingdom of Chaos.

"A great battle. One great battle. Surely I can arrange that. Rebellion within England mayhap?" A plan burst forth in Roanna's mind. A good plan that would give her control of the demon before he dominated her completely with his reminders of her guilt and moments of weakness. She had vowed never again to be used by another.

One battle is not enough. Murder de Guise first! Murder her now.

"Tansy, I think. Not a deadly dose at first, but it has a cumulative effect. Each time she resists us, she gets a stronger dose." And if someone caught Roanna administering the common road weed, she had the excuse that it killed intestinal worms. Or better yet, regulated the queen's menses now that she aged beyond childbearing years.

"She will give in. Or she will die. We will break the circle of her diplomatic logic."

The road to London, 1 January 1559

On a cold and clear New Year's dawn I rode out of Kirkenwood on the horse I had ridden into the castle. I did not stay for the exchange of gifts among the family. I did not stay to celebrate one final Mass in the chapel. I took with me only the few personal possessions I had brought from France and Raven's staff. I doubted I'd use it to focus my magic, but I cherished the memory of her carrying the tool, pounding it into the floor for emphasis, poking me with it when I was slow at my lessons. It would come in handy if I had to abandon the horse and walk throughout Britain on my journeys for my bishop.

I could have had Excalibur strapped to my hip as well. 'Twould make my eventual battle against the Demon of Chaos easier.

But I had to find a better way. Any use of violence only added to Chaos. I was a man of the church. A man of peace.

Helwriaeth followed me, her female pup gamboling around her feet—the other pups now bounced through the kennels with the working and breeding dogs. Within a few yards of the castle gates my familiar cuffed Newynog with one of her massive paws. Immediately submissive, the two-month-old youngster trotted in her footsteps, eager for the coming adventure.

Donovan had left for London within days of receiving news of Elizabeth's ascension, so he could not interfere with me taking Newynog with me. No one interfered. No one said good-bye. When I reached the standing stone marking the eastern edge of the village, I paused and looked back at Kirkenwood, afraid this would be my last view of my childhood home.

Moisture blurred my already damaged vision. I took a deep breath and then another. A small figure came into focus atop the watchtower. Sunlight glinted on golden hair confined by a copper caul. Meg. She held up the baby and waved Betsy's tiny arm to me. Someone would miss me. A lump choked my throat as I returned the wave.

At that moment the sun topped the surrounding hills, sending long rays onto the standing stones. The black crystal atop the staff caught the light and refracted into a myriad of rainbows. The face of the Merlin in the stone facing west lit when the prismatic display struck it. He seemed to smile at me.

What is the Pendragon but the next generation of the Merlin, bound to wander this land, gathering news, teaching, and imparting wisdom and justice? Raven's voice took on a husky masculine tone. It amplified and seemed to contain a dozen voices.

Go in peace, my son. The voice settled into the gruff tone of an ageless, yet tireless man—a lot like Father Peter's. The raven at the well took flight and croaked a counterpoint to the benediction.

My dogs and I set our path for Oxford and Dr. John Dee with new lightness in our hearts and an affirmation of our mission.

Chapter 20

London, 20 January 1559

DONOVAN surreptitiously checked the contents of his purse. Queen Elizabeth threw a handful of coins to the players of the masque as they took their bows. A number of nobles joined her in showing their approval. Donovan tried to look elsewhere, become inconspicuous in the crowd. Granted, the cunning actors had worked the mechanical unicorn, representing the queen's virgin status, and the lion, representing her princely heritage, with remarkable precision. He could almost believe that the allegorical beasts truly danced together in harmony. The play had demonstrated an admirable theme of virtue triumphing over base sins. The actors and director should be rewarded. But this was the third masque this week. At each performance Elizabeth's attending nobles were expected to bestow alms on the poor, reward actors and musicians, and purchase costly gifts for the queen herself.

Briefly, Donovan was almost grateful to Kate for dying. Mourning allowed him to wear simple unadorned black. He'd go bankrupt if he had to dress to the latest fashion with heavy gold or silver embroidery, satin or velvet decorated with jewels, froths of lace, and ridiculous padding in his breeches.

He feared he might have to go to the Jews and seek a crippling loan against next year's wool crop if he stayed in London any longer.

"My Lord of Kirkenwood," Elizabeth hailed him from the dais. She beckoned him with her long fingers—each heavily bejeweled to emphasize their length and grace.

Donovan bowed and limped over to her side. He wished he'd brought his crutch, or Raven's staff to support his still-painful wound. *As soon as I get home, I'll make Raven's staff my own. Much more dignified than a crutch.*

He bowed again over her hand. "Gracious Majesty, how may I serve you?" he murmured, hoping he uttered a correct phrase of adoration.

She inspected his hand closely while playing with the ropes of pearls about her neck. More pearls adorned the delicate caul confining her hair. He withdrew his hand quickly, embarrassed by the lack of riches displayed there.

"We had hoped you would honor us with a galliard later." She quelled the laughter that always seemed to bubble just under the surface.

"I regret, Your Majesty, that the wound I received defending your border against Scottish incursions still grieves me," Donovan demurred. Another disaster to be grateful for. He'd been tripping through country dances around the maypole with willing maids for years, but he'd never had occasion to learn the elaborate court dances. The only other time he'd come to London, for Mary's last Parliament, dancing, masques, and enjoyment of anything had not been on the agenda.

"We had hoped to discuss border matters with you. More privately, Lord Donovan," Elizabeth said softly. Her tone implied that she had more to discuss than just the border.

Donovan chanced a glance into her big brown eyes. A keen intelligence glittered there, giving beauty to her rather plain, oval-shaped face framed by a mass of red curls. If her skin were not so swarthy—a heritage from her mother—she might be considered beautiful. He decided she was handsome rather than beautiful. And much too forthright for his taste.

He liked his women more subtle, more dependent, less complicated. Elizabeth filled any room with her personality. Sometimes she didn't leave enough air for the rest of the court to breathe.

She had endured years of revilement for being a bastard and daughter of a whore after Henry VIII executed her mother on trumped-up charges of adultery and treason. Anne Boleyn's only sin was that she had not given Henry the son he craved. Malcontents had rebelled against Mary in Elizabeth's name, without the princess' knowledge or consent. Elizabeth endured years in prison under Mary's reign.

Always she survived, moving cautiously all her life, never

committing herself to any faction, any cause, or any man, so that her half sister—or Mary's husband Philip of Spain—had no reason to condemn her. After each travail she emerged stronger and a greater symbol of England's steadfast fight against foreign oppressors.

Outwitting, or even matching Elizabeth intellectually might prove a very interesting, and very dangerous game.

Behind her Robert Dudley, her Master of the Horse and constant companion—lover?—scowled at Donovan's attentions to the queen.

Donovan swallowed a smile at the man's obvious jealousy. He'd best get used to it. The queen was now the most sought-after marriage prize in all of Europe, and Dudley was already a married man.

Elizabeth rose to her full and glorious height, only an inch shorter than Donovan. Every man in the room dropped to one knee. The ladies sank into deep curtsies. "Come, Milord Kirkenwood. I wish to take the air." She held out her hand for Donovan.

He came up from his bow awkwardly, having to put too much weight upon his injured leg. He tried not to show his pain. Elizabeth must have seen it anyway, for she took his hand and helped hoist him upright. "You must consult my physician about that wound. I would hate to lose one of my most valuable assets in the continuing border war with Scotland."

"I would be honored, Majesty." Donovan grunted, not capable of saying more until the fire in his leg eased. Even those few words took great effort. He just hoped the physician did not charge princely fees to lesser nobles.

Dudley and a flurry of Elizabeth's ladies, all dressed in white, fell in behind them as Elizabeth led the way to a large anteroom. Dudley and two other courtiers Donovan did not know shooed out all those who lingered there. Without the press of people and hundreds of candles giving off heat Donovan breathed easier. Still the queen dominated the room. He dared not look anywhere but at her.

Elizabeth turned on Donovan the moment they had relative privacy. No man would ever be truly alone with this woman, he realized. Mischievously he wondered how Dudley managed to creep into her bed with all of her attendants on constant watch.

"My Lord, one hears rumors of your family."

"There are always bruits about the nobility," he countered.

"Whispers of magic and dealings with the devil?" Elizabeth arched one eyebrow in a gesture reminiscent of Griffin.

Donovan immediately resented being reminded of his rift with his twin. "Of the devil, my only knowledge is the Demon of Chaos the Scots bring with them when they try to burn my pastures, slaughter my sheep, and rape the women under my protection. As for magic, I have none I assure you, madam." His tone became chill. He couldn't help it.

Elizabeth responded to him with laughter. Some might call her mirth bright and cheering. Chills ran up and down Donovan's spine.

"We appreciate your candor, milord. Let us be equally candid. You do not wear the ring of the dragon rampant."

"My grandmother did not bequeath it to me." Alarm increased the chills, contrasting sharply with the fire in his wound. What did the queen know of his heritage and the role of the Pendragon in history? The Kirkwoods did not advertise their heritage.

"We have the right to know who has inherited the talents and wisdom of the Merlin," Elizabeth insisted suddenly sober and very dangerous. "We received a letter by private hand mere hours after our sister's death. Did you know that in our father's last days his only companion was his fool, Will Somers? We remember Will well. He always wore green." Elizabeth dropped into a moment of silent reverie.

Donovan waited impatiently for her to return to the point of the conversation. He'd rather be riding across the moors on this cold and clear night, watching the stars march across the heavens in their endless wheel. But here, in London, in the presence of the queen, he dared not even tap his foot in his restlessness.

"Our father entrusted a letter to Will for us. He wanted us to know certain things about your family should we ever come to the throne. He trusted no one else in those final days of his life. Will's family continued to honor that trust."

Donovan touched the ring suspended upon a fine gold chain under his shirt and doublet. The queen and all of her retainers watched him with caution and suspicion. Donovan pulled out the ring, letting it dangle before their eyes. Dudley's gaze and one of the ladies' became fixed upon the shining gold signet. Were they susceptible to a trance? Donovan dared not find out here and now. But later . . . ? He might not have magic, but he knew a few tricks.

"A pretty bauble," Elizabeth said, not at all influenced by the sparkle of the dangling signet ring. She reached forward to cradle it on her hand.

Donovan did not release it from its chain. "When my grandmother passed at the last Equinox, she told me to give this to my son. I have as yet no legitimate son. I am only custodian, not the wielder of power."

"Do you tell us that England is without a Pendragon?" Dudley and the ladies shrank back away from the queen when she spoke.

"At the moment."

"And if you wielded the power of your ancestors, Lord Donovan, would you withhold those powers and wisdom from your queen as your grandmother did from our sister?"

"Mary rejected Raven's offer of assistance in the matter of maintaining the peace. Raven could not support the Popish Church. Mary could not accept anyone not of the Popish Church." Indeed, Raven disapproved of any church, preferring private worship and an individualistic approach. Donovan agreed with her, but dared not say so. Easier to attend Mass—Anglican or Roman—publicly and perform other rituals privately.

"And did you change your allegiance during our sister's reign?"

"I survived, Majesty, with my people and lands intact. I survived to protect your border with Scotland. What I believe privately had to remain private these past five years."

"An attitude that many took, Majesty," Dudley reminded them. He didn't add that at one time Elizabeth had demanded instruction in the Catholic faith to placate her sister.

"Well said, dear Robin," Elizabeth laughed. She held out her hand to Dudley. He kissed it. She slid her fingers up to caress his bearded cheek. Her caress lingered.

Lovers, Donovan decided. If not now, then sometime in the past.

"But that does not solve the problem of Britain without a Pendragon. We sorely fear that we will have need of the wisdom of the ancients to preserve England from her enemies in the days to come."

Donovan kept his silence. A few weeks ago, before he had endured nearly two weeks of London society, he might have volunteered to share with the queen all of the knowledge that Raven had given. He might not be able to work the spells or control the forces of nature, but he knew *how* it could be done by one of talent. But now? He couldn't afford to stay in London two more days and Parliament did not meet for another four. Nor did he wish to linger longer away from his daughter. He missed Baby Betsy with every breath.

Elizabeth would have to find another solution.

"We would keep you close to us, Lord Donovan. We will visit the most learned Dr. John Dee within a few days. Mayhap you and he can devise a plan to assist us in finding a new Pendragon."

Donovan's face turned cold and his leg hurt abominably. How could he pay to stay so long in the capital?

"Yes, Majesty," he replied tersely.

"Mayhap, we need only find him a new wife to beget the son who will inherit the ring," Dudley said. He looked as if he tried to swallow his mischievous grin. He didn't succeed. His jealousy of Elizabeth's attentions was so obvious his skin almost turned green.

"In time, dear Robin. We will find him a proper wife in time." Her smile at Donovan suggested that she considered herself a candidate for that role. "For now, we will keep him close. Find him a room at court."

That would save Donovan a few pennies each day. But it might cost him more if he had to outfit himself to the latest fashion. He'd cling to the simple black as long as possible. Even the queen must respect his mourning.

"And now, dear Donovan, you shall regale us with stories of your ancestors and their mighty deeds. Does the dragon rampant ring contain magical powers?" Elizabeth offered her arm to Donovan, expecting him to escort her back to the dancing that had begun as soon as the masque ended.

Chapter 21

The road to Stanhope, January 1559.

" 'TAINT no reason on God's green earth we have to accept the bastard Elizabeth as our queen!" a man dressed in the furred cloak and bonnet of two generations past harangued a gathering at the village well. A merchant, I guessed, since he looked more prosperous than the smocked farmers leaning forward to catch his every word.

Men and women alike mumbled agreement with the speaker, about two dozen in number.

I didn't even know the name of the village nestled snugly between two fells on the track to Stanhope. All I wanted was food for myself and my dogs, rest and water for the horse.

The speaker intrigued me. This was evidence of Catholic support in the north for Marie Queen of Scots, information my bishop needed.

I dismounted and tried to listen unobtrusively at the back of the gathering.

"Well-armed troops await us at the border. We need only rise and follow them. England must be liberated from the Godless whore who presumes to don the crown!" the speaker continued. A slim young man, with a northern burr in his voice, he commanded attention. I could not decide how he drew people to him like iron to lodestone.

And then he lifted his gaze to mine. Compelling gray eyes penetrated my very soul, anchoring me in place and driving independent thought from my mind.

On and on the young man spoke, exacting promises from one and all to take arms with hayfork, shovel, and scythe if they had no other weapons.

And then he mounted a spirited gelding and rode out of the village. A chill ran up my spine as he passed me. Helwriaeth barked sharply and pressed close to me. Newynog, her pup, tucked her tail and hid beneath her dam.

The audience remained in place murmuring, "Elizabeth must die."

"The Protestants will steal our children and sacrifice them on their Satanic altar," a woman wailed, throwing her apron over her face.

"The Southrons will take fire and sword to our homes and fields," a man cried, shaking his fist.

The phrasing of the last comment shook me free of the speaker's enthrallment. The words fell into the cadence of one who spoke Scots, not English.

Had we stumbled upon the Demon of Chaos' host? More chills racked my body.

"I did not smell sulfur upon him, Helwriaeth," I said quietly. "All the accounts say that sulfur will taint whomever the demon touches."

Helwriaeth snarled, baring her teeth.

"We have to follow him. Stop him from starting a war." I set one foot in my stirrup.

Helwriaeth remained rooted in place.

"We'll rend our enemies limb from limb."

"London will burn."

"Elizabeth will dance the traitor's death at the end of a rope. She'll be cut down a'fore she dies, her belly slit open and her entrails burned before her eyes. And then we'll rip out her heart with our bare hands, lop off her head, and quarter her body." A great laugh from one and all accompanied that statement.

"Her adulterous lover Dudley will suffer the same fate!"

"Death to all disbelievers!"

The villagers began to shout as they gathered closer together. An aura of violence spread through them like a smoky miasma.

Something vicious clamped around my gut. My talent shrank from the blood these people suddenly craved.

I had to stop them. Violence would only begat more violence. All England would be in flames and the Demon of Chaos loosed if I did not stop it here and now.

"Good Englishmen, listen to me!" I cried from the lip of the well, the exact spot where the demon in human guise had stood. "Listen to yourselves."

Eight men turned upon me, snarling their displeasure.

Helwriaeth took her station before me, snarling and snapping at the first man to approach too close.

"Are you prepared to die deposing a woman who has not yet declared for one faith or another? Are you prepared to die advancing the cause of Scotland?"

" 'Tis the Southrons who will die!" A woman flung a half-rotted apple at me. It hit me square in the chest.

I stood my ground.

" 'Tis you who will die!" I said quietly, calling upon every skill I had learned in the pulpit and in Raven's lair to make these people listen.

"Open your eyes and your ears to the truth, to your own truth." I waved Raven's crystal-topped staff in front of them to gain their attention. The movement seemed to break an almost tangible tether that chained them to their alien thoughts and emotions.

An unnatural quiet descended upon the villagers.

I made the sign of the cross over an abandoned bucket of water on the lip of the well. "Bless this water and all that it touches," I prayed. Then, I dipped my hand into the chill water and shook my fingers dry over the crowd.

Droplets of water seemed to steam as they touched the clothing and hands of the villagers. One by one, those people shook themselves clean of the spell cast by the demon.

"Who is this man who exhorts you to leave your homes and families unprotected upon the mere promise of support from Scotland?" I spread more of the blessed water—not true Holy Water, but the closest thing available. "Who is this man who promises only death and destruction?—probably your own." I dampened the staff's crystal and shook it like an aspergillum, the brush used to spread Holy Water during Mass. "Who is this man who pretends to speak and think for you?" The silence deepened as the villagers began looking at each other in puzzlement.

Several shook themselves as if the water droplets were heavy and needed to be shed.

"He's one of our own!" a brash young man called, brandishing a shepherd's crook. He stood at the back. Not much, if any, of the blessed water had touched him. The demon's spell still held him in thrall.

"Is that man one of your own?"

"I never saw him before," a woman said quietly, shaking her head as if clearing water from her ears.

"He 'taint born of anyone I know," an elderly man mumbled.

One by one, their eyes cleared of the glaze of compulsion.

"Nourish peace in your hearts, my friends. Peace and unity begin here." I breathed easier as I moved among them. I made the sign of the cross over each one, ignoring the faint blue trail that followed my hands.

Exhaustion made my limbs heavy. I hadn't realized how tiring persuasion could be.

"What possessed us to listen to a stranger?"

"Who be you, stranger, that you speak contrary to t'other?" An elderly man detained me with a firm grasp of my arm.

"I hail from Kirkenwood, little more than a day's ride from here."

"One of the Merlin's get?" the man asked, narrowing his eyes in speculation.

The old woman at his side opened her eyes wide in awe. She dropped a curtsy and crossed herself.

"I'm just a man who wants to avoid the chaos of war."

"God bless you, boy," the old man said. "We all here will spread the word. That messenger of the devil will find his words falling on deaf ears."

"Send your people north and west. Ask the priests for help. I'll follow the man." The thought of climbing upon my horse sent shivers of fatigue up my spine.

"Be careful, good Father. That messenger of the devil is very dangerous," the old man warned.

"Will such a messenger stand up to the truth?"

"Let us pray he cannot."

I followed the slight frame of the persuasive merchant for three days. For three days I blessed villagers and broke the compulsion of violence. For three days I chased chaos, never quite catching up to him. Then he disappeared. Not even my dogs could catch his scent.

We turned south, bone weary, with growling stomachs.

But we left the area clear of the demon taint. Holy Water and burning sage helped open the path of truth in clogged minds, but my words and my connection to Kirkenwood did more. A few hotheads with more energy than sense might have left to join the Scottish troops on the border. I could not stop those determined to engage in violence. All I could do was negate the influence of a demon with the truth and with faith. I hoped it was enough.

Mortlake, west of London, late February 1559.

"What a marvelous crystal," Dr. John Dee cried even before I had dismounted in the courtyard of his mother's house at Mortlake. The Thames-side cottage needed new thatch and plaster but looked snug enough for the foremost astrologer, scholar, and mystic of all Christendom.

Dr. Dee grabbed my staff from its resting place in a special sheath—where knights of old had carried their lances. He examined the crystal set into the top with avid curiosity. I might not have existed.

Helwriaeth merely looked at me, mouth open in a doggy grin. She knew the man was harmless. Little Newynog dozed across the pommel of the saddle, unaware of the stranger in our midst.

Hesitantly I cleared my throat. "I wrote to you, sir, requesting the opportunity to study with you."

"Yes, yes, go in and get warm. I'll be along in a moment. Mother will see to you. First I must see all there is to see in this glorious crystal under natural sunlight." He waved me inside without lifting his gaze from the crystal. He hadn't even asked my name.

I studied him as I climbed off my horse. Every muscle in my back and legs protested the movement. I'd traveled long and hard. Newynog stirred as I lifted her down. She opened a sleepy eye and squeaked as I set her down at Helwriaeth's feet. They began nosing about the courtyard.

Dr. Dee stood middling height, a full head shorter than myself. About ten years older than me, his sandy hair had grayed prematurely. I guessed that his posture stooped naturally after all his years of peering at ancient and modern manuscripts. He also had a reputation for trying to peer into mystical realms. Tangled and thinning, his hair drooped from beneath a black skullcap. When had he combed it last? At least it was clean. Threadbare black scholar's robes covered him from neck to toe. His elbows nearly poked through the stained cloth. A bruise marred his forehead. The oblong injury was still bright red in the center, indicating a recent blow. Varying shades of purple, green, and finally yellow radiated out from it. A new wound on top of several old ones. What had he knocked it against? Repeatedly?

The door to the cottage remained open. I followed his instructions and stepped inside, having to stoop almost double to get through the door. "Stay," I told Helwriaeth when she tried to follow me. I wanted her watching Dr. Dee and my staff.

The passage to the lower rooms was blocked by a locked door—the doctor's laboratory? I climbed a narrow and twisted stair, having to turn myself sideways to get past the steep turns. At one point, I nearly crawled to avoid banging my head on the ceiling—undoubtedly the cause of Dr. Dee's semipermanent bruise. The stairwell opened into a parlor. Mistress Dee sat by the window plying her needle. Six lights, panes of glass, blocked out the cold day while allowing the noon sunshine in. This close to London, glass should be much more affordable than the extravagant window Donovan had installed—the window that had allowed demon arrows to penetrate Kirkenwood and kill poor Kate.

I crossed myself in memory of Donovan's wife. She hadn't deserved to die so young.

A bright fire in the hearth warmed the room and set my damp coat to steaming—it had never truly dried since the last rainstorm two days ago. I smelled of wet wool, tired horse, and weeks of travel dirt. I sincerely hoped I could beg hospitality from the Dees. Hospitality that included a bath and a real bed instead of a straw pallet. The dormitories at seminary had been more comfortable and cleaner than some of the inns I had stayed at on the journey here. Oftentimes, I'd ended up in the stable because the inns would not allow the dogs inside and I refused to be sepa-

rated from them for an entire night. I needed them to warn
me if the demon returned to the villages I cleared of his
taint. Here in the safety of Dr. Dee's home, I might make
an exception.

"Griffin Kirkwood, at your service, madam." I bowed to
the lady of the house. From her thin gray hair and wrinkled
skin I guessed her to be Dr. Dee's mother. Her prominent
nose and broad forehead spoke of a close blood relationship to the man I had come to learn from.

She nodded acknowledgment of my entry, but peered out
the window into the courtyard where her son twisted my
staff about, gazing at the crystal and the lovely rainbows it
cast forth in the sunlight. The dogs continued to sniff
around the courtyard, making wary circles around Dee.
"Now what is he up to? I swear that boy will catch his
death standing out there in the cold."

She stood up and rapped upon the window with her
knuckles. From over the top of her head, I watched Dr.
John Dee ignore his mother. What was so fascinating about
the crystal? I began to feel a bit possessive about the staff.
I wanted it back—intact.

Helwriaeth must have sensed my unease as she narrowed
her exploration of the courtyard to Dr. Dee's feet. She'd
not let him get far with the staff. Newynog continued to
sniff every cobble, herb, and wall of the outbuildings, intent
upon only her puppy curiosity.

"Excuse me, Master Griffin. I'll fetch him in and serve
us all mulled wine. You need som'at warm in yer belly
'bout now, I figure." She bustled out of the room in quick,
birdlike movements. The narrow bend in the stair posed
no obstacle to her slight frame.

I continued watching through the window, half expecting
the lady to grab the renowned scholar by the ear. She didn't
grab his ear, but she did shake her finger under his nose
as if he were still an errant schoolboy or apprentice. Eventually he looked up from his examination of the crystal—
at least he hadn't removed it from the staff for better
viewing—and stared at his mother, blinking as if he
couldn't remember who she was or why she berated him.

As soon as I heard the sounds of them entering the cottage,
I backed away from the window. Dr. Dee clumped up the
stairs without his mother. Helwriaeth and Newynog followed

him. My dogs did not want to be separated from me any more than I liked having them wander beyond my sight.

A thump told me that Dr. Dee knocked his head on the ceiling as he negotiated the turn in the stairs. "*Mary's teats, that hurts!*" he cursed.

He emerged from the dark well rubbing his forehead with one hand and carrying my staff ahead of him as he would a torch.

"You the Griffin Kirkwood, the one who wrote to me?" Dr. Dee asked, peering at me closely.

I bowed to him.

"Yes, yes, a scholar. Studied in France by your accent. But a native of the north of England." He returned his attention to the crystal as if the mysteries of the universe lay within the matrix of the rock. "A priest, I'm guessing, or you wouldn't have needed to go to France. Griffin. Griffin. *Griffin Kirkwood?* The Pendragon?" Finally he looked at me through clear hazel eyes. The clouds of preoccupation dropped away, his posture straightened, and he smiled. He became instantly the dignified scholar and scientist, a worthy teacher.

"Alas, I must disappoint you. My grandmother was the Pendragon, she did not pass the dragon rampant ring to me." I faced him forthrightly, wondering if my lack of ancestral authority would lessen me in his eyes.

How had he heard of us? Villagers in the north had old traditions and older memories. We announced ourselves to the current monarch—most of the time. The Wars of the Roses had disrupted communication and many traditions. No one else had the need to know that Merlin's descendants still tried to fulfill his mission.

Helwriaeth sat on my foot and leaned into me, begging caresses. Newynog curled around her dam's feet, tugging at the feathered fur of her tail. As long as they remained relaxed, so did I. The staff and crystal were in no danger.

"One hears strange things among the alchemists of the world, and reads stranger things in ancient manuscripts," he replied to my unvoiced question. "Merlin was the first great alchemist. The exploits of his descendants have been followed by scientists for many generations."

I nodded acceptance of his explanation.

"The ring is of no importance." Dr. Dee shifted his attention from me back to the crystal. His eyes glazed over as if he fell into a trance. " 'Tis the magical heritage, the years of schooling, and . . . and this marvelous crystal that matter. Tell me, do you understand the language of the angels?"

"The language of the angels?" I felt stupid never having heard of that particular tongue. I spoke English, French, Latin, and Welsh. I read Greek and German (and some Anglo-Saxon). Of Spanish, Italian, and Russian, I knew some.

"Enochian, the language of the angels," he replied, somewhat impatiently. "Do you hear it?"

I shook my head, still puzzled. "As far as I know, Dr. Dee, Latin is the official language of the church. Would not angels speak to us in a language we could understand?" A tiny fear began to nag at me. He must speak of an allegorical language, not one of the accepted tongues that an angel would choose as fitting for communication with mere humans.

"No, no, no, no. The angels have a language all their own, and only a few special souls have the ability to hear them. You do. You must. You are the Pendragon. Surely if the angels speak to anyone in this troubled land it is you."

"I—I—" Did I dare confess my magical talent to this man? He was a reputed magician, but he dealt with alchemy, the science of magic, not with the forbidden talent that ran in my family. I decided to take a chance. "God grants me visions from time to time."

"Then certainly you can hear angels. You just can't understand them yet. This crystal may open the secret places in your mind that will allow this. I have waited for one such as you for a long time. Come down to my laboratory. We will begin teaching you the language while we delve deeper into the crystal." He started back down the stairs without waiting for my consent.

"But, Dr. Dee, I came here to speak to you of astrology, to learn that skill."

"Bah, anyone can gaze at the stars and compute the mathematics of their movements. Only a gifted few can truly interpret the signs. And those few are the only ones with a chance to hear and understand the angels. Why waste time working up a chart, wandering through circles within circles, when one can get the same information directly from the angels?"

Chapter 22

Mortlake, England, spring 1559.

WINTER flowed into spring. The dogs and I stayed at Mortlake with Dr. Dee and his long-suffering mother. I spent endless hours in front of the window lights studying the convoluted grammar that Dr. Dee claimed belonged to Enochian. I spent an equal amount of time working and re-working the mathematical calculations of astrology. Any night that the clouds dissipated I peered at the stars, trying to distinguish one from the other. Gradually the constellations began to reveal their secrets to me. I wished the mathematics were as clear.

Donovan would have untangled the numbers with ease.

Neither the stars nor the angels gave me insight.

Dee moved back and forth between his home and court, seemingly at random. I gleaned much information from him regarding the current state of politics, economics, and diplomacy. This I passed on to my bishop.

Mistress Dee delighted in the dogs and spent much of her time playing with Newynog. Mother and pup followed her into the village each day as she did her shopping and visiting. I think they became bored by my hours of study and deep conversations with my mentor.

Many of the study problems Dr. Dee left for me while he traveled to London revolved around Elizabeth's horoscope. I saw nothing unusual in the signs and portents of the stars surrounding her. Strife would beset her at times. Great grief and loneliness as well. Nothing specific.

Marie Queen of Scots had many of the same portents in her future, but of greater intensity. My dreams told me more of her fate than the stars.

For the first time since entering seminary, I did not resist the visions and dreams. Meg featured often in the too-real images. I feared for her life. Under Dr. Dee's urging, I began to sort out the symbolism. Meg represented more than just my younger sister. She was an innocent. And perhaps God had chosen her to impart special messages to us because of her innocence. An angel on Earth? Perhaps her cryptic chants and words were the true Enochian language.

But the symbolism of the flaming swords and triple crowns of the vision that had changed my life and sent me to seminary puzzled Dr. Dee. He did not agree with my interpretation. The three crowns represented my ancestor Arthur in current and ancient heraldry. Surely the vision meant that I was to become a warrior like the renowned king.

I did not tell him of the offer of Excalibur from the Lady of the Lake. That was a private matter between me and the Lady. Nor did I speak of the recurring waking vision of towering waves smeared with blood and a headless Marie Queen of Scots walking through them as she led men to the gallows. Those images were too frightening to consider.

Then in March, during Lent, word came to London that Pope Paul IV had decreed that all those faithful to the true church had the right—nay, the duty—to depose by any means necessary, a monarch convicted of heretical acts and philosophies.

He had pronounced a death sentence upon Elizabeth. The Demon of Chaos had a rich new harvest to feast upon.

Dr. Dee returned from London that day, trembling all over as if he had taken a chill. I took him down from his horse and carried him into his laboratory where we kept a brazier going nearly all the time. For once, the dogs were about. They curled up against my mentor and friend, giving him their warmth. He clung to Helwriaeth's neck ruff for balance even while sitting.

"Parliament and the people are outraged," he finally said over a cup of mulled wine. "They threaten the homes and shops of known Catholics with violence. Even those they only suspect of Catholic sympathies are not safe. You must flee, Father Griffin." That was the first time he'd addressed me as a priest.

"The people of Mortlake are my friends. I celebrate Mass for them every Sunday." I had been surprised how many came to receive the Eucharist from my hand when I sought only to celebrate Mass for myself. A goodly number of people in England clung to the Catholic faith even though they now had the option of falling away into the Protestant ceremonies.

I had to share the village church with the Protestants. Each day before I celebrated Mass, I cleansed the church with burning sage—I could not afford the costly incense prescribed by ritual—and resanctified the altar. I was certain the Protestant priest performed the same cleansing ritual when I left.

Helwriaeth nudged my hand, concerned. I did not know how much she understood. Certainly she read the doctor's agitation.

"I must pray on this," I said as I rose from a crouched position by his chair.

"Not in the church! They'll look for you there."

A thrill of power surged through my body. A spell of invisibility begged me to use the power. I took a deep, cleansing breath and purged my body of the unwanted magic. "My flock will not betray me."

"You do not understand, Father Griffin. The people of England love Elizabeth. Through all the terrible years of Bloody Mary's reign, when the slightest indication of Protestant sympathies led to the rack and the stake, our only hope for freedom from the oppression of the Inquisition was Elizabeth. Many true Catholics renounced the church because of Mary's harsh rule, made harsher at the urging of her husband Philip of Spain."

I bowed my head in sadness. I had witnessed Father Manuel's attempt at persecution. He had failed because the people of Kirkenwood loved their lord and their freedom more than the church.

"We will do all that we can to protect Elizabeth," Dr. Dee continued. "You must flee. The people here know you for a priest. Even your friends and your flock may turn on you."

"For the safety of you and your dear mother, I shall depart."

"Where will you go? No place in England will be safe for you."

"Best you do not know who offers me shelter next."

London, late March, 1559.

"We must outlaw the Mass," Donovan insisted to three of his colleagues in Parliament. They gathered around a small table against the back wall of a tavern deep within the wynds and alleys of London. White rings from slopping beer mugs marred the table along with nicks and dents from decades of hard use. But the table did not wobble when Donovan pounded it with his fist to emphasize each word.

The noise of dozens of patrons partaking of the new beer gave them as much privacy as anyone could hope for in London these days. Everyone seemed to know what everyone else did, aided by the penny broadsheets sold outside St. Paul's Cathedral.

"Lord Kirkenwood is right," Master Joseph, a mercer from Lincoln, agreed. He represented his parish in the Commons. "We must do everything possible to keep Catholics out of England. We cannot allow the Bishop of Rome to rule our lives or dictate who will be our queen. But we must also ensure loyalty to the Church of England. Outlawing the Mass is the first step. And a fine for every soul who does not attend Anglican Mass each Sunday."

Donovan almost blurted out his disagreement with that practice. He'd had too many years of required attendance at Catholic services. Freedom from Rome should also mean the ability to choose to go to church or not.

"Both measures are well and good," Michael, the brewer from Stratford, agreed. "But securing our church will do us no good if the Catholics succeed in assassinating Good Queen Bess. Who will reign after her?"

"Marie of Scotland," Donovan breathed the name. "We'd be trading Spanish Catholics under Bloody Mary for French Catholics under Marie."

"Aye. She's the great-granddaughter of Henry VII by his eldest daughter Margaret. She is next in line," Joseph agreed. He took a long pull on his beer, then raised his hand to order a refill from the barmaid.

"Elizabeth has other cousins. Protestant cousins," Michael added.

"All women," Joseph argued, shaking his head.

"Not all. Lord Henry Stewart of Darnley is descended from the same Margaret, by her second marriage. By primogeniture, he is the next male in line." Michael took to pounding the table now.

"What about the Earl of Huntington? He claims descent from Edward III, an older, purer line than the Tudors," Donovan interjected. For that matter, his own family had as many kings in the family tree as any other in England. But all of his royal ancestors were bastard born and ineligible.

The barmaid finally heeded their summons, ignoring the demands of several less important customers in the noisy tavern. Donovan gave up hope that their conversation would remain private for more than two minutes.

As the barmaid reached to refill Donovan's mug, he held his hand over the top. He'd rather have ale, but since the ready availability of hops from Flanders, beer had become all the rage in London, ale almost forgotten.

"But if we outlaw Catholics, then Marie would be an outlaw in our land. We could bypass her and her line and put one of the Grey lasses on the throne," Donovan interjected. "They, too, are of noble descent from Henry VII from his younger daughter Mary—the Rose of England."

He was surprised at how easily he imagined England without Elizabeth. For all of her flirtations with him (mostly to evoke jealousy in Dudley), her favor at court, and her preference for Donovan's company, he did not personally like the woman. Her forthrightness, her ready curses, and her convoluted logic that kept everyone guessing irritated him no end. He couldn't wait to return to the simplicity of border wars at Kirkenwood.

"Aye, young King Edward, bless his soul, named Lady Jane Grey his heir—bypassing Bloody Mary. She ruled for nine days. That gives her sisters as good a claim to the throne as Marie of Scotland." Joseph half rose from his

chair in his enthusiasm. At the end of his speech he realized
that a number of eager tavern patrons eyed him curiously.
He sat abruptly and took another long pull on his beer.

"Better than the Greys, we need Elizabeth to marry and
get a son," Michael said. He narrowed his eyes and pursed
his lips, making his long face with the prominent nose and
sunken chin resemble a sly fox.

"If Parliament demands she choose a husband, Elizabeth
will only cry and dissemble and stall once more. She has a
talent for making petitioners feel guilty for making a request rather than admit that she stalls," Donovan spat.

"She stalls until she can find a way to free Dudley of his
loveless marriage," Joseph added. "Do we want that Gypsy
as our king?"

"He's as black of morals as he is of face!" Michael spat.
"An opportunist who will rob you blind while stabbing you
in the gut and smiling the entire time. Son of a traitor. We
can only expect him to be one as well."

Donovan almost protested the man's contradiction. Dudley's father had been the Earl of Northumberland and protector of the young King Edward. He'd married his eldest
son to Lady Jane Grey and then advised or coerced Edward
to name the lady his successor. If one supported the claims
of the Greys to the throne, then the Dudleys were heroes.
If one preferred the claims of Mary and Elizabeth Tudor,
then certainly Dudley had been a traitor. Robert Dudley—
the queen's dear Robin—had spent time in the Tower for
his father's crimes.

Donovan could not remember if Elizabeth had been in
the Tower at the same time.

"I hear that Amy Robsart, Dudley's wife, ails." Donovan
decided to refocus the conversation. Everyone in the city
knew that a cancer ate at Amy Robsart's breast. How much
longer could she live? Too long if she kept Elizabeth from
taking a husband.

"A diplomatic marriage might intrigue Queen Bess more
if Dudley keeps her waiting much longer," Donovan added.
"Arran of Scotland perhaps? He has strong ties to England
and is Protestant. Mayhap he'd end the border war."

" 'Tis not our place to put forth candidates," Michael
said sternly. "She can find her own husband."

"As long as she does it quickly and settles on a Protestant. We'll have no more foreign Catholics ruling our Queen and our land." Joseph pounded the table this time. All of the mugs bounced, slopping more beer on the already stained table.

"So we are agreed. When Parliament meets tomorrow, you two in the Commons, and I in the Lords, put forth the bill that the Queen must outlaw the Catholic Mass and fine her citizens for nonattendance at the Anglican Mass. Then we put together a delegation of both Commons and Lords to demand she marry and secure the succession." Donovan looked to each of the men.

They nodded, firming their chins and gritting their teeth.

And you, brother Griffin, will have to leave England along with your Catholic demons and your claim to the dragon rampant ring.

Chapter 23

Edinburgh, Scotland.

ROANNA fished a single tansy button out of the spices that collected at the bottom of the cup of mulled wine. She looked over her shoulder to make sure no one saw her quick movement. The traverse, or small anteroom to the queen regent's solar, remained empty. She flicked the button into the brazier. With a sigh of satisfaction she approached the inner door.

Every bone in her body ached from Tryblith's constant prodding. Her mission to incite rebellion in the northern shires of England had failed. Once more Griffin Kirkwood had interfered with her spells. Just like that first time at Kirkenwood . . .

Roanna walked carefully around the full perimeter of the standing stones at Kirkenwood. She tried touching the stones, but lightning crackled between them and her hand every time she came too close. They would allow her entrance only through the eastern portal. Villagers and farmers from outlying areas flocked to the market, also entering and leaving only between the two easternmost stones. The locals seemed to make a point of touching one or the other of those stones for luck upon each passing.

While Gran watched from the other side of the ditch, Roanna walked boldly through the portal. Nothing stopped her, but the stones to either side of her continued to crackle with repulsive energy whenever she came within touching distance.

Roanna retreated outside the stones. She looked over her shoulder toward Gran for reassurance that her ideas might work. Gran pointedly looked elsewhere, neither condemning nor confirming.

Then Raven appeared amongst the throng of people at the market. The lady of the manor drifted from booth to stall to paddock, sniffing the spices a merchant brought from York, testing the texture of a weaving, tasting small bites of mutton presented to her on a stick. She talked with men and women, hauled a child out of the way of a rearing horse, and smiled at everyone. Her black hair with its distinctive white streak and her startling blue eyes made her stand out in the crowd as much as her proud carriage and fine clothing. But the most distinctive thing about her in Roanna's eyes was the staff she carried. Taller than herself by a head and a half with a black crystal affixed to the top, she never loosed her grip on the polished oak of the shaft.

Instinctive animosity rose in Roanna. Raven Kirkwood represented all that Roanna would never be: educated, powerful, full of authority and grace. 'Twas her son and grandsons who led raids across the border and defended this castle against all comers. 'Twas this lady who stood between Roanna's clan and prosperity.

"I must separate the lady from her staff," Roanna mused. A sensation of warm approval flushed her neck. Quickly she looked around to see who might have heard her words. Gran smiled at her broadly.

Roanna's idea blossomed and gave fruit. She rummaged in her basket for what she needed. Then she followed Lady Raven through the market for a time until she could safely remove one hair from her head. Raven slapped at her scalp as if swatting an insect, but made no other acknowledgment of Roanna's presence. Then Roanna retreated beyond the ditch to prepare.

Sometime later, tired but flushed with a sense of accomplishment, Roanna walked the perimeter of the stones once more. This time she spread a fine powder in her wake, not much, just enough to attack Lady Raven's heart when she left or entered the stones. As soon as the spell found its target, the residue would vanish, no longer having a purpose.

Taking a deep breath, Roanna entered the circle. She met a wall of resistance. More a sense of revulsion emanat-

ing from the stones. They reminded her sharply that she
intended to take a life.

"I have to do this!" she told the stones.

They did not listen.

Once more Roanna stalked her quarry. Every time she
came close to the woman, she whispered a tiny compulsion
toward her. Not much, just enough to urge her to go home.
No matter which direction she chose, she had to cross the
path of the spell.

Step by step, Raven edged closer to the eastern portal,
where Roanna had spread her powder in the heaviest concentration. Anxiety built in Roanna's chest. Her heart beat
fast and heavy.

Three steps from the portal stones, Roanna ran past
Raven, knocking the staff to the ground with a seemingly
casual foot. Raven kept moving, guided more by Roanna's
compulsion than anything.

Two steps more. Then one step.

"Raven!" a young man called as he pelted through the
thronging villagers. One of the Kirkwood twins. Donovan
or Griffin, Roanna could not tell. "Raven, here is your
staff." He politely lifted the staff from the ground and
placed it back into his grandmother's hand.

"Thank you, Griffin," Raven said quietly. She seemed to
shake all over a moment, then lifted her head and stared
at the portal. "Will you escort me home? 'Tis nearly sunset." Her eyes crossed a little and she looked about warily.

"Sorry, Raven. The dancing is about to begin, and Laurel
promised to partner me." Griffin straightened his blue doublet, kissed his grandmother on the cheek, and dashed back
into the center of the village. The first strains of music
drifted across the green.

"Stupid boy, haven't I taught you anything these last
eighteen years!" Raven stamped her foot and pounded the
staff into the ground once. Then she turned to face the
portal. She waved the staff in front of her path, once, twice,
thrice, scuffing the powder Roanna had spread there. Then
boldly, she took that last step beyond the stones.

She paused, gasping in pain. "Stupid boy, couldn't even
detect this simple spell," she muttered and marched along
the path back up to the castle.

Roanna sat down hard. How could she have been so
stupid? The forest of stone she had glimpsed in her scrying
bowl must have been the castle, not a city. She'd never
seen a city before and presumed no place else could boast
so many walls piled so very high. Griffin Kirkwood had not
been in Carlisle; he'd been here all along. Here and close
enough to give Raven back her staff. The staff had given
the woman enough strength to withstand the spell.

"I failed," she sobbed into her apron. But secretly she
rejoiced because she had not succeeded in taking a life.

"Partial success, Roanna," Gran said quietly, coming up
behind her. "You hurt her. But 'twill take longer and more
work to bring her down. Perhaps this is more fitting for
the bitch of Kirkenwood. She'll suffer long." Gran almost
drooled with her greedy need to see the end of Raven.

"What must I do now?" Roanna asked, drying her tears.

"You will devise a new spell."

But she hadn't had time. Less than two weeks later, the
Kirkwoods brought a rain of fire and death to her village.
Gran had been one of the first victims.

Now Griffin had succeeded again in negating her spell,
because she had underestimated him and not recognized
him following her.

Only a few stragglers had rallied to the Scottish flag at
Jedburgh. Marie de Guise had dispersed her minimal invasion force. Without huge numbers of Englishmen to augment her troops, she hadn't a prayer of success.

Now Roanna and Tryblith punished the queen regent with
poison for failing to pursue the war they needed. Roanna
really wanted to poison Griffin Kirkwood. Make him suffer
for this failure. 'Twas more his fault than Marie's.

"What did you put into the queen's wine?" Lord Moray
asked, stopping her with a heavy hand upon her shoulder.

Where had he come from? Even if he used magic to
appear and disappear at will, she should be able to sense
his presence. More likely he knew of a secret passage that
she had not yet discovered. Holyrood Palace was riddled
with them.

"Cinnamon, nutmeg, honey, a touch of cloves and . . ."
she rattled off the standard ingredients for mulled wine.

"And what you dropped into the coals of the fire?"

"Something to clear Her Grace's bowels of worms." Roanna looked up into his eyes, keeping her own expression clear and innocent. She'd learned how to lie successfully years ago.

"Or to plant other worms in her body that eat away at her health?" He smiled evilly. For the first time since Roanna had met him, his enjoyment reached his eyes.

She did not trust that genuine smile. She knew how to deal with his false smiles that left his eyes cold and assessing. Warmth from this man—even in bed—seemed alien. He took her without passion to relieve his itch, nothing more. But he did reward her with ever more expensive clothing. Her latest gown was embroidered with gold and garnets which she planned to sell as soon as she found a richer or more powerful lover.

"Her Grace requested a remedy . . ." Roanna batted her eyelashes trying to maintain a guise of innocent vulnerability.

"Come, now, Roanna. We both know you are anything but innocent. How much poison have you given the queen?"

Roanna gasped rather than say anything.

"How much? Her hands and feet swell enough to make her clumsy. Her face bloats, and she complains of aches and pains. Your poisons have done this to her. How much longer before she dies and leaves me to rule Scotland?"

"Milord, I love the queen. I would never . . ."

"You would and you have. Answer me, slut!" He raised his fist as if to strike her.

She stood firm. She'd endured worse beatings from Lord Douglas—elder and younger.

"The queen's doctors tell her she has dropsy. The mulled wine eases her aches," she protested, refusing to cringe away from him as an ordinary maid would.

"Dropsy, eh?" Moray dropped his fist to stroke his beard in contemplation. " 'Twill kill her eventually. How long?"

Roanna shrugged. He'd never know from her that tansy mimicked the disease. She would not give him information that made her vulnerable to manipulation. If anyone found out she had poisoned the queen, she'd hang or be burned at the stake for witchcraft. The Protestant Church elders pursued witches most vigorously these days.

"Double whatever you give her. I want a treaty with England. No sense in wasting valuable men and resources on this continuing border war. Her Grace refuses to negotiate a treaty, so she must be removed from opposition."

"Milord, I could never . . ."

"What do you want as a reward? Money? Jewels? A new lover?"

An estate of my own! she thought wildly.

War! Tryblith nearly shouted at her. *Death, blood. I must have blood. Eliminate him before he stops the wars altogether. Murder him. Here. Now.*

"Roanna!" Marie de Guise called her from her private solar. "Roanna, where is my wine?"

"Coming, Your Grace." Roanna dipped a perfunctory curtsy to Moray and ducked inside the solar without further argument.

The premier lord of Scotland had suddenly become a very dangerous man for her to know. Just yesterday she had considered him a protector. What could she do to eliminate him from the circle of power? Marie had to continue funding the border raids. Roanna had almost manipulated her into a position of needing to press the war more completely, turn the raids into full invasion.

"Your Grace." Roanna placed the wine on the queen's dressing table. Then she picked up the silver-backed hairbrush and began the soothing ritual of dressing her silver-streaked tresses.

Marie de Guise drank the wine greedily. Color came back to her pale cheeks—fuller every month that Roanna served her. She flexed her fingers as if they ached. They, too, looked bloated. On some days her hands hurt so badly, she could barely hold her fan. None of her rings fit anymore.

"Another," Marie ordered.

"Your Grace, are you certain? You do not wish to appear drunk before the court. You hear petitions today. The wine may blur your clear thinking." The tansy did enough of that.

"I shall not appear at all if you do not prepare another dose."

"Yes, Your Grace." The next dose of poison should

go to Moray. Marie was more valuable to Roanna and Tryblith.

"And send Milord Moray to us. We must discuss the treaty negotiations with him."

"The treaty with England, Your Grace?" Roanna stopped with her hand upon the door latch. She needed to kill that treaty as dead as Lord Moray.

"Aye. We would leave Scotland at peace for our daughter when we die."

"Surely you are not so ill as to court death, Your Grace." Roanna clutched her throat and opened her eyes wide. Mayhap she could substitute wild parsley in the wine to negate the effects of the tansy. With renewed vigor, the queen would denounce the loathsome treaty.

"We ail most grievously today, Roanna. Only your special recipe for mulled wine eases the pains." Marie de Guise sighed heavily.

"Will it be true peace, Your Grace, if the English use the treaty to take over your government? They will steal Scotland from your daughter with their sorcerers, their merchants, their well-armed troops. They lie with every breath, Your Grace." Roanna allowed her eyes to cross, inducing a mild trance. Colors jumped into sharper focus. Everything in the room developed a bright halo of energy. She drew this into herself on a deep breath. As she exhaled, she blew lightly across the queen's hair into each ear. Her words found the vulnerable spots in Marie's mind, attached with tiny fish hooks, penetrated, and became one with the queen's thoughts.

"Can you detect a sorcerer in their midst?"

"I might, Your Grace. The visions God grants me sometimes tell me when another works magic."

"Then you shall accompany us to the negotiations. We would know if they try to twist the truth to their advantage."

Roanna went rigid, staring at nothing. She fought the urge to blink. She made her hands tremble and then she began to sway, forward, left, back, right. She made three circles widdershins.

"Roanna! What ails thee, child?" Marie stood and backed away from her soothsayer. She clenched her fist against her heart, breathing rapidly.

Roanna collapsed her knees and fell to the floor, careful to brace herself with her shoulder when she made contact. She lay there moaning a moment while Marie screamed.

"No, Your Grace, do not summon help," Roanna whispered harshly. She paused to swallow deeply and watch the queen regent's reaction. She seemed frightened, but not hysterical. "Your Grace, I have been granted a vision. I must speak to you alone, before the memory of the images deserts me."

"What have you seen, child?" Marie knelt near Roanna's head, her skirts billowing out into a wide puddle of priceless royal blue brocade. Between her tightly corseted waist and the iron strips in her farthingale, she'd need help getting up. Roanna didn't mind lifting her, as long as she listened first.

"Your Grace, I have seen betrayal at the negotiating table. They will try to trick you. You must approach the ambassadors from a position of strength."

"Obvious."

"Wait, there is more. I saw you riding into battle, flags flying bravely, pipes skirling. I see soldiers from northern England flocking to your banner. They all carry a white rose. I see . . ." Roanna peeked at the queen through lowered eyelashes. Marie seemed sufficiently fascinated.

"What else do you see, Roanna? Tell us! We must know the future before we approach the English dogs with words of peace."

"The vision is gone, Your Grace." Roanna slumped back against the floor, affecting exhaustion.

"War," Marie said flatly. "I would do much to avoid war. How may I know this vision is true?"

"Elizabeth cultivates the love of her people in the south. She ignores the north. The Pope has now authorized any true believer to depose or assassinate a heretical ruler—Elizabeth. Many Catholics remain in the north. Catholics who know your daughter is the true queen of England. They will rally to your flag."

"They did not this past winter."

"In deep winter all men huddle close to their hearths. Spring heats their blood now and makes their feet restless."

"Mayhap you are right."

"If you go to the treaty negotiations already in posses-

sion of all England north of York, the English must respect
the sovereignty of the ancient kingdom of Scotland. It is
clear: The white rose is for the House of York." Roanna
did not know if York was the red rose or white. It did not
matter. Marie probably did not know either. She'd been
raised in France.

"York. We must pray upon this. Prepare another dose
of mulled wine, Roanna. Then you will accompany me to
chapel."

But Marie de Guise had fallen deeply asleep and would
not rouse when Roanna returned to the solar.

Good. She'd not negotiate peace today.

Now you will kill Moray, Tryblith reminded her.

"Now I will convince the other lords that Moray seeks
to wear the crown of Scotland himself. Let them kill him.
I'll not have more blood on my hands." Like the blood of
her sister.

*But you must kill him yourself. I need the blood to sur-
vive! I need the blood to grow stronger, to teach you more
magic. I know a spell for turning water solid so that you
and you alone can ford rivers in spate.*

"Useful if I have to flee. How much blood do you need?
What if I slaughter a chicken?" The back of her neck stiff-
ened, the cords twisted painfully as they always did when
Tryblith frowned.

"Is a pig enough?"

I need you to kill a man.

If only she could find Griffin Kirkwood, she would gladly
kill him.

Chapter 24

Mortlake, England, March 1559.

"MURDERING Catholic dog!" the vicar of the Anglican parish shouted at me, throwing a stone.

The stone went wide, but my horse shied and sidestepped. With knees, hands, and determination, I curbed his impulse to rear. Another stone flew from the hands of the grammar tutor, one of the men who brought his family to celebrate Mass with me every Sunday. The draper, one who felt the Anglican Church had not purged itself of enough Catholic trappings to be the pure faith, threw another stone. It hit the horse in the flank. The beast reared and then bucked, trying to rid himself of me.

Helwriaeth turned and bared her teeth at my pursuers. I heard her deep, throaty growl. Then a higher, more nasal growl. Newynog stood with her mother in my defense. The pup had grown to nearly her adult height, but not the bulk of a mature wolfhound.

Another stone flew over my head. My heart leaped to my throat. I gave the horse his head and let him gallop in any direction he wanted. "Helwriaeth, Newynog, heel!" I ordered the dogs.

One of them yipped in pain. I wheeled the horse around, ready to tear out the heart of the man who dared hurt my dogs. Before I could race back into the village with murder in my heart, both hounds loped toward me. Helwriaeth carried her left hind foot high about every sixth step. I saw no blood. She was hurt but not dangerously so.

Angry villagers poured out of their shops and homes. I decided upon the better part of valor and retreated. I heard a few stones land in the dust, but no more came close enough to threaten me or my dogs.

Still, my heart pounded in my throat and panic rode my back like a gibbering demon. My hands trembled, and the horse took advantage of my weakness. He took the bit between his teeth and ran in a new direction, toward a line of trees.

Instinctively, I ducked, flattening along his neck so that the first low branch did not knock me out of the saddle. A quick check showed the dogs following at a slower pace. I trusted them to catch up.

"God, help me know your purpose in this," I pleaded even as I took back control of the reins and slowed the horse to a bone-shattering fast trot.

No one answered. Not God, by whatever name he/she answered to these days, not one of Dr. Dee's angels. Not even Raven.

I scrunched my eyes closed a moment. After several deep breaths I knew only that I must go on. The dogs would find me.

Gradually I gained control of the horse and guided him south and west. Eventually I'd come to a ferry that would take me to the north side of the Thames. I'd wait for Helwriaeth there. Where would we go then?

Sunset found me nearly at Windsor. Too close to the royal castle for safety. I made camp by a small stream near the south edge of the park in a thick copse of oak trees. The dogs limped in shortly thereafter, tired, footsore, thirsty. I dared not light a fire. I'd be hung for poaching if anyone found me in the royal hunting preserve with two wolfhounds.

But I had to tend Helwriaeth's injury. She limped heavily now, not putting any weight at all on the left rear paw. Both dogs collapsed beside my saddle and panniers, tongues lolling and eyes drooping in exhaustion. They'd been bred for long runs like this in hunting and in war, but Newynog was still young and Helwriaeth aging. For all their vitality and intelligence, our wolfhounds were not long-lived: eight to ten years, twelve at the most. The pup licked her mother's paw listlessly, trying to help her without the energy to do much. I held them both close for a moment.

When I had rubbed down the horse and hobbled it where it could reach the stream and fresh grass, I knelt beside the dogs.

At my first touch to the injured foot, Helwriaeth snarled. Her teeth came perilously close to taking off my hand.

"Easy, girl. You know I have to do this." I stroked her ears and back.

She whimpered and laid her head on her paws, keeping one eye on me suspiciously.

Carefully I ran my hands along her spine, along her hip and thigh and finally down her leg. The thick muscle above the knee joint felt hot to my touch. My familiar yipped, but did not snap.

"We've a long way to go, girl. I'll have to treat this. But how?"

A spell is nothing more than a prayer, Raven's voice reminded me.

"I thought you had stopped haunting me when I left Kirkenwood." I sat back on my heels and addressed the woman who had taught me everything I knew about life and love and the importance of family as well as magic.

Our wolfhounds are family.

"I need water and liniment and a fire."

Silence.

I sighed, knowing what I had to do, but not liking it. Neither dog could hunt for a meal tonight—even if poaching in the royal preserve didn't bring the death penalty. So I threw them each a goodly portion of dried meat from my supplies. Newynog could drink from the stream. Helwriaeth shouldn't move. So I brought her water in my little cooking pot.

When she turned her head away after drinking most of the water, I refilled the pot. I bathed the bruised knee and thigh in cold water with a roll of bandages I kept for the horse's sensitive feet and legs. Helwriaeth sighed and closed her eyes.

"Feels good, old girl. Takes away the fire." I murmured soothing words to her as I soaked her leg. Some of the swelling eased.

I had some horse liniment in my bags—no man traveled without it. This particular potion—taught to me by Raven—needed to be warm to work best.

"No fire," I said again. Prayer would have to suffice. "Not for myself, Lord, to help another." I cradled the pot in both hands, almost as I would a communion cup. Imploring words flowed from my lips. I begged God for forgiveness for my cowardice, for my need to return harm to those who hurt my dog. I beseeched any number of saints to intercede for me. Time flowed around me. The night air remained gentle with only a little mist that soothed and hid rather than chilled.

'Twas not the night that warmed my blood, but the fire in my hands. My own hands brought the pot of liniment up to the desired temperature.

Feeling lighter, freer, and much more tired than before, I massaged the potion into Helwriaeth's leg. When she drowsed lightly and I could flex the limb without disturbing her, I wrapped the knee in the bandage I'd used to bathe it earlier. The cloth, too, had warmed, though it remained moist.

A rustling in the bushes roused Newynog. She growled softly, taking seriously her sentry duties since her mother could not.

" 'Cor! What you doing with that there dog?" a rough voice asked.

My eyes, sensitized by contact with the dogs, discerned a stooped man in ragged clothing hiding behind a clump of ferns. Even in the darkness I knew his frightened eyes showed more white than iris.

"You poached a meal for them animals, magician?" the man accused.

Game wardens! I thought, my heart in my throat. I stood slowly, hands out to my sides, showing that I carried no weapon. All the while, I scanned the undergrowth around my oak tree seeking other wardens, or an escape route.

I held my staff, not knowing how it came into my hand.

More rustling in the brush caught my attention. Two big-eyed and scrawny children crouched behind my horse. They eased forward, set upon removing the hobbles and the horse while their father engaged me.

I stepped back, keeping the children within my field of vision.

Another presence off to my left. A woman with a babe in arms trembled behind a tree.

"You are not a game warden," I stated flatly.

"Nay, but you fear them as much as we do." The man stepped out of his concealment. His leather knee breeches and jerkin had worn to buttery softness, thinning at the knees and elbows. His shirt had seen many washings, none recently. But it was his face that arrested my attention. Hollow cheeks, narrow nose, strong chin cleanly shaved, but his skin carried the dark flush of more exotic climes than England. A few lines of silver highlighted his blacker than black hair.

"Be you a 'Gyptian?" I had never seen any of the legendary travelers. But I had heard of them and been taught to fear them.

"That is what the *giorgi* call us." The man nodded in acknowledgment.

"How many of you are there?" Should I try to retrieve my dirk from the panniers? Gypsies never traveled alone. The law restricted them to two adult males in each group, but the law could not limit those it could not find.

Newynog got up and prowled over to the horse. Low rumbles came from deep in her chest. So far she kept her teeth covered. She'd prevent the children from stealing the horse. In a fair fight, I could handle the man. I stood half a head taller than he and outweighed him by at least two stone. I'd been well fed for months on Mistress Dee's bounty. This man probably hadn't eaten a full meal in the same amount of time.

"Just those you spy, magician." He, too, held his hands out to his sides, palms up, indicating he had no evil intention toward me.

I did not relax my vigilance. The title "magician" was almost as dangerous as "priest" these days. Perhaps a little less so.

"We seek only the company of another traveler, magician. Neither me nor mine wish you harm." The man took a step closer to me. I remained firmly by Helwriaeth's side. She still had her teeth and three strong legs. She could take care of herself, but I felt safer with my foot touching her back.

"Why do you seek me out? You could have remained hidden, our paths never crossing."

"Your magic called to us."

"I work no magic. 'Tis forbidden by the Church."

"Call it what you will, but 'tis magic. Magic that can protect my wife and babes from those who hunt us."

"Who hunts you?"

"Those who throw stones first and ask questions later." *Mayhap something neither of us can fight.*

His thought came to me unbidden. I made the sign of the cross and reached for my rosary.

"The mortals who hunt you fear what they do not understand or what is new to them." I finished the statement for him. But I did not mention the immortals he truly feared.

"Aye. We are English born and as loyal to the crown as any other. But because our customs differ, we are hunted, tortured, and enslaved."

"Torture is forbidden in England."

My visitor merely raised his eyebrows, letting me draw my own conclusions. I could not turn him away.

"I have no fire and few provisions, but you may settle here for the night. The dogs will warn us of the approach of intruders."

"And noble dogs they are. Tell me how a wandering magician comes to possess such magnificent beasts?"

Helwriaeth snorted. She recognized banter meant to disarm as well as I did.

"They are my inheritance. And your children will each lose a hand to the pup if they do not desist in their attempts to steal my horse."

The man barked a single word in a language I did not recognize. The woman and her tiny babe emerged from the gloom, her children edged away from the horse and Newynog. None of them looked as if they'd eaten well in a long time.

The boy, having perhaps five years, produced a rabbit, holding the still furred carcass by the ears. The girl, she might be three or six, showed me some turnips caught in the basket she'd made of her skirt.

Newynog sat by the horse's feet, unwilling to give up her guard post.

"I have dried meat and some greens I gathered by the side of a stream. But a fire will alert the game wardens to our presence." I shrugged, content to make do. But my heart went out to these people. They needed more. More food, more clothing, more love. I could not give them enough.

"We know how to shield a fire from giorgi eyes, magician." The Gypsy barked a few more words, and the family scattered. A few moments later they wheeled a handcart packed with a mound of bedding, cooking utensils, and odd tools into the little creekside glade. They laid a fire in a depression, then erected a metal tent over it. The man looked at me expectantly. I did not offer to light the fire with my mind, though I knew I could if I wanted to.

He sighed, putting all the disappointment of the ages into his expression. Then he pulled out flint and iron to strike a spark into the kindling.

"Do you have a name, Master Wanderer?" I asked as he set about skinning the rabbit.

"The giorgi named me Micah when they baptized me. Among the Rom I have another name. An older and more respected name," he replied. "And you, Master Magician, what name do you answer to?"

"F . . ." I hesitated to give him my priestly title. "Friend Micah, I am called Griffin."

"Not a Christian name."

" 'Tis not a name found within the pages of the Bible certainly. But also an old and proud name." The Kirkwoods had been known as the Griffin clan until the death of King John three hundred and forty years before. Since then the oldest son was always given the name Griffin, whether he became the Pendragon or not.

"And you, too, have another name, I sense. One that you keep secret from all but those who dwell within your heart," Micah said under his breath. Then he nodded and grunted as he peeled away the last of the rabbit skin. He gave it to his woman. She immediately began scraping and cleaning it. When properly tanned and added to others of its kind, it would make a nice wrap for the baby.

"And do your wife and children have names?"

"The boy was baptized George. A farmer's name," Micah spat. "They thought we'd settle and become tied to the Earth. As if any man can own the Earth the Goddess gave to us all."

We stared at each other for a long time. He volunteered no information about his wife and daughters.

I stilled, uncertain how to proceed. This man's religion was obviously pagan, even though he'd accepted baptism. I screwed up my courage and asked the inevitable question. "If you do not believe in—" how to phrase this? "in the Christian God, His Son, and the Holy Ghost, then why did you accept the sacrament of baptism?"

"The priests gave us a choice, let them wash our brows with water or they would brand and enslave the women of my clan and hang the men. Queen Mary's laws were very harsh."

"I do not think life will be much different for you and me under Elizabeth. They have begun persecuting Catholics with the same zeal they persecuted Protestants under Mary."

"Men will always look for someone to persecute. Those who look different, live different, or believe different. So long as they are different."

"I fear you are correct."

Questions about my own life and faith began pounding in my temples. I had much to think on this night. Men of my own faith and church had persecuted these gentle people, coerced them into accepting baptism without instruction and without faith. I could preach any number of soothing phrases about the rightness of those actions. All souls needed to be baptized. Or so the Catholic church taught. But I knew that the continued persecution of the Gypsies pushed them farther and farther away from the Catholic church. Why couldn't a Christian choose the life of wandering? Why must people throw stones at them for their dark skin and ragged clothing before offering Christian charity?

If these people stole and poached, they did it to survive when no good Christian would allow them the right to purchase food or dwell under a proper roof.

Why had my own flock driven me out of Mortlake when they knew me incapable of the violence necessary to assassinate the queen?

Faith and the teachings of my church slid slightly apart in my mind.

Chapter 25

Wandering the roads and byways of southern England.

FROM Windsor, I made my way west by northwest to Oxford. Some nights Micah and his family joined me. On others I camped alone without fire and only a single blanket and my dogs to keep me warm. Newynog always seemed to know when we would meet up with the Gypsies or some other wanderers. On those days she brought in a rabbit or a brace of grouse to add to the stewpot that night. She and Helwriaeth always received a share of their own kill.

Some of the other wanderers, not Gypsies, came to my camp seeking solace more than a meal. I prayed with them, blessed them, and offered them what I could from my dwindling stores. They usually departed before dawn, leaving a token in payment, a fish, a few turnips, or once, just a bead from an old and broken rosary. Vagabonds were illegal in England. Everyone must pay for hospitality in some way.

But travelers have their own community, their own method of communication, and their own sense of honor. Word must have passed among them where and when I moved. They found me of their own volition.

Helwriaeth recovered slowly. I kept our pace gentle, allowing Newynog in her puppy enthusiasm to roam and bound around us as sentry.

Eventually I came to Oxford. No one paid much attention to another scholar leading a footsore horse through the streets. My student robes from Paris—that I had stuffed into the bottom of my pack because they had been a part of my life for so long I could not imagine traveling without them—looked like the garb of every third man in the city. I could have walked into one of the colleges and found sanctuary for many days.

But I sought a different sanctuary.

Outside the city walls I found the sprawling manor of Edward de Vere, Earl of Oxford. Quietly, I presented myself at the back door, the one used by servitors. The steward greeted me with wariness. "Benedicte." In a low voice I gave the standard Latin greeting used among Catholics.

"You cannot stay here," he hissed at me just barely above a whisper. "Milord Earl is in London attending Parliament and winning every tournament the queen hosts. I have not the authority to grant you hospitality. Go. Quickly before the others suspect who you are."

"But I am merely a wandering scholar seeking research within my lord Earl's library," I protested.

"Not giving a Latin benediction to an uneducated servant. You are a priest and not welcome in England. Not now. Not while the country seethes with the news of the Papal Bull. Now go." He slammed the door in my face.

"Where now, Helwriaeth?"

She turned away, slouching her shoulders in a doggy shrug. She still favored her hind leg too much to satisfy me. I wished we could stop for a few days or a week to let her recover.

"Maybe the Duke of Norfolk will have a place for us in his household," I told her encouragingly. We turned east and kept walking.

I did not tell her that at our current pace, Bury St. Edmunds was a good two weeks away. Norwich, where I'd more likely find the duke, another week beyond that.

"Master Scholar," a feminine voice whispered to me from beside the well house. "The candlemaker by the north gate will give you a meal and maybe a bed. He won't ask questions if you tell him Millie from the manor sent you."

I nodded. Mentally I added two names to a new list of sympathizers among the commons. My bishop might not think such a list important—he wanted only the names and resources of the nobles who would support an overthrow of the Protestant government—but I knew 'twas the commons who would be the foot soldiers in such an uprising. Without faith of their own, they would follow their lord into battle, but without enthusiasm, and they would retreat at the first setback. I would not allow a demon compulsion to replace faith.

The candlemaker, Jonathan by name, gave us food and a place to sleep in the back of his factory for two days. Twice during that time, men wearing the livery of the town constable stopped and asked Jonathan about a Catholic magician masquerading as a priest. Twice he denied knowledge of me. For some miraculous reason, no one had yet connected the dogs to the man they sought. Two wolfhounds were a mite hard to hide.

After the second visitation by the constable, I departed Oxford in the quiet hour before dawn. Helwriaeth limped less and began the day with more energy than any since we had left Mortlake. The horse, too, walked with surer feet. Newynog nearly exploded with suppressed energy and brought me two rabbits and three grouse for my supper. I willingly shared them with Micah and his family as well as another Gypsy family of two brothers, their wives, and children.

Never did any of them introduce their women. Yet they treated their wives, daughters, and sisters with tender respect bordering on reverence. Did "civilized" men honor their women as well? Most of them reserved that kind of treatment only for Mary, Mother of Jesus. Women in general had fewer rights and respect than a man's horse or dog. Englishwomen had more respect and freedom than most of their gender on the Continent. Yet these Gypsy women held places far above any woman I had yet encountered—even Catherine de Médici and Marie Queen of Scots.

The camp settled around a single banked fire in a rough circle. I lay awake watching the stars progress through the night sky in their endless wheel of time. My thoughts flitted from star to star, from idea to idea, settling on nothing. A faint silver crescent moon, Queen of the Sky, dropped low, making the stars more brilliant.

Perhaps I dozed, perhaps I merely lost myself among the stars. A faint moaning drifted to me on the breeze. A portent of storm? I looked about, expecting dark clouds to gather to the west. The sky remained clear, the breeze barely there, certainly not enough to set the trees to moaning in their upper branches.

The hairs on the back of my neck rose in atavistic fear. Helwriaeth lurched to her feet, facing west and the source of my unease. Newynog joined her. Both dogs bared their teeth and lifted their hackles.

"What?" I asked them in a hushed whisper.

And then I heard the pounding of hooves. A hollow sound not really there, too loud to be merely my imagination. Questions raced through my mind too quickly to answer. All the while something deep inside me shouted for action.

An unearthly glow of blue-white light filled the copse of trees to the west. The racing hooves grew louder.

I had to seek protection from these otherworldly visitors.

"Awake, awake!" I called to the Gypsies and other wanderers gathered around my campfire. "Gather in a circle. Hold the little ones. Cover your heads. On no account look up."

I grabbed my staff and planted the crystal into the ground. Methodically, breathing as deeply as I dared, I drew a large circle with the crystal in the earth around us, our beasts, and the fire. With each step I recited a new prayer. Panic drove all the magical incantations I knew from my brain. All I had left at the tip of my tongue were the petitions of the rosary. A circle of beads to count the prayers. I drew a circle of protection, chanting prayers.

Before I closed the circle, I sensed the presence of unwelcome visitors. I dared not look up.

Newynog barked loudly in warning. I called her to heel, fearful she'd leap outside the circle. Helwriaeth joined her daughter in bugling her alarm.

At last the crystal met the starting point of my circle. The unholy glow increased around me, as bright as the brightest full moon. Curiosity, stupidity, enthrallment, I do not know what made me look up when I knew 'twas to invite death to walk beside me.

Beautiful men, tall, straight, fine of feature and beautifully pale in the strange light. Pale hair, pale skin, pale eyes. Pointed ears and slanted eyes only enhanced their beauty. They wore sumptuous clothing in the brightest rainbow colors. Raven would have found their garb fashionable in her youth. Each elf rode a ghostly pale horse of the finest Andalusian breeding. Their bridles jingled with fine silver bells; rich velvet covered the saddles.

Near heavenly music tinkled from the bridle bells. A

brief flash of fear made me wonder if Dr. Dee truly sought
the bright illusion of elfin music, mistaking it for the voices
of angels.

Silver hooves struck sparks from the earth they barely
touched as they followed the hunt.

A ghostly white fox raced ahead of the mounted elves,
who numbered about a dozen. The leader dug silver spurs
into his steed's flanks. The elves raced forward. Trailing
behind them on mundane horses of dun and chestnut and
splotched colors, rode ordinary men, driven to exhaustion
by the compulsion to follow the hunt until they died.

I knew an urge to mount my own horse and follow them,
to find eternal beauty, everlasting wealth, immortality,
something special just beyond my mortal reach. I needed
to sing along with the bridle bells, to join my voice with
the angelic beauty of it all.

My dogs raised their own voices in an unnatural counterpoint. Their howls were filled with pain straight from hell.

Or sanity.

I bowed my head in prayer instead, wishing I'd never
looked upon this wild elfin hunt. Safety for all those in my
charge lay in keeping their heads down and their eyes
closed. Any who looked upon the elves would die before
dawn.

The fox led them around and around my circle.

In their very paleness I knew who called me to the other
side of life.

I dug in my staff and raised my voice in psalm. "Yea,
though I walk through the valley of the shadow of death,
I will fear no evil; For thou art with me; Thy rod and Thy
staff, they comfort me." I raised my own staff to the heavens. The black crystal caught the eldritch glow and cast a
giant shadow. A trick of the light and trees and shrubs bent
the shadow into a semblance of a dragon rampant.

The elf king pulled his speeding horse to a violent halt
before entering that unnatural shadow. His steed reared
and pawed in fright at the shadow creature of legend. The
entire hunt stopped as well. Disorder entered their ranks.
Ghostly horses shied and milled and bumped into each
other.

Two of the mundane followers fell from their steeds in

an exhausted faint. I longed to run to them, to save their souls before the elves regained their senses.

With a sublime mastery of hands and knees and subtle magic, the elf king brought his horse under control.

"Who dares intrude upon our hunt?" His voice echoed and boomed across the land. A vague hollow emptiness froze my panicked heart and fluttering innards.

I replied not. The psalm continued to hum in the back of my throat. I gave it life. "Thee preparest a table before me in the presence of mine enemies; Thee anointest my head with oil; My cup runneth over. Surely thy goodness and mercy shall follow me all the days of my life; And I will dwell in the house of the Lord forever."

"Amen," Micah and the other men whispered in chorus.

"Amen!" I shouted.

The elf king loosed his sword and slashed at the shadow. The image held. His horse reared and backed away. The elves behind him milled aimlessly. Even the ghostly fox stopped his endless run.

"Beware, Pendragon." The king pointed his otherworldly sword at my breast. He slashed at my circle. Blue sparks bounced back into his eyes. "Beware that you defy me no more! We do not treat lightly those who interrupt our hunt. Your soul is forfeit next time we meet." The elf king gathered his forces and rode around the dragon rampant shadow.

Two more stragglers managed to dismount and fall upon their knees, foreheads touching the earth.

"Pretty!" Micah's young daughter cried. "Pretty horsie." She wiggled out from her father's desperate grasp and ran after the deadly hunt.

Chapter 26

I LUNGED and missed the child. Her left foot rose, bare inches from the circle I had drawn in the turf. If she scuffed it in any way, our protection would vanish. We'd all lose our souls to the hunt.

Helwriaeth grabbed the little girl by the neck of her gown, as if picking up one of her own pups. They stopped a scant finger's length from the circle. The girl wailed her displeasure.

I panted, willing my heart to slow its frantic drumming.

Newynog ambled over and laved the child's face with a raspy tongue. She screamed again, then giggled as Newynog repeated her ministrations.

Helwriaeth kept a firm grasp on the child's gown.

"Oh, *chavi*." Micah's wife ran to rescue her daughter. She caught her up in a ferocious hug that elicited more screams.

"Doggie." The little girl pointed to Newynog. "Play doggie."

Micah joined his wife in hugging the child.

I rolled over and stared at the sky once more, too tired to think or even to rejoice. Helwriaeth joined me, flashing me a doggy grin of triumph at a good night's work.

"Build up the fire," Micah ordered.

One by one, each of the wanderers rose up and joined the others in a tight circle about the fire. Hands shook as they added fuel to the flames. I saw how their nostrils pinched and their eyes darted about. They left places in their circle for me and the dogs. Wearily I half walked, half crawled over to them, closing the gap. Uneasily we kept our backs to the dangers and temptation of the rest of the world.

I drank the *usquebaugh* they poured into my cup in three gulps—no matter how shaky their hands, they spilled not a drop. I held out the cup for a refill.

"Many thanks, Father Merlin." The unknown wanderer tugged on his cap as he filled my cup to the brim with the strong liquor.

"I am not the Merlin," I mumbled.

"Who else could have saved us all from the undeath of the king of the elves?" Micah asked. Awe tinged his voice. He, too, tugged on his billed cap in respect.

I looked all around the circle. Every one of the half-dozen adults and as many children stared at me as if I presented them with miracles.

Perhaps I had.

"Are we all here?" I asked rather than dispute them. I didn't think I could have won that argument.

"Aye, all hale and whole, thanks to you, Father Merlin." Micah caressed his daughter's dark curls, making sure she hadn't wandered off and been replaced by an other-worldly changeling.

"What about them?" The other Gypsy male asked, pointing with his cup to the four men collapsed outside the larger circle.

Two of them stirred and looked about in bewilderment. Their horses browsed nearby, seemingly recovered from their ghostly ordeal. I feared the first two who had fallen from their horses had died. I needed to go to them, say the last rites for them, bathe them in holy water and oil.

I dared not disturb the circle yet. Dawn was a long way off.

Slowly, with protesting joints, I stood up, using my staff as a crutch. Carefully I smudged the circle a little, close to the men. "Enter," I invited.

Hastily they joined us. When they were safely within the circle, I closed it again using the crystal as my knife.

One look confirmed that the remaining men had indeed died. They would have to wait for morning. Perhaps then their wandering souls would find their bodies again and I could send them on to heaven intact.

We all sat up for the rest of the night, keeping the fire blazing and our guts full of drink. We sang old songs and made up new ones. Music soothed our troubled souls and gave us a way to rejoice that we all lived.

At dawn, we broke camp, each going in a separate, silent direction. Micah and I buried the two unfortunate men using his tools to break the hard ground. I prayed all the while that the king of the elves had not succeeded in stealing their souls as well as their lives.

My dogs and I proceeded east. Each night a growing number of wanderers joined us. Each night I drew a circle of protection around us.

They called me Father Merlin.

Inspired by the example of my ancestors, I began a journal, recording the events of the days as well as my philosophical musings. I also kept track of the gossip I encountered. Travelers and villagers alike kept me informed of Queen Elizabeth's latest romp with her favorite courtier. Rumors of an illegitimate child born to the queen frequently slipped into the gossip. Villagers also knew the actions of Parliament almost as soon as they made a decision. I heard more about the bill to outlaw the Mass and fine citizens for nonattendance of Anglican services. I would not write that sad news to my bishop until I knew that the laws had been passed by Parliament and ratified by Queen Elizabeth.

My journal helped me keep track of the passage of days. Good Friday found me near Huntingdon. I considered entering the town for the solemn rituals of the Holy Days. The original castle of the Locksley family had fallen into ruin and been replaced by a more comfortable manor. The Locksley family, too, had fallen upon hard times, and Henry Hastings now held the title of Third Earl. A descendant of Edward III, Hastings had a claim to the throne and was married to a sister of Robert Dudley, the queen's favorite. Was he Catholic or Protestant? Would he welcome me as Robin Locksley had welcomed my ancestress Resmiranda Griffin when she fled King John's tyranny?

I sought instead the old stone circle where Resmiranda had presided over a meeting of truce between King John and his adversary Robin Locksley, Earl of Huntington. The Robin Hood of legend had matured and become respectable by the time of that meeting in 1213, but he was still at odds with John. Both men had needed to cooperate during the rebellion of 1213–1216 that led to the Magna Carta.

Suddenly I knew that I must discover if the circle remained intact and restore it if it had not. I set my path for the castle ruins and the tor above them. The tower keep had lost its roof and the curtain wall had been breached in three places. Many stones had gone missing, probably to be found in the foundations of other buildings. The moat was just a ditch now, and the gates probably became a wall in a village house or firewood. Most lords had abandoned the damp and uncomfortable castles for more modern manors, except along the border where medieval warfare still ruled our lives.

Part of me was saddened by the passing of a way of life that had produced the code of chivalry, the Magna Carta, troubadours, and heroes like Robin Hood and King Arthur. Another part of me rejoiced that we had stopped fighting among ourselves long enough to outgrow the need for castles designed more for defense than comfort.

But had we? Would the tension between Protestant and Catholic break out into another civil war that must bring the castles back to life? Civil war would unleash the Demon of Chaos once more upon the land.

I had to help England keep peace. But my bishop and the Pope actively sought civil war to depose Elizabeth.

As the sun dropped toward the horizon in the western sky, I skirted the moat and headed up the massive tor. A path of sorts still existed, probably made by sheep. A stream cascaded down the rocky slope with wild abandon. I thought I saw a hut near the base of the last little waterfall before the creek and the land leveled out. I considered stopping there and begging hospitality. Maybe tomorrow. Tonight, on Good Friday, the most solemn of Holy Days, I had more important things on my mind. An old woman pushed aside the leather curtain that covered the low doorway. She came out and stood beside the water, staring at me for a long time. Her scraggly, white-yellow hair covered one side of her face. Age and time had stooped her shoulders and gnarled her hands. At one time she might have been tall and statuesque. Her dark eye burned in her weathered face. The mass of wrinkles around her eyes and

mouth might have been a map of a river and its tributaries—
the river of her life. She carried a long staff—taller than
she by a full head—made taller by a crude sculpture of a
raven perched atop it.

Newynog bounded over to her, licked her hand, and
loped back to me. I waved my own staff at the crone by
way of greeting and proceeded up the hill.

She grunted something and continued to watch my
steps intently.

The sun had not yet set but lay in shadow behind the
tor. The twilight gave me enough light—my vision seemed
strangely more acute than before, but still not fully recovered from my battle with the demon—to see the path that
wound upward in long switchbacks. I lost sight of the old
woman. Yet I sensed that she still watched me. Friend or
foe? The dogs roamed slightly ahead of me rather than
guarding my rear. I trusted their judgment.

At last I crested the hill just as the sun reached the distant horizon. Its dying rays caught the tips of a circle of
small boulders, lighting them with green fire in a web that
connected each to its neighbor and all of them back to
three fallen stones in the exact center. The creek began
there, springing forth from the earth in a musical bubble.

I stared at the broad plateau in awe for long moments.
The sun dropped below the horizon and still the web of
green fire lit the stones.

Helwriaeth splashed into the stream where it exited the
circle between two slightly larger stones on the eastern
boundary. She trotted through the water toward the center
with Newynog at her heels.

"I guess I need to follow the same route," I muttered
and stepped into the water. I guessed that sunrise on the
Summer Solstice would appear between these two stones if
one stood atop the triptych surrounding the birthplace of
the spring. The moment I passed the portal stones, a sense
of safety, almost a homecoming, wrapped around me.

I turned in a circle, arms out, symbolically embracing the
stones. From here I could see for miles in every direction.
But I could detect no sign of the old woman and her hut
at the base of the falls.

Newynog dashed out of the circle at the eastern portal
and raced around the entire circle before pouncing on a

nesting pheasant. I let the dogs eat two of the eggs and the bird. The rest of the eggs I saved to break my morning fast.

Helwriaeth brought me twigs and branches from all over the tor that boasted much grass and few trees. We made camp and then I set my altar on the center stone and kept my Good Friday vigil of prayer and meditation through the night.

On Saturday I rested, ate a little, and read from my devotional. Then I kept vigil again through the night.

Chirping birds muffled by fog roused me from my prayers as light began to filter through the mist. Hastily I washed in the creek and then sanctified all three of the stones. I had not celebrated Mass since leaving Mortlake. Today I would sing the glories of Easter morn at sunrise.

I lit two candles and a tiny morsel of incense salvaged from Kirkenwood's chapel. Then I raised my eyes and my voice. "Alleluia! Christ is risen," I shouted in Latin and then in English.

"The Lord is risen indeed!" a chorus of voices replied in Latin and then again in English. I recognized some of the wanderers in the group from my camps along the road. Most I had not seen before, but I recognized them as Gypsies and other vagabonds by their ragged clothing and their certain gait over uneven terrain. One by one they entered the stone circle by the eastern portal, cleansing themselves ritually as they stepped in the creek.

I accepted that cleansing in lieu of confession.

"Welcome," I called to them around a lump in my throat.

They brought wine and bread as their offering. Together we celebrated the wonder of our Risen Lord. The familiar phrases in Latin rolled off my tongue as the English translation could not. My impromptu congregation replied enthusiastically at the proper places with the proper phrases. They might not understand the language, but they knew the ritual of the Mass by rote. The English translation used by the Anglicans contained many obscure words and awkward phrases, probably less understandable to the average Englishman than the traditional Latin Mass.

Together we joined the faithful throughout Christendom in the same ritual, as it had been celebrated for centuries. The web of green light intensified, binding us all to the land, to God, and to every other Christian celebrating this most special day with the same words and motions.

My heart swelled to near bursting.

"God and his blessed Son Jesus Christ are here with us today," I began my homily. "Let us reach out and embrace our brothers in Christ with the same enthusiasm we greet our Risen Lord."

Unplanned words flowed from me. I preached love and forgiveness, tolerance, and brotherhood. "Only by forgiving and respecting each other can we join together to fight for light within the world," I finished. The words I had spoken did not remain in my mind, but the message did.

'Twas the message of all the Pendragons of Britain. I needed to spread this wonderful sense of unity to all of England, indeed all of the Continent. I had begun the task. How to continue?

Communion wine had never tasted so sweet, nor had Communion bread nourished my soul so well. Our humble offering became more than just a symbol of the body and blood of Christ. As I raised my hands in blessing, I knew that God, Christ, and the Holy Spirit had truly been present in our humble offering of adoration.

No matter what name you give to God, know that she is listening, Raven reminded me.

Every member of the congregation—men, women, and children, villagers, wanderers, and Gypsies—all shook my hand as they departed to their homes and camps and the rude feasts that ended the Lenten fasts. They smiled and wished me well, then became lost to my view in the clinging fog that persisted beyond the stones.

When I was alone, I loosed a sigh of satisfaction and turned to clear the altar. The ancient crone from the hut by the falls blocked my path. Through the curtain of hair on the right side of her face, I thought I discerned a mass of scar tissue where her eye should be.

Had her right eye been plucked out by a demon in a battle more fierce than my own confrontation with Tryblith?

"I be Deirdre, keeper of this place."

"Are you a priestess of the old gods?" I asked.

"Matters not what you call your God. You teach the message of the light," she said. "Been a long time since we had a Griffin presiding up here. The stones need the ceremonies and rituals to stay alive. You will always be welcome here. The stones will harbor you."

The raven sculpture atop her staff stirred and croaked. Then it flew off, due east. The old woman stepped into the creek and disappeared into the fog.

"You learned long ago that no matter what name you give to God, she hears our prayers," the old woman said through the fog.

Or was it the raven who croaked the message?

Chapter 27

Norwich, England, Home of the Duke of Norfolk, spring 1559.

"YOU shall be my chaplain, Father Griffin." Thomas Howard, fourth Duke of Norfolk embraced me with enthusiasm. A thin and bitter young man of sallow complexion and nervous demeanor ushered me and my dogs into his private solar mere moments after my arrival. His constantly fluttering hands and nail biting set my nerves jangling. I wanted to back away from him, along with my dogs.

"By law, I am not allowed to celebrate Mass, either publicly or privately," I reminded him, still wary of his too anxious greeting. The dogs had backed away from his rough hands on their ears. The hairs on my back prickled, much as Helwriaeth's ruff stood on end.

"Elizabeth does not listen to me," Norfolk ranted. "She listens to no one of any breeding. The only advice she seeks is from that . . . that commoner Dudley. He has no title or estates of his own, and he doesn't even sit on her Privy Council. At best she seeks advice from her upstart of a Secretary of State, William Cecil. But me—England's only remaining duke and her maternal cousin—she ignores. She will not have me, me her *cousin,* anywhere near the Privy Council."

Then he turned his small, cunning eyes upon me. "You must help me turn Elizabeth back to the true faith, Father Griffin."

I backed a step farther away from this angry and ambitious man. Norfolk would not be the first man to use a stranger as a weapon in a personal battle against the queen.

"I shall ignore the queen's illegal decree about the Holy Mass," Norfolk announced.

He was mistaken about the law. Parliament had passed it and Elizabeth concurred. She did not peremptorily decree matters of such importance.

"I am *the* duke. Her maternal grandmother was sister to my father. She cannot fine or imprison me." Norfolk waved his hands in dismissal.

A sharp burn surged up my spine into my skull. My vision fractured between colors and gray tones as if only one of my damaged eyes worked at a time. I saw huge ocean waves crashing over me as I flailed in the surf. The water foamed with blood and the duke joined Marie Queen of Scots in walking across the water toward a headsman's block. The queen held a wedding ring in front of Norfolk's nose, enticing him forward to his fate.

"Father Griffin, are you ill?"

I emerged from the sense-shattering vision gasping for air as if I truly had been drowning.

"A long and dangerous journey, Your Grace. If I could rest and sup before commencing my duties as your chaplain . . ."

"Of course, of course." He rang a little silver bell to summon his steward. "We begin tonight. I must introduce you to some like-minded men. You will bless our endeavors by serving us Mass at midnight. But first we will dine and discuss plans for ending Elizabeth's misguided tyranny. We will show her the error of her ways and bring her back to the true faith or find another to sit upon her throne. Her cousin Marie of Scotland."

"Have you met Marie Queen of Scots?" I asked. Though Catholic and a probable heir to the throne of England through her grandmother Margaret Tudor, I could not be certain her temperament was suited to the strong-willed and rather independent English. Could any monarch, male or female, unite them under one church after so many years of schism?

"I hear that Her Majesty is a lovely young woman, superbly educated. She is our true queen."

"She is a shallow woman who thinks clothes and jewels give her power and that her beauty will conquer all obstacles," I said quietly.

"All the better for good English nobles like myself to

guide her through the intricacies of politics. We shall return to the days when the nobles ruled and the monarch merely sat in judgment. Then and only then will England prosper in true peace and faith." He slapped my back as if I were a long lost friend instead of a newly met priest.

"Or we shall dissolve into civil war that will leave us vulnerable to invasion from foreign powers and the Demon of Chaos," I muttered.

The self-absorbed duke did not seem to hear me.

Norfolk's leaps of logic bothered me. If Marie of Scotland survived long enough to add the crown of England to those of Scotland and France, she'd likely show her gratitude to Norfolk with pretty smiles and gifts of jewels. But she would listen to her French uncles, a cardinal and a duc, not her English citizens.

An evil thought pushed into my mind. Had Pope Pius IV issued his Bull upon the urging of the French? Or perhaps Philip of Spain had insisted upon the wording to countenance the aggression of his Inquisition.

My faith rocked. I had trouble maintaining my physical and mental balance for a moment. I must have swayed upon my feet because Helwriaeth pressed herself hard against my hip, giving me something to lean on. She bared her teeth at Norfolk as he, too, reached to support me.

"Come. A hot bath, a cup of wine, and a sleep will cure you quick enough of whatever plagues you. Can't have my priest taking ill just before we begin this great venture in the name of the church."

The Pendragon of Britain must find a better compromise than regicide.

At the time of judgment, would I favor Britain or my faith?

At supper that night, I met Thomas Howard's Catholic friends. Charles Mattingly and Mathew de Lisle, younger sons of Protestant lords with no chance at inheritance under the current regime, were dressed in the height of fashion, dripping lace and jewels. Their sullen expressions spoke more of their disgruntlement at being younger sons than of their faith in the Catholic cause. Sir Bartholomew Digby and Lord Edward Binghampton approached me with honest and open faces. I almost trusted them. The dogs would have told me more, but both had been banished from the intimate supper offered by the duke. Three others came late; I did not learn their names.

No musicians entertained this group (I missed them sorely after my vagabond friends had brought music back into my life), and the servitors left the room after presenting each remove. Discussion stopped abruptly any time the door opened to admit menials who carried gossip as easily as their trays of food. Norfolk's conspirators drank more than they ate and they consumed soup and bread, fish, game, and mutton, as well as a treacle tart apiece that almost gagged me with its sweetness. They argued and complained loudly about Elizabeth's usurpation of power—they seemed more disgruntled that she was female than about any one thing she had done. Their discussion accomplished nothing.

And then at last, when the men were too drunk to understand the implications, Norfolk stood up with his glass raised. His eyes glittered in the candlelight. I thought I detected avarice in his gaze. Perhaps only malice.

I sensed Helwriaeth and Newynog scratching and whining at the locked door of the suite of rooms I had been given. They needed to be at my side.

"Then we are agreed, gentlemen," Norfolk said without a single trace of drunkenness. "Unless Elizabeth agrees to marry me and return to the true faith, we will depose her by any means possible and put Marie Queen of Scots on the throne."

I had not heard any such agreement! I'd heard nothing of the sort through all the long supper.

The assembled malcontents raised their glasses and mumbled something that might pass for consent.

"Your Grace," I said quietly, "I cannot countenance regicide, murder, for surely that is what you are proposing."

"Not murder, priest. Execution. By Papal decree, the faithful are duty bound to remove a monarch who practices heresy. Elizabeth is a Protestant and therefore a heretic."

"But you would marry her, violating the laws of consanguinity. She is your blood cousin."

"If she returns to the true faith, those objections can be dealt with."

"Would you force her to accept our faith or guide her to true conversion?" I almost shook with suppressed outrage.

"Whatever. A toast, gentlemen. A toast to the return of England to a true path and the priest who will help us accomplish it."

"Hear, hear," the men chorused, looking at me through bleary eyes.

"What do you propose I do?" I asked through gritted teeth. I had to stop him if he intended murder.

"Whatever is necessary to bring the true faith back to England." *And put me on the throne.*

The duke's thoughts came to my mind unbidden.

I had just become the Duke of Norfolk's scapegoat. Should anything go wrong with his plots and treacheries, I was certain I would take the blame. He'd make sure I burned at the stake or suffered a traitor's death, the gruesome drawing and quartering, while he walked free.

Kirkenwood Castle, 15 June, 1559.

"How could you let your brother steal Raven's staff!" Donovan yelled at Fiona. "Not only the staff, but Helwriaeth's only female pup as well!"

He'd returned from London and Parliament last night soaking wet, on a horse made skittish by thunder and lightning. While the capital and the southlands warmed and basked under bright sunshine, Kirkenwood remained in the grip of a storm worthy of the Vernal Equinox. By midmorning he still had not warmed all the way through, and everything smelled of mold. His leg hurt abominably.

"Our *brother* Griffin did not ask permission. He just left. And you did not tell me that he had no authority to take them," Fiona returned, facing him in a broad stance with hands on her hips. "And he is more your brother than mine. You two shared the same womb as well as the same mother and father. I only share a father with you." A very annoying smirk twitched the corner of her mouth upward. She had always found amusement in his foul moods.

Donovan wanted to wipe the smile from her face. His sister reminded him too much of Elizabeth and her cunning ploys to divert her courtiers, advisers, and Parliament from policies she did not like. She rarely disagreed, but strewed confusion in her wake while she stalled and dissembled and kept people waiting for a decision.

"Methinks the time has come to find you a husband, Fiona, if any man would tolerate your sauciness," he grumbled.

"Go spend some time with your daughter. Your foul temper certainly isn't helping me run your household. As for finding me a husband, I've found the man I like and have waited only for you to come home from your life of luxury in London to give us your blessing." She flounced off before he could reply.

"As uppity as the queen," he muttered to the empty air behind her.

Betsy squirmed again, holding her hands out to her father, no longer afraid of him.

"A lesson to be learned in this," he mumbled.

Betsy studied him with big solemn eyes the color of the deepest part of the lake in sunshine. Donovan felt as though she looked into the bottom of his soul, reached in and yanked out many of his hurts.

"Griffin needs the staff to guide him. He can't see where he's going," Meg said in her adult voice. She, too, examined her brother with fathomless eyes. But the blue depths did not reach all the way into rationality. Quickly they fogged, and she turned her attention to one of the hunting dogs that roamed the Hall, a big male wolfhound that tolerated her vigorous hugs. It must be an aging one that had become more pet than working animal.

"I did not realize Griffin had gone so blind," Donovan muttered. "He seemed to cope well enough around here." A moment of concern melted some of his bitterness. But then lightning flashed across his mind and he remembered how vulnerable Griffin had left the family, indeed all of Britain, by renouncing his claim to the Pendragon when he became a priest. The Catholic and Protestant churches alike condemned magic. In order to be an effective Pendragon, a man had to have the freedom of conscience to wield whatever powers the gods gave him to protect Britain and the family.

"Griffy not blind," Meg sang in her five-year-old voice. "Griffy just can't see where he's going."

That stopped Donovan's lean toward sympathy.

"He's as blind of heart as he is of eye."

While he's stumbling around in the dark, I must do what I can to maintain the tradition of the Pendragons, Donovan thought.

"Come, Betsy, I'm going to show you a special place full of wonderful treasures." Gently he carried the little girl up the stairs toward the secret door that led to the lair. But first he must retrieve some books from his luggage. The printing presses in London produced many marvelous volumes on a daily basis, including books every church wanted to suppress. Books of alchemy and magic.

He'd spent every pence of the £5 of Elizabeth's stipend on books. He'd even consulted Dr. John Dee on the best method for commencing his experiments.

The magic Raven could not awaken in him could be duplicated by science. The lair seemed the best place to set up his laboratory.

Chapter 28

Norwich Castle, Home of the Duke of Norfolk, early spring 1559.

"THE watch bell is about to ring midnight," the Duke of Norfolk announced. "We will hear Mass now."

My inner sense told me that the moon had set and midnight was long past. But the watch bell had not rung. Had the duke given orders to still it until he was ready for it to be midnight?

The vain young man, not much older than myself, yet quite childish in his expectation that the world ordered itself to please him, was as bright-eyed and energetic as if he'd just broken his morning fast rather than having dined on heavy meats and heavier wines.

"Your companions are in no condition to receive the body and blood of Christ with a pure heart. Their sins are not confessed and their minds hardly receptive to the Holy Spirit." I remained seated beside Norfolk at the small dining table. In the back of my mind, I heard the dogs scratching and whining for release from their confinement. They wanted to come to me, protect me from Norfolk's plots and subterfuges.

I could not flee. My bishop depended upon me to remain in this hotbed of Catholic rebellion.

"Perhaps we'd best postpone our celebratory Mass till the morrow." Norfolk stared at his bleary-eyed coconspirators. Mattingly and de Lisle snored lightly while sitting up, eyes open, mouths slightly agape as if words hesitated upon their tongues. "You will listen to our confessions in the morning, and then we will all partake of Mass. So good to

215

hear the blessed words of the sacrament in Latin again, in the language of God."

The language of God. Briefly I had memory images of Dr. John Dee waiting patiently for an angel to speak to him in any language, even in the obscure Enochian tongue. Wishful thinking. Much as Norfolk's vision of a Catholic world with himself at the center was naïve and shortsighted.

By midmorning when Norfolk and his companions stumbled out of bed, the dogs and I had explored a goodly section of the lands around Norfolk's country manor. Newynog ranged far afield, startling grouse and barking at hawks flying above. Helwriaeth strolled at my heels, content to sniff at wildflowers and nose an occasional mole hole. I touched her whenever I could, relishing our time together. For, surely, her detachment from the life bursting within this pasture meant that her days drew to an end. I would miss her. She had given me Newynog to replace her as my familiar, but no one could replace Helwriaeth.

When I paused at the crest of a knoll, she sat on my foot and leaned into me. I ruffled her ears, and she closed her eyes in doggy bliss.

"What shall we do about the young duke?" I asked her. "I doubt the sincerity of his cause. I think if Elizabeth had stayed a Catholic, Norfolk would become Protestant, just to oppose her. He wants power without accepting the responsibility that goes along with it. Nor is he willing to learn the arts of diplomacy and politics. He wants the easy path handed to him by others." For the seven years that Helwriaeth and I had been together, we had talked through our problems in this manner.

I talked. She listened patiently. The process helped me order my thoughts and find alternatives.

There are always alternatives. Raven's voice was made husky by time and distance. Or was it truly her voice? Perhaps all of my ancestors haunted me, using her voice to convey their wisdom to me.

Must I add Deirdre of the raven staff to that list?

"Alternatives. Norfolk bears watching. He offers me shelter. From his household I will hear much of politics, religion, economics. From here I can report to Bishop Eustachius du Bellay with the sanction of my host. But I do

not have to trust Norfolk or approve his plans. Perhaps I
can teach him a little caution.''

Helwriaeth sighed her approval. Newynog bounced back
to us, tongue lolling around a huge grin. I petted her enthusiastically. She tugged on my sleeve, begging for rougher
games. I tossed a stick for her. She brought it back but
refused to drop it. We tussled for it at length before she
consented for me to throw it again.

I wished Donovan could be here to enjoy these brief
moments of companionship. I sighed in resignation. Too
many bitter words had passed between us.

By the time we returned to the manor, Norfolk's companions had limped home, holding their heads against monstrous hangovers. The household servants came to me
eagerly with every bit of gossip. My sympathetic ear heard
much of how the lords spoke among themselves with plots
to kill the queen, but not in conjunction with Norfolk.

Indeed, I had much to watch and report from this nest
of discontent.

I stayed with Norfolk through the long summer. Queen
Elizabeth took a progress through the southlands. Anyone
who could escape the city during the summer did so. The
crowds and the heat had, in years past bred the plague. No
one wanted to take a chance that this year would be the
one London remained safe during the hot months. The
queen's court visited many of her lords, some whose loyalty
needed rewarding, others whose loyalty needed to be
boosted. She did not venture toward Norwich, and Norfolk
made no move to join her gay festivities.

I celebrated Mass every day in Norfolk's beautiful
chapel. None of the services matched the Easter sunrise
Mass in the open for shared intensity.

In July, I received word that Henry II of France had
finally died. His eldest son became Francis II, king of
France. He and his wife, Marie Queen of Scots, openly
quartered their seal with the Arms of England as well as
France and Scotland.

Norfolk's spies at Elizabeth's court reported that the English queen had received the news with a laugh, but letters
of protest against the young couple's claim to England left
Secretary of State William Cecil's desk posthaste.

Then in the heat of the summer, the Archbishop of Canterbury died. All of Europe held its breath waiting for Elizabeth to appoint a new head of the Church in England. My bishop urged me to hasten to interview all of the candidates. He wanted me to press Elizabeth to choose a man with Catholic leanings.

How did he expect me to gain the queen's ear when my presence in England bordered on illegal? I could only report that Elizabeth chose Mathew Parker to fill the post, a man of even temperament and moderate political views. But still a Protestant. She played a waiting game, keeping an uneasy balance. She sought to please her people, yet at the same time she must not offend the Catholic powers of Europe by appointing one of her bishops who leaned toward the radical Puritan interpretation of the English Bible.

By the time the autumnal rains had washed the danger of plague out of London, Norfolk's temper had cooled and he packed up his household to return to the capital, eager to reestablish his preeminence at court.

I sensed the need to move my observation post closer to the hub of political and religious activity. Norfolk would continue his plotting there and perhaps introduce me to men who could truly be counted upon when the time came to bring the church back to England. I strongly discounted Norfolk's usefulness for other than conceiving wild plots. Others with more level heads must carry them to fruition.

The more I listened to the Catholics in England, the more I became convinced that only when all of Europe was once again united in the same church would we have peace. Protestant sects chipped away at the authority of Catholic monarchs all over the continent. But before England as a whole would accept Catholicism, Spain's excesses, in the form of the Inquisition needed to be halted.

When first we arrived at Norfolk's Thames-side house outside the city, I removed myself from the bustle and confusion of unloading luggage and household goods. Servants had come ahead to lay the fires and restock the pantry. But furniture and beds came with us. My first mission was to seek out the family chapel.

I wandered through numerous richly paneled rooms with low ceilings that would keep the heat during the coldest

winter months. In some, the paneling had been painted
white with lovely flower decorations to brighten the rooms.
Many leaded lights had been set into the windows. I mar-
veled at the expense and found myself staring at the way
the glass transformed light—even the diffuse light of a rainy
day near sunset. The crystal atop my staff refracted bright
light into many colors. These window panes transformed it
into something liquid, nearly tangible that shifted to reveal
and conceal hidden depths.

I could lose myself in a trance staring through these windows at the rain.

The dogs were content to sniff out every corner while I
stared for long moments at the wonder of light and glass.

Finally I broke away from my contemplations to wander
into an inner room without windows. I lit a candle at the
entrance and held it high to reveal the chapel. An ordinary
dark room with unpainted walnut paneling. About a dozen
people could stand here to hear the Mass. Three or four at
a time could kneel at the altar rail to receive the Eucharist.

I sought the sacristy behind the altar. The door swung
shut on silent hinges behind me, as it should, keeping the
room private for the priest in attendance. Intent upon
counting candles and examining linens, at first I did not
notice the shrouded sculpture atop a pedestal in the corner.
Newynog bumped into it and set it rocking. I dashed to
keep it from falling. The dark linen shroud dropped away.

My candle showed the luster of fine marble. My fingertips
caressed the sculpture where my eyes could not penetrate
the shadows. How had Norfolk managed to salvage this
exquisite piece from the ravages of the Reformation?
Something in the contours of the face and shoulders sent
me to light more candles. When the room was ablaze with
enough light for my damaged eyes to see clearly, I gasped.

Before me stood the most beautiful Madonna I had ever
seen. The sculptor had caught the woman's expression of
love and wonder as she nursed the Holy Babe. The artist
had also found something more, the sadness of knowing
the child would grow and find a destiny too awesome for
a mother to comprehend, a sadness at knowing the child
would come to manhood only to die. A mother's love and
a mother's grief. And more.

My sister Meg's face looked down upon the Holy Child.

"Helwriaeth, hold the door open," I commanded the dozing wolfhound. She roused enough to push at the panels with her nose and then plopped herself down so that she wedged it open.

"No, Newynog, I do not need your help," I said sharply as the mostly grown pup nudged the pedestal with an over-eager paw.

With Newynog at my heels, inspecting each step I took, I wrestled the sculpture out into the chapel. The ethereal grace of the piece belied the weight of the marble. I strained and struggled to lift the thing. By comparison, the pedestal moved easily.

"What are you doing?" Norfolk demanded imperiously from the doorway. He took a belligerent stance with narrow chin thrust forward and thin neck extended to the point the cords bulged out, giving him the pop-eyed look of a rooster about to lose his head.

The image rocked me. My sight blurred but did not descend into the dangerous realms of vision. *How long?* I asked myself. *How long before his plots are discovered and Elizabeth executes him for treason?*

"I am bringing forth this sculpture into the light. It is too beautiful to remain hidden." I covered my momentary distraction with caressing the marble, surprised that the texture, so close to living flesh in appearance, should actually be cool stone. It was like looking upon my sister restored to sanity.

"My father and grandfather put it away during old Henry's reign. I left it hidden because it is too beautiful and detracts from the beauty of the Mass." Did the young duke actually blush? His eyes never lingered more than a few seconds on the naked breast of the Madonna where the Holy Child suckled.

"I should like to leave it here by the door, where it can remind us that Our Lord took flesh and became man, but is out of line of sight when all eyes should be turned to the altar."

"Do . . ." Norfolk hesitated while turning his eyes away from the Madonna and Child. "There is to be a public punishment tomorrow. Some old woman is having her ears cut off. The entire household is going. I thought 'twould be a good opportunity for you to meet some sympathizers."

"What was the woman's crime?" I had never learned to accept gory punishment as entertainment. I'd seen enough blood spilled in battle against raiding Scots.

"Gossip, of course. Should have her tongue removed instead of her ears."

"Serious gossip for such a serious punishment."

"She spread tales that Elizabeth has borne Dudley a son. The queen cannot tolerate an accusation of adultery. Not with the man she wants to marry as soon as his wife dies."

"Rumors often have a basis in truth," I replied.

"But the child had to have been born before Elizabeth became queen. Since her ascension she is surrounded by maids and courtiers and retainers all of the time, even in her bedroom," Norfolk mused. He tugged at his dark beard and began to pace the length of the chapel.

"Elizabeth fears this woman and the tales she spreads. If she does not marry soon and produce an heir, any child—even a mythological and illegitimate one—could become the focus for rebellion," I commented offhandedly, still fussing with the exact placement of the Madonna.

"A child?" Norfolk's eyes lit up with excitement. "If Elizabeth's child were raised in the true faith, then we would have a monarch to replace her when we depose her. We would not have to invite the French to invade with Marie Queen of Scots at the head of the army. We would not have to accept Spain's Inquisition. We must find this child, Father Griffin. *You* must find him and bring him to me."

Chapter 29

Edinburgh, the Grassmarket, 15 February in the Year of Our Lord 1560.

ROANNA peered through the eyeslits of her black hood. The noise of the crowd rose around her like a roaring surf, building with each wave. She waited another heartbeat and then one more. The excited babble took on a surly tone. The mob wanted blood.

In front of her the condemned thief sobbed and cowered.

Her heart beat harder. Tryblith gibbered in her mind, more greedy for blood than the crowd.

When she could contain the demon no longer, she released the rope on the counterweight. The thief squealed as the noose tightened and drew him upward. He kicked helplessly for long moments. His eyes bulged and his tongue swelled. And then his bowels released and he went limp.

The crowd bellowed approval of this marvelous entertainment.

Power surged through Roanna. Every mind in the crowd opened to her. She knew their hopes, their disappointments, their lusts, and their hatreds. She sent bolts of lightning into the numerous fire barrels placed around the market for the comfort of the merchants. Greedy flames danced upward. Those who paid for the privilege of warming their hands retreated from the sudden blast of heat. The magic within Roanna retreated to manageable levels.

The same thing happened every time she disguised herself as an executioner. Death and power had brought her back many times over the course of the winter.

She jumped off the gibbet and disappeared into the cheering mob. With a few deft gestures she transformed from the black-clad executioner into a solemnly dressed merchant. No one suspected that the grim duty to make an example of Edinburgh's criminals was performed by a woman, especially not a woman with entrée to the palace. Tryblith needed death. This was the safest way to give it to him.

Once inside the shadowed wynd between the Grassmarket and the Royal Mile, she pried a sack containing her gown and petticoat from behind a loose stone in the sagging wall. On execution days she eliminated the farthingale and corset Queen Marie deemed proper attire.

Roanna breathed a little easier as soon as she donned the feminine garments over her doublet and breeches. Every extra layer of clothing distanced her further from the black-masked executioner. Every extra layer of clothing also helped block out the cold wind and damp air. February in Edinburgh seemed more bitter than the winters spent at Hermitage Castle, or even her memories of the months huddled in Gran's drafty cottage as a child.

Once her transformation was complete, she crept through the narrow wynd to a tiny close. Here she roused the real executioner from a trance. He mumbled and shook his head. She implanted into his memory the scene of her latest execution. He would truly believe he had tightened the noose and pulled the rope. By the time he opened his eyes and looked out upon the world with sanity, she was gone.

"Are you satisfied now?" she asked the demon while she waited in the shadows for the executioner to go about his other duties.

I will not be sated until there is war between England and Scotland, he replied.

"I'm working on that. Marie de Guise will veto the newest treaty again today. Instead of banishing French troops from Scotland, she will hire more. The English will have to attack to protect their border."

You could have killed the treaty completely if you had murdered Moray as I told you to.

"An impossible task. He is too well guarded." She had stalked him for months. He seemed to sense menace and had banned Roanna and every other woman from his bed. Every time she got close enough to the lord to slip a knife between his ribs, her opportunity for escape evaporated. She refused to murder the man only to be caught, tried, and executed immediately afterward. She preferred being the executioner.

As long as Marie remained regent for her daughter, the other lords allied themselves against her. Lord Moray provided a convenient rallying point. Roanna had not been able to seduce or coerce any of them into assassinating Earl Moray for her. Not that manipulating others into acting for her would satisfy Tryblith.

She dared not put into words, or even coherent thought, her dissatisfaction with the demon. She sensed she had learned all the magic he had to teach her. His jolts of pain became stronger and stronger each time she resisted his manipulations. As soon as she dared, she'd cast him off and order her life to her own liking. Never again would she allow herself to be manipulated by others.

And she would not kill again.

Roanna found Marie de Guise still in bed while the Privy Council read the treaty.

"Your Grace, you must stop this outrage," Roanna pleaded. "The Protestant Lords are selling Scotland to the English acre by acre." She bustled about the room helping the maids prepare the queen regent's clothes for the day.

"We cannot," Marie croaked. Her bloated face showed few traces of her former beauty or vivacity. Her once lustrous black hair was limp and streaked with yellowish white. "But we must." She heaved herself onto her side and slid her legs to the edge of the bed in preparation for rising. There she paused, groaning heavily.

Roanna rushed to her side to assist the queen regent in rising. She had not given the woman a dose of tansy in months, indeed she'd given her every antidote she could think of. Something else ailed her.

You killed her with the tansy, Tryblith said. His voice was strong today, having fed on the energy of death in the Grassmarket. *The early doses were strong enough to damage her innards beyond recovery. 'Twill be a slow and painful death.*

Roanna could almost see the beast rubbing his hands together in glee. A wave of disgust rose in her. *God's wounds,* she liked Marie de Guise. A strong woman who surged forward with determination, she allowed no man to stand in the way of her vision of the truth. Roanna wanted the same kind of strength for herself.

She'd never have it as long as Tryblith haunted her. His usefulness had passed. But how to rid herself of him? How to make coherent plans without him learning of it through her thoughts?

"We'll take this slow and easy, Your Grace," Roanna crooned to the ailing queen. "If you will just sit, then you can rest against me until you have the strength to stand. Your ladies will wash and dress you. Then you will feel better. If necessary, I'll call two footmen to carry you in your chair to the Council Chamber."

"You are so good to us, Roanna. We give you the black onyx ring with the diamond in the center. Take it now before the greedy crows on the Council have a chance to contest our will." Marie patted Roanna's hand lovingly.

"Perhaps an infusion of wild parsley and hibiscus flowers in your wine, Your Grace." Roanna thought furiously for remedies that might help the queen live long enough to oppose Lord Moray and this new treaty.

"Your Grace." A lady in waiting dipped a curtsy within the doorway. "Milord of Moray has come to have speech with you."

Before Marie could deny the earl access to her bedchamber, Moray swept into the room, nearly knocking the lady in the doorway off-balance.

"You need not bother coming to the Privy Council, Your Grace. We have signed the treaty with England. Your French troops will vacate our lands within the month."

"We shall veto the treaty," Marie said. A measure of strength infused her voice, and her spine straightened from its weak slump. But she still leaned heavily upon Roanna.

"We of the Council have overridden your veto, Madame. *We* do not wish foreign Catholics to rule our land any longer." Moray leaned forward, almost nose-to-nose with his father's widow. "You, woman, are helpless against our unity. If you live long enough, I'll have you on the first ship sailing to France along with your hired soldiers."

Marie swayed and lost the little bit of stiffness in her

spine. She gasped, as much in pain as in outrage. "You dare speak so to us, your queen's duly appointed regent!" Her voice carried not her former conviction.

"Yes, I do. You are too ill and weak to perform your duties. This day, as we signed the treaty, the Privy council appointed me to fulfill your duties. I am now regent of Scotland."

"My daughter . . ."

"Your daughter has not set foot in Scotland since she was five years old. She knows nothing of us. As long as she remains in France, she has nothing to say that has meaning to me or my Privy Council."

He turned and stalked out of the bedchamber. At the door he paused and spoke over his shoulder. "Your pet witch is now banished from Scotland as well as your soldiers. If she is seen in the city after tomorrow dawn, she will be arrested and burned at the stake." His gaze locked with Roanna's, and his upper lip curled into a sneer.

Silence hung heavy in the room, an unwelcome companion that no one dared oust.

At long last, when the maids and ladies began fidgeting nervously, Marie whispered. "You must take the ear bobs that go with the onyx ring. Take them and flee this night, Roanna. Go to our daughter in Paris. Tell her . . . You'll know what to tell her. We trust you, dear child. We trust you with the welfare of all Scotland."

Norfolk House, near London, spring 1560.

I did not attend the public punishment of the gossip. Instead I began my search for information about Queen Elizabeth's life before her ascension to the throne. My questions took me all through London and the immediate environs over the next few months. With every question, my conviction deepened that Norfolk must never find a child that could be passed off as Elizabeth's illegitimate get. I searched to protect the child, not to give him to the duke.

Those who had served Elizabeth had nothing but praise

about her sweet nature, her generosity, and her modesty. Her detractors could say nothing good about her, claiming her a pinch-penny, vicious to those who crossed her, and a whore.

Bit by bit I put together a picture of a very intelligent woman who walked carefully between the paths of freedom and imprisonment. She had asked many questions but never truly committed herself to any cause or any person—except for Dudley. From their first meeting they had been devoted to each other, best friends and confidants. No one could or would point to a time when either had the freedom to indulge in an affair of the body as well as the mind and heart.

But gaps appeared in the story. Long months had gone by when Elizabeth was in the Tower under her sister's tyranny. Then many more long months when she lived in near exile at Hatfield. A discreet woman could lace her corsets to conceal a pregnancy for four, even five months. Then she could retire quietly to the country during a long summer, when the city was unsafe, to await the birth.

As spring swelled the ends of tree branches with new leaves, and the grass grew vibrant with green, I prepared to make a trip to Hatfield and the surrounding villages.

I stopped at the chapel for incense, candles, and a few spare linens against having to sanctify a rude altar in the wilderness. A woman blocked my entry into the chapel. She stared at the lovely Madonna, crooning a song to the marble statue.

"Meg?" I asked.

My younger sister turned to look at me with a big smile, never interrupting her song. I longed to sing with her. Norfolk had little taste or time for music.

"Meg, how did you come here? Did Donovan bring you to the capital? Why have you sought me out?" I rushed to embrace her, as if by enfolding her in my arms I could protect her from all the evil in the world. What was Donovan thinking, bringing our sister to London? Innocents such as she needed to be cherished and protected, not exposed to the vices and filth of the city.

"Pretty Mary has a baby," she said, still smiling. She cupped the head of the sculpted Holy Babe as if caressing a living child. "Meg had Baby Betsy." She wrestled out of my hug to go back to the statue and sing again. The lilting tune had no true words, merely baby sounds that meant nothing to anyone but Meg.

"Where is Baby Betsy now, Meg?" I tried to coax information from her.

"Betsy walks now. Betsy talks now. Betsy needs her da. Doesn't need Meg anymore."

"Is Betsy with her da in London?" I'd heard that my twin had come back to court to help Elizabeth and Parliament implement the sweeping economic reforms that would help pay off Mary Tudor's massive debts and put England back on a strong economic footing.

"Betsy walks now. Betsy talks now. Betsy doesn't need Meg anymore."

I sighed in exasperation.

"Can Meg have Mary's baby?" She pointed to the beatific infant at his mother's breast captured in the marble.

"No, Meg. Mary must keep her baby." Did my sister even know that the sculpture represented the Holy Mother and Babe?

I could not leave my innocent, bewildered sister to Norfolk's untender mercies. Donovan would denounce and imprison me if I took Meg to him in the city. I had no choice but to take her with me.

I penned a quick note to my brother telling him that I protected Meg.

Perhaps God had led her here to help tend Elizabeth's child should I find it. I trusted Meg more than the duke. I did not tell him or Donovan where we traveled to. I had a feeling we would not return to Norfolk house for a long time.

Chapter 30

Hatfield, England, spring 1560.

MEG and I rode into the village of Hatfield on a Friday afternoon. She had a mount and saddle of her own from the Kirkenwood stables. She still could not or would not explain how she had come to me at Norwich.

Throughout the journey she had alternately prattled and remained so silent I had to look to make sure she still followed me. But the dogs had adopted her and would not have let her stray far.

I reined in at the parish church. Church records were an uncertainty. If the local priest was literate and interested, he detailed every baptism, funeral, and marriage he performed. Too often the priest was nearly illiterate and could barely write his own name. In such cases he had learned the Mass and his duties by rote as an apprentice to a previously illiterate priest.

The Protestants and the printing press had changed much of that. Books of Latin grammar had become available for the increasing number of grammar schools opening in villages and towns. Elizabeth's economic reforms kept more money in England rather than squandering it on foreign wars. Having money to spend upon educating the masses seemed a true measure of the prosperity of the times.

I hoped that during Catholic Mary Tudor's reign the local vicar had not reverted to the old style of ignorance, believing the written word contained traps laid by the Devil.

Catholicism had thrived for many centuries on ignorance.

My family knew that ignorance was not bliss, that the traps of demons and devils preyed upon those who did not

229

use their minds to think for themselves and explore alternatives.

In many ways the Catholic Church had perpetuated ignorance and illiteracy, giving over decision making entirely to the church.

I sat back on my horse abruptly as this new, nearly blasphemous thought crept into my mind and took root.

"Let's see what kind of records the priests here have kept." I dismounted before the lych-gate of the churchyard and looped the reins around a stray sapling growing in the decaying mortar of the low stone wall. Meg followed my example, turning bright eyes up to mine.

"We're going to find Meg's new baby," she lisped.

I wondered if she'd be happy with a life-sized doll. But then, she'd been very good with Betsy, changing her nappy, bathing her, playing with her, singing her lullabies and number songs.

What went on in her traumatized mind that made her need a baby so desperately?

"I'll look for clues here, Meg. We may or may not find a baby." What would I do with a bastard child born to Elizabeth and her lover Robert Dudley if such a child existed?

I could not turn over an innocent child to Norfolk to be used as a pawn in his twisted dynastic games.

Few questioned that a child of Elizabeth and Robert Dudley might exist.

Elizabeth repeatedly referred to Dudley in public as her "Sweet Robin." She allowed him great liberties, often discussing serious governmental matters in her bedchamber while she dressed for the day.

From the moment they first met at court when her young brother Edward VI was king and Robert's father the Lord Protector of Edward, Elizabeth Tudor and Robert Dudley had demonstrated their friendship and their mutual attraction. For a time there had been gossip of a marriage between the two while they were still teenagers. The match could have made the Dudley fortunes for all time.

But the Earl of Northumberland banked on a different royal alliance. Elizabeth was strong, intelligent, and determined to maintain her independence. Northumberland would not have remained in control of England for long once Elizabeth ascended the throne. So he married another of his sons, Guilford, to Lady Jane Grey, a royal cousin known for her sweet nature and deference to stronger personalities to make decisions for her. Jane was descended from Henry VII by his youngest daughter Mary. Each of Edward's Tudor sisters had clouds of questions regarding their claims to legitimacy. Mary was a Catholic; her mother's marriage to Henry VIII had ended in divorce and declaration of Mary's illegitimacy. Elizabeth's mother had been executed for adultery and treason. She, too, had been declared bastard so that Henry might marry again to beget the longed-for son.

Northumberland had persuaded Edward on his deathbed to bypass the claims to the throne of Edward's two sisters, Mary and Elizabeth, in favor of Jane.

Mary Tudor and Elizabeth led all of England in rebellion against Northumberland and Jane. The earl had lost his titles and his head, and so had his son and daughter-in-law. The rest of the Dudley family had been stripped of honors and many of them imprisoned—including Robert.

Now there was talk that Elizabeth would restore an earldom to the eldest remaining Dudley brother. Possibly she would ennoble her favorite as well so that she might at long last marry the love of her life. But not before his wife, Amy Robsart, died of the cancer that ate at her.

So I searched for a child born of the youthful passion and lifelong love of Elizabeth and Dudley. A child that should never ascend the throne, but who could be used as a pawn in Norfolk's power-hungry games.

The vicar met me in the porch of the squat stone church with its square Norman tower.

"*Benedicte*," I greeted him, bowing slightly.

"May the Lord be with you," he replied in English. He was Protestant, refusing to acknowledge my Latin greeting in kind. I had forsaken my French *soutane* and the English cassock Norfolk had given me in favor of lay clothing. The man would know me for a Catholic, but not necessarily a priest.

I suppressed a sigh. I should have guessed that in the village Elizabeth had called home, the people who remembered her kindly from her tormented youth would remain sympathetic to her cause and her religion.

"Father, may I examine your parish records? I have a bequest for a child who may have been born here."

He looked at me skeptically. I had already identified myself as a Catholic in our greeting. He had little reason to trust me at a time when he was ordered to report and exact fines upon all those who failed to attend Sunday Mass or partake of the Eucharist in the Anglican parish.

"I have a letter from the Duke of Norfolk identifying me as Griffin Kirkwood, a gentleman scholar in his employ, and requesting your cooperation." I produced the document from my scrip. I hated using Norfolk's authority when I knew I would not take the child to him. But if I could find the child, so could another. I had to use whatever tools came to hand to secrete the child away from prying eyes before Norfolk's plans could come to fruition.

The priest took the folded parchment with Norfolk's gaudy seal impressed in green wax upon the bottom. He read the carefully worded plea I had penned and my sponsor had signed.

"My lord has also instructed me to make a donation to the poor box as well as to the church itself," I added, producing two gold coins. They were the new mintage, smaller than the ones that had been debased during Mary Tudor's reign but of purer metal and more valuable. The priest's eyes widened.

"Of course. I have done my best to keep accurate records of the sacraments performed here. Alas, I have only been here two years and my predecessor's handwriting is nearly illegible from a shaking hand and there are gaps. His memory failed him near the end. I suspect he also felt some need to encode his records lest they fall into unsympathetic hands during troubled times."

"I understand, Father. May I have the honor of knowing your name?"

"Thomas Greene." We shook hands. I guessed him to be a Cambridge man from the cut of his robe and the colors in the lining of his hood.

"Father Thomas, I will do my best to decipher the records. I have some experience in ancient documents written in a variety of bizarre scripts and languages. If you like, I can reproduce them in a fair hand that can be read by all.

But first, is there a place where my sister may rest while I look through the records?"

"I believe the lady has found an occupation."

I looked over my shoulder to find Meg seated at the base of a rowan tree in the graveyard making a chain of the tiny daisies that looked like pearls strewn across the lawn. The two dogs sprawled at her feet, tongues lolling, eyes blinking in near sleep. We both smiled at the lovely picture of innocence she made.

"Meg has the ability to find joy in all that touches her life."

"If she tires of her chore, my wife will find refreshment for her."

We moved into the sacristy where he produced a huge book bound in fine leather and stored in a lovely metal box gilded and ornamented with jewels. "Knock on the door of the rectory if you need anything." He shoved a stool at me and wandered off, content to leave me with his precious book.

I settled in for a long afternoon of reading in dim light with my eyes already tired from road dust and constant searching of the landscape for outlaws and enemies alike.

While looking for a place to lay my staff so that it would not roll and possibly damage the crystal, I remembered Raven focusing candlelight through a glass vial of water to increase the amount of light when her eyes began to fail. Would the crystal serve the same function? I moved a rack with a branch top designed for hanging damp cloaks. A decorative tin basin at the bottom would keep the drips off the floor. With a little maneuvering and fussing I managed to stand the staff so that the crystal lay between a rushlight and the pages of the book where it rested on a pedestal. Amazingly a circle of brighter light illuminated a segment of the writing. By shifting the book up and down, right and left a few inches, I could refocus the light to the area where I read.

Hours later I looked up from the faded script and rubbed my eyes. A headache pounded behind them, reminding me of the demon arrow that had blazed so brightly and damaged them beyond repair. So far, I had found naught of interest. I had searched through a number of years brack-

eting the times when I knew Elizabeth inhabited the
royal manor.

Nothing of interest. I had ferreted out the names of almost every servitor and retainer in the princess' household.
Some of the ones who had followed Elizabeth to court had
gladly spoken to me, mostly in praise of their royal charge.
All of Hatfield seemingly loved her. But of Kat Ashley,
her governess from early childhood, confidante, friend, and
surrogate mother, the one person who would know all of
Elizabeth's secrets, I could learn little and could gain no
access.

Tired and a bit discouraged, I turned back to the faded
ink and wobbling script of a time just after Elizabeth's release from the Tower and before her ascension to the
throne. The first words I read leaped out at me with new
clarity:

Baptized this eleventh day of August in the year of Our
Lord 1557, an orphan child. Christened Robert
Ashley. The name given him by the woman who left him
to the care and generosity of the parish.

In the margin beside the entry, another hand had written
an addition in a tiny flourish. I peered closer, trying desperately to focus my aching eyes on the flowing feminine hand
that had scratched the entry. The words remained a blur
to me. Frustrated beyond measure I ran my fingers over the
dried ink. I wished and prayed for insight into this cipher.

And then, as if my fingers had grown eyes, I knew the
meaning of the addition. Someone had written them in the
archaic Secretary hand. Up until that entry I had been reading only the modern Italian form of script and so failed to
decipher anything different. Carefully, I peered again at
the words.

my dearest robin

Chapter 31

Mortlake, England, spring 1560.

"ARE you certain you cannot hear the angels whispering their divine message?" Dr. John Dee peered at Donovan intently.

Donovan gritted his teeth. Every time he visited the astrologer, he asked the same question.

"My grandmother, we called her Raven, told me I had magical talent, but I have not the control to access it." Donovan gave the same answer he had given the last three times he came to Mortlake. Ostensibly he came today with a message from Elizabeth requesting (demanding) Dee's presence at court. She had a mission on the Continent for the learned doctor, and a desire for a new horoscope.

Donovan always sought the opportunity to play Elizabeth's messenger to Mortlake. He hoped to learn the art of scrying from the famed magician. He didn't trust Griffin to care for Meg properly. Only by scrying their whereabouts could he know for certain that Meg thrived. He would not enter Griffin's mind—probably the easiest form of magic since they had employed that medium of communication as children.

Hopefully, Dee might drop a crumb of knowledge that would release Donovan's magical talent, before he disappeared into the political intrigues of France, Spain, and the Holy Roman Empire.

"Yes, yes, of course," Dee mused more to himself than to Donovan. "The angels hover near you, but you do not know how to listen to them. Your brother has the same problem. He has talent and refuses to use it. You want talent and cannot access it. And the two of you as alike as two peas in a pod. Two people, one soul. A strange puzzle."

Before the obsessed scholar could wander off, Donovan grabbed the sleeve of his threadbare scholar's robe. "Perhaps, Dr. Dee, if I could discover the Philosopher's Stone, I could use it to bring forth my talent."

"Perhaps." A light seemed to ignite behind Dee's eyes. They cleared momentarily of the perpetual glaze of distraction. "Perhaps there is another way. I have been experimenting for her majesty's agents. A fascinating puzzle. They seek the perfect poison—odorless, colorless, with a delayed effect." Dee seemed unconcerned that Elizabeth's agents sought a tool for assassination. He saw only the "fascinating puzzle."

"Some of my concoctions," Dee continued, "are worthless as poisons but do have interesting effects upon the body. Some of them release the mind."

Donovan stilled for a moment. "I have hoped for drugs as a remedy for my lack of talent. But Grandmother Raven could not or would not train me in the uses of exotic herbs." She had told him many times that her knowledge of plants was for healing only. She did not consider his lack of talent an ailment needing medicine.

"Are you familiar, milord, with the Oracle of Delphi?" Dee peered again at Donovan as if he needed to be nose to nose in order to see clearly.

"Someone ancient and Greek, I think." Donovan had studied a little of the Greek mythology but found the dimensions and architecture of their temples more interesting. Griffin, on the other hand, had immersed himself in the legends as well as the language.

"More than that. The Oracles were the messengers of God—human priests and priestesses. They drank barley wine to make themselves receptive to the gods." Dee anxiously grabbed Donovan's shoulder and propelled him toward the house. "I have experimented with barley wine myself to no effect. But I have a new fermentation waiting in the cellar. Last autumn's harvest was worthless for grain. Too damp a year and much of it rotted in the field. But it makes an excellent wine."

Once inside the snug dwelling, Dee steered Donovan

toward the locked door on the ground floor rather than to the stairs that led upward to the living quarters.

"Is this your laboratory?" Excitement heated Donovan's blood. His own haphazard attempts at alchemy had met with many disappointments. Perhaps, at last, Dee would show him the secret of searching for the Philosopher's Stone, the key to all magic and power. Donovan was certain he could find the elusive key to all the secrets of the universe if only he knew where and how to begin.

"Yes, this is where I work. I must ask you not to touch anything. I have many delicate instruments and the slightest disturbance will disrupt months of observations." Dr. Dee paused before he twisted the massive iron key in the eye-level lock. The keyhole looked big enough to pass a rolled parchment through. Donovan had caught glimpses of the mechanism before the alchemist thrust the key into it. He was certain he could pick the lock with a few mundane tools. Anyone who really wanted to spy upon Dr. Dee or disrupt his experiments could easily do so.

"I guess a big lock like that is as strong as the massive walls of a keep," Donovan muttered.

"Precisely. The locksmith assured me that this is the largest lock he has ever made. It will hold against a battering ram." Dee smiled proudly as he thrust open the door.

The lock might hold against a battering ram, but the door and hinges wouldn't. A man handy with his hands could pick the lock in a matter of moments. The locksmith should know that. Perhaps he planned to do just that and ransack the laboratory for gold and other precious items used in Dee's experiments. He might also pick the lock for pay. The queen's enemies, the Puritans, or rival alchemists would offer much for access to this supposedly secure room.

The moment the door opened, Donovan strode into the low dark laboratory with only one high window for light. He aimed purposefully toward the rows and rows of shelves containing dozens of glass vials, each carefully labeled with glyphs in a language he did not recognize. One looked like it might contain sulfur. He reached to bring it into better light for closer examination.

"Don't touch that!" Dee said using censorious tones that made Donovan feel like a small boy caught stealing apples from the root cellar.

Hastily he dropped his hand, content to use his eyes only to discern the ingredients. Below the vials stood wooden boxes full of rocks—not just any rocks he guessed. Each must contain an important mineral. He'd have to study them much closer to learn their properties—Raven hadn't cared much for rocks. She liked herbs better than minerals for her potions and spells.

"Sit there, on the stool by the distillery," Dee ordered while he fussed with a stack of crates near the door.

Donovan looked around for the assembly of beakers and flames and tubes that might signify the presence of a distillery. He knew what to look for only because he had seen a drawing of one in a book. The author, a Continental alchemist, had proposed distilled spirits to increase the potency of some potions and magical concoctions. Donovan suspected that distilled grains or *usuqebaugh*—the water of life—fortified the alchemist more than the concoction.

He took the stool beside the contraption and examined each part of it. The machine seemed to be of a standard with no innovations.

"I know I have a special goblet here somewhere," Dee muttered, shifting crates around. The fussy man gave the impression of harmless absentmindedness. But Donovan suspected that the scholar observed everything with keen insight, using his image to disarm others. He'd make a perfect spy for Elizabeth.

"Is that it on the shelf at your left elbow?" Donovan asked.

"Of course! How observant of you. I always use this goblet for my experiments. I had it made by a witch down in Cornwall. She claimed descent from Merlin of old and infused it with special power." He wiped out the interior of the mud-colored pottery with the end of his much-abused sleeve.

"Indeed?" Donovan replied. What else could he say to such blatant falsehood. He knew of no relatives in Cornwall. Merlin had had only one child, Arylwren. Her daughter Deirdre had begun the tradition of meticulous records of each birth, death, and marriage—or lack thereof. Of course, some of the far-flung family might have sired a bastard or three while campaigning in the area. Even so, most of them knew the importance of the family record and tried to keep track of all their get.

"Now for the wine. I'll be right back." Dee bustled out of the door, carefully locking it behind him. Was he afraid that Donovan would steal something and flee? He couldn't even think of a use for most everything here, let alone its value.

And he thought himself well on the way to being an alchemist.

He looked about the room for several moments, attracted by the textures and colors within the rocks on the shelf. One looked like marble with veins of blue. Did lapis grow in marble? He didn't know and vowed to find out.

Within a few moments, Dee returned with the goblet brimming with the straw-colored wine. He thrust it into Donovan's hands, slopping several mouthfuls on his robe. "Drink it up, milord. Fast is best so you don't notice the taste if it's gone vinegary."

"Isn't there a ritual involved?" Donovan looked at the brew skeptically.

"Oh!" Dee stared at him, his eyes glazing over once again. "I never thought . . . what do you suggest?"

"Each of the four elements must be invoked. The participants and the working area must be ritually cleansed, and . . . a chant to alert the angels that we listen."

"Yes, yes, of course. We will take the time to prepare. But not too much time. I must hasten to London at Her Majesty's behest."

"Is there an open area where we can work?" Donovan had never heard of Raven even trying a spell indoors. She needed fresh air and intimate contact with the elements.

"But it isn't safe out there," Dee protested. He looked toward the window apprehensively.

"Of course it is safe. We won't leave the yard," Donovan said. "Come, I will show you how to protect a circle. We need symbols of Earth, and Air to accompany a Fire. The wine, of course, represents Water." He picked up the blue-veined marble. "This is Earth. At the appropriate moment, I'll drop it into the goblet. We'll light a Fire to heat the wine. The Fire creates smoke, binding it with Air."

He marched out of the laboratory, leaving Dee to lock up and follow as he chose. At the back of the garden grew a twisted maple tree that offered ample shade and shadow. Donovan set the goblet into a slight hollow between two roots that nearly protruded from the ground. He twisted off a partially broken branch and used the withering leaves to sweep clear a level spot between the rows of herbs and the tree. He gathered a few sticks and kindling into a tidy arrangement ready for a spark. Then using the other end of the branch he began drawing a pentagram large enough for the two of them to stand within the center. Around the pentagram he drew a circle but did not close it until they both stood within.

Dee's eyes grew huge inside his pale face. "You invoke witchcraft?" His chin and hands trembled.

"I invoke the elements. This is a ritual of white magic, intended for enlightenment and understanding. Hardly black magic. We will touch no demons with this." If it worked. He'd probably just get drunk. "Come inside the pentagram, Dr. Dee. You must stay within the sigil if you hope to understand and record what transpires. Once I close the last line of the drawing, we will be obscured from view." If the ritual did not need a magical talent to trigger it.

Dee gulped and took one long stride to put himself inside the drawing.

Donovan closed the last line. He took a deep breath and reached for the flint and steel in his scrip. Raven would light the fire with a thought. Griffin could do the same if he wanted. Donovan had to use mundane means. Would that lessen the impact?

He knelt by the kindling reciting a prayer Raven had taught him as a child.

Pridd, ground and support my quest.

He slipped the blue-veined marble into the center of the kindling.

Awyr, breathe life into my search.

He moved his hand in a quick circle above the kindling to stir the air and let it reach into every corner of the spell.

Tanio, fire, light my way.

He struck his first spark into the waiting tinder. It

grabbed hold of the tiny morsel of flame and gave it a home.

Dwfr, water, control us and bind us together.

With the last words he dribbled a little wine into the fire. It sizzled and reached hungrily for new fuel.

His fingers tingled as if he had actually accomplished something.

Slowly he stood up from his crouch by the fire and lifted the goblet toward Dee in a silent toast. Then he downed the liquid in two huge gulps. The alcohol burned all the way into his gut, flushing his face and making his head too light to stay attached to his shoulders.

A sour aftertaste lingered on his tongue. The sensation brightened, grew more acidic and enticing. It tasted . . . yellow.

He opened his eyes. Dr. Dee's nose was within inches of his. Every pore grew larger, deeper, filled with interesting bits of dirt and tissue, inviting deep investigation. Donovan blinked and looked again. The pores on Dee's nose had shrunk to normal size but turned richly purple surrounded by a yellow aura.

Auras. He needed to look at auras to see if any of them hinted at angels hiding behind them.

His eyes looked up at the tree. The leaves pulsed with green life, a green so deep and bright it defied reality. The twisted bark became a map of the rivers and roads of England, Scotland, Wales, and Cornwall. If he looked a little more closely, he could see the towns and the people, the castles and the nobles. He could find Griffin and Meg and track their coming and going. He could follow the map into the future to glimpse his own destiny.

He drifted closer to the tree, intent upon seeing where his life path led. Would he become the Pendragon? Would this marvelous wine open the closed doors of his talent?

An occasional flash of the future would be enough. He need only demonstrate a little talent to justify the wearing of the dragon rampant ring.

Seeing angels would be better. He could gain knowledge and wisdom from angels.

He shifted his gaze to slightly beyond the scholar's right ear, as Raven had taught him to look for auras, the layers of energy that surrounded every living thing. Each layer should be a different color and a different intensity giving clues to health, emotion, state of mind, and any number of other things if one only knew where and how to look.

Sure enough, a little being made up of light and pale blue flames sat on Dee's right shoulder. It laughed silently and danced about, soaring up on transparent wings. It twisted and twirled in convoluted loops, circling Dee's head, tugging at his scraggly hair, brushing his other shoulder and landing back where it started.

An angel or a faerie? He'd never seen a faerie, though Griffin had told him often enough when they flitted about the lake beside the kirk. But he thought faeries should be bright colors, miniature replicas of humans except for the rainbow wings. This creature was all white and gold and brightness. The patterns of light only hinted at a body hidden within the layers of energy.

He blinked against the too-whiteness radiating out from the delightful angel. Then it opened its mouth to speak.

A dozen voices boomed into Donovan's head, shattering the illusions of colors and brightness. Brittle shards of light fell about him, like a broken piece of glass. Beautiful. Deadly. Worthless. He grabbed his temples in a desperate attempt to control the noise pounding inside him, demanding to get out.

The noise grew. It took possession of his heart, forcing that beleaguered organ to beat erratically. His blood boiled, shifted course, gagged him. The noise grew fiery. He watched his skin blacken and char, melting away from his bones in silent puffs of ash.

He screamed in pain. His own voice became one with the noise of angel voices overwhelming his senses, burning him alive from the inside out.

On and on the pain enveloped him.

Over and over he prayed for death to end this terrible pain. To silence the noise.

He sobbed and fell to his knees. He buried his head in his arms. If only the noise would go away, he could think, he could find a way out of this terrible, terrible pain.

Blackness crept into his vision as it, too, burned and turned to ash. With the blackness came numbness, and finally . . . nothing.

Chapter 32

Hatfield, England, spring 1560.

I STARED at the entry in the parish records for many long moments. Would anyone but Elizabeth have penned that tiny endearment next to the name of an orphaned infant?

My gut told me I had found proof of the existence of such a child.

Now what?

Instinctively I reached for Helwriaeth's head. I needed to touch her, draw strength and inspiration from her solid presence. She must have wandered in sometime while I was lost in concentration, for she butted my hand with her nose, reassuring me. A moment later, another damp nose nudged my left hand. Newynog. Helwriaeth's baby, the one she could not abandon. Neither could I. But we both knew her other pups, the males, would all be treated well, trained for the hunt or for war. They would be well fed, given shelter, their ailments tended.

But would anyone love them as I loved Newynog?

Elizabeth had abandoned her child. I could almost see her tears as she put the infant into the arms of someone she hoped would shelter and care for her dearest Robin. But would anyone love him?

The child would be nearly three years old now, if he lived. Had his young life already been warped by cruelty and neglect? I had to find out. I had to make certain the child thrived with love even if his adoptive parents were poor. I could ease the adoptive parents' burden so long as they loved the baby.

Otherwise . . . Meg had known I would need her on this

quest. She desperately wanted a child of her own. She
would be a wonderful and loving mother.

Hastily I searched the remaining parish records for funer-
als of an orphan baby or any small child. The terse entries
told their own stories of grief. This girl had died of croup.
That boy had run under the wheels of a cart and been
crushed. Too many babies died young. None of them were
named Robert or Robin. All of them had companion bap-
tismal records.

Adoptive parents could have moved out of the parish.
This registry made no mention of those who left the district.
The priests recorded only the sacraments they presided
over. But good priests had long memories.

I left the sacristy and sought my host. Both dogs trailed
after me, constantly touching me, needing reassurance and
comfort as much as I did. Outside in the churchyard I gathered them both close in a hug. They licked my face and
ears with exuberant, unconditional love.

Meg entertained Father Thomas and another lady—
presumably the rector's wife—with laughing anecdotes beneath the spreading rowan tree in the graveyard. Meg's
skirts spread about her in a puddle of blue wool. With the
spring sunshine cascading through the oak leaves onto her
golden hair that never stayed captured by her cap and veil,
she looked much like the marble Madonna come to life.

I paused to study the gay picture the three of them made.
My eyes refused to focus clearly after the long hours of
reading under uncertain light. I saw shadows and echoes of
each person spreading out in layers around them. Father
Thomas and his wife glowed with honesty and integrity.
Neither had anything to hide. Meg, however, masked a
layer of black that alternately fell behind the bright yellow
of joy and broke through to dominate all of her life force.

Until she faced the terrible things that had been done to
her, she would never totally dominate that dark layer of
her life; her mind would not heal.

Did I want her to heal? Perhaps the wisdom that crept
out of her innocence was a gift to all of us that I should
not tamper with.

"Master Kirkwood, have you completed your search?"
Father Thomas stood and dusted off his robes. His wife

remained seated beside Meg, the two of them intent upon the construction of yet another daisy chain.

"I have found the entry in question. I have not yet completed my search," I replied.

"Your sister tells me that you, too, are a priest." Father Thomas bent to stroke Helwriaeth's back rather than look me in the eye.

"I have no parish at the moment, only a quest."

"You are attached to the household of the Duke of Norfolk."

I nodded. The duke had never hidden his preference for the Catholic faith. He adhered to the law only by reluctantly paying his fines for not attending Angelican Mass each Sunday. Not everyone had the economic means to pay the fines or the courage to face potential martyrdom.

"The day grows late. Will you accept hospitality from me and my wife?" Father Thomas sighed. We both knew I was Catholic and he Anglican. But the custom of hospitality still prevailed. Neither of us threatened the other. And since I had never admitted my faith out loud to him, he was safe from persecution for dealing with a Catholic priest.

"We have the means to pay for rooms at the inn. We would not wish to burden you."

"Nonsense. Beatrice and Meg get along famously. You will not be an imposition upon us." He assisted his wife to her feet and introduced her.

We smiled and nodded to each other.

Meg scrambled up with the eagerness of the child she pretended to be. The dogs went to her, expecting caresses.

"Perhaps we could discuss your parish while we dine?" I cocked my head, wanting to trust this man, yet unsure how to go about asking after one orphan child named Robert Ashley.

"We are not a large parish. In the two years I have been here, not much has transpired that has not come to my attention, either through confession or gossip." We began walking toward the rectory, a snug cottage behind the church with a built-up loft beneath the thatch that could accommodate several bedchambers or one very large nursery. Giggles and splashes up there told me that at least two youngsters washed up for the evening meal in a loft bedchamber.

" 'Tis the children of the parish who interest me. As I said earlier, I have a bequest for an orphan from relatives who have only recently learned of his existence.''

"We have no orphans in this parish. Any child who finds himself without parents is quickly adopted. We take care of our own.'' He set his mouth and chin in a stubborn expression that reminded me of Fiona.

If he knew the true identity of the child I sought, he would not reveal it to me.

If I had any hope of fulfilling my role as the Pendragon of Britain, I must ensure the safety and well-being of that child, and protect his identity from others who could do the same research as myself.

The next morning, I positioned Meg and Helwriaeth at the village well. All the women came there at least once a day. All the gossip of the village passed around the well. Many of them brought their children, mostly those too young to work the fields, or be apprenticed to their father or another tradesman. Most of the boys should attend the grammar school, and indeed I saw no boys between the ages of seven and eleven.

I sat outside the public house, nursing a tankard of beer and listening. Newynog took up her position at my feet. Part of me heard the gossip of the old men and ne'er-do-wells who also sat outside the pub nursing a tankard of beer or ale. Another part of me remained connected to Helwriaeth and thus to whatever Meg heard. I could not trust my sister to pass on the information coherently.

We heard about the new coins—how could Englishmen trust coins that were smaller than the old ones? Nothing wrong with the old ones, the oldest pub denizens grumbled. Others complained about the fines for nonattendance of the Anglican Mass. Shouldn't they be able to choose to stay away from church if they disagreed with the new vicar as long as they didn't attend a papist—spit in the dirt—abomination?

As the day wore on, complaints and whispers turned to more local matters. This woman was stepping out with that man and wouldn't there be a hasty wedding very soon. The baker cheated on his measures of flour in the bread. The publican added strange things to his beer along with extra water to stretch the number of tankards each barrel filled. The exotic ingredients masked the watery taste for certain. One woman at the well knew for certain that one of the additives in the beer was rotten barley. Surely that caused the midwife to dance jerkily all over the village, shaking each limb as if unconnected to the rest of her body. Spittle ran down her chin and then didn't she roll her eyes to heaven and die right over there by the blacksmith's forge.

I set my tankard down and stared at it suspiciously. Rotten barley was as dangerous as rotten rye.

The next piece of news pricked my ears. I signaled Meg to listen more closely to the women at the well.

"Disgraceful how Vicar lets that woman live in the village. Doesn't every man who doesn't find comfort in his own bed seek hers?"

"I hear she's expecting again. Her with no husband living."

"But she starches and presses the laundry until it gleams in the sunlight better than any woman in the village," one young woman defended the miscreant.

The other women glared at her.

"She's more children than she knows how to feed and clothe decently."

"But she takes in orphans no one else wants," her stout defender continued.

"To what end? Slow starvation and freezing to death because she can't afford the children she has. Better the orphans are left out in the cold to die quick, afore they know what they're missing." The speaker snorted.

"Who says any of them are truly orphans?" another woman asked slyly. "Could be they are all hers and she just tells us they're orphans so's we won't oust her from the village for being a whore."

"Which she is, of course."

"Vicar lies and tells us she takes in orphans. Gives her money from the poor box to feed them."

"Vicar probably sleeps with her, too. Wouldn't be surprised if those 'orphans' are really his get."

"And his sweet wife never suspecting."

"We need a new vicar. An honest man!" This time the woman who seemed to lead the malicious gossip stalked off, snapping her fingers calling her own brood of three to follow her. The children ranged from just barely walking to a five-year-old girl who carried the youngest.

A fourth child I had presumed belonged to her remained playing in the dirt next to where the woman had stood for much longer than necessary to gather two buckets of water.

I let a little time pass. The filthy child remained by the well as the women came and went. Some returned for more water. None of them even looked at the child. A gentle nudge from my mind sent Helwriaeth sniffing at the creature.

"How does one find the laundress?" I asked the crowd of idlers around me. If indeed she served the function of town prostitute, these men would know her.

"Just look for the smallest hut with the most young'uns hanging around," a grizzled man with few teeth and less hair laughed raucously. "Got a claim to one or two of them meself."

"Ah, you ain't got the stick to jump that one!" another man proclaimed. They continued their bawdy jokes for several minutes.

"Is that child one of hers?" I pointed to the little one who protested Helwriaeth's determined face washing with her tongue. The child ducked away from the dog and shoved a fistful of dirt into its mouth. Helwriaeth, good mother that she was, batted the baby cheek with her muzzle until it spat out the noxious meal—possibly the only food it had taken all day.

No anxious mother ran to protect her child from the ministrations of a wolfhound three times its size.

"Probably. She turns the lot of them loose to fend for themselves while she washes clothes of them's too lazy to do it for themselves."

"Does she boil the laundry in her house?" I threw a small coin onto the table for the publican. He bit the new one that looked too small to be worth anything. When he examined the coin for tooth marks and found none, he nodded his head that I was free to go without prejudice.

"Sometimes she works at home, but you won't get no joy from that'un while she's working. Best you wait for night to fall." All the men laughed and slapped each other on the back.

"Could be she's down by the river pounding sheets and things with a rock to get out certain stains from the bed of the knight's son. Heard tell he bedded the last virgin in town last night." More laughter and back slapping.

I ambled over to the well and scooped up the child. It cried and reached for Helwriaeth. "Sorry, Helwriaeth's back isn't as strong as it used to be. Otherwise I might let you ride her." No telling which gender or true age. It was small and weighed a lot less than a three-year-old should.

The child didn't care about the strength of Helwriaeth's bones. It wanted my dog.

"I'll let the dog be your nanny." I lifted the child over my head and jiggled it until it giggled. "Come along, Meg. I think we found someone who might answer some questions."

Meg hastily dipped her kerchief into the bucket of a passing adolescent. The grammar school had dismissed for the day and now the older children fetched water for their mothers. Then Meg washed the face and hands of our small charge. The child squirmed and fussed until she finished.

Then my sister, the unfulfilled Madonna, took the child from me and cuddled it lovingly, crooning to it in a baby language I could not translate. It settled into her arms contentedly, singing back to her.

"Is it a boy or girl?" I asked my sister, feeling vaguely guilty for referring to the child as "it."

"Baby boy. Meg's baby boy." She made some squeaking noises like a little bird. The boy repeated the sounds back to her. "Meg's baby bird. A baby Robin."

I took a deep breath, wondering if she knew the significance of the name she assigned to the boy.

He opened his mouth in a riotous giggle, showing most of his teeth. If I remembered correctly the nights Donovan, Meg, and I walked the floor with our younger siblings when they teethed, he shouldn't have that many unless he was over the age of two.

A well-trodden path beside the river led us to a deep pool surrounded by boulders. A lone woman knelt beside one, pounding the life out of a swathe of white linen. It did indeed gleam in the spring sunshine. From the embankment all I could see was the curve of her slender back and the curl of lank, medium brown hair from beneath her cap.

"Madame." I stopped several yards from the woman. From the slenderness of her shoulders and the strength she exerted to pound the sheets with rocks, I guessed her to be young, not much older than myself.

She turned to us. However old she truly was, her face showed the creases and deep furrows of worry, not enough food, and abuse of her body. She could have been anywhere from twenty to fifty summers.

Then she spotted the child and her face lit up, shedding years of care. I guessed her closer to five and twenty. Her shift beneath her threadbare bodice was damp and clung to her ample bosom. The laces of her bodice gaped near her waist, giving the suggestion that perhaps she carried yet another child.

"Robin, where have you been?" She held her arms out to the child. He giggled again and buried his head into Meg's shoulder. A game? Or did he cringe from the woman who perhaps meted out discipline with a heavy hand?

"We found him playing by the well. No one seemed to be looking after him. No one came to feed him at noontime. No one cared when he ate dirt." I spoke a little softer than I'd intended.

Tears filled the woman's eyes. "Poor little tyke ain't had nothing else to eat since sunup." She turned away from us and returned to her washing. Baskets of shirts and undergarments awaited her attention once she finished with the sheets.

"Is the child yours?" I asked.

"Aye and nay. No one else wanted him. The old vicar could barely keep himself, suffering from the bone disease and a rotten stomick. I took 'em in rather than let him starve." She pounded a new stain with renewed vigor.

"Is he faring any better under your care, Madame?"

"I feeds all of 'em sommat every day. They sleep together warm. His clothes start out clean each day. Bettern' a lot of folks who has t' take to the road."

I knew that life. My Gypsy friends might have taken on the care of an orphan. But life on the road was as hard as this woman's. I made my decision on the spot, not caring if this Robin was the "dearest Robin" I sought, though I felt it likely.

"My patron has just learned of this child's existence. He

thinks the mother might be a distant cousin of his. He feels responsible for its upbringing." Partially the truth. But my "patron" would never, ever, get his manipulative hands on this innocent child.

"Will he have food and a warm bed, a chance to go to grammar school? Will your patron love him?" She turned haunted eyes up to me.

"I love him," Meg replied.

"My patron has authorized me to pay you for the services you have rendered to this child." I held up a handful of small coins. None of them gold. She'd have a hard time disposing of gold without question. "I wish it could be more."

The haunted eyes widened at the sight of twenty good coins, mostly shillings and a few ha'pennies.

"Perhaps this will allow you to find a husband or at least bear no more children out of wedlock," I said sternly.

"No decent man'll take the likes o' me to t' church porch." She hung her head, but no blush marred her complexion.

I fished a single gold coin from my scrip. "Will this allow you to refuse the men who come to your door each night?"

She stared at the coin and gulped. "Aye, m'lord. 'Twill be enough for me to refuse even the knight and his son when they summon me. For a time."

"Take this money and travel north with your children, to Kirkenwood." My impulse shook me. I had to save this woman when no one else would, as she saved the children when no one else would. I gave her directions to the border castle. "Tell Fiona, the laird's sister, that we sent you. That we beg her to give you shelter and honest employment."

"I don't take charity. I work for what I gets."

"Fiona will find work for you."

The woman nodded abruptly.

Part of me quailed at presuming upon Fiona's hospitality. I couldn't save all the homeless and distressed of England. But I could help this one woman, give her children a chance at all of life's opportunities.

"And the little 'un?" She gestured with her chin toward Robin and Meg.

Should I keep the child?—presuming I could get him away from Meg. Or send him north with his foster mother?

He'd be anonymous with her. But Norfolk would hunt the child when he realized I had not returned to his household. He'd look in Kirkenwood first.

"Meg and I will guard him carefully, give him the education he deserves. We will love him." My heart swelled as if I had laid claim to my own child. This little one had already wormed his way into my heart.

Meg rooted around in her scrip and came up with a sprig of an herb I half recognized. Raven had planted a bed of it in a sunny corner of her garden. I'd asked about it several times. She'd always promised to tell me its secrets later. When I was older. When someone I knew needed it.

"Take this, when your courses run two days late," Meg said quietly. "You'll not have any more unwanted mouths to feed."

The woman took the plant skeptically. "Does the church forbid this?"

"Don't ask." Meg turned back to talking in baby gibberish to Robin. The boy giggled and tugged on her hair. The dogs frolicked around her ankles eager to join the game.

"Robin has a blanket that came with him. He cain't sleep at night without it." The laundress pocketed the herb. She'd say no more about it to me or anyone else.

"Where is this blanket?" I asked.

"Blanket's right here. Meant to wash it with the rest of the children's clothes." She held up a blue blanket, the right size to wrap an infant. In one corner, the remnants of some dark embroidery spelled out the initials ET with tiny roses and crowns around them.

Elizabeth Tudor, crown princess of England at the time of the boy's birth.

Chapter 33

Mortlake, England, spring 1560.

A VAGUE awareness of cool slipped beneath the folds of darkness that enveloped Donovan. With the sensation came an urgency. He had to do something, say something. But he could not remember what.

He latched onto the cool as something tangible in the nothingness where he floated. Heaviness followed the ice forming around the edges of his being.

A tremendous weight pressed against the center of the cool.

Something shook, dislodging the cool. Bone-deep aches followed the sensation. He could not succumb to the urge to retreat back into the blackness. What demanded his attention. His actions?

Then he realized he had a body and it trembled with chill, and weakness, and . . .

He retched. Deep convulsions turned his body inside out. A gentle voice soothed him and delicate fingers caressed his brow as he continued to fill the chamber pot held beneath his face.

"You can turn him onto his back again, Mother. I need to talk to him," Dr. John Dee said, much too loudly.

Donovan cringed beneath the assault of sound, expecting a repeat of the angels roaring at him in deafening waves of meaningless noise.

Something about a conversation with angels. Information he had to impart. What?

Another convulsion rocked Donovan's slender hold on consciousness and sanity. The coolness came back. Was it merely a damp rag across his eyes and brows that felt as heavy as rocks?

"Did you see the angels, Milord Donovan?" Dee asked impatiently.

Donovan reached up and grabbed the front of Dee's robe, guessing the scholar leaned over him from the nearness of his voice. "One comes with deceit in his heart. You must not heed his words though they sound as wisdom. They are but an idle breeze trying to sound like a great gale." Donovan fell back against pillows, exhausted.

The sense of urgency left him. He'd given his message. But where had it come from? He hadn't planned the words. They just spilled out of him as water from an ewer—the ewer being no more cognizant of the water than Donovan had been of the words.

Griffin spoke in riddles after a vision. Donovan hadn't had the glory of a vision to tell him why he spoke, nor of what. This whole wretched mess must be nothing more than a hangover from the barley wine.

"You spoke with the angels," Dee insisted.

Donovan sensed the man leaning closer yet. He could smell the fennel seed Dee used to sweeten his breath. But he hadn't yet the courage to open his eyes. "I know not what the angel said. I only heard a great roar that near ruptured my ears."

"Can you repeat the words? Even if you know not the nature of the words, I can translate from the Enochian language."

"Leave off, Johnny. The man barely lives," Mistress Dee insisted. She must have pushed her son away, for the smell of fennel receded.

"But we must transcribe the ephemeral experience right away before it drifts into the mist of forgetfulness."

"You'll be late for your appointment with Good Queen Bess. Now, leave the boy be and get to London."

Dee mumbled and fussed, but eventually Donovan heard a door close. Then the sounds of rustling cloth and dripping water.

"Now we'll see about getting you well. I only hope my son in his zeal has not poisoned you beyond repair." Mistress Dee clucked and soothed, replacing the cool damp cloth on Donovan's brow.

"Has he done this before? Wine made from rotten barley?" he croaked.

"Only drunk it himself and with less dangerous results. He merely had a hangover."

"I saw something special," Donovan murmured. "I saw auras as well as spirits. The barriers in my mind almost collapsed and opened my talent."

"Well, barley wine isn't the way to do it. Any more potent a brew would kill you. Less potency and you'd only get drunk."

"But there might be another way. An herb, a potion that will open my mind."

"You could try ghostweed," Mistress Dee suggested. "I've heard tell of midwives of old using it to calm hysterical women. But the dosage has to be carefully measured lest you think you can fly and step off a rooftop to your death."

"Mayhap next time I'll be able to soar with spirits rather than be deafened by them."

"Not for some time yet to come, Milord Donovan. You must recover from this brush with death first."

Hatfield, England.

"We need a place to hide," I said to Meg as we rode away from Hatfield. We had stopped at the rectory only long enough to gather our few belongings and saddle the horses.

"Sanctuary," Meg replied. She looked at me with clear eyes, expecting me to know what lay within the layers of defense she had built up over the years.

"Sanctuary," I repeated. A heaviness lay in my heart. When King Henry VIII had broken with Rome, he had dissolved the abbeys, convents, and monasteries throughout England. Many lay in ruins or had been sold and converted to manors for the king's favorites. Scotland had followed suit shortly thereafter. As the altars were desecrated and ripped out, so, too, had vanished the right of sanctuary. Remaining churches had converted to the Anglican reforms. They did not offer the same right of protection as the tradition of old.

Thomas Cromwell, Henry VIII's henchman, had passed specific laws ending the right of sanctuary in all but a few places, especially in London where protected gangs of criminals terrorized the city and then retreated to sanctuary. Violent criminals were exempt from protection within the few remaining places where sanctuary was still recognized.

The practical part of my mind recognized that Henry VIII and Thomas Cromwell had corrected a badly abused system that had grown beyond its original purpose.

"Norfolk will not violate sanctuary even if he finds us," Meg reminded me.

"Where?" I pounded my fist into the pommel of my saddle. My first instinct was to retreat to Kirkenwood. Norfolk would look there first for me and the child. Donovan would not welcome me there. And my duty to my church and Bishop Eustachius pulled me back to the capital and its environs.

"London." Meg continued to speak sanely, but seemed as cryptic as Raven could be at times. Meg's eyes—or did Raven truly observe me through her granddaughter?—penetrated my soul and found me wanting. Her cheeks lost the babyish roundness, and a woman of strength and intelligence engaged all of my attention.

Whitefriars, Raven's voice broke through the loop of confusion and question in my mind. But the words came out of Meg's mouth.

I looked more closely at her. The moment of clarity vanished from her eyes and expression. She looked once more an overgrown five-year-old.

"Whitefriars, of course," I repeated. "The Carmelite monastery just outside the walls of London." The last place in England to offer sanctuary to the dispossessed, political refugees, and debtors. Why that place had remained exempt from the cleansing by Thomas Cromwell, I did not know. But to Whitefriars I must take Meg and Robin.

We reached London just before sunset on a rainy evening. The lamplighters lit torches at the Ludgate and Newgate of the old city. But the inner city remained dark, with houses and shops keeping their lights tightly shuttered within. We skirted the ancient confines of London, crossed the River Fleet (little more than a muddy sewer) and angled back toward the Thames. The land gates to Whitefriars remained firmly shut against the cold, the dark, and official intruders. Were the river gates more welcoming?

I dismounted wearily and pounded on the doors. The dogs were wet and bedraggled. Meg and Robin huddled together beneath her cloak, shivering. I suppressed a bone-racking yawn while I waited impatiently. Had Joseph felt the same sense of urgency to avoid pursuit and find sanctuary when he and Holy Mary fled to Egypt with the infant Jesus?

At last a small panel within the door slid back to reveal a single brown eye surrounded by pale, wrinkled skin. I couldn't tell if the owner of the eye were male or female. I guessed the person to be old and careworn.

"Whatcha want?" a creaking voice asked. Male, by the broken bass rumble.

"I seek sanctuary for my sister and her babe. Myself as well, if there is room," I replied politely. I even affected a little bow of respect for the place if not the inquirer.

"What they wantcha for?" He barely blinked and revealed no more of himself or the interior.

"I flee from . . . from a noble who disliked the horoscope I cast for him." True enough. Norfolk had asked me to tell the future for him only once. I hadn't needed to consult the stars and my charts to tell him that his current quest for power would end in disaster. Any quest for power by that man would lead him to the headsman's block. The duke had stalked away from me, blaming me for everything that had gone wrong in his life, including Elizabeth's preference for other councillors than himself.

"And the woman?"

"An illegitimate babe sired by . . . by someone of great power and influence." The truth again. "The child is a threat to an inheritance." A common enough story. In an age when more and more estates became entailed to the male line, noblemen had been known to adopt and legitimatize their bastards when their wives produced only girls. Better that a bastard of their own get inherit than the male spawn of a rival branch of the family.

"Tell it to the queen. Let 'er protect you." He began slamming his eye portal.

"Wait!" I protested, much too loudly. "I can't go to the queen. I'm a Catholic priest."

The portal stalled, halfway closed. The gate guardian paused a long moment. "A priest, eh? You willing to give us the sacraments?"

"I can deny no true believer who is repentant and comes to the altar seeking forgiveness for his sins."

"What about your sister? She willing to serve us as well?" He chuckled lasciviously.

"No."

"Ah, well, 'twas worth a try." He partially opened the door.

"Will my sister be safe from the inhabitants of this place?" I firmly blocked the door, keeping the guardian inside and away from Meg. "She has been hurt by men, and I will not risk her again."

"Safe enough. We got women—men with families. Some of 'ems' willing. Most belong to summun. This 'un belongs to you." He shrugged and opened the door a little farther. "Come along, then. Supper's almost ready. We eats together, works together, piss together. But nearly everyone's got their own sleeping place. Them horses'll bring a pretty penny at market."

"I might need them again."

"Cain't keep 'em here more'n a day. No room. No fodder. Too much shit."

Resigned, I took Robin from Meg's tired arms while she dismounted. As soon as she stood on her own, she snatched the boy back again, as if afraid she'd lose him forever. I led the horses through the gatehouse tunnel into the open quadrangle. Meg followed slowly, peering deeply into every shadow we encountered.

She mistrusted this place. I trusted her instincts. The dogs kept close to my heels, grumbling deep in their throats.

A blast of heat, as from the fires of hell, hit me full in the face.

"Norfolk will come with fire and death, hotter than these fires," she said quietly. "But not for a time. Robin and Meg will find a new home before then."

Chapter 34

Whitefriars Abbey, London, 1560.

I IGNORED the intense heat from two furnaces to stare at Meg. She bounced Robin in her arms and talked about a hot stew with lots and lots of turnips.

Her pronouncement about Norfolk bringing fire and death had vanished from her mind.

Despite the strength-draining heat, I shifted my staff to a defensive position and looked around the Whitefriars cloister, assessing potential danger.

Two dozen people, dressed in the light summer wear of peasants, milled about the open courtyard. Most ignored us. A few wide-eyed children paused in turning the well wheel to stare back at me and my sister. A woman scolded them in harsh tones. They began pushing the shafts around and around again, pumping water into a huge trough.

Across the cobblestone yard, three men tended a huge oven. One shielded his eyes with a padded mitt while opening an iron door with his equally protected free hand. Another man dipped a long shaft into the roaring brightness. He withdrew the shaft with a glowing blob on the end.

"Metalwork?" I asked the gate guardian who hovered nearby. But where were the anvils and the ring of hammers against the molten iron?

"Glass," the guardian replied. A kind of awe tinged his voice. "We all work at something in the factory. Glass gives us the coin to keep us fed and sheltered. Also keeps the queen's guards from sniffing too close to the gate. Too many people want to buy our glass for them to risk threatening us, no matter that most of us can't leave the abbey for fear of arrest. I be Ralph." He thrust a gnarled hand toward me.

I clasped his hand. My apprehensions faded. Meg had said Norfolk would come. But not for a while yet. We had time to rest and plan.

Meg and Robin seemed undaunted by the waves of hot air radiating out from the furnaces.

"I am Griffin, this is Meg, and her boy Robin."

Ralph—he swallowed the "L" and hardened the "A"—jerked his head toward one wing of the ancient monastery. "Supper be ready soon. When the bell rings. Strip your belongings from the horses. They go to market at dawn. Fine beasts like this will fetch more than we'd gain by eating them."

I patted the horse's rump with affection. He had served me well since I bought him in Edinburgh nearly two years ago. I'd miss his steady pace and fine stamina when I left this place. As I must leave eventually.

Ralph chuckled. "None of us can leave, our lives depend upon staying put." He slapped my shoulder much as I had touched the horse. "Your cells is this way. Separate ones for now. You'll have to share come winter, though. Cold weather always brings extras. This time o' year they take to the road and find work on the farms. Bunch a' Gypsies stayed two full weeks during the last of the winter's storms."

"Was a man named Micah with a son George and their family among the Gypsies?" I asked, suddenly needing to know if my friends from the road continued to find safe haven.

Ralph shrugged. "You be the one the Gypsies call the Merlin? Heard tell of a miracle of life on a Wild Hunt." He peered at me closely.

I held my breath, not answering.

Finally Ralph shrugged and continued, "Gypsies don't always give a name. They just come and go as the whim takes 'em. You'll say the grace at supper. Ain't had a proper grace in ages."

"Our Lord dined with prostitutes and criminals. Who am I to deny you whatever blessings you can garner from life?" God's grace did indeed reach out to us in mysterious ways.

As I inspected the narrow cell Ralph showed me, I

breathed a deep sigh of relief. I could find peace here in
the stark surroundings. Men and women had sought the
simple life within a cloister for many centuries. Perhaps
here, with hard work and prayer, I would find answers to
my many questions, a clear path to stride forward into
the future.

Meg's cell was across the cloister from mine. Mostly single, unprotected women lived on that side. Single men lived
near me. After our days on the road together, I didn't like
her being so far away. If anyone ever suspected Robin's
true identity and tried to steal him, or worse, kill him, I
could not get to her in time.

I looked to the dogs for inspiration. The three of us stood
in the doorway to my room for several long moments of
indecision. Newynog pressed close to me, needing me to
ruffle her ears. Helwriaeth heaved a tremendous sigh and
ambled across the cobbled enclosure to Meg's door.

Her leaving felt almost like a permanent separation. As
if she walked to her death. "Good-bye, Helwriaeth," I
whispered, hugging Newynog close. I knew with the certainty of a vision that my beloved familiar had not long to
live. But as long as she breathed, she would fulfill her duty.

Palais de la Louvre, Paris, France, 16 June, 1560.

Roanna clamped her mouth shut on the news that bubbled from Tryblith. A sour aftertaste would not leave her
tongue. She fussed uselessly with the garments within the
wardrobe chests of Marie Stuart, Queen of Scots, wife of
the King of France, and Pretender to the crown of England.
Five days ago Roanna had awakened fighting for breath,
with a heaviness in her lungs and her limbs. Images of
huge amounts of water blotted out every thought. Towering
waves, spilling blood, pelting rain; the element of water
drowned her—drowned the fire of her magic. When consciousness and morning light finally banished the encroaching darkness of death, she knew that Marie de Guise
drowned in the fluids of her body. The tansy Roanna had

given the Queen Regent of Scotland had done its work
at last.

For several frightening moments, Roanna had shared the
death with her victim. This was different from executing
criminals she had never met before. She *liked* Marie de
Guise, admired her inner strength and unwillingness to be
cowed by men simply because she was a woman.

Then the power built within Roanna. Her body tingled
with energy. She reveled in possibilities. She could banish
Tryblith back to his netherworld, free at last to take charge
of her own destiny, as Marie de Guise had done for many
years before Roanna and her demon brought her low.

The power continued to grow in Roanna, but so did the
bitter taste in her mouth that could not be banished. And
as she gained in magic, so did Tryblith. He remained firmly
rooted in her mind, triumphing at her inadequacy. Five
days she endured his taunting. Five days of being able to
compel all those around her to do her bidding—even forcing a titled lady of the royal bedchamber to empty Roanna's chamber pot—but not finding the right spell, the right
combination of elements to force Tryblith to leave.

Now the messenger with the official news rode into the
courtyard upon a near foundering horse. Instead of bursting
forth with the news, Roanna retrieved a black gown sparkling with jet beads from the armoire.

"We want to wear the green, Rose." Marie stared at
Roanna with stunned indignation. She had Frenchified
Roanna's name as she did most words that had their origins
in Scotland or England. "We spend enough time in mourning for this official, and that relative. 'Tis time to bring joy
and gaiety to court." She laughed lightly, filling the room
with her infectious mood.

"Forgive me, Your Majesty. My hands sought this gown
of their own volition. I know not why." Roanna ducked
her head in false meekness. Inside she grinned. She had
worked her way into a position of trust and confidence in
this royal household as easily as she had in Edinburgh,
despite the monstrous layers of protocol and formality the
French applied to everything.

The huge palais was staffed with hundreds of servants,
many assigned only a few simple chores a day. But protocol
demanded they perform no others and that no other ser-

vant perform their duties. Thus, one maid cleaned the shoes and caps for the queen, another fetched them to the mistress of the royal wardrobe for inspection. Yet another servant carried them into the royal presence on the day she chose to wear those particular items. Still other servants saw to the cleaning and mending of a few particular items of clothing.

The royal budget could easily bankrupt itself on servant salaries, housing, and feeding alone. Soon the numerous courtiers who depended upon royal bounty for their livelihoods might have to face bankruptcy so that the court could maintain their protocol and the servants who upheld it.

The studied orderliness was only a mask for a system that lent itself to ripples of chaos. Tryblith delighted in creating delays in the orderly progression of events. Roanna couldn't count the number of ambassadors and church princes who had to reorder their days because she and her demon had sent one person sprawling on a slippery stair.

But with so many people with limited authority, interested only in protecting their limited authority, a cunning stranger could walk in and insert herself in the queen's bedchamber with ease.

Marie de Guise's onyx ring had helped only when she confronted the queen. No one else recognized it.

"Have you had another vision, Rose?" Queen Marie asked, glaring at the offensive black gown of mourning. Concern played across her lovely features, softening the royal hauteur.

Roanna suppressed another grin. Marie's biggest vulnerability lay in her empathy with those beneath her, and her willingness to trust those who seemed as sincerely caring as herself. She had not the ruthlessness to deal with the independent and fractious lords of Scotland. But Earl Moray did. Marie's absence from her homeland gave Scotland more peace and stability than her presence would.

The time was coming when Roanna would have to push Marie to go home. Her adherence to the Catholic faith would stir up tremendous trouble amongst the firmly Protestant nobles of Scotland. First things first.

Roanna opened the door two heartbeats before the page

with the grim message knocked. She stared at the folded
and sealed parchment for a long moment. Then with a
quick look over her shoulder to ensure an audience,
Roanna gasped with her hand over her heart and promptly
collapsed in a puddle of velvet skirts held in perfect circles
by the tin hoops of her farthingale. If she'd worn a bloody
corset, she wouldn't be able to bow her back in a further
display of unconsciousness.

Several of Marie's serving women rushed to Roanna's
side. They made soothing noises, dabbing at her brow with
kerchiefs moistened with perfume. Roanna nearly gagged
at the intense scent, but she needed to complete her performance. She allowed herself to rouse partially, keeping her
eyes closed as the mistress of Her Majesty's kerchiefs and
veils cradled her head in her lap.

"Chaos, blood. So very much blood. Smoke and fire.
True believers burning at the stake. Chaos. War. Defeat."
She uttered each word carefully and individually so that
there would be no mistake or misinterpretation of her
vision.

Tryblith giggled almost loud enough for the other women
to hear him, if they could hear anything over their own
hysterics.

Roanna fluttered her eyes to indicate her return to
reality.

"Give our Rose a few sips of watered wine, Lily," Queen
Marie said. She gave off an aura of calm, but her voice
came out more husky and breathless than usual. Roanna's
"vision" had penetrated Marie's frivolous mind.

Hesitantly, Marie reached for the missive, still resting
upon the page's pillow. She examined the seal with her
fingers for long moments. Then, carefully, she broke the
wax and unfolded the parchment.

All of the women in the room waited with barely a
breath to disturb the eerie silence.

Except for Tryblith's chortles of glee inside Roanna's
head. She was getting tired of the demon.

At last Marie read the terse message sent by her half-
brother James Stuart, Earl of Moray. She gasped, and fat
tears spilled down her pale cheeks. She crossed herself and
murmured a prayer in Latin.

You need to teach me that tongue! Roanna admonished Tryblith.

He remained stubbornly silent. Roanna suspected the demon had never learned the Roman language, despite his years of running free in Britain before a Pendragon witch and his consort had imprisoned him in his current tomb.

A dozen women rushed to comfort Marie. The mistress of the queen's kerchiefs and veils barely bothered to set Roanna's head down on the floor before abandoning her for the queen.

"My mother has died. The doctors say 'twas dropsy," Marie cried. Women helped her to the bed, patted her back, and proffered watered wine. "I must go home. My brother will lead my people farther away from the true faith. Scotland needs her queen!" she wailed.

At last! Now we will have war. An all-out war of extermination between England and France, Tryblith proclaimed.

"And I will be free of you at last," Roanna murmured. No one heard her. All attention was centered upon the queen in her distress. But a swift stab of pain at the base of her neck told her that Tryblith heard her. He heard everything she said and most everything she thought.

"Marie?" King Francis II, Marie's husband wandered into the chamber through the privy door that led to his own quarters. "Marie, my ear hurts." The king pouted like a small child. He stood several inches shorter than his wife, a frail and pasty figure against her bright beauty.

"Sweeting." Marie held out her arms to her husband. In all the months that Roanna had lived in the palais, she had never known the king to seek Marie's bed at night. Nor had he done more to govern France than affix his signature and seal to decrees his mother wrote and proclaimed. These two young people remained cosseted children with no responsibilities beyond planning what to wear at the next banquet or masque.

"Sing to me, Marie. Make the pain go away with your lullabies." The king lay down next to his wife and put his head upon her breast, more a child seeking comfort from his mother than a husband needing nursing from his wife. His mother had certainly done little to comfort either of them as they matured.

The crowd of ladies and maids might not have existed. The world centered around King Francis II and his childhood companion.

"Francis, my sweet, I must return to Scotland. My mother has died, leaving my government in the hands of unbelievers."

"But you can't go, Marie. I need you here. I need you to make me well."

I need you to divert Mother away from me. She frightens me. His next thoughts came through to Roanna as if Francis spoke them aloud, but his mouth remained firmly closed in a pout. What had Catherine de Médici done this time?

"I won't be gone long, Francis. But I must set my government in order and find a proper regent of the true faith." Marie stroked Francis' hair and neck as she spoke in soothing tones.

"No, Marie. I forbid it!" Francis half sat up. " 'Tis my right as king and . . . and as your husband. I forbid you to leave me even for a day." He lay his head back upon her breast, whimpering with the pain in his ear.

"No, I will not leave you, Francis. I will stay here as long as you need me." Tears rolled down Marie's cheeks, as she silently grieved for the mother she had not seen since she had been spirited out of Scotland at the age of five.

NOOOoooooo! Tryblith wailed, stabbing Roanna's mind, joints, and gut with white-hot pincers.

Chapter 35

Whitefriars Abbey, London, England.

BEFORE supper that first night at Whitefriars, I watched the men work the glass. One man dipped his long, hollow pole into the fiery furnace lined in white clay and withdrew a gather of molten glass. Sweat trickled down his face and plastered his shirt to his back despite the chill drizzle and evening wind. His muscles bulged and flexed easily as he swung the pole in graceful arcs, right and left. A big man, who had probably done heavy manual labor all his life. I wondered what had sent him to the sanctuary of Whitefriars.

From the blazing furnace he proceeded to the workbench with his treasure. Gradually the white-hot blob elongated. The last swing flipped the rod onto the bench. He sat down astride a bench, then put his lips to the cool end of the metal and blew.

The glass blossomed, becoming a misshapen tube. Then another man took wet wooden paddles to the glass as the blower rolled the rod back and forth. The tube took on straight lines. I wondered what it would be when finished, a large bottle or decorative piece?

I could see the glass change color as it cooled. From molten white, with tinges of red and yellow around the edges, it turned more orange.

The shaper stepped away from the glass and the blower took it to a second furnace.

"That's the glory hole," one of the children said as he carried a bucket of water to the workbench. His words came out in a nasal rush that was barely understandable to my French-tuned ear. He sloshed water as he walked. I reached to help him lift the burden that was obviously too heavy for his slight frame. Proudly he jerked it away, slopping more water.

Newynog bit at the falling drops. The children at the well laughed.

"I kin manage," the bucket boy said proudly. "Got to build my strength so I kin work the glass when I'm tall enough to reach the gather and the glory hole."

"Why does he reheat the glass in the glory hole?" I asked my informant.

"It's cooled too much to work proper. Got to keep it hot while he's working or it'll crack. Once he's done, the glass gots to cool real slow—in the annealing oven overnight—or it gets too brittle." The boy placed his bucket next to the workbench, transferring the tools from the bucket of steaming water already there. The water that had been heated by immersing hot tools into it was returned to the trough to cool.

"What's he making?" I followed the boy as he performed his chores.

"Windowpanes today. Most days. Big call for lights in the houses of the swells. The glass is clear today. Tomorrow we add minerals to what's left over and make colored vials and small bottles. When the gather is as empty as we can make it, we shift to another furnace." He pointed to the opposite side of the courtyard to a similar array of brick-and-clay ovens where a man poured sand into one of them. "Once this furnace cools, it's got to be scrubbed out—that'll be your job since ye're new—and restoked. You'll haul charcoal up from the river barges, too. New ones always get the worst jobs. Next step up is to fill the gather with the proper mixes. Brother Jeremy—he's the owner—tells you how much of what goes in each day. If you stay long enough, you might get to do some real work." He shrugged his shoulders and returned to turning the well wheel with other children, boys and girls, all too young to work so hard.

Everyone here must have sought the place for a reason, entire families forced to flee the law. The big glassblower with the bulging muscles—skilled as he was now—might very well have made his living as a hired thug before he sought refuge here. What had I let myself and Meg and Robin in for?

Newynog pranced after the boy, chasing the children around and around as they pushed. The dog stood nearly as tall as the tallest among them. She probably outweighed them all by a stone or two. With a grin, I acknowledged the chore that would be given to my familiar. She'd probably think being harnessed to the wheel and chasing the children around a game.

I turned my attention back to the glass workers. Apparently the windowpane was now hot enough to finish the work. The blower returned it to the table. He rolled the pole while his coworker shaped it a little more. They repeated the heating and shaping routine twice more before moving the glass to a table covered in warmed metal. Here another man waited for them with a different set of tools.

Almost quicker than I could watch, the small, wiry man who had the reflexes of a pickpocket broke off the closed end of the tube with a padded mallet. Then he separated the open tube from the end of the rod with a tool that looked like scissors with short, fat blades. Almost before the pole was withdrawn he whipped out another scissor tool with longer, more slender blades. With these he slit the tube. Another man jumped in with a rolling pin and flattened the pane of glass with the skill of a fine baker. (Why was he here?) He squared the edges and rolled it again. I thought I saw markings on the metal table to show him the precise size of the finished pane.

Already the glass cooled enough that I could see it clearing from dull orange to bluish white. One of the workers, hands protected by huge padded mitts, scooped up the still hot pane with a flat tool and slid it onto a small tray. Gingerly he carried it to another opening in the brick wall beside the furnace. He tucked the glass into its hidey-hole and closed a door over it, with a flourish as if presenting the queen with a missive upon a velvet pillow. (Had he been a refined servant caught stealing from his master?) This must be the annealing oven where it would cool gradually overnight.

I breathed deeply, feeling a tremendous sense of accomplishment. Very shortly I would be a part of this exciting enterprise.

A criminal among criminals, I had to remind myself. I had celebrated the Latin Mass and elevated the host in the

Roman tradition. I spied for a foreign bishop. Therefore I
was subject to permanent exile or prison if caught by Her
Majesty's loyal citizens.

The bell rang for supper. I searched for Meg and Robin
in the crowd that moved slowly toward the refectory. Each
person finished whatever he or she was doing, set aside the
tools carefully—probably in prearranged places, and drifted
toward this well deserved meal. They took pride in their
work. They were probably well fed, too, if finishing was
more important than the next meal.

I had trouble believing any of them the thugs and thieves
who reportedly sought refuge here.

Meg emerged from her cell with Robin in tow. He clung
to her hand and toddled behind her, thumb stuck resolutely
into his mouth. Immediately, a gaggle of women surrounded her, babbling questions in accents that ranged
from the Yorkshire dales to London stews. Some of the
women laced their kirtles from bottom to top—a signal of
availability. Only prostitutes did that.

I shuddered, wondering again what kind of influence
these people would have on vulnerable Meg and very
young Robin.

"Give me strength, Lord," I implored silently. Instinctively I clutched the rosary at my belt and recited a quick
Pater noster and a Hail Mary.

One by one, each of the women drifted away from Meg
to join with a man, often gathering a child or two to her
side. They seemed a parody of loving families.

"Father Griffin!" Ralph hailed me from the gate. "You'll
say the blessing. Brother Jeremy has asked you to sit beside
him on the dais." He joined me, looping his arm through
mine.

"Brother Jeremy?"

"Aye. We call him that. The last remnant of the good
brothers what used to own this place, 'afore Bluff King Hal
ousted all of the thievin' church."

"I am a priest of the church that King Henry ousted," I
replied flatly.

"Aye. But you ain't a thief. Just a good man needin' a
place to hide 'cause Good Queen Bess don't like your
style."

"I've never met the queen."

"Don't matter. Neither have any of us. But she don't like our style of livin' neither!" He laughed uproariously at his own joke.

"Why are you here?" I had to ask. Had to know if I had put Meg and Robin in more danger by coming here, than we would face on the road.

"Just a bit o' debt. Couldn't pay my taxes and protection money to the gang what kept my cobbler shop safe from fire. I paid the protection money. Tax man didn't like it and confiscated everything I owned and still said I owed more."

I breathed a little easier. Debtors were criminals but not violent. Just honest men run afoul of the system.

"Brother Jeremy," Ralph called across the cloister in stentorian tones.

A short, round man, clad in a dirty monk's robe that might once have been the white of the Carmelites, looked around for the source of the summons. His tonsure was ragged and spotty—more natural than shaved. The rest of his mud-colored hair hung in long, limp tangles below his shoulders. The robe didn't fit, being much too long at sleeve and hem. From the open throat I caught a glimpse of a fine linen shirt. No monk would have put a barrier between his skin and the rough woolen robe of his calling.

"Father Griffin, meet Brother Jeremy, our savior."

"Benedicte," he said in the worst Latin accent I had ever heard. Even Donovan had spoken better the first week Raven taught us the most prevalent language in the civilized world. The stout man extended his hand in a most secular greeting.

"Brother Jeremy set up the glassworks. He's the one what taught us all the right skills and found places to sell the glass. Without him, we'd be just a ragtag bunch of criminals stealin' what bread we could and fightin' 'mongst ourselves. If'n we ever git out of here, we've got a trade we can work anywhere there's sand to melt into glass."

"I admit I saw this as a means to a fine profit from my own exile from civilization," Brother Jeremy said quietly. His voice would always be soft and quiet. "But these people have become my family. We help each other through good times and troubles." He held my gaze with a forthrightness far stronger than his voice, daring me to find fault with him or his factory.

Without his industry and thoughtfulness, this sanctuary could be more dangerous than any prison or life on the road.

"Benedicte," I replied. I blessed the man, making the sign of the cross over him.

"Thank you, Father." He bowed his head in acceptance of my blessing. "We are all pleased to share our sanctuary with you." He extended his arm again.

I clasped his elbow, and he gripped mine.

The world went white, the ground tilted beneath my feet. My hands grasped only his skeleton. He grinned at me from an eyeless skull. A few wisps of long white hair clung to the bones. Behind him, scrawny, hungry men and women tore at each other for a few scraps of bread; children lay dying in the open cloister; armed troops of the queen pounded at the gates ready to kill all those inside.

Brother Jeremy would die soon, leaving all of these people directionless. Without him, the sanctuary of Whitefriars would become a pit of violence and starvation.

Richmond Palace, the court of Queen Elizabeth, a few moments before dawn, 30 June, 1560.

Donovan sorted the herb packets he had collected over the course of the winter and spring. He'd haunted every apothecary in the city as well as a number of hedge witches in the villages surrounding Elizabeth's residences. The aromas—sharp, spicy, acidic, or sweet—each promised something different. None of them would give him a safe vision of angels or faeries or whatever being he had encountered while under the influence of barley wine.

But in combination? He needed time and privacy to experiment.

He was anxious to go home. Hopefully, Griffin had returned Meg to the sanctuary of Kirkenwood. Donovan had nightmares about what might happen to his sister should she find herself abandoned by the irresponsible Griffin. Griffin was good at abandoning his family and responsibilities.

Once home, Donovan could indulge in his experiments, perhaps find some of the elusive ghostweed in Raven's garden. He knew that if he could distill the correct potion, or brew the proper combination, he'd be able to force his dormant magic to come forth to his aid.

Then and only then would he feel entitled to wear the ring of the Pendragon. Then and only then would Elizabeth seek his council as a wise magician rather than as a foil to make Dudley jealous.

A rap on the door startled him out of his contemplation of rosemary, thyme, oak bark, and essence of pine. He didn't trust the essence of mummy. Too easy to substitute a charlatan substance for the real thing.

Quickly, he stuffed the packets into his saddlebag. Ten more minutes and he'd have departed the court for home. He was always the first to leave before summer heat brought outbreaks of the plague and other maladies.

"Enter," he growled. How quickly could he dispatch whatever business came to his door before the sun roused the sleepiest of heads.

"Milord." A page in Elizabeth's green-and-white livery bowed as he proffered a silver salver with a folded parchment atop.

Donovan recognized the stylized rose seal pressed into red wax. Elizabeth. What could she want with him so early? Didn't the woman ever sleep? She'd been up dicing and dancing until long after midnight. Now she summoned him a few short hours later.

Grumpily he grabbed the missive from his queen. The page hesitated at the door, still holding out the salver. Donovan threw a few coins at him. The brats learned early to garner whatever they could from the lords because Elizabeth was as tightfisted as a miser with her money.

But because she refused to spend money, England was once more prosperous and near to ending the massive debts incurred by Bloody Mary Tudor.

"Will there be a reply, milord?" the page asked, eyeing the coins skeptically. He bit one of them and peered at his tooth marks closely. Then he pocketed the pence. He finally lowered the salver but made no move to retreat, despite Donovan's foul mood.

"A moment, please." Donovan made to close the door

in the boy's face, but the page stood his ground. Seemingly, he had more rights and privileges in the queen's household than her courtiers.

Donovan broke the seal and scanned the queen's words. She wrote in small, cramped letters, as if hiding something within the words. Elizabeth with a secret was a dangerous person. She had the power of life and death over her courtiers and could easily cast any one of them into the Tower for minor transgressions.

"I don't suppose I could bribe you into telling Her Majesty that I had already departed for the north?" Donovan raised an eyebrow in query.

"No. Milord. Her Majesty commands all my loyalty. I would not lie to her. Not for any price."

"Very well. Tell Her Majesty that I will attend her shortly."

The boy cleared his throat.

"What!"

"The letter commands you to attend her immediately."

"May I wash and shave first?"

"Immediately, milord."

Sighing and rolling his eyes, Donovan straightened his simple leather doublet and crammed his feet into the long leather boots he wore when riding. His hose were old and patched—fine enough for riding pell-mell for home. The queen would have to accept him as he was, an impoverished northern lord of simple taste.

Elizabeth was still in her bedchamber. She'd partially dressed in her gown, but still selected sleeves, hose, veil, and shoes.

Dudley sat in a padded chair beside her dressing table, commenting on her choices. "The silver veil, I think, Bess . . . er, Majesty." He quickly corrected his familiar form of address as soon as he spotted Donovan.

Elizabeth's ladies—all dressed in black or white to provide a suitable backdrop for the queen's magnificent gown of green and silver—tittered. They swore frequently that the queen slept alone. But Dudley was always attending her before anyone else arrived.

"Ah, Milord Kirkenwood." Elizabeth turned her approving smile upon him. For a moment her eyes actually twinkled with delight. She was up to something.

Donovan bowed low, using the moment to search the room for hidden traps. Only Dudley's grin threatened him.

"Your Majesty, you rival the morning sun in brilliance. How may I serve you?" Donovan hated the ornamental language of the court. But he'd learned to use it to avoid Elizabeth's notoriously short temper.

"Kirkenwood, we have a surprise for you." Elizabeth held out her beringed hand for him to kiss.

He did so, still keeping a wary eye on Dudley.

"Just viewing your dazzling beauty is enough to please me, Majesty."

"And yet you are so eager to leave us?" She pouted a little, eyeing his rough leathern clothing.

"Business calls me home, Majesty. If I am to pay my taxes and tithes, I must tend to my lands upon occasion. I also must hasten to my sister's wedding."

"Ah, yes, young Fiona, isn't it?" Elizabeth raised one eyebrow as she struck a familiar listening pose, hands clasped at her corseted waist. Her position emphasized the swell of bosom atop her gown as well as the extreme slenderness of her torso. Donovan knew that each of her poses was a study in attracting admiration.

Dudley obliged her by ogling her attentively.

"Yes, Majesty. Fiona is pledged to marry the younger son of a neighboring barony. A good match. They will dwell at Kirkenwood and manage my affairs during my absence. But I still must return home occasionally to oversee."

"Yes, yes. We will not detain you long, Milord Kirkenwood." Again that sly grin that boded no good for Donovan.

He bowed again, as required by protocol.

Elizabeth smirked as she clapped her hands lightly.

The door behind Donovan opened. He swallowed heavily and turned to face . . .

A plain woman of medium height and middling years—perhaps thirty by the lines radiating from her bulging pale eyes, neither truly brown nor blue, just . . . pale, like the rest of her. Her mousy brown hair lay smooth against her skull, affixed into a severe knot at her nape. The heavy court gown of sober brown and gold drained the color and animation from her face. She might be passingly attractive if she wore the right color in a lighter gown and loosened her hair.

She dipped a hasty curtsy to the queen, never taking her prominent eyes off of Donovan.

"We wish to introduce Martha, Lady St. Claire, widow of Sir Wilfred," Elizabeth said around a smirk. "We have chosen her to be your bride, Milord Donovan of Kirkenwood. An admirable alliance of wealth and land, of old titles and new. We will host the wedding when the court returns to London in the autumn."

Chapter 36

Richmond Palace, London.

"I HAVE no desire to take another wife," Donovan muttered.

"You have mourned your bride for nigh on two years, milord," Dudley reprimanded him. His earlier smirk had dissolved into a serious frown.

Elizabeth tapped her foot beneath the wide skirt of her farthingale, making an odd counterpoint to the pounding of Donovan's heart. She'd thrown men into the Tower for less defiance than this.

"The Barony of Kirkenwood is too valuable to leave heirless." Elizabeth made the statement sound like an order. "You will marry at Michaelmas, milord, and get an heir on Lady St. Claire as quickly as possible. We will not allow your section of our border to fall vacant, without a protector."

"I am young yet, Majesty. Surely I have time to . . ."

"To what? To sire a passel of bastards who will tear the barony to pieces claiming their piece of it? You have had long enough to mourn your child bride. Now 'tis time to get on with securing the future."

Donovan met the queen's gaze with determined defiance, ignoring Martha, Lady St. Claire. The Tower be damned. He would control his life. "I have a daughter, Majesty. Betsy shows promise of becoming a true heir to my heritage." He left the implied reference to the Pendragon deliberately vague. Raven may have instructed him to give the ring of office to his son, but he could defy her, as he defied his queen.

Both had been known to make an occasional mistake.

"A titled woman becomes the source of much jealous controversy." Elizabeth's face became a stern mask. "We know how ambitious men leap to use a woman of property and prestige." Momentarily the queen turned her back on Donovan. Her hand reached to touch Dudley's where it rested on the arm of his chair.

Donovan couldn't help but remember the short-lived and bloody rebellion in Elizabeth's name shortly after Mary took the throne. Elizabeth had no knowledge of the plot and had not sanctioned it. But her name on the lips of the discontented had sent her to the tower.

"Save us, please, from war," Dudley pleaded. "A violent contest for your daughter's hand will leave the border vulnerable to attack by the Scots." The queen's lover grinned once more. His strong white teeth made a mocking slash across his swarthy face.

"Does Her Majesty agree that a woman alone cannot protect her own? My grandmother governed more than just Kirkenwood with grace and wisdom for many years before her marriage and after the deaths of her three husbands."

"Your daughter is too young to risk that she will be as strong as the revered Raven. You will marry Lady St. Clair as we have commanded." Elizabeth turned back to Donovan, her composure restored.

Donovan opened his mouth to protest, but Elizabeth jumped in before he could gather the words.

"Furthermore, we believe your marriage will be more . . . more amiable if you and your bride become better acquainted away from court this summer. She will travel with you to Kirkenwood and you will both return before Michaelmas for the nuptials. Leave us." She dismissed Donovan and his new lady with a wave of her hand.

"With luck, their son will be born shortly after the nuptials," Dudley chortled in an intimate whisper to the queen.

No. Donovan promised himself. *I will not give Dudley the satisfaction of proving him right. I'll not bed the lady until after the marriage. Perhaps not even then.*

Donovan marched through the various anterooms toward his own. "I ride out of Richmond within the hour," he snarled at Lady St. Clair.

She kept up with his long-legged stride, barely half a step behind him.

"I want this marriage no more than you, milord," Lady St. Claire said quietly when they finally cleared the streams of courtiers waiting for Elizabeth to emerge from her private quarters.

Donovan stopped abruptly. "Then why?"

"Because Elizabeth commands. I assure you, I have no need of your wealth or title. I have sufficient to live a gentle life. I care not if I produce heirs to my property. I have nieces who will need dowers."

"Wealth?" Donovan snorted. "What wealth? Living at court drains away whatever cash I can put together each summer. Soon I shall have to sell off my sheep—or my sisters—in order to support myself in the rudest of rooms in the city."

"Then why stay here? Why agree to the marriage?" she returned his question. A tiny sparkle of good humor flashed across her eyes. But it was gone almost as soon as she said the words.

"Because Elizabeth commands," he gave back to her. He allowed himself a tight smile. "You may follow me to Kirkenwood as best you can. I presume Elizabeth cares not if you summer in the barren north or not, so long as you absent yourself from court." He had noticed that the only ladies in the massive entourage who followed Elizabeth from palace to castle to manor were the few who attended her personally. Other titled ladies or the wives of her courtiers were not welcome. They might prove more beautiful than she and thus detract from the adoration the males of the court gave her.

"I shall ride with you, milord," Lady St. Claire stated.

"I ride fast and alone, without servants or furniture."

"Then I shall provide my own maid and we will both ride with you with a minimum of baggage."

"Can you not observe the hint that you are not welcome, Madame?"

"Whether I observe it or not, Elizabeth has commanded that I travel with you to Kirkenwood. Therefore I shall, rather than risk royal wrath."

"Women!" Donovan stalked off toward his room. "First Raven, then Kate and Betsy and Meg, and let us not forget meddling Fiona. Now Elizabeth and Martha St. Claire. They will be the death of me yet."

"I hope not. Since Elizabeth demands I marry, I intend to get a son from you and possibly a daughter before I am widowed yet again."

"More likely life in the north will kill you 'ere it touches me," Donovan said quietly. Suddenly he didn't like the tone of this conversation. "My castle is simple and cold, the land stark, the climate harsh, and war with the Scots threatens with every raid."

"I have lands and a goodly home in Kent. You may visit me there each winter while you attend the queen and Parliament," she replied heartily. "For this summer, I shall survey Kirkenwood and what you bring to this marriage." She lifted her skirts a bit and stalked ahead of him as if she brought him an ancient title and proud heritage dating back to King Arthur.

You won't be able to control her any easier than you can control your breathing or the four elements, Raven's voice chuckled in the back of his mind as if she stood directly behind his left shoulder.

A private manor, Paris, the end of June 1560.

"Bonjour, ma petite!" Charlotte de Guise, Countess Lafabvre cried enthusiastically to Roanna.

" 'Tis my honor to be your guest this evening." Roanna curtsied deep and long before the sister of the most powerful duc in all of France. The queen had granted Roanna leave to visit a de Guise relative this evening. All of Paris now sought the queen's soothsayer as an ornament at their gatherings. Roanna attended with or without permission.

She used the *salons* and *musicales* to learn all she could of the latest gossip. She needed to find a way to pry Queen Marie away from France and force her to return to Scotland. With or without King Francis' or Queen Regent Catherine's sanction.

"Ah, ma petite Rose." Countess Lafabvre grabbed Roanna by the shoulders until she stood straight and tall, then kissed her cheeks with the same vigor as her original greeting. Her ample bosom jiggled as she talked, clear evidence that she wore no corset, probably for shedding clothing with ease in the presence of her chosen lover for the evening. "We shall have such sport tonight. I have invited Bishop Eustachius du Bellay as well as my brother, Francis de Guise. They shall provide us with much heated debate—Brother Charles the Cardinal is far too self-important to add to the *salon*. But what is this simple ropa you wear? If you are to become my brother's newest mistress, you must wear something that will attract him. I will outfit you as will suit your position at court."

"Merci." Roanna bent her knees slightly in another acceptance of the lady's generosity. She and the countess had planned the seduction of Francis de Guise for many weeks. The duc had discarded his latest companion and been surly to one and all since.

"But your brother can bed any lovely lady who invests her money in silk and jewels and artifice to bedazzle a vulnerable man's senses. Mayhap, the good duc seeks someone different, with simple tastes but an intellect worthy of his political acumen?" She gave the duchesss a tiny, shy smile.

Charlotte laughed loudly and long. "Of course! Such simplicity. My brother will not know what has hit him." She flung her arms out in a flamboyant gesture, inviting the eye to survey her round figure. The countess was running to fat. But then some men preferred their women plump.

Roanna opened her mind a tiny fragment to make sure Tryblith listened to the countess' plans. She had almost no education and dabbled in politics only enough to know who needed to be assassinated in order to stir up trouble. She'd have to rely on the demon to give her the words to keep pace with Francis de Guise.

"*Mon Dieu,* but I shall enjoy watching my brother outwitted by a woman. When will men learn that women control true power. As long as they do not realize their brains rest between their legs, men are vulnerable. Imagine, at this very moment, France, England, and Scotland are all ruled by women, no matter how much men delude themselves that they control the world."

"But Scotland is truly ruled by the queen's brother, and Catherine de Médici rules France in her son's name,"

Roanna countered. "Therefore, the men believe these
countries are allied and ruled by men. This is why they
resent Elizabeth so much. She rules openly in her own
name. Philip of Spain, the Pope, even your brother, all feel
threatened by her. If she succeeds, they might have to acknowledge the other women of power in their world and
thus a diminishing of their own supposed control."

"Precisely. For now we shall allow them their little
delusion."

"And we shall manipulate them into doing exactly as
we wish." Roanna smiled despite the nagging pain Tryblith
twisted at the base of her skull. The demon was essentially
male. Let him seethe. He'd learn who manipulated whom
when she was finally able to break free of him.

"Just do as we planned, and I shall find you a nice boring
little lord for you to marry—one who will not object to you
wielding power in the beds of the mighty." Charlotte de
Guise flounced to her *chaise lounge*. Her girth spilled over
the narrow couch in places. She reclined carefully, ever
mindful of the limitations of her gown. No sense in
exposing too much too soon. In a studied pose she awaited
the remainder of her guests for the evening.

Roanna seethed. "A boring little lordling indeed. I'll find
my own husband, Your Ladyship," she muttered. "Perhaps
yours will oblige me?"

Yesssss! Tryblith hissed.

Roanna could almost see him rubbing together his hands
(Claws? Paws? She had no idea what form he took).

Half a dozen guests arrived together in a flurry of activity. A playwright with a better appreciation for the beauty
of the language than a story line pranced in alone. A wild-
eyed priest with no congregation but the rabble he roused
with his sermons in the *rues* of the roughest quarter of the
cité slithered in followed by three equally wild-eyed and
rudely dressed acolytes. A member of Catherine de Médici's Privy Council who had no love for the king's mother
came next, accompanied by three minor courtiers. Then a
pretty young man Roanna had seen about the court wandered past the countess almost unnoticed. His only claim
to fame or power was an infatuation with the king. Some
claimed he had access to the king's bedchamber. Roanna

knew the king had no interest in sharing his bed with anyone, male or female.

A few moments later a footman announced Eustachius du Bellay, Bishop of Paris. An unremarkable man of middle height, middle years, and growing middle, a person Roanna would bypass in a crowd as a nonentity, he seemed dwarfed by his purple robes and the great pectoral cross of amethyst and pearl. Two men, looking out of place in the fashionable garb of the laity, scuttled behind him. These men must be some form of escort or bodyguards, probably priests or monks trying to pass in public as ordinary people.

Appearances can be deceiving. Remember Griffin Kirkwood. Who would have thought him able to deflect your demon arrows, Tryblith reminded her. *Du Bellay is a mighty prince of the church. Do not underestimate him.*

"He is soft. Too tolerant of the Huguenots who plague this land with their religious reforms," Roanna retorted. "That is why our hostess seeks to persuade him to join with her brother and his Holy League: to shore up his sagging faith. At least in public. And add his voice and power to the nobles who want a total restoration of Catholic supremacy."

Do not underestimate him. His faith does not sag as his belly does. The fanatics of the Holy League are dangerous to you. But this man in his steadfast tolerance can find peace in France and be our undoing.

"Madame, *je suis très enchanté.*" Du Bellay kissed his hostess' outstretched hand, lingering several heartbeats too long.

"Aha!" Roanna said to herself. "The good bishop is not so steadfast in guarding against the sin of lust. I wonder if he has broken his vow of celibacy?"

The footman cleared his throat discreetly. The crowd hushed in anticipation. Duc Francis de Guise swept into the room.

Roanna gasped. She'd never seen a more handsome man in her life. The duc had absented himself from court for several months so she had not seem him to recognize him. That time two years ago when she disguised herself as a wild Highland prophet, all of her attention had been on Griffin Kirkwood, not the courtiers surrounding Marie.

Rumor had placed de Guise in Spain recently, conspiring with Philip against the de Médici regency.

"I think I'm in love," she whispered. Tall for a Frenchman, but not nearly as tall as Griffin Kirkwood, de Guise almost vibrated with energy. His aura filled the room, crowding out the personalities of every other person there. Wings of gray at his temples stood out in sharp contrast to his black hair. His features were larger, firmer versions of his sister's, the former regent of Scotland. The deep brown eyes, that had been soft in Marie de Guise, took on a burning intensity in her brother. Francis de Guise seemed to look through the artifice of clothing, skin, and bone deep into one's soul. In middle age, he retained his youthful figure and vigor.

Roanna's breasts grew heavy, her sense of smell grew keener, seeking this one man's musky allure. A weakness in her knees and moisture between her legs made her reach blindly for a chair, a stool, or table, anything to rest her weight against.

You thought Griffin Kirkwood the most handsome man in the world, Tryblith reminded her. His voice took on the sharp edge of one who seeks vulnerability in his prey.

Roanna had no doubt she was the demon's prey. At the moment she did not care. She could not take her eyes off the duc.

De Guise surveyed the room. His gaze lit briefly on his sister. He nodded to her and continued inspecting the assortment of personalities she had collected for the evening. He passed Roanna by, then stopped abruptly and returned his attention to her.

Had he peered past her inner self to find the demon who always resided in her mind?

One brief glance at her plain ropa, devoid of lace or embroidery, a few red curls artfully peeking from beneath her cap and veil, and his eyes snapped with a decision. He approached her with extended hand. She curtsied and kissed his ring, respectful protocol she had not given to the bishop.

"And where did *ma soeur* find you?" His voice sang to her, heating her blood until it moved in harmony with the timber of his vocal caress.

"I am but a simple Scottish lass seeking refuge from the

Protestant lords who now rule my land, Your Grace."
Roanna kept her eyes lowered demurely. She didn't dare
look at this man, lest he see her lust and use it against her.

"A sad tale, how Scotland has fallen into the ways of sin
along with England. My niece needs to send all of those
barbarian disciples of Satan to the gallows." His words condemned, but his tone continued to seduce her. His fingers
curled intimately around hers.

"What can Marie do? She cannot leave France. The Earl
of Moray has signed a treaty with England and sent all of
Marie's troops home to France. Her Majesty cannot correct
matters alone, from Paris. She needs your help, Your
Grace. She must return to Scotland to secure her kingdom
and the alliance." Roanna's voice sounded breathy with
anticipation to her own ears.

Use him as others have used you, Tryblith reminded her.
*Use his attraction to you to gain our ends. Marie must start
a war with her own lords and then with England.*

"This is a discussion that requires much serious thought
and a great deal of time—without interruptions. Perhaps
later?" de Guise asked.

"Later," Roanna promised. He hadn't even asked her
name.

De Guise tucked her hand into the crook of his elbow
and patted it twice. His gaze lingered on her lips a moment
and then he turned his attention back to his sister, the
hostess for the evening.

Roanna stayed at the duc's side the entire evening. She
listened intently to the political discussion. She ignored the
fanatical priest. His following was too uncertain of numbers
and permanency. The playwright she also dismissed as
being of little consequence. He was interested only in re-
writing the phrases uttered by the other guests so that they
tripped more eloquently from his tongue than theirs.

But the bishop and the duc both presented arguments
for and against tolerance and reform. Bishop du Bellay's
sincerity seemed to sway the Countess Lafabvre. But then
she had shown her prejudice the moment the cleric arrived.
De Guise, on the other hand, held the attention of all those
present—even the fanatical priest—by the force of his
personality.

"We must stand fast against the Protestants. Only by

adhering to the Holy Father's ruling can we hope to preserve the true faith and peace within France. Without internal peace we cannot maintain the strength to protect our beloved country from invasion from the south as well as from across La Manche," de Guise argued. "Philip of Spain has the right of it. We need an Inquisition to root out heresy in all its most subtle forms. No one must even think of veering from the path set for us by the Holy Father in Rome." He looked around the room, capturing the gaze of each eager listener in turn.

Had anyone noticed his lapse in logic? Roanna wondered. At the same time he wanted to protect France from Spanish invasion from the south and implement the Spanish Inquisition.

"The very severity of Philip's Inquisition drives true believers into the arms of the Protestants," du Bellay countered. "Look what happened in England during Mary Tudor's reign." He spoke calmly, rationally.

Roanna sensed the mood of the room shifting in favor of the bishop.

"The Inquisition failed in England because Elizabeth bewitched the populace. She is Satan's spawn and no true heir of the Tudors!" de Guise spat. "Magic runs rampant throughout England, unchecked by the church. Indeed, Elizabeth has the audacity to send her most famous magician, Dr. John Dee, as emissary to our own regent. He says he has come to negotiate on behalf of the treasonous Treaty of Edinburgh. The English demand we sign away the lawful rights of our queen, Marie Stuart, to claim the throne of England. I say beware one and all lest this man cast his evil eye on every member of the Privy Council to force them to sign the vile document. The only way to eradicate the spells and enticements of the Protestant wizards is to restore our troops in Scotland, and invade England from there."

No one spoke. The hush remained unbroken for many moments.

"Perhaps you should be regent for Francis and Marie instead of Catherine," Roanna suggested quietly. In the unnatural silence her voice sounded loud, almost proclaiming. "You are aware of the dangers Dr. Dee presents. You can nullify his powers with your faith, Your Grace.

You can lead France to victory in both the physical and spiritual war against the English."

De Guise looked down upon her. He held her hand tightly where it still rested in the crook of his elbow.

"Perhaps you are right, my dear. Catherine is weak, a woman, prone to vapors and Dee's unnatural influence."

"But, *mon cher frère,*" the countess added, "you must take up the reins of government soon. Your claim to the regency is through Marie, your neice, wife of Francis. But Francis is weak, often ill. If he dies while his mother holds power, then she will continue as regent for her second son, Charles."

Later in the dark of night, when the city slept, Roanna whispered into the ear of her duc. "I know how to assassinate Catherine. She is heavily guarded while in public, has a taster check every meal for poison. But Dr. Dee is an alchemist. He knows the secret poison of the Borgias." French alchemists claim he'd also found the Philosopher's Stone that gives the possessor unlimited magical power. Roanna intended to steal the stone from him as well as the poison formula. "He knows of the poison that is tasteless, odorless, and delays acting upon the victim for three days so that no one can trace the poisoner or the time of the poisoning. If I can get the formula from him, I can introduce it to Catherine's wine at any time."

"No need, *chérie.* I already have plans for Catherine." He caressed her face, trailing his fingers down to her naked breasts.

Heat flooded through Roanna once more. She leaned closer to him, weak with wanting.

"Use the poison on Elizabeth, sweet Rose. She is the greater enemy. You sail tomorrow at dawn," he whispered. Then he heaved himself over onto his side and began to snore heavily.

Chapter 37

Whitefriars Abbey, London, England

AT the Whitefriars Abbey glassworks, I found a respite from the anxious questions I could not answer for myself. After an adequate supper of thin, meatless stew and a thick, coarse rye bread—it satisfied far more than the soft fluffy stuff served in France—I cleared an area near the altar within the original chapel. Casks of minerals, sacks of charcoal, and barrels of foodstuffs filled most of the nave. Before I could resanctify the broken altar, Ralph wandered in.

"Would you hear my confession, Father?" he asked, looking at his shuffling feet.

"Gladly." I fished my stole out of the box of Holy Water, incense, oil, and candles I had brought with me. A stillness came over me as I kissed the cross embroidered at the center of the long strip of fabric—since I had only one set of vestments, I had chosen a white stole as appropriate to all occasions.

The confessional was still buried under supplies, so Ralph settled on the step of the dais. I plopped down with my back resting against the altar. We each made the sign of the cross. My rosary came to my fingers. And I listened.

One by one, the refugees trooped in, seeking solace in the knowledge that God forgives the truly repentant. As each story unfolded, of petty theft, violence, debt, suspected witchcraft because the woman was attractive and alone, and sometimes no greater sin than being orphaned, or bastard born, and thrust out onto the streets at a tender age, I murmured prayers for all such refuse of life in the city. Had any of my family been so callous as to treat our people with so little regard that extreme poverty drove them to such desperate measures? I hoped not and prayed for my own forgiveness.

None of them had rosaries to count the prayers I assigned them for the minor offenses. I wondered if Brother Jeremy would allow his glassworks to make a consignment of beads and crosses.

Near midnight, when I should ring the bell to recite the office of Matins, a young woman, younger than Fiona and in the final stage of pregnancy waddled in, supported by the hulking brute I had watched blow glass this afternoon. His tender concern for her welfare showed in the way he touched her hair when she paused for breath at the foot of the altar. She clutched at the bulk of the baby with a spasming fist.

Brother Jeremy trooped after them, concern written all over his face.

I scrambled to my feet, alarmed at the girl's pale face and sweating brow.

"Father, will you marry us?" the girl gasped.

"Are you in agreement of the match?" I asked the man.

"Aye, Father. I wanted to go into the city and search out a priest months ago. But she wouldn't let me leave Whitefriars," the man replied in an accent that shouted of his origins among the moors and heather in the north.

"Please, Father. I do not want this child born a bastard," the girl insisted, pausing twice in her short speech to breathe.

"I agree, Father Griffin. I consent to my daughter's marriage," Jeremy added. He added his arm to support her as her knees nearly gave way under another contraction.

"We have not much time." I tugged a missal free of my belt where it normally rested.

Meg must have followed them into the chapel, knowing their mission. She slipped between the sacks of sand and the casks of cobalt, a silent shadow who needed to be there but did not want to intrude. I presumed she had left the dogs with Robin.

Ralph hovered near the door. A second unrelated witness to make the marriage legal. I would begin a new parish book this night to record the ceremony. My neglected journal would get a fuller accounting.

The bride breathed deeply, nearly doubling over in pain. Meg stepped up beside her and presented her with a single yellow flower of wild endive. The weed grew rampant in the cracks and crevices of the cloister. My sister smiled and a halo of light seemed to grow out from the two candles I had lit. The aura enshrouded us in its beneficence.

And so I married Gareth and Carola. Their daughter came into this world moments later with only Meg to help. Jeremy retreated with Ralph while Gareth and I recited prayers throughout the mysterious and miraculous process.

But the baby's skin was blue, and she made no sound as she opened her mouth.

"What's wrong with my baby?" Carola wailed.

Gareth choked on his sobs.

"She drowned." Meg looked at me, helpless as she held the baby, still attached to her mother through the umbilical cord.

The infant continued to open and close her mouth, making no sounds, taking in no air. I had seen this same helpless gesture before. Back home, when a village child had wandered away from his mother and fallen into the lake beside the kirk. What had Raven done to save the boy?—for even now he worked with the sheep of Kirkenwood.

I grabbed the baby away from my sister, balancing her facedown on my palm. With my free hand, I thumped her back gently. A faint gurgling sound greeted me. She did indeed drown in the fluids from within the womb. I stuck my finger into her tiny mouth, circled and crooked it slightly and withdrew a long rope of thick mucus.

The baby gagged. I thumped her back again. More of the goo dribbled out of her mouth. Clear and thump. Clear and thump. At last she seemed to be free of the choking liquid.

Still she did not breathe easily.

I flipped her over, pinched her nose and breathed into her tiny mouth. Once, twice, thrice. A thin wail finally erupted from her.

Carola sobbed. Gareth fell to his knees, crossing himself repeatedly. "A miracle. You've performed a miracle," he proclaimed with each cross.

"Only common sense," I insisted.

Meg merely smiled and delivered the afterbirth.

"A miracle," Carola agreed.

"No miracle. Experience and God's will." I placed the babe into her mother's arms.

"Like Merlin of old, he commands the forces of nature to work God's will," Jeremy said quietly from the doorway. I hadn't realized he had remained. But then a concerned father needed to know the worst, or the best, during the birth of his grandchild.

"Merlin . . ." Gareth said. "Merlin the Magician from the King Arthur tales. I remember the stories. Me mam used to sing to us of their wondrous deeds."

"Uh . . ." I replied. "I'm just a man. A priest," I protested.

"Are you, Father Griffin?" Meg asked. Sanity shone through her gaze.

Kirkenwood, high summer 1560.

"Must you follow me everywhere, woman?" Donovan asked Martha for the umpteenth time. He had approached the gallery by a circuitous route, stopping in the nursery for a visit with Betsy and her two older, illegitimate brothers. Then he had gone into the bedchamber, supposedly to rest his leg. He'd feigned a more severe limp than necessary as part of his ruse. When he thought no one was in either the hall or the upper rooms, he had crept silently toward the hidden door on stockinged feet.

"I thought you were resting that old injury," Martha St. Claire said. Her very stillness told him of her determination to ferret out every last one of his secrets.

All he truly wanted was a modicum of talent, a spell, a potion, anything that would help him find Meg. She had wandered away from Kirkenwood and not returned. Griffin had written that he cared for her. But Donovan couldn't trust Griffin. His twin was as likely to abandon their sister as sell her to the stews in London when he tired of the responsibility of her—as he tired of his responsibility to the family heritage.

"Your pain could portend a thunderstorm," Martha suggested. "Though not a cloud mars the sky." Her eyes narrowed in suspicion.

"God's Bones!" he exploded. "This is my home. And you are not yet my lady wife. I do not have to report my movements to you." He sat down on one of the stools left behind by the wandering minstrels who had earned their supper with an evening of song last night. Jerkily he pulled on his boots.

No wonder Elizabeth had been so anxious to send Martha St. Claire to Kirkenwood. The two women were both bossy, stubborn, and convinced every decision they made was right.

Each pack of wolfhounds had one leading female or one leading male. Challengers either left or died in battle. Elizabeth and Martha would have killed each other if Martha had to stay at court.

"If I am to be your lady wife, then I have a right to know everything about the management of this place, including what lies behind the secret door over there." She pointed directly to the wood panels that hid the entry to the tunnel and the lair.

Donovan minded not if she discovered his alchemy laboratory. But what if she sniffed out the journals and records and magical grimoires from ages past? The Kirkwoods did not actively hide their descent from King Arthur, neither did they advertise it. But they rarely mentioned as close a link to the Merlin. Their heritage as the Pendragons of Britain was known to only a few highly placed members of the royal family and their chosen confidants. Knowledgeable magicians and wise men like Dr. Dee knew, but more from their own research than common gossip.

Security lay in never drawing attention to the true antiquity and power of the family. He certainly was not about to share with this nosy woman all that he knew.

Martha must have spied upon him two days ago when he left his bed in the middle of the night. He'd spent several happy hours blissfully alone with his books and his potions and his star charts. He had discovered a reference to ghost-weed in an old grimoire as part of a spell to subdue demons. Now he needed to learn how to identify the herb.

Maybe then he could converse with angels and open himself to his true talent. Surely the ghostweed would reveal Meg's whereabouts and help him expel the demon church from England.

Not while this woman watched his every move. He liked her as well as he liked Elizabeth—not at all.

"I'm going hunting." Donovan rose and stalked toward the stairs, not acknowledging the secret door by glance or thought.

"Then I shall have to delve into the secrets of this place by myself. Would you please hand me that rushlight, milord?" She turned calculating eyes upon him even as her stubby fingers probed the crease made by the joining of two wooden panels in the wainscoting. As she bent over to look closer, her skirt—minus the blasted farthingale required for court dress but rarely at home—rose up to reveal an enticing amount of ankle. He admired the view for a few heartbeats, then caught himself.

"What did I do to deserve you?" he asked the air, rolling his eyes upward.

"You made Dudley jealous by attracting Elizabeth's attention." Martha threw the comment over her shoulder as she continued her inspection. Her twisting body shifted her bodice a trifle, pushing her breasts above her corset.

He'd gone too long without a woman. Too long indeed if he found Martha St. Claire enticing.

Maybe he could distract her with sex and soothe his itch at the same time.

He ran his hand up her exposed ankle. She sat back on her heels and stared at him with suspicion, and—and something else he didn't want to put a name to.

"You can delay my investigation, but you cannot stop me." Her voice came out a little breathless. Her breasts rose up, nearly freeing themselves of the corset.

"Can't I?" He resumed his seat on the stool, close enough to grasp her shoulders and bring her into his lap. He traced the edge of her bodice with a delicate finger, following with a trail of kisses.

"Milord, we are not yet wed," she protested. But only mildly.

"Short of killing you, or murdering Elizabeth, we might

as well be." He moved up to claim her lips before she could protest again. Fire ignited his loins. He deepened the kiss.

She opened her mouth as she threw her arms about his neck, pressing her enticing bosom against his chest.

His hand sought her neatly turned ankle beneath the voluminous skirts.

She traced his ear with a delicate fingertip. And then she kissed it, blowing gently against the sensitive organ.

Tingles ran up his spine.

Eventually they broke free, drawing deep breaths. She clung to him. He gathered himself to carry her into the bedchamber.

"But 'tis broad daylight! The household . . ."

"Is busy about their own business."

"But . . ."

"You have nothing to fear, Martha. I'll not hurt you. Indeed, I shall teach you to enjoy the experience as your first husband did not."

She had confessed that the elderly Lord St. Claire had barely consummated the marriage before taking ill and requiring her to tend his needs for years until he finally succumbed and died.

Donovan's own marriage, with Kate's youthful verve and imagination, had been happy enough while it lasted.

Martha had proved an astute observer and economical manager, even if she was argumentative and too curious for her own safety or his peace of mind.

He kissed her again. As long as she pressed her bosom against him, he could ignore the fact that he did not truly like her. As long as he accepted and did not think, they'd deal well enough together.

The alarm bell tolled long and loud from the watchtower.

"God's arse, not now."

"What is it, Donovan?" she asked. Confusion clouded her eyes.

"Someone comes. Probably raiders. They'll want the barley harvest." He set her down abruptly, not telling her how unusual it was for the Scots to attack in broad daylight. "I must go."

He stalked toward the stairs, already reaching for the sword he must strap on. Memories of the last raid shuddered through him. He stopped and returned to where she stood, swaying a little.

To hell with his secrets and his pride. "Hide yourself," he ordered, triggering the hidden latch for the door. "Close the door and latch it from inside. Even if the Scots breach the walls, they'll not find you in there."

"My place is by your side, milord."

"Dammit, woman, just this once do not argue with me!"

She clamped her mouth shut, but set her chin in a determined expression he knew meant defiance.

"I have not the time to tie you up. But if I find you dead at the end of this day's work, I'll . . . I'll . . ."

"You'll what?"

"Women!" Donovan threw his hands up in the air and went about the business of protecting his castle and his people. He had no doubt that Martha St. Claire followed in his wake, joining the women in their assigned tasks.

"I'd better not find you dead at the end of this day," she said quietly as they descended the stairs.

Whistling a jaunty battle song of old, Donovan strapped on his sword and rushed into the bailey, shouting orders as he ran.

Chapter 38

Kirkenwood.

HACK, slash, parry, thrust, withdraw, lunge. Donovan pushed his way through the village, felling the desperate Scots right and left. The poor sods hadn't a chance. Must be an extremely bleak harvest after a hard winter. They faced starvation unless they could liberate grain and live-stock from across the border. These raids had almost become a ritual.

A Scot with a crude ax screamed a hoarse battle cry and hurled himself at Donovan. Vaguely he felt a hot slice across his ribs followed by a gush of warmth. He ducked and thrust beneath the man's frantic rush, jabbing his sword into his gut as he rolled. He came up covered in gore and the stink of death.

His sword skewered a wild-eyed Scot with a gaunt face beneath his ragged beard. Donovan's gaze locked with his enemy's. For a moment he understood and sympathized. Next year he might be the one risking a desperate daylight raid because hunger overcame the good sense to wait for midnight at the dark of the moon.

"If you'd asked politely, I might have shared a bit with you," he said through clenched teeth. Then he slammed his left fist into the man's face.

His opponent reared back and fell to his knees.

Donovan rebalanced, preparing to kick the man sense-less.

But the tall, bony Scot fell forward, eyes rolling up.

Donovan looked around for another raider to engage. The few left standing retreated as rapidly as they had come.

The fight drained out of Donovan all of a sudden. His

knees wobbled, and his face was cold and clammy. And yet heat spread from his ribs outward in a consuming fire. Darkness crowded the edges of his vision.

"Not yet. I can't give up yet," he whispered to himself. Rousing a little he braced himself on his sword, like a cane, and surveyed the wreckage of the village: two fires, and the door of the grain barn hung open like a great maw. Women and children huddled in the shadows. Soldiers and tenants alike stared at the wreckage, taking deep breaths of relief.

"Give them decent burial. Have Father Peter say Mass."

"Milord?" one of the soldiers from the castle asked. "They're filthy, thieving Scots!"

"They were hungry men, desperate to feed their families. They died with honor. Next year we might be raiding them in the same circumstances. I would hope they'd have the decency to bury us with respect." His last words trailed off into a whisper as his knees gave out and the darkness slammed into him like a horse kick to his chest.

"I thought I told you to take care of yourself," Martha admonished Donovan.

He opened heavy eyes to find her bending over him, that determined thrust of her chin hiding an almost trembling lip.

"Did not," he mumbled. "You said 'I'd better not find you dead.'" He closed his eyes again, too weary to do aught else. Vaguely he realized that he lay in his own bed and that something as stiff as a corset constricted his breathing.

"If you can quote me so precisely, then I presume you will live." Martha sniffed.

Donovan risked opening one eye a crack. "I'll live. But did you have to bind me up with this devilish device. I can't breathe properly."

"The wound is deep. We feared the ribs cracked. But I did not see any air bubbles in the blood, so I presume your lung was not pierced," she replied. "Are you in a great deal of pain?" Her tone softened.

"God's wounds, it feels like fire every time I take a breath."

"I found some ghostweed in the herb garden. It will help you sleep." She half rose from the edge of the bed before he stopped her with a firm grip on her arm.

The effort to hold her brought a new wave of pain and dizziness. He fought it. "Did you say ghostweed?" he asked through clenched teeth as he rode the wave of fire in his chest.

"Aye." She looked at him questioningly.

"Dr. Dee suggested I try ghostweed."

" 'Tis a marvelous sedative, but dangerous. Too much brings delirium and death."

"I need it for my experiments."

She said nothing, staring at him, challenging him to say more.

Dared he?

"I'm an alchemist."

"Dr. Dee is also a noted magician. What do you need ghostweed for?" A note of accusation crept into her voice.

"Dr. Dee thinks the drug will open my mind to speak with angels."

"More likely devils and demons. The weed is also called Devil's Trumpet. Mayhap I should destroy it, burn out the roots."

"No. I need the ghostweed to free my mind of mundane walls."

"I have heard rumors and legends about your family. Are you really all magicians of great talent? Does Elizabeth show you favor because she fears your curses?"

"Elizabeth doesn't fear anything, least of all me." Neither did Martha.

"Answer my question, Donovan. Are you a magician?"

"No, I am not. But my brother is. And I need to be to claim . . . to claim . . ."

She continued staring at him with that stubborn chin, demanding the truth by her silence.

"God's death, must I give you the entire family history?"

"Will it take that to explain yourself?"

"It will. Not many know the full truth of the Pendragon. They know only rumors of great magic. But it is more. A great deal more."

"More? As in the faces in the standing stones that stare at me with accusations? Why do they think me an intruder and usurper?" She almost sobbed.

" 'Tis a long tale, but we have time. We have all the time

in the world." He pulled her down beside him, cradling her against his side.

Whitefriars Abbey, London England, summer 1560.

Over the next few months I learned to make glass beads for rosaries. Brother Jeremy dug out a few tools for me from his hoard. They'd come from his family glassworks near Chester on the Dee estuary. I didn't ask why he had been exiled from them to this sanctuary for criminals. At first my efforts were clumsy, lopsided blobs that clung perversely to the mandrels, the fine metal rods that kept a hole in the middle. These I broke off and sent back into the gather to remelt for another attempt. I could not see the delicate work except in the strongest light. But gradually I learned to feel the proper rotation of the mandrel, guess at the chill marks when I touched a bead too long to my marver, the heat-proof working surface.

The simplest method of bead making involved long canes of hollow glass. These we cut at precise intervals then tumbled together while still warm to smooth off the edges. But the tumbler broke, and no Gypsies presented themselves at the gate to mend it.

Meg strung my finished beads on twine, with decorative knots between the beads. Crosses we carved of old wood from broken casks. Crucifixes proved too much for my limited artistic abilities, though Gareth made a crude mold for a larger Celtic cross to place on the altar. By the end of summer my flock had rosaries to help them count their prayers.

I continued making beads for the joy of the creation. Brother Jeremy taught me to make glass into solid canes. I stuffed a blob of molten glass into a mold and cooled it enough to remove the mold. A thorough reheating and our leader attached a second rod to the other end of the disk of glass. We then walked in opposite directions, stretching the cane to the proper dimension. Then we broke them into convenient working lengths. With canes, I could work in different colors regardless of what came out of the gather furnace that day. I began experimenting with multiple colors in the same bead.

Color led me to experimentation in size, shape, and decoration. True liberation of my creativity came with an order for a set of fine goblets and a decanter in ruby red with gold foil decoration. While Jeremey and Gareth struggled to find the proper mix of gold in the gather to create a true ruby color, I played with the foil on the surface of my beads. The tiniest bit stretched and became a glittering mosaic.

A merchant bought a handful of the decorated beads for his wife and took them to a jeweler to be strung on fine gold wire. After that, my beads became a regular source of income for Whitefriars. The merchant and trade classes who could not afford to deck their clothing in fine jewels substituted glass beads that glittered and caught the light.

I could work glass in the dim gray world my eyes often gave me. Glass cooled to its own color regardless of what I did to it. I could determine shape and size in the strong light cast by the ovens. A sense of accomplishment blossomed within me. My journal filled with notes of color mixes and mandrel diameter rather than the politics of Church and State.

While I waited for the end of the day to scavenge the last of the glass for my beads, I learned the value of cleaning the furnace, sweeping the ashes from the fire into a bucket for soapmaking, and breaking free the cooled glass that adhered to the sides of the oven. The white clay lining of the gather and glory hole reflected heat and light back into the mix, making it hotter than mere heating by charcoal. Hard work. Mindless work that allowed me the mental freedom to plan my next sermon, a catechism class, ways to seek pardons for some of the refugees who had committed minor offenses and certainly done penance through the years of hard labor in the glassworks.

Eventually, cleaning the gather oven and restocking it with sand, potash, and lime and whatever additives Brother Jeremy dictated—cobalt for blue, copper and iron for greens, took only half the workday. Hauling charcoal, sand, and other ingredients for the ovens from the river barges up through the old abbey to the chapel strengthened muscles I did not know existed until they ached beyond movement.

Meg helped mind the children. Helwriaeth kept a watchful eye on the toddlers, occasionally hauling them away from dangerous fires and scalding tools by grabbing the wanderer by the seat of the pants in her gentle jaws. I'd watched her carry puppies in much the same manner. Newynog's boundless energy found outlet at the well wheel as I had predicted. She thought it a great game as long as I stopped to scratch her ears every time I passed her. Gruff and scowling characters, filthy enough and mean enough to belong only in children's nightmares, followed my example and provided both wolfhounds with enough rough affection to keep them satisfied.

Whitefriars had an amazing effect on all of us. Something about the hard work isolated from the pressures of the city that lay just beyond our walls, gave us all a measure of inner peace. The time for reflection had made changes in all of us.

Removed from politics and the quests for power and control, I watched true faith blossom within my little flock. They cared not for theological arguments, did not question dogma. We all worshiped simply, united in a quest for divine inspiration and guidance.

The Pope in Rome and my own bishop in Paris seemed much too far away to have importance to any of us. I suppressed my guilt that I neglected my mission.

Despite the isolation of Whitefriars, the locals heard about "The Merlin" and his miracles. They flocked to hear my sermons.

One bright Sunday, as summer reached its height, I lounged upon the grassy bank between the river gate and the water's edge, chewing on a piece of grass and letting the sun soak into my aching body. Gareth sat beside me with his infant daughter in his lap. I'd baptized her Faith three days after her birth.

"I never thought I could love anyone as much as I love this little scrap of life," Gareth said, gazing at the sleeping babe with amazement. "I love Carola. I know that. I'd die

for her. But this one . . . this one eats at my soul and ties
it in knots. I worry about her living here, a criminal condemned for what I did, not for any fault of her own.''

"What did you do?" I asked. Gareth had not yet made
confession to me. A number of men had not, as if they
believed themselves beyond forgiveness.

"I killed a man."

I sat a little straighter and stiffer. "I, too, have taken a
life," I confessed. "Years ago. I lived up near the border.
Raiding the Scots and being raided by them was a way of
life. In the heat of battle, I killed, more than once." But ever
since my magic had truly awakened under that awesome vision of triple crowns and a legendary sword, I had shared in
the death of those around me, guiding them beyond their
fears into the light. I could never willingly take another life
again. I feared I'd have to follow them into whatever afterlife
awaited them, heaven or hell, or extended purgatory. I had
no fear of dying, my faith promised much, but I wanted the
fate I had earned and not someone else's.

"Aye. I know what happens when your blood is up. Your
mind and your soul close down," Gareth agreed.

We fell into a painful silence, each reliving past moments
we'd rather forget.

"How did it happen?" I finally asked.

"I was young. I got drunk at harvest. My best friend was
drunker. He insulted the lass I lusted after. I hit him."

"Not so great a crime."

"But I kept hitting him. Me with my great fists and the
strength of my shoulders. Him just a scrawny thing with
barely a muscle on him. I hit him until he pleaded for
mercy and then I hit him again. His face was a bloody pulp.
He stopped screaming them. My da had to break my arm
to pull me off him even after he was dead." He held up
his right arm with an ugly knot in the forearm I had
thought scar tissue from a burn. Every glassworker had
burns of some degree or another. Even me. Gareth's broken arm had healed, but not exactly right.

Silence again. I didn't know what to say.

"There is no sanctuary for murder," I finally said quietly.

"No one who cares about Geordie's death knows I'm
here. The queen's men don't search this place for criminals,
even if they know the one they pursue lodges here.''

"That's why Carola wouldn't allow you to leave long enough to find a priest to marry you."

"Your coming was a miracle, just in time. Life will be hard enough for our little Faith without the taint of bastardy."

I reached over to caress Faith's downy fluff of light brown hair. The moment my fingers touched her, flashing yellow-and-red light blinded me. Shudders ran through me, twisting my belly in knots. My knees shook and my mouth went dry. I saw the infant grown to womanhood, skin so soft she looked kissed by dew, fine hair bound up in jeweled combs—not jewels, but sparkling glass. She wore a simple dark gown edged in lace and stood before an altar, facing a priest I did not know. Beside her stood a nervous man, eager to take his wedding vows and end this endless ritual. Candlelight on vivid altar vestments, scintillating prisms refracting from glass, life as bright and clearly defined as I thought it should be but could never quite see.

The over-bright colors of the vision faded to the dusty grass and cracking mud of the riverbank, made duller by my damaged vision. "Faith will prosper, my friend," I said. Something in the vision was not quite right. But since I could not decipher the queasy feeling in my gut, akin to extreme apprehension, I said nothing more to the father of the lovely baby.

"Can you truly see the future, Father?" Gareth asked in awe.

"Sometimes. When God grants."

"Then you truly are the Merlin?"

"Nothing quite so simple, nor so complex. I am but a priest trying to do God's will." And attain the right to call myself the Pendragon, one of Merlin's descendants. Only then could I justify the presence of magic in me.

But to act as the Pendragon I'd have to leave this haven, go out into the world and actively seek peace and prosperity for Britain.

My vision of the future required that Britain become unified in one religion, behind one strong monarch. Until Catholics and Protestants came to an accord, we faced civil war that would leave us weak and vulnerable to invasion.

I had to leave this place of peace. But where would I go? How would I ensure Robin's safety and keep him from becoming a focus for rebellion?

"Father Merlin! Father Merlin," a child cried as he pelted across the cloister and through the river gate. I think his name was Michael. I hadn't had time to learn all of the children or identify them by family grouping or as orphan. "Father Merlin, there's a woman at the gate asking for you."

"Asking for me, or asking for the Merlin?" I scrambled up from the embankment, dusting my soutane free of grass and dirt.

"For both," Michael panted. "She told Ralph she must speak with the priest, Father Griffin, who is known to one and all as the Merlin."

A chill ran up my spine.

I approached the gate cautiously, hoping Ralph had had the sense to keep the woman outside our walls until we learned her identity and mission.

"Father Griffin, we meet at last." A gentle voice with an accent that spoke of wild heather, misty moors, and a perpetual wind—of home—greeted me.

I looked closely at the mourning-clad woman who stood just inside the gate. Her big gray eyes opened wide. I nearly fell into their depths, losing myself in the mysteries of life that she could share.

For the first time since taking my priestly vows, I experienced a deep longing for hearth and home, wife and children.

"How may I serve you, madam?" I shook myself free of the spell she wrapped around me.

" 'Tis how I may serve you. Bishop Eustachius du Bellay sent me with messages and a new commission."

The fine hair along my spine stood up in warning. All traces of lust and longing vanished within me. My bishop would never have used a woman as a messenger.

"Whom may I thank in my prayers for delivering the message?" I asked warily, holding out my hand for a written missive. Eustachius du Bellay would not rely upon someone misinterpreting an oral message. He'd write it down, in code if necessary.

"Roanna de Planchet, widow of Giles, Count de Planchet." She nodded her head graciously and held out her left hand bearing an elaborate signet ring. Still no sign of a written message.

"Demons. She smells of demons!" Meg screamed. She stood in the center of the cloister tearing her hair, gouging the skin of her scalp with ragged fingernails. Around her, the youngest children took up her cries of fright. Their walls rang around the stone walls of Whitefriars as if demons had indeed been loosed.

The dogs howled their distrust.

Chapter 39

Whitefriars.

SO, it was true, Bishop Eustachius du Bellay had made Griffin Kirkwood his pet spy in England. Roanna almost laughed. Duc Francis de Guise had known whom Roanna must find as well as where she would find him, two of the bishop's most trusted secrets.

Was there no end to the man's power?

But the duc is not the most handsome man in the world. Griffin Kirkwood, the Pendragon of England is, Tryblith whispered into her ear. *He's a priest. Think of the power his fall from grace will give us. Seduce him. He's already half in love with you.*

Seducing the priest might give Tryblith magical power, but Francis de Guise could give Roanna temporal power. He'd already given her a title and a pension by marrying her to one of his retainers in a proxy ceremony. The fact that the retainer had died two days before the wedding ceremony did not bother the duc. They had consummated the marriage for the deceased count. And oh, what glorious, decadent heights of ecstasy Francis had given her aboard ship as they sailed down the Seine to Rouen. She could still taste the slightly salty, slightly sweet mix from licking wine off his cock.

Would Griffin Kirkwood taste so fine? She doubted it.

The duc had said upon ripping her wedding clothes from her back, "I'll leave chastity to my wife. But God gave men needs that must be relieved, therefore he also created women like you to minister to us. No reason we both cannot enjoy the essential."

For the first time in her life, Roanna had reached climac-

tic ecstasy. Not just once, but every time he entered her.
She'd never taken a more exciting and interesting lover.

Seducing Griffin Kirkwood meant more than using his
body. She needed control of his mind as well. Even Tryblith
would gain power from just watching Griffin Kirkwood assassinate Elizabeth of England.

First she had to stop the mindless blonde woman here
in Whitefriars from screaming the truth and ruining the
entire mission.

*Kill the screaming bitch and the bevy of children clinging
to her skirts,* Tryblith commanded as if bored rather than
apprehensive that the woman had actually sensed the
demon's presence. *Kill the dogs, too. They annoy me.*

"The noise," Roanna protested, clutching her temples.
Surreptitiously she rubbed her eyes to redden them. She
allowed herself to sway a little. Her skin burned inside the
cloister—some kind of ward against demons. But she and
Tryblith were stronger than Griffin Kirkwood's halfhearted
splashes of holy water. If he had truly wanted to keep
demons away, he would have used magic as well.

"Helwriaeth, guard!" Father Griffin commanded. A monstrous wolfhound sprang from her place behind the priest to
stand in front of the screaming woman and the brood of
children. The dog snarled and drooled into her gray-mottled
beard. Her teeth glistened in the sunlight. The tension in
her hind legs showed the wolfhound was prepared to leap
upon anyone who threatened her charges.

A second wolfhound joined the first. This one was more
lithe, less gray, and taller at the shoulder. A war dog with
the scent of the enemy on the tongue.

Roanna recoiled.

Tryblith at last recognized them as a threat and vacated
Roanna's mind.

Suddenly free of the weight of him, she reeled slightly;
had to clutch Father Griffin's cassock to retain her balance.

The dogs and the woman ceased their noise.

"Are there truly demons lurking in the shadows?"
Roanna opened her eyes wide, hoping she looked innocent
and vulnerable.

"Only in my sister's mind," Father Griffin said quietly.
But he looked strangely at the dogs. "Come, share our
supper and join us for Mass later. We deny refuge to

none." He swept his arms out to encompass the entire cloister where perhaps two dozen adults in ragged clothing lurked. The stoop-shouldered man in the corner, whose arms nearly touched his knees, could have been the legendary hunchbacked demon that haunted the bell tower of Notre Dame de Paris. A gap-toothed woman of ancient years had milky eyes that certainly could throw curses right and left with ease. And the children! Filthy, ragged imps of Earth, Air, Fire, and Water bent upon causing trouble with every thought.

Roanna swallowed the unaccustomed fears and stepped boldly to Father Griffin's side. "We have much to discuss, Father Merlin."

He cringed at the title. And yet she noticed a glint of pride in his eyes and a settling of his shoulders as if welcoming a responsibility.

"Bishop Eustachius has joined with the Duc de Guise and the Holy League. We need a miracle worker with a strong faith to end the tyranny of Elizabeth the Bastard so that France may sign a treaty of peace with England."

"Is there a plan or just rhetoric and postulations?" Father Griffin headed her toward one of the buildings. Their path took them directly in front of the madwoman whose screams had subsided to incoherent mumblings. The dogs continued to growl as they lifted their noses, sniffing and baring their teeth in confusion.

The demon they had been trained to sniff out had left.

"First Marie Stuart must return to Scotland and restore order to her barons," Roanna outlined her plan. "When the Queen of Scots is poised to claim her rightful throne in England, the Holy League will act." Roanna shied away from the madwoman. Father Griffin looked puzzled.

"Use your magic to see the truth, brother," the madwoman hissed. "See the demon that sat upon her left shoulder where death should reside. It is gone now, but she still stinks of sulfur. She brings death. She reeks of death and chaos."

I looked for the demon, holding my staff above my head
defensively. I scented nothing out of the ordinary. Only
Countess Roanna's delicate, floral scent wafted across my
nose. I breathed deeply of her, bewildered and confused
by Meg's rants and the apparent absence of a demon.

The black crystal atop the staff pulsed redly. But that
could be merely a reflection of the fires in the glory hole.

Today was Sunday, the fires lay quiet.

What had set off Meg's raving?

After my last encounter with Tryblith, the Demon of
Chaos, I wanted to run away screaming and hide until the
next century. I did not care. Too many innocents stood
between me and the enemy of England.

How had the beast found me? Who hosted it? From
everything I read, I believed the demon male, therefore it
would have to invade the mind of a male of its own descent.
My ancestress, Resmiranda of blessed memory, had killed
the last known descendant of Tryblith with the great sword
Excalibur. The sword I had refused. My fingers itched to
wield it to slay the demon I could not find.

Who among us could host the demon? Neither Meg nor
I had seen it since arriving at Whitefriars. Logic dictated
Tryblith would have come with Countess Roanna de Plan-
chet, the only stranger among us.

But she was female and not of Tryblith's get. And the
demon had left. I did not think a demon could desert its
host.

Who, then?

Perhaps the demon had followed her but sulked beyond
the still open gate. It could not enter sanctified ground. I
had blessed the entire abbey with holy water soon after
taking refuge here.

"Is it gone?" Countess Roanna asked quietly. She removed her hands from her ears as Meg's protestations died
to wild mumbles. My sister still clutched Robin tightly in
her arms and the dogs stood at guard.

"I sense no demon," I replied. "Come to the refectory.
I must read the missive from my bishop, but later in private." So far she had made no effort to put a parchment
into my hands.

Still wide-eyed with fear, the countess preceded me
toward the refectory that took up nearly one entire wing

of Whitefriars. She paused only briefly to glance at the quiet ovens and the rows of glassmaking tools.

For the first time since my arrival at Whitefriars, the children shied away from me. Neither of the dogs responded to my command to return to my side. They kept close to Meg and Robin. I scowled at them, trying to force them to obey through the bonds of love and magic that kept us together. Newynog looked confused. Her growls reverted to a puzzled whine. Helwriaeth stood her ground. I decided to leave them with Meg until their manners returned. No sense in frightening Countess Roanna further.

My bishop would not have trusted a message to one who harbored a demon.

"We dine simply here," I explained as we dished turnip stew onto bread trenchers. I found an extra spoon for our guest as she seemed out of the ancient habit of carrying her own. We had reverted to ancient times in our refuge, cut off from much of the world around us—everything but the gossip.

"I have known hunger. A simple meal is often more rewarding than sumptuous fare with exotic sauces. French cooking is too rich, and troubles the stomach after a time. Stew and bread trenchers remind me of home, of why I returned." The countess kept her eyes cast demurely down.

I wished she'd look up at me again. Something about those big gray orbs drew me into her soul, invited me to share . . . My body stirred with lust, and I had not the will to suppress it.

She was looking at my staff where I had laid it on the floor between us. Was that greed that hardened her features and narrowed her fabulous eyes?

"You must truly be a magician to possess such a wondrous staff," she said quietly. "I have not seen one like it since . . . since my gran took me to visit an old woman at a fortress in the extreme north, nearly on the border."

I stilled. "You met my grandmother?"

"We met a woman named Raven many years ago. My gran needed a poultice to heal a boil on my father's back. Gran's eyes were failing and she needed me to guide her."

I relaxed. No wonder this charming woman looked familiar. I'd probably seen her as a child.

But Meg was rarely wrong. Even in her most insane moments she made sense in a twisted way. I had only to look deeper into her meaning rather than her exact words.

A demon sits on Roanna's left shoulder where death should hover, Raven said in Meg's voice.

Chapter 40

Oxford, 8 September, 1560, just after midnight.

"THE rumors that Queen Elizabeth carries Dudley's child persist throughout London," Roanna told the Earl of Oxford. Idly she sucked on her finger, making certain the flamboyant earl watched her movements with every bit of lust she could project to him. Then she ran the wet digit round and around the rim of the Venetian glass goblet in a deep ruby red—the color of blood—decorated in gold foil. A slight ringing sound accompanied her gesture. She hummed a harmonic counterpoint in the back of her throat.

Oxford's eyes glazed over as his gaze locked on her finger. He swallowed convulsively but did not look away.

Only then did Roanna continue. "The rumors spread beyond the city until they come alive. They are now more truth than fabrication." She'd barely escaped the cloying atmosphere at Whitefriars before being forced to take communion with common criminals. Tryblith had prodded her, convinced they were strong enough to withstand the sanctity of the bread and wine.

She did not want to take the chance. Deep waves of self-loathing made her hasten away from the chapel. Tryblith would never understand how soiled she felt whenever she encountered a church. So she had fled with the excuse she needed to find lodging in the city before nightfall. Griffin, of course, had offered a cell in the old abbey. She needed more than a pallet on a stone slab.

She needed a bath to wash away the burning on her skin from his holy water. At first it had been merely an annoying flush, but it had grown to a maddening fire. She feared her hands would blister if she stayed any longer. Next time she would better prepare to withstand Father Griffin's spells.

Roanna also rejected the sanctuary because she needed the freedom to move about the country without explaining herself to Griffin Kirkwood at every step. Oxford was only one of a long list of conspirators Francis de Guise had given her.

"Elizabeth cannot marry Dudley," Oxford protested, gaze still fixed upon Roanna's circling finger. "Robin Dudley already has a wife."

"Amy Robsart is very ill, has been for years. A cancer in her breast. They need only wait for her to die naturally."

"But if she lives longer than expected? She has already lasted more than two years," Roanna prodded.

"Amy Robsart must die before Elizabeth can no longer hide the pregnancy. The queen and her Master of the Horse surely plot to murder Amy." Oxford completed her statement for her, completely trapped by her spell.

Just yesterday in Windsor, Roanna had used similar tricks to make Bishop de Quadra, ambassador from Philip of Spain, believe that Elizabeth had confided in him about Amy Robsart's imminent death. When all the reports were made to Oxford's justices, Elizabeth would appear to have advance knowledge of the murder.

How fortunate that Amy Robsart had taken up residence in Oxford's shire where a Catholic sympathizer would sit in judgment of a murder trial. Elizabeth frequently visited Dudley at Kew, the manor she had given him. Her rival was not welcome in her presence, so Amy had had to seek lodging with friends elsewhere.

"Elizabeth cannot commit murder and remain our queen," Oxford said quietly as if he had memorized lines in a play—lines that Roanna had written for him.

"The Duke of Norfolk is ready to throw them both into the Tower. They will not live to face trial. Marie Stuart will be free to claim the throne and rule England, Scotland, and France from London. England and Scotland will be Catholic once more."

"What must I do?" Oxford asked, again as if by rote.

"William Cecil, Lord Burleigh, Elizabeth's Secretary of State, is your wife's father." The lady had obliged them by taking to her bed with "the headache," a polite euphemism for menstrual cramps. Roanna had no patience with wom-

en's weaknesses. She'd never suffered a cramp in her life
and didn't intend to now. "You must convince Burleigh
that he can only retain his political power if he assists you
and Norfolk in seeking justice once Amy Robsart is murdered. Justice must be served. Elizabeth and Dudley must
both die as criminals deserve."

"Elizabeth must die."

"There is a priest in the sanctuary of Whitefriars. He
must be the one to slip the knife between Elizabeth's ribs
once she is in the Tower. Only a priest can cleanse her of
the taint of the Protestant heresy."

"The priest in Whitefriars."

"Now go to your wife's bed and make her forget that I
came to see you."

"But . . ." Oxford started to rouse from his trance and
rise from his chair.

Roanna increased the hum in the back of her throat in
an odd counterpoint to the hum of her finger on the glass
goblet.

Oxford settled into the comfortable pads of his oversized chair.

"Does she truly bleed, or merely dislike you in her bed?
Go to her. Teach her the delights of succumbing to her
husband. She cannot deny you your rights."

"My rights."

Roanna followed Oxford to the door of Lady Anne's
bedchamber. She implanted the image of Oxford tying his
fifteen-year-old wife to the bedposts. The coddled chit
needed to learn the realities of marriage. Roanna left them
to it. She had a long ride ahead of her and much to plan.

Many villages had celebrated the Lady Fair yesterday,
one day early, on Queen Elizabeth's twenty-seventh birthday. Abington, south of Oxford, retained the traditional
date. Amy Robsart resided with friends at Cumnor Place
between Oxford and Abington. All of her servants would
depart the manor for the fair early in the morning.

Roanna had no intention of allowing the cult of Elizabeth to replace the cult of Mary, mother of Jesus, known
throughout the Catholic world as Our Lady. By this time
next year, Elizabeth would be dead. No one would celebrate her birthday for good or ill, and religious war would
unleash chaos throughout the island of Britain.

Then and only then would Roanna be free of Tryblith's manipulations and demands. Many would die, but she would slay no more.

Between Oxford's bedchamber and the stables, Roanna transformed into a slightly drunken gentleman companion of the earl's. She collected her three footmen—all thugs hired from the docks of Southwark with an unwillingness to work at anything that hampered their natural aggression. Roanna allowed these thugs free rein when encountering obstacles in her path. They seemed to adore her for it and protected her fiercely.

Oh, she loved the privileges that came with a title and money.

They rode hard for the village of Abington where she stationed the thugs. Once the servants from Cumnor Place arrived, her men must keep them there by fair means or foul until Roanna returned from her errand. The same applied to Anthony Forster and his wife who owned Cumnor, and their other guests: Mr. William Owen, his wife, and mother.

A large oak tree provided Roanna with an almost comfortable perch with a full view of the rambling manor that had been a retreat for the Abbot of Abington before Henry VIII, Elizabeth's father, decided the Catholic Church owned too much land in England, hoarded too much wealth, and had more power than the crown.

Dawn came. Cumnor's owners broke their fast early. Right after, a crowd of lesser servants emerged from the back gate of the grounds. Laughing and singing, they walked merrily toward Abington and their holiday.

The sun rose higher. Roanna began to sweat beneath her heavy black doublet and hose with her black gown stuffed into them. She often giggled at the ludicrous padding men stuffed into their breeches and how they ballooned out in improbable silhouettes. Now she blessed them as excellent cover for her disguises.

Noon came and went. At last, the swells had dined and departed the front door while the last of the servants crept out the back.

Roanna jumped down from her perch and shed the mannish clothing, hiding it in a fork of the tree. She donned her heavy black cloak and pulled the hood low over her

face. In her left hand she carried her staff. Not as elegant
as Griffin Kirkwood's, but it was hers. Gran had sacrificed
the goat whose skull adorned the top. Wrapping a cloak of
magic about herself to misdirect the eye of any observer,
Roanna approached the back of the house and slid into the
cool shadows of the kitchen. She opened all of her senses
to listen to the entire house.

I hear only one heartbeat, Tryblith said.

Roanna could almost see him drooling in anticipation of
the coming death. She walked silently through room after
room, moving upward toward the place where she expected
to meet Amy Robsart.

"Halt!" Amy called from the top of the staircase. She
wore a light ropa that hung loosely on her wasted frame.
Her skin looked as pale and as translucent as one of Griffin
Kirkwood's blue-tinted windowpanes. Her once lustrous
dark hair hung limply on her shoulders. Her pale scalp
showed through her thinning tresses. Her hands looked like
parchment wrapped loosely around a collection of mis-
matched bones.

Death did indeed sit heavily on her left shoulder.

"Why did you beg me for a private meeting?" Amy
asked, not moving from the banister across the gallery. She
waved Roanna's letter in her left hand.

"You know who I am, Amy Robsart." Roanna made the
skull atop her staff appear human and lit a red light behind
the eye sockets.

Amy gulped and nodded.

"You have expected me since Robin first felt the lump
in your breast and deserted you. You are already dead to
him. He has not returned to your bed since, and seeks the
love of another."

"No," Amy protested on a sob. She held the parchment
of Roanna's letter away from her. "Robin loves me. 'Tis
that witch, Elizabeth. She keeps him from me. She is to
blame, she . . ." Choking tears cut off any further protests.

"Come to me, Amy Robsart. Come to Death with an
open heart and a free mind. Come now, for I am the Grim
Reaper," Roanna cooed to her victim.

Amy sidled away from the protective banister. Not far
enough.

"Give up your dreams, Amy. Robin will not return to

you. He loves another. He has always loved another." Roanna added a layer of compulsion to her words. "End the pain, Amy. End your loneliness. Come to me. Come to Death." She held her arms out as if to a lover.

Amy drifted to the top of the stairs and stopped. "I cannot. I must see my Robin one more time."

"Come!" Roanna demanded. A rope of magic shot from her fingers and tangled with Amy's ankles.

Pull, Tryblith directed. His voice sounded breathless, as if viewing the naked body of his lover.

Roanna hesitated. Then Tryblith's hairy paws seemed to reach through her hands and yank hard upon the magical rope.

"Help me!" Amy screamed, tumbling down the thirteen steps. Her arms flailed, her legs buckled, and her back arched. Over and over she screamed.

At last she lay limp upon the last stair, head down, legs tangled at odd angles. "Help me," she gasped, reaching a skeletal hand toward Rosanna in entreaty. "Help me live to see my Robin one more time."

Roanna reached down and clamped her strong hands about the woman's neck. One quick twist. The fragile bones snapped.

"Your heart is already broken, Amy Robsart. No sense in letting it break further with your husband's continued perfidy."

Chapter 41

St. Claire dower lands, Kent, 9 September, 1560.

DONOVAN and Martha viewed the small manor above the village of Ide Hill near sunset two weeks after leaving Kirkenwood. The fading light added a rosy glow to the honey-colored stone of their new home. The sitting of Parliament, Michaelmas, and their wedding approached.

Donovan leaned across the small gap between his horse and Martha's to steal a gentle kiss. Behind them a servant smothered a giggle. "The manor looks snug and warm. I wager that gentle breezes do not penetrate the walls, the chimneys do not smoke, and those many mullioned windows allow the summer sunshine to warm and brighten the large rooms," Donovan said around another kiss. "Bliss," he added. He let Martha guess whether he meant the manor or kissing her.

"You may have one of the attics for your laboratory," Martha said around another quick kiss. Then she gathered her reins and cantered across the village green toward the manor.

Before noon the next day, Donovan unpacked his vials and packets, his small distillery, brazier, and star charts. Martha puttered happily in her rose garden, leaving him to his experiments. He sighed blissfully the first time he lit a fire beneath one of his potions and the flames did not flicker and die. For the first time in several years, the damp did not penetrate to the bones of his weak leg.

Every time the wound ached, he relived his guilt over Kate's death. He should have remained at Kirkenwood that night instead of riding recklessly over the moors. If he'd stayed home to fight the Scottish raiders, he'd not have killed the demon/priest, might have been able to protect his wife. He'd do better by Martha. She deserved better.

She had shown little enthusiasm and less imagination than Kate for bed sport. But he could talk to Martha, dream with her, and explore ideas. Already she showed signs of producing a child. A few more weeks would see them married and the child legitimate. He asked nothing more from life at the moment.

A great stillness settled on his shoulders. For an instant he felt he could reach out and touch the universe.

Another moment of this inner peace and his magic might blossom; he could discover the Philosopher's Stone, he could find Meg. Once he knew she was safe, he would rid England of the demon Tryblith. Until then he had only his powers of persuasion in Parliament to keep at bay the Catholics who harbored the demon. His magic would augment those powers of persuasion. England would unite and grow peaceful under his guidance.

His fingers curled around the packet of ghostweed Martha had brought from Kirkenwood. Raven had indeed planted some of the rare herb in her garden. Weeds had hidden the delicate green leaves and white trumpet flowers from casual view.

So far, he had not found the time or courage to experiment. Perhaps now on a Monday afternoon when most of the servants made themselves as scarce as possible—nursing sore heads from yesterday's Lady Fair—he could try the drug with Martha's supervision.

But with this tremendous *stillness* within him, did he need the ghostweed? The question disrupted his peace and sent his insides into a restless quaking once more. Almost like a portent.

"Milord." Martha appeared in the doorway to Donovan's new lair. She curtsied and kept her eyes cast down.

"Yes, milady?" Why the formality? Who was the shadow just behind her, eavesdropping on the conversation of a man and his betrothed?

"A messenger from the queen." Martha's voice remained more cool and distant than usual.

Donovan's hands began drumming on the counter before he could stuff them into his pockets. He wanted to pace, to run his hands through his hair, pluck at the dust motes in the air.

"Enter," he finally remembered to command the courier in Elizabeth's green-and-white livery.

The man strode forward purposefully. "Her Majesty, Elizabeth Regina, Queen of England, Ireland, and France, commands your presence, Milord Donovan Kirkwood, Baron of Kirkenwood," he recited as he handed Donovan a roll of parchment.

Donovan broke the seal without hesitation. Elizabeth's own bold hand had written in haste, summoning him to Windsor immediately.

Now Martha took up drumming the tabletop with her fingers, a habit she had picked up from him over the summer.

"Inform Her Majesty that I shall attend her tomorrow as she breaks her fast." That should give him enough time to unpack his court clothes and bed Martha one more time before his duties to Elizabeth parted them. If Martha had not quickened already, he intended she would by morning.

"Her Majesty commands your presence now, milord. You are to return to Windsor with me posthaste."

"Why? Surely Her Majesty must allow me time to prepare for such an august summons."

"I shall order your horse saddled, milord, while you bid farewell to your betrothed." The courier turned smartly on his heel and exited the attic.

Martha rushed into Donovan's arms, the moment the courier disappeared down the staircase. He kissed her temple and held her close.

"Will . . . will she throw you into the Tower?" Martha asked. Tears choked her.

"I have done nothing to displease her."

"Who knows what will displease Her Majesty."

"Aye. Who knows. But if the Tower were my destination, she would have sent a much larger escort than one lone and discreet courier. Lord Burleigh or one of his clerks would have penned the missive rather than Elizabeth herself."

"True. You will be careful, say nothing untoward?"

"Always."

She looked at him skeptically. "And don't fidget. It

shows your impatience and need to be elsewhere. Elizabeth demands the total attention of her courtiers. If you fuss and pace, you insult her beauty." She fussed with the fold of his sleeves.

"Yes, milady." He kissed her cheek again. "You'll not forget me and marry another?"

"Not while I carry your little one." She cupped her belly.

"Do you carry for certain?"

"Nothing is certain until the child takes his first breath of air and screams his displeasure at being born." She smiled that special smile reserved for when mothers shared secrets with their babes.

"I'll return before Michaelmas, even if for only a few hours, long enough to say our vows. I'll not have this child born illegitimate." One brief squeeze of her shoulders and he followed the courier down the stairs.

Several hours later, the gloomy round tower of Windsor Castle came into view. Donovan pulled his horse to a halt for a much needed respite from the constant jouncing pace set by the courier. Both horses bowed their heads wearily.

"Do you know the reason for the queen's urgency?" Donovan asked the still nameless courier for the twentieth time.

"The queen commands. I obey," he replied and set his spurs to his horse's flanks once more.

Donovan followed at a more subdued pace. He had no interest in killing this horse—unless he rode in the other direction, back toward Ide Hill and Martha.

Only Griffin had been a better and more sympathetic listener than Martha with intelligent replies and probing questions that made him dig deeper into his own mind for answers.

Suddenly he missed his twin so much his midregion became an aching void. He needed Griffin's perspective on Elizabeth's mysterious summons.

The queen was pacing the long garden impatiently when Donovan was shown into her presence. The fine drizzle that heralded the beginning of autumn did not slow her or drive her indoors. Ever mindful of her coiffure and her sumptuous wardrobe, Elizabeth rarely tolerated changes in the weather—unless on progress when she needed to make herself available to the commons, show them her love for them by braving the elements. Good Queen Bess among her people was an entirely different person from Queen Elizabeth at court.

For once she was alone. None of her ladies hovered about, nor any of the mass of courtiers and officials.

Where was Dudley? The man rarely took a piss more than three feet from his queen.

Donovan walked up to Elizabeth and went down on one knee into the mud her pacing had churned in the finely cut grass. She extended her left hand with her coronation ring. He kissed the symbol of her sovereignty.

"Oh, get out of the mud, milord," Elizabeth admonished him impatiently.

"How may I serve you, Majesty?" Donovan rose gratefully. The grass had stained his hose. If he'd been given the opportunity to change to riding leathers, he'd have withstood the cold, damp ground better.

"Amy Robsart died yesterday." Elizabeth blurted out without any of her usual dissembling or convoluted twists of conversation. Her hands fluttered about.

"I grieve for Robert Dudley at his loss." Donovan bowed his head. "Though Mistress Robsart's illness was grave and lingered long, death always comes as a shock, even when expected."

"You do not understand, Donovan. Robin killed her!"

Donovan went still with caution. "Were there witnesses?" Not once did he doubt Robert Dudley capable of eliminating Amy Robsart so that he would be free to marry Elizabeth. But the man was not stupid. He would have arranged for an assassin, or a subtle poison. Or why not wait a few more months until the cancer in Amy's breast took her naturally?

"No. No witnesses. She was alone in the house. All of the servants were dismissed to attend the Lady Fair. When they returned, they found her at the foot of the stairs, her neck broken." Elizabeth recited the events as if reading from a report. "My poor Robin. I must go to him. I will stand at his side as he faces his accusers."

"Dudley may not have pushed her." Donovan stood in front of his queen, keeping her from dashing toward the castle and her lover. "Where was Robert Dudley yesterday?" Donovan offered Elizabeth his arm and led her in a new round of pacing the garden. She accepted it. Nearly of a height with him, they did not have to incline their heads to insure their whispers reached no other ears.

"At his home in Kew."

"And his wife?"

"With the Forster family at Cumnor Place near Oxford. They and their other guests seemed to have absented themselves from the house as well. Mistress Forster believed Amy awaited a secret visitor."

"In her weakened state she might have simply fallen."

"Aye. She might. But everyone whispers of Dudley's foul deed. My sweet Robin is accused and condemned without benefit of trial. And . . . and in the city they link my name with his in the deed." Elizabeth looked near to tears. "I must go to him."

Donovan had never seen this formidable woman give in to her emotions. Usually she feigned strong responses to manipulate the men around her. These tears seemed genuine.

"Please, Majesty, think before you act. This is one time when you must be a prince, think with a prince's logic and not with a woman's heart. One of your enemies might very well have entered the house and murdered Amy Robsart simply to blacken your name. If they planted evidence to implicate you and your lover . . ."

Elizabeth opened her mouth to protest his presumption.

Donovan held up his hand to cease her words. "Please, Majesty, I repeat only the words that will surround this episode. Others create them. I only lay them before you for examination. If such evidence has been placed at the scene, then by your own laws you must cast yourself and Robert Dudley into the Tower to await trial. Your enemies will place another on the throne regardless of your innocence."

"You believe this . . . this . . . travesty!"

"I present possibilities. The Catholics here in England and in Europe might very well stoop this low to place Marie Stuart, or Katherine Grey, or even the Earl of Huntington on the throne." And loose their demon Tryblith.

"What can I do to prevent this?" Elizabeth increased her

stride. All trace of her tears vanished. Her eyes took on the hard glitter of determination. Donovan had to stretch to keep up with her.

"First you must acknowledge the situation and appoint an impartial team to investigate. Hiding it will only add guilt to the speculation. Then separate yourself from the investigation and Robert Dudley. You must not receive him until his name is cleared."

"I value your advice, milord. You must stay close to me. You are my Wolfhound as Robin was my Eyes."

Donovan cringed. Once Elizabeth settled a pet name upon a courtier, she never loosed him from her court or her side.

"Send for Lord Burleigh, Majesty. As your Secretary of State, he should be your most prominent adviser. I have other commitments."

"Ah, yes, your betrothal. We must postpone the marriage. I cannot bear to be separated from you. My Wolfhound. My companion and protector, loyal and fierce."

"But, Majesty . . ." Donovan withdrew his arm from her grasp.

"Postpone the wedding or end the betrothal, I care not which. You may not leave court."

Donovan stared at her in defiance.

"Would you rather take up residence in the Tower?"

"Majesty, I seek only to serve you." He bowed his head while she stalked back into the castle. He needed Martha's calm logical advice.

What would Griffin do?

Help me, my twin. If you are listening, I need you right now almost as much as I need my Martha.

Chapter 42

Whitefriars Abbey, London, autumn 1560.

LONDON roiled with rumors regarding the death of Amy Robsart. We never knew from one day to the next if the populace sided with Elizabeth, Dudley, or those who would condemn them both.

We heard that Elizabeth was pregnant with Dudley's child and that he killed poor Amy so that he could marry the queen and make the child the legitimate heir to England. We heard that the justices appointed to investigate the matter would shortly arrest both Dudley and the queen and throw them into the Tower. We heard that in the wake of the scandal, the Earl of Huntington (who had as good or better claim to the throne through Edward III) was poised at Nottingham with armed troops to take London and crown himself king. We heard that French troops massed to cross the channel and invade on behalf of Marie Queen of Scots.

None of it came to pass.

We heard everything. We believed less. We watched the city panic as each rumor took hold and found a life of its own, only to wither and die in the face of the next rumor and panic.

But Elizabeth seemed to be handling the problem with wisdom and discretion. Through it all, the queen remained quietly at Windsor or Richmond or Greenwich. Dudley remained at Kew, virtually under house arrest.

And through it all I sensed an urgency in the air and a desire to consult with my twin. He sat in Parliament, he escorted the queen to masques and banquets in Dudley's absence. Elizabeth called him her Wolfhound. He had the information my bishop needed. And I think he needed me.

How to be sure? Did I dare leave the sanctuary of Whitefriars to seek him out?

The justices eventually declared Amy Robsart's death an accident and Dudley free of any guilt. He returned to court subdued and repentant as befitting a widower. But Secretary of State Cecil—now Lord Burleigh and father-in-law to the Earl of Oxford—had replaced him as the queen's confidant.

I listened eagerly, recorded much, and came to no conclusions except that the death was too convenient. Dudley's fall from grace came just when Elizabeth, Parliament, and the people seemed ready to accept Dudley as her consort. Many gained in power and favor from Amy's death. None of them Elizabeth or her favorite who were accused most frequently of the murder.

Roanna de Planchet chose not to remain at Whitefriars after Meg's insane accusations. I could not blame her. She had money enough to rent lodgings. The hue and cry had not been raised against her.

Her gracious manner, her intelligent responses to my questions, and the warmth she generated in my belly lulled my suspicions that she carried no written missive with Bishop du Bellay's signature and seal. I filled my journal with endless praise for her beauty.

So I listened to Roanna de Planchet, hoping to learn who had truly sent her.

Her plans were based upon a sound foundation. Marie Stuart must return to Scotland. As long as Francis II remained alive, she would not leave her husband's side.

I shied away from the implication that an anointed king, faithful to the true church, must die. Countess Roanna hinted that Marie's marriage had never been consummated, that 'twas no true marriage at all. Marie must leave the unfruitful union, request annulment, and find another husband.

No vision came to me to guide my actions. I clutched my staff and gazed long and hard into the black crystal. It remained a simple crystal.

There was something about the way Roanna had stared so longingly at my staff with her gray eyes, open wide, alert, greedy, and observing and yet so innocent and beguiling. . . .

Over the next months, Countess Roanna came to Whitefriars often. She attended Mass frequently, along with a growing number of tradesmen, merchants, and even a few nobles. She always left a donation in the poor box, though she had yet to seek me out for confession and my memory of pressing the bread of the Eucharist into her hand was always fuzzy and vague.

I looked forward to our meetings, enjoying her wit and intelligence as well as her piety. Her big gray eyes drew me to her time and again. Then I shied away, dangerously close to the sin of lust.

For the first time in many years I questioned the purpose of a priest's vows of chastity. I questioned the vision that had sent me to the church. Had I truly seen my vocation? Or perhaps I had misinterpreted. Three crowns for Arthur's shield, the legendary sword he had commanded . . . perhaps I should . . . ? What would I do without the church?

Meg and the dogs always found something else to do, somewhere else in the abbey to be, when Roanna came. Often they disappeared before she entered the gate.

My lords of Norfolk and Oxford, one an open Catholic, the other a secret follower, remained absent from Mass with my congregation. But then, they might not have been aware that I, Griffin Kirkwood, was the priest referred to most often as Father Merlin of the sanctuary of Whitefriars.

If Norfolk came to me now, I would have to lie and pretend failure in the mission to find Elizabeth's illegitimate child. Then I would have to spin more untruths to explain why I had not returned to his household and reported that failure.

My disappearance from his court could only mean death or betrayal. I hoped he would forget me and the child in view of a new plot to give him power over his cousin Elizabeth. Possibly the scandal over Amy Robsart's death was one of his ploys.

Michaelmas came and went. We approached All Hallows. Whitefriars became crowded as the homeless and the wanderers came to us seeking the warmth of the glass ovens. Meg shared a cell with two prostitutes looking to find a new occupation. I worried that they might revert to their

old ways and drag Meg with them. But Helwriaeth chaper-
oned them. Neither Meg nor Robin would be allowed to
stray far.

My own cell overflowed with two other young men of
Gypsy extraction, neither of them from Micah's clan. They
sheltered with us through the first fierce storms of autumn,
repairing tools, making new molds, sharpening knives,
whatever metalwork needed doing. I let them share the
bed, I slept on the floor with Newynog to keep me warm.

Part of me missed Helwriaeth terribly. We'd been together a long time, seeing each other through persecution
and adversity. Newynog must replace her as my familiar
when she died. She eased the separation by beginning it
now. But as long as Helwriaeth lived, we were bound together by more than love, more than magic.

"Will you hear my confession, Father Merlin?" a young
woman asked one cold November day as I sat before the
glass ovens, shaping and ornamenting a carnelian bead with
cross-hatched grooves.

I looked up from my work, struggling to refocus my eyes
from the extremely close work to the near distance. I saw
only the shape of a dark cloak and hood pulled low around
a pale face. So many new people crowded Whitefriars I did
not know them all. But I thought I should recognize this
face if it had appeared within our sanctuary before.

"Go into the chapel, child. I shall follow you in a moment." I had to finish the bead before the glass cooled
beyond working malleability and was ruined. My priorities
had shifted. Confessions would wait. Glass would not.

Inside the dim chapel, the woman awaited me, still
cloaked, still anonymous. She stood in the center of the
nave, turning her head back and forth, seeking the protection of an enclosed confessional.

"Have no fear, I will protect your anonymity, Madame.
We have not the luxury of closed doors and screens to
separate us." If penitents could not see the confessor, they
could pretend they spoke directly to God and not to a mere
man. I didn't like my parishioners making me so special a
being as a substitute for God. I was a man with a man's
weaknesses and mortality. *A man's lust for Roanna de Planchet.* In the Sacrament of Confession I provided a conduit
to God; I did not become him.

The anonymous young woman hesitated.

"You may keep your hood up," I conceded. We both needed the extra layer of wool in the chill stone building.

"For what I am about to ask you, Father Merlin, I may as well reveal myself to you now as later. She folded back her hood, revealing long, soft waves of Tudor red hair—blonde and pale red mixed together. Her pink-and-white complexion and soft brown eyes reminded me of Marie Stuart. But she did not have the height of the Queen of Scots, nor the harshness of her cousin Elizabeth.

She shrugged. "Call me Kitty."

Kitty—Katherine—Katherine Grey, younger sister to the ill-fated Lady Jane Grey. A Tudor cousin with a close claim to become Elizabeth's heir, I knew who she must be. But for the confessional, I needed only her Christian name, not that of her family.

Her temper tantrums when Elizabeth downgraded her and her sister Mary from Ladies of the Bedchamber, positions they had held under Mary Tudor, to Ladies of the Privy Chamber had provided Londoners with much gossip. Katherine had embraced the Catholic faith under Mary despite her Protestant upbringing. She had also been known to associate with one Spanish ambassador after another—perhaps plotting Elizabeth's downfall. Rumors of a betrothal to the King of Spain's son, Don Carlos, had reached us in Whitefriars, so they must have reached Elizabeth as well. There had been other rumors, of a betrothal to the Earl of Arran in Scotland to unite Scotland and England, or a betrothal to the Earl of Huntington.

Elizabeth had restored Katherine as a Lady of the Bedchamber to pacify the girl's ambitions, had kept her close and showed her much favor, regardless of their differences in faith. But the queen had not yet named Katherine heir or made plans for a marriage of benefit to all of England. Perhaps she only kept the girl close as a means of watching her ambitious plots and thwarting them.

I raised an eyebrow in query to her but did not speak.

She returned my gaze stolidly, adding nothing to her brief introduction.

I nodded to her. "I am Father Griffin." I pointedly kissed the cross embroidered at the center of my stole to seal the confession and sat on the dais with my back propped up against the altar. She settled gracefully on the step below me, keeping her back to me. "I prefer Father Merlin. If no one knows your true name, you cannot be accused of treason."

"I am a Catholic priest. I celebrate Mass daily in defiance of Her Majesty's laws. Is that not treason already? You have come to confess, my child?"

"I have come to beg a favor of you, Father Merlin."

"Within the privacy of confession?"

She nodded again. "I have fallen in love, Father."

"The love between a man and a woman is a pale reflection of the love God bears his children." *Her* children? The image of the old woman at Easter morning service blessing me in the name of her ancient goddess flashed before my eyes.

No matter what name you call God, be sure that she *is listening.* And then I experienced again the tremendous sense of being a part of the marvelous whole of existence. I could reach out and touch anyone, read their minds, once more join my mind to my twin's. I was one with God and all of his/her creations. My faith alone connected me to God, the church was but a crutch.

I buried that blasphemous thought hastily, along with a need to connect to my twin. He would not welcome me. But my thoughts continued to nag at me, popping back into my mind without conscious wish.

"When one is born with the wrong blood, love is not allowed." Katherine's—I could not think of this dignified woman by her childish nickname—words brought me back to reality with a jolt. "Until Elizabeth herself bears an heir, none of her relatives—no matter how distant—can be free to follow our hearts and destinies."

Elizabeth has a child, I almost blurted out. An illegitimate child she could never acknowledge and I must protect from the machinations of ambitious men.

"If you marry according to your heart and bear a child, both of you could become the focus of rebellion," I reminded Katherine. I reminded myself as well. Little Robin faced the same dilemma as she. "Both you and your betrothed are in danger from Elizabeth's enemies as well as the queen. By the laws of Henry VIII, those who carry royal blood may marry only with the permission of crown and Parliament. If you wed without permission, you commit treason. You are doubly in danger if your betrothed is a foreign national."

"Edward—Ned is as English as I. I will not make the same mistake as my cousin Mary in inviting the Spanish Inquisition into England. Not when I love another."

We both breathed a sigh of relief. "I am willing to take the chance if you will perform the wedding ceremony. You put yourself at risk if you agree. Do not take this request lightly.

"I . . ." Dared I defy the queen further? I had to remind myself that I owed my loyalty to God and my bishop and then to England (somehow the Pope and the church in Rome escaped my deliberate attempt to prioritize my loyalties). My mission was to bring peace and unity to England through a single faith. Only then could we conquer Tryblith, the Demon of Chaos. As long as Elizabeth stood so solidly behind the Protestant cause, by definition of the church that ordained me priest, she was my enemy. If I performed a simple Nuptial Mass—a sacrament I truly believed in—was I truly committing treason?

She has not given you her true name, the cowardly portion of my mind whispered. *You can always claim you did not know her true identity.*

"Does your betrothed believe as you do?" I asked.

"Yes. 'Twas he who suggested I come to you."

"I would meet the young man before agreeing."

"He awaits you outside the gate. But he will not give you a name."

"Bring him to me." I shrugged. "What is in his heart is more important in the eyes of God than who he is." Neither the Catholic nor the Anglican Church might agree with that statement. When it came to royal heirs, both churches demanded total command over unions.

I thought I knew Katherine's intended already. Rumor had placed Edward Seymour, Earl of Hertford as one of many devoted swains who followed Katherine about the court. A popular young man with a winning smile, he had the best title and fortune among the lady's worshipers.

Very early the next morning while the queen hunted and Katherine remained at Whitehall with a supposed toothache, I crept out of the sanctuary of Whitefriars for the

first time since coming there. The smells of the narrow
street, human and animal waste, dank river, and rotting
garbage rose up to greet me in malevolent waves. I almost
retreated to the clean warmth of the abbey. Instead I
stepped forward into the rain, wearing my winter coat with
the hood pulled low over my brow, my clerical robe safely
hidden within the folds of dark wool. I clutched my staff
as a talisman against the evil of the city. So must the friars
of old have faced the world after the quiet sanctuary of
their abbey.

Briskly I walked up to Fleet Street and turned left toward
Westminster and Ned's hired rooms on Cannon Row.

At last I came to the narrow house Katherine had directed me to. Upstairs, she and young Ned—the Earl of
Hertford—awaited me with three companions to witness
the brief ceremony. The woman who stood beside Ned
must be his sister, Lady Jane Seymour, one of Elizabeth's
Maids of Honor. I could not distinguish the faces of the
two men in the shuttered and ill-lit room. Just before entering the small, shadowy apartment I paused to lower my
hood. My association with the petty criminals of Whitefriars
had taught me caution and suspicion. The two men stood
before the hearth, speaking ardently in hushed tones.
Something familiar about the posture of the more mature,
dark-haired, one caught my attention. Then he turned at
some creaking of the floorboards.

Norfolk! The one man I could not afford to meet again
face-to-face. Every moment I remained in his company endangered Robin. Endangered the peaceful course I hoped
to find for England.

"I dare not tarry, milady." I lowered the timbre of my
voice and kept my hood pulled low. "We must begin and
end quickly." Without further preamble I brought forth my
stole and missal. Habitually I would have draped my rosary
across the open pages of the little book that guided the
ceremony. Norfolk had seen me carry the distinctive ivory-
and-gold prayer beads. This scene must remain anonymous.

Raven would have known how to disguise me with a
little magic. I was not yet so desperate to endanger my soul
for my own and Robin's safety when discretion served the
same purpose.

Heart beating a little rapidly, sweat breaking out on my

brow and back from the close quarters and bright fire, I began. "Dearly Beloved."

Norfolk and the other man—a noble by his sumptuous clothing and proud demeanor—took their places beside the bride. Lady Jane stood by the groom. Norfolk stared at me with curiosity and puzzlement. I ducked my head, dropping the hood of my cloak lower across my eyes. With luck, only my mouth and chin showed. I had been clean shaven when I served in Norfolk's household. Now I wore a beard—even the price of my beads did not extend to expensive razors.

With luck I could hold the gruffening of my voice. With luck . . .

"Do I know you, Father Priest?" Norfolk asked.

I swallowed and shook my head. "Do you, Kitty, take this man, Ned . . ." I plodded on through the vows. As I raised my hands for the final blessing, I looked up. How could I seal this solemn sacrament without looking my charges directly in the eyes? The cloak shifted away from my upper face.

But Norfolk was gazing fondly upon Katherine Grey, the woman he undoubtedly hoped to use in his plans to depose Elizabeth. Katherine was young, beautiful, with only a moderate education, but as ambitious as Norfolk himself— I was surprised he had not married her himself. But perhaps he had grander plans. He would want her to be raw clay in his hands, easily molded to his image of dutiful and respectful queen.

Mayhap, I should say, she would be molten glass in his hands. One slip and he would burn and she would shatter.

Before Norfolk could look back at me and recognize the man who had betrayed his trust, I mumbled the last "Amen" and left more silently than I had come, one step closer to the hangman's noose than I had been an hour ago.

Chapter 43

London, late autumn 1560.

ALL the way back to Whitefriars, I listened intently for
sounds of pursuit. Private armies had been outlawed under
the reign of Henry VII when he finally ended generations
of civil war by uniting the red rose of the Lancaster lords
with the white rose of the House of York. Norfolk tended
to live above and beyond the law. His retainers openly
swaggered through the streets heavily armed, wearing the
duke's yellow livery. Anyone who impeded their way or
misstepped in the soldiers' path fell victim to their violence.

I had not heard if any had died at their hands. Many had
been injured.

Was Elizabeth so powerless in her own capital that she
could not curb the arrogance of these men? More likely,
she used them to police the streets at no cost to herself.

I hated to think of the street brawls that would follow if
any other lord allowed his men to roam so freely. Especially a prominent Protestant lord whom Norfolk would
delight in bringing low.

Right now I had only to worry that the Duke of Norfolk
might send his retainers to follow the mysterious Father Merlin. I prayed that my distant ancestor's reputation might
frighten him into believing I came out of time and mist to
perform yet another miracle and was not truly a mortal man
who could be captured, tortured, beaten into submission.

I retreated hastily to the sanctuary of Whitefriars, grateful for the warm welcome my people reserved for me.
Katherine Grey and her new husband must face the slings
and arrows of their fates without me. I was done with them.
Done with venturing beyond my safe walls for a time. Per-

haps in the spring, when I knew for certain that Meg and
Robin were safe, I would once more journey through England seeking the information my bishop needed and finding a way to return my land to the true faith.

For now I must content myself with reporting the gossip
of the city.

Had I given Katherine Grey and Edward Seymour the
means to usurp Elizabeth and provide England with Catholic heirs?

Within two weeks of the clandestine wedding, Queen
Elizabeth's courier waited patiently at the Whitefriars gate
with a summons for me and a promise of safe passage
through the city to her palace at Whitehall.

Dared I refuse?

Sanctuary no longer extended to treason, murder, or violent robbery. Elizabeth had every right to send troops into
Whitefriars and remove me to the Tower.

She sent a solitary squire with a written missive. I had to
trust her safe passage. I took Newynog and my staff with me.

I walked the streets outside the walls of London with the
silent messenger in green-and-white livery at my side. The
houses here were more spacious, and the streets wider than
within the city, but they still crowded atop each other, and
abutted the cobbles. The squire steered me around noisome
puddles and yanked me away from the contents of a chamber pot slung from an upper window without warning.

Shopkeepers, merchants, beggars, and prostitutes all bowed
to me, blew kisses, or reached out to touch my cloak or staff
for luck. The route became more and more crowded with
well-wishers. Some formed a parade behind us.

I grew nervous at this obvious adulation in the presence
of a royal official. I did not deserve it. It might provoke
Elizabeth's notorious jealousy.

"Bless me, Father Merlin." A one-eyed and toothless
crone who smelled of sharp herbs and sharper chemicals
knelt in the road at my feet. Her one eye, as dark and
piercing as a raven, pinned me in place. I read in that eye
the knowledge of death, her own and those around her.
She'd die in her own time, sooner rather than later, no
matter what I did or said. God called to her.

My escort reached for the hilt of his short sword. I shook
my head. She must hail from some respectable household

since she covered her missing eye with a patch. Her clothing was worn but not shabby or patched. Gently, I touched the old woman's head. "Go in peace, Old Mother. May your life brighten your descendants and all who touch you."

Newynog added her blessing of a sloppy tongue on the crone's folded hands.

With tears in her eye, the woman scuttled away on her knees, through the midden at the center of the cobbled street. Her once-fine gown was ruined with night soil, but she seemed to glow with pleasure and peace.

My escort surreptitiously crossed himself. The ancient gesture of prayer remained instilled in the people no matter what the monarch decreed was the true religion. My hope for an England united by the true faith soared.

At the Royal Palace of Whitehall, my silent, now wide-eyed, escort left me in a small anteroom. No fire to warm me from the November chill. No window brightened the gloom. The room was barren, courtiers did not sit while awaiting the queen. Only a single oil lamp burned in the corner to keep me from bumping into the walls. I forced myself not to pace, reaching deep within myself for that place of stillness that formed the core of my prayer and meditation.

Newynog sat at my side, head leaning heavily into my thigh. I ruffled her ears and she sighed/moaned in doggy contentment.

Shortly thereafter Elizabeth herself threw open the door between my anteroom and her solar. She wore riding clothes in rich, dark green velvet with a matching feathered hat that cocked to one side of her bright curls—redder than Katherine's or Marie Stuart's and curled tight against her head rather than long and flowing. An older, firmer version of Marie Stuart, she nearly vibrated with energy. Everything about her was brighter, more determined, more alive than the Queen of Scotland and France or the new bride who defied her queen. I think I smiled at the commanding image she presented, even slightly windblown by her recent ride.

And yet Roanna's image haunted me with her sweet smile. I always felt her presence as a subtle shift in my heartbeat. Elizabeth seemed to take all of the light and air in the room and concentrate them within her.

"You!" she gasped.

"Your servant, Your Majesty." I bowed with my right leg extended and my right fist clenched over my heart, as

I had been taught during that long-ago time I trained to become Baron of Kirkenwood, a peer of the realm.

"So, my Wolfhound has brought me a wolfhound." She offered her hand to Newynog for a sniff.

The dog looked at me for permission before approaching this stranger. She was now old enough to have a few manners—upon occasion.

"I think you mistake me for someone else," I demurred, keeping Newynog at my side with a gesture.

"Kirkenwood?" She cocked her head prettily. Her brown eyes softened in puzzlement.

"Perhaps you mistake me for my brother Donovan."

"Then it is true?"

"What is true, Your Majesty?"

"I summoned the Merlin. A Kirkwood responded."

I bowed my head, almost a nod, but not quite an admission. At times I welcomed the association with my ancestor as proof that I was indeed the Pendragon of England, even without the ring of authority. Other times, I cringed away from the magic people expected of the Merlin.

She stared at me silently for several long moments, examining my rough clothes, the long, crystal-topped staff, and the dog that would intimidate a lesser woman.

"Enter, Lord Merlin. I have need of your services." She backed away from the doorway into a large spare room full of light from large windows despite the gloom of the day. I recognized the slight bluish tint of the panes as coming from the Whitefriars furnace. Our source of sand always added blue to the mix. Another factory nearby turned out greenish window lights.

A small door in the right inside corner of the room led elsewhere. It remained firmly closed. The courier must have exited from there. Did he listen through the panels? Elizabeth and I seemed to be alone.

Elizabeth settled herself on a high-backed bench before the hearth, also on the right-hand wall. No other chairs or seats littered the room, though two writing tables and three cupboards did. I stood silently before her, hands folded inside the sleeves of my cloak, staff tucked into the crook of my arm. Once more I reached into that quiet still place, waiting patiently for the queen to speak. I kept Newynog close to my side, though she looked at the fire with longing.

"The resemblance is remarkable," she said, examining my face minutely. "But I can see you are not my Wolfhound. He could not stand so still this long."

I think I smiled, remembering Donovan's restlessness, his wild rides across the moors, his scattered thoughts.

"You may speak, Father Merlin. I will not lop off your head for impertinence this day."

Again I nodded. Waiting for her to come to the point.

Elizabeth fiddled with the texture of her riding gown, shifting her gaze from the fire, to the velvet, to the dog, to my face. "Release the dog, priest. At least allow her the comfort of the fire though you take none of it. Why is it you Catholics take delight in inflicting discomfort upon yourselves?"

I shrugged. "I like a fire on a cold day as much as any man." With a snap of my fingers, Newynog relaxed and scooted toward the hearth. She stretched out to her full length with a heavy sigh. I noticed that her head came enticingly close to Elizabeth's knee, inviting a caress. Unlike Helwriaeth, who did not like to be touched by any but me—or possibly Meg and Robin—Newynog was a glutton for affection.

Elizabeth obliged the dog. That occupied her for several moments.

I had never known a woman to refrain from speech for so long a stretch. From the look she gave me, obviously none of her courtiers could allow silence to hang within a room this long. With half a smile I waited.

"You do not ask why I have summoned you," she said at last on a sigh of . . . of satisfaction?

"You will tell me when you are ready."

"God's breath, man, you exasperate me," she said on a laugh, eyes rolling upward. "And you delight me. You do not prance and pose to gain my attention. Nor do you come to me with false tales against another."

I shrugged again rather than speak.

"Are you certain you are twin brother to Milord Donovan Kirkwood?"

"Yes, we are twins, birthed on the same day from the same womb."

"He is the elder, I presume, since he inherited the title and you entered the church. The wrong church, I might add."

Again I kept silent. I gained nothing by contradicting her statement.

"But you . . . you are the one who has visions and performs miracles."

"Some call it so." I thought of little Faith, the delightful baby who held her arms up for me to hold her every time she saw me, who laughed when I tickled her and ceased her crying at my touch. She would have died if I had not known how to clear her lungs at her birth. Her parents called my actions a miracle. The only miracle I saw was God's direction to guide me to Whitefriars on the precise day my knowledge and experience were needed.

"But you do not call them visions and miracles?"

"Only God can work a miracle."

"I do not need a miracle. I need a vision."

"So did your cousin Marie. I was not able to help her. The visions come when God needs me to know something." I'd had a vision that day at Marie Stuart's court. But not one I could impart to her. The memory of bloodstained waves crashed over me once more, and through the waves I saw wide gray eyes laughing at the death and destruction. Who?

"Are you having a vision now, Lord Merlin?" Elizabeth half stood, hand out to catch my swaying body.

"No new vision, Majesty. Just a painful memory."

Roanna! Roanna's gray eyes had stared at me on that day, more than two years ago. Roanna? Some relative of hers must have been the wild Highland creature who prophesied doom if Marie did not return to Scotland. But my vision had promised doom if she did.

I needed to sit and mull this over.

Elizabeth kept me standing.

"What did my cousin need to see when last you came to court in France," she asked eagerly.

"Your sister, Mary Tudor, was dying at the time. Queen Marie asked for a vision of guidance."

"As do I."

I waited for her to continue.

"No questions, Lord Merlin? You are the strangest man I have ever met. And the stillest. I feel I must reach out and touch you to make certain you are not a mere statue, or a figment of my imagination."

I almost laughed with her. But too much hung in the balance. I dared do nothing that might drop my guard. I had too many secrets.

"A smile—or half a one. I have hope that you are human, after all."

"A man, Your Majesty. A simple man."

"A simple man who has visions." She scratched Newynog's ears. The dog leaned into the caress, moaning her pleasure. Then, with an abrupt change of demeanor from light and friendly to deadly serious, Elizabeth threw her next words at me almost as an accusation. "Will my cousin return to Scotland now that her husband has died in France?"

"Francis has died?" I could not help the words flowing free of me. "I knew that he ailed; has always ailed. But dead? So young?" Barely eighteen, if I remembered correctly, and I doubted that I knew for certain when the young king had been born.

"A putrid ear felled him not ten days ago."

"I grieve for Marie. She loved him dearly."

"Will she return to Scotland?"

"Catherine de Médici will try to keep her in France, under her control, possibly marry her to another ally."

"But will Marie return?"

Once more, the flirtatious young queen walked across my memory, leading men to the gallows and the headsman's block. Bloodstained waves crashed over us both. She continued walking. I gasped for breath and swallowed seawater.

"Sit, you stupid man." Elizabeth guided me to the floor beside my dog. Newynog put her head in my lap and whined an inquiry.

"I see war, Madame. A terrible war at sea. A war that will destroy England if we do not unite the land and people before then."

"My land is united," she insisted with a cold edge in her voice.

"But the people are divided by your church."

" 'Tis your church that disrupts our peace and prosperity." She almost stamped her foot in frustration. Almost. At the last moment she restrained herself, maintaining her regal demeanor.

Marie Stuart would not have maintained such restraint.

We stared at each other for several long moments. I looked away first, almost nauseated with the dizziness of my recurring vision.

Chapter 44

London, and Whitefriars Abbey, winter 1560.

OVER the next few months, Elizabeth sent for me at least once a week. I found myself looking forward to our time together. Her intellect challenged mine. We discussed religion, politics, classical scholars, economics, religion, and more religion. We touched upon mystics and a spiritual life. Our conversations raised many questions, and I longed for the collection of documents in the lair at Kirkenwood. In one rash moment I wrote to Fiona and asked that she send the copies I had made of the Synod of Whitby, references to the Knights Templar, and the Culdee Church.

My journal overflowed with my arguments with myself and speculations on the true nature of the church and faith.

Elizabeth had been well educated in both the Protestant and the Catholic faiths. She spoke and read classical and modern languages. Often she would switch tongues, searching for the best phrase or concept. I was hard pressed to follow her leaps of logic and language.

Donovan remained absent from our presence though I knew he resided at court and often counseled the queen now that Dudley's star waned.

Hesitantly I suggested to Elizabeth that Donovan be consulted on a matter of economics—a subject he understood much more readily than I. She flatly refused.

"Nay, milord priest, I must weight your differences of opinion separately," she said and changed the subject.

If ever Donovan and I were to reconcile, we must do it on our own. Elizabeth would not be our agent.

Every time I visited the queen under safe conduct, Countess Roanna de Planchet awaited me in the chapel upon my return. She would rise from her devotions and ask for the minutiae of my conversation with Elizabeth.

"I ask for Bishop du Bellay and the Holy League," she explained herself. "Bishop Eustachius de Bellay and the Holy League need to know when Elizabeth will return to the true church. Have your teachings brought her closer to that time? If not, she must die. Have you foreseen her fate? Whose hand will deal the death blow? They need to plan. What did you see in your visions or in the stars for Elizabeth's fate?"

When I did not answer to her satisfaction, she stormed out of Whitefriars like a jealous wife. Sometimes I caught a whiff of sulfur on the wind with her passing.

The room always felt empty and chill without her. I longed to clasp her close, keep her beside me.

And then came the day when I found fault with Elizabeth's logic. And my own.

"Father Merlin, can you honestly tell me you believe in the . . . the magic that transforms the host into the body of our beloved Christ at the moment of Eucharist?" Elizabeth threw up her hands in exasperation.

"Madame, can you deny it?" I replied with the freedom our arguments gave me. We had agreed on many spiritual issues and often discussed the difference between the individualism preached by James the Just, first Bishop of Jerusalem, and by saints Peter and Paul with their emphasis on unity within one church organization. Both had their merits. While an individual quest may prove more satisfying without a church organization, the faith would have died without an organized church to bind the faithful together at the fall of Jerusalem in the first century.

No longer did I fear Elizabeth would throw me into the Tower for an impertinent statement. She enjoyed our arguments too much.

As for my defiance of her laws, I always celebrated Mass within the sanctuary of Whitefriars where she could not touch me. She had yet to learn of Katherine Grey's marriage, and she had no other evidence of my treason. I dreaded the moment she questioned why her Lady of the Bedchamber gained weight and frequently lost her breakfast. Would Katherine or Ned or any of their witnesses betray me?

"Explain yourself, priest." Elizabeth's appellation carried the bite of venom as she challenged my argument. I had the right to counter her statements, but only with logical arguments; logic was my only antidote.

I jerked back from my memory of Norfolk's questioning stare at me. "You consult me for visions. You refer to me only as the Merlin and not by name. You *expect* magic every time we meet, and yet you deny that God can perform *magic* during one of our most holy sacraments."

"The bread and wine are but symbols of the Last Supper!"

"They are the essence of our communion with God. Jesus Christ himself said, 'Take, eat, this is my body given for thee,' and then he took the cup of wine and said . . ."

"I can quote scripture as well as you. Is it not obvious that the Last Supper was but a symbol? Christ did not cut up his body and drain his blood for his disciples to cannibalize him. He offered symbols for the sharing of His word and His spirit."

"I would refute that, Your Majesty."

"If you believe so strongly in the *magic* of the sacraments, why will you not share with me the *magic* of your visions? I know you have had more since first we met."

"God grants my visions on His agenda, not mine. What I see is meant to help a few individuals." Like the one-eyed crone who asked for a blessing, or Brother Jeremy who must die and leave the community of his glassworkers to founder on their own—I had shared that one with him and even now he trained Gareth to carry on as leader—or my vision of little Faith who would prosper and marry well. That one gave her father the hope of escape to shoulder more and more responsibility. "I share with those concerned. No one else." Except for that one vision of blood-stained waves and Marie Stuart leading a parade to the gallows. That vision involved all of England and Scotland. Possibly the rest of Europe as well. But I could not speak of it yet. Not until I understood my role in the disaster.

"I need to know how to deal with my cousin," Elizabeth insisted. "She seeks permission to land at an English port before making her way to Edinburgh. She brings French troops with her. *Catholic* French troops that will just as easily menace my northern border as defend their queen."

Elizabeth surprised me. Rarely had she asked for advice or counsel, only for a spirited argument or a view of the future.

"You have denied Marie permission to land at one of your ports."

"I have neither given nor denied permission." Elizabeth was famous for dithering in indecision until events shifted to her preference.

I shrugged, a now familiar gesture when dealing with this exasperating, puzzling, delightful woman. If only she would embrace the true faith, I knew she could unite England to withstand all of the terrible events fate would throw at us. And I knew they would come. Mayhap not today or tomorrow. But come they would. As long as Tryblith ran loose in an unknown host, chaos would eat away at England's peace and prosperity. I had not the power or authority to actively root him out of his lair and destroy him. But the time was coming when I must choose between saving my soul by denying my magic and saving all of England.

"You see something, Father Griffin," Elizabeth insisted, leaning close to me.

I sat up straighter—she allowed me to sit in her presence now, a rare privilege—and fought the chills that racked my body. "Nothing new. Nothing specific. Just war from without and within. England must unite in one faith to combat the Demon of Chaos as well as foreigners who seek to render us poor and powerless." New words that more clearly defined the future I had seen in countless visions.

"We are united in the true faith. 'Tis traitors like you who invite foreign bishops to rule us," she hissed.

My skin grew cold and clammy from the implied threat as well as the chill of my vision.

The church tended to canonize visionaries and mystics of the past and burn those of the present.

"The Holy Father in Rome unites us all in the true faith," I insisted, perhaps a little too vehemently, to reassure myself more than her.

"And yet Pius IV cannot stop war between other countries who look to him for spiritual leadership. Spain seeks to conquer Holland. France battles the Spanish on her southern border. The Holy Roman Emperor—who seeks my hand in marriage—is neither Holy nor Roman, but another Hapsburg puppet of his uncle, Philip of Spain. The Bishop of Rome is but a church leader. He has no special endowment of sanctity just because he commands Rome. He is not God's right-hand man any more than you are."

"Neither are you, Madame."

I resisted the urge to cross myself in counter to her statement. Blasphemy. But part of me listened to her. Part of me condemned the men—kings and bishops—who sought Elizabeth's demise simply because she was female and defied them. I wondered if the Holy League was motivated by faith, by politics, or by wounded self-esteem that a woman could best them all.

When I returned to Whitefriars that evening, Countess Roanna awaited me in the chapel as usual. She rose from her prayers all eagerness, big eyes shining just for me.

"I need a drink," I stated, too weary from my arguments with Elizabeth to express the emotions my questions provoked.

Roanna took my arm. "Come. The others have finished their supper and gone to their beds, but there is some stew left. And I think I can find an unopened cask of beer for you." She took my arm and escorted me out of the chapel.

"I need something more than new beer." I broke free of her, feeling immediately bereft. I ducked into the sacristy and poured some wine from my sacramental cask into a pitcher. On second thought I filled a second one as well.

Roanna refilled Griffin's cup. The last dregs of the wine plopped into the ruby liquid. She passed her hand over the cup, adding something more. He'd barely touched the stew. But he had emptied an entire pitcher of wine into his gut. He drained his cup again and plunked the cup down on the table.

"More," he groaned. His eyes looked haunted, but not glazed. How much could the man drink before he passed out?

"You have had too much already, Father Griffin. Perhaps

you would benefit from confession and prayers, much as
your flock," she said sweetly even as she poured from the
second pitcher.

"There is no one in England who would understand my
confession even if I indulged in that greatest of comforts."
He buried his face in his hands.

"Perhaps, I . . . ?" She added another dose of herbs and
wine to his cup before pushing it beneath his hands. Gently
she wrapped his hands around the wooden vessel.

"Roanna, dear heart." He paused a long moment.

She shivered in delight at the intimate address. Her potion worked. The spell she had woven around him with
painstaking care since she first came to him at Whitefriars
was finally complete. His downfall was imminent. She
would have her revenge for everything that had ever gone
wrong in her life. Then she could discard Tryblith and get
on with the business of living.

"I have been strong in my faith and my mission for many
years," Griffin mumbled. "But now . . . now I have doubts.
Queen Elizabeth has asked questions that make me question things I have held surely in my heart. I have read
proscribed documents and consider heresy."

"The queen is a Protestant witch." Roanna ventured to
trace with a gentle fingertip the shape of his hands where
they clutched the cup with a desperate strength. The
wooden vessel would not ring as did the Venetian glass of
the Earl of Oxford. But she had other means for inducing
a trance. She held her breath, waiting for him to pull away
from her touch, as he always shied away.

His hands remained in place beneath hers, accepting the
sensuous circles of her fingers upon his own. She became
bolder, widening her caress to the backs of his hands and
wrists.

Had she given him enough of the potion? Too much?
The best alchemists of Europe and hedge witches of England and Scotland could not agree upon how much of this
aphrodisiac would drive a man to wild exploits of ecstasy
and how much more would render him uselessly asleep.

"Roanna, I . . ." he broke off his next words to stare
longingly into her eyes.

"Yes, Griffin." She returned his gaze, moistening her lips
provocatively. She shifted her posture to push her breasts

above the edge of her gown. Thankfully, she'd given up trying to wear a corset. So much easier to undress.

"Roanna," he breathed. He lowered his mouth to capture hers.

She leaned into his kiss. Her breasts grew heavy. Hot honey wandered into her veins. She cupped his face, holding him close for an extra moment of delicious languor.

Ooooh, he succumbs. What glory, what power in the seduction of a priest, Tryblith crowed.

Shut up, demon.

Too bad he does not come to you of his own volition. 'Twould be twice the power if you did not have to drug him or encase him in spells.

Shut up, demon. I'll do this my way or not at all.

Or not at all! Tryblith's laughter faded as if he wandered off. But a twisting in the back of her neck told her he had not gone far.

"Oh, Roanna, I should not have done that." Griffin licked his lips, hovering too close. They rested their foreheads against each other, prolonging the moment.

"I do not object, Griffin."

"But . . ."

"Drink the wine, Griffin." She pushed the cup up to his mouth. Obviously, if he could question one kiss, he had not had enough of the potion.

As he downed the next cup of wine, Roanna lifted her hand to his shoulder. "You are so tense, Griffin. Allow me to rub the knots from your neck." Without waiting for permission, she shifted to stand behind him.

"That feels so good. Roanna, you are just what I need." He clasped her hands as they drifted down his chest and across his broad shoulders. He kissed her palms, and then her wrist. "The Culdees of Ireland embraced marriage, even for their priests. They were heretics, but their tradition is older than Rome. Thomas the Doubter wrote a gospel. The Church calls it apocrypha, doubtful of authenticity. Yet his writings are two generations closer to our Lord than the accepted Gospels. Who am I to believe?" he mumbled, just barely audible. He leaned his head against her chest, between her breasts.

Roanna melted. This was what she was born for, to seduce this one man.

And then he tugged until she sat in his lap and he kissed the inside of her elbow. She wrapped herself around him, kissing him with rising passion. Moisture hit her loins, swelling her womb. She clenched as if holding him inside her.

"Come, Griffin. This is no place for us to pursue this matter." Gently she extricated herself from his grasp. "Come." She caught up both of their cloaks and led him into the courtyard, then down through the gardens to the river gate. A tiny gatehouse offered them modest protection from the wind and rain.

"The monks did not provide much comfort for their porter, but I think the remains of his pallet are still upstairs."

"Upstairs," Griffin repeated. He only slurred the word a little.

She had to hurry. Anticipation flushed her face and all the way across her newly sensitized breasts. Only his hands molding her to fit against him would relieve the heavy ache.

He stumbled twice upon the turret stair as she led him to the upper chamber. She had to push his head down to keep him from knocking himself out at the low places. At last they emerged into the small square room with a straw pallet and blanket in the exact center.

Roanna lit the tiny brazier beside the pallet with a thought, barely pretending to strike a spark. She had prepared her love nest many weeks ago. Her blood pounded almost as hot as the fire. She had waited all winter for this moment. She wanted to linger, savor the moment of triumph of robbing this priest, this Kirkwood, of his most solemn vow to the church. She needed to feel the weight of him atop her, thrusting again and again in mindless rut.

He swayed and his eyes began to close. She had to hurry.

A few flicks of her fingers sent her gown tumbling to the floor. Chill air drew her nipples into tight knots. Her shift clung to them in perfect outlines. Tauntingly she circled them, holding them high and prominent for his gaze.

He reached for the ties of her shift. The fine linen slid off her shoulders and caught on her hands where she still cupped her hands beneath her breasts.

With anxious fingers and an impatient gasp he fumbled with the fabric until he had exposed her to his sight. His hands replaced hers in molding, kneading.

A deep sigh of longing escaped her lips. She leaned into his firm touch. As he lowered his head to lick her nipples she fumbled with his doublet, easing it away from his shoulders, stroking his back down to his tight butt.

And then they were stretched out on the pallet, his clothing discarded in haste and only a little torn. "Let me look at you," he mumbled, raking her with eyes and hands. At each point his gaze lingered, he paused to kiss her body with his wonderful, questing, inquisitive mouth.

Pressure built inside her. She shifted her hips, inviting him to explore more intimately. He thrust up her knees, opening the essence of her femininity to his tongue.

Ripples of pleasure coursed up her in expanding waves. Her back arched. Sharp gasps escaped her.

Just when she thought she must explode or die, his full weight came down upon her chest and he filled her. Together they rode the storms of passion. Upward in tight spirals they climbed, all the way to the starbursts spangling the firmament.

He collapsed upon her. She continued to shake in an ongoing orgasm, pulling his seed deep within her.

At last he stirred. "Griffin?" she whispered.

"Roanna, my love. My only love." He kissed her hard and long.

And then he snored.

"Just like every other man, only concerned with your own pleasure," she snorted. Tears of disappointment clouded her eyes and sent her chin quivering. She needed to bask in his embrace, talk to him, share her life with him.

She wiggled out from beneath him. The smell of him lingered on her body, in her hair, and indelibly in her mind.

"Remember this night, Griffin Kirkwood. Remember and know that I am the instrument of your fall from grace." She wrapped her cloak tightly around her and retreated down the stairs and out the unguarded river gate where her own bodyguards awaited her.

But will Griffin Kirkwood, priest and Merlin, remember this night after all those drugs? Tryblith chortled.

"Shut up, demon."

Will he even know that he has broken his sacred vow of celibacy?

"Shut up!"

Chapter 45

Whitefriars, the next morning.

I CRADLED my head in my hands, unable to face the breakfast porridge Carola plunked down in front of me. My head felt as if demons stabbed at my eyes from the inside.

Why had I drunk so much last night? I hadn't indulged in so long a drinking bout since before the seminary. I had trouble remembering the last time I had been so drunk that I lost a clear memory of my actions. It must have been the night of my sixteenth birthday, the day Da considered Donovan and me to be men. We'd drunk long into the night and then . . . and then Da had brought two of the scullery maids to us. We'd shared the girls as we shared everything. Our room had erupted in wild giggles until nearly dawn. In the morning neither Donovan nor I had much memory of our initiation into the rites of manhood.

Da would never know we had already experimented with those same two girls. We were precocious brats; unthinking of anything but our own pleasure. Only Raven's conscience made us acknowledge the sons the girls produced as our bastards.

So why had I awakened in the porter's room above the gatehouse down by the river? I smelled of my own musk, wine, and sweat. And something else. Something else haunted my senses along with a peculiar lethargy and contentment even with the demons tying the cords of my neck into impossible knots and jumping up and down in my stomach, I was content with myself and the world.

"Eat. 'Tis the only cure," Carola commanded me sternly. She stood with hands on her hips, glaring at me as if I were one of the erring children.

"Drown the demons," Meg added. She brought a pitcher of well water to me. "Demons don't like water. Drown them, then wash them away." She sang the phrases as if a nursery rhyme.

Robin picked up the tune, "Drowning demons!" He danced in wobbling circles with the two wolfhounds—bigger than he by half. They eventually collapsed into a puddle of giggles and fur and slobber.

I smiled at his childish joy in all things. My face ached from the unfamiliar exercise.

Painfully I obeyed the two women. And I did feel better. A quick wash helped more. Though a long soak in a tub of hot water would have banished more of the unfamiliar aches and pains. But Whitefriars did not boast a bathtub or the means to heat copious amounts of water.

And then I discovered long scratches upon my back and upper arms. They looked as if a demon had truly run his talons all over my body.

"Foolish imagination. I probably scratched at fleas a little too enthusiastically. I was so drunk I didn't know when to stop."

A little more slowly than usual, I went about my duties, unable to banish the silly smile that creased my face.

All morning long I kept looking toward the gate expecting Roanna to come. Rarely did a full day pass that she did not visit us, bringing special treats for the children, gossip for the women, and beautiful smiles for the men.

Bright halos of energy caressed all living things within my view with special blessings. The day seemed brighter than usual, the sunshine warmer, the budding plants awaiting spring and Easter more beautiful. Had nearly a year—or was it two—passed since I celebrated Easter in the center of the faerie circle with a congregation of Gypsies and vagabonds?

At noon, I celebrated a full Mass of Sext as usual. As I joyfully administered and partook of the bread and wine of the Eucharist, I missed pressing a morsel into Roanna's hand.

I tried conjuring the memory of my fingers pressing the bread firmly into her palm. The image remained as fuzzy as my vision from my damaged right eye.

And I remembered my argument with Elizabeth the pre-

vious day. Deep in my heart I knew that God was present
each time I celebrated the Eucharist. I offered up more
than mere symbols of the Lord's passion. This was an essential ritual for our communion with God.

*No matter what you call God, remember that She is lis-
tening!* Raven's voice came to me as clearly as if her ghost
had spoken aloud.

I looked around the chapel, seeking evidence of her
presence.

Only Roanna stood in the back of the room, silent, hesitant. I had never known her to hold back. The rest of the
congregation passed out of the chapel in search of their
noon meal. They parted around her like a creek separates
to circle a boulder.

With my vision sensitized by the hangover I saw her aura
clearly. Dark splotches and red sparkles circled her head
in a turbulent whirlwind.

Every part of my being froze.

The hairs on the back of my arms rose. Newynog growled
low in her throat, uncertain. Roanna was now a familiar
presence. And yet . . . ?

She handed me my cloak and staff, as solicitous as a wife.

But she was not my wife. Nothing more than a friend
and colleague. A messenger from my bishop.

A messenger who had never delivered a written missive,
only spoke of vague plots.

"We have had news in the city this day. Marie returns
to Scotland!" she cried with the eagerness of a child. An
eagerness at odds with the turmoil of her aura. "The church
will return with her."

"War will return with her," I replied quietly, clutching
my staff as if my life depended upon it. "War in Scotland
first. Her barons will never accept her or her church. France
must come to her aid. Spain will join the fray, eager to
catch the spoils. Then the war and chaos will spread to
England."

Yes! A harsh, spitting, male voice echoed through my
head.

Not Roanna's voice. But no one else was present. Just
that strange growing aura of black with red starbursts.

She caressed the oaken shaft of my staff, gazing longingly

at the crystal. The layers of red sparkles around her swirled faster. The black clouds within them grew larger, spreading to fill the chapel. I tried pushing her out into the narthex, suddenly not wanting her inside my church. She resisted.

In a swirling moment of dizziness, I was back in the Palais de La Louvre in Paris, sparring words with Marie Stuart. A wild Highland prophet burst in upon us. Not a prophet, Roanna in disguise. I had not mistaken her eyes. I had seen them before.

And not just in Paris. I had seen them on the night of my vision of fire and swords and crowns in a nameless Scottish village. 'Twas she that Donovan attempted to rape while she stared at my astral self above my body. Then again I had seen those eyes outside Kirkenwood as she flung demon arrows directly at me. 'Twas then I had first seen Tryblith within a whirlwind of sparkling red flamelets and known him for the Demon of Chaos. She could not be his host. And yet those eyes . . .

Cautiously I sidled closer to the altar. This demon was strong, growing stronger if it could tolerate its host inside a sanctified chapel.

Had I ever administered the Eucharist to her? I did not think so. I had merely deluded myself because I was trapped within the aura of chaos and lust she cast about me.

Nor had she ever entered into the seal of the confessional.

" 'Tis my staff, Roanna. You will never possess it." I withdrew the tool of magic from her touch. My stomach fluttered and bounced in anticipation of what I must do. I needed the staff to banish the demon. Could I lay it to rest once and for all?

Or did God need to find someone more worthy?

Not here, not now. I had not prepared. I knew no safe place to send it that would hold it for more than a moment. And if I failed, when the demon exited Roanna's body, it might inhabit another, one of my friends and compatriots. Perhaps an innocent like the baby Faith.

This would be easier with Excalibur. But I had rejected the sword of my ancestors in favor of peace and compromise.

The time for peace and compromise had run out.

Only then did I realize that Roanna carried her own staff, a thinner, shorter tree branch topped with a small goat skull. Why had I never seen it in her hands before?

Even as I asked myself the question, her staff faded from view. She kept it hidden with magic. But I had seen it before. In the hands of the wild Highland prophet in Paris.

"Yes, your staff." She continued to stare at the crystal with lust. "It carries Elizabeth's scent. You have weakened her with your magic," she said in a quiet monotone. Someone else, the demon probably, gave her the words. They did not come from her heart. "She is vulnerable to you. You can end the Protestant menace once and for all. Next time she summons you, you can kill her with ease. Marie is on her way, she will step into Elizabeth's place and return the popish faith to England."

Now she looked directly into my eyes, trying to lay upon me the same trance the demon laid upon her.

Without thinking I grabbed the staff and retreated to the altar in two steps. A small Celtic cross stood upon clean white linen. Gareth had fashioned it of slag glass—mixtures of several colors at the end of the day when there wasn't enough of any one in the gather or in the colored canes to make a single decorative vial, bottle, or goblet. Made with love for his daughter's christening, and sanctified by many Masses and Eucharists in its presence, the cross offered me more protection than metal armor.

I grabbed it and held it in front of me with one hand, the staff in the other.

"Begone from this place, demon. I name thee Tryblith and command thy body." The ritual words sounded hollow.

Roanna laughed. A deep rolling laugh that came from deep in the Underworld and not from her own throat. "You cannot command me, priest," she spat in deep guttural tones. Red-and-black flames shot from her fingers.

I ducked and rolled. But the night of drinking slowed my reactions. The hellfire caught my upper arm, branding me.

I gritted my teeth against the pain. No time. Think! What will banish a demon?

My faith, shaken by questions, might not be enough. I needed a circle, the four elements, herbs, and minerals.

I had none of those things.

"By the Earth of my bones, the Air that I breathe, the Fire of my spirit, and the Water of my blood, I banish thee, demon. In the name of God I banish thee!" Raven's voice echoed the words as I spoke them. Other ancient voices joined hers, giving me the strength and control to do what I must. I chanted the words over and over, holding the cross and staff before me as I approached Roanna and the demon.

"You and your pitiful magic cannot banish me!" she screamed and let loose another blast of fire. It flowed around me, blocked by the shield of my faith and my magic.

"In the name of the things I hold most Holy, I banish thee from my presence. Begone from Whitefriars forever and a day."

She gasped as if I had burned her. Another stream of fire shot from her hands. This time it hit the barrier of my magic and backlashed. She screamed, holding her arms over her face as she ducked away from the flow of her own demon fire.

I took two steps forward. She backed up three. Her flames died. I advanced again. She retreated. Step by step I herded her out of the chapel. Out in the open courtyard she stretched and seemed to grow taller, wider. Her hands became arched talons, her eyes turned yellow and slit vertically. Her bared teeth sharpened into miniature daggers. "You cannot command me!" she screamed once more. But her voice returned to the normal soprano of a woman in distress.

"Begone, Tryblith, Demon of Chaos, and darken our gates no more." I walked slowly toward Roanna, still carrying the cross and staff. The air thickened and darkened as I closed upon my quarry, as if I walked beneath muddy water. Each step came heavier and more difficult. My words felt slurred and slowed, as thick as the air.

The cross and the crystal began to glow blue and red—my signature color and Raven's. Their eerie light pulsed, throbbing up my arms into my head. Images of death and blood pounded within my mind. Each blow against the inside of my skull demanded an avenue of escape.

"Begone, Tryblith!" I repeated, forcing the words past thick and numb lips. Each syllable sent new pain up my spine into my head and the backs of my eyes. I saw everything outlined in blood red instead of the usual shades of gray.

Tears poured from my eyes and the film of gray slid away with them.

The onslaught of colors nearly blinded me. Everything within sight, people, weeds, stones, the ever-present glass, all pulsed with bright auras.

Roanna's aura doubled and tripled in size. Each layer became a wilder swirling torrent and took on a darker shade of blood.

With one last shriek, Roanna rose up from her huddled crouch in the center of the courtyard. She hissed, vertically slitted eyes turned as red as her aura.

Crimson lightning crackled. It shot through the abbey in deadly bright arrows.

Thunder crashed. Echoed. Compounded.

I dropped to my knees, hands over my ears, eyes clenched closed. And still I saw the flashes of light and heard the roar of thunder louder than the crash of surf against a storm-tossed beach.

My tears dampened my cassock, shiny bright red in my restored vision. They took on the texture of ruby glass beads, made brighter by a golden aura.

The dogs barked, chased Roanna. They ran circles around her, creating the magical enclosure I had not had time to do.

And then Roanna spun into a whirlwind and disappeared. A circle of charred stone showed where she had stood.

Where did she go? Would she come back? Did the demon go with her?

She left behind the stink of burning sulfur and a huge hole in my heart.

Chapter 46

*The Mendip Hills outside the city of Wells, deep winter
1560.*

ROANNA crept through an abandoned circle of stones.
An eerie green fire sprang to life, rimming the entire circle
the moment she entered. Tingles of power—old power just
awakening after a long sleep—drifted toward her from the
stones. Her own ball of cold light grew brighter in her hand.

The circle had not been desecrated.

Before her, the tall dolmens marking the entrance to an
ancient cave barrow rose up out of the stormy gloom.

Tryblith had promised her shelter to nurse her bruises
and damaged magic after her duel with Griffin Kirkwood.
So far on this long journey to the west of England, she had
found little warmth and less food. At least the cave would
allow her to light a fire—provided she could find dry fuel
and tinder. A little moldy bread and cheese would help her
recovery, but she doubted she'd find that here. Later, when
the storm abated, she'd creep into the nearest village and
steal what she needed.

Other than the occasional direction, the demon had remained silent this entire journey. None of his usual painful
prods had directed her, only the word *home* said with great
longing and loneliness.

Griffin Kirkwood had given her this grief. 'Twas his fault.
When she recovered, she'd take her revenge upon him and
his house, beginning with the ones he loved most. Other
men who had used and discarded her faded from her memory. Only Griffin remained. Everything that had ever gone
wrong in her life was his fault. Beginning with the raid
upon her village when Gran had died and the Douglas had

kidnapped her, and ending . . . she'd end it all with Griffin's death and not before.

Water crept through the broken sole of her shoe. Rough turf and stone shards had cut her feet repeatedly on this mad flight from London. But here in the circle the grass grew thick and clean, the wind lessened, warmed with the promise of spring and the coming dawn.

Heartened by the lessening degree of misery, she approached the man-made arch. The light of green fire that rimmed the stones winked out as she stepped out of the circle. Only her own ball of cold white light cupped in her palm remained. It did not penetrate the archway.

Inhaling deeply, she took the next deliberate step into the thick shadows of the barrow. The air resisted her passage. She pushed with all of her strength and her exhausted magic. It felt like walking through mud as high as her head. Gibbering fear assailed her. She nearly retreated. Tryblith awoke long enough to prod her forward with a sharp twist to the cords in her neck.

As she passed beyond the barrier, the air seemed to pop within her ears. Instantly her light sprang higher, illuminating the chiseled entry stones that towered above her, higher than the soaring ceiling of the chapel at Whitefriars. Taller than Countess Lafabvre's three-story town house in Paris.

Another magical barrier kept her light from penetrating beyond the stones into the cave proper. Marshaling the last of her resources, she waded through this density with more trouble. She fought for air while the barrier crushed her chest. At last the magical shield released her. She stumbled forward, almost dropping the precious ball of light.

Treasure! True treasure. Firewood, tinder, flint, and iron. FOOD! Aged cheese and dry flatbread, jerked meat and thick meal for porridge. Who knew how long it had been here? She did not care. Fire first. Then food. Then thought.

Warmth and a full stomach made Roanna's eyes heavy. She wrapped up in a beautifully preserved blanket and slept before her fire. She dreamed that Griffin Kirkwood slept beside her, wrapping her in the protective warmth of his arms.

When she opened her eyes, sunlight streamed through the opening of the cave. Griffin's absence felt like a gaping hole in her belly.

She watched the slight distortion of light through the magical barrier for a long moment. But food, sleep, and warmth had restored her body if not her mood. She slid easily through the barrier this morning as she sought a convenient bush as a necessary. Going back into the cave she encountered the resistance again. A one-way barrier to discourage intruders.

Once conquered, she barely noticed her second passage through the magic.

After a meal of boiled grains and dried fruit, she decided to explore the cave more deeply. This time she lit a torch, also stored in the interior along with the fuel, food, and blanket. Stepping carefully around the numerous puddles she walked deeper into the cave.

Home? Tryblith woke up. His presence in her mind became a light joy rather than the oppressive weight she had carried for nearly seven years. *Home!* he shouted again, nearly deafening her with physical sound as well as mental dominance. She clamped down on his enthusiasm, easily mastering him. Since the duel with Griffin Kirkwood, he had lost strength.

Despite Griffin's betrayal, she had to thank him for that small advantage over her demon.

Secretly, she smiled to herself. Tryblith must not know what she feared, hoped, did not know how to verbalize.

The cave forked into two equal-sized tunnels. "Which way, Tryblith?" As much as Roanna hated turning to the demon for anything, she had to ask. She sensed that if she wasted time exploring the wrong avenue, Tryblith would regain his strength before she was ready.

Right. Turn right.

A tingling in Roanna's right hand added to the demon's command. But this power came from without, not of Tryblith's making.

A few steps farther the brittle bones of two skeletons, nestled together in death as they must have been in life, reached out to trip her. She gasped and jumped back in superstitious fear.

"Who?" she asked the demon as well as any ghosts that might haunt this ancient cave.

My grandson. Murdered by Resmiranda Griffin. Curse her and all of her descendants!

The name meant nothing to Roanna. "And the other?"
She stooped to examine the bones. A few tatters of elegant
cloth clung to the frame in places. The first skeleton,
Tryblith's grandson, still held a rusted sword of antique
design clenched in his fist. The other skeleton gripped the
ends of a rotting knotted cord embedded in the throat of
his victim.

"Is he one of my ancestors? Is that how you came to my
bidding so easily?" Born of anger, fueled by a battered and
bleeding body, the spell had cost her much strength. For
days afterward she had been the easy toy of both Lord
Douglas and his son, Jamie.

*Your guilt for murdering your sister laid you lower than
your pain and exhaustion,* Tryblith reminded her.

"I did not murder my sister. She begged for death because she could not live with the humiliation Jamie Douglas
thrust upon her. She would have died a slow and painful
death if I had not mercifully dispatched her."

If you say so. Tryblith pressed hard upon her neck and
shoulders.

"Enough. Tell me who is this grandson of yours and why
I could call you so easily!"

*You descend from an old and noble line, the line of the
other man, but not mine or that of the Pendragons. The
Pendragons call themselves Kirkwood now, but in Blakely
Radburn's day, they hailed by the name of Griffin.*

"As in Resmiranda Griffin, the woman who warded this
cave and murdered your grandson. So what is my old and
noble lineage?" She knew. Gran had told her one dark
night as she held Roanna and whispered secrets to keep
her from fearing a vicious thunderstorm.

Roanna examined the second set of bones more carefully
but not enough remained to tell her much other than he
had contributed to Radburn Blakely's death.

*Keep going deeper into the cave. Soon you will come to
my portal and we will be free.*

"What is my family line?" Roanna planted herself firmly
in place.

The portal. You must take me to the portal!

"Not until you give me knowledge of my family." She
took another step toward the entrance.

Nimuë, you come from Nimuë's line.

"Who in hell was she?" Roanna took one step in the direction the demon prodded her.

Tryblith heaved a tremendous sigh. *Nimuë's father married the daughter of King Arthur's Merlin. Nimuë then seduced the Merlin to get a child by him. But she was banished when the old magician died. She died in turn when Arthur tried to take back his kingdom from usurpers. But her son lived. He went into hiding and fathered a long tradition of secret witches. You and your gran before you have inherited the magic. You must pass it on to your own child or grandchild.*

"And the Kirkwoods are descended from the Merlin's daughter and Nimuë's father. Griffin Kirkwood is a cousin of sorts. I seduced my cousin!" she laughed. But Gran had hinted at an even closer relationship. She had seduced Raven's father—Griffin's great-grandfather. No one in the village ever remembered that Gran had married, only that she had borne a girl child. A tingle of delicious power crept through Roanna at the near forbidden relationship. "I do not think the Kirkwoods have listed me in their much esteemed family tree." Roanna took a step beyond the skeletons.

Ayrlwren betrayed her husband and slept with Arthur. You are not related by blood to the Kirkwood clan.

"But you said Nimuë's child was fathered by the Merlin."

She wanted the world to believe it so.

"Who sired the child?"

Silence.

Roanna retreated two steps.

My portal!

"Who sired Nimuë's child?"

Her own father.

"A child of chaos! A child of power. No wonder you love me."

Take me to my portal! Tryblith insisted with a series of white hot probes into her mind.

She should have felt resentment against the demon. "We can conquer the Kirkwoods once I regain my full power," she promised her demon. *And I will have Griffin in my power. Together we will beget the greatest magician of all time, greater than even Merlin of old.*

Yessssss! Tryblith hissed with joy. *Free me and we will become invincible.*

Roanna said nothing. She explored deeper into the cave until she came upon a bronze door sealed with rusted iron hinges and bosses. And something more. Magic held the portal closed as well. Magic she could break.

If she chose.

But the cost of opening the portal was too high. She'd lose the only important thing left in her miserable life.

Chapter 47

Tryblith's portal.

ROANNA ran her fingers delicately over the line of green fire that marked the magical seal. The green matched the light that had rimmed the circle of stones and within the barrier at the cave entrance. Whoever had sealed Tryblith behind iron, bronze, and stone had set up many subtle layers of magic. Each one must be broken separately and in sequence.

"Very fine work. I could learn from this magician."

Resmiranda Griffin died three hundred years ago as must every mortal die. As you will die if you do not release me. Here. Now!

"I think not." Roanna stepped back from the portal. She admired the graceful magic from a slight distance. "She really did fine work. A pity to break it after so long." Work so subtly strong it lasted through the chaos of the Wars of the Roses and the religious disruptions of the last century.

Release me or I shall kill you and find another more willing creature!

"If you could kill on your own, you would not need me to do your murders for you." Roanna deliberately walked away from the portal. "You cannot forsake me until another summons you, Tryblith. 'Twas my spell that gave your spirit the ability to come forth. The rest of you must wait behind the portal until either I break the seal or all-out war in Britain weakens it beyond repair."

Tryblith screamed incoherently in the back of her head. Sharp pains stabbed at her eyes and neck. He was strong here so close to the portal. But she was stronger. She had more to protect.

"And I believe the war must be on British soil. A foreign war has little effect upon you, unless I, your host, am present and participating."

More screams. More stabbing pain.

She returned to her campsite, step by painful step. Methodically she gathered the last of the food into the blanket, kicked dirt over the fire, and approached the first barrier.

"I think a pentagram drawn within the circle of stones, an animal sacrifice—a rabbit should provide enough blood—five fires, one at each point of the sigil . . ." she mused out loud. The spell to free herself of the demon once and for all took shape. This close to the portal she should be able to banish him back to his netherworld. He'd only come forth again with a summoning. Next time she needed a demon, she would include his name in the spell. She would control the relationship next time.

Come back for me! Tryblith demanded. He sent a particularly hot pain into her extremities.

Roanna fought to keep her knees from buckling. She could not show weakness now. She had the strength to overcome the demon if only she ignored him a while longer.

Cold sweat broke out on her back as she pushed through the first barrier of magic. Her feet felt leaden, and her legs became too liquid to support her weight under the onslaught of pain.

You'll need to kill something at least as large as a goat or a pony. A human sacrifice would be better. Then you would have a new skull to place upon your staff and give you greater power.

Tryblith's sending of pain weakened a little as she approached the second barrier. She reviewed the elements of her spell like a litany against his control.

"A human sacrifice can be arranged." The thought of slicing Griffin Kirkwood's throat and spreading his naked body out in a pentagram of its own—his gorgeous naked body—sent a delicious thrill through her. Maybe she'd mount him once she'd staked him out. The final humiliation would destroy his soul before she destroyed his body. "I think a rabbit has sufficient blood to fuel the spell for now. At least then I'll have my dinner when I'm done."

If you do this now, you kill your unborn child. It cannot

survive the forces that must course through you to break our bond.

Roanna froze in her steps. How did Tryblith know?

I know everything about you. Including your need to rid yourself of me so that you think you can regain control over your life.

"I will control my life."

You are a mere woman in a world ruled by men. A world where men fear strong women so much they call them witches and burn them at the stake.

Roanna almost sobbed at the truth of Tryblith's statement.

There is much I can still teach you, Tryblith coaxed.

Roanna smiled. "There is little of magic left for you to teach me. I have learned English and French and the ways of the court. What more can you give me that I cannot find on my own?"

I can give you the ring and staff of the Pendragon, but only if you do not send me back behind the portal. If I am summoned forth under the control of my name, I will not show you how to gain these items of power. I will not protect you while you are big and clumsy and vulnerable with pregnancy.

Whitehall Palace, London, March 1561.

"Where has your brother taken himself, Kirkenwood?" Queen Elizabeth demanded. "His compatriots refuse my messenger entrance to Whitefriars. They say the Merlin has disappeared."

Resentment burned inside Donovan at his brother's blatant use of the ancient title that the family kept hidden from all but a few. On the other hand, he rejoiced that at last he had to a clue to Meg's whereabouts. *Are you still safe, Meg?*

A warm glow centered in the back of his heart. The clearest reply he'd had from any of his wild mental quests to find his sister.

"I do not know where Griffin Kirkwood has taken himself," he replied rather than vent his anger at his brother. More likely Griffin had tired of whatever game he played with the queen and coerced his comrades-in-crime to lie for him. He tried locking his gaze with the queen's. Raven had taught him that even the most obtuse of the mundanes could be made to see the truth in his eyes.

Elizabeth watched the soft rain on the window lights. She gazed at the fire. Her hand reached to scratch the ears of a large dog that was not there. She fussed with the pearls adorning her gown when she realized no wolfhound responded to her caress.

"You must know where he has taken himself. You are his twin, so alike to look at, in voice and posture, in education. And yet so different in attitude, religion, and politics." Finally she looked at him. Her eyes pleaded with him.

" 'Tis the differences that separate us, Your Majesty. I have not seen or spoken to Griffin the Priest in over two years." He'd heard of his brother's quiet visits to the queen. Everyone at court had. They gossiped about the new lover who had supplanted Dudley. Rumors linked the mysterious man with the enormous wolfhound at his side as ambassador for the marriage suit of the Earl of Arran, or the French king, or the son of Philip of Spain—though who would willingly marry the insane heir to Spain, Donovan could not fathom. The young man was rumored to love inflicting pain on others, the more helpless the better.

Donovan doubted all of the rumors about Elizabeth's marriage, she'd never marry anyone if a husband would reduce her power one little bit.

But Griffin was another matter. He probably sought to seduce Elizabeth back to the Catholic faith, make her vulnerable to demons. Donovan vowed to hunt down and kill his brother himself before he allowed the Catholics to unleash their demons upon England again. He had to fetch Meg away from the criminal enclave at Whitefriars, whisk her away to safety.

"You must bring the Merlin back to me, Milord Donovan. I miss him terribly already." Elizabeth's hand reached for the absent wolfhound again.

Jealousy brushed Donovan's shoulders. He'd never had

a familiar. He'd never touched the dog that accompanied Griffin every step through London.

"Perhaps a wolfhound from my kennel would help to ease your loneliness, Majesty. I can send to Kirkenwood this day for a pup."

Her eyes brightened a little.

"Consider it my gift to you upon my marriage to Lady St. Claire." Months had passed and Elizabeth still refused them permission to marry. The babe grew big in Martha's belly. Big enough to be twins. The midwife of Ide Hill predicted a boy, a son to inherit Kirkenwood and the ring of the Pendragon. Only if the marriage took place before the birth.

But time ran short. The Vernal Equinox was nearly upon them. Two months after that would see Martha in labor—less if she truly carried twins and they came early as twins often did.

"The time is not right for you to marry, to take you away from the court, Kirkenwood." Elizabeth's eyes narrowed. She stood from her chair and proceeded into the next chamber, her bevy of white-clad Ladies in Waiting trailing in her wake. The courtiers and officials who littered the receiving chamber followed.

Elizabeth had ended the interview. She had said nothing further about accepting a dog. She'd take no gift rather than give tacit permission for one of her courtiers to marry.

Donovan spotted a pale and subdued Katherine Grey among the ladies. Rumors had begun to circulate about her and the Earl of Hertford.

Time to take matters into his own hands as Katherine had.

Chapter 48

Whitefriars Abbey, London, March 1561.

HOW could I have been so blind—literally and figuratively? I had welcomed the Demon of Chaos and his host into Whitefriars. I had looked at Roanna de Planchet's aura and not seen the layers of red flamelets within the black energy of evil. I had looked upon her and thought only as a man falling in love.

Something of import must have transpired the night I drank so heavily to open my inner vision to her true nature. What?

Even Elizabeth's keen intellect and bright wit had not dulled my interest in Roanna's quiet beauty and homely comforts. I loved Elizabeth's mind. Every part of my being longed for Roanna. Elizabeth . . .

No I must not think upon the queen, must not visit her, lest my actions give the demon and his assassins entrance to her palaces. For Elizabeth's death would surely bring about the war and chaos the demon needed to run free throughout the land.

I needed more information about demons, about Resmiranda's duel with Tryblith. I had been approaching the conflict as a matter of faith. Faith was no longer enough. I needed access to all of the journals and chronicles hidden in the lair at Kirkenwood. The few documents I kept with me offered guides toward a path of enlightenment. They did not acknowledge demons from the netherworld.

Yet I feared to leave the sanctuary of Whitefriars. Here I knew myself to be safe. Meg and Robin were safe. Gareth and Carola, their daughter Faith, Brother Jeremy, and old Ralph, all of my friends here in the sanctuary must remain safe from the demon.

How long would my banishment of the demon from Whitefriars hold? I set wards of ancient origin augmented with Holy Water at every corner of the old abbey.

Dr. Dee should return soon from his diplomatic mission to Paris, Vienna, and Rome. I could ask his advice. He would help me find the portal that confined Tryblith's physical body so that I might seal it once more.

To seal it I would need to unleash my magical talent. More magic than I had used already to banish Tryblith.

Magic had restored my vision. Magic had expanded my perceptions by revealing auras of every object I viewed. I could not shield myself from the constant assault of color and energy. In those auras I read emotions, health, and truth—or lack thereof. In the auras I saw around every rock, tree, blade of grass, and animal, I saw a oneness with God.

I shuddered.

My confrontation with the demon had shown me that my immortal soul, by the use of magic, must be sacrificed in order to save England. The church would condemn me. Would God? Who was I without the church?

Could the Catholic Church truly unite England? We English needed Elizabeth's calm grasp upon affairs of state. We needed her intelligence, her political acumen, and her ability to manipulate the powerful men of the world, temporal and clerical.

She had given me as much food for thought as I hoped I had given her.

She had remained a true friend. Roanna had betrayed me. That betrayal hurt more than the aching muscles and mind left over from my blast of magic after so many years of disuse.

I was afraid. My faith did not give me as much courage as I thought.

The fierce storms of the Equinox descended upon southern England as if trying to maintain winter's cold grip on the land—or unleashed by demons. All of us huddled in the refectory around the hearth. We spoke quietly. Even the children remained subdued. Except for Faith and Robin, who laughed and cooed, delighted with their lives.

As I watched the little boy play with the growing infant, a

vision rocked me. Again I saw Faith grown to womanhood, healthy, happy, approaching her wedding. This time her groom came into focus. Robin, grown tall and strong, with a quick temper and a quicker smile. He would adore her as an adult as he delighted in her giggles now.

And I knew what was wrong with the first vision I had of that blessed moment. Neither Faith's father nor I would live to see them joined in happiness.

The gate bell clanged like thunder, rousing me with a jolt. All of us jumped, darting glances into the shadows. Ralph crossed himself, clutched his rosary, and trudged to the gate. Gareth and another well-muscled glassworker followed. Each of them selected a club from the firewood. Reluctantly, I grabbed my staff and joined them.

The storm nearly blasted me back into the snug warmth of the refectory. I shuddered in the chill and longed for my cloak. I left it behind in favor of freedom of movement should the confrontation at the gate become a brawl with Elizabeth's soldiers, or worse, a fight for life and soul with a demon.

Chances were it was merely another benighted traveler who sought refuge here. But for the safety of all, those who arrived after sunset must pass the scrutiny of more than Ralph's aging eyes.

Newynog raced ahead of me to be the first to encounter our visitor. Helwriaeth remained with Meg and the children.

I lagged behind the others, fighting the wind, gathering my inner strength.

When I slipped into the relative shelter of the gatehouse, I stopped short. My own face stared at me from beneath the dripping cloak of our visitor. I blinked a couple of times, not trusting my restored eyes. The visage remained the same. Dared I hope that my twin had sought me out to reconcile our differences? Several times in the last year I had sensed a gentle questing on the wind that might have been Donovan's mind seeking mine. I had dismissed each occurence as wishful thinking.

Dared I hope now that he had sought me for a reconciliation? United, we could defeat the demon. United . . .

Donovan's stony glare ended my hopes that we could ever unite in anything except recriminations. Ralph and

Gareth stood beside the newcomer, jaws flapping in won-
derment. They crossed themselves repeatedly.

"*Benedicte,* my brother." I finally greeted Donovan with
my hand extended in friendship.

He stared at my outstretched hand. A myriad of emotions crossed his face too quickly for me to read.

"Fetch Meg to me, and I will take her to safety," he
finally said in resignation.

I dropped my hand. "Our sister is safe and happy."

Gareth and Ralph nodded their heads in agreement.

"She be the best nanny any of us could hope for. All the
children love her. That great dog of hers protects them
better than we could. Please, milord, do not take her away
from us," Gareth pleaded.

Donovan's face became a blank mask as he struggled
with more emotions.

"Are you sure?"

"Very sure, brother. Even if I have to leave here, she
will stay and be an extra mother to the children. 'Tis the
life she chose."

"If you must leave this place, you must send to me, I
will watch over our sister."

I nodded my agreement.

"Come, Martha, we must seek another solution. I
thought I could put aside the years of bitterness, but I
can't." Donovan turned on his heel to brave the storm
once more.

"We have no other choice, milord," the cloaked figure
beside him clutched at his arm. "Any other priest in the
city will hasten back to Elizabeth. He is the only one we
can trust." She spoke softly, but her voice carried an edge
of iron strength. Her determination must match my brother's. Whatever their relationship, it must prove volatile at
times.

"Why do you truly seek me, brother?" I asked. My
knuckles turned white where I gripped my staff. Bitterness
and jealousy had filled our last parting with grief. As much
as I longed to hold my twin close to me again, to share our
thoughts and dreams, to plan the future together, and fight
today's enemies together, I dared not hope that Donovan
had changed his attitude one ort.

"Queen Elizabeth commanded us betrothed. Now she

has ordered us to postpone the wedding indefinitely." The woman—Martha, Donovan had called her—flicked her cloak aside to reveal the huge swelling of her belly. "We came to the priest in this sanctuary seeking a private wedding that will not reach Her Majesty's ears until too late."

"Even then she may throw us both into the Tower for defiance of her pleasure," Donovan spat.

"Is our queen so capricious?" I knew she could be when crossed. Deep inside, I knew she never acted impulsively but always calculated closely the effects of each action.

"Elizabeth is jealous of all of her courtiers. She binds us to her with tricks as well as commands. None of us may bring our ladies to court lest we pay them more attention than we do to her. She is spiteful," Donovan said more quietly. "We would gladly return to Ide Hill or Kirkenwood and be quit of her."

"Lately, the queen has shown great preference for Milord Donovan," Martha added. "She leans on him much as she used to lean upon Robin Dudley."

"I have heard as much." She welcomed my visits for the intellectual challenge and the love of conspiracy. But she rarely asked my counsel and I doubted she heeded it when given. She asked for my visions of what would be, not what she should do. "For the love of the child about to be born, I will assist you. Gareth, show them to the chapel. I must have a few moments to prepare." My fingers ached from where I gripped the staff too tightly. I could not yet relax them.

Donovan's eyes seemed to follow my thoughts to the staff with the black crystal. "I will not submit to this man for the sacrament of marriage," he announced. "He is Catholic. He has stolen much from me." Donovan straightened his shoulders and firmed his chin.

As he changed his posture, I detected a subtle weaving within his aura that should not be there.

Roanna! She had driven the wedge between us with magic. With the realization, I felt much of my own bitterness drop away as a dog shakes raindrops from her coat. Could I break the hold my enemy still had upon my brother?

"I merely keep the staff and the dogs in custody for your son, as bequeathed by our grandmother."

"Donovan, there is no other priest we can trust, Anglican or Catholic. In three months this is the first evening you have been able to steal away from court. You might not have another chance before . . . before . . . ?" She laid a hand upon her belly.

"You are correct, my dear. As usual." Donovan sighed heavily and offered her his arm. "The marriage is more important than who recites the words over us."

Gareth led them toward the chapel.

"Be he truly yer brother, or some demon in your saintly face come to haunt us?" Ralph detained me.

"Milord of Kirkenwood and I sprang from the same womb on the same day," I told him. I breathed heavily, and my hand finally eased off the staff. The tips of my fingers tingled, working away from numbness. "Until we were eighteen, our lives, our thoughts, our souls, were two halves of one whole."

"What happened then, Father Merlin?"

"I had a vision and he did not share it."

"Who be the elder?"

"I am. By less than an hour."

"Looks to me like he ended with more than he had a right to expect. He got the title and the lands and the money. And the woman. You got a life of trial and tribulation, of exile and poverty."

"But my life is rich in friends and faith."

"Can you perform the sacrament of marriage with one such as he? He is unconfessed and unshriven. Anger boils from him as steam from a damp cloak near the fire."

"For the sake of the woman and the child she carries, I must take it on faith that he enters this marriage with love and good intent. More than can be asked of most nobles who face an arranged marriage."

Ralph accompanied me back to the sacristy where I gathered my stole, bread, and wine for the Nuptial Mass. I recited a new incantation over Holy Water and anointing oil. Then I prayed for forgiveness that I used the holy rite to work magic.

You seek to break evil magic only. That is a task your church sanctions, Raven reminded me.

Meg and the dogs bounded into the chapel ahead of me, eager to greet Donovan and meet their new sister. Robin planted his face shyly into Meg's shoulder. Donovan raised an eyebrow at me in question over the presence of this unknown child in our sister's arms.

"You know, Meg. She always has to adopt whatever stray child crosses her path." I shrugged.

"She looks hale and happy," he agreed on a sigh.

I nodded. "Dearly beloved," I began the ceremony, gathering my motley congregation to share in the blessed sacrament.

The gate bell pealed once more. Ralph and Gareth exited, grumbling.

I hastened through the ceremony, sensing unwanted disruptions.

As I pronounced Donovan Kirkwood, Baron of Kirkenwood, and Martha, Lady St. Claire, husband and wife, I crossed each of their brows with the oil, murmuring prayers in languages more ancient than Church Latin. A blue tinge glowed in the shape of a blunt cross on Donovan's forehead and my thumb. A commotion rose in the doorway of the chapel. Startled, I smudged Donovan's anointing. The blue tingle in my hands stopped abruptly.

"Let me through, you filthy peasant!" the familiar tones of Thomas Howard, Duke of Norfolk, shouted above the protests of Ralph and Gareth.

I froze.

Meg ducked and blended into the shadows, taking Robin with her.

"Ah, Kirkenwood," the duke called to my brother by title. "I have come to share this blessed evening with you. My cousin Bess must not be allowed to keep you two apart any longer." He embraced both Donovan and Martha heartily. "Now who is this elusive priest who has visions and performs miracles for all of London?"

Norfolk looked me directly in the eyes and blanched. "So this is where you hide, traitor," he hissed.

Chapter 49

Whitefriars, London, late March 1561.

THE wind howled through the old abbey, begging me to make use of its power. Desperate to keep Norfolk from finding Robin through me, I raised my hands and gathered the moving air. I wrapped it around me. It whirled in ever-tightening circles. Debris, dust, and magic swirled to add their power to the wind.

Norfolk would try to follow me. He would not look for Robin just yet.

I no longer cared that I used magic to achieve my ends, ends that were strangely at odds with the mission assigned to me by Bishop du Bellay. Roanna had betrayed me. She was my enemy now and the enemy of all of Britain, not the Protestant cause that divided Europe.

I stepped behind my artificial cyclone. All eyes remained where I had been. Two more steps took me to the crypt stairs. I stumbled down the confined space. My breath came hard and fast. The still circling wind robbed me of air. Exhaustion weakened my limbs and blurred my vision.

As I landed in a foot of water at the base of the stairs, I remembered to call Newynog to me.

But my faithful familiar knew me well and had followed right on my heels. Her rough tongue on my face revived me a little.

"I've learned something, friend." I wrapped an arm around her shoulders, gathering her warmth and strength deep within me. "Magic takes muscles, much like hauling charcoal. Unless I use those muscles frequently, build upon them and keep them strong, the effort robs me of everything."

Newynog showed her agreement by wiping chilling sweat
from my brow with her tongue.

I rested my head against the dog for another long moment. "Come, Newynog. We have to find a different sanctuary and a place to plan our next move."

Whitefriars.

Send Martha and Meg to Kirkenwood. Now. Tell no one.
The words echoed in Donovan's mind as if Griffin had
spoken aloud. But he hadn't said a word. He'd just . . . just
disappeared in a cloud of blue smoke that smelled of wet
dog, wet wool, and burning charcoal.

The younger wolfhound had gone with him.

Donovan shook his head to clear it of the echo of his
twin's mental command. He could not trust Griffin, a Catholic who harbored demons.

But Griffin had sheltered Meg and given her the only
thing that made her truly happy: the care of a child.

"Where did the bloody magician go?" Norfolk screeched.
"He can't do this to me!"

"Looks to me loik 'e just did," the old man who tended
the gate said. He idled against the doorjamb, half blocking
it. The looming bulk of the other gate tender filled the rest
of the chapel entrance.

Donovan searched the shadows for his twin. He saw only
Meg holding the child. The older wolfhound stood before
her, braced for attack, teeth bared but silent. His sister and
the dog quaked in fear, barely trusting in the dark and
Norfolk's blustering sense of superiority to hide them.

The dogs had not deserted Griffin. Wouldn't the wolfhounds of Kirkenwood *know* if their chosen man had deserted the cause of light and life, even if only mistakenly?

"I'll have the man's head before this night is out!" Norfolk proclaimed much too loudly and too insistently for the
confines of this small building and the ears of the petty
criminals. He never did anything by half measures. And
never to help anyone but himself.

Donovan became wary. If Norfolk chased Griffin, perhaps the demons rested on Norfolk's shoulder and not Griffin's.

He needed time to sort this out. He needed to talk to Martha about it.

"You draw a weapon in this sacred place in the presence of the sanctified host and wine?" Donovan protested, placing a firm hand upon Norfolk's sword arm.

The duke turned wild eyes upon Donovan. For a moment he feared for Norfolk's sanity. No one except Elizabeth crossed England's only duke and lived.

"You dare lay hands upon me! You . . . you . . ."

"As a baron and peer of the realm, Your Grace, I request you respect the sanctity of this place. We were in the middle of a nuptial Mass. But your precipitous accusations have deprived us of the priest."

Send the women to Kirkenwood! They must take the child so that Norfolk never finds him. Griffin's voice came to him once more.

The child? Donovan asked himself and his brother in the same mental voice they had used in their youth. A voice that Griffin had always commanded and initiated. Donovan thought he'd never share that sweet communication again.

He trusted that mental voice.

Griffin did not respond.

"I'll bring your brother to trial for witchcraft," Norfolk grumbled, fully drawing his sword, despite Donovan's restraining hand. His retainers in their yellow livery followed suit. "He shall be punished for his defiance of me."

More was at stake here than just Norfolk's displeasure. Something to do with Meg and the child. What was so important about that child?

"Please, Your Grace, return to Ide Hill with me and my bride. Share a cup with us to celebrate this marriage. You will be godfather to the babe when it comes, won't you?" Donovan kept his hands upon Norfolk's sword arm, willing him to put aside his anger. His hand grew hot as Norfolk struggled to maintain the emotions that propelled him.

"Retire to Hertford's rooms in Cannon Row. I will seek you there after I have found the traitor and brought him to justice!" Norfolk stalked out of the chapel, sword at the ready.

Get the women to Kirkenwood before Norfolk decides to hold them hostage. He must not discover the child!

What child? Silence again. This time Donovan felt a deliberate emptiness in his head. Griffin kept silent for a reason.

"If I am to protect them, I must know why," Donovan muttered to himself and his brother.

Who should he obey? Norfolk, the declared Catholic who put obstacles in Elizabeth's path at every turn? Or Griffin, the Catholic priest who sought . . . What did Griffin seek?

One of these men had brought the demon Tryblith into England. Which one? Who profited most by Chaos?

He could not decide. Not here. Not now. He inclined toward trusting Griffin.

He followed Norfolk into the open courtyard of Whitefriars. The full force of the storm dumped rain and wind upon him.

Griffin? Do you hear me? I will not send my pregnant wife north into the teeth of this storm. 'Twill kill her and the babe.

Donovan looked about for traces of his brother. Surely he hadn't used magic to disappear from Norfolk, a fellow Catholic. He saw only sheets of rain threatening to drown the shielded lanterns at the gatehouse.

Now what?

Do not go with him. He will betray you. Send the women to Kirkenwood. Tonight. No more delay lest he follow you.

No.

Meg and Helwriaeth will protect Martha. Send them as soon as Norfolk is safely away. Get him drunk. 'Tis the easiest way to distract the blackguard.

"Norfolk drunk won't get me answers. Let him find you. I'm taking my wife back to Ide Hill before the queen misses me."

Whitefriars crypt.

Newynog and I waded through the flooded crypt of Whitefriars. This time of year, so close to the Thames, the water level rose dramatically down here. "We picked a devil of a time to explore this forgotten corner," I said through clenched and chattering teeth. We had looked here briefly once last summer, just enough to know that it offered a means of escape.

My dog whimpered at my side, half in agreement, half in need to retreat to the warmth of the fire in the refectory. I'd left my cloak there. No time to go back for it.

A dull ache pounded behind my eyes. I'd used too much magic in the escape.

If Norfolk found Robin, then he would use the boy to usurp the throne from Elizabeth. No matter whether he succeeded or not, innocents would die—possibly Robin himself. Chaos would follow. The demon Tryblith would win regardless of where the crown landed.

It might very well land on a bodiless head in the midden. I could not conceive of a government without a crowned head leading it in God's name.

The time approached when I would have to use all of my talents, magical and mundane, to stop the chaos.

And Roanna? What would become of her?

I couldn't allow myself to care.

My newly awakened magical senses told me that Norfolk searched each cell of the abbey proper. I felt his need to find me like a cold knife in the back of my mind.

The pain in my head increased. But I had to allow him to burn through his anger in a fruitless search, distract him from finding Robin.

Donovan's desertion of me hurt more than the pains of my body. Reopening the channels between our minds and weakening Roanna's spell of separation hadn't changed his stubborn heart.

Fire lanced from my knee up my thigh and down to my foot. Then I noticed the pressure against my leg. I had banged against a stone tomb. Something alien brushed my hand. I yelped and yanked my arms free of the rising water. I crossed myself instinctively as a ward against ghosts or ghouls. Then I heard a rat squeak. More than one. Dozens of the filthy creatures prowled the dark and forgotten place.

"Can you see to lead us, Newynog? There should be a little stair at the far end that leads up to the river gatehouse." I spoke in the soothing tones I wished someone would utter to me.

My dog whined a negative. Even wolfhounds need some trace of light to navigate through the dark. Too many new scents confronted her nose for her to find a blind path.

Reluctantly I brought a ball of cold light to my hand. I had already damned my soul by using magic to escape the chapel and to banish Tryblith. Another little spell could not condemn me further.

The rats fled. Their beady eyes glowed redly in reflected light. I shuddered once more. If one had bitten me or Newynog.

No time to worry about small perils, I had to flee this place into the city before Norfolk thought to search for other exits than the main gate. I had to find a safe haven and someone to help me get Meg and Robin away from Norfolk's prying eyes.

For tonight I could only hope that the angry duke did not recognize Meg as my sister and a likely coconspirator in hiding Elizabeth's illegitimate son from him. She would have to hide Helwriaeth to do that. Norfolk would recognize the wolfhound.

I prayed he would not hold all of the children of Whitefriars hostage against my return.

The ball of cold light illuminated only a few feet around me. It kept me from banging into any more tombs. The bruise from my previous encounter still hurt, but I could walk without a limp. I plowed forward through the deepening water by dead reckoning. Racked by chills and the pounding headache, I forced myself to place one foot in front of the other. I wondered if I would reach the stairs leading up to the little gatehouse before I had to swim. I couldn't hold the ball of magic light and swim, too. Newynog had already lost her footing, and she did not like it.

"Just a little farther." I coaxed her along, hoping I was right and we would not end up joining the dead who inhabited this place.

Newynog snorted a mouthful of water and her distrust of my statement.

"So I'm whistling in the wind to keep my own fears at bay. Indulge me."

She snorted again.

At last I caught a glimpse of a narrow step ahead. Its fellows wound upward out of sight. Being careful not to bang my knees again, I crawled out of the cold water and immediately chilled more. Newynog edged me aside and climbed ahead, pausing only long enough to spray me with more water as she shook herself warm and dry. She smelled almost as horrid as the rest of the crypt.

Shivering, headachy, and exhausted, we finally climbed up to the small nook beside the river·gate that was an excuse for a porter to stand out of the wind when summoned. We of Whitefriars locked this gate, but did not post guards here. The room above would offer more protection, perhaps an abandoned brazier, blankets, and a pallet. My mind shied away from that place as if avoiding a white-hot poker.

From the loud voices and banging I heard from the main portion of the abbey, I guessed that Norfolk still violated the sanctuary in his single-minded search for me.

Whose authority could stop him? No one in the realm outranked him except Elizabeth herself. He rarely listened to her or obeyed her commands. He'd listen only to a prince of the church, and none lived openly in England anymore.

Where should I hie from here? I knew a number of people in the city who would shelter their Father Merlin. They might even find a change of clothes and a cloak to send me on my way. None could afford a horse.

Gritting my teeth and bracing myself against the wind, I forged out into the remnants of the storm.

For once Newynog did not complain. She trotted ahead of me, certain of her path and the necessity of leaving the only place we had called home in a long time.

Chapter 50

Whitefriars Abbey, near dawn.

"HE'S gone, Your Grace. No sense in searching further."
Donovan tried one more time to end Norfolk's angry
search of Whitefriars.

The duke turned wild eyes upon him. His hair was disordered and he'd tangled his beard with constant tugging.
"I have to find him. He has stolen something very precious from me. Madonna and child. Lovely marble Madonna and child. Child . . ." His words drifted off into a
quiet mumble. Much of the man's energy vanished. He
seemed smaller, much less imposing without violent emotions propelling him.

"Come, Your Grace. The storm abates. I must take my
wife home now. You and I are both expected at court
early." Donovan tugged at Norfolk's sleeve. Together they
walked out of a small cell on the north end of the abbey.
He guessed that several women dwelled here, judging by
the brightly colored garments strewn about. A familiar subdued and much washed blue gown had caught his attention.
Some residual sense of urgency behind Griffin's mental
commands kept Donovan from blurting out that his sister
Meg resided here.

Where was she? And who was the child Griffin felt
obliged to shelter from Norfolk?

They found Martha dozing upon a settle in the refectory.
Someone had draped an extra blanket over her. An aging
wolfhound crouched beneath the high-backed bench, out
of sight to all but the most observant. Donovan spotted
Meg in a corner with several children and a bevy of chattering women.

Which one was the child Griffin had ordered him to send to Kirkenwood with the women? Why? All of the babes looked Gypsy dark. He could not imagine anything special about a Gypsy.

Something to do with Norfolk. That meant something to do with the queen.

Dudley is Gypsy dark, Raven's voice reminded him.

No. Not possible. He shook his suspicion away.

He pointedly ignored everyone but Martha.

Norfolk hovered beside him. "I shall dispatch two of my men to escort your lady back to Ide Hill. You and I had best repair to Whitehall. No sense in alarming Her Majesty with our absence." The duke seemed suddenly anxious to be away. He fidgeted with his sword hilt—now safely sheathed—looked around with darting and furtive glances, and shifted his weight from foot to foot like a small child needing to find the necessary. Finally his eyes lighted upon Meg, the only blue-eyed blonde in the group of dark women. Would Norfolk recognize the stubborn thrust of the Kirkwood chin and the depths of midnight blue in her eyes?

"You!" Norfolk stalked over to the women.

All conversation in the refectory ceased abruptly. Donovan's ears rang in the sudden silence.

"What crime brought you to the sanctuary of Whitefriars?" Norfolk asked Meg accusingly.

"Crime?" Meg's eyes took on the cloudiness of confusion so prevalent in her life. "Crime is. Sanctuary is."

"What kind of answer is that?" Norfolk clenched his fist as if ready to strike.

"Your Grace, the girl means nothing to you. We should go." Donovan tried to intervene.

"A highborn lady I guess, by her posture, the clearness of her skin, and the fine bones of her face. She hides in the only sanctuary left in England. I would know why."

"You should seek sanctuary, milord," Meg replied meekly. She kept her eyes lowered.

"What!"

"Seek sanctuary from death, milord. Death stalks you as surely as you stalk power."

"I will have the truth from you, girl!" Norfolk strode forward, fist raised.

The Gypsy women rose as one, making a solid barrier between the volatile duke and Meg.

"She is nothing, Your Grace. Why waste the time questioning her? Elizabeth expects us to break fast with her." Donovan clung to the duke's upraised fist.

Martha sat up, clutching her distended belly. "Milord, I think first we'd best find a midwife," she whispered.

Norfolk glared at her. "Not now, woman."

"Time and tide as well as babes wanting to birth wait for no man, Milord." She grimaced.

Donovan abandoned Norfolk to kneel beside his wife. "Are you certain, Martha?" Too early. The baby came too early. 'Twas only seven months. Perhaps seven and a half.

"Aye, Milord. The babe comes. Now." She grimaced again.

Immediately the six dark women and Meg crowded around her, edging Donovan away. "It's too early," Donovan protested. "We need a midwife. A doctor. We need help."

Norfolk tried to detain Meg with a hand upon her sleeve. She stared at his hand as if it were some offensive spider that needed squashing.

"Your hand is marked by death. Remove it from here immediately lest it taint the babes about to be born," she stated haughtily.

"Babes?" Donovan pushed the duke away to confront his sister.

Meg grinned impishly. The carefree mischief of her youth brightened her eyes.

"How can you be sure?" Donovan pressed her.

"Our Meg is always right," one of the Gypsy-dark women replied. "Best take yourselves off and wait. We will send word when babes and mother are safely delivered." She shooed the men out of the refectory.

"I must be at court. 'Tis too early for the babes." Donovan's thoughts scattered. He couldn't leave Martha and his babes in the hands of strangers. She needed her own bed, the comfort of a familiar midwife.

He needed to get Norfolk away from here.

"Go." Another woman joined the first in pushing him and Norfolk toward the doorway. "We will send word. This is no place for men, especially a father who will interfere."

"I'll send a litter for her, and her midwife," Donovan said.

"We're all midwives," a middle-aged woman declared. "And she shouldn't be moved." All the women giggled as they pushed him forcibly out the door.

From the river gate, I plodded eastward along the rough beach of stones and mud to the first landing on the Thames. Already boatmen readied their craft for a day of ferrying goods and passengers up and down and across the Thames. Their faces, lit by an occasional shielded lantern, took on the gruesome sharp planes and shadows of ghostly masks. I recognized none of them, and therefore trusted none of them.

Wrapping cold shadows around me like the cloak I longed for, I sidled up the embankment beside the steps. Newynog slunk within my shadow, as invisible as myself. But one of the boatmen always seemed to be watching the stairs. I needed a diversion.

Once more, a ball of cold light came to my hand, more easily than the last one. Either I was flexing my magical muscles or the respite in the gatehouse had given me strength. With a quick flick of my wrist, I sent the ball scudding over the water toward London Bridge.

All eyes in the vicinity followed the darting light long enough for me to clamber up to the street. Shadows flowed with me to the Fleet Bridge and across the muddy stream. From there, the Ludgate was only a few more steps. In this section of town, much of the ancient wall that protected old London from raiders remained intact to protect the city from unpaid tolls and taxes. The watchman knew me and waved me through without question. A single coin—the last one in my pocket—ensured that he would tell no one of my passage. I'd need the bag of coins in my cell, but couldn't go back for it.

Up Paternoster Row to Cheapside I wandered, seeking inspiration or a familiar face. Most of the people I served at Whitefriars were denizens of the night, their lodgings

over near Fenchurch Street or East Cheap in the shadow
of Tower Hill. Did I want to take shelter so close to the
fortress that could easily become my prison should Norfolk
discover and denounce me? I suspected that Tryblith had
planted the seeds of chaos in his vulnerable mind. Neither
Norfolk nor the demon that prodded him would rest until
they had destroyed me and brought England to her knees
in chaos.

Would Elizabeth protect me against charges of witchcraft
and treason?

I could not trust her good will. The queen was indeed
capricious—but only as her change of mood would serve
England.

All of my being longed for the north. I needed to go to
Kirkenwood, to consult the journals and grimoires of my
ancestors as well as renew my strength and spirit. But not
without Meg and Robin. To get them out of Whitefriars, I
needed help.

From Cheapside, I worked my way back toward East
Cheap, through narrow lanes overhung by dwellings built
above shop fronts. The closer I came to the river and the
Tower, the less respectable became the buildings, the
thicker the miasma of ill humors rising from the river and
the open sewers. A man in good clothing with a full purse
would fear walking here alone in the dregs of the night as
torches guttered and thieves sought one last mark before
retreating from the light of dawn.

I had no fear, for I had nothing left to lose except my
life. The desperate poor of the district recognized one of
their own in me.

Behind me, on Carter Lane and Cannon Street, I heard
the rumble of carts headed to market. More and more details of the rotting buildings came to life as the sun sent its
first rays of light above the horizon. The last tattered remnants of the storm clouds fled. Today promised to be clear
and cold.

I shivered again and clamped down on my teeth to keep
them from chattering. I had to find shelter soon before I
took chill and could not free Meg and Robin in time.

The broad thoroughfare of Gracechurch Street that led
to London Bridge loomed before me. In the distance I
heard the rumble of the mint pounding away within the

walls of the Tower. A lion from the royal menagerie roared his protest at the rising of the sun and the noise from the mint. More people, rich and poor and merchant alike appeared on the street. A flash of bright yellow livery stopped me. Norfolk's men.

I had to cross Gracechurch to reach East Cheap and the homes of the people I knew.

Stupid with fatigue and hunger I turned and ran back the way I had come.

A shout rose up around me, grew, and surrounded me. The clatter of many booted feet followed. And then I heard the distinctive scrape of swords pulled free of their sheaths.

Only then did I realize my mistake. If I'd remained still and let the men pass, they would not have noticed me. A running figure drew attention. Something to remember the next time. Presuming I lived long enough for there to be a next time.

I ran up Watling Street toward St. Paul's. The cathedral offered many hiding places, but no true sanctuary. If Norfolk would violate Whitefriars in his search for me and my secrets, then Anglican St. Paul's would deter him less.

I circled the cathedral. Printers were already setting up their booths in the forecourt. A penny would buy copies of the latest ballads, poetry, gossip, or criminal trials. More importantly, the tangle of stalls presented a maze to confuse the men who drew ever closer upon my heels. I dove behind a substantial booth with dozens of broadsheets tacked to its frame.

"Here now, what's the bother?" the proprietor peered nearsightedly at me. Ink stained his hands as well as his leather apron. Years of manning the bulky presses made his arm muscles bulge beneath his shirt.

"Hide me," I whispered. "For the love of God and England, hide me from them." In a fight I was certain he could hold his own. I prayed it would not come to a fight.

"Can't do that. Not worth my license to sell." He beckoned toward the men in yellow livery.

I scrambled upward and out of the booth, tipping it as I pushed away from its interior.

More cries followed my progress through the maze. The printer had raised the hue and cry. Nowhere in the city was I safe.

I plunged on, darting and dodging as best I could. My breath came in sharp pants. Fire burned upward from my lungs. Running warmed my body. Hunger and exhaustion made me stumble. Norfolk's men gained on me.

Frantically I searched for a refuge. Any refuge. Apothecary Hall came into view. I had no guild membership, but I had consulted some of the herbalists there and sent some of my flock to their members. Perhaps.

I put on a burst of speed. A corner blocked my pursuers from view. I turned another corner and raced up the steps of the guildhall. Inside the foyer, I paused to catch my breath and assess my surroundings.

Clawlike fingers clasped my wrist. I gasped and tried to jerk free.

"In here, Father Merlin," an ancient voice creaked.

"Who?"

"One you have blessed." The one-eyed crone I had encountered on my first visit to Elizabeth showed herself. She hobbled into an alcove off the foyer, using a long staff to aid her. A carved raven sat atop the aged walnut shaft. "Into the cellar with you. I'll send my grandson to you when it is safe."

"If it is ever again safe for the Merlin in London."

Chapter 51

Whitehall Palace, London.

"HAS your wife safely delivered?" Norfolk asked Donovan in hushed tones.

Donovan searched the milling courtiers for signs of someone who might hear the duke. Norfolk had whispered, but in the maze of rooms opening into each other, sound carried in the strangest ways. If Elizabeth found out that her "Wolfhound" had married without permission, she'd throw him into the Tower, possibly annul the marriage and declare the new baby, or babies, illegitimate.

"Let us retire to the balcony for a breath of air," Donovan suggested, draping a firm arm about Norfolk's shoulders. The gesture was a presumption upon the duke's elevated rank, but necessary to ensure he came. Once they stepped into the open air, Donovan closed the long window and latched it.

The cool air refreshed him after the long and traumatic night. But his face felt puffy and his eyes gritty. He'd not recover until he slept. And he could not sleep until Martha was safely delivered and Elizabeth no longer required his presence.

"Is your lady wife safe?" Norfolk asked again. This time he made no pretense to keep his words quiet.

Donovan wondered if the queen's cousin set out to entrap Donovan into an admission of defiance of the queen's orders.

"Word arrived a few moments ago. The labor pains stopped."

"Is that good?" Norfolk had lost a young wife in childbirth about the time of Elizabeth's coronation. He must know the dangers Martha faced.

"The midwife says yes, 'tis good. 'Tis too early for the

babes to come. The longer they wait, the bigger and stronger they will be." Donovan clenched his hands and found himself silently praying to whatever god or goddess might listen. He didn't do that often. Didn't believe enough to pray during the good times. "I hated to leave her. But better I live apart from her than risk Elizabeth's wrath and end up dead upon Tower Hill."

"You must get Lady Kirkenwood away from that awful place. 'Tisn't fit, nor safe for her to linger." An edge came into Norfolk's voice. His eyes narrowed in calculation. And yet he retained a sense of wild disorder in his posture and compulsive digging and yanking at his beard. If he kept it up, he'd likely pull out the hair in ugly patches.

Donovan looked at him sharply. What was the wily duke up to? Was he even rational?

"I have ordered a litter for milady, to take her back to Ide Hill. She'll be more comfortable there, with her own midwife, in her own bed, with her own servants." He'd also ordered his men to bring Meg and the child she cared for with them.

"Aye. A good plan. When will she be gone?"

Why was Norfolk so anxious? Surely he had little personal concern for Martha, never having met her before yestereve. Nor had England's only duke made any overtures of friendship to Donovan, a minor lord from the border country and one of Elizabeth's favorites. Norfolk abhorred everything about his cousin the queen—especially her favorites.

"I do not know for certain," Donovan hedged.

"Best you find out and get your lady gone from Whitefriars," Norfolk hissed. "Her delicate condition was all that kept me from torching the place last night. By midnight, that festering sore will stand no longer."

He seeks something, or someone other than Griffin, Donovan mused. *Meg!* Donovan nearly screamed his sister's name. *He seeks Meg and the child she has adopted.*

"Surely, Your Grace, 'tis drastic action. You of all people in England, a true Catholic, must appreciate this one last church sanctuary, an ancient and honored custom of yo . . . the church."

"A traitor to me and mine harbors there. A magician of the foulest kind. There is no sanctuary for betrayers and heretics."

"The priest abides there no longer. We searched the place

high and low last night." A hollowness of fear expanded in
Donovan's middle. If anything happened to Griffin, would
he, Donovan, survive as well? Last night's intimate mind-to-
mind communication had shown him just how much of his
soul was bound up in his brother's body.

But he could not think beyond Martha. He had to get her
to safety. He needed to take her home. To Kirkenwood.

If only he had some of the ghostweed extract so that he
could fly to her side. Fly away from the intrigues and politics of court. Living at war upon the border seemed quieter
and safer than enduring Elizabeth's whims.

"A magician of Griffin's caliber can hide in plain sight.
Only fire will root him out. Whitefriars burns tonight," Norfolk continued.

Donovan jerked back to the conversation, away from his
musings about home. "Her Majesty will not thank you for
taking the law into your own hands, Your Grace. She toler-
ates Whitefriars. She must have reasons."

"Her Majesty will eventually thank me for ending the
tyranny of criminals who hide there by day and wreak
havoc on London by night, only to retreat beyond the arm
of the law when confronted."

"There is little evidence that crime in the city centers on
Whitefriars. Her Majesty believes in the law and evidence
and trials." Donovan had trouble following Norfolk's logic.
Was the man insane or just blinded by his own ambition
and sense of self-importance?

"Evidence? I do not need evidence to know the truth.
Whitefriars burns tonight. Get your lady to safety today or
watch her burn with the rest of the whores and heretics."

Apothecary Hall, London.

I slept most of the day in the dank cellar beneath Apothecary Hall. I stripped off my sodden clothing and wrapped
in the blanket provided by the one-eyed crone who, I
learned, was mother to the head of the guild and grandmother to many of the younger journeymen and appren-

tices. Near sunset she brought me hot broth and clean clothing. Two of her grandsons listened to my lungs and inspected my fingers and feet for signs of illness. I succumbed to their eager ministrations, recognizing the lesson the old mother gave the boys. But I knew how to hide the symptoms they overlooked due to inexperience and a tendency toward haste. Only when they were satisfied that I thrived did they allow me solid food.

Hot bread, fresh from the oven, nearly melted in my mouth. The cheese was soft and fresh. The mutton stew tasted like ambrosia. The tart dried apples, sweetened with honey and fortified with walnuts, reminded me of how long it had been since I had eaten anything close to the nourishing foods I had considered essential in my youth.

I drank a lot of newly brewed beer to keep the scratchiness in my throat from betraying the deep cough that sat like a slumbering wolfhound on my chest.

When I had eaten every crumb and wiped my mouth free of foaming beer, I spoke to the boys more than to their grandmother. "I must go back to Whitefriars. My sister and her child are no longer safe there."

Good thing they were not familiar with my voice, or they would recognize the building congestion and confine me to this cellar for days, dousing me with noxious potions of dubious worth.

"No one is safe at Whitefriars tonight," the younger boy mumbled.

"What do you mean?" The cough grew heavier as my throat tightened with fear.

"Rumors only, Father Merlin."

"What kind of rumors?"

The boy looked anxiously to his grandmother. She nodded. He swallowed heavily, his oversized throat apple bobbing in his scrawny adolescent throat.

"The Duke of Norfolk gathers all his men together. They relish violence and speak openly of burning traitors and magicians," the older boy whispered.

Me.

Norfolk would destroy the entire abbey tonight to force me out into the open with Robin in tow.

"He must be mad!" I blurted out.

"Cunning. Mad. Hungry for power. What be the difference?" The old woman shrugged.

"I must go," I said upon a wheeze. Wearily I stood and swayed.

The older apprentice apothecary placed a cool hand upon my wrist.

"You burn with fever. You cannot go." He pushed me back to a sitting position.

"You do not understand. My sister. A child. I have to save them." Not to mention all of those who depended upon me.

"We will warn your people. Bring your sister and her child here." The younger boy bounced up eagerly. Newynog leaped to her feet to join him.

"I will not endanger anyone else," I stated firmly. Clenching my jaw until it hurt, I focused on that small pain so that I could ignore all of the small aches brought on by the fever. My eyes focused. The fever burned only slightly.

"My boys go with you," the crone said, recognizing my determination. Meg called it stubbornness. So did my bishop for that matter.

I nodded my acceptance of her verdict.

"May I know the name of my benefactress, Old Mother?" I asked as I gathered my staff and wrapped the blanket about my shoulders in place of a cloak. I thought I knew, but needed confirmation of my ally.

"Old Mother will do, boy. You blessed me and gave me hope to live a while longer. May you find peace and bless the lives of all you touch." She placed her withered hand upon my forehead in her own benediction.

Goddess go with you. Raven's gentle voice joined hers.

We left then, walking boldly out of the Apothecary Hall and turned directly for Ludgate and across the Fleet, the shortest path to Whitefriars. Newynog snuffled every shadow, ranging a few feet ahead of us, but always returning to my side to shove her head under my hand. We only had to stop once for me to cough my lungs clear.

I prayed every step of the way that the chill I had taken would pass quickly. If I'd the time, I knew how to rid myself of the foreign humors through meditation and an inner search. I didn't have the time. With each prayer I cast out my senses in search of hostiles in pursuit. The dichotomy of my actions no longer

bothered me. I'd worked magic yesterday—damning my soul or
saving it, I no longer knew. Until England was safe from the
seeds of chaos planted in Norfolk by Roanna and her demon, I
had to use every tool available to me.

I felt a gathering of violence in various parts of the city.
Part of the nightly ritual of desperate people emerging from
their lairs? Or was it Norfolk gathering his men and a mob
to torch the abbey?

Whitefriars lay quiet in the gloom of a cloudy twilight. I
expected a vision of smoke and flame, panic and death. All
I saw was the bulky silhouette of ancient buildings waiting.

Ralph passed us through with only a lifting of his
eyebrows.

"Brother Jeremy?" I asked quietly.

"Sleeping."

I'd only been gone a day. It felt like a year.

I made my way toward the leader's cell with my two
helpers and Newynog on my heels. The boys looked around
curiously. Coals still burned under the glass furnace and
the glory hole. The now familiar acrid scent of molten sand,
burning chemicals, and charcoal filled the air. I breathed it
in deeply. The boys wrinkled their noses.

"Brother Jeremy." I shook the man awake. He roused
instantly, alert and ready to jump to the newest crisis that
demanded his attention. I suspected he'd not been truly
asleep, merely resting; something he rarely did. His energy,
night and day, kept Whitefriars alive.

"Brother Jeremy, you must evacuate the abbey. Everyone must leave immediately by the river gate. His Grace
of Norfolk plans to torch Whitefriars."

"He can't," Brother Jeremy said quietly. "We are a legal
sanctuary, honored by Her Majesty."

"The duke counts himself above the law. He obeys only
when the law suits his likes. At the moment he does not
like me and will gladly sacrifice innocent lives to flush me
out along with the secrets I protect."

"We will not leave our home. The queen promised us
that, as long as we commit no further crimes and provide
her with the glass she needs, she will respect the ancient
tradition of sanctuary."

"She does not know about Norfolk's quest for vengeance." But I could tell her, if I could get to her in time.

"He cares not for the consequences. Elizabeth's crown is still too new and uncertain for her to bring low her cousin, the premier peer of the land."

"We will not leave our home," Jeremy insisted as he sat up. He rested a long moment. "We will defend ourselves and our home against unlawful attack," Brother Jeremy said with resolve. He stood and reached for his boots.

"With what? You have no trained soldiers, no weapons." I did not have Excalibur.

"We have weapons aplenty in our tools. We have fire to make them white hot and as deadly as any sword. We have determination and a home and loved ones to protect." He grinned. His face became a grimacing death's head to my sensitized vision. Was tonight the night of his death? I already envisioned Gareth assuming the reins of leadership.

"To work, then," I agreed. "Boys, you'd best take yourselves home, away from the dangers of the next few hours." I gestured the boys out of the cell.

"Not worth telling Grandmother we left you behind," the older boy, Michael, said.

"She'd skin us alive and box our ears," his cousin Jonah agreed. They both grinned at me.

"Then take yourselves to the infirmary. We'll send the injured to you."

Brother Jeremy and I stomped out together, shouting orders right and left.

Stoke the fires of both furnaces. Fill them with sand, potash, and lime. Lay all of the tools close by. Get the children and women into the chapel with its slate roof and access to the crypt and escape.

If only I had Excalibur, or any sword, I'd feel more confident.

Too soon, shouts of anger clanged at the gate demanding entrance. Ralph left the porter's peephole firmly closed. But ancient and rusted hinges only delayed the mob outside for a short time.

Two dozen men in Norfolk's distinctive yellow livery stormed through the breached gate. We met them with molten glass flung from the tips of blowing pipes. We met them with pincers and pokers heated white hot at the tips. Quilted mitts for holding hot tools provided extra protection against slashing blades.

Men screamed. Swords clanged against iron tools, reverberated and amplified to a deafening din. Newynog menaced men from behind, ripping legs and arms with strong jaws and wicked teeth.

I saw Norfolk directing the erection of three tripods at the gate, each one a stand for an arquebus. One blast of the weapons could fell my people from a distance. I rushed the guns with my pincers raised high. The white hot tip had dulled to glowing red. Still hot enough to inflict dangerous burns. Gareth and another big man followed with blowing pipes just dipped in the gather.

A beefy soldier stepped authoritatively in front of the gunners, protecting the valuable equipment and men from us. He drew his sword. His stance widened a fraction. He knew how to fight.

But so did I. *"En garde,"* I called to him, holding the pincers as if I wielded the Lady's Sword of magic, power, and legend.

"Engagé!" he replied.

Lunge, thrust, parry, retreat. I drew him away from the gunners. Out of the corner of my eye I caught a change of movements. The gunners loaded the arquebus. We hadn't much time.

Gareth drew back his arm and flung a mighty glob of hot glass into the middle of the three weapons.

Sound and rushing air threw me backward. Dimly I realized that Gareth's molten missile had ignited the gunpowder. I shook my head to free it of the ringing in my ears. My eyes cleared a little.

A hot whoosh of air felled me once more.

The thatch on the stable caught fire.

Newynog grabbed my collar in her teeth, urging me up. A man in smoke-grimed yellow lunged for me. I rolled away from his sword. Sparks flew when the blade met the cobbles. My pincers still glowed red. I swiped at the man's legs. He stumbled. Newynog sank her teeth into his thigh. He howled and dropped to his knees, beating at the dog with his hands. She darted out of his way, seeking another victim.

The bleating of goats and the cackle of panicked chickens added to the uproar. Women rushed to douse the fire. We men and Newynog held our ground and beat back the intruders. And finally Norfolk's men retreated, taking their wounded and dead with them.

"Norfolk?" I asked whoever might be near me as I rested my pincers on the ground and gasped for air. Smoke clogged my lungs. I longed to cough and cough for a long time. Each breath tightened the bands constricting my chest.

"First out the gate, as soon as you attacked his gunners," Gareth said. "Coward." He spat into the ground.

A quick look confirmed that most of the meager livestock milled around the courtyard, getting underfoot, squalling loud enough to wake the dead. The thatch still burned in places. Most of it was too sodden from the rain and the women's efforts to control the blaze to do more than smolder.

"How many did we lose?" I asked.

Gareth grinned broadly through his soot-blackened face. "None."

"Hurt?"

"None." His grin grew even broader.

"Teach the arrogant bastard to violate our sanctuary!" Ralph chortled.

Relief weakened my knees. A choking cough did nothing to loosen the tightness in my chest.

"Then I must take Meg and Robin and leave here before Norfolk thinks up another plan," I said weakly. While the others cleaned up the courtyard—globs of cooling glass everywhere, smoke and smoldering thatch, animal droppings, and the remnants of the abandoned guns and tripods—I dragged myself to the chapel. Meg would be with the children. She and Helwriaeth would protect them at all costs.

Inside my church, lighted only by the altar candles, I searched for one bright head of blonde hair. Shadows within shadows hid identities from me. Not as many women as I expected. Many were in the courtyard. Others had taken to the road again with their families.

"Meg?" I called. "Helwriaeth?" My words trailed off into a bone-racking cough. Newynog pressed close, giving me what strength she could.

I opened my senses as far as I could with the constriction in my chest and fever weakness. I tapped into Newynog's sensitive nose. She sat on my foot. She could not smell her dam or my sister. Robin was only a distant echo to us.

Chapter 52

The River Hag Inn, Carmelite Street across from Whitefriars Abbey, London.

ROANNA watched the bowl of water from the safety of her room above the tavern across Carmelite Street from Whitefriars Abbey. The image of Griffin Kirkwood channeled volley after volley of magic through his pincers. He kept his weapon white hot long after a mundane tool would have cooled.

Norfolk's men retreated from him, arms shielding their eyes from the blasts of energy he unleashed. "You don't even know the pure strength of magic that responds to your thoughts," she whispered. "You will force yourself to believe that the intensity of your faith alone saves your friends within the abbey."

What was faith but another form of magic?

Roanna reared back as a blob of hot glass ignited the gunpowder. But the images in the water did not blast through to burn her. Tryblith giggled at her instinctive shying away. He drank in Norfolk's chaotic energy.

We did this to him! We made him violate all of his convictions by invading the sanctuary.

And then the battle was over. Norfolk retreated, too cowardly to see to the safety of his own men.

Not a very good military leader, Tryblith chortled.

Roanna had to clench her teeth together to keep the demon from growing still stronger as the screams of the dying men reached her physical ears from outside the tavern.

She had to maintain a delicate balance of strength and control. If Tryblith became too strong, he would taint the baby. If she dominated him too severely, he would replenish his strength from the baby.

398

The flickering light of the burning stable thatch turned the flimsy half-timbered walls of the inn garish shades of red and orange. She turned her attention back to the images in the water. The crystal at the bottom of the crockery bowl grew more visible through the scene. She had not much time.

"Cords bind tight. Squeeze life away. Choke him, choke him, choke him," she chanted as she slowly clenched her fist.

Griffin Kirkwood doubled over in a spasm of uncontrolled coughing.

I told you the spell would work. Tryblith sounded very superior and pleased with himself.

"I know the spell works."

She smiled and sat back in her straight chair. But she kept her eyes on the images in the water. They grew fainter, more transparent. Her strength waned. She wanted nothing more than sleep.

You've done this before. You killed the Douglas with this same spell. Tryblith wanted more violence. *Kill him and the staff is yours.*

Roanna wasn't about to give the demon everything he wanted. "We will meet again, Griffin Kirkwood. I'll have your staff on my terms."

Griffin revived some. A sigh of relief escaped her. She wasn't ready for him to die yet. He needed to realize his fall from grace when she showed him the consequences of his actions.

His twin she could dispatch without regard. But first she would make sure the petty rift between them grew into an uncrossable chasm of despair.

Griffin began his mad search for his sister. What was so important about the insipid creature with only half a mind? The girl was useless. Much like Roanna's sister, lost so many years ago. She hadn't the courage to live when faced with rape. Roanna had the courage, and the fortitude to use the pain as a magical weapon. She had used that pain to summon Tryblith, her salvation and her doom.

"I'll have the secret of the importance of your sister from you, Griffin Kirkwood. Secrets are power." She tightened her fist once more. Griffin's collapse into a coughing fever drained her of the last of her energy. "Remember that you lust after me, Father Griffin. Remember that you lost your immortal soul the night you lay with me. Together we could have ruled the world. But you betrayed me."

Together you and I will rule the world through chaos, Tryblith consoled her.

"First we find the sister. Then I steal the staff."

Ide Hill Manor, a few days later.

"Where is Meg?" Donovan asked Martha as he sat on the edge of their bed, holding her hand. He had stolen a few hours from Elizabeth's demands to visit his wife. He wondered if Elizabeth suspected that he had married without royal permission. Not only did the queen bind him closer and closer to her, barely allowing him time enough alone to use the privy, she had removed the court to Richmond, miles farther east from Ide Hill than Whitehall. The move had taken place mere hours after the clandestine wedding. Donovan had had the devil's own time getting away for the extended ride home.

"Meg?" Martha turned her head toward him. Her eyes looked tired, her face drawn, reflecting new hollows and dark shadows. In contrast, her belly seemed to swell by the day.

"My sister. The woman at Whitefriars who said you carried twins." Donovan squeezed Martha's hand.

"She is your sister?" Martha tried to sit up. She always preferred to look Donovan in the eyes. But the bulk of her pregnancy made every movement awkward. At least the labor had stopped. A few more weeks would give the babes a much better chance at life.

"Yes. Apparently she traveled with Griffin to the sanctuary. She has a child in her custody. Griffin thought the child important. I would question her."

"I barely remember the woman. Only that she had eyes of the deepest blue I have ever seen. More intense even than yours, my sweet. And she seemed to have a halo surrounding her."

"That's our Meg." He drifted off in pleasant memories of home and growing up in the crowded, bustling family. "What happened to her?"

"I do not know."

"I sent word with the litter that she should accompany you back to Ide Hill."

"Only the servants you sent with the litter returned with me. I was told of no other message."

Panic rose in a lump to Donovan's throat. Norfolk had attacked Whitefriars. He'd been forced to retreat. But there had been a fire. Norfolk boasted to Donovan privately that he had killed the traitorous Griffin along with numerous other violent criminals.

Donovan doubted the duke's story. He would have sensed Griffin's death as surely as he had felt both Da's and Raven's passing. Besides, if Norfolk had killed so many at Whitefriars—including the nearly legendary Merlin of the abbey—why had he been forced to flee like the coward he truly was? A few discreet inquiries among the servants revealed that many of Norfolk's men had suffered horrible burns. Had Griffin truly used magic to fend them off? Three had died on the scene, two later. Six more men might well die or be maimed and scarred for life.

Had Meg been one of the victims among those in sanctuary? Or had Norfolk captured her? If he had, then the demon Tryblith surely guided his actions.

"May you burn in hell, Norfolk. I'll kill you with my bare hands if I can't get you convicted of treason."

Apothecary Hall, London.

Roanna crept up the shadowed steps of Apothecary Hall. She wrapped her cloak tighter around her, as if chilled by the wind. With her own staff in hand, she bent over and shuffled her slow steps, presenting the illusion of an ancient woman in need of help.

On the third step, a young man offered her his arm. "How may I help you, Old Mother?" he asked solicitously.

"Something for the joint disease. All this rain." She coughed and extended her right hand for his inspection. A mild illusion showed the skin wrinkled and spotted, every knuckle swollen to three times its normal size and the fingertips twisted at odd angles.

"My grandmother has shown me how to make a wonderful salve that will warm the ache out of you. It uses extract of mummy." The boy nearly bounced with enthusiasm.

"You may fetch me some," Roanna commanded in a voice that cracked and wheezed.

The moment the boy ran off on his errand, Roanna slipped into a shadowy alcove beside the door. Her scrying bowl had shown her Griffin Kirkwood writhing in a fever in this building. Where?

She cast out her senses. Confusing waves of magic engulfed her. They filled the building, swelled and circled around her as if she were their source and destination.

Slowly she circled in place, arms extended, seeking. Seeking.

More circles, more confusion.

You're standing directly on top of him! Tryblith chortled.

"The cellars," she breathed. A quick assessment of her surroundings revealed a trapdoor with a steep ladder in the corner of the alcove, as if this little ell had been added as an afterthought solely to give access to the lower levels.

A quick check of the central hall showed the apprentice apothecary happily grinding away with a mortar and pestle. A middle-aged man peered over his shoulder, offering advice. From the look on the boy's face the advice was unwanted. They'd be occupied with the salve for some time to come.

Roanna swung onto the ladder and descended into the gloom below. The scent of damp earth, mold, and disease nearly smothered her. She gagged, clenching both hands across her mouth. The little bit of breakfast she'd been able to swallow threatened to come up again.

"Not yet. Not here, and not now," she ordered her body to behave. Slowly, her stomach settled as she became inured to the smell.

Once more she opened her magical sense. She found the corners and ceiling of the small room where she stood. More rooms led off of this one. Then the waves and circles of uncontrolled magic flooded her senses and took on color—all tinged with blue. Griffin's signature color.

Left, Tryblith prodded her. The twisting in the back of her neck nearly brought up her breakfast again. She was tempted to let it fly, let her weakness become the demon's.

Left, he said more quietly, without any painful prodding.

Roanna turned left into a series of storerooms. The array of scents from various apothecary ingredients masked the offensive odors. Until she came upon a decaying corpse wrapped in bands of linen. The mummy. Pieces of the dead man had been removed for whatever arcane process distilled the essence of mummy so touted by doctors, scientists, and apothecaries as a cure-all.

The sound of a deep, bone-racking cough farther along the maze of rooms made Roanna forget to gag. She'd found Griffin Kirkwood.

Silently she crept through three more rooms, each one a little higher than the last. The earthen floor became drier, the walls shored up with stone rather than timber, the scents less pervasive and noxious.

At the doorway to the last room, Roanna risked a tiny flame of cold light on her fingertip. Sure enough, Griffin Kirkwood lay on a dry mattress covered in clean linen sheets. Three blankets, at least, covered him. A small pot of something slightly sweet, slightly acrid, and not unpleasant bubbled on a brazier in the corner. A little daylight filtered through a high window in the outer wall.

The dog kept guard beside the mattress. She raised her head and growled low in her throat. Her exposed fangs dripped drool into her beard. She gathered her muscles, ready to leap on any who intruded upon her master.

Roanna wrapped a sleep spell around Griffin's familiar. The dog resisted, nearly as immune to spells as her master. With Tryblith's aid, Roanna sang a soothing lullaby, deepening her initial spell. Newynog growled once more. But her eyes drooped. Then without further fuss, she dropped her head upon her paws and snored lightly.

Roanna waited and counted a dozen heartbeats to be sure the dog truly slept. Even as she watched, Griffin coughed again, flailing his arms and kicking at the confines of the blankets. Fever flushed his cheekbones and made his hands pale. He trembled all over with chill.

There! Beside him on the floor. The staff! At last the staff is ours, Tryblith gasped. For the first time, a touch of awe tinged his voice.

"The staff is mine," Roanna corrected him. She bent to retrieve it.

Griffin coughed once more, nearly gagging on his own phlegm. Roanna gently turned him on his side so that he would not choke, and tucked the blankets around his shoulder once more.

Then she fled with the staff.

Next we steal the ring.

For three days I thrashed with fever. For three days demons clawed at my sanity through my dreams. I saw Tryblith, full-bodied, taller than two men, with hideous fangs springing from distended dragon jaws. Long hairy arms extended far beyond the proportions of his potbellied body. He reached for me with extended talons as long as my open hand. Several times he crushed me against his black-pelted, potbellied body, robbing me of breath. The malevolent odor of sulfur, burning hair, and another bitter chemical smell gagged me as I fought for air. He ground his outsized genitals against me in a hideous perversion of the sexual act.

My manhood shrank and shriveled as it had the moment my magic came into full bloom and I shared in the humiliation of Meg's rape and my brother's failed attempt to ravish the nameless girl in that burning Scottish village. Nameless no more. I knew her now as Roanna. My wild Highland Rose.

I knew a moment of bliss as I lost myself in Roanna's beautiful body. Then I burned with guilt that I had lusted at all, let alone for the host of the demon.

I dreamed of Meg. Meg as a bright and spirited adolescent with a talent to match my own. Meg as a pseudo-child, escaping from her memories into nursery rhymes. Meg as the Madonna, the marble statue in Norfolk's chapel come to life. Robin as the child who must be sacrificed.

No! Protect Robin. *Meg, save the boy. Keep him from Norfolk's greedy plans.*

Images of Meg and Robin faded away from me on an astral wind.

Then I saw Roanna again, more beautiful than ever. She whispered to me in soothing tones that turned to vipers in my ear, spreading painful poison through my mind.

And all the time Tryblith tortured my body, wrenching my arms and legs out of joint, burning me with his breath. He tortured my mind as well, digging in his claws of disorder, pain, fear.

But at last I woke, weak and shaking, soaked in sweat. The acrid scent of damp charcoal in the brazier reminded me of my nightmares. I sneezed myself free of the herbs my two apothecary apprentices had burned there. The two boys, Michael and Jonah, knelt by the dying fire, bickering quietly about the contents of the next potion they intended to feed me. They agreed only upon the inclusion of extract of mummy in both the potion and the mustard plaster upon my chest.

"I need no more of your noxious brews," I croaked. "Small beer to quench this raging thirst is all I want." I sagged into the straw pallet, exhausted by those few words. How many times had the boys changed my mattress and bedding when they became soaked with my sweat?

When I opened my grit-filled eyes again, barely a moment later, I swore, Michael stood over me with a tankard of the requested beverage. Jonah propped me up while I drank greedily. Too soon they took the tankard from me.

"Not too much at once, Milord Merlin," Michael admonished. "Too much will overtax your stomach and bowels and make you more ill than before."

He had the right of it. But that did nothing to ease the burning in the back of my throat.

"What happened? Where is my sister?" The words came out a little firmer than before, but still rasped harshly on my ears and throat.

"The fever and cough grew worse by the hour. We brought you back to Apothecary Hall, Milord Merlin," Jonah said quietly.

"My sister? They call her Half-wit Meg. She has a child . . ."

"Brother Jeremy at Whitefriars says that she left," Michael said. His eyes slid away from me in uncertainty.

"Left? When? Where?" I tried to sit up but found Jonah's bony adolescent arm stronger than my need. He pushed me back onto firm bolsters.

"We do not know," Michael replied. He offered me the tankard of beer to pacify me.

I drank again, a little slower, savoring the moisture as I swirled each gulp around my mouth before swallowing.

"Bring me my staff," I ordered. I thought I had enough strength to use the crystal to scry my sister's location. Keeping her away from Norfolk and Tryblith seemed more important than endangering my immortal soul by using magic.

Newynog whined from the floor beside me. I dropped my hand to her ears. She pushed up against my touch. Some of her strength flowed into me.

"Rest now, Father Merlin. Later, after you've slept and maybe drunk some of Grandmother's broth, we can discuss this."

"Now, boy. I cannot wait to find Meg and the child. All of England cannot wait for me to recover." I tried fixing the boy with my gaze.

He avoided me by staring at his feet as he traced idle designs in the rushes with his toe.

"Michael, Jonah, what is going on?" I demanded.

"You boys, take yourself off and find Father Merlin some soup and bread." The ancient one-eyed crone shuffled into the room, using her raven-topped staff for balance. Her grandsons fled eagerly.

"Good Mother," I greeted her weakly. Suspicion and outrage crept through me, giving me more strength than Newynog had. But the old woman returned my stare levelly and my newfound will to charge out and slay any who stood between me and Meg faded all too quickly.

"Stay where you are, boy. You'll not find your sister this day."

I raised an eyebrow in question, too depleted to do ought else.

"She's truly gone, Father Merlin. Gone as can be from Whitefriars."

"Where did she go?"

"Away."

"You are as cryptic as she."

" 'Tis the privilege of wisewomen."

"Then give me my staff. I would use it to find her."

"Not today."

"When?"

Silence.

"When, Good Mother?"

Another long silence. Then she heaved a tremendous sigh. "The staff with the black crystal is as gone as your sister."

Chapter 53

Apothecary Hall, London, Spring 1561.

STILL weak from fever, not entirely free of my dreams, I looked more closely at the old woman. She wore no patch today and her yellow-white hair was neatly pulled away from her face. The folds of scar tissue seemed to peel away from her missing eye. Decades of ill health, care, and worry sloughed off. She was once more tall and straight, with piercing blue eyes and a cloud of curly dark hair.

"Do I know you, Old Mother?" I didn't think anyone outside my immediate family had eyes of such a deep blue—like a midnight sky above a full moon.

The dream image of the crone faded before my eyes. I saw her as she was now, not as she had been decades ago at the height of her beauty and power.

"Mayhap you do know me. Them what didn't fergit called me Deirdre."

"Deirdre. I know that name. And that raven atop your staff." She nodded agreement. "Why are you in London if you are the keeper of the faerie circle above the ruins of Huntington?"

"Rest now and regain your strength." She urged me to lie back upon my pallet. "You've demons to fight but not right now. Not until you've set your feet and your heart upon the right path," she continued. "Sleep, boy. Sleep and be well when you wake." She touched my eyes with her age-twisted fingers.

I slept long and deep without dreams. When I woke again, I ate and climbed out of the bed to use the chamber pot. My wobbling knees wouldn't carry me as far as the privy. Then I slept again.

Seven days I recovered from the fever that had lasted three days. Seven days I fretted over the loss of my sister and the loss of my staff. I recorded my troubling dreams in my journal. But writing them down did not make them easier to decipher. I vowed that as soon as I regained my strength, I'd use whatever magic came to me to find my sister and my grandmother's staff.

As soon as I could, I gathered what I needed from the Hall: a large crockery bowl and an agate representing Earth, common herbs to burn in Fire, their smoke was Air. For fresh Water from a spring or creek, I had to dispatch the two apothecary apprentices. Well water would work, but for a spell of this importance I did not want to trust the static nature imposed upon the element by a well.

The boys, eager and curious about everything, like barely-weaned puppies, wanted to observe the spell. I sent them scuttling from the room with a glare. Only Newynog would watch over me, giving me the strength to repress my lingering coughs.

One by one I dropped the herbs into the fire, chanting in archaic Welsh over each. Smoke filled the room, seeking out every corner and crevice, cleansing the Air and myself of impurities. I breathed deeply, free of congestion for the first time in many days. Only then did I fill the bowl with fresh water. When it lay still and smooth as the surface of the Lady's Lake back home, I dropped the agate into the exact center, keeping my gaze fastened upon the ripples. I merged with each wavelet, sending my mind outward in ever widening circles seeking . . .

Nothing. The image of Meg I held in my mind remained in my mind. I could not see her in the here and now, only in my memory. Why?

I tried again and again until exhaustion claimed me. I tried again the next day and received a faint impression that she lived. Only that one scrap of vision. I held it close against my heart, accepting that she had hidden herself so well that I could not find her. Or someone with powerful magic hid her.

On the third day, I sought a vision of Norfolk. If he had my sister and Robin, he'd not be able to disguise his triumph from me. Unless Roanna and her pet demon had corrupted him. I suspected he was one of their tools but refused to believe he had enough magic in him to hide Meg. His aura

had always been small with thin, petty layers. Roanna's
aura—or any true magician's—had broad, complex layers of
light and energy pouring out of them.

I burned the herbs, dropped the agate, watched the ripples,
and . . . Thomas Howard, fourth Duke of Norfolk, paced his
Hall at Norwich rapidly, with uneven steps. I had found his
aura. Today it sparkled with vibrant red in wild fluctuations
of size and intensity.

"Where is he?" he screamed. "I have torn London and its
environs apart, and no one has seen the Merlin in over a
se'nnight. No man can just disappear like that. Not even as
powerful a magician as he!"

"You need another magician to sniff out his magical trail,
Your Grace," Dr. John Dee replied distractedly. He studied
a document written in his bizarre Enochian language.

When had he returned to England? Where had he found
the document? I recognized the script now. The Knights
Templar of old had used it to encode their secret documents.

The doctor's betrayal of me stabbed deep in my soul.
I thought we were friends. But Dee had no true friends,
only his star charts and his quest for speech with angels.
He studied the problem of my disappearance, as he would
any problem, as an exercise in logic and tactics rather
than emotionally.

"A magician such as you, Dr. Dee?" Norfolk asked. Hope
brightened his face into a handsome young courtier, a visage
too often marred by his scowl of discontent.

"I have not the magic for such a task. Best you find someone else. I have more important work."

"I know just the person." Norfolk smiled slyly.

"Who? Have they enough magic to speak with my
angels?"

"My wild Scottish Rose has no need for angels. She has
the devil's own demon at her command."

Roanna. She and Tryblith had tainted Norfolk with the
seeds of chaos. That explained the expansion of his aura, and
the sparkling red. The magical images in my scrying bowl
revealed the truth. I saw Roanna's life energy surrounding
the duke, not his own.

Only Roanna and Tryblith had reason to steal my staff.

I closed and grounded the scrying spell before my own
emotions scattered it. Norfolk did not have Meg. If he did,

he'd stop looking for me. Robin was his true quest, and Meg would not allow the boy to be taken from her. She loved him as her own.

I needed a new course of action to save my sister and all of England from the chaos of Norfolk's schemes.

That afternoon I left Apothecary Hall wearing my cloak and carrying my pack with Newynog at my heels. Nothing of me or mine remained at Whitefriars.

I felt naked without the staff. A fine spring mist dampened the entire city. Droplets of water glistened on the yellow petals of daffy down lilies. On another day, in another place, I might have stopped and admired the beauty of the flowers, drunk in their perfume and renewed my soul in delight of God's handiwork. Today, I trudged on.

I could not go back to Whitefriars. As long as the people of London could come to me as priest, magician, counselor, they would call me the Merlin and speak of me in public. Norfolk or Roanna would hear and return for me. They would not abandon their search for Meg and Robin in favor of other plots.

I headed north, toward the home I longed for. Perhaps Meg had taken Robin and Helwriaeth there. I knew they lived, felt it in my bones, but I could not find them. Without the staff, I felt lost, empty. I had no control over my future.

I'd sent a note to Donovan at Ide Hill, begging him to keep his mind open to me. So far I'd received only echoes of my own sendings to him.

Just outside the city environs, a family of Gypsies awaited me. They had their own mysterious ways of knowing things that evaded other folk.

"Father Merlin," Micah tipped his cap to me. His wife and daughter curtsied, keeping their eyes lowered as was their custom. "We would be honored if you would travel with us."

In that moment I knew that no matter where I traveled in England, Norfolk would hear of me. He would continue seeking me and seeking Robin. I had to leave England if Meg and Robin were to stay hidden.

Set your feet upon the proper path first, Raven and Deirdre reminded me. The sheaf of apocryphal documents in my pack seemed to burn through to my heart.

"Micah, I travel out of England for a time. While I am gone, I charge you with finding a woman and her child. You must protect them as you would protect your own wife and children." I laid a hand on the man's shoulder, begging him with my eyes to accept my mission.

Even Norfolk's obsessive searches would not consider Gypsies worthy of his attention.

"Aye, Father Merlin. Gladly."

Quickly I described my sister's bright blonde hair and midnight-blue eyes, her lithe figure and her tendency to speak in circles.

"A special wisewoman," Micah agreed, nodding. "We honor those touched by the Goddess."

I stilled a moment, recognizing the truth of the man's statement. My sister had indeed been touched by God, no matter what we called Her.

"She is protected by a dog such as mine, but the dog ages and has not the strength or stamina she used to. Find her, please, and let not my enemies know of her." I opened my mind to let Donovan know that I sent others to seek out Meg. I hoped he heard me.

I parted amicably from Micah and his family with blessings and good wishes all around. I felt better about leaving, knowing that someone would look out for Meg—if they could find her.

The road to London, south of the city, spring 1561.

Roanna sat atop one of Norfolk's mettlesome geldings square in the center of the road. Her extended senses listened to the pounding hoofbeats of Donovan Kirkwood's horse grow closer and closer. Her black Jesuit cassock chafed her skin and weighed heavily upon her shoulders. Her back itched from the coarse wool in places she could not reach.

"I wish you could make yourself useful and scratch," she sighed.

The demon raked her back with ghostly, palm-length talons, much as he stabbed her mind in his efforts to control her. Her skin erupted from the inside. The itch became a burning scratch.

"Not so hard," she admonished him.

He laughed in the back of her mind. Since stealing the staff of the Pendragon from Griffin, he'd taken on form and some substance and now existed as a phantom image that stood beside her—distended dragon jaws level with her head atop the horse. She had trouble believing the disembodied voice that had lived in her head for years came from such a huge and ugly being.

Her own powers seemed to have increased as well. She and the demon were still balanced. Her baby was still safe.

She rested Griffin Kirkwood's staff against her stirrup as a soldier would carry a lance. Tryblith could not have stolen it from the Merlin. He was still only a transparent image, not a true figure. Nor could he assume the proper disguise that would accomplish her next task. She controlled their plans.

Her physical ears picked up the steady cadence of the Baron of Kirkenwood. He traveled alone and he traveled fast. Elizabeth must expect him back at court.

Roanna could use his preoccupation and his roiling frustration against him.

He rode down an adjacent hill at breakneck speed. She steadied her horse with her knees. Atop the knoll directly in his path, she waited, a solitary silhouette against the dying sun.

She pulled the visage of the fallen Jesuit from her memory and draped it across her face. What had been his name? Manuel. The Spanish spy for the Inquisition. Remembering his name and his mission brought the image of his face into focus. She sharpened the image adorning her face.

That little bit of magic cost her much in strength. The crystal-topped staff did not accept or channel her magic as easily as the staff she had inherited from Gran. But the black crystal gave her more power. The skull atop her own staff had lost potency. She should have replaced it with the head of the slain Jesuit. But at the time she hadn't needed it. Now Father Manuel's bones rotted at the bottom of a river. The skull of her ancestor in Tryblith's cave barrow might have helped some, but she was reluctant to disturb his tomb. Getting another sacrificial victim would prove difficult. In this day and age she would have trouble hiding a ceremony of such magnitude, and keeping her victim a secret from the overly long noses of the law.

The crystal would give her enough power. It just had to get used to her style of magic.

The sun dropped a little lower, casting her shadow long and low down the hill.

Donovan rode into the semidarkness of her shadow. Only then did he look up from his study of the road and his horse's mane. He slowed his pell-mell pace, letting the horse find its own speed up the steep slope.

"Out of my way," Donovan commanded. "I ride on the queen's business."

"And I stop you on the business of Pope Pius IV and the Inquisition of Philip of Spain," Roanna intoned with what she hoped was a Spanish accent. She lifted the staff and threw back her hood so that the late afternoon light caught the illusion of the face she projected.

"You!" Donovan crossed himself superstitiously. "How can it be you? I killed you three years ago!"

"And for that you must face justice!" Roanna leveled the staff, pointing the crystal directly at her prey. Her magic channeled through it in a line of dark fire, taking much of her energy with it.

Donovan's horse reared and screamed. He clenched the reins with white-knuckled fists. But his knees were weak. He bounced around in the saddle, unable to control his terrified mount.

Roanna sent another blast of magic toward him. She doubled over gasping for air, fighting the dizziness of extreme fatigue.

Tryblith popped into view beside her, adding his beastly roar to frighten the horse. He opened his huge maw in a parody of a grin at her. She had not the strength to control him.

The horse screamed and reared again. Its eyes rolled, showing too much white. Then it laid back its ears and pranced anxiously, lifting its hooves high and placing them down with sharp thuds.

Donovan clung to the horse's neck with both arms, hands hauling on the bit in an effort to master the steed.

"Dismount and face holy justice!" Roanna intoned. She let loose one last blast of power. Her hands trembled with the effort.

This time the horse bucked, kicking its heels back. Donovan landed flat on his back. The horse took off for London at a wild gallop.

Donovan gasped painfully, fighting for air. He flailed slightly in panic as his chest refused to breathe. He wheezed again and again, trying to force more air and control into his body.

Roanna dismounted painfully. Every joint in her body ached from the effort of throwing the magic through the alien staff. She wanted nothing more than to lean against the warmth of the horse and sleep a few moments or a year.

But she had work to do. Fighting to keep the slain Jesuit's face from fading, she approached Donovan cautiously.

"Do you recognize this staff, Donovan Kirkwood?"

His eyes grew wide. The intense, compelling blue was overwhelmed by black pupil. He nodded, still fighting for air.

"I relieved your twin of this artifact. He worked magic and condemned himself with the act." She allowed the alien visage upon her face a feral smile, showing black and broken teeth. Sulfur tainted the foul breath she added to the illusion of diseased teeth. "Griffin will never work magic again. And for your crime of murdering a priest of the true church, I claim the ring of the Pendragon!"

"Never," Donovan choked out. His hands went automatically to his throat.

She had to hurry. If he had enough air to speak, he'd recover soon.

"You betray the location of the jewel even as you protest." Roanna bent and fumbled with the ties of his ruffled shirt collar. He wore the ring on a leather thong about his neck. She yanked it away from him. The thong resisted. Donovan grabbed it with both hands.

A vibration ran through her booted feet. More horses approached. No time for subtlety. No strength for magic. With one vicious swipe she rammed the crystal on the staff into Donovan's temple. Blood trickled from the rapidly bruising wound. She slit the thong with her knife, caught up the ring and fled.

He's not dead, Tryblith sounded disappointed.

"But he will be soon. Or his brains are so rattled he'll never again speak sense. Now, with the ring and staff, the girl and the brat will not be able to hide from us."

Chapter 54

Richmond Palace, spring 1561.

"SO, my Wolfhound sees fit to open his eyes," Elizabeth said on a snort. She did that often to hide her true emotions.

Donovan peered at her through tiny cracks in his heavy eyelids. He could barely see her outline in the dim room. She loomed over him, her tall figure elegant even as she stooped her shoulders in concern.

"What day is this?" His voice came out a bare whisper. Fierce drums pounded in his head, neck, and shoulders. He didn't even want to think about moving lest he set off new waves of pain and nausea.

"Tuesday. What day do you think it should be?" she replied.

Donovan searched the limits of his vision for anyone else. Dudley stood nervously by the door. He should have known that the queen would not visit his rooms alone. Whatever transpired here would be known throughout the court within an hour of her leaving.

He swallowed heavily and licked dry lips. Best tell Elizabeth his news now. If she decided to throw him in the Tower, he couldn't hurt any more than he already did. "I left Ide Hill on Sunday eve," he said cautiously. "Martha." His eyes finally opened fully. "I must go to Martha. She is near her time. I have to save her and the babes from the demon." He tried getting out of bed.

Dudley started toward him. But Elizabeth pushed Donovan easily back against the bolster. Dudley retreated to his post by the door.

"You, milord, go nowhere until your broken pate

mends," Elizabeth said in her usual imperious tone that half-joked. "We always suspected the Kirkwoods had especially hard heads. The blow was meant to kill you. If my courier had not found you on the road within moments of the attack, you would have died. Dr. Dee saw an omen in the stars that I should summon you from your little love nest at Ide Hill." She sat on the edge of his bed and gathered one of his hands in both of her own. "Now tell us, Wolfhound, about this demon that left you for dead upon our highway."

"I . . . ah . . ." How could he tell her that he had encountered the ghost of a Jesuit priest he had killed three years ago, that the same ghost had condemned him to an eternity in a fiery hell? Elizabeth may have espoused the Protestant cause, but she still highly respected priests, any priest.

"Send someone to Ide Hill. Please, Majesty. I must know that my wife and babes are well."

"Wife?" Elizabeth stood abruptly, dropping his hand. Indignation stiffened her spine more than the steel corset.

Donovan braced himself against the waves of motion within the mattress as well as against the queen's wrath.

"Your wife!" Elizabeth said again, on a slightly softer note.

"My wife. The babes will be legitimate. I will have my heir."

"To Kirkenwood and to the Pendragon ring," Elizabeth said through her frown.

Donovan reached instinctively for the thong about his neck. His fingers encountered rough and broken skin where the demon had ripped it from him.

Gone. The demon had stolen the ring of the Pendragon from him. Gone. His heritage. The gift of the past and the future he must pass on to his son and heir. Gone.

And the demon had Raven's staff with the black crystal. The ring to grant authority and the staff as emblem of power. The demon ruled the Pendragon magic.

He wept.

"Oh, I'll not throw you into the Tower, my Wolfhound." A low chuckle radiated out from Elizabeth, beginning deep within her chest. "As tempted as I am to make an example of you to the rest of my wayward courtiers . . ." She cast a sharp glance toward a shadow in the corner. "I have need of your services in Scotland."

"Scotland? Majesty, I cannot leave until Martha delivers."

"That must be your punishment for disobeying a royal order, Milord of Kirkenwood. You shall leave your mousy little wife while you join our ambassador and agents in Edinburgh. You will be there when our cousin Mary Queen of Scots arrives. You will insinuate yourself into her court and report everything to me. Do you understand, Donovan Kirkwood?"

"Must I report every time she takes a piss?"

Elizabeth laughed heartily. "Aye, milord. If you think it significant. Especially if she meets a lover in the privy."

Donovan suppressed a laugh. His head hurt too much to let forth with mirth to match Elizabeth's. Dudley remained strangely silent and frowning in his corner.

Elizabeth sobered too quickly.

Wariness prickled up Donovan's arms. His brain began to cloud with fatigue and an urgent need to sleep right when he needed to be most alert.

"Your brother sent me a message," the queen said abruptly. She pulled a roll of parchment from her sleeve.

Donovan took it from her. His eyes did not want to focus. The words swam before him. He forced himself to concentrate on one letter at a time. The familiar script bounced and took on cohesive form.

Norfolk seeks to find and control an orphan child I found in the village of Hatfield. He sows the seeds of chaos in his wake.

It was signed with a small drawing of a Merlin falcon.

"He speaks the truth," Donovan nearly choked on the words. Griffin was not his enemy, probably never had been. He gulped back a pricking moisture from his eyes. How long since he and his twin had exchanged letters—even embittered ones? How long since they had embraced in true affection?

But Griffin and his Catholic followers had brought the

Demon of Chaos to England a small voice in the back of his head argued. Hadn't they?

No. Donovan asserted control over the nagging voice. The Spaniards and their Inquisition had brought the demon. But Griffin was not one of them.

He couldn't sort out the questions of the demon possessing the staff and claiming to have killed Griffin and who was guilty of Catholic heresy and who not.

"You know of the child and Norfolk's search?" Elizabeth leaned over Donovan. Fierce emotions played over her face so quickly he could not read them.

"I saw him briefly. I also witnessed Norfolk's attempt to tear Whitefriars apart in search of him and those who protect him." The need to sleep nearly overwhelmed Donovan.

"I must know the child is safe!" Elizabeth insisted.

Dudley finally moved. He clasped Elizabeth's hand and kissed the fingertips in an oddly intimate gesture. She turned her hand to cup his face in her palm.

A suspicion pushed aside the waves of sleepiness within Donovan. Could the child be hers? Born illegitimately before she ascended to the throne? Before Dudley's wife died under mysterious circumstances?

Would Norfolk dare use an *illegitimate* child, raised in the Catholic faith by Norfolk himself, to usurp Elizabeth? Norfolk would hold sway over the child, possibly reign as regent.

He dared much. Risked more.

Shudders ran up and down Donovan's spine as if a ghost walked there.

Meg had the child. She'd not likely give him up. If she could be found. He had to find her and protect her.

He had to go home to Ide Hill, be with Martha through the ordeal of the birth.

"I do not know where my brother has hidden the child. I know only that my sister loves him as her own. As long as Norfolk seeks, he does not have the child as his tool for flinging chaos about the land." Donovan drew in a deep breath. "Now, Majesty, I must see to the safety of my own wife and babes. The Demon of Chaos will not stop with felling me."

"Your skull is too thick to succumb to mundane weapons, milord. And 'twas only a mundane weapon that felled

you. Rest a while longer. I will send messengers and guards
to Ide Hill. You will depart for Scotland as soon as you
can sit a horse without falling off."

"I will wait until the babes come."

"You will go to Scotland or to the Tower. Make your
choice. I have many courtiers who would welcome the gift
of Kirkenwood should I decide to divest you of your
honors."

The manor of the Duke of Norfolk, Chelsea, near London, spring 1561.

"You failed again!" Norfolk screamed at Roanna. "Griffin
Kirkwood stole a child from my custody. I will have that
child and Kirkwood's death!" His eyes rolled, showing
more white than brown iris as he tore his hair. Tryblith
prodded him with small stabs of needle-fine pain all over
his skin. Norfolk swept a table clear of parchment, pens,
penknives, ink, and sealing wax. The ink pot shattered,
spraying the contents over the duke and the fine carpet
from Persia. It mingled with the dyes, taking on the color
of old blood.

Roanna grabbed the lit candle with her mind, keeping it
firmly in place. She liked her luxurious apartment and did
not want it set afire. She liked being able to manipulate
Norfolk without having to bed him. Soon she'd not be able
to bed anyone and needed a different method of control.

She leaned away from her scrying bowl—the finest silver,
filled with a clear yellow wine and a cut crystal dropped
into the center. Norfolk would not allow her to use any but
the most expensive and regal tools to seek the illegitimate
child of Elizabeth Regina. She'd have had better success
with plain crockery, fresh spring water, and a stone polished by that stream.

"Temper tantrums will not aid my spell," she said
sternly. A thrill of power coursed through her as Norfolk
dropped his hands away from the expensive Venetian glass
decanter and goblets in cobalt blue before he broke them.

Not Venetian. She recognized the design. Someone at Whitefriars had imitated the best glass in the world and done it admirably. She probably knew the glassblower, had shared a meal with him.

And now she shared . . . best not think of that.

"Forgive me," Norfolk said sheepishly, running his hands through his hair and beard. He only mussed them further.

Roanna rose and produced a comb from her scrip. Like a mother with a troublesome child she fussed until he presented a semblance of neatness. Norfolk accepted her authority meekly. As he had when she came to him with the staff and the ring some days ago.

"The woman and the child remain hidden, shielded. Her magic is very strong. Stronger perhaps than that of her brother Griffin Kirkwood."

"Then why didn't she possess the ring and staff of the Pendragon?" Norfolk asked. His temper threatened to rise again.

"Because her mind is warped. She wanders in and out of sanity without prediction. But she loves little Robin fiercely and will protect him with every tool available. Give up the search, Your Grace. I have another plan that will put you even closer to the throne of England than regent for Elizabeth's illegitimate son. I can put you on the throne itself."

"How?" Norfolk breathed. Awe and wonder lighted his face, erasing deep care lines and decades of frustration.

"You will wed Mary Queen of Scots. Then you will use her—with my help—to overthrow Elizabeth."

And I will have war at last!

Glastonbury Tor, spring, 1561.

Before I could leave England, I had to set my feet on the proper path. Both Raven and Deirdre had commanded it. In the ancient traditions of Britain and the original Merlin, a path usually meant some kind of labyrinth or ritual progression.

Walking the labyrinth cleansed the soul and cleared the mind. I'd been foundering for years, seeking answers and guidance from the church. I needed to look deep within myself.

As a youth, Raven had instilled in me the firm belief that some places on this Earth hold great sanctity. Inevitably, the shrines the Druids had believed ancient and worthy of worship had been usurped by the Romans. The invaders had been tolerant of local religions and merely given them the names of their own equivalent deity. When the Roman Empire fell, the Roman Christian Church had stepped in to fill the void, stabilizing governments, economies, and trade. They had also converted many of the Roman temples to their own use, homing in on the sacred sites that had been revered through many transitions.

Our own kirk at Kirkenwood lay upon just such a place.

Another secret branch of Christianity had perpetuated many of the older traditions in the form of mystery schools. The best known of these was the order of the now heretic Knights Templar.

I should not have been surprised as an adolescent when Raven took me to an obscure Scottish chapel that abounded in Templar symbolism as part of my initiation into the mysteries of my heritage. There, south of Edinburgh, Raven had been treated as an equal by the custodians. There she had taken over the guardianship of many secret documents. Among them the Gospel of St. Thomas, the Templar Documents, and the study of the Irish Culdees that I had found in the lair.

The time had come to begin my own pilgrimage.

I turned my feet west and hiked to Glastonbury Tor. Long tradition and legend held that Joseph of Arimathea had brought the Holy Grail here soon after the Crucifixion, returning to a site Our Lord had visited in his youth. The red-and-white springs at the base of the tor had been considered sacred for many, many generations before that. The place had Arthurian connections as well.

Glastonbury called to me. I hoped to learn something from the pilgrimage.

Traveling quietly and secretly whenever possible, I met few interruptions on this quest. A long week of walking brought the massive hill with its single tower atop into my view. Generations of farmers and shepherds had drained the swamps around the islands that were now hills. Unlike my ancestors, I could walk into the town at the base of the major tor without having to hire a reed boat.

I approached the tor at sunset, shading my eyes. As the last bright ray of light touched the verdant grass, the terraces of the hill came into view. I had found a path.

The ruins of the old abbey at the base of the hill offered me shelter from the wind. I made a rude camp within the bakery—the only building left with a roof—within sight of the rumored grave of King Arthur. I knew he was not buried there, but as long as the world believed him here, they would not desecrate the crypt of Kirkenwood. Newynog prowled restlessly all night, sniffing out the ghosts of the place.

Otherworldly voices disturbed my dreams. At dawn, I rose, barely rested, but filled with purpose. Those ghosts had shown me the beginning of the path. I bathed my face and hands in the waters from the Chalice Well that flowed redly and evenly all year. Newynog spat out the bitter, mineral-laden water. Then, together, we followed a well-trodden track around and up the tor. Pilgrims had not forgotten this place even if they did not speak of it openly and the Anglican Church no longer considered it any more holy or sacred than a number of desecrated abbeys and monasteries.

A magnificent church had stood atop the tor before Henry VIII broke with Rome. Earthquakes and zealots had destroyed most of it. The tall tower of the Church of St. Michael, all that remained, was visible throughout the long journey, a guide and a goal.

We began at a brisk pace, Newynog bounding ahead and back to scout the way. Soon enough we slowed, feeling the effects of the night's unbroken fast. My familiar walked ahead of me but never beyond my sight or the next turning.

Around and back, ever upward with each spiral turn and switchback, we walked. I fingered every bead of my rosary, but familiar prayers did not come to me. They seemed strangely out of place on this prehistoric ritual path. Instead I concentrated on my quest, to rid England of the Demon of Chaos once and for all, to still the convoluted plots of power-hungry men who would destroy peace and unity solely for their own need to control.

I nearly stopped in my tracks. Holy Mother Church in Rome seemed to have the same quest. Destroy England rather than let her stray from their rigid unquestioning dogma. Questions and doubts plagued me. The only path to answers seemed to be upward. I plodded on.

Each terrace took me higher, lifting a little more of the heaviness of doubt. By the time I crested the tor and faced the tower of St. Michael, I thought I knew what I had to do.

A little old man, wearing the brown robes of a Franciscan monk, minus a tonsure, leaned heavily upon a staff, guarding the doorway to the tower.

" 'Bout time you showed yer face here," he admonished me without preamble or greeting.

Newynog barked at him and clung to my heels.

"We came . . ."

"I know why you came and why you must leave."

"I need answers."

"You need to know what questions to ask. Read and compare. Look for contradictions. You'll find it quite a Revelation." Shakily he inched around and disappeared into the shadows within the arched doorway of the ruin.

"A revelation," I mumbled.

Shrugging my shoulders I retraced my steps back to the abbey and the town. The next day I traveled to Bristol where I bought a very expensive copy of the New Testament in English before taking ship from there to the continent. I read the book of The Revelation of St. John the Divine three times before I realized what I was meant to find there.

Chapter 55

Greenwich Palace, outside London, Spring 1561.

"ELIZABETH said I did not have to leave until I could sit a horse without falling off," Donovan muttered to himself. He affected a wobbling gait as he wandered about his rooms at Greenwich Palace for the benefit of the servant the queen had provided him—undoubtedly a spy who reported every nuance of Donovan's recovery, or lack thereof. Elizabeth had moved him with the court in her endless wandering from palace to manor around London. Soon she would set off on her annual Progress around the southlands. She never ventured very far into the sparsely populated north.

Donovan only hoped she would not leave until he had word that Martha was safely delivered. He was determined not to begin his journey to Scotland until then, no matter how well recovered he actually was.

He wrote to Martha every day begging for news and a packet of ghostweed. He bribed other servants heavily to make sure his missives were delivered and not destroyed by Elizabeth or one of her minions.

After a week of walking crooked lines and faking the severity of his headaches, a folded parchment bearing Martha's seal finally arrived, carried by Martha's own steward. Donovan tore open the unbroken wax. The letters in Martha's precise hand swam before his eyes at first. He blinked hard, forcing himself to focus on the words.

"Two small boys, twins, born yestereve!" he crowed to the ever-present servant. "Griffin and Henry we name them. Both nurse lustily and cry loud and long when dis-

425

pleased. Do you hear that, man? She gave me two boys first time out!''

The servant nodded politely and edged toward the door. Donovan let him go, knowing he'd report immediately to Elizabeth or Dudley that the Baron of Kirkenwood had no more reason to feign illness and would be leaving for Scotland soon.

Donovan managed to write a happy reply to his wife before Elizabeth's page arrived with a summons for the Baron of Kirkenwood to the queen's presence. He implored his wife to remove their children to Kirkenwood as soon as they were strong enough to travel. He had a much better chance of stealing away from his new assignment and traveling to his home than making the long journey between the two capitals. Already he ached to hold his sons. He and Betsy had been so close those first months of her life, he longed to share the same bond with his sons. Even now, he centered most of his letters home in messages to his lovely, solemn-eyed daughter.

As an afterthought of his soaring joy, he sent out a happy mental message to. Griffin. He needed to share the news with the one man who would appreciate the specialness of twin boys as heirs to everything the barony of Kirkenwood and the Kirkwood family represented.

A soft feeling of approval grew in the back of his mind. But the return was distracted and short-lived. What was Griffin up to that he could share nothing more than this brief emotion?

The next morning, before dawn, Donovan, three servants and a cartload of baggage began the tedious journey toward Edinburgh by the Great North Road. Against orders from the queen, he stopped at Kirkenwood for three days. Three short days in which Betsy, Peregrine, and Gaspar were never out of his sight. Once more he wrote to Martha, begging her to come north.

He tried to think of several plots to take his children with him. None of them were practical. When they grew a bit perhaps, but not this year.

More lonely than he thought he'd ever be, he made his way to Edinburgh.

Thomas Randolph, Elizabeth's agent in Edinburgh, awaited

him. Together they discussed the mountain of correspondence Elizabeth had sent with Donovan outlining her policy toward her sister queen, Mary Queen of Scots. (Elizabeth refused to Frenchify her cousin's name.) Typical of Elizabeth, her policy was vague and open to many interpretations. Lord Burleigh's instructions were more specific. Be cordial to Mary, but never ever allow her to think she had a valid claim to the English throne while Elizabeth lived.

Two days later, Donovan and Randolph joined the throng of nobles awaiting the moment Mary Queen of Scots (like Elizabeth, her nobles, too, seemed intent upon eradicating anything French about their queen) set foot upon Scottish soil for the first time since she was five years old.

No other Englishmen had been authorized to witness the event.

They met the queen's ship on the strand at the harbor of Leith along with the Earl of Moray, Mary's half brother, and a gaggle of other lords on a cold and windy afternoon.

The salt-laden air cut through Donovan's courtly clothes. He'd grown soft in the warm southlands. He needed to renew himself and his contact with the land and people up here in the cold north. If he ever quitted this dark and grim city, he'd return to Kirkenwood and never dabble in politics again.

But that won't end the tyranny of the demon Tryblith, Raven's voice reminded him. Why did his grandmother's voice carry nuances of Meg and Griffin?

He shivered and pulled his coat closer about his shoulders.

A preternatural chill ran up his spine on top of the one coming off the North Sea. He lifted his head seeking the scent of sulfur his reading had told him must accompany this premonition of evil.

Nothing. Just salt, moisture, fish, and the dank smell that always permeated a harbor.

He searched the crowd of nobles and their retainers looking for the source of that warning of evil.

"What?" Randolph clutched at Donovan's arm.

Donovan looked into the shorter man's clear and pale eyes. "Something is wrong," he whispered. "I don't know what. Someone uninvited and unexpected, mayhap. An assassin would please some of these grim nobles too used to ruling without their queen."

Randolph looked carefully through the crowd, nodding to this person and that one as he made eye contact. "I see no one I do not know."

"Just because you know them, does not mean they do not belong here." And then Donovan saw her, a willowy woman of his own age, with flame-colored hair and a strong chin lifted to the elements. Her deep gray eyes seemed to draw all the warmth and light of the day into her, where she kept it close, leaving the rest of them to freeze in the gloom of the overcast.

He knew those eyes, deep, impenetrable, easy to lose one's sense of self in them. Where had he seen her before?

James Stuart, Earl of Moray seemed to have the same questions. He peered at her anxiously, then returned his attention to John Knox, the leader of the Scots congregation, and the grim-faced nobles beside him. But Moray's gaze kept returning to the woman.

Donovan took a moment to study her beyond her eyes. Her attention was fastened upon the small boat working its way from the large French galleon, through the chop of the harbor, toward the cobbled beach. But the man standing beside her, holding her arm solicitously, couldn't rest his eyes on any one person or thing for more than a few heartbeats. Something about his posture beneath his hooded cloak reminded Donovan of anxiety, distress, frustration.

Slowly, unobtrusively, Donovan shifted so that his back was to the couple in question. "Randolph, who is the woman over there?" He gestured slightly with his head. But he needn't. She was the only female present, at least until the queen landed with her ladies.

"Probably the mistress of the man she's with, hoping for a position at court to give her status and proximity to her lover."

"And the name of her lover?"

"Thomas Howard."

"Norfolk!" Donovan whistled through his teeth. "God's teeth, what's he doing here?"

"Norfolk." Randolph rolled his eyes. "Didn't think about the why, just the who."

"Does Elizabeth know he's here?"

"I am willing to bet this year's wool crop that Elizabeth did not give him permission to be here."

"Should we tell her?"

"Let us wait a day or two to see what he's up to."

A murmur rippled through the crowd. Mary Queen of Scots' small boat, well laden with luggage and too many ladies grounded on the gravelly bottom with several feet of water between it and dry land.

The queen stood bravely in the prow of the boat, clad in an inadequate white velvet cloak and gown, cut undoubtedly in the latest fashion from the court of France. She blatantly carried a rosary on her belt—illegal in Scotland for more than thirty years.

She looked a lot like Elizabeth. Haughty, stubborn, determined. Donovan hardened his heart against this new queen. And yet softer touches of femininity made her much more beautiful than her older cousin.

No one moved to haul the boat closer to land or to assist the queen. Not even the French sailors manning the oars.

Donovan strained to understand the quiet French words spoken within the boat. He had never had Griffin's facility for languages and often pretended understanding when Elizabeth conducted conversations in French. But then Elizabeth often drifted off into Welsh, German, or Italian as well just to keep the flock of popinjays around her off-balance.

The conversation in the boat became strident.

Moray folded his arms across his chest and glared malevolently at his half sister.

John Knox lifted his Bible to attract attention away from the woman in distress. "Whore of Babylon, know ye we will tolerate no idolatry in brave Scotland."

"I'll not have her interfering with *my* government," Moray muttered. "She doesn't land until she agrees."

An accompanying murmur arose among the nobles in the harsh Scots tongue that combined English and Gaelic into guttural nonsense to Donovan's ear. The men looked at each other questioningly. No one moved.

"C'est impossible." Mary's sweet voice drifted across the water between waves.

"Doesn't anyone here have any respect for the woman's title, if not for the woman herself?" Donovan asked the air. He stomped into the waves and offered his arms to carry Mary to the beach. "Settle your differences face-to-face, Moray, like a gentleman."

"*Merci,* milord," Mary said around a wide smile. She dropped easily into Donovan's arms.

He held her high so that her long legs and longer skirt would not trail in the water as he trudged toward the shore. He refrained from looking at her. Respect, he told himself.

He deposited her next to Moray without ceremony. They both stood, straightening clothing. Then they looked up at the same moment, standing eye to eye. Mary's gaze caught Donovan's.

They stood staring at each other for endless heartbeats. Her soft brown eyes smiled at him.

Something like lightning passed between them.

Donovan's heart skipped a beat or three.

Her beauty commanded attention without squeezing the air out of those around her just to make room for her personality.

"Your Grace." He finally remembered to bow. Thankfully he did remember that in Scotland, monarchs ruled by the Grace of God and not their own majesty. Moray might have thrown him into the dungeons of Edinburgh Castle for a monstrous breach of protocol if he dared use the word, "Majesty." The regent might anyway for his audacity in bringing the queen ashore.

Mary smiled prettily and extended her hand for him to kiss. "My gracious thanks, milord," she said in broken Scots.

Donovan held her fingers a moment too long and never allowed his gaze to stray from hers.

"*Mon pleasir, Madame,*" he whispered in the first French phrase that came to him. He knew his accent was terrible, but at least he'd made the attempt.

And then the crowd erupted around them with men rushing to be the next in line to greet their queen. All except Moray and John Knox.

Donovan found himself eased away from the striking woman. But her gaze remained locked with his until he felt his spine prickle with a ghostly presence. The strange woman with Norfolk stared at him with malevolence and bitter hatred. And something like . . . like triumph.

Who was she?

Roanna breathed in short shallow gasps. She should not have nearly fainted the moment her eyes rested upon him once more. But the man in close conversation with Elizabeth's agent, Thomas Randolph, could not be Griffin.

She faced Donovan, Baron of Kirkenwood, not Griffin. Why was the man not dead? These Kirkwoods were destined to haunt her both alive and dead.

She shivered again under the assault of the wind off the North Sea. The beach was wide open, barren of cover to protect her from the wind or from Kirkwood. A deep core of anger burned through her.

"Griffin loves Elizabeth more than he loves me. You shall love Elizabeth's dire enemy. Because you love two different queens, two different enemies, you shall never find peace with your twin again." With a gesture and a rope of magic she bound Donovan to Mary Queen of Scots.

"Love her well, Donovan, even after she breaks your heart. As your brother broke mine."

Blinking her eyes against sudden tears, she moved to the back of the crowd, thrusting Norfolk into the milling mass of nobles eager to greet their queen. "You must make an impression upon her," she whispered into the duke's ear. "Make her love you instantly so that she will consider marriage to no other."

Instantly she regretted her impulsive love spell between Donovan and Marie. It would have served her better binding Marie to Norfolk. Another spell atop the first would negate both. She had only politics and persuasion to force the queen to marry the duke.

Do as you are told, Thomas Howard, so that I may be free to return to France and my duc. I must lie with him again so that I can obliterate the memory of Griffin Kirkwood's hands upon my breast, of his breath against my ear, of him deep inside me spilling his seed.

Norfolk stumbled forward, an awkward schoolboy in the presence of the beautiful young queen who stood half a head taller than he. Moments ago he had been his usual arrogant, sophisticated self. Now he shuffled his feet and looked everywhere but at the woman he needed to woo.

Before Norfolk could overcome his shyness, Earl Moray had bundled everyone onto horses—no litters for gently bred ladies in this harsh land—for the return to Holyrood Palace. There, Mary headed first to the abbey beside the palace. The place had been pillaged and stripped bare in 1544, but retained its roof and right of sanctuary. Mary knelt at the naked altar. Her priest stepped onto the altar dais and began to recite the Latin Mass. Her French entourage joined her.

"Madame, you could at least have the decency to thank your God for your safe voyage in the privacy of the chapel provided you," Earl Moray snorted in offense. He retired into the dark warmth of the palace, cursing and stomping loudly.

Mary continued her prayers.

"Go, kneel beside her. Show her that you, too, follow the true faith," Roanna hissed at Norfolk. An agitation in her stomach made the words come out too angry.

He pouted and frowned at her. "But it is raining and the roof leaks," he whined.

He should not have been able to defy her. Tryblith's controls were deeply embedded into his mind. She closed her fist, drawing the demon power into her. Then with a tight circling motion, kept hidden beneath her cloak, she wound a new tendril of power around his mind. "Remember why the abbey roof leaks. All of these people are fiercely Protestant. They do not truly want Mary here, or her religion. She needs a strong husband to guide her and keep her true to Rome. Go. Kneel as close to the queen as you can. When she arises, be the one to offer her your hand. Else she will remember Kirkenwood better than you."

Norfolk's eyes became glassy as he succumbed to her will. Woodenly he turned on his heel and stumbled into the abbey, oblivious to the loud echo of his boots on the stone floor. When he tripped over an unmended crack and nearly fell headlong into the queen, Roanna released the chain of power a little. She needed him whole and hale, until he married Mary and produced a son. A son to rule both Scotland and England under Roanna's influence.

Then she turned abruptly and sought the warmth of the palace.

Moray awaited her just inside the doorway. Shadows draped around him like an extra cloak. "So, you have returned, little witch," he said flatly.

Roanna turned her eyes up to his, opening them wide in feigned innocence. "Do you address me, milord?" she lisped, allowing a French accent to shape her words. She pouted in an imitation of Mary's ladies at court.

"Aye, Rose, I speak to you. I exiled you once for your crime of witchcraft. This time I will burn you."

"I have committed no crime, milord."

"Yes, you have. I saw the way you entranced Norfolk. I rule here in Scotland. If I bring you to trial, my testimony will convict you."

"You threaten me, milord?" Roanna prepared another tendril of power to shoot through the earl. "I believe that you rule no longer. Her Grace, Mary Queen of Scots has returned to claim her throne." Too bad she had to kiss Moray to regain control of him. To accomplish that, she'd have to raise up on tiptoe and even then, she'd have to pull his rigid neck down to her level. The remembered feel of his slobbering, demanding kisses nearly made her gag. Everything made her gag lately. Griffin's kiss had been dry, heated, sharing. She wanted to just shoot Moray, with a pistol, or an arrow, as well as the power. His head would look very nice atop her staff. He should pay for his crime of sending her into exile in France.

But if he had not done so, she would never have met Duc Francis de Guise, never have earned her title and her income. She'd never have come so far in her mission to take control of her life away from Tryblith.

Griffin Kirkwood had nearly made her forget the duc who had given her so much, and the earl before him, and the baron before that.

"Be gone, witch. Leave Scotland this night or burn at dawn." Moray wheeled about and retreated into Holyrood Palace, the folds of his cape swirled in heaving waves, creating chill drafts. Roanna's stomach roiled in the same imitation of a rough sea.

"I shall depart on the next tide, milord. But not for the reasons you think."

Chapter 56

Rouen and Paris, France, summer 1561.

THE last few coins in the purse Bishop du Bellay had given
me three years ago did not cover passage from Bristol to
the disputed port of New Haven, Le Havre to the French,
in the province of Calais. My strong back—from hauling
charcoal and sand from the river to the abbey—was worth
more. And so I worked a leaky barque to Rouen.

Once upon French soil I donned my soutane and displayed my rosary upon my belt.

"Wouldn't 'a let you board if'n I knowed you was a
Papist," the grizzled captain muttered and spat from the
deck of his ship behind me. He held his right hand with
the two middle fingers clenched, the others extended to
ward off the evil eye.

I ignored him. Newynog pointedly lifted her leg on the
man's boots before trotting over to my side—she had always been insistent about asserting her dominance, even
over the male dogs we occasionally encountered. The boat-
man cursed volubly and shook his fist at us.

Three barges awaited passengers and cargo upon the
Seine, headed for Paris. All looked full. I hesitated.

"Father, bless my poor boat." The first captain approached me with cap in hand over his ample belly and
bowing repeatedly on spindly legs.

"A blessing, certainly." I raised my hand in the traditional gesture to make the sign of the cross over the vessel.

"More than that, Father. Will you grace the voyage with
your presence?" The captain smiled around broken teeth.
"We will make good time upriver. Nine, ten days at most."

"You seem overladen already." The barge sat low in the

water. A strong wake from a larger boat slopped over the sides as I watched. "I will seek passage with another less burdened." I bowed and made one step toward the next barge.

"No problem, Father." The captain shouted orders in a patois that resembled French in the crudest form. Three burly sailors grabbed a plump merchant, his plumper wife, and their three scrawny servants by the arms and escorted them across the plank.

"Here, now, I paid my passage. Good coins, not base metal!" the merchant protested in a high tenor voice that did not match his girth.

"Take your coins." The captain pressed three gold pieces into his hand.

Our tenor merchant widened his eyes briefly, then narrowed them in calculation. I felt sure the coins represented more than the original fare. And he wanted more.

"My cargo. I paid extra to travel with my cargo."

"Don't you trust the priest to see your goods safe to Paris?" the captain sneered.

"Priest, uh, no. Don't want to offend a priest by doubting him." The merchant bowed deeply to me, dragging his wife with him.

"I do not want to put this man out. He needs to be with his cargo." I tried backing away again only to stop in my tracks at the aghast looks on all of their faces.

"No, Father," the merchant protested. "Take our places. Please. Honor us." He grabbed his wife's arm and dragged her to the next boat.

Such blatant deference to an unknown priest bothered me. The garb and the rosary had always commanded respect. But this? Something had changed in France during my absence. Drastically changed.

"Forgive me, but I must hasten to Paris. I shall hire a horse at the nearest inn." I urged the merchant back aboard the barge.

Newynog bounced aboard the barge without hesitation. I called her back. She looked very disappointed, but I had not the time to indulge her passion for watching moving water—as long as she didn't have to bathe in it, she loved water.

"Allow me to ease your passage," the merchant begged,

bowing to me as he crossed himself three times. He pressed
three of the largest coins from his handful into my palm.

"Monsieur, 'tis not necessary," I objected.

"But I want to do this, Father. I am always generous to
Holy Mother Church."

Such obvious attempts to ensure the goodwill of a priest
and therefore the church must speak of extreme tensions
between traditional Catholics and Huguenots, the French
sect of Protestantism.

I hurried to the nearest hostelry. Newynog and I pressed
forward all through the day and the night, stopping only to
refresh ourselves and rest the horse. Dawn of the second
day found me at the Cathedral of Amiens. How had I arrived there? Some instinct I did not care to examine had
drawn me far north of my target.

While the horse and my dog ate and rested at a nearby
inn, I sought the shrine within the oldest portion of the
beautiful building. As I expected, my senses brightened as
I knelt in devotion at an altar that was old when Druids
had come here for a similar purpose.

I remembered again the little monk who had greeted
me at Glastonbury. He had led me to study the Book of
Revelations. I found there a passage referring to the Lord's
brothers. The Church declared repeatedly that the Holy
Mother Mary had remained a virgin to the end of her days.
A blatant lie.

What would I learn here?

As if in answer to my question, a wizened monk in a
dusty gray robe stumped through the chapel, using a walking staff for support. The length of oak was a near replica
of my own.

"Read any Good News lately, Pére Griffin?" he asked
as he made a clumsy obeisance to the altar. Then he continued on his path.

I could not be certain, but I thought he walked through
the cavelike wall of this subterranean chapel.

"Read any Good News?" The phrasing was clumsy, unfamiliar. "Good News. The Gospels."

I jumped up from my prayers and went in search of a
Latin Bible.

Through the last leg of my journey to Paris, I read all
four Gospels from the back of my plodding horse. Rich in

metaphor and glowing with lessons of peace, love, and unity, I found hints of other truths. Truths the Vatican denied. Questions that could not be answered by church dogma. "No wonder they never wanted the Bible printed in the vernacular. They did not want anyone to *read* it!"

Guilt flushed my face. I had studied for five years for the priesthood and never read more of the Bible than assigned lessons; each carefully chosen and often taken out of context. The Protestant cause had set loose more changes than just reform when they printed the Bible in common tongues and made it accessible to any who chose to think for themselves.

At sunset of the third day, we wended our way through the alleys of Paris toward the cathedral.

The arguments of scholars, the cries of street vendors, the pleading of the denizens of the evening passed over me as water. I didn't know these people anymore. They did not call me Father Merlin and treat me as one of their own. I was just another priest to be placated or spat upon depending upon one's political and spiritual leanings.

I stopped at the cathedral to pray. There in a deep dark chapel within the crypts, another wizened monk wandered past me. "James is Just. He deserves justice," he muttered. "Justice for James should be Good News."

What did that mean? I knew of no Gospel of James. Or did I? The Book of Revelations mentioned James as brother to Our Lord. Had he written a Gospel?

Frantically I skimmed all of the pages within my pack. Buried within the pages of a dissertation on the Culdees of Ireland I found a single quote attributed to James the Just, first Bishop of Jerusalem and brother of Our Lord.

Pay attention to the Word. Understand knowledge. Love life. And no one will persecute you, nor will anyone oppress you, other than yourselves.

I grew almost faint. This ancient father of the church, the first church, assured me that God would not persecute me for reading, for exploring ideas, for thinking for myself.

But my own kind, the fathers of the present church would.

I stumbled out of the cathedral barely aware of where I walked, only that I needed time to think. I needed to talk this through with someone. I could not find Donovan with my mind.

My steps took me to the public rooms outside Bishop du Bellay's salon deep within the maze of his palais. A bevy of clerics held court there, juggling ledgers, scribing the bishop's letters, and sorting through the petitioners who awaited a moment of the man's time. Elizabeth had a similar retinue of officious beings who protected her from the masses.

I pushed my way to the front of the crowd. Newynog nipped a few heels to clear the path. The secretary who had put up violent arguments against sending me to England two years ago saw me coming. He bodily barred the door.

"I have important information for His Grace," I hissed as quietly as possible.

"You are supposed to be in Eng . . . elsewhere. We did not give you permission to leave your current assignment."

"But . . ."

"Put it in your report and send it by trusted courier," the secretary replied. He crossed his arms and glared at me as if I had just crawled out from under a rock.

I checked his aura. He harbored only the demons of his own fanaticism, directed toward his bishop rather than his faith.

Newynog growled at him. He growled back. She sat and looked at me in puzzlement.

"Please. This is too important. I must see the bishop tonight."

"If it waited for you to sail from . . . wherever you came from, it will wait for you to submit a report through proper channels."

"What is this noise?" Bishop du Bellay threw open the door behind his secretary.

"Your Grace," I bowed my head, but only after I made sure he knew who addressed him.

"Father Griffin! Enter. Your news must be important to bring you all this way." He yanked me into his private room, past the gaping secretary.

Instinctively I checked his aura for signs that chaos had tainted him. Soft layers of healing blue-and-yellow concern met my slightly cross-eyed gaze. No red sparkles. The only black was the tiny dot of death above his left shoulder. Everyone carried that omen to some degree.

"Your Grace, will you hear my confession?"

"Is that necessary, Father Griffin? Your reports, sporadic and sparse as they were, indicated nothing . . ."

"Will you hear my confession, Your Grace?"

He nodded and retrieved his stole. The moment he kissed the cross at the center of the green scarf I breathed a huge sigh of relief. I needed allies. Du Bellay was trustworthy, especially under the seal of the confessional. I fell to my knees beside his chair and began the familiar litany. I included my doubts about the church, the existence of documents declared heretical that approached the questions of faith and spiritual development from much more logical positions than the church in Rome. I questioned that the church had become a barrier between me and God. And lastly I brought forth Holy Scripture: the Revelation of Saint John the Divine. "Mary was the mother of Our Lord. She was also the mother of James the Just, first Bishop of Jerusalem. The church denies this and yet it is recorded in the Bible. The church lies, dissembles, and seeks only control, not faith," I blurted out.

Du Bellay bowed his head sadly but said nothing.

"Proceed my son," he said at last. "You bring forth dilemmas I am not prepared to answer."

As my narrative poured out, du Bellay stopped me occasionally to ask questions. Mostly he sat silently, absorbing the whole of my adventures and my questions.

"You were right to hasten away from England, Griffin."

Every bit of me froze. Gone was the title of my priesthood that I had cherished. I sat back upon my heels, relieving my aching knees.

"You have grown much in these three years. I do not know how to address your confession," he mused, tapping his fingers upon his lips.

"What penance do you give me for the sin of working magic?" I asked. I expected the lash, banishment to a distant monastery, silence for the rest of my life. But that would do nothing toward conquering Tryblith and the chaos he brought to us all. I was prepared to add disobedience to my list of transgressions.

"Say a novena if you must." Nine days of fasting and prayer. "By the time you finish it, I shall have a new mission for you. We cannot allow these problems to go unaddressed. I must consult with some experts."

"More expert than the Merlin?" I bit my lip against my own audacity.

"More expert than myself." The bishop chuckled. "An exorcist, one learned in demonology. Historians as well. Oh, do sit, Griffin. Pull the chair behind you closer while we talk. My aging knees ache just watching you."

Gratefully I rested upon the straight chair with carved arms and a tall back. "Then I am not excommunicate for my sins?" I closed my eyes with my head leaning back upon the chair, afraid to look at him.

"*Sacre Bleu!* What made you think I would take such drastic action against one of the church's best weapons against evil?"

"The church . . ."

"Is sometimes blinded by its own ignorance and fear, Father Merlin. You have begun a path toward spiritual enlightenment that I may not follow. But I can offer you sanctuary and respite between your tests and trials."

"How dare you exclude me!" a new voice shouted in the outer office.

Both the bishop and I sat straighter, wary. Du Bellay put away his stole with haste, but not forgetting to unseal the confessional by kissing the cross once more. I had no fear that what we had said would remain private.

The door flew open and Francis, Duc de Guise, posed a moment within the frame. His brother the Cardinal of Lorraine stood behind him like an unwelcome shadow. The duc's handsome face and fine figure clothed in the latest fashion might have won him friends and influence at court and in the salons, but here he looked out of place. The cardinal, who did belong among the princes of the church, plainly did not want to be there.

Francis de Guise paced into the bishop's privacy, brushing aside the protesting secretary and slamming the door in his brother's face.

Before he opened his mouth to speak again, I cringed away from him. A sparkling red-and-black aura preceded him.

Roanna and the Demon of Chaos had tainted the most powerful noble in all of France. And possibly his brother the Cardinal of Lorraine.

Chapter 57

Edinburgh and Dunbar, Scotland, summer 1561.

ROANNA fled Edinburgh. She paid for passage aboard a ship bound for France, then sent a serving wench from Holyrood to take her place. The girl had orders to deliver Roanna's trunks to the home of Francis de Guise. Then she was free to do as she pleased.

Dressed in the wench's sturdy clothes, Roanna bought a horse, a placid mare without much speed but a smooth gait and a great deal of stamina. She spent the first night at an inn near Dunbar. The innkeeper charged her an exorbitant fee for a private room. Roanna paid from her dwindling purse with gritted teeth and muttered curses. She'd steal the money back in the morning. But for now she had to have privacy.

Tryblith respected neither her determination nor her privacy. She felt him looking over her shoulder, sharing every image she pried out of her scrying bowl.

She saw Griffin Kirkwood in Paris, wrestling with his own personal demons of faith. He'd not interfere.

"What do you fear, Tryblith?" she asked the bowl.

Nothing, the demon replied. His answer was too quick and edged with bitterness. The same bitterness he'd exhibited when he related Roanna's family history, and his own, in the cave barrow outside the city of Wells in the west of England.

"You fear peace. You fear those who work for peace, like Griffin Kirkwood." And Griffin's ancestress, Resmiranda Griffin; the woman who had sealed the portal so completely only generations of civil war and religious strife had weakened her spells enough for the demon to respond to Roanna's summoning.

"A web of green fire lit the circle of stones outside the barrow. I wonder where else she brought a circle to life with her essence?" Smiling lightly, Roanna bent over her crockery bowl and dropped a pebble into the center. She kept an image of green fire lighting a web of Life firmly in her mind.

The standing stones of Kirkenwood jumped into her view. But the green was gone, replaced by Griffin Kirkwood's distinctive blue: the same color as his eyes.

You'll not find a sanctuary from me! Tryblith exploded with anger. He twisted the cords in the back of Roanna's neck into tight knots. *I can break any spell, any barrier you erect.*

She ignored the pain he inflicted upon her and fished the pebble out of the water. Tryblith relaxed his grip on her. She almost saw his grim smile of satisfaction. Then she dropped the pebble again.

Before Tryblith had a chance to react, the circle of boulders outside the cave barrow came into view. Green light still gave life and power to the circle.

Too close to the portal for safety. Roanna retrieved the pebble and dropped it once more. This time, Tryblith nearly blinded her with pain. Her head jerked back in reaction to his talons raking her neck and back.

But she kept her eyes open and upon the wavelets and ripples in her bowl. Another circle came into view. Bigger, stronger, atop a tor, above a ruined castle.

Silently, Roanna fixed a tether of magic to the image. The slender thread vibrated lightly. It would lead her to a place where she could safely give birth. Her baby would be safe from Tryblith.

You cannot escape me.

Paris, France, and Rome.

Before I could finish the novena—nine days of prayer, fasting, and meditation—Bishop du Bellay bundled me off to Rome. I protested mightily the abrupt transfer. I had been making my own decisions for too long to obey without question.

But the bishop and I were allies against the chaos spreading around us.

Eustachius du Bellay, scion of a house as noble, if not as old, as mine cut off my arguments. "De Guise has been tainted by the demon. Through Roanna de Planchet he has contact with the Duke of Norfolk, who has also been tainted. We cannot allow them to find you here. They *will* use you, take innocents hostage, sacrifice others, anything to get their hands upon you, Griffin Kirkwood, Pendragon of Britain . . . Merlin."

His use of my claimed title and referring to all of Britain as my province instead of just England, told me more of his respect and honor than anything else.

"I consider you my equal in authority, Father Griffin, possibly my spiritual superior; your priestly vows of obedience to the church notwithstanding. Please think this through on your road south. But go. Now. Without protest."

"I have much to learn about history, demons, and exorcism. There are experts and archives in Rome," I demurred.

Once more I saddled the fine mount I had purchased in Rouen.

"Use your magic wisely and sparingly," Bishop du Bellay whispered to me as he pressed a wallet fat with documents and a purse heavy with coin into my hands.

"Then I am absolved of my crime against the church?" I asked, more than a little bewildered by the haste of my departure and the bishop's urgency for me to be gone.

"I do not know, Father Griffin. I do not know much of your destiny except that we both work for a higher power and a grander purpose. We work for peace in France and Britain. Both countries need to remain stable and strong enough to counter the excesses of men who would use the church to further their greed for power. The Inquisition will rob us of more of the faithful than it will return the lapsed to the fold."

Something in his soft brown eyes spoke to a deep need in me. They reminded me of Raven in expression and intensity; though no one not of Kirkwood blood could match

Raven's eyes in midnight-blue color. His hooked nose resembled the beak of the cranky old raven who haunted the
well of Kirkenwood. My ancestors spoke through him,
much as the standing stones of Kirkenwood held their
visages.

"There has to be a better way to unify the church," the
bishop finished with echoes of Raven's voice. "Find that
better way, Father Griffin, away from the boiling emotions
that consume Paris. I fear that tomorrow you and your
wolfhound familiar will be the catalyst for witch hunts and
religious persecutions. Already I hear whispers of fear because of your visions. The Demon of Chaos uses de Guise
to foster these rumors and the spread of violence. Find
safety and answers in Rome."

So I rode out of Paris on a fleet horse, headed south into
the lush hinterland of France. My road took me to the
shrines at Chartres where I walked the labyrinth set in the
stone flooring of the nave, Orléans where I was directed to
a bookseller who sold me a slim volume of the *Book of
the Secrets of Enoch,* a work much revered by the Templars, and finally Toulouse where I was left to meditate on
my own on the lessons of the previous four pilgrimage sites
of old. In each site I found a sense of peace absent in Paris
and London. In each place, my extra senses perceived the
ghosts of other pilgrims, some seeking enlightenment, some
merely seeking inner peace.

Each night I gazed into a bowl of water triggered by an
agate. I scried for my sister and Robin with no luck. I scried
for my twin and his bride and learned of their separation
forced by Elizabeth as well as of the birth of their children.
And I watched events in France as the seeds of chaos
took root.

Roanna and those she had tainted remained hidden from
me. Where was she? Who did she infect with chaos now
that she had tainted powerful nobles in both England and
France.

And so I traveled across the Alps to Italy, frustrated that
I could not yet return to Paris or London and act upon the
growing tension between Catholic and Protestant.

I was given quarters and the duties of making fair copies
of deteriorating documents in the archives of the great Ba-

silica of St. Peter at the Vatican. But each of the copyists was given only every third or fourth page of texts so that none of it would make sense. My mind had a great deal of free time to puzzle out translations I was not supposed to have access to. When pages from the supposedly lost transcript of the trials of the Knights Templar in 1314 came across my desk, I found ways to access, copy, and translate in coherent chunks. My fellow clerks cared not what they wrote, merely copying letters without comprehension. Substituting my work for theirs was too easy.

The charges of heresy and witchcraft against the Templars were unfounded and the evidence nonexistent. Still the Order was declared heretic and all of their extensive assets forfeit—the same tactics used by the Inquisition today. Since the day of the execution of the Templar leaders on Friday 13, 1314, any Friday that fell on the thirteenth day of the month was associated with bad luck and witchcraft.

Learning Italian, honing my Latin, visiting the many neighborhood churches filled a few of my ponderous free hours. I sought out priests skilled in exorcism and found I knew as much or more of demons and devils as they.

I prowled through Rome at odd hours with my wolfhound, seeking, constantly seeking to renew my contact with the people—the heart of a land and of the church. People did not greet me as they had in London, nor did they ask my blessing. They spoke in odd accents I had trouble deciphering—reading a foreign language was much easier than listening and speaking. The food tasted strange, their hot spices burned holes in my stomach. Everything smelled of rotting garbage and garlic. Refuse fermented under a too hot sun. My clothes were too heavy and my skin too fair for the climate. Even with my broad-brimmed hat my skin turned red and blistered. My eyes ached from the glare.

I worried constantly about my sister, my twin, the state of England and of France.

And every day my heart and my mind returned to Roanna. I burned at her duplicity. Ached to hold her. I wept that she was damned as long as she hosted the demon Tryblith.

Later in the year, I learned that Katherine Grey deliv-

ered a son, in the Tower. Elizabeth had thrown both Katherine and Ned into the prison and annulled their marriage.
Katherine would never be named Elizabeth's heir.

Elizabeth continued to keep the world guessing about
how she intended to secure the succession.

William Cecil Lord Burleigh took on the awesome task
of raising Katherine Grey's son in the Protestant faith and
protecting him from ambitious men who would use him as
a pawn. The child was born illegitimate under English law.
But in the eyes of the Catholic Church, the boy stood in
line to inherit Elizabeth's throne. Would Norfolk turn his
attention to this child and away from Robin for his
power games?

Huntington, summer of 1561.

The thread of magic vibrated strongly. Roanna stilled the
rest of her body and listened to the harmony as her tether
to a stone circle atop a tor hummed louder and louder.
She had searched for this place for a long time. Perhaps
too long.

We cannot go there, Tryblith said offhandedly, as if the
stone circle meant nothing to him.

But she sensed the tension in him, felt her neck knot
as he cringed away from the one place he could not follow her.

Silently she dismounted outside the ruins of the old castle. She had to support the bulk of her growing belly with
one hand in order to stretch her feet to the ground.

Ancient Huntington fairly reeked with a haze of green
magic. She should shrink away from here, turn around, and
flee to Duc Francis de Guise. He would protect her from
mundane perils. But then her child would become yet another victim of Tryblith's chaos.

"I dare you to follow me!" she called out as she marched
through one of the gaps in the curtain wall of the castle.
She disturbed only crows and rats nesting in the ruin.

Come back here! Tryblith screamed. *We are bound to-*

gether for all time by your summoning. You cannot escape me.

"I don't need to escape you, I only need to erect a barrier between us." However temporary.

On the far side of the castle, Tryblith awaited her. He materialized as a misty image, as if he were made of glass and the light flowed through him. He reached for her throat with dagger-length talons. Part of her cringed away from his choking grip. But she kept her feet on the still discernible path and walked right through him.

Her heart returned to a more normal rhythm, if a little louder than usual. The baby kicked her hard. She couldn't tell if the child protested her action or triumphed with her at this minor success.

The path twisted and climbed a little until it neared a creek. The water flowed free, making joyful noises as it bounded over stones, traveling toward ever bigger streams until it reached the ocean. Roanna thirsted after her long journey. Road dust clogged her throat and smeared her face. If only she could stoop and drink from the water. Just a sip or two would help. But she dared not leave the path. Tryblith would reclaim her the moment she strayed from the time-honored processional way.

The path steepened. She shortened her steps and took deeper breaths. Tryblith paced beside her, berating her. He whined, threatened, and pleaded with her. She closed her ears and her mind to him. His image became more and more transparent until it faded to nothing along with the sunshine.

The climb took longer than she expected. At each turn, the path almost disappeared. She had to stop and peer intently at each sprig of bent grass and packed earth for clues. One false step and she'd not be able to return to the path. She and her baby would be at Tryblith's mercy.

The demon knew no mercy.

At last she crested the tor. As the last rays of sun set beyond the horizon, green fire lit the tops of hundreds of rough stones set into a perfect circle. At the center of the circle, three large boulders rested together, each as flat as an altar. The little creek sprang to life among them and exited the circle to her left, at the exact position of east. She knew in her bones that if she stood upon the center altar at dawn on the Summer Solstice the sun would rise between the two easternmost stones, turning the water fiery red.

The creek is off the path. If you step into the creek, you will once more be mine. You cannot escape me. Step off the path, or return to your horse. Either way you are mine, Tryblith chortled as if he knew what he was talking about.

"Stupid demon, the creek *is* the path." Roanna sat on the path to remove her boots. The bulk of the baby prevented her from bending over to perform the chore. Then she arose clumsily and shed her skirt and kirtle. Clad only in her shift and barefoot, Roanna stepped into the creek.

The chill water made her feet ache and her teeth chatter. *The chill isn't good for the baby. You'll harm the baby if you continue,* Tryblith babbled.

Roanna ignored him. One step after another she followed the creek bed, letting the water ritually cleanse her. Her body felt lighter, but Tryblith continued to taint her mind.

The moment she passed between the stones, into the circle proper, the demon became a faint echo, as if he called to her from far away. He twisted the cords in her neck, a faint reminder that when she left the protection of the circle, as she must one day, he awaited her.

"We knew you'd come. We've built a wee hut for you." An ancient one-eyed crone straightened behind the altar stones. Sure enough, a circular mound of twigs and sticks came into view.

"How . . . ?"

"We knew. We've been building layers of protection around the entire tor for months now. No one can find you by means magic or mundane. No magic can penetrate the circle, and you can work no magic of your own while here." The woman fussed with the placement of one last stick in the hut's woven walls.

"How . . . ?" Roanna felt stupid asking the same question. Stupid with relief. She didn't have to go through this alone.

"We knew. 'Tis part of who we are, who we were, and who we will be. Rest now, dearie. You are safe and so is the babe. The circle will protect you, as long as you work no magic. But only until the birth. We cannot hold out against the demon any longer than that. When this business be finished, ye must return to your demon."

"But the babe will be safe? I may leave it with you for proper raising?"

"Your daughter will be tainted no further by the demon. Mayhap we can cleanse her of the chaos you have exposed her to."

"A girl?" Roanna cupped her belly, cherishing the thought of a daughter. A little girl to follow after her. To carry on the magic of Gran's line. But clean of the anger and bitterness that had always colored the women descended from Nimuë.

Her entire body shuddered with chill and release of the tension of carrying a demon on her shoulder for so many years.

"May I ask your name, Old Mother?" Roanna finally stepped out of the chill water. But she could not stop shaking.

"Some call me by all sorts of names, foul and fair. Witch or bitch in the same breath. Some calls me Deirdre when they needs to be respectful."

"My daughter shall be Deirdre, too. In honor of the help you give us both."

"We'll see. Now wrap up in this blanket afore you take a chill. 'Twill rain by moonrise. We need you indoors, fed, and warm before then. We'll see how long we can keep the demon outside the circle. Remember, you must work no magic, not even to scry the child's father."

Chapter 58

Rome.

FOR almost a year I wandered Rome, feeling like a mother must feel while carrying a child: waiting. I knew that important events were about to happen, but I could do nothing until others made decisions and took action.

Perhaps I should have returned to Paris. I could have gained entrance to court and salons with my message of peace and unity through diplomacy and compromise rather than bloodshed.

Would anyone listen to me, a mere priest of dubious credentials?

I began to write. Letters, pamphlets, essays, whatever came to mind. I found another wizened brown-robed monk who spoke in cryptic messages haunting the archives of the Vatican. He often pointed me to texts I needed to read. Through him I made contact with a network of other Christians on the path to enlightenment. They took my critiques and copied my writing, distributing them by secret pathways to men of influence throughout western Europe. I was not surprised to find Dr. John Dee near the bottom of the list.

The summer of 1562 Duc Francis de Guise and his Holy League began a holy war against the Huguenots. The Huguenots fought back fiercely.

Catherine de Médici sat back and watched the fray. I wondered how she could allow the extreme violence to continue. I wondered how anyone could watch the slaughter of innocents and not grieve.

Pope Pius IV also sat back and watched. He could have mustered troops to end the civil war.

They both tolerated a religious war for political reasons rather than because of their abiding faith.

I made three trips to Paris that summer, secretly, and without Papal permission. With a replica of the dragon rampant ring, I gained entreé to Catherine de Médici.

"Majesty, please stop this horrible war," I begged.

" 'Tis not in our interest to sue for peace," she replied. With a wave of her hand, three heavily armed men escorted Newynog and me from the Palais de la Louvre. For once my familiar minded her manners and did not attack the guards.

From the palais I made my way to the leaders of the Huguenots, Prince de Condé and Admiral de Coligny. The light of fanaticism burned fiercely in the eyes of the Admiral. He envisioned a new Jerusalem; France ruled by a Protestant priesthood with himself presiding. The prince spoke of strategic towns and wealthy provinces. He wanted a crown. They treated my pleas for peace with less respect than had the queen.

The war raged for nearly a year before I convinced the two sides to talk. Nearly a full year of death, countless innocents maimed, land ruined, and trade come to nearly a halt. The latter I was sure was Catherine's motive to accept peace overtures from the exhausted Protestant cause.

I helped write the treaty. I presided over the signing, prodding a reluctant Admiral de Coligny to affix his name and seal.

Duc Francis de Guise refused to join us at the peace table.

The peace held uneasily for two weeks. I returned to Rome convinced Catherine de Médici would enforce the truce, at least until trade and prosperity resumed for a time.

A month later the war erupted again. Defeat exhausted and deflated me. I returned to the copy rooms at the Vatican.

And then one night I dreamed of Helwriaeth. She came to me, her ghostly paws making no sound on the cool tile floors so prevalent in Italy. She licked my hand and rested her great head beside me on the bed a moment. A great doggy sigh of relief escaped her.

I awoke with a start. Newynog paced round and round the bed, whining in bewilderment and distress.

My hand was wet, as if a dog had licked it.

Helwriaeth had died.

Depression hung heavily on my shoulders. Many days I had trouble forcing myself out of bed because I knew nothing but defeat. Even my tentative contact with Donovan seemed to evaporate. I had not the energy to pursue anything, least of all my magic.

Another year passed while I copied text in a variety of languages. Eventually I found enough interest in something to scheme for access to whole texts and complete copies of documents. All of them were supposed to be lost or destroyed because they challenged church dogma.

Strange that the archivists kept the documents and carefully preserved them even though their superiors proclaimed the writings the works of Satan, lies, forgeries, and many other foul names.

I took up my writing and correspondence where I had left off, now including Francis de Guise, Catherine de Médici, and the Prince de Condé on my list of recipients.

Kirkenwood, late February 1563.

"You have not tried the ghostweed," Martha said.

Donovan ceased sorting his court clothes. The unadorned blacks he had worn at Elizabeth's court for so long were hopelessly threadbare and outdated. Though Mary presided over a more sober court than her cousin, Donovan felt the need to cast off the black in favor of brighter colors.

He felt at home in Edinburgh. The city and the young queen seemed to reach out and embrace him with respect and honesty. He understood the politics of the Scottish court. London and Elizabeth's court seemed alien lands speaking a coded language that could never be deciphered.

Each time he returned to Martha at Kirkenwood, he wondered what fascinated him so about Edinburgh. It was cold, windy, damp, and grim. Martha was his wife, the love of his life.

Martha, on the other hand, greeted him with deeper and deeper frowns at each homecoming. She retained her somber wardrobe from before their marriage. She hadn't even asked for a new gown. She had come north to Kirkenwood two years ago when the twins, Griffin and Henry, were but a few months old. Each of the five times Donovan had come home for a full month she had asked when they could return to Ide Hill with the twins. Were Betsy, Peregrine, and Gaspar included in that request or not?

He found himself longing for a return to Edinburgh and Mary soon after each cold homecoming. He almost felt as if the vibrant young queen tugged on a short leash that drew him home, much as he trained dogs to come to heel.

When Elizabeth had summoned Parliament last winter, the English queen had begged Donovan to remain in Edinburgh as her agent and spy. Martha had voiced her disappointment quite loudly and removed herself from Donovan's bed. Her diatribe had been even louder and shriller when Robert Dudley had excluded Kirkenwood from the celebrations in London for Elizabeth's restoration of Ambrose Dudley to the ancient earldom of Warwick, including Warwick Castle and huge tracts of land.

Later that same winter, when Donovan considered taking Martha south for a few months, just to quiet her, smallpox ran rampant through the capital. Elizabeth was stricken and near to death. The entire court and most of the wealthier population left London in undue haste to avoid contamination. Only Robert Dudley stayed at the queen's side to be named Lord Protector should Elizabeth die heirless.

Even as death stalked her, she would not name an heir, not even Katherine Grey, her former favorite, or Katherine's newborn son. And definitely not Mary Queen of Scots.

Now Martha sought to keep Donovan from Edinburgh with the bribe of ghostweed. A bribe he could not resist.

"Ghostweed." Excitement blossomed in Donovan's chest like it had not in years. Not since Elizabeth had summoned him away from his experiments to stand at her side in Dudley's place. "Ghostweed."

"It will release your magical powers. You will have the ability to become the Pendragon," Martha coaxed.

He could find Meg. He could open mental communication with Griffin.

"Our son Griffin is destined to be the Pendragon, not me. I will have a new ring of authority commissioned for him when he is ready." Donovan wasn't sure why he suddenly felt leery of Martha's eagerness to try the drug.

"But how will you teach him to use his powers if you have none yourself?"

High-pitched giggles interrupted his response. One of the twins ran into the lord's bedchamber, chubby legs pumping. Behind him, his duplicate careened into the doorjamb at a less steady gait.

"Da!" both boys squealed. "Da!"

"Da!" Betsy chimed in, clapping her hands. "Tell us a story." She enunciated each word more clearly than most four-year-olds could. The little girl also talked about pretty colors that circled people's heads. She saw auras.

Donovan envied her. He wished he could see Martha's aura and figure out what emotions drove her. She acted jealous. Of what?

He loved her dearly. She had no rival. Even as he thought this, he felt his heart tugging him back to Edinburgh and Mary Queen of Scots.

In one quick movement he scooped Betsy onto his shoulders and grabbed the boys, one under each arm. He danced about, laughing with the children until they tumbled onto the broad bed, wrestling and tickling. That brought a smile to Martha's face, lightening her countenance.

As the children quieted, Martha's smile drooped. "Ghostweed," she said again. "You'll stay long enough to try the ghostweed."

"I'll meet you in the lair in an hour," Donovan replied. "And, Martha?"

"Yes." She paused in the doorway, back to him and their brood.

"Thank you for our children."

Her shoulders lost a little of their droop and she exited without comment.

The boys found an interesting bug crawling in the floor rushes. Betsy tugged on his fingers. "Da."

"Yes, Betsy." He wrapped his hand around her possessive fingers.

"Da, Auntie Meg says you mustn't go to Dun Edin." Her childish voice took on the deeper tones and cadence of adulthood—a lot like Meg when she spoke in childish riddles while a full-grown woman.

Something deep inside Donovan chilled. He forced himself to still his instinctive need to pace and prowl.

"Auntie Meg speaks to you, Betsy?"

"In my dreams, Da. She has such a pretty halo, all gold and white."

"Does Auntie Meg have wings as well?" Donovan's face grew alternately hot and cold. Meg had never come home. None of his requests for information about her, sent by trusted courier throughout England, had provided one scrap of rumor about her or the aging wolfhound who had deserted Griffin for her. She seemed to have stepped off the face of the Earth.

Maybe she had. Maybe she showed herself to her beloved niece in angelic form.

Betsy could not possibly remember Meg from the first few months of her life. Nor did the child have any reason to refer to Edinburgh by its ancient name. This message must be a true sending.

"Wings? Like a butterfly? Butterflies have pretty colors in their wings, they don't need colors around their heads."

What kind of answer was that?

"Tell me what Auntie Meg told you, Betsy. Every word." He had no doubt this tiny girl child could repeat the message verbatim. She already recited long ballads and Bible lessons.

"Dun Edin shelters doom. Dun Edin rises higher with each death," Betsy sang in the same tuneless chant Meg had often used.

"You have truly been blessed by angels, poppet." Donovan kissed her temple where soft golden hair curled—the same color as Meg's. "Now your da must learn to speak with angels."

He left the children with their nanny. Peregrine and Gaspar studied diligently with their tutor in an adjacent room. Donovan wanted to linger, monitor their progress, but instead he made his way to the lair, at the end of the secret tunnel through the curtain wall. "You aren't sitting here, waiting for me, Martha," he remarked absently to the empty room.

Dust coated everything. No footprints disturbed the covering. He hadn't been here in nearly two years. Neither had anyone else. Even Martha.

Ever restless, he set about sorting the dried herbs hanging from the rafters, searching old journals for references to the ghostweed, lighting the brazier against the chill of the ages trapped in the stone walls and for burning whatever was needed for the potion. Absently he fingered the pouch of dried weed he had left here.

Impatience began to twitch in his fingers and itch along his spine. Where was Martha? Did he really need her for this experiment?

Another thought followed close behind that. A treacherous and disloyal thought. Did he really need Martha now that she had provided him with his heir, and a second boy should something happen to the first?

Mary had showed a decided preference for him. She needed him to guide her through the tangled paths of running a kingdom fractured by religious differences and clan warfare.

He sat down hard on the high stool, oblivious to the dust.

"Martha," he said quietly. "You are my friend. My lover. Why do I have these traitorous thoughts?"

His thoughts tangled and looped back upon each other.

The ghostweed seemed to hum an alluring tune within its sachet.

"I think I need to talk to the angels. To find Meg. To sort this all out."

Resolutely he placed a cup of water atop the brazier. He and Martha had decided months ago to try an infusion of the leaves first. Easier to limit the dosage and add to it gradually as needed to produce the desired effect. He'd know in a few moments if his magic could be released, if he could assume the responsibilities of the Pendragon until Baby Griffin came into his powers and wisdom. Saints only knew where the boy's uncle and namesake had taken himself off to. He certainly wasn't guarding Britain with magic, or seeking solutions to the religious war in France. He had abandoned his responsibilities. As he always had.

"Griffin, you are a coward!"

The water began to bubble. Donovan dropped a pinch of dried ghostweed into it and removed the cup from the brazier. Too impatient to seek out a cloth to protect his hand, his fingertips burned against the hot crockery. He blew on them and danced about a bit. Finally, when he could wait no longer, he added cool water to the mixture. This time he tested the infusion with just a touch to his lips.

It didn't burn. But his lips began to tingle, just from that brief touch.

"Just a sip at first. We agreed on just a sip." He drank a large gulp and set the cup down on the first flat surface he could find.

The mass of cobwebs strung from bookcase to ceiling to doorjamb jumped into view as a vast network of spun silver. He reached to touch them, verify their metallic content. They dissolved under his fingers, replaced with bright eight-petal blooms of impossible colors. Too-vivid reds and yellows and greens. He circled the room, examining everything with new vision, new clarity of thought.

"Resmiranda Griffin knew the answers to all questions magical. I must read her journal. I must understand her spells." He reached for the bound book of his ancestress' writings.

And stopped.

The skin on his hand dissolved. He watched the muscles work, the blood pulse through them in tiny vessels, the bones flex. Awestruck at the marvelous, efficient structure, he traced his hand with his other fingertip. A trail of blue-green light followed the path of his musings.

"Magic. I've unleashed part of my magic," he gasped at the sight of the aqua light. *The color of the Mediterranean Sea,* a voice that might have been his own, perhaps Griffin's, told him. Then his normal hand returned to his view, complete with skin, absent of blue light tracings.

"More weed." He gulped the rest of the cup of ghost-weed infusion.

His arm floated up above his head, too light to remain at his side. The other arm drifted up as well. His feet wanted to follow, but the ceiling was too low.

"I must fly!" Exultant at this marvelous manifestation of talent. "Griffin can't fly, but I must. I am a better magician than he."

He ran up through the walls to the highest rampart of the castle and spread his arms like wings. "Meg, do you have angels' wings?" he asked. "I must speak with you, Angel Meg. Join me in flight as I spy out your hiding place."

Chapter 59

The ramparts of Kirkenwood Castle.

"DON'T fly to me, Donny. Don't find me. Hide and seek. Oyez, oyez in cummin' free." Meg sang to Donovan. "All ye, all ye in come free." Trumpets and harps accompanied her melody.

"Are you with the angels, Meg? Do you fly with angels? I would fly with you." Donovan balanced on one foot. The wind caught his sleeves, buoying him up. Light and free. He longed to soar like a bird, like the cranky old raven who roosted on the well. Only that old raven never flew, never did anything but complain.

Some of the lightness and elation left him. The drug was wearing off, and so was the magic.

"Meg, I need to talk to the angels. I need to know where my magic is buried so that I may root it out."

The angelic music drifted up to the clouds. The fluffy white blobs shifted and firmed becoming a choir of angels with Meg floating in the middle. But she didn't have any wings.

Directly behind the angels lurked Tryblith, the Demon of Chaos. Its huge dragon maw opened, exposing row upon row of sharp teeth. Blood dripped from its jaws. It pushed aside the heavenly protectors in its quest to grab Meg, to keep her from radiating peace throughout Britain.

"Meg! Don't move, you'll fall. I'm coming to you."

He started to launch into flight, confident of his ability to save his sister.

A black flying demon sped into his face, raven beak open. "Crooack!" it protested his action. "Crooack."

Not a demon, the raven from the well.

Donovan teetered backward, flailing his arms.

The raven flew at him once more. Donovan fell sideways, bounced, tumbled back. A loud thud told him he'd landed solidly, but nothing hurt. Perhaps he had flown back to the tower parapet.

Slightly dizzy, he retreated into the tower toward the tunnels and the lair. Each step sent him careening from a wall to its opposite. He bounced back and forth like a child's toy. He giggled.

"One more dose of the weed and I will know how to find Meg. I'll fly with her, and magic will open before me like an unfolding rose.

If Tryblith doesn't catch you first, you fool.

Who was that? Who spoke to him as if he was yet just a boy?

"Donovan!" Someone called his name from above.

"Coming, Meg. I'm coming for you as soon as I take my medicine." He staggered onward, not paying attention to the turns in his path or to the side branches. All he knew was that he descended down, down under the castle, into the bowels of the earth. Dark. Dark.

Light seemed unimportant. He knew the way. He'd traversed it in the dark many times as a child, sometimes on a dare, sometimes secretly following Raven and Griffin.

The stone walls and floor became packed earth. Still he continued. Phosphorescent pools glowed before and behind him. He saw Meg's face and angelic aura reflected there.

At last the pathway branched in three different directions, and he knew he was lost. Slowly he turned in a circle. Back the way he had come was only darkness piled upon shadow piled upon regret and loneliness. Martha would be very upset with him for not waiting. She'd want to share this experience with him. But she'd been late. He couldn't wait. Had to move forward.

Forward? Which forward. He had three choices.

When in doubt, listen to your heart. Your heart will recognize the light, Raven reminded him on a snort.

"There is no light, Raven." So far he had not questioned how he could see anything without a light to aid him.

There is a difference in the darkness. Listen to your heart.

Donovan stilled every portion of his body. An alien feeling. He ignored all of his urges to twitch and pace and move forward no matter the cost. His heart beat loudly in his ears, the only sound in this forgotten cave save the drip of old moisture into the strangely glowing pools.

Another sound. What?

He heard only the echo of his own heartbeat. But it seemed to come from without his body, belonging to another, beating in near harmony with his own. He plowed on straight ahead, certain that the darkness was less dark there, that someone he could trust awaited him.

A sense of openness surrounded Donovan. A brief sense of fear washed over him. Without definable walls, anything could emerge out of the darkness. Tryblith could await him. Had he heard the demon's heartbeat echoing his own?

Was he the host for the Demon of Chaos?

Pain behind his eyes and in the back of his neck nearly blinded him. The chill of the cave penetrated his clothing. His sense of here and now, up and down deserted him. Reeling in near panic, Donovan reached out for the nearest wall. He encountered only air.

Listen to your heart! Raven commanded. *Remain still long enough to know that your heart still beats, that your lungs still breathe, that life continues down through the generations.*

Reluctantly, Donovan obeyed. He wanted to run wildly in panic until he found an exit. Years of obeying Raven's overt commands had made compliance a habit. He might ignore or disobey later. But in her presence he had to be respectful and obey.

Once more he forced his muscles to still. He breathed deeply, counting each inhalation and release. In, one, two, three. Hold, two, three. Release, two, three. Hold two, three. Again. And again. And yet again he practiced the breathing exercises Raven had tried so hard to beat into him.

Then he heard it. First only the sound of air moving in and out of his lungs touched his ears. Then his heartbeat, then its echo.

He turned right and faced a large cavern glowing with otherworldly light. A golden cauldron seemed to hover in the center of the room. Bright tendrils of life in a myriad of colors spilled forth from it. And beneath it stood a magnificent stone tomb.

Other sepulchers surrounded the dominant edifice, crowding against it. He knew where he was now. The crypt behind the kirk. A crypt full of his ancestors. No new burials had taken place here in three or more generations. No one visited here anymore. But he knew the place from bedtime stories related by Raven.

This tomb belonged to King Arthur, the first Pendragon. Beside him resided his lover, companion, friend: Arylwren, the daughter of the Merlin.

Donovan traced his lineage back to these two. He crept toward them, hesitantly, reverently. The bright tendrils of life spilling from the cauldron wove around him, touching him, including him in the pattern.

The gräal of Celtic myth. The Holy Grail of Arthurian legend.

He united with the tapestry of life as never before. He felt as if he touched the face of God. This must be what Griffin experienced every time he celebrated Mass. This was what drew Griffin to the church.

As Donovan rested his right hand on the inscription atop Arylwren and his left on the carving of Arthur resting atop the stone coffin, the cauldron of life faded from his view. But he remained connected to the pattern of life and saw for the first time all of his own strengths and weaknesses. He knew who he was and what his purpose in life was.

'Twas the light of the Holy Grail that had led him onward without his knowing.

Weary and elated at the same time he sank down to sit beside Arthur and the love of his life.

And then he listened beyond his frail body to the harmonic vibrations of the Earth. His magic stretched, hummed, faltered, and finally joined the music of life.

Hours later, Donovan roused from his cramped position in the tomb. Only then did he become aware of aches and pains all over his body. When he fell from the ramparts, he had jolted every joint. But he'd been too much under the influence of the ghostweed to notice. Now when he tried to stand, he found his weak left leg would not support his weight, the knee swollen to three times its normal size, and his right shoulder throbbed and ground bone upon bone when he tried to move it.

"Did I discover my magic only to be trapped down here unable to help myself?" he muttered. He knew his newly awakened magic would not extend to healing these massive hurts.

His sense of oneness with his ancestors and with the Earth did not allow him to despair long. Drawing in a deep breath, he cast out his senses.

Another mind hummed along with his. Griffin. Griffin deep in thought as he penned yet another missive urging compromise and diplomacy upon the French. Donovan smiled, content that his brother had not deserted the cause of light over darkness, peace over chaos.

But Griffin was in Rome, much too far away to be of assistance.

Another mind hummed in tune with him. *Betsy?* he asked of the childish voice singing a lullaby to herself as she drowsed, hugging a ragged baby blanket to her cheek, nearly ready for her nap. *Betsy, I need your help.* Gently he showed the little girl mental pictures of the secret door in the gallery.

Her laughter nearly exploded in his mind. She already knew of the door, had explored the first few steps downward before Peregrine and Gaspar hauled her back to the nursery.

Follow the tunnel to the first forking, Betsy. Then turn right. Bring a light and Da's old crutch. Donovan felt her acquiescence just before exhaustion claimed him. He, too, dozed.

"Here," Peregrine said with authority. He shoved the crutch at Donovan.

"Oh? Where is your sister, young man?" Donovan asked sleepily. In the dim light of an oil lamp, he saw Gaspar behind his brother.

"Betsy said you needed help," Peregrine replied, very serious in his new grown-up role. "Nurse said Betsy must nap and would not let her come."

"I found a dead bat," Gaspar reported, holding up the corpse by a wingtip. "And I found this strange rock. It broke off one of the white columns hanging down from the ceiling. Can you use them in your experiments, Da? Can I help?"

"I can see 'tis time to expand both of your educations. Help me up, boys. I seem to have taken a bad tumble."

Donovan held up his left hand to them, not trusting his damaged right shoulder to support his weight.

"Have you broken anything, Da?" Peregrine asked, running his hands up Donovan's good arm as if he knew what to look for.

"I don't think so. Just wrenches and sprains. The other shoulder may be dislocated. Father Peter will help set it." With many grunts and shifts of balance, Donovan and the boys managed to get him upright and leaning on the crutch.

"I do not believe you will be able to climb back through the tunnels, Da," Peregrine said.

"Nor do I. There is another exit. Through the kirk. I think we'll find Father Peter there." Donovan's senses told him the family priest returned to the kirk from visiting a sick family in one of the outlying farms.

The three of them stumped awkwardly back into the main cave and around to the locked gate. Donovan had to crawl up the seven steps. He rattled the gate in frustration.

"One of you will have to go back and around to have Father Peter unlock the gate," he said wearily.

"You know how to unlock it yourself, milord," Father Peter said sternly from the other side of the barrier.

"And so I do. I just do not know if I have the strength left."

"One last chore and then you can rest. Maybe Raven will cease to haunt me once you prove yourself," the priest sighed.

"She haunts me, too. But I don't think she'll give up until . . . until a new Pendragon is chosen. An undisputed Pendragon to take her place." Donovan gasped in amazement at his own deductions.

"You've the right of it, milord. Now unlock the gate so that I can help you up and dress your hurts." Father Peter stood, hands on hips, chin thrust out in Kirkwood determination.

Donovan peered at the lock, imagined the levers that must be pushed aside, the ones that must be flipped to a new position by the key, the bolt sliding back . . .

The lock clicked and the gate swung free.

The alarm bell clanged long and loud.

"Milord." Father Peter scurried to scoop Donovan into

his arms. "A courier rides through our gate posthaste. He wears Elizabeth's green-and-white livery."

"Peregrine, run and tell your mother to greet the man, give him refreshments. I'll join them in a bit. When I've recovered from my fall."

"Aye, Da. Does this mean you will be leaving us again. Going to Edinburgh to be Queen Mary's lover?"

"Where did you hear that?" Donovan stopped his son from pelting out of the church.

" 'Tis common gossip, Da."

"Do you know what the words mean?"

"N . . . no." Peregrine looked at his feet and shuffled them a bit.

"Has your tutor informed you of the punishment for repeating idle gossip?"

"Yes, Da."

"So why did you repeat it and risk a caning?"

"Because Lady Martha said it, too. It must be true if your wife repeats it."

"My wife is your mother."

"No, she isn't," Gaspar chimed in. "She told us never to call her mother. Not Perry, not Betsy, and not me."

"We'll see about that." Donovan set his face in a blank mask rather than let his boys see his agitation. The hum of his magic behind his heart stuttered into an unharmonious whine. He stilled his body once more. "I shall not return to Edinburgh. I will stay with my family and mend the hurts I inflicted upon Martha," he muttered. "I'll take the whole family to Ide Hill to be with her."

The tug on his heart to return to Edinburgh and Mary sprang to life. Only then did he recognize it for what it was, a thread of magic imposed upon him.

Who would do such a thing? Who wanted to destroy everything he held dear?

Dudley jumped to mind first. But no, the man need not be jealous of Donovan anymore. Martha claimed his heart.

An image of a gray-eyed woman standing beside the Duke of Norfolk on the strand awaiting Mary Queen of Scots' boat. The woman . . . he'd seen her before. She must have cast the spell. He'd have to consult with Griffin to identify her. Griffin would know how to find the woman with or without magic.

"I need to get back to the castle, Father Peter. Please help me."

"I'll mount you on my own donkey, milord."

But when he rode in through the castle gates, the courier waited impatiently.

"The missive carries Lord Burleigh's signature," Donovan said to Father Peter after scanning the carefully written words. "The quest for Mary Stuart's hand in marriage has become a heated race. Her Majesty commands me to hasten to Edinburgh and assist her cousin in choosing her consort wisely." Which meant there were to be no more unpleasant incidents as when Mary's French secretary, Pierre de Chastlard, was found under the queen's bed and summarily executed by her barons last February.

"Which means, in her carefully vague language, that you are to stall and keep the Queen of Scots from marrying anyone until Elizabeth chooses for her." Father Peter tapped his teeth with a long finger while he thought the matter through.

"I am especially commanded to discourage Her Grace from making a foreign and Catholic alliance. Don Carlos, the son of Philip of Spain is mentioned three times as a particularly distasteful bridegroom."

"We must advise milady to pack. I'll not return to Edinburgh without her," Donovan said. "We'll order new gowns for her. I'll introduce her to everyone." A warm glow filled his heart at the thought of finally including his wife in his life at court.

"But, Da." Peregrine tugged at his sleeve. "Lady Martha left for Ide Hill with the twins nigh on three hours ago."

Chapter 60

Rome, late February 1563.

ROANNA and the red sparkles of her aura returned to my scrying bowl. Thinking back I knew she and her demon had been instrumental in ending the uneasy truce in France last year. I wrote to my bishop, demanding permission to return to Paris. I did not know if anyone would listen to me, but I had to try, had to have the backing of the church.

Bishop du Bellay refused to recall me to Paris or send me back to England where I belonged.

Elizabeth sent troops to France to aid her fellow Protestants. They occupied the port of New Haven. I suspected she used the port as a staging ground to repossess the entire region of Calais more than to foster peace in France.

The war escalated.

I wrote to everyone, Elizabeth, Mary of Scotland, Catherine de Médici, Prince de Condé and his cohort Admiral de Coligny, Pope Pius IV. I begged all of them to find a way to end the war. When those failed, I implored Francis de Guise to cease his persecution of Protestants. If I had ever had an introduction to Philip of Spain or his nephew the Holy Roman Emperor, I'd have written to them as well. By the end of the second year I had thrown caution to the wind and signed my letters as the Pendragon of Britain, sealed with a replica dragon rampant ring.

My failure to achieve anything preyed on my conscience. The longer letters to the Pope and the bishops delayed intervening in France, the more I questioned their rights to govern the faithful. Over the past two years I saw the church as a political entity relating rarely to the people who worshiped in their buildings.

Our Lord Jesus Christ taught us to forgive, to turn the

other cheek, and to love our enemies. The politics of religion seemed to have forgotten this.

How could I obey a church that sanctified torture, persecution of innocents, and civil war, all for the sake of politics and not for faith? If I could not obey the church, I could no longer consider myself a priest.

Could I live with myself if the church defrocked and excommunicated me for my failure to obey?

Would I ever again feel united to the entire world through God as I did when I celebrated Mass with my humble congregation of wanderers in the midst of a faerie ring at Huntington?

I couldn't live with myself if I failed to try to stop the war.

I needed to be in France seeking peace. I needed to be in England thwarting Norfolk's plots, especially now that he sat on the Privy Council. Elizabeth had appointed both Norfolk and Dudley last winter, after she recovered from smallpox. One to balance the other—or one to spur the other to violence.

Then Bishop du Bellay wrote to say that Roanna was once again seen in the company of Duc Francis de Guise. I knew that already. He ordered me to move more cautiously lest I draw the demon to my side.

Du Bellay's orders no longer interested me. I did what Christians with doubts had done for centuries. I took a pilgrimage to St. James at Compostela in northwestern Spain, a stopping place on my way overland to France. My journey was easier than in earlier centuries. The roads had been improved and clearly marked. I had maps and spoke enough Spanish to keep the locals from cheating me out of the generous purse I carried—Bishop du Bellay kept me well supplied so that I was free to pursue my studies of heretical and apocryphal documents.

The object of a pilgrimage is the spiritual growth while enduring the journey rather than the destination. But I felt as if I had already journeyed far and learned much. The answers were within me, I just had to acknowledge them and set them free.

In only a little over a month I reached the bustling town surrounding the ancient shrine and received a scallop shell

as symbol of completion of the quest. The carnival atmosphere of the town, centered upon entertaining and provi-
sioning pilgrims, as well as selling them worthless souvenirs,
offended me.

I prayed and meditated within the quiet chapel dedicated
to James the Less, or James the Just, within the crypt of
the greater building. No wizened monk in a brown robe
appeared to offer me a clue. I had only a sense of restless
unease. This was not where I belonged.

I retreated into the hills beyond the town where I found
a monastery. Cool breezes and tall trees gave me a small
sense of home despite the dry grasses and pervading scent
of juniper and olive. The silence of the place soothed my
nerves. Newynog loved the journey, running freely hither
and yon. She disappeared for hours and usually came back
with her own dinner.

I ate with the brothers, observing the rule of silence. At
sunset I sought the solitude of a natural grotto in the hills
beyond the walls. A spring and waterfall cut deep into the
rocks, forming a moist half-circle with a deep pool at the
base. Other penitents had set up a prie dieu there. A finely
sculpted, black marble Madonna and child blessed the out-
pouring of water—a near twin in face and form to the white
marble Madonna in Norfolk's chapel.

And I knew that both sculptures had found their way to
places I would meet them.

I knelt in front of her beside the pool, seeking Meg's
face in hers as I had in another chapel too long ago. She
listened to my confession without comment, as Meg would
have. I felt freer, lighter, closer to answers than I had for
many, many months.

My eyes followed the fall of drops from ledge to ledge
and down into the pool. Ripples flowed outward. Sunlight
glinted on the surface, reflecting the plants and ferns, rocks
and cloudless blue sky. Ripple after ripple after ripple. The
reflected images shifted subtly. I saw another cascade down
a steeper hill, along a broader creek, in a greener landscape. Meg knelt in the pool, catching the falling water in
her hands. She scooped it over her face and hair. Robin,
grown taller and sturdier than last I saw him, crouched
in the shallows, eager to catch any fish that chanced to
shelter there.

I sighed heavily in relief. My sister and the child she protected thrived. Somewhere. Somewhere in England judging by the lush greenery.

The images shifted again. The stream became a blinding streak of light. It darted across my vision, back and forth like one of Robin's fish seeking escape from his artificial confines. The sword Excalibur slashed the stream of light. It tumbled and dropped, embedding itself in the flat altar stone before me. It quivered upright, becoming the cross of Our Lord's crucifixion and yet still a sword.

I was reminded that I had rejected the gift of the sword. Would I have accomplished more toward maintaining peace if I had accepted it? No. Violence breeds violence. I needed to reject the sword and the warrior's life it represented.

No more must the Pendragon of England be a warlord.

An angelic choir sang the hymns of passion in response to my inner revelation. But they were not all the angels of our teachings. The twelve Apostles stood shoulder to shoulder with the prophets of the Old Testament and each of them wore an aspect of one of the old gods and goddesses. Reigning above them stood Mary, Mother of Jesus, in the guise of the ancient Goddess, first among equals, mother to us all.

Together they all sang the truth of love and forgiveness, of living together in peace and harmony without prejudice for individual differences. Never again must one of them die in sacrifice so that we mere mortals might live forever in God's love.

The triple crown of my first vision split into three separate diadems encircling Our Lord's head in place of the crown of thorns. The crowns split again becoming six, and again becoming twelve, and again becoming twenty-four. They spread outward like one of the ripples in the pool becoming a broad circle hovering above a field of gold.

Monarchs appeared beneath the crowns. I recognized Elizabeth and her near-twin cousin Mary. Behind them, belonging to neither of them stood a boy child, heir to both, but not yet. Beside them stood Catherine de Médici and her two remaining sons. She wore the dominant crown, the boys and their diadems mere reflections of her strength and resolve. And behind the boys a young woman, their sister married to the Protestant Prince of Navarre. Beyond the heirs of France, Philip II of Spain, his rival from Portugal, the Holy Roman Emperor, the Pope, and a dozen others I did not recognize, knelt in prayer before the crucified Christ. Then their councillors, their critics, rebels, politicians, and priests encircled them, becoming a solid wall separating them from Our Lord, from their true faith, from God.

And Jesus whispered, "Father forgive them, for they know not what they do."

As he breathed his last, pain stabbed my wrists and ankles. I looked and saw the blood of the stigmata. His wounds became my wounds. I suffered the torture of the whip across my back, the thorns slashing my brow, the spear piercing my side.

My life's blood flowed freely into the lovely grotto pool, staining it red that darkened to black. The blackness of a hell on Earth without the love of God.

The blackness of a church that made itself more important than God and faith.

Chapter 61

The hills beyond the Shrine of St. James at Compostela, Spain, 1 March, 1563.

BY whatever name you call God, be certain that She is listening. Raven's voice echoed and rolled through the blackness.

I awoke to a fine drizzle on my face and Newynog standing protectively over my supine body. My arms stretched out to either side as if I lay upon a cross about to be erected. Remnants of fiery pain still lashed my back and pricked my brow. I dared not roll to my side for the lingering ache of a deep wound below my heart.

The holes in my wrists and feet had stopped bleeding. I feared the slightest movement might start them draining my life away again.

The world shimmered in a new light. A web of blue fire connected every living and inanimate thing within my view. A golden cauldron spilling the tangled threads of brightly colored life hovered just beyond my reach, if I dared move. It fed the web of light shimmering around every animate and inanimate object in creation.

I'd had inklings of this connectedness. The Easter Sunrise Mass within a faerie circle at Huntington the strongest of my glimpses into the mystery of life. I cherished this moment, almost relishing the pains in my body because the entire world shared in my pain as well as my joy. I was not alone.

I need not fear that I would never again touch the face of God, by whatever name I called Her.

Newynog growled with uncertain menace. I risked turning my head to the left. Eight brothers from the monastery waited

there in their patient silence. Five of them knelt in awe, crossing themselves repeatedly, their lips moving in prayer. One
of their number crept forward, hands open to Newynog to
show he posed no threat. I recognized the infirmarian.

"Newynog, off," I commanded sternly. My voice came
out a hoarse whisper.

My dog growled once more as she backed away three
steps, just far enough to allow her to sit beside me and
supervise the monk's attention to my wounds.

In short order he bathed and bound the worst of them,
clucking his dismay. Six of the brothers carried me down
the hill to their cloistered retreat, one ran ahead to prepare
a bed for me. The infirmarian worked the beads of his
rosary as he led the way.

At sunset, the prior came to my side straight from Ves-
pers. "This is a true stigmata, Father Griffin. Those who
will it upon themselves put the holes in the palms," he said
quietly as he checked my bandages.

"Artists take liberties with anatomy," I replied, thinking
of the great masterpieces in the Vatican that showed Christ
crucified with the nails in his palms.

"*Si*, Padre. The bones of the hand will not support the
weight of the body upon the cross. The bones in the wrist
are less fragile."

"I know." Raven had taught me anatomy better than
most surgeons. She'd taught me all I needed to know, and
I had ignored her to find my own path. A path that led me
straight back to where she wanted me.

Memories of my revered grandmother sent my thoughts
along another path. Then I began to laugh. A low chuckle
at first, then louder and louder until I could no longer contain the mirth.

The infirmarian looked at me with alarm and disbelief.

"The stigmatum is nothing to laugh at, Father Griffin."

"I do not mock these incredible markings, Brother. I
laugh at myself and my awkwardness." Lost deep in my
memories of the shrine in Scotland that Raven and I had
visited so long ago was a lesson. Hundreds of scallop shells
from the shrine at St. James de Compostela filled a niche
of their own in one of the chapels there. A path. Those
seeking enlightenment through the secret pathways of the
wise began their spiritual journey at Compostela, passed

through a total of seven stages, or mystery schools at equivalent shrines, ending at that obscure chapel in Scotland.

I'd done it backward, as I did most things in life, stumbling in the dark seeking my path.

No more. I knew where I needed to go now.

"Will you remain here, to bless this hallowed shrine?" the infirmarian asked.

"I cannot."

"The Lord has blessed you with the stigmatum, a rare sign of your devotion and worthiness to serve Him."

"He has given me a different mission, Father." And a curse. The stigmatum was a powerful symbol that I, too, must prepare to sacrifice myself in the cause of peace and understanding.

"I will write to the Holy Father requesting an honorable escort for you back to Rome."

"No."

He paused in silence that came easier to him than words.

"I must leave here alone, in secrecy."

"God works in mysterious ways, Father Griffin."

I did not correct him for the misuse of the honorific. I had no right to celebrate Mass or distribute the Eucharist any longer. My parish extended far beyond the limits of the church, far beyond artificial boundaries of countries.

The infirmarian insisted I rest for three days, feeding me fortifying broths and small beer to replenish the blood I had lost. Newynog barely left my side, and then only long enough to patrol the grounds, marking the infirmary as her territory and me as her pack to be protected at all costs. Cook brought her bones and chunks of meat that the brothers rarely ate.

Then in the dead of night I slipped away from Compostela with my bishop's money and my counterfeit signet of the Pendragon, leaving behind my soutane and sandals, and my stole. But I took my rosary.

In the summer of 1563, I sailed to England. I severed my connections to Rome and the Catholic Church by that one act of disobedience. How long before a bull of excommunication followed me?

I told myself that I did not care. The church had no hold over me. I answered only to God. And yet . . . I loved the majesty and communal bonding of church ritual. People needed that sense of connectedness. I reveled in the magic of the Eucharist becoming the flesh and blood of our Lord. I held the hymns of joy and praise deep in my heart.

I slipped into London unnoticed and took shelter once more at Whitefriars. My friends greeted me with love and relief that I lived. They had feared the worst for me. I was delighted to see Faith grown and toddling about, the joy of all who knew her. Brother Jeremy still blustered through the glassworks, defying my vision of his death. Ralph continued to growl at the gatehouse. Gareth and Carola expected another child in the spring. I regretted that I'd not baptize this one.

The faithful among them begged me to celebrate Mass with them. I had to decline. The church might never hear of this transgression, but I would know I had no right to preside. Already I had heard of Jesuits following me with orders to return me to Rome, in chains if necessary.

I sent word to Queen Elizabeth of my return as soon as I had greeted my friends. My polite but urgent missive requested a private audience. Her courier returned within the hour with an extra horse to carry me to Windsor.

She embraced me warmly and invited me to sit by the fire with her. Newynog obliged her by parking herself within easy ear-scratching distance. For once I took the offered chair, making certain the cuffs of my plain shirt did not ride up to reveal my partially healed scars of the stigmatum.

"Will you take orders in the Anglican Church?" Elizabeth asked me as soon as I had informed her of my decisions and plans.

"I serve all churches and none," I replied.

"Once more the Merlin?" she cocked her head prettily.

My heart swelled with warmth and my mind brightened, knowing she would tear holes in my logic and force me to find my own truth.

"I was chosen to be the Pendragon of Britain by an ancient and noble line." My gaze rested on Newynog. She lolled her tongue in silent laughter. She and her dam before her had chosen me. The ring and the staff were mere symbols to convince ignorant people of the choice.

I interpreted the stigmatum, a symbol I could not ignore as I had more subtle reminders, as evidence that God, too, needed me to take up the office.

"I can no longer ignore my heritage."

"It seems you will follow your own path regardless of what I say or do, so why have you sought this secret assignation?" Her expression turned stern. Courtiers and nobles alike had quailed before her when she made that face. I had to be made of sterner stuff to succeed.

"At this time, I ask first for travel papers. Give me the freedom to come and go as necessary. Then, when the time is right, I ask that I be allowed to help negotiate a peace treaty between England and France. You will have to sacrifice my claim to Calais to win peace."

"I already sacrifice my troops. War still rages. There can be no talk of peace as long as Catholics persecute Protestants."

"The war is fueled by stronger forces than the politics of religion. I will do what I can to bring peace. You must do what you can to maintain it. Give up Calais." I doubted peace would come until I had defeated Roanna and exorcised her demon. If I did not survive that encounter, I must extract Elizabeth's promise now.

"You ask much, Griffin Kirkwood. England will never relinquish her last hold on the continent. Calais is all that remains of our right to the French throne. We will not give it up."

I met her impatient glare with silence. Either she granted me what I needed, or she didn't. I'd move about as I saw fit, outside the law if I had to. I would stand behind her diplomats, whispering terms of peace in their ears—as a ghost if necessary. I would rather do it with her sanction.

The silence stretched on so long that Newynog grew impatient and butted her head beneath the queen's hand.

"Your familiar has overruled me, Merlin!" The queen let loose with one of her wonderful, explosive laughs that seemed to enhance the light in every room in the castle. "Very well, I shall send the travel papers to you at Whitefriars but I will not give up Calais."

"I would prefer to leave with them now, Your Majesty. We will discuss Calais again. I will make you see the sense of it. But I dare not linger too long in such a conspicuous place as Whitefriars. The Jesuits pursue me." And possibly a demon.

"I have given no leave for any Jesuit to set foot in England, neither priest nor their poisonous literature."

"Nevertheless, they come. In small numbers now. More will come later," I said with the surety of a vision.

"They will be greeted with the law."

Again I kept silence. I knew, even without a vision, that the order of Jesuits would campaign with militant fervor to bring England to her knees rather than let her remain Protestant. They would come in droves, flooding the populace with books and pamphlets. Preachers and inquisitors alike would flock to their ranks, all because they could not see beyond the church into true faith.

"Go now with our good wishes, Father Merlin. But I will not sue for peace, and I will not return Calais to the French."

From Windsor I made my way to Kirkenwood, with Elizabeth's passport. The time had come to breed Newynog. The line of familiars must continue. Since I had denied Newynog the chance to breed prior to this, I expected her to run through the entire kennel, mating with every male she encountered. Not so my Newynog. She chose one dog only to sire her litter, the leader of the entire pack who boasted a distinctive coloring and admirable proportions.

Neither Donovan nor Martha was in residence at Kirkenwood; only Betsy, Peregrine, and Gaspar kept court in the nursery. My sister Fiona had moved to her husband's properties. He had been a third son, without expectations of inheritance and quite happy to act as Steward of Kirkenwood. But with one brother lost to smallpox last winter and the other dead of a hunting wound gone septic, they now anticipated their own titles along with their first child due at any moment.

I drank in the cool damp air of home. The wind greeted me like an old friend. All of the scents and sounds were right. But not I. Henceforth all of England was my home. I could not stay here long enough to see Newynog's pups born.

I hoped I had learned enough of Roanna's deceptions to recognize her and her demon without the help of my familiar.

Important matters drew me back to France. I left without my dog, my staff, or the original ring of the Pendragon.

Chapter 62

Paris, spring 1563.

PARIS was a city besieged by terror. Huguenots and Catholics held alternating neighborhoods. They blocked passage between with manned barricades. From one day to the next, one did not know which street would run red with blood from brawls and battles. Beyond Paris, armies met on the field of battle. Too many lost their lives. Persecution and war convinced no one to convert to the rival faith.

But church leaders, politicians, and fanatics would never agree with me on that issue.

As I made my way toward Notre Dame and the bishop's palace, I cloaked myself in shadows that sent an observer's vision scattering in every direction but mine. The magic I expended bothered my conscience no more. My visions had shown me that I had grown beyond the artificial limitations of the church.

Without the staff or Newynog (Holy Mary, how I missed my familiar like a gaping hole in my heart) to focus and strengthen my spells, the magic took its toll on my bodily reserves. First my muscles became heavy, sweat trickled down my back, and then my stomach growled in desperate hunger, almost betraying me to the wary guards at a crucial barricade.

But I persevered, determined to complete my mission.

Once inside the Episcopal Palace, I continued my magical cloaking, keeping to shadows and scuttling about to attract as little attention as possible. I found Eustachius du Bellay hurrying from his office toward his saddled horse in the courtyard. The usual bevy of clerics surrounded him.

Mind-to-mind communication between Donovan and myself had been easy when we were children, an essential part of us almost from birth. Reaching into these alien minds to send

477

them on other errands took more control and a delicate touch, but at last, still within the colonnaded cloister, I rid the bishop—no longer *my* bishop?—of their annoying presence. I partially dropped my magical cloak so that he could recognize me.

"Griffin!" Du Bellay nearly jumped into one of the tall columns that supported the roof and separated us from the openness of the courtyard.

"You no longer address me as 'Father,' " I said flatly. Communication between Paris and Rome traveled swiftly.

"What are you doing here? I expected you to be lording it over Elizabeth's court as a newly converted Protestant." The bishop flicked his riding crop against his palm, as if he wanted to flog my back with a longer, lead-tipped whip.

I hid my flinch. Did he know of the stigmata? The prior of Compostela had no reason to keep it secret.

"Have you given up magic? I see not your familiar at your heels." He kept his eyes carefully averted from mine.

"Magic is part of me, a part of my heritage, and the tool God has given me to work toward peace."

Silence stretched between us, stretching our trust of each other thin, near to breaking.

"Queen Catherine has de Coligny and Prince de Condé, the Huguenot leaders, cornered. Without them, the resistance will disintegrate as mist in sunshine," I began telling him why I came.

"I hasten there now, to negotiate their surrender and terms of peace." Du Bellay stopped his rapid progress toward his horse. "Why do you seek to delay me? Do Elizabeth's troops break free of Le Havre?"

I recognized that he could negotiate as fine a treaty as could I. He had authority and integrity all would acknowledge. In France the Merlin was still an unknown, still a mythical creature.

"No. She waits, as only Elizabeth can wait. She has other motives."

"Such as?"

Again silence became my tool. After several long moments—he could use silent patience as well as I—I continued with the speech I had planned for a long time. "France at war with itself benefits only a few."

"And which few are those?"

"The members of the Holy League and the fanatics who seek to bring the Inquisition to France."

"De Guise."

"Catherine reached an uneasy but workable peace last summer with the Huguenots." I knew because I had been there, pushing all parties to sign the agreement. "De Guise ended the truce with the brutal torture and murder of a suspected Protestant, a man who had fought for neither side. I believe he was a baker who sold his excellent bread to Protestant and Catholic alike."

The news had reached me by convoluted pathways. It had sent me into a deep depression. "As long as there is war in France, de Guise undermines Catherine's authority. He seeks the regency for King Charles; possibly a marriage with his niece Mary of Scotland. Politics motivates his fanaticism, not religion."

"As it does to many who claim to be faithful."

"You and I, we both seek a better way."

"And yet you disobeyed all orders from myself and from the Holy Father in Rome. Don't tell me that your own faith is not dictated by politics."

"I refuse to allow my religion to put a barrier between me and what is *right!*" At last I voiced the truth that had driven me to this point in my life. "None of us can allow religion to separate us from God and His higher purpose," I said more quietly.

"Amen." Du Bellay crossed himself and bowed his head. "Do you know that the light nearly shines through you, Father . . . Merlin?"

"I . . . ?" What could I say? I had trod an ancient path he might recognize, but I doubted he'd step away from dogma far enough to see it.

"De Guise must be stopped." I brought the conversation back to its purpose, away from an examination of me and my beliefs. "Now. This very day. We cannot allow him to start the war again. Nor can we allow him to come to power. He will invite the Spanish and their Inquisition into France. Chaos will follow."

"*Oui.* Your Demon of Chaos has been loosed in France."

"With every death, every drop of blood shed, he gains power." And if Roanna was in France now, then the demon might be very close to separating from her, taking full form in this world. I had to find her and exorcise Tryblith back to the netherworld before that happened.

Roanna might not survive the exorcism. That thought stopped me more than the immensity of my task. Could I sacrifice her? I would accept death when I accomplished my task. But to kill her, too? The safety of her immortal soul had to outweigh my personal emotions. It had to.

And yet I hesitated.

"I ride to meet with Catherine's troops now," du Bellay broke into my musings.

"Your Grace, I beg of you, do not try and execute these Protestants as heretics. You will only make martyrs of them."

"And how would you have me deal with them, Griffin Kirkwood? You tread close to defrocking and excommunication yourself. I could turn you over to the Jesuits and send you back to Rome for trial."

"Treat the Huguenot leaders as traitors to the crown. Bring them to justice for breaking the king's peace."

Du Bellay paused, deep in thought. "An elegant solution. They have no defense against the charge."

"But they would deny the charge of heresy. To them, you are the heretic and have no right to bring them to justice."

"*Oui,* I will do my best. Catherine is shrewd. *Peut-être* she can be persuaded. *Peut-être que non.*"

"Try, Your Grace. For the love of God, make her see sense."

"For the love of the church."

"There should be no difference. But there is."

We stared at each other another long moment. On this point, at least, we agreed. Trust had stretched thinner than the gold wire I wrapped around beads. It held.

I reached out and touched his forehead in silent blessing. My connection to him grew stronger as he, too, perceived bits and pieces of the web of light and life that brought us all together.

And then a vision rocked me. He would fail in this mission. His failure would eventually lead to his own separation from the church he loved.

He opened his eyes in wonder.

"Who are you?" he gasped in awe.

"I am the Merlin of old, the Merlin of now, and the Merlin yet to come. We are all one." And suddenly I understood how Father Peter at home could remain so ageless through multiple generations of service to the family. He, too, had walked the path of enlightenment.

"Do not fail, Your Grace. France cannot afford to have you fail."

"I must hasten to Catherine, to end this terrible war."

"And I must hasten to de Guise." I took a deep breath, seeking calm in the face of the tasks I knew to come.

"How will you stop him?"

"I do not know."

"Have you enough conviction to execute him if necessary?"

"I am no Jesuit armed with Papal writ." And if I managed to assassinate the duc, I would die with my victim. My magical senses would not allow me to do otherwise.

Chapter 63

Holyrood Palace, Edinburgh, Scotland, spring 1563.

"YOU are sympathetic to my cause," Norfolk hissed into Donovan's ear. He clasped Donovan's arm with strong clawlike fingers that bruised through the many layers of clothing. The duke led him away from the line of courtiers waiting for Mary Queen of Scots to emerge from her chambers.

Donovan had to think fast to remember which cause. Norfolk had so many—most of them short-lived. But the duke's Catholic faith and his need to depose Elizabeth dominated all of them. Donovan shrugged his shoulders rather than admit to a treacherous sympathy out loud. He wasn't the only spy at this court. Every second man reported to Elizabeth, or Mary, or the Earl of Moray, or Philip of Spain, or one bishop or another, including the Bishop of Rome.

And Donovan resented every moment away from Martha at Ide Hill. Her steward responded to his letters with a bold refusal to receive him at her home or speak to him ever again. But at night he heard his sons crying with missing him.

"Her Grace, Mary, likes you. She will attend your words if you present my suit." Norfolk's face grew soft, pleading, like a child eager for a treat. Donovan preferred the bitter man who cunningly calculated everyone's motives. That man was more honest.

Donovan went still inside. He saw wild layers of light surrounding Norfolk's head. His aura appeared in fluctuating layers that grew and condensed by the moment. Red tinged the outermost layer and dominated the flares, clear evidence of his strong emotions. Donovan needed to figure out why Norfolk's aura was speckled with red while others remained pure, like a stream of water pouring from an ewer.

"I must think on this," Donovan said. "How will England profit by your union with a foreign monarch?"

"We all profit by presenting a united front against Elizabeth. She is a heretic and a bastard. She leads England to hell."

More likely Norfolk's selfish ambition led both England and Scotland there.

A ripple of voices and movement among the courtiers told them that Mary's door had opened. Donovan used the commotion to avoid answering Norfolk. The man was still powerful, still a duke, and a member of Elizabeth's Privy Council—when he bothered to remain at court. Donovan had to walk carefully.

Mary's ladies emerged first—all named Mary, and all dressed in bright colors. Her courtiers, men and women alike, bowed deeply.

Then Mary glided graciously into the anteroom. Tall, lovely, and gentle, she commanded men through love, where Elizabeth demanded obedience through intimidation.

Mary wore black, studded with diamonds and jet, still in mourning for her husband, Francis. Knowing Mary, as Donovan had come to know her, she would respect the custom until she wed again. She had made her wishes quite clear, she would wed again. Then she would burst forth in a wardrobe as varied and dazzling as an exotic bird.

Edinburgh needed color and life. He wished Mary and Elizabeth would get on with the business of selecting husbands for themselves or each other. Maybe then he could convince Martha to return to his life with their sons.

Mary raised the court from their bows with a bright, musical laugh and a clap of her hands. She greeted many of them by name, inquiring after children, estates, favored dogs, and sick relatives. Elizabeth never stooped to such familiarity.

When Mary reached the far end of the room and her demithrone, she sat, so that she no longer towered over most of the nobles. Elizabeth rarely sat, as restless as Dono-

van used to be. She made certain all of her court knew
how tall and how powerful she was.

Mary's expression sobered as quickly as if she had
donned a mask. "Milords, distressing news has reached us
from London," Mary announced. A little bit of French accent remained in her speech, making her lisp a little. Otherwise, she had learned to speak her native Scots almost
flawlessly.

The room waited for their queen to speak. Donovan
edged closer.

"What news, Your Grace?" the Earl of Moray, Mary's
illegitimate half brother asked. As highest ranking peer of
the realm 'twas his duty to speak first. He actually managed
most of the day-to-day business of governing Scotland,
leaving Mary as a glittering ornament of the court. How
long would she allow that to continue? Certainly if Norfolk
wed her, he'd find a way to remove Moray from power
immediately—probably through assassination.

"Her Majesty, our cousin Elizabeth, has once again denied to name us heir to her crown," Mary announced.

" 'Tis wrong, your Grace," Norfolk jumped forward and
dropped to one knee.

Donovan feared he would propose marriage on the spot,
followed by a declaration of war.

"But our cousin has offered a bone to her poor northern
cousin." Mary chuckled lightly, ignoring Norfolk. "Elizabeth offers to choose our next husband for us. She suggests
that when we marry to her satisfaction, then and only then
will she name us her heir."

"Suggests?" Donovan asked. For all her intelligence
Mary remained remarkably naïve about the lies and innu-
endos that accompanied political decisions. Elizabeth would
never name a Catholic heir to England. She wanted Mary
married to some mewling coward whom Elizabeth could
manipulate, thus keeping Scotland weak but allied to England. She sought this marriage to keep France or Spain
from using Scotland as a back door to invade England.

"We trust our cousin to choose wisely for us," Mary asserted sternly. "But she will take her time."

At least Mary recognized the truth of that.

Norfolk rose from his knees, making sure he remained
at the front of the crowd.

"And until our cousin makes a decision," Mary continued, heedless of Norfolk's attentions to her, "We will have a little game here in the court, which our cousin feels is barbaric and incapable of making a logical and safe choice. We will bet five pounds that Elizabeth chooses one of her own rejected suitors for us. Now each of you must bet an equal amount naming the one!"

"And the winner takes all?" Donovan asked.

"Your Grace, I will bet one hundred pounds that my cousin Elizabeth gives your gracious hand in marriage to me." Norfolk placed his clenched fist across his heart and bowed his head.

"The Earl of Arran is the only acceptable candidate Elizabeth can choose," Moray said, arms crossed, a deep frown marring his handsome face.

"Wishful thinking, Milord Earl," Donovan muttered. "Elizabeth wants Scotland subservient to her, not united against her."

Mary gestured for a scribe to record the bets.

"My five pounds names your brother-in-law, the Duc d'Anjou," Earl Maitland suggested, naming the youngest of Catherine de Médici's royal sons. The boy was only about eight or ten and would not be ready to marry for some years yet to come.

"Henry Stewart, Lord Darnley," Thomas Randolph added.

Donovan raised an eyebrow at his suggestion. Darnley was still a teenager and yet rumors had already circled Elizabeth's court about his cruelty to horses and dogs—and mistresses. Rumors also said he liked young boys as much as frightened virginal girls. A descendant of Henry VII, the boy had royal blood, but as a Catholic, Parliament would never consider allowing him near the throne.

The English people would never acknowledge another monarch who would persecute them as Mary Tudor had.

The church might also have objections, for Mary and Darnley shared a grandmother, Margaret Tudor.

Several other candidates were named before Donovan found the courage to speak the truth.

"I will bet that Elizabeth names someone totally unsuitable so that you choose not to marry under her conditions and thus she has a reason to delay naming you her heir."

A round of tittering laughter followed his statement.

But Mary did not join the merriment.

"I think that Milord of Kirkenwood speaks the truth. But we shall see. Shall we put a time limit of one year on the bets?" Mary raised a slim eyebrow with her query. Murmurs of agreement followed.

"Milord Kirkenwood, will you take a turn around the garden with us?" Mary held out her hand, expecting Donovan to assist her in rising from her demithrone. She had no fear of standing next to him, for she did not stand taller than he.

Donovan bent one knee—the one that wouldn't support his full weight—so that his left arm was within easy reach of her slim, white hand.

The full court made to follow them, the Ladies Mary in close accompaniment to their queen. At the stone archway of the queen's private rose beds, Mary waved off the entourage. "We wish to speak to milord in private," she whispered to the ladies.

They stood firm where they were, making a solid barrier between their queen and the court. Mary and Donovan remained in full view, but their words should not be overheard.

Intrigued, Donovan hastened his steps, leading Mary deep into the knotted pathways. Grass muffled their footsteps. Only the cooing of pigeons along the roof ridgeline broke the silence.

"Milord, we have a small problem," Mary said quietly, looking at the grass beneath their feet.

"How may I assist, Your Grace?"

"This is somewhat delicate, milord."

"I shall respect your privacy, Your Grace."

"My nobles, my people, Elizabeth, the church, everyone expects me to take a second husband. I prefer a state of wedded bliss to the single life." In dropping the royal "we" she indicated her trust in him. She made herself vulnerable and expected him to respect her privacy.

"Yes, Your Grace. You have a responsibility to secure the succession with an heir of your body."

"I look forward to matrimonial bonds. But a second husband would expect that the first . . . that I . . . that we . . ."

Donovan went still again. There had been rumors, of

course. Francis had been ill most of his life. He and Mary had been very young, childhood friends more than lovers.

"Do you mean, Your Grace, that you and your husband never . . . um, God's life, Madam, how do I put this delicately? You and His Majesty of France remained . . . friends. You never . . ."

"We never."

"And whatever man Elizabeth chooses for you will expect you to have experienced . . . um . . ."

"Experienced, yes. This next husband of mine would know, would have reason to proclaim my marriage to Francis was invalid, Scotland's long alliance would be in jeopardy from the scandal. The Queen Regent of France would love an excuse to make war on Scotland, to destroy me. She would ally herself with Elizabeth the Heretic in order to destroy me."

"And you wish me to . . ."

"Remove the evidence. Tonight, after midnight."

A special flutter behind Donovan's belly quieted, opened, blossomed. He'd remained faithful to Martha for a long time. His many months of celibacy preyed upon his mind and body.

Remnants of the love spell the woman with gray eyes had inflicted upon him still hummed in response to Mary's nearness.

Out of the corner of his eyes, he caught a flicker of light. A small tracery of blue fire seemed to connect the roses to the grass to the trees, to the walls, to the people awaiting them by the archway.

When he turned his head to look more closely, the web of light vanished.

But a morsel of common sense overrode the wonder of the possibilities Mary suggested. He forced her chin up so that he could see into her eyes.

"Was your secretary, Pierre de Chastelard, hiding under your bed for a similar purpose when your nobles, led by the Earl Moray, found and executed him without trial?"

"Oui," she said sadly, closing her eyes and biting the inside of her cheeks.

"And if your overly-protective nobles discover me in your bed?"

"We will announce our betrothal." Finally she looked at

him. Honesty and determination shone there. "You, milord, are an acceptable suitor. I made a mistake with Pierre. He was a commoner, and though I was fond of him, I never thought to marry him."

Her thoughts spun into his mind. He felt with her the excitement of forbidden love as well as the nervousness of a true virgin.

"I am a married man, Your Grace." He dropped her chin and stepped slightly away from her.

Her eyes opened wide in bewilderment.

"You are? You never mention your wife, never bring her to court."

"Martha prefers life in the warm southlands to our harsh northern climate."

"You are estranged. You do not desire to continue this marriage?"

"I . . . ?" He swallowed heavily. "Elizabeth ordered the marriage. Then rescinded her orders. We wed in secret to ensure the legitimacy of our children. Now my wife chooses the estrangement."

"Reason enough to end an unlawful union."

"I must think on this." And get the hell out of Edinburgh before this woman trapped him in a conspiracy against Elizabeth.

He kissed her fingertips in seeming token of compliance.

"And if we are not discovered? Would you still marry me?" Donovan asked. He needed to report this assignation to Elizabeth. Posthaste. And then he'd settle in Ide Hill with Martha and all of his children forever.

Griffin's emotional turmoil slammed into Donovan's consciousness as he stalked a demon through the rues and alleys of Paris. His concentration on Mary and her "problem" shattered.

Griffin?

"What, milord?" Mary asked anxiously.

"A private matter, Your Grace, that must be attended immediately."

"We have been alone too long. Gossip will prevent our *assignation* tonight."

"We must be discreet, Your Grace." He bowed stiffly and escorted her back to the palace. He stiffened his back and his face into a mask of rejection. All the while he wondered how she would react when he did not present himself at her door tonight.

Griffin, how can I help? What is my role in this drama? Griffin? Why do you not answer me, Griffin?

Chapter 64

Paris, France, spring 1563.

"ON pain of His Majesty's extreme displeasure, We order you to refrain from perpetuating the religious conflict . . ." Duc Francis de Guise read the edict from the King of France out loud to Roanna. "Bah! Charles never wrote this. 'Tis his mother's doing. She is more interested in peace than faith." He paced an anxious circle around Roanna's apartment that occupied nearly an entire wing of his palais.

"Then you must ride immediately to join His Majesty's troops when they imprison the Huguenot leaders. You must make certain that neither Catherine nor the Bishop du Bellay succumbs and allows the heretics to escape their proper punishment." Roanna conveyed Tryblith's advice.

She no longer had the heart to pursue violence with the same fervor as her demon. Not since . . . Deirdre had shown her a different way, if only she would grab it.

Until she made a decision, she had to keep Tryblith in France, away from England and his portal, the source of his power. In England he could separate from her. She'd be rid of him, but at what cost to herself and her daughter?

She could not dwell on the fact that the politics of the current war seemed a waste of vitality that France sorely needed to husband. She could not think logically if her heart bled at the thought of the tremendous waste of war.

With so much money and manpower going into battle, crops had not been properly planted or harvested, marauding armies had burned out entire towns as well as their stores and fields. Neither Tryblith nor her duc saw anything but the war as a means to achieve their desires. Power.

The nearly two years of religious war—the most vicious

kind—had given Tryblith the power to become nearly tangible. Only the most stubbornly mundane could not see him when he chose to reveal himself. The terror he inflicted by showing himself only fed him more power.

But he was still tied to Roanna; must remain within a few feet of her until she returned to England and his portal. A few more weeks of war, carefully fostered by their protégé, Francis de Guise, would give the demon the final spurt of energy to go his own way.

A few more months of warfare and Catherine de Médici would fall as regent for her son Charles IX. De Guise nearly had all of his key players in place for him to walk into the Privy Council and seize the regency.

And Roanna could make a life of her own. A life far different from the one she had originally dreamed of. A life with . . .

No she must not even think it, lest she curse and taint her future by wanting it too much. Tryblith would jump upon her vulnerability and destroy her dreams even after he separated from her. She must protect her daughter at all costs.

"You must ride with me, *ma chérie, Rose.*" De Guise lifted her chin with gentle fingers and planted a kiss upon her cheek. His free hand strayed to her breasts, tracing their rounded tops, fuller than a year ago.

Delicious tingles swept over Roanna. She did love this man. As long as he touched her so, she could forget Griffin Kirkwood. But Griffin had fathered her daughter . . .

"Don your riding clothes, *cherie.* We ride as soon as the horses are saddled." The duc stomped out of the salon, full of righteous purpose, or driven by Tryblith's prods, she could not tell which. "Those presumptuous heretics will burn tonight. They do not deserve trial."

And in burning they become martyrs. Their followers will not allow the war to end! Tryblith crowed, stroking his engorged genitals.

Roanna turned away in disgust. *God's death!* She was tired. Tired of fighting every moment of every day to retain control of Tryblith.

Wearily she dragged herself into her dressing room, ordering her maid to prepare the midnight-blue velvet riding habit—the same color as Griffin Kirkwood's eyes. The same color as the eyes of the child. "Soon," she promised herself. "Soon I shall be free of him."

"Madame?" the maid asked, holding up the yards and yards of the riding skirt. "Surely you do not wish to be free of His Grace the duc. He is kind to you. He does not beat you as he does his wife."

He wouldn't dare. He knows I would blast him with so much magic he'd die trying. She loved him, but only so long as he treated her with the respect she had earned. And the duc loved her. Griffin Kirkwood did not. Griffin Kirkwood did not even remember their one night together.

Tryblith reveled in the pain of others. But he quailed and whimpered and shrank when pain came to Roanna and thus himself. He'd almost lost all form and visibility last year when she labored so long and painfully. That little bit of weakening had given Roanna an edge of control over her demon when she finally emerged from the faerie circle. With that control she had traveled quickly back to France with Tryblith—away from his portal, and away from her daughter.

"You attend the salons with *le duc,*" Céline continued. "He has given you *entrée* to court. You cannot hope for a better position."

And Roanna owed him much for all he'd done for her. Money, title, respect, comfort. But he was no Griffin Kirkwood in bed. Nor in her heart.

" 'Tis not His Grace I wish to be free of, Céline. 'Tis another who haunts me. Now hurry. His Grace will not wait patiently."

But he would wait. He and Tryblith had no choice.

Armed peasants and merchants still thronged the rues and alleys of Paris. The de Guise soldiers rode through the crude barricades of hay bales and overturned carts, clearing a path for their duc. They slashed at all who resisted with swords and lances.

A surly woman, a prostitute by the amount of bosom she revealed without embarrassment, flung a mass of offal from the gutter at the duc and his horse. The beast shied and reared. But Francis de Guise mastered his mount.

"Seize that woman," he commanded as he wiped the goo from his face with a lace-edged square of linen. The cost of the handkerchief would have kept the woman in fuel and lodging for a year.

Two armed men grabbed her by the arms and dragged her back toward the ducal palais. She screamed curses upon the head of the duc and all Catholics.

"Flog her and then burn her!" Francis de Guise commanded. "I'll have no heretics in my city."

Roanna shuddered. But for the kindness of the duc, she might be that slattern.

Tryblith, of course, loved every moment of the fray.

At the next barricade, the men politely removed obstacles from the duc's path. They cheered him and pelted him with flowers.

Roanna breathed a little easier. Most of the city's denizens loved their duc and their church. When the time was right, they'd cheerfully depose the king and his mother in favor of de Guise.

A premonition chilled her to the bone. That day was coming. But not soon and not for her duc. For his son.

She began to search the crowd for signs that not all was as cheerful and loyal as it seemed. Her eyes detected nothing untoward. She engaged her magical sense, drawing upon Tryblith's strength to enhance her talent. She cast outward in wider and wider circles.

There! To her left, about fifteen yards away, she felt a hot knot of hatred. The emotion radiated outward, enveloping all those it touched. The mood of the crowd shifted subtly. Behind that enveloping emotion she found a familiar heartbeat. Griffin Kirkwood. Her nemesis, her lover, approached with murder in his mind. He had no thought for his own safety or future, only in ending the war.

"Your Grace." Roanna edged her mount forward, grabbing at de Guise's reins. "Your Grace, you must take shelter, immediately. I sense . . ."

Before she could finish the sentence, an explosion of gunpowder deafened her left ear. The crowd shrieked and ran in two dozen directions, careening into each other, lashing out in fear. The horses reared. Their heavily shod hooves came down upon the heads of the disorganized crowd. Soldiers drew their weapons and circled in place seeking the enemy.

And her lord slumped forward, blood streaming from his mouth and the bullet wound through his heart.

Chapter 65

Paris, spring 1563.

A GUNSHOT exploded near my left ear. Once more I relived the nightmare raid upon the Scottish village. The terrible sense of failure swamped my wide-open magical sense. Once more I felt death and knew I must follow a soul to its destiny.

De Guise. I had shot the premier peer of France before he could stop du Bellay and Catherine from ending the war.

I had brought death prematurely. My soul needed to follow him into death.

Not yet. I couldn't die yet. I had to send a demon back to the netherworld.

I reached out with both my magical and mundane senses seeking an anchor to reality, trying desperately to keep my soul and my body intact. A short, hot stab made my heart stutter, gasp, stop. My knees collapsed. Darkness encroached from all sides. The halos around the people manning the barricades and crowding the streets intensified, nearly blinding me with the too-vivid hues.

My hands clutched my chest. I forced myself to look at them, expecting to see blood gushing from a gaping bullet hole. No wound. No blood. Only shared pain and a journey into the unknown.

De Guise soared forward. I reached a hand to latch on to him, guide him in this last terrible journey. Red light swirled in a gaping hole open beyond this reality to the next. De Guise hesitated. The unknown frightened him.

Calmly, knowing I had no other choice, I led him up to the blinding gates. We need only take one more step through . . .

Hold on to me, Griffin! Donovan's voice came through

the red haze covering his eyes. *Hold on, climb out of the hole of death.*

De Guise lingered before his destiny. I had to push him through. I had to guide him as far as possible.

I latched onto my twin's mental command. His strength came flooding back into me. Not enough to fully restore my vigor, but enough to keep me conscious. With his help I pulled back from the need to follow someone else into death.

One breath. Two, and then a third. My heart fluttered. Three more deep breaths, controlled, steady, measured. A ragged thump against the walls of my chest assured me I lived.

But I still had not the strength to stand. Donovan was too far away to do more than keep my mind intact. I knelt there in the back alleys of Paris, waiting.

I had killed a man. I deserved to die.

"You!" Roanna stood before me, magnificent in her fury. Red hair, hanging loose about her shoulders, lifted in the breeze, stirring into a bright halo. Her pale face stood out as a moon on a dark autumn night surrounded by the velvet midnight of her gown and bonnet. Strong emotions contorted her expression.

"Roanna." I reached out blindly, begging her help. There was a time . . .

Then I saw the gloating demon behind her left shoulder, where death hovered, ever-present, waiting impatiently, greedy for blood and death and yet more chaos. The crowd in the main rue screamed and dashed about madly, seeking shelter from this newest round of violence.

I had to remain anchored in this reality to combat the Demon of Chaos.

"You filthy traitor, you murdered him!" Roanna raised her hands. Red light sparkled around the edges of her fingers.

I knew she channeled magical power in preparation for a devastating spell.

"Please, Roanna," I gasped, reaching a pleading hand to her. I knew not what I asked for, only that I needed help.

"You murdered my lover!" The red sparkles increased. The demon moved closer to her. The bonds between them had thinned. He was near to separation.

I had to stop them.

I dragged in three more deep breaths, seeking control. My chest was on fire; my knees water. A small amount of power was mine to command if I would but use it. I could lunge, wrap my hands around her throat and squeeze. The magic would intensify my hold of her, press my fingers deeper and crush her vulnerable life artery. And I would die with her. I had not the strength to resist death again.

But the demon? The demon must be vanquished before Roanna's death, or her pain and death would release it to wreak havoc where and when it pleased. I had not the strength or preparation to take down the demon first.

Donovan was gone from my mind, separated by a thousand miles and his faltering talent. Newynog remained at Kirkenwood awaiting the birth of her pups. Roanna carried my staff. I was on my own.

But magical power still tingled within me. My vision cleared a little. Auras took on more natural colors. The darkness retreated.

Another three breaths should restore my control. I could withstand whatever she threw at me.

Fire engulfed me.

"Die, you traitorous bastard," Roanna screamed. "Die and go to hell for your betrayal of me." Another blast added heat to the first.

I sank all of my power into keeping the flames at bay and breathing.

"I saved France from devastation this day. How did I betray you, Roanna? Tell me how this action affects you." If I could keep her talking, delay her spells just for a little while, I could recoup a little more.

"Your staff does not work!" She broke the previously hidden length of wood over her knee. Half rolled away into the midden. The other half, with the crystal, wobbled closer to me. If I could just touch it . . .

"And the ring of the Pendragon has no power!" She threw the piece of jewelry into my face. "You lied to me and then you murdered my duc just to weaken my power!"

"No, Roanna, you delude yourself. I did not fire the gun to weaken your power or harm your lover. I assassinated a man bent on the total destruction of France and its people rather than allow another to control the government and the church." I had to let her work her spell. I had to know her magic as thoroughly as I knew my own. Only then would I know how to destroy the demon.

"Liar." She paced a wide circle around me, scattering powdered sulfur and something else my nose could not identify. The circle would trap us both within her magic.

I had not the strength to move and shield myself from her next onslaught. Every step she took weakened me further. She alone could not kill me, but with the demon adding his strength to her spell? I had to hang on, to survive. Roanna must not die before the demon. The demon must not gain enough strength from my downfall to release the tether that bound him to Roanna.

The tether was visible to me, a black umbilical. As I concentrated on Roanna, I realized that her umbilical of life, that should have connected her to the rest of the world and to God, was black as well and ran back to the demon rather than outward into life. She was alone, unconnected, her soul lost.

Could I save her? In this life or the next?

"You lie now as easily as you did the night you took me in the gatehouse," Roanna screeched. She ran her hands through her glorious hair, nearly tearing it out of her scalp. "You lie like you did that night your men razed my village and your brother tried to rape me. Lies stream from your heart more easily than the truth." Her insanity alarmed me. Her spells as well as her thoughts would not follow normal patterns. She could utterly destroy me.

She closed the circle. A small snapping sound in the back of my mind sealed my doom—or perhaps only hers.

I rose out of my body. My spirit self sought the black tether. It stretched and thinned, ready to snap any moment. Carefully, I wrapped my ghostly hands around the weakest points. Heat poured from my stigmata scars through my hands as if I were the furnace and this strand of demonic life the gather of glass.

My hands burned in my spirit and my body. Every nerve and muscle shrank from my task. I persisted until the tether became like a cane of glass ready for the molding. Bit by bit I folded the tether back on itself, splicing it, strengthening it, building up layer after layer of resistance.

The demon opened his great maw. He looked about in

confusion. He must sense my astral presence. But he focused his vertically slit eyes on my body, not my spirit. His dagger-length teeth glistened with venom. One bite would send my body and my spirit into the Netherworld without hope of redemption. I despaired of my own redemption now that I had willfully taken a life. But I could not die until I had sent this demon back to the Netherworld.

Roanna's circle looped around Tryblith, enclosing all three of us in the spell.

But what had she said. I took her? When? Where?

I slammed back into my body with the shock of realization.

And then the memory flooded through me, aided by the entrapping circle. My roaring need to get drunk overwhelming the bitter taste of the wine. Her insistent prodding to drink more. Always passing her hand over my cup after filling it. Sensuous pleasure, a need to share everything with her, my thoughts, my magic, my life. And then the intimacy, love. We had loved. She had been the seducer. I had not "taken her."

Something very *clear* about the memory told me the truth.

I fought for control, for a source of power. Every joint in my body ached from my abrupt transition from spiritual to corporeal. My hands ached with old burns. The stigmata trickled blood. If I could just reach the remnants of the staff . . .

"Ah, I see you finally remember. Bad enough that you betrayed me. Bad enough that you fought me and banished me from my home in Whitefriars." She began walking a new pattern within the circle. Glowing red lines followed her footsteps making the design clear. A pentagram.

My heart froze.

"But you did not even remember your perfidy," Roanna continued. "You fell asleep! And you snore."

"Now you lie, Roanna." I gasped. "I do not snore." The numbness in my limbs retreated a little. My aches faded a little. De Guise had made his decision. The soul that had dragged me toward death had passed, leaving me behind. Leaving me weak but whole. I could recover. I had but to survive.

"Liar!" She let forth another stream of flame. The demon stepped closer to me. The black tether held!

" 'Twas you who seduced me, Roanna. You drugged my wine. You loved me as wholly as I loved you." I threw up my arms to shield my face from her fire. I smelled smoldering cloth and smoke. The fire touched not my skin.

"Liar. Murderer!" A sob broke through her fury. She shuffled her feet and smeared one line of the pentagram. She could not admit her own complicity in the misadventure. Her need to blame others for her own actions still blinded her.

If ever I was to banish the demon, I must first make her admit the truth and take responsibility for her actions.

"I loved you, Roanna. 'Twas your wine and drugs that made me forget."

No, he is incapable of love or the truth. He cared so little about you that he chose not to remember. The demon reached for me with foot-long talons and hungry teeth. His eyes glowed blood red. But the tether that still bound him to the one who had summoned him kept him from reaching me.

I scuttled sideways, closer to the broken piece of staff blessedly within Roanna's sigil of power. The partial lines of the pentagram flowed with me. "Think back with honesty, Roanna. Think and remember without the cloud of demons separating you from the truth, separating you from true life. You know me. I do not give my heart or my body lightly. I loved you. And you loved me as you could not care for de Guise. The duc was but a means to an end for you. But you *loved* me. I know you did."

"Liar!" She walked three more steps. Another six would seal the pentagram.

"Ask yourself if perhaps the demon placed the veil of forgetfulness over me, just to keep you from acknowledging the truth. He needs to keep you angry."

She paused for three long heartbeats. Her feet shifted anxiously, weakening the pentagram.

He lies. He is a priest and incapable of telling the truth. He wants only control and will do anything to keep you from thinking for yourself, Roanna, the demon said. But he backed off one step. The original circle kept him from moving farther from me and the truth.

Roanna's eyes glazed. Confusion reddened her pale cheeks. The demon controlled her thoughts and her words, just as he accused me of doing.

"You shall not escape my vengeance, Griffin Kirkwood. You murdered Duc Francis de Guise. You killed the man I love above all others. For this you must die a horrible, lingering death." She walked five more steps. I moved as far from her as I could, still on my knees. The pentagram took on a lopsided imperfection. My sensitive perceptions found the weaknesses in the sigil. The black crystal was almost within reach.

Could I negate her magic?

She closed the sigil with one last decisive step. The cobbles beneath my knees spat fire and heaved. The stone buildings around me trembled. Rubble flew through the air.

I ducked, covering my head and neck with my arms. Prayers and incantations shielded me from the debris. But my spell and talent was in tatters from the death of another so close to me and from my astral projection. I had nothing left to fight her with.

Roanna's screams and the whirling debris attracted attention. Armed men ran toward us. Their booted feet rang hollowly upon the cobbles. Their shouts came to me as from a great distance.

A flying rock struck me near the temple. I heard distant bells ringing. Black stars formed before my eyes. Shouts. Confusion. The clash of metal weapons upon stone. The thunk of something heavy landing near me.

And then darkness.

Roanna ran. She did not know or care where. She just ran from Francis' dead body. From Griffin and his accusations. She ran from her memories, and the truth Griffin had made her look at. She ran from herself.

Breaking the circle and the pentagram took three sobbing moments. She rushed through it, scattering magic to the winds, ungrounded, incomplete, wild and hungry for blood.

But she could not run from Tryblith. He loped easily beside her on his fat, lizard legs covered in scales and ending in talons that scraped noisily along the cobbles.

The sound grated on her ears, shattering anything resembling coherent thought.

So she ran. As far as her aching body could carry her. And then some.

You will not be welcome back at the palais now that the duc is dead, Tryblith reminded her. *His wife and son rule there now.*

"I must go back to Scotland." She continued sobbing uncontrollably. All she could think of were the misty green hills, a warm peat fire, and Gran's little hut in the now flattened and dead village.

To England. We can find refuge in England. In my barrow. The demon prodded her forward now. Peace would come to France now. No longer could they reap the harvest of chaos here.

"To England. There I will wreak havoc among everyone and every place that Griffin Kirkwood loved. None of his family shall survive my wrath. None of them!"

What about his daughter? Tryblith laughed.

Chapter 66

A back alley, Paris.

GRIFFIN! Donovan's voice prodded my consciousness. Griffin, wake up. A sense of urgency in the voice pierced the red fog that kept my eyes closed and my magical senses in retreat.

What is wrong? Griffin, I can't find you!

"I'm alive," I replied through swollen lips and a throat dry as the dirt clogging my nose.

Where are you? The relief in Donovan's voice flooded us both. With the easing of tension in my back, a new series of aches and burns, scrapes and bruises replaced it.

Cautiously, I assessed my surroundings. Better not try to move anything else yet. I didn't truly want to know what Roanna had done to me.

"A back alley of Paris. Drizzle. Late at night. The moon has set. Fires all around. Cheering and drunken songs in the distance."

You are too far away. I cannot come to you.

"Where are you?" I wondered briefly why Donovan suddenly had enough magic to communicate. Hadn't I always had to open the channels of mind-to-mind contact?

But the questions took too much effort.

In Edinburgh. The smile that came through his voice eased my headache a little.

"Perhaps I should ask whose bed you share."

You would not believe me if I told you. But I'm not in her bed. Just considering possibilities.

"Well, go back to your lover. I'll contact you when I do not hurt quite so badly."

The demon?

"Gone for now. I don't know where. Something scared Roanna off. The demon had no choice but to follow her. They are still tethered together. For a time."

I think I can scry for him.

"No!" I spoke too loudly and the noise hurt my ears as well as my chest. "He'll know he's being watched and follow your magical trail. He'll kill you."

And will he not do the same to you when you follow him?

Now Donovan was reading my thoughts as well as speaking to me.

" 'Tis my destiny, not yours."

Perhaps it is our destiny. Hie yourself back to England. I will meet you at Kirkenwood.

"Say good-bye to your lover. I have a feeling she is as dangerous as mine."

What is that supposed to mean?

"I'll tell you later." Gingerly, I eased my chest off the cobbles. One of my biggest aches faded. I looked down, moving my head in tiny increments to keep the headache to a minimum. A black crystal winked at me in the firelight. I had fallen atop the remnants of Raven's staff and beside it lay the ring of the Pendragon, Raven's ring, not the duplicate I wore on my right hand. Perhaps the crystal had facilitated Donovan's mental search for me. Perhaps it saved my life.

But it left a horrendous bruise.

When I had achieved the tremendous effort of sitting, I scooped up the crystal, amazed that it had not shattered. I pocketed the ring as well. I could not focus my eyes closely enough to gaze into the crystal and track Roanna and Tryblith. Later. For now, I concentrated on standing and then walking. Bishop Eustachius du Bellay's Episcopal palace was miles away. I had no place else to go.

Between here and there, I also had to find a way to negate all of the magic Roanna had raised within her circle and then scattered to the four winds without regard. Her spell had sought my blood. The magic would also seek blood. Whose? Would it care?

At the first crossing, where the alley met a larger street, a fire burned out of control in the thatch above a cobbler's shop. It chuckled as it gobbled up each new morsel of fuel, then roared with delight when dry thatch exposed solid rafter. It behaved as fire is wont. But something about it was different.

I tried to engage my magical sight and found the effort too great. But even without the extra senses I knew this fire had begun in the Netherworld. The colors were too intense, the smoke roiled with tormented figures writhing within. Some of Roanna's magic had found a target.

Frantic citizens threw buckets of water on the blaze from the well in the center of the next crossroad. They could fight this fire more effectively than I in my weakened state. Even otherworldly fire must drown eventually. It just took longer.

I stumbled on, encountering other fires. Roanna's element must have dominated the magic she unleashed.

And then some of the rejoicing in the crowds filling the main rues filtered through my foggy brain. The war was over. De Coligny and de Condé had been captured, the Duc de Guise had been assassinated. Without the leaders, the energy to feed the war fizzled.

Tryblith would find little chaos to feed upon in France. He and Roanna would have to seek a new source of conflict. Where would they go?

In asking the question, I knew. They would go home. I had to follow them. Tonight.

Holyrood Palace, Edinburgh, Scotland.

"Good-bye, Your Grace." Donovan planted a gentle kiss on Mary's cheek. "I cannot stay with you tonight."

Rain drizzled against the window lights of her private chamber. All else was quiet in the palace at this midnight hour.

He looked at the undisturbed bed with longing. So did she.

"Stay," she whispered. She returned his kiss with passion and longing.

"I wish I could." He pulled away from her eager embrace. Her scent, her warmth, her eagerness swamped his senses. "Duty calls me."

He brushed a wayward strand of red-gold hair from Mary's brow; let his fingers linger on her milky skin; tracing one lazy finger down her neck toward her generous bosom, covered only slightly by the translucent lawn of her night shift. At the last moment he captured a curly tress and kissed it with the passion he wished he could give back to her.

"Let my ladies find you here in the morning, Donovan." She tugged him toward the bed. "We would rule together, Donovan. Together we could put the Earl of Moray, my bastard brother, in his place. I need you by my side and in my bed."

"I am needed elsewhere, Your Grace, for the good of England and Scotland." The warmth of her body and the earnestness of her pleas inflamed his body. He wanted to give in to her. But only . . .

Forgive me, Martha, he pleaded with her mental image.

Mary cupped his neck with a delicate hand and drew him closer for another kiss.

He held back a little, letting her know the importance of his mission by the stiffness in his neck.

"We have more between us than just one night of service, Donovan. We have a true passion of the heart and a meeting of our minds," she pleaded, trailing kisses across his cheek toward his ear.

"I am still married. I will consider marriage with you—if it benefits both England and Scotland as well as ourselves. But I would annul that marriage before I come to you, keep all trace of scandal from you." His sympathy suddenly jumped to Robin Dudley. How many nights had Elizabeth's favorite avoided the bed of his one true love to prevent scandal?

"If we are to be together, it must be for more than a few clandestine meetings. I would have all of you all of the time, even if you did not offer me a crown." One more quick kiss and he stepped backward, out of her arms. The extra inches of separation cooled the heat of his lust. Lust, that was all he truly felt for this bewildered queen. His heart truly belonged only to Martha. "I shall return to you, Your Grace, but this is very important."

"Your absence from court will be reported to Elizabeth. She will be very angry with you if you leave without her permission. Or mine." Stern lines creased Mary's mouth. She screwed up her eyes just like Betsy did when she prepared a temper tantrum.

"I am sorry to distress either of my queens. But your crown as well as Elizabeth's may depend upon what I do in the coming weeks. I cannot do it from here." Or from the Tower. But with his senses wide open to Griffin, he knew that no prison could long hold either of them.

"Do not do anything foolish, Mary, while I am gone," he whispered.

"Then stay. Be my husband and lover. Help me rule this volatile land and gain my rightful throne of England. Our sons will rule both countries, united under one crown."

The truth of that statement rocked him like a vision. His son by Mary. No. Not tonight. Another night would conceive the child who would unite the two kingdoms and end the border warfare that had shaped so much of his life.

The bright face of a squalling infant rose up before his mind's eye. Demanding, determined, cunning, and strong. He knew his next son even before his conception.

At the same time, a sense of urgency from Griffin pulled him away from Mary's warmth and open, loving embrace.

"I have to go before a demon is loosed." With determination he opened the door a crack and peeked out for sign of observers.

"Does this have something to do with the Pendragon of Britain?"

"You know about that?" He paused, keeping his back to her.

"Rumors, legends. A letter from my father, written only a few days before his death, was delivered to me by secret courier the day I returned to Scotland. I was told to consult with the senior member of the Kirkwood family of Kirkenwood should I ever need 'special' assistance."

"Elizabeth received a similar letter, entrusted to Will Somers, her father's fool." Had Mary Tudor, Elizabeth's older sister? If she had, she had never consulted with Raven. And when Raven approached her directly, she rejected all magical intervention. Indeed, Raven's letters had probably triggered Mary's assignment of Father Manuel to Kirkenwood as a spy for the Inquisition.

"Has my cousin consulted you, my Pendragon?"

"I am not truly the Pendragon, Your Grace. But, yes, Elizabeth consulted me. I was not able to help her at the time."

"And do you rush to help my rival now?"

"I rush to save all of Britain, regardless of who wears a crown for any part of it. Now I must act as the Pendragon against the forces of evil."

"I will wait for you, Donovan Kirkwood, my Pendragon."

Another vision rocked his perceptions and his joy. If he left now, Mary would be forced to wed another.

But he would sire her child.

Donovan! Griffin cried to him. *God help us both, Tryblith and Roanna have fled. I cannot find them.*

"Good-bye, Your Grace. Whatever happens to me, to us, I beg you never consider Norfolk as a suitor. He seeks only his own power and knows nothing of love, nothing of a monarch's true role in nurturing the well-being of the people and the land. By all that you hold holy, swear to me that you will not marry Norfolk."

She bit her lip. The silence stretched a long time between them.

"Norfolk cannot give you what you need. His ambitions will destroy you as well as himself," he pleaded.

"I swear, Donovan Kirkwood, Pendragon of Britain. As long as you live, I swear that I will not marry Norfolk." She crossed herself solemnly.

Donovan nodded just before quietly closing the door between them.

Regret hung heavy upon him. Mary might not be his wife, his soulmate. But she could give him much. The house of Kirkenwood united with the crown could bring lasting peace to this island.

Our destinies are shaped by forces greater than our own. We cannot allow our own desires to create a barrier between ourselves and what is right. The Pendragon is not meant to rule, only to guide and advise.

Raven's words stiffened his spine and banished the last traces of regret.

Donovan crept through Holyrood Palace without looking back. His first act before returning to Kirkenwood would be to make certain Norfolk left Edinburgh as well. Tonight. He'd use what magical persuasion he could. Then he would write letters to Elizabeth warning her of the duke's ambitions. That should keep him in England, under Elizabeth's careful scrutiny for a while.

Together, Donovan and Griffin would find a way to stop the man and his plans, just as they would stop the demon. He whistled a jaunty battle song of old, confident of success. He and his brother would be united once more.

Chapter 67

The streets of Paris, spring 1563.

OF COURSE life never proceeds as planned. I was halfway
across Paris, facing a blaze large enough to block all of the
detours around it, when fatigue and hunger nearly knocked
me flat on my face. Yesterday I might have contained the
fires, possibly wiped them out entirely. Today, after the
trauma of nearly dying with the Duc de Guise and of battling Roanna and her pet demon, I had nothing left.

But the war had ended. I had to cling to that success just
to keep going.

The power tingled in my fingertips and died. I could endure a great deal of privation, but eventually the weakness
of the body catches up with the strength of the spirit. As I
cast around with my senses open to anything out of the
ordinary, I encountered only mundane sights, sounds, smells,
taste, and touch. I could not even see auras, the most fundamental of all magical skills.

I had no hope of finding Roanna and Tryblith quickly.

My feet found a new direction, back to the Episcopal
palace. But Bishop du Bellay was not there to shelter me,
or advise me. His officious secretary cast me out without
hesitation.

Exhausted, hurt, and confused, I made my way toward a
student hostel. I slept for a full day. When I awoke, raven-
ously hungry, my feet felt like lead and my limbs like porridge. I purchased bread and wine and cheese at a nearby
market, ate every crumb, and slept again.

The next time I crawled from my blankets, the sun shone
brightly, on a city intent upon returning to a normal way
of life after more than a year of warfare.

I sought and found solace and regeneration in the cathedral. This magnificent edifice was one of the seven ancient shrines that symbolized the stages of enlightenment.

While I basked in the quiet, I recorded my battle and my thoughts into the journal I had nearly forgotten. So much to set down for future generations to read and learn from. So much I wanted to tell the Pendragons to come about life and light. I still had to learn how to spread them throughout the world. So far I had reached only a few of the common folk. Any influence I had on Elizabeth remained doubtful.

Donovan had probably done more to influence leaders and politics and economics without using magic. Together we might have made a formidable Pendragon. Separate . . . ?

Separated by mistrust and Roanna's magical intervention, we had nearly failed.

Bishop du Bellay returned to his palais. He paced his office in a rage. "She cannot see beyond the political expediency of washing her hands of responsibility!" he proclaimed the moment I walked into his office—despite the secretary's protests.

"She?" I asked. Fatigue still made my face puffy and my movements wooden.

"Catherine." We both knew there was only one Catherine whose name could make him spit with contempt.

"And what has the queen regent done this time?" I edged toward a chair, willing to risk a major breach of protocol and sit before being invited. Otherwise I might fall flat on my face. I kept my black cap firmly planted on my head for warmth. My recovery was not as complete as I had hoped.

"She refuses to try the Huguenot leaders for treason, or a breach of the king's peace. She insists that since the war was religious in nature, the church and only the church may bring them to justice."

"Even if their deaths for heresy bring about a new conflict?"

"She will not look that far into the future. This way the Protestants who survive have no grievance against her."

"Only against the church. What does Pope Pius have to say about this?"

"No word yet. The missives are still en route."

"Then stall."

"Easier said than done. Catherine is most anxious to be done with this conflict."

"As is France. Can you gain me entry to the palace? I would have a private word with the queen." Another chore before I was ready to hold my eyes open for more than few moments.

Two hours later, I stood before Catherine in private audience. No audience with a monarch is ever truly private. Charles de Guise, Cardinal of Lorraine, two members of the Privy Council I did not know, and young King Charles IX sat with the queen regent around a large square table with a green baize covering—later it could be used for billiards.

"Majesty." I bowed as low as I could without growing dizzy. "On behalf of all those who seek a lasting peace in France, I beg you to drop the charges of heresy for de Condé and de Coligny," I began my prepared speech.

"We have listened to you before, Pére Griffin. The truce you urged upon us last spring did not last as long as it took the ink to dry," Catherine replied. Her plump face hid her emotions. Even her heavy-lidded eyes showed me nothing of her true thoughts.

I'd have to use other persuasions. Once I might have quailed at this invasion of privacy. Today I cared only to end the war, permanently. Slowly I unwound a tendril of power. I stared directly into her eyes, seeking an entry for my persuasion.

"Charges of heresy will make martyrs of the Huguenot leaders. One martyr is stronger than a thousand armed troops. The war will never end. Try them for treason alone," I said quietly. My words followed the pathway opened by my magic.

Catherine nodded, blinked slowly, as if falling asleep.

Then my own words crashed back into my own mind. She'd erected a barrier in her mind and forcibly rejected my suggestion. Perhaps someone else had put the blockage there against the possibility of lasting peace.

Someone like Roanna.

I needed more time and energy to break down that barrier. Perhaps I could slip around her resistance with another tactic.

"If you must try them for heresy, then let the prisoners languish in prison a while. Tempers will cool, the pain of past wrongs will lessen. Their death throes will be more an afterthought than a rallying cry."

Catherine nodded at that statement. "We will take this under consideration. The church has prison cells that will make their confinement more unpleasant than their death and descent into hell." She returned my stare with malice. "Now leave us, Pére Griffin, before I decide that your petition stems from a heretical sympathy with the prisoners rather than a desire for peace."

"As long as a single Protestant lives, we cannot have peace," Charles de Guise, Cardinal of Lorraine, added. "Look what they did to my sainted brother! He is the true martyr in this case."

I left. Some battles could not be won. But perhaps I lessened the impact.

Bishop du Bellay patted my shoulder in commiseration when I returned to him and related my interview.

"She gave us time. You must do your best to wear away at her resolve." I heaved a tired sigh. Perhaps if I had not been suffering so from fatigue, I could have succeeded.

Fanatics do not hear logic. They listen only to what they want to hear, Raven reminded me.

"*Oui,* sound advice, my young friend. I shall speak to the queen regent again in a few days, and a few days after that. When did you become so wise?"

I took off my cap and scratched at my scalp, feeling totally filthy as well as tired and hungry.

Du Bellay looked at me closely then. The ravages of the past few days must still show clearly on my face. "Sweet Jesu! Boy, what have you done to yourself?" He pushed me into his own padded chair by the window and rang a silver bell summoning refreshment.

"I battled a demon to a stalemate. It escaped and now I cannot find it. I faced an angry queen and failed in my arguments."

"You were lucky to survive." His gaze remained fixed upon my head, making me uncomfortable.

"What?"

"Your hair, Griffin. Stark white. Your skin, as thin and pale as old parchment. And your stance, off center, hesitant. Like an old, old man tottering toward his grave. *Mon Dieu!* You nearly glow with otherworldly light."

My hands reached instinctively to touch my hair and skin, as if my fingers would verify what my eyes could not. I certainly felt old today.

Bishop du Bellay pressed a goblet of wine into my hands. The fine ruby glass nearly sprang to life with the light streaming through the window. I think I smiled at the memory of my small success in treating Tryblith's black tether like a cane of glass. With new peace surrounding me in the glow of colored glass, I drank. A few sips at first, then deeper. The liquid spread warmth from my stomach to my toes to my fingers. I sighed.

"I must follow the demon home to England." I stood shakily, longing for a staff, even a nonmagical one. I had the crystal, secreted in my doublet. All I needed was a length of wood. I also had the original ring of the Pendragon, as well as my substitute.

Could I muster the strength to find Roanna and her demon within the crystal and to banish them?

"If you meet them in battle again, you will die, my friend," Eustachius du Bellay said quietly. "I should regret to lose you."

"I shall not die until the Demon of Chaos is banished. And then I can pass in peace, knowing my mission in life fulfilled." I did not need my magical senses to know that I would never see my bishop, my friend, again.

"And your heritage? Who will follow you as the Pendragon?"

"There is another."

"Your twin?"

"Perhaps. The wolfhounds know. They will choose."

France and London, summer 1563.

I scried in the black crystal. Roanna and Tryblith had taken ship to England from Le Havre, the economic heart of Calais. I hastened after them.

Elizabeth had not removed her troops from the port. She had sent her army overtly to assist the French Protestants in their battle against Catholic oppression. But she truly wanted to reclaim Calais—an English toehold on the continent.

Protestant and Catholic alike in France quickly put aside enough of their differences to rally to a common cause. They resented the continued English presence in their country regardless of religion. They besieged the port and city. Angry, frightened, armed men turned me back at the city gates. Rumors of plague within the city had begun to circulate through the army, a more fearsome enemy than English cannon trained upon them from the fortified walls. I could not catch an English packet in New Haven for a quick sail back home.

As I contemplated my next move, I scanned the walls for a possible way into the city and a ship home. Blood seemed to sparkle within the mortar of the dressed stones and between the cobbles of the street. Roanna and Tryblith had been here.

Had the demon sowed the seeds of plague?

If he had, then the chaos I feared had begun. I had to get home quickly. The demon would seek his personal portal to the Netherworld for his moment of full release from his human host.

I'm looking! Donovan's thoughts broke into mine. *Do you know how many chronicles and journals and record books are in the lair? I can tell you how many bushels of barley were harvested in 1315 or how many lambs were born in 1485 but no references to the demon or his lair.*

"Go back farther," I pleaded with my twin. "Go back to another civil war."

Before the Wars of the Roses?

"Aye. 'Twas the chaos of that dynastic struggle that loosened the seal on his portal. Look at the chaos between King Steven and his cousin the Empress Matilda. Look at Matilda's son, Henry II, and how his sons rebelled against him. Those are the years Tryblith ran rampant over all of England."

One of the few comforts that sustained me now was Donovan's open communication. Mind-to-mind, we aired our differences, examined the source of our bitter separation, and realized that we fought for the same end, the elimination of the Demon of Chaos. Bit by bit we became close again. Bit by bit we reforged the bonds that made us two halves of one whole. Together we could make a formidable Pendragon.

Only this time, he had the strength and the talent and I had the restless frustration.

"You must warn Elizabeth. No ships from Calais can be allowed to land. They carry plague."

I ride on my fastest horse within the hour, his voice finally broke through the heavy silence.

"No, Donovan. You must continue the search for Tryblith's lair. You cannot risk yourself. I need you hale and whole. England needs you hale and whole."

Martha has my sons at Ide Hill.

"Send your most trusted messenger, first to Elizabeth and then to Martha. She must take the boys north as soon as possible." A vision flashed before my mind's eye. The older twin, Griffin, would become the next Baron of Kirkenwood, but not for a long, long time. By the time my twin died, the laws and the monarchs would shift. Only males would inherit Kirkenwood from that point on, by law, not just tradition or chance.

A strange sense of peace settled upon my shoulders. I'd not be there to see the changes. But someone else of my blood would watch in secret. Who?

I knew but dared not admit it to myself yet.

Elizabeth should receive news of the plague about the time I landed in England. Could we stop the plague ships in time? Could I find Tryblith in time to defeat him before England collapsed in the chaos of disease, famine, and the power struggles that would follow?

A leaky fishing boat dropped me rather unceremoniously on the rocky beach near Hastings—far away from Portsmouth and the plague-ridden ships of returning soldiers. The sailors heaved me and my small pack of belongings onto the shore and returned to the open sea with extreme speed, away from English customs agents and armed patrols. But I'd lined their pockets with about half the gold given me by du Bellay.

·

The month past the Summer Solstice brought truly warm weather that bred the plague. The disease spread far and fast.

I hastened northwest toward London even as people fled to the healthier air of the coast.

But what of those too poor or too stubborn to flee?

As much as I longed to run to the far north and Kirkenwood, to seek out information on Tryblith's lair, I knew my place was in London, to help those who could not help themselves.

Once again, I found quarters at Whitefriars. Once again my friends pleaded with me to hear confessions and celebrate Mass. Reluctantly I obliged them, speaking in their native English, invoking whatever God would listen to our prayers. These people needed their Merlin more than a church-approved priest.

All summer the plague raged. Some weeks three thousand souls succumbed to the disease. I had read the works of Michele de Notre Dame, or Nostradamus, in my years of study. He alone had found some success against the black death. Following his dictates I washed my entire body each day in a lime solution. I stood over a small fire of applewood and herbs to let the smoke cleanse me. I preached the faith of cleanliness to any and all who would listen, especially in Whitefriars. I set the children to fashioning rat traps and to replacing pallets and straw mattresses often. We burned the old ones and washed the bedding. The women scrubbed the walls and floors with the same lime we bathed in—in much stronger doses.

But even those measures could not keep the seeds of the black death from creeping over the walls of Whitefriars. Brother Jeremy succumbed first. My vision of his future had been true. His quick death shocked us deeply. Of all of us, he was the most robust, bursting with life and creativity. Sadly, his son-in-law, Gareth took up the reins of authority over the glassworks. No one else sickened for many days. We hoped we had beaten the plague. But one by one the little ones, and the old ones took to their pallets and died. I mourned old Ralph with a heaviness in my soul. When hearty Gareth's face turned black and he died within hours, my little community lost heart. The glassworks shut down. I smuggled Carola, her new baby son, and little Faith out of the old sanctuary. They headed north to Kirkenwood with directions and a few base coins to help them on the road. My vision was clear. Faith would thrive, but not if I allowed her to stay. She must survive to fulfill my early vision of her future. Something good and gracious depended upon her.

Farmers refused to deliver foodstuffs to the city, and there was famine as well as disease in the city. The river level dropped dramatically, wells ran dry and brackish. New diseases crept upon us besides the black death. The smoke of funeral pyres blackened the sky every day for months. Communication broke down. Only my mental contact with Donovan let me know that the world continued to spin through the heavens in its normal path despite the disease we battled in London.

Each day I went into the city with what food and medicine I could find. Each day I heard confessions and blessed the dying, giving their souls the comfort denied to their bodies. My soul tried to follow the victims into death. From somewhere deep inside me I found the strength to remain intact, sending only my prayers with the departed. God listened to our prayers and opened Her arms to those who passed this mortal realm.

These were natural deaths, brought about by a hideous disease. But the disease itself was a natural part of the world. The demon had not created it. Tryblith and Roanna merely used it to spread chaos.

All the time we struggled and fought and despaired I felt Roanna in the back of my mind, laughing. *I'll have my revenge on you, Griffin Kirkwood. One by one, all that you hold dear will be stripped from you and your brother.* I felt her grip tighten on my heart.

Somehow, our destinies were bound up together like the mythical Gordian Knot.

Each day, my reflection in the polished metal mirror showed more years of age and care upon my face. Each day my magic grew in strength, helping me keep disease and hurt from infecting my body. But none of my talents could end the devastation.

At last the days cooled. In early October I awoke to find paving stones slick with frost. The number of new cases of plague dwindled and ceased. By the middle of the month

I had the freedom to continue my quest for Tryblith. On the day I left Whitefriars for the last time, I turned first to the east. My twin needed to know how his wife and sons fared.

I found Ide Hill abandoned. The dead lay where they had fallen. Recent deaths, probably the last to succumb to the ravages of the disease. I recited my prayers, anointed brows, and burned those I found. I paused over Martha's stiff body. She had barely touched my life, and yet I grieved with my brother. He'd lost a friend and a companion more than a wife. Her blood mingled with the Kirkwoods. One of her sons would succeed to the title and the lands. Would he become the Pendragon as well?

I searched out two half-starved, frightened little boys. My blood called to their blood. They lived. I found them wandering the grounds crying for their mother, eating dirt and freezing in ragged, filthy clothes.

I have found Tryblith's lair, Donovan came through to me so clearly I thought him standing behind me instead of many miles away in Kirkenwood.

"I cannot leave yet, dear brother."

Chapter 68

Kirkenwood, 22 October, 1563.

DONOVAN stared Newynog in the eye. Any normal dog would look away, unable to hold a man's gaze for more than a few moments. "I suppose you and that unruly pup of yours will insist upon coming," he said flatly. Griffin's familiar had weaned her litter weeks ago. The males and the other two female pups had gone into the kennels for training. Except for the first female pup born, the one that dominated all the others in the litter.

The mother wolfhound's steadfast gaze spoke volumes of determination.

"Very well. But make that puppy behave. And keep up." He stalked to his horse. A small party of soldiers and retainers, including a nanny for his twins, had already mounted the fastest steeds in the stable. What little baggage he allowed them must fit into a single pack apiece. One extra horse carried panniers stuffed with books and scrolls from the archives as well as food and extra blankets. He estimated the trip south would take five days. With luck, Griffin's trek north with the twins would shorten it by a day, possibly two.

Six rainy days later, they met on the road outside Oxford.

"Griffin?" Donovan stared at his twin as they embraced. "You are truly aged." Their mental conversations had not prepared him for the extreme change.

Newynog and her pup leaped to greet Griffin, worming their way between the brothers. The mother wolfhound rose up on her hind legs, placing front paws on her master's shoulders. Years of care faded from Griffin's countenance. He hugged the dog with tears in his eyes.

519

Donovan looked away to avoid the emotions that clogged his reason. The sight that greeted him froze every muscle and thought. Two little boys huddled together beside the road, thumbs in mouths, eyes cast down. They clung to a bedraggled toy, a horse sewn of leather and stuffed with wool. Donovan had given identical ones to each of them. But only one remained.

He took one hesitant step toward his sons.

"Easy, brother." Griffin held him back with a strong arm. "They are frightened and bewildered, responding little to anything but each other."

Slowly, Donovan approached the boys and knelt in the mud of the roadside. He held out one hand for them, hoping they would respond as the dogs did, to his scent. Hoping they would remember their da.

They reared back, clinging to each other fiercely. "Do you remember me, Griffin, Henry? I'm your da. I've come to take you home. We'll have hot baths and warm blankets, and fresh milk from the sheep we keep in the byre."

No response. Their startling blue eyes opened wide, half-glazed with fear.

Then one of them—impossible to tell which—blinked. "Da?"

"Yes, son. I'm your da." He held out his arms to them. Every scrap of his being ached to hold them close, feared he'd drive them away with fright. He bit his lip to keep his chin from quivering and the tears from forming.

He had to remain still, solid, reassuring.

"Da!" the other boy launched himself into Donovan's arms, followed reluctantly by his brother.

As he folded them close to his heart, Donovan allowed the tears to flow, allowed his breaking heart to heal.

He did not need a familiar. He needed his children. All of the lost children he and Griffin had gathered at Kirkenwood.

"Now, which one of you is Griffin?" he asked, half laughing through his tears.

The twins looked at each other. Each pointed to the other and said, "Griffin."

"Well, then. Which one of you is Henry?"

The boys kept their fingers pointing at each other and said, "Henry."

Donovan rolled his eyes upward and caught Griffin's smile.

"Oh, you two will be more of a handful than your Uncle Griffin and I were. We'll straighten this out later."

"I have friends near Oxford. They'll give us rooms for the night and a hot meal," Griffin said, gathering his pack. He kept one hand on Newynog's head as if afraid to be separated from her again.

The pup hung back, not bonding with either Griffin or one of the twins. Perhaps these things took time.

"We have much to plan." Donovan rose, still clutching his sons, one in each arm. He buried his face between their shoulders, drinking in and memorizing the feel of them. For the first time, since the arousal of his magic, he knew fear. What would happen to his sons' fragile hearts if he were killed in the coming fray? Like Meg, they might not recover emotionally to take up the reins of governing Kirkenwood as a mundane baron, or guarding Britain as the Pendragon.

Oxford, England, 30 October, 1563.

The more I studied the journal of Resmiranda Griffin in the year 1213, the more I feared the duel to come. She had hidden the text of her own battle with Tryblith's host beneath layers of magic. What looked like an accounting of fleeces, barley, and hay became a description of how she had discovered the demon lair the first time in 1208 while fleeing King John. Five years later she returned to end the tyranny of Tryblith and his host Radburn Blakely. Blakely had been the king's most trusted adviser and led John in one disastrous action after another.

I shuddered when I realized how close Roanna had come to a similar position. Through deceit and guile she had served Mary de Guise, regent of Scotland, Mary Stuart as Queen of France, and become mistress to Francis Duc de Guise, the most powerful man in France, second only to

Catherine de Médici. She also had some kind of control of Thomas Howard, fourth Duke of Norfolk, a member of the Privy Council and the premier peer of England.

Impossible to trace Roanna's bloodlines over three hundred years of obscurity. But she could not have summoned the demon unless she was descended from a previous host. Possibly she named one of my own ancestors in her lineage. The Kirkwood men had never restrained themselves, especially when crossing the border on raids.

My vision rocked back to the last raid I had ridden upon. My twin and I had driven her to summon the demon.

We must be the ones to vanquish it.

The risk was great. Could I ask Donovan to take that risk when his sons needed him so desperately?

"I think we need to be inside the stone circle that protects the barrow." Donovan broke into my musing.

"A stone circle. Yes. A circle has no beginning and no end. Each path leads back to the starting point." The standing stones of Kirkenwood beckoned. The presence of my ancestors would strengthen my spells. But home was too far away. Too many innocents lived within the circle. I needed the most powerful stone circle in all of Britain.

With that thought, I knew that only I could shoulder this responsibility. Donovan must live to nurture his sons and the next Pendragon. He had found his magic. He must now use it to nurture rather than vanquish. Our roles in life had reversed.

"I've worked out a ritual," Donovan continued.

I clamped down on my thoughts before he could read them.

"Show me."

Donovan handed me a scroll. From the markings around the edges, I guessed he had added to or amended an older one. The first lines were written in the old Secretary script by a feminine hand. Resmiranda again?

She had described a pentagram within a circle, fires at the center and each of the five points which must touch the circle. Herbs and incantations in archaic Welsh followed.

Then in Donovan's more modern Italian script, bolder, less precise, but just as important, a ritual for attracting the demon and feeding the power with the celebrant's own blood. My face grew cold and clammy.

"We could use goat blood, but Raven always told us never to take a life for a ritual. That would open the door to evil, make us vulnerable to the temptations of the demon," he placated me.

But his words and tone did not work.

I had a vision of the Holy Eucharist, the sacrament I had performed so many times, the bread and wine transfiguring into the body and blood of Jesus Christ. Donovan's ritual was another form of Eucharist, a sacrifice of body and blood for the good of all.

Our ancient ancestors had practiced a form of this sacrament with ritual sacrifice. One brave and dutiful person to give up his life for the health and well-being of the entire tribe. Christians believed that Jesus had done the same for all mankind, for all time.

But other sacrifices must be made. God's work must be continued by men. I rubbed at the scars of the stigmata hidden beneath my shirt.

"This will work, brother. All the elements are here. Now show me on the map where the lair is located."

At midnight, I crept out of the house with my pack, the scrolls and maps and Newynog. Her pup followed close on her heels. The unnamed young dog would not choose me. She must find another. Curious that she had not chosen one of the twins. Our grandmother had prophesied that Donovan's son would succeed her as the Pendragon.

She had been wrong. The dogs chose me. God chose me to fight the demon and keep Britain safe.

Until the dogs chose another, the pup could not leave her mother's side. I was gratified that Newynog at least would survive this night.

In the back of my mind I felt Donovan stir. Our bonds were close. He already missed me.

Regretfully I erected a solid barrier against him. He must not find me yet.

The sun rose high in the heavens on a cold windy day as I rode along the Avon and over the slight rise that led to the Giant's Dance. The stone circle had been abandoned upon this windswept plain aeons ago, its builders long since forgotten and lost to history. Its isolation made it the perfect location for the night to come. Roanna and Tryblith would not hesitate to meet me.

But first I had to summon them.

I unsaddled the horse and left him to graze or roam free. I had no more need of him. Newynog and her pup sniffed out the perimeter of the massive upright stones. The formal entrance to the stones lay at the east portal. I stepped through, solemnly, aware of the sacredness of this place.

No matter what you name your God, be certain that She is listening, Grandmother Raven whispered to me in an intimate secret. I smiled in response and set about arranging Donovan's ritual. When it was all done but for lighting the fires and triggering the circle of power with my blood, I sat upon the altar stone, opened my being to the cosmos, and prayed.

Breathe in three counts, hold three, breathe out three, hold three, repeat. My lungs expanded, my heartbeat slowed, my sense of self flew outward, grew, exploded into a million bright points of light. The great wheel of stars and planets circled above me, heedless of my existence, and yet I became one with them, joined with them in a glorious dance of life that continued in greater and greater circles. No beginning, nor an end.

I heard the soft music of the heavens and understood why Dr. Dee searched so long and diligently to hear the angelic choir. Yesterday I had sent to him a book I found during my wanderings. A book of secrets originally penned by Enoch, a prophet of old revered by the Templars and the mystery schools. Perhaps there he'd find the origins of the Enochian language. I pointed the way for him to look for his own path of enlightenment.

I felt the grass grow, the earthworms work their way beneath the turf in endless circular tunnels. I touched each portion of the stones around me, became a part of them and added my soul to the energy of the power they radiated, to the other stones they connected to, and the other lives that joined with them. My ancestor, Myrddin Emrys, the Merlin, his daughter Arylwren, her children by King Arthur Pendragon, their descendants, Resmiranda Griffin, her descendants, Grandmother Raven. We all joined together in the endless circle of life magnified by these stones.

After an endless time, I returned to my body, refreshed, accepting, my magic and perceptions enhanced by the presence of stones and all the Pendragons who had come before me. I was at peace for the final bits of ritual.

Faeries flew a ring around me, chirping their glee at my return to them. I called one to my hand. A tiny green male settled upon my palm a moment. Perfectly formed, he smiled at me and bounced back into the air after only a moment. He and his companions laughed brightly at something. But then, faeries laughed at everything.

Their joy brought a lightness to my grim purpose and gave me hope. I set about completing what I had started.

I called upon Tanio, the element of Fire, and coaxed it to ignite each of the five outer fires of the pentagram and the central one, the heart of the ritual. I called upon Awyr, the element of Air, my element, to send word to my enemies that I awaited them. I called Pridd, the element of Earth, to rise up within the stones to become a sealed arena for this battle. Lastly, I called up Dwfr, the element of Water, within my blood, to fuel the other elements and seal the ritual.

When I looked out among the stones, I saw Roanna, clearly visible but still tethered to Tryblith, circling the great monument. The splices I had made in the tether shone as bright spots of glass reflecting light.

My enemies, my destiny, poked and prodded between the uprights, seeking an entrance. At last they came around to the east and stepped through into my world.

"I see that all is ready, Griffin Kirkwood," Roanna said. Her words came out in a long hiss, like a serpent tasting the air for prey.

"And so it begins," I replied, sheathing my bloody knife. I held my right hand over my left wrist where blood dripped into the fire, sizzling with each drop. I did not heal the wound. I still needed my blood to seal another circle.

The power rose up in a solid wall keeping others out of the circle—except possibly for Donovan, the other half of me and thus a part of this—and the three of us trapped within.

None of us would leave until at least one of us died.

Chapter 69

The Giant's Dance, Salisbury Plain, England, All Hallows Eve, 1563.

ROANNA felt the wall of power snap closed behind her. She should have been the one to seal the arena. She needed to be in control of every aspect of this duel. But Griffin had beat her to it. He had anticipated every move she made, as a lover anticipates the needs of his partner.

She banished the images of Griffin lying naked beside her, enticing her to new and glorious heights of pleasure. No other man had touched her heart and soul as he had.

No other lover had given her a child. The child she kept hidden from her life and her demon.

No matter. She clung to her anger, forgetting her weariness with life. This night she killed Griffin, and with the death of the Pendragon of Britain, Tryblith would finally break free of her. She would have control of her life and her heart at long last. She would have her revenge for everything that had gone wrong with her life, the deaths of all those she cared for.

Once free of Griffin and Tryblith, she would raise her daughter to inherit the great heritage of both mother and father, without interference from a demon, or a father, or the church.

Griffin had set the stage. A stage she knew well, for she would have set the same one. He had chosen the huge magnificence of the Giant's Dance. She was more at home in the small, intimate circle outside the cave barrow. The extra room gave her more freedom to maneuver.

He did not flinch when he cut himself to draw blood, Tryblith gibbered. He sounded frightened.

"No, he did not flinch. He is determined. Solid in his convictions. As he has always been. We must attack his faith, his belief in what is right." She knew Griffin Kirkwood intimately. As intimately as a lover.

But she did not know the man who gazed at her with midnight in his eyes and a crown of faeries circling his prematurely white brow.

Had she inflicted old age upon him? Her heart ached, no matter how hard she tried to thrust her emotions aside.

The wind howled around the stone circle. Wild hoofbeats sounded in the distance. Fox hounds bayed. A cloud of blowing leaves, grass, and dirt circled the circle. And within that circle rode a host of ghostly elves. Waiting to gather the soul of the loser.

She vowed that she would not be the one to join their endless chase.

Could she condemn Griffin to that fate?

"What will your precious church think of this pagan circle, your pentagram, those elves, these faeries?" Roanna taunted. She focused upon the anger she had harbored for so many years as she began walking a circle that included both the circle Griffin had drawn with his new staff, the altar stone, the entire inner horseshoe of uprights.

"What do you think the church will think?" he replied. A curious half smile lit his face, but not those incredible eyes. If she looked too long into them, she'd lose herself, her sense of purpose.

I do this for the future, for my heritage, so that tomorrow I can follow my heart, free of demons and lovers, she reminded herself.

"You condemn your immortal soul, Griffin Kirkwood. You consort with faeries and dark magic. Blood magic. The church won't take you back."

"So be it."

He was too calm. What did he know that she did not? She knew everything about him.

Or did she?

"Your oh so merciful God allowed me to murder twenty thousand innocent souls with a breath of plague from my demon. Why do you put up with the nonsense preached by His church?" Her circle was almost complete. At the last moment she pushed Tryblith to the inside of her ritual line. She needed his strength, his pure evil to combat this man.

"But you did not kill them. You did not even sow the seeds of the plague. I guided many of the dead to the other side, none of them bore your mark. The plague was already in Le Havre when you arrived. Your demon only left his mark to make certain I hastened to follow you."

"The ploy worked."

"But the twenty thousand deaths in London did not aid your demon, did not add to his strength. All of those lives wasted!"

All of those deaths wasted! The demon screamed. He clawed at the tether that bound them, trying to get to Griffin.

Roanna remained at the edge of her circle, keeping the demon in check. She'd loose him when the time was right. Not yet.

Her ears roared as she took the last step to close the circle. The faeries yelped and winked out of sight. The dogs growled and hunkered close to Griffin's feet. A double wall of power now enclosed them, his and hers.

As the entire world should have been his and hers to enjoy together.

"I will be free of you and the enchantment you cast upon me as well as the choking tether of this demon," she muttered.

"A tether that robs you of as much as it gives you." Griffin raised his hand, circled it as if gathering a dog's leash tight.

A hot brand encircled her throat, choking off her air, dragging her closer to him.

She gasped and fought the magical collar. Tryblith scratched her throat with long dragon talons. The choking spell vanished. She dragged in long gulps of air even as she prepared her first spell. Griffin stood bare inches away from her. She needed more room, more air. She stared into his eyes, seeking the window into his soul. He had to reveal his next move to her.

Instead she found herself staring at her own mistakes, her own anger, her own sadness. And delusions. Tryblith had clouded her mind, made her blame others for everything she did to herself.

She had to break the connection with Griffin or lose all that had propelled her thus far.

"Fire from the skies, bathe this man in your unholy light!" One arm up, the other pointed directly at Griffin, she pulled energy from the heavens. Lightning flashed. Thunder rolled. Fire leaped from the tops of the stones, through her in a long chain.

The elves rode faster, cheering at the merciless fire.

Griffin jumped aside and rolled. The dogs sprang in the opposite direction. Newynog screamed as the lightning caught her hind leg. Her high-pitched keening echoed and amplified within the containing walls of power.

"For hurting my familiar, you seal our fate, Roanna." Griffin spun in a tight circle. Wind whipped around and around them, catching up chalky dirt, bits of turf, small stones, and scattered leaves into a vicious whirlwind. It grew taller, expanded, aimed directly at Tryblith. The demon pressed himself backward, trapped by Roanna's wall of power. The whirlwind followed him about the circle. It gained strength as circle compounded circle.

The demon jumped upon the altar stone, hunching down. The wind caught him, enclosing him, pelting him with the debris of life it had gathered in its circuit.

Each pelting stone, biting bit of dirt, and suffocating onslaught of leaves Tryblith suffered, inflicted itself upon Roanna. She batted at the sympathetic assault. Air bled from her lungs. Her skin was on fire. Red haze blinded her mundane vision.

Griffin spun a second whirlwind, milder this time. He was losing strength.

Now, the new dust storm enfolded Roanna and Griffin within its calm eye. As Tryblith's pain weakened her, Griffin reached out and clasped her left wrist with his right hand, then ran his own left arm along hers to clasp her elbow in a parody of a formal dance. Fire burned along the path of his hand.

She looked down to find blood dripping from his fingers. A burr or tiny blade on the underside of his signet ring had cut her. While she stared gape-mouthed at the mundane wound, he slid a matching signet ring upon the fourth finger of her left hand.

"Blood of my blood, breath of my breath. With this ring

we are wed to each other, Roanna. With our mingling blood, we are bound together for all time in a dance of life and death." The band of the dragon rampant upon her hand shrank and molded itself to slender fingers. It should have been big enough to fall off.

"Now it is just we two, Roanna."

"As it was ordained from the time we first met," she choked out the words.

"Whatever you inflict upon me, you inflict upon yourself."

"No. You will not control me. I will not allow anyone to control me." Desperate for breath, she broke free of him, spinning her own circle. She raised a firestorm. Griffin's ritual fires blended with hers. He pointed at each in turn, muttering an incantation. They did not obey. Fire was her element, not his. It obeyed her will, despite the blood he had used to control all four elements.

His skin reddened.

The heat seared *her* face and hands.

Smoke rose from his clothing.

She coughed.

He squelched a scream of pain.

She gathered the pain and enhanced her power as Tryblith had taught her. "I must have control."

Griffin shrank within himself. Dying.

Her heart withered and broke.

The dust storms dissipated.

Tryblith broke free of the pelting debris. He leaped through the firestorm, raking Griffin with his talons. But the strength of Griffin's whirlwind had drained him of power. The demon barely drew blood on his victim's throat.

Roanna's throat ached and burned with sympathetic scrapes.

Tryblith opened his great maw full of dagger teeth for one last fatal bite.

One last death to give him the power to break free of Roanna's summoning. One more death to unleash his chaos upon the world. One bite to kill Griffin. And herself.

"Noooooo!" Roanna doused the firestorm. She rammed her staff into the demon's mouth. Her shoulder wrenched, straining every muscle in her back as she added power to her blind thrust.

Time slowed. Her weapon drove deep, deeper into the vulnerable tissue of the demon's mouth. The ragged goat skull shattered.

The broken bits rammed deep into Tryblith's throat like so many vorpal daggers. The largest fragment pierced his brain.

The demon yanked desperately at the shaft. It broke at his mouth. Without enough leverage to free himself, he collapsed in a pool of green ichor.

A horrendous cloud of sulfur rose. Tryblith faded into a faint outline, malevolent yellow eyes lingering in long moments of silence. His gaze promised revenge when he broke free of his portal once more.

Roanna stared, stunned, at what she had done. She did not see Griffin's fist connect with her jaw. Felt only the sharp pain. Saw winking black stars before her vision. She staggered backward. Bounced against the wall of power and crumpled to her knees.

Still dazed, she tried to gather her magical shields against his next assault. She had to survive. Her daughter . . . She couldn't allow it all to end this way. Griffin stood over her, staff in hand. A terrible grimace of physical pain and something else crossed his face.

She braced against the magic he channeled through his staff. Her shields had no defense against the sharp black crystal atop his staff as it crashed into her temple.

Blood trickled from his own head.

As blackness gathered around her vision, she let loose one last blast of power.

Moments later, or was it hours, she roused a little as Griffin cradled her head in his lap. He dribbled something moist into her mouth—wine. Sacramental wine. His Latin prayers for her soul came in short gasps, as if they traveled through the depths of great pain.

"Do you . . . renounce . . . the devil and all his works . . . and his dominions, Roanna?" he gasped. His fingers weakly caressed her brow, soothing her hair away from her eyes. He traced the sign of the cross on her forehead with holy oil.

"Wh . . . at?"

"Renounce . . . the devil and . . . his minions, Roanna. Please. You. Must. To save . . . us all. To make sure

Tryblith . . . stays . . . trapped in the Netherworld." He slurred his words. He was hurt nearly as badly as she.

"Say the words, Roanna. You. Must say. The words. Say it and be free of Tryblith. Say it and take control."

She drew one sharp shallow breath that stabbed her heart. "Christus Domini," she sighed.

A new lightness gathered around her. The lightness of freedom. The last trace of Tryblith's control evaporated as mist in sunshine.

"Thank you, Roanna." Griffin's breath came in ragged spurts.

She breathed again and felt something break in her head. Warmth dribbled from her temple. The chilling cold in her limbs eased into numbness.

"Find our daughter, Griffin."

"We have a child." He did not sound surprised. Just determined beneath the weariness and pain.

"I have hidden her where only you can find her. Her name is Deirdre. Sorrowful one. Baptize and bless her. Raise her well."

"I love you, Roanna." He held her hand and kissed her brow.

A blinding white light opened before her, leading them onward to a better path.

"GRIFFIN!" Donovan screamed. He whipped his horse to greater speed. The blown beast shied at the ghostly horses that circled the Giant's Dance. He jumped free of the beast as it stumbled and collapsed. Donovan was on his feet and pelting across the plain in one movement. He made certain he kept his eyes on the ground and away from the influence of the elves.

The silvery energy of the elves threw him backward. He drew his sword, held it by the blade so that the hilt made a cross. "By my faith, protect me from this unholy visitation. By my strength, free me from their quest. By my magic banish them to the Netherworld of their beginning," he shouted to the four winds.

A break in the continuous stream of elven guarding

opened. Donovan did not question, did not hesitate. He dove through and came up whole.

"We care not for your soul, Donovan of Kirkenwood," the king of the elves said. His voice sounded as if he spoke through a long tube a long way away. "We came for the Pendragon only. But he is passed beyond our reach."

Donovan's spine itched as one by one, the elves peeled out of formation and rode across the hills in search of other prey.

Donovan scrambled across the defining ditch toward the standing stones of the Giant's Dance. "Griffin, no, you can't die. Not now. Not when we've just found each other again."

He sobbed as he pounded against the barrier between the uprights. At last he came to the Heel Stone at the east. The portal resisted him. He pushed hard against it with hands and magic, with his soul screaming to rescue his twin.

The barrier shattered in a thousand points of light. Donovan shredded the last of it with his hands, heedless of the glass-sharp shards of energy that lashed his palms and threatened his eyes.

"Griffin." He slid upon a noisome green puddle of demon gore to stop upon his knees beside his brother. The smell of sulfur gagged him.

"Donovan." Griffin stretched a feeble hand from where he crouched over the fallen demon witch. Her flame-red hair spread about her shoulders like a molten pool of glass. Peace and a terrible beauty graced her countenance.

"Is she . . . ?" Donovan didn't know what else to say. Griffin's ravaged face and hands, the huge bruise and blood at his temple that matched the one on the witch's face, his broken posture and ragged breath fairly shouted how poorly he fared.

"She died in a state of grace," Griffin gasped. His mouth worked as if he had more to say, but had not the strength form the words. "Bury her in sacred ground."

"Griffin, lean on me." Donovan shifted so that he could ease his brother back to rest in his lap. Much as Griffin cradled Roanna.

"She was so beautiful," Griffin wheezed. "I loved her." He blinked back tears. "Our love was forbidden by the church. If I could have reached out to her honestly, I might have saved her."

"She was evil through and through, Griffin. She summoned a demon. She murdered at will."

"She was a victim."

"What of the demon?"

"Gone." Griffin sighed heavily. His body grew limp.

"Don't die on me now, brother." Donovan frantically fumbled at his belt for the flask of wine, for strengthening herbs, or a miracle.

Griffin seemed to rouse a little with the few drops of wine. "You must seal the portal once more, Donovan. Travel to the lair and seal it with the same ritual Resmiranda used. Pour all of your strength and magic into it. He must not break free again."

"We'll do it together."

"No." Griffin breathed shallowly for several long moments.

Newynog limped over to them, whining her distress and loneliness. Her pup followed, hesitantly. Both bewildered. Newynog licked Griffin's face and sank down beside him.

He seemed to rouse a little as his hand found her ears and scratched. "There is a stone circle atop a tor behind the ruins of old Huntington Castle. I celebrated Easter Mass there to a congregation of wanderers, people lost to all but God. Bury me there, dear brother."

"You aren't dying, Griffin. I won't let you die."

"Roanna had a daughter. My daughter. Deirdre. Find her for me, Donovan. Find her and raise her as you would the next Pendragon. Give her the rosary." He fumbled, pressed the ivory-and-gold beads into his brother's hand. "And my journal."

Griffin shuddered beneath Donovan's touch. He drew in a long, ragged breath, expelled it upon a cough. His face drained of color and animation. He looked as peaceful and blessed as a marble statue.

"Teach all of Britain the vision of the Pendragons. Teach them that no matter what name we give to God, She listens." He breathed his last.

The stones of the Giant's Dance joined the stones of Kirkenwood, joined the wolfhounds, and all their ancestors in a mourning cry of anguish.

Epilogue

I TOOK Griffin's body to the tor above the ruins of Huntington Castle. Numb to all but my task, I rooted out the foot of the processional way that led up to the plateau and the stone circle. Off to my right, a stream cascaded down the tor beside a decrepit circular hut. An ancient one-eyed crone ducked out from behind the cloth curtain of a doorway. She hobbled a few steps and waited silently, with the patience of the ages for our slow cortege. She propped herself upright with a long staff topped by a carved raven.

"May I bury my brother in the circle up there?" I asked bowing reverently to her.

"Aye. The Merlin of Britain belongs there. He were good to me and blessed me one time when the rest of the world shunned me for having the evil eye." She touched the webbing of scar tissue over her missing eye.

"Thank you, Old Mother." I couldn't say more. My throat closed on my grief again. As it did nearly every hour on the long, slow journey from the Giant's Dance to here.

And then, miracle of miracle, Meg appeared behind the crone. She emerged from the one-room hut built into the base of the hill, as a diving bird breaks the surface of the water.

Meg, tall and proud, graceful as a breeze and gentle as a feather, she smiled upon me with her brilliantly clear eyes.

"Meg!" I rushed to embrace her.

She gathered me close, comforting me. A sob broke in my chest, burst forth into the tears I had not allowed myself to shed.

"A burden shared is half the weight," she whispered

through her own tears. "He was a great man. We shall miss him."

We clung together another long moment before I could look around. Two children trailed behind my sister. She would never be without motherless children.

"Master Robin." I bowed slightly to the boy with Elizabeth's long face and Dudley's dark curls.

He nodded regally and examined me with big solemn brown eyes that saw all my flaws and faults and calculated how to use them—just like his mother.

But the little girl toddling in his wake took most of my attention. She had a mass of dark auburn hair and midnight-blue eyes. Kirkwood eyes.

"Deirdre," I gasped.

Her eyes danced with mischief as she stuck a thumb into her mouth. For a moment I was transported back to the days when Griffin, Meg, and I cavorted all over Kirkenwood, playing pranks, getting into trouble, and loving each other fiercely.

"Her mother came to us for help and protection, Donovan," the old woman explained. "We cared for her within the power of the faerie circle. The demon could not touch her or the child. Within hours of the birth she crawled away with her demon. We presume she left so that her death would not taint the wee one."

"She died, but she crawled away so that her life would not taint the child." I did not know how I knew that, only that the truth circled my words.

Gulping back a new spate of tears I knelt before the little girl. "Deirdre, a very special man asked me to give this to you." I fished the gold-and-ivory rosary from my belt and held it out to her. She fingered the shiny treasure with awe before looking to Meg for permission to take it.

My sister nodded, new tears forming in her eyes.

"And you, Meg, how did you come here?" I asked, rising from my crouch to confront her.

"Deirdre came to me at Whitefriars when Griffin was so ill. She brought Robin and me here for safety. She knew that the child's mother would need us both. We built layers of secrecy here from the first day. No one could find us here, except the one who needed us most. No one could hurt Robin or the babe here."

"Not even Griffin or I could find you."

And then Newynog limped into the little circle of our reunion. She batted her wayward pup across the nose to get her attention. She pushed her daughter toward Deirdre. Reluctantly, the unnamed pup trotted in the direction commanded by her dam. Without further direction, she sat at Deirdre's feet, almost as tall as her new mistress. She licked the child's face, her tongue nearly covering her from ear to ear.

Instead of crying in fright, Deirdre hugged her puppy and laughed uproariously. "Coffa!" she cried in delight. "My Coffa."

"Coffa, Remembrance," the crone said quietly. "Aye, we shall remember our Merlin."

"When this final chore is done, Meg, come back to Kirkenwood," I pleaded. "Our home overflows with motherless children. We need you there."

My sister nodded her agreement. A half smile tugged at her mouth.

"You, too, Old Mother. You are welcome at our home as well." I bowed to the crone.

"Nay. I must remain here and tend his grave."

Griffin's vision of a peaceful and united England had a chance now, thanks to him. We would all make pilgrimage to his grave to honor his dedication and sacrifice.

On that note we trudged up the hill toward the sunset. A band of Gypsies joined us, singing their mournful songs guiding Griffin into the arms of whichever God awaited him.

Historical Note

On April 11, 1564, England and France signed the Treaty of Troyes, bringing hostilities between them to an end. Elizabeth relinquished all future claim to Calais.

In 1564, Eustachius du Bellay resigned as Bishop of Paris. Many resources leave the years of his tenure blank.

On June 2, 1572, Thomas Howard fourth Duke of Norfolk was beheaded on Tower Hill for the crime of treason. He had attempted in at least three conspiracies to marry Mary Queen of Scots and usurp the throne of England in her name.

On February 8, 1587, Mary Stuart, Queen of Scots, having been held hostage in England for nearly twenty years after Protestant Lords placed her son James on the throne of Scotland, was executed for treason against Queen Elizabeth I of England.